The Tremble of Love

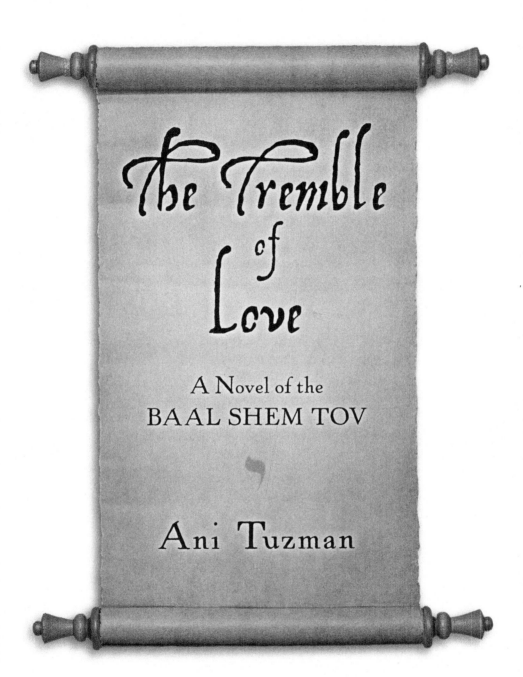

The Tremble of Love

A Novel of the BAAL SHEM TOV

Ani Tuzman

DANCING LETTERS PRESS
MASSACHUSETTS

Published by Dancing Letters Press
60 Depot Road, Hatfield, MA 01038.

Printed in the United States of America

Cover design by Laura Duffy
Interior design by Karen Minster
Map design by Annie Bissett

Tuzman, Ani
The Tremble of Love: A Novel of the Baal Shem Tov/ Ani
Tuzman.—1st ed.
546 p.; 6x9"

ISBN 978-0-9974844-1-0 (Hardcover)
ISBN 978-0-9974844-0-3 (Paperback)
ISBN 978-0-9974844-2-7 (E-book)

FIRST PAPERBACK EDITION

Dancing Letters
PRESS

To B.

with infinite gratitude
for the gift of meditation.

CONTENTS

POLISH-LITHUANIAN COMMONWEALTH

PODOLIA REGION ❧ 1703–1760

• Mezritch

 • Brody

Polnoyye •

• Lemberg

Medzibocz •

• Satanov

 P O D O L I A

Dniester River

• Tluste

Horodenka • Iwanie • Kamenetz-Podolsk

Okup

Carpathian Mountains • Kuty

• Zabie

Area
of
map

Black Sea

• Constantinople

• Salonika

OTTOMAN

•Smyrna EMPIRE

Mediterranean Sea

• Safed
• Jerusalem

— — —
Modern Day
Country Boundaries

PREFACE

The Tremble of Love, A Novel of the Baal Shem Tov is an historical novel inspired by the life of Rabbi Yisroel ben Eliezar who became known as the Baal Shem Tov, the Good Master of the Name.

Born in 1698 in the Polish-Lithuanian Commonwealth, the Baal Shem Tov was a healer and spiritual guide. It is said that everywhere he went he encountered the *Shechinah,* the Sacred Presence. The Baal Shem Tov's life is swathed in legends and tales of miracles. He wrote no books and asked his followers not to write down his teachings, but instead to live them, through their loving actions and their joy.

The intention of this book is to bring the world and heart of the Baal Shem Tov to life and to convey the essence of his teachings. While events reputed to have occurred in the rabbi's life are woven into the tapestry of this telling, the novel is a fictional account. A number of the book's characters are based on people known to have been or believed to have been in the Baal Shem Tov's life; others have been inspired by my study and my inner relationship with the master.

The Tremble of Love, A Novel of the Baal Shem Tov tells the story of a rare teacher who saw love everywhere and beckoned it forth from the hearts of rag pickers, ruby merchants, midwives, and murderers. It is said that to tell and listen to stories about a great soul evokes blessing. May it be so.

Ani Tuzman
Massachusetts, USA

AUTHOR'S NOTE

That which is nameless and beyond description is called by many names: Source. Oneness. I AM. God. Adonai. Allah. Christ. Shechinah. Shakti. Tao. Love. In Hebrew alone, there are at least 72 different names for God. If one name, or no name at all, finds favor with you, please feel free to substitute accordingly wherever a name for the Nameless appears in the following pages.

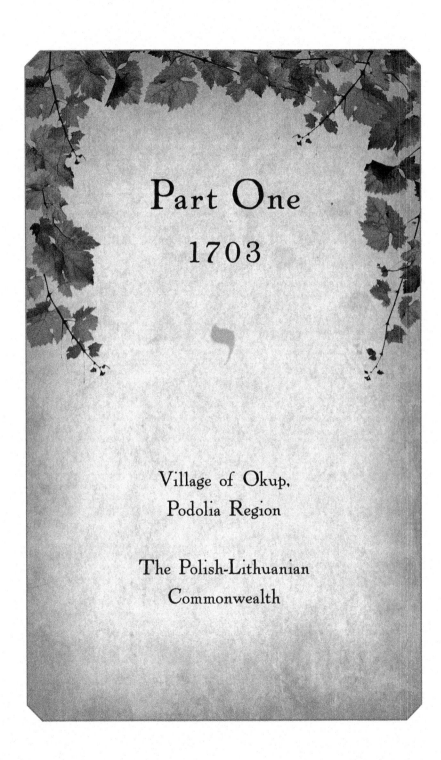

Part One
1703

Village of Okup,
Podolia Region

The Polish-Lithuanian
Commonwealth

"Caring for that child is like trying to tame the wind," the butcher's widow lamented, unaware that Srolik was near enough to hear her. The gentle widow huddled close to her friend under the baker's tin awning, waiting for the hard rain to ease so she could make her way through the marketplace before the Sabbath's descent.

"We have done what we could to honor the memory of the boy's holy parents," the baker's wife assured her companion. "The righteous Sarah and Eliezar would surely forgive us for giving up an impossible duty."

There was nothing to forgive, Srolik thought, crouched for shelter under a nearby, empty cart. The villagers of Okup had cared for him as best they could these past three years. It wasn't the villagers' fault that his parents were dead.

"Your strange ways are no surprise to me," the tinsmith had chided early that morning, dragging his cart past Srolik. "Your parents bore you in the midnight of their lives—little wonder your mind is wrapped in darkness."

Srolik had kept his gaze lowered as usual, continuing to walk slowly toward no particular destination. He hadn't understood what the tinsmith meant but felt relieved to hear him say it. Maybe this explained why Srolik seemed to move in a different world than others around him, a world quiet and vast, as if it had no end. Often when his neighbors spoke to him, he watched their lips move and hands gesture, as if he were deep inside his own body, looking out at them. That was why he preferred to walk with his head lowered, rarely looking into people's eyes or addressing them. He hoped they would not address him either. Better they talk about him as if he were not there.

He wasn't afraid of them, though some thought so. It was just that when his father had drawn his last breath, it seemed as if he had taken Srolik's voice with him.

Srolik was six years old when his father Eliezar died. A handful of village men crowded into the room where his father lay in the dim light of their single oil lamp. Srolik watched from the foot of the bed. It was the bed he and his father had slept in together since the day he'd been born, the same bed his mother had died in, holding him. The towering shadows of the men rocked back and forth while Malach Hamoves, the Angel of Death, waited patiently in a dark corner.

Reb Eliezar lifted a gaunt hand to call Srolik to his side. Leaning over him, Srolik felt his father's coarse beard on his cheek and heard the rasping of the old man's breath. When Reb Eliezar started to speak, Srolik held his breath. He wanted to listen with his whole body and let the tenderness of his father's words wash over him.

"Do not be afraid, Srolik," Reb Eliezar whispered hoarsely.

Srolik was afraid, but he did not say so. He wiped his tears with his sleeve, though he knew his father would not mind him crying. When he turned back, he was surprised to see joy in his father's eyes.

Reb Eliezar took Srolik's small hand in his trembling grasp, lifted his head slightly, and looked straight into Srolik's eyes. "You will not be alone, my son. God is with you."

Then he lowered his head as if its weight were too great and closed his eyes, his large hand suddenly heavier in Srolik's. Reb Eliezar did not move again. Srolik tried not to move either, hoping he might see the quiet Angel of Death take his father's soul.

Since that day, the Jews of Okup had cared for Srolik, passing him from home to home, inviting him to their tables for a bowl of kasha, beets, a cup of parsnip soup. He slept squeezed into a bed with their own children or wrapped in an overcoat as close to the hearth as he could be without catching fire. Recently, just in time for the coming colder nights, the butcher's widow had passed on to him a worn black coat with one button left and sleeves that hid his hands.

"The donor doesn't wish to be known," the kind woman told him.

When Srolik looked up, wordlessly, to thank her, she seemed startled by his eyes.

"The blue of your mother's," she said. "You're sturdy like your mother Sarah, too." She recalled the beauty of his mother's hair unbound in the women's ritual bath. "She had hair the color of amber and thick with waves. Like yours, Srolik."

It pleased him to imagine his mother alive.

Later, Srolik overheard that the coat had belonged to the sons of the departed butcher. After his father Eliezar's capture by Cossacks when he was a young man, Srolik's mother had moved in with the butcher's widow and her five sons. Maybe Srolik had been given the old coat because of his mother Sarah's many kindnesses to the butcher's family.

Decent boots were the most difficult to find, since good ones were passed from father to sons with little use left in them after that. What a surprise then when a rag picker, mumbling his apology, presented Srolik with Reb Eliezar's old boots.

"Here are your father's boots, boy," the man said, handing them over, "even though they'll be boats on *your* feet." The rag picker had taken them from his father's deathbed, he confessed, thinking them of no use to Srolik. But seeing the boy in the village, dressed like a beggar, he had felt sorry for the orphan.

Srolik did not mind that his clothes were ill fitting and tattered. And while the villagers may have felt otherwise, they kept it to themselves. At least the boy keeps himself clean, the good Okupniks said, told by the woodcutters that Srolik bathed in the forest streams. What the townsfolk didn't know was how happy Srolik felt dipping naked into the moving currents when the sunlight made the water gleam, reminding him of his father's eyes.

What we need comes when we need it, his father used to say. Look for miracles and you will find them everywhere. The sun rising is a miracle.

Teeth to chew bread, another. Feet to walk. Our narrow bed. The memory of your mother—although the memory of his mother was not a miracle Srolik could share with his father. Reb Eliezar told Srolik that a miracle had returned him to his wife at the age of forty-eight after thirty years as a prisoner in the Ottoman Empire. But he died before telling Srolik about the miracle that brought him back.

Passing the stable now, Srolik heard his name spoken and right after it the word "burden." He didn't want to be a burden, to make the lives of the kind Okupniks harder—but he didn't know how to change his ways.

Someone tapped his shoulder. Srolik turned around to see a man wearing a shtreimel, a wide rimmed fur hat, as if it were the Sabbath not an ordinary weekday. The stately man motioned that he follow him to a building where four other men seated at a long table were waiting. The man with the shtreimel joined the others at the table. Srolik stood before them.

"Srolik, do you know what the *Kahal* is?" the fur-hatted one asked.

Srolik shook his head. He did not repeat what he'd heard the tin-smith say: "The Kahal is a group of Jews *better off* than the rest of us, but not better."

"The Kahal," the man continued, "is a council elected by the Jews of Okup to govern them. We collect taxes from each Jew according to his earnings and use the money to pay for things that benefit the community like rent for the prayer house, the Men's Study House, the *cheyder* for boys, and the town's ritual bath. We pay the salaries of our rabbi, our sons' teachers, and the one who performs ritual circumcisions. I am the head of Okup's Kahal."

Srolik gazed at his father's boots, listening.

"The Kahal also makes decisions on behalf of the Jews of the village," the leader said. "Today, we have a decision to make concerning you." Without telling Srolik more about the decision, the men started to argue with each other.

"He is almost nine years old," one stated as if this were a serious problem, "two years past the age to begin learning."

"It would please his righteous parents, Peace Be Upon Them, were the boy to learn," a second asserted, interrupted by a third who insisted, "The orphan should be put to useful work."

After further disagreement, a man appointed by the community council to oversee the affairs of orphans was called upon to rule. Rising from his chair and clearing his throat, the "Overseer" made a declaration in a booming voice as if Srolik were not standing right there.

"Srolik shall accompany the other boys to cheyder. Even if the child is not able to learn anything," the Overseer commanded, "better he go to school than roam unheeded among Polish woodcutters and farmers."

Srolik would have been happy to continue roaming, but no one asked him what he wanted.

IN THE SMALL CLASSROOM, Srolik squeezed together on a bench with four other boys sharing a prayer book. That it was upside down they learned only when the teacher passed by and turned it around. The students were told to look at the page before them. All Srolik could see were black flames dancing wildly as if they wanted to escape the flat page.

Morning after morning Srolik tried to see what the other students saw, then stopped trying. Instead, he listened to the beautiful melodies of the older boys praying, his gaze drawn to the single window in the cheyder beyond which the tall meadow grasses and trees prayed without words.

One morning, the teacher told a story about a father's sacrifice. Srolik felt as if he were walking right behind that father and son, watching Abraham lead a confused Isaac up the mountain. When the father raised his knife, commanded by God to kill his son, Srolik could not fight back his tears. He was sorry for Isaac, but more sorry for Abraham.

Even after Isaac was spared, Srolik couldn't stop crying.

The good people of Okup said that Srolik's saintly parents had sacrificed their lives for him. Since then, the villagers of Okup had made countless sacrifices on his behalf. *All this for a simpleton,* many complained. Why hadn't he been sacrificed on the day he was born, not his mother?

His father had never showed even a trace of regret that Srolik lived. Reb Eliezar told him that life is a gift from the *Ayn Sof,* the One Without End. He took care of Srolik as if Srolik was a gift.

What if, when the tinsmith's sons say Srolik is worthless, they are wrong?

IT WAS BECOMING HARDER for Srolik to remain still on the classroom bench. His mind wandered as if something was calling him beyond the walls of the cheyder to the forest.

One morning, his body followed. When the teacher ordered him to come back, Srolik's legs continued walking. In the woods, he found his way to the bank of a stream where he watched the water roll over boulders. He had no idea how much time had passed when he made his way back to his place on the bench.

In the days that followed, Srolik tried to refuse the forest, but its call was too strong. Soon, he was wandering out of the cheyder every morning. When he began to stay overnight among the trees, the smoldering feelings of the townspeople became an angry blaze.

"I have no patience left," Srolik heard his teacher report to the Overseer of orphans at the end of one morning's studies.

After that, Srolik stopped making his way to the small schoolhouse, and no one insisted any more that he study. He was rarely invited to eat and sleep in the homes of Okup's Jews. Srolik had begun spending time with Alta Bina.

~

BINA STRAIGHTENED, PRESSING HER HANDS INTO the small of her back. A fortnight had passed since she had first offered steaming broth to the boy rumored to be untamable, more animal than child.

It had only taken two days for him to draw closer and receive her offering. Since then, each morning, Bina prepared a soup enriched with herbs and roots, placing the clay bowl on a smooth boulder in the field that stretched between her cottage and the narrow river that flowed toward the broader Dneister. It pleased her that the boy came to eat.

Her cottage, little more than a hut, sat on a hill a few kilometers distance from where the rest of the Jews' homes huddled together in the shadow of a large citadel. Abandoned now, the citadel had been built by the Polish king to defend against Turkish invaders. But the fortress had failed to protect the village. Bina had been a young woman when the Ottoman Empire took control of the Podolia region in 1672, so unlike many in the village, she remembered Turkish troops conquering and ravaging Okup.

Were she not hunched by age and habit, the *Alta*, the Old One, as Bina was called, would tower over most in Okup, Jews and Polish citizens alike. Her white hair, covered by an old red kerchief, was never properly bound. Most hung down her back, the passing breezes weaving through it, giving her pleasure.

Bina knew she was considered mad and gifted, that she was both disdained and revered. The Okupniks said her mind was a moon only partially lit. But they sought her when the ones they loved were suffering. They came, or when too sick to walk, sent emissaries to her precarious hut, perched on the rise of an abundant meadow that yielded all manner of healing herbs and flowers.

That she was ridiculed did not matter to her. What mattered were the growing things: their roots, leaves, bark, their fragrances and powers.

When Bina trusted that the child would stay if she drew closer, she brought her own bowl out and sat on a tree stump a short distance from her door. She watched the boy.

Although he was surely quite hungry, the boy didn't devour the meager meal in a few gulps. Instead, he cupped his hands around the clay bowl, lifted it close to his face, and paused, letting the steam wash over him before bringing the rim to his lips. He sipped slowly, savoring the broth. Bina knew that a person could take more or less nourishment from food, according to his state of mind and heart. Maybe this was why the boy looked so healthy despite his modest, irregular fare. He was receiving all the goodness the food had to offer.

The child began to visit her more often and at unpredictable hours. He was no longer coming only for broth and stale bread.

THE LATE SPRING SUN still hung high in the sky when Bina motioned Srolik closer to where she was bent over a copper tub of soapy water. She gestured that he extend his arms to receive the wet fleece she'd been kneading into thick pieces of felted wool. She stood and led him to the screens woven from dried stalks, showing him how to spread the fleece to dry there. Silently, the boy began to help her.

Resting in the shade of a large oak, she let him take over her work. He lifted and spread the fleece slowly, with care. She was struck by his complete absorption in the task, not unlike how he ate.

As the boy lifted the last of the wet wool from the tub, Bina thought of the peasant woman who had brought the fleece in exchange for herbs that might heal her husband Kovel's relentless wheezing. The woman had confided that she sheared the fleece from an old ewe discarded by the *szlachcic*, the wealthy nobleman to whom her husband was indentured. She begged Bina not to tell anyone that she had come, saying "Kovel would refuse remedies coming from a Jew as poison, and would beat me for fetching them." Bina gave the timid Polish wife a decoction to help her husband, along with cuttings and seeds so the woman could grow the beneficial herbs herself rather than risk a future beating.

After Srolik helped Bina empty the tub, she led him to the black currant bushes that grew at the edge of her field. There he kneeled beside her, collecting them in a wooden bucket. When the Alta sat back on her knees to ease her spine, Srolik continued to pick each of the tiny berries as if nothing in the world existed but this single shrub and its delicate fruit.

Bina recalled the impatient *Kabbalist* who, a few years earlier, had also helped the Alta gather the tiny currants. The man, anxious to hasten the preparation of a tincture for his inflamed throat, had crushed most of the small berries between his large fingers, with few currants making their way whole into the clay bowl Bina had given him. Turning to watch Bina, he had asked how it was that she could pick the berries with such reverence "as if each were a letter in the ineffable Name."

Back in the hut as the currants boiled, the weary traveler had confided that for years he had studied the Kabbalistic practice of focusing on the individual letters of the divine names hoping to draw closer to God, but that he had never experienced the promised elevation of his spirit. Yet here was Bina, an illiterate herbalist, who seemed to have attained what he sought. Bina said nothing, continuing to measure the vodka needed for the man's tincture.

Now, she wondered what men such as this one might learn from this unusual boy.

SROLIK BEGAN to come each day during the hours the sun was overhead. He helped Bina gather leaves from the rosettes of young woad plants. From the blue woad leaves they made indigo dye in which Bina then soaked the felted wool.

Together the old woman and the boy gathered roots, leaves, and flowers from the flourishing plants. Bina taught the orphan about the simple dandelion whose flower, leaf, and root were all of benefit. She introduced him to plants and shrubs clustered on the riverbank and to those hidden in the cool, moist shade of the forest. Sometimes Bina would call their names—milk thistle, goosegrass, meadowsweet—and speak of their healing properties. Srolik listened.

When the days became shorter and the air cooler, Alta Bina instructed Srolik to lower himself into a hole more than half his height deep and as wide as he was tall. As a young woman, she had taken weeks to dig the hole, lining it with rows of logs to keep its walls from caving in. It had become painful to squeeze herself down into the space, so Srolik received from her hands what was to be stored for the winter. Doing as she told, he placed the turnips, beets, and white radishes on the hard packed soil, the carrots in bins of sand. The roots of cabbages harvested with their outer leaves were attached with hay rope to logs laid across the top of the hole. This would then be covered with layers of straw and packed snow.

"Burdock," she stated, holding the dark brown hairy root in both her hands like a sacred offering before handing it over to its winter nest. "For diseases of the kidney and to remove boils from the eyelids."

Srolik did not ask any questions, nor did he repeat her words. But Bina knew he was taking in the knowledge she offered.

As the cold began to kneel with them in the field, Bina led Srolik to a stack of firewood left at the forest's edge by a Polish woodcutter in exchange for a compress for his daughter's lungs. The hunched woman and the boy carried the birch and oak logs closer to the hut and stacked them in a small shed nearby.

Bina invited the boy into her hut for shelter from the winter. When they were not working or sleeping, Srolik sat on a stool across from the tilted chair in which she liked to sit. That three-legged chair was where Bina's young mother had nursed her until the day the Cossacks attacked. Bina had been told the story by the old woman, some said a sorceress, who had saved Bina's life and later taught her the ways of the growing things. When Bina was old enough, the sorceress Henda told her what had happened to Bina's parents.

Bina's mother had been raped and murdered in a Cossack raid and the infant Bina left to die in the devastated hut. Henda, coming to visit with herbs for the new mother, found the infant just barely alive. She fed Bina the milk of a goat that had survived the attack. Then she went with the child in search of her father. Bina's father's body was found with the bodies of other men that had been rounded up and mutilated in the center of the village. Henda kept the infant, feeding her goat's milk until she could eat the softened wheat that Henda chewed first. As Bina grew, Henda shared her knowledge of the plant world as willingly as she shared other sustenance. The time came when the sorceress sent Bina to restore the hut long abandoned by her parents and to harvest what was growing wild there.

Bina and the orphaned child had more in common than he might imagine. Perhaps it would comfort the boy to know this.

"Srolik," she called his name into their shared silence. "Like you, I never got to know my mother. Nor did I know my father. You and I were both left without parents when very young."

"Did you know my mother and father?"

It was the first time she heard the boy speak. He was looking directly at her for the first time, too. Bina kept his gaze. The earnestness in the child's eyes pierced her heart as few things did anymore.

"Did you know them?" he repeated.

"I did not know them well, Srolik, but I knew of them. I can tell you what I know, if you wish."

The boy nodded.

"Your father Reb Eliezar was captured in a raid by invading Cossack horsemen, the same raid in which my mother and father were killed."

"Why?" he blurted out.

Bina wondered if he was asking why the Cossacks captured his father or why they killed her parents? Or was his question why the Cossacks raided in the first place? Bina realized the answer to all was the same.

"Most of the Cossacks were runaway peasants, angry at the szlachta, the Polish noblemen who were their masters. These peasants, farmers who were little more than slaves, fell prey to leaders who promised them freedom and then used them for their own ends. The peasants were led to see Jews as the enemy—"

"Why?" Srolik inserted. "Why the Jews?"

"The landowners employed Jews to manage their estates and still do. Jews are put in charge of collecting taxes for the noblemen, enforcing their laws, and implementing their whims. Jews are easier targets for the peasants than the szlachta, whose manors and palaces were built as fortresses."

"Reb Eliezar was not one of the Jews who managed the noblemen's land, granaries, or taverns," Bina continued. "But this didn't matter to the embittered Cossacks. When the horsemen rode into Okup, your father, instead of fleeing or hiding, remained to protect other innocent Jews. The enraged Cossacks seized him. But instead of killing him, the Cossacks took him captive, probably because of the courage he showed. The Cossacks were known to sell their captives to the Turks. They must have thought a man like your father would be worth a lot."

Srolik lowered his head. Bina could feel him taking in every word.

"Your dear mother Sarah, despite her neighbors' discouragement, never lost faith that her beloved Eliezar would return. She went daily, no matter the weather, to stand on the banks of Dniester River in a patch of sun kind enough to find her. There she would wait for your father."

"After *thirty* years, Srolik, your father returned. He was dressed in a brocade caftan bound by a silk sash embroidered with tulips. All but his cherished Sarah were shocked."

"All marveled at his story as we learned that Reb Eliezar had been sold by the Cossacks as a slave to a vizier, a high ranking political advisor to the sultan. In the vizier's service, your father had a number of dreams, foretelling attacks and revealing strategies for victory, which he conveyed to his master. When it became known by the sultan that your father was the source of the vizier's wise advice, Sultan Mehmed made Eliezar his trusted advisor."

Srolik lifted his gaze and stared openly at Bina.

"How your good father survived and was able to return to Okup is a mystery and a miracle—which was followed by the great miracle of your mother bearing a child so late in her years. You, Srolik, were the fruit of your parents' faith."

The orphan's eyes fill with tears.

"Srolik, you are the fulfillment of your parents' love."

〜

HEAVY SNOWS gradually bent and buried the dried stalks left in the field. Bina and Srolik worked from dawn to dusk at her hearth or at the unsteady oak table.

She taught the boy to prepare tinctures from herbs mixed with vodka, to make infusions and decoctions from leaves, roots, and bark. She guided him in making poultices of crushed comfrey and peppermint oil to draw out infections, syrups of boiled fennel seed mixed with honey from the hives they tended, and salves using pine resin and beeswax.

These were powers she respected and knew how to release. She knew when and how to plant and to harvest, how to crush, boil, and combine the growing things with each other to bring healing. Even when the villagers believed death was certain, they came for relief in their last days. Just so, earnest Aryeh the blacksmith had come, tender and mournful, hoping to find healing for his wife Dvorah.

When Aryeh first came, it was to save his cherished wife. He pleaded with the old woman as if she were the Creator herself.

"She must live," he insisted, tears flowing freely. Nothing was more important than keeping his Dvorah from the grasp of the Angel of Death. As if such a thing were possible.

The Alta recognized the blacksmith's grief, but she knew she could not make miracles beyond the powers bestowed upon the herbs and plants by the Creator. Bina had stared into Aryeh's moist eyes. Not everyone could receive the old woman's gaze. Aryeh had.

"We can try to help her suffer less," the Alta told him. "This much we can do."

Before taking ill with pneumonia, Dvorah had come often to the Alta's hut. The dark-haired beauty brought a sweet noodle pudding one week and someone's feverish child the next. She came seeking poultices to soothe the burns her beloved husband endured at his irons, and remedies for neighbors too prideful to be seen approaching the old one's hut.

Dvorah had brought her newborn daughter Rifka to Bina, the seventh week after the girl's birth, eager to place the child in the Alta's furrowed arms. The women exchanged no words. Bina had cooed softly into

Rifka's tiny ear, then dipped her bony fingers into a clay urn from which she drew several drops of fragrant oil, which she rubbed gently into the baby's crown. Someone else might have been frightened or even angered by Bina's actions. Instead, Dvorah had expressed her gratitude—with her eyes and her silence. Bina knew that were Dvorah alive now, she, too, would take an interest in this wandering orphan.

After their work, the boy slept on a straw mat near the hearth, while Bina, who had grown accustomed to no more than three or four hours of sleep, leaned into the circle of light cast by her oil lamp and made sleeves of indigo felt.

When winter lifted, the woman and the boy worked side-by-side, turning over the yielding earth to prepare for planting.

SROLIK TRUSTED Alta Bina. He believed her when she said he was the answer to his mother's prayer rather than a curse.

He watched the Alta place seeds tenderly in the ground, speaking softly to each one, telling it to grow and offer itself for healing. When the Alta harvested, before removing a single leaf, plucking a berry, or pulling a root, she spoke to the plant. Each time she greeted a plant—even the third chamomile of two already greeted—she thanked it for the blessing it would bring for the tailor's headaches, the butcher's son's chest pain, or the lonely widow's indigestion. She never stopped thanking the growing things, no matter how many times she lowered her stiff body in front of yet another barbed and windswept shrub. The Alta took no living thing for granted. At her side, Srolik learned that each part of creation blesses the world, even the beetles nibbling holes in the leaves of the Alta's cherished plants.

The last time Srolik had felt such tenderness was when his father had stroked his face during one of their last sleepless nights. He had not remembered his father's touch until he watched Alta Bina bend over her newly planted seeds in their narrow furrows. He watched her wizened hands become agile, as they held and placed delicate seeds. The Alta was given different hands for planting.

Bina and Srolik celebrated his becoming a bar mitzvah one morning in her meadow. Some might judge it wrong, maybe even a sin, that he was honoring his coming of age as a Jew in a field with a white-haired woman, rather than in the synagogue among a quorum of men. But there was no one here to judge.

"Remember as you grow older, " the Alta instructed him, "your duty is to care for living things as if you were God's eyes and hands." Then she toasted him, both of them raising cups of sweet beet juice.

How could he not feel that his life had value?

SROLIK HAD COMPLETED three rounds of planting and harvesting with Alta Bina when autumn again took summer's place. He sensed, even before she told him, that it would be time for him to leave her soon.

One chilly morning, after Bina had finished her steamy groats, she drew close to him, putting her large hand on his shoulder.

"I have arranged for you travel to Horodenka, Srolik. A man named Ibrahim will be expecting you there."

He did not ask the Alta to explain more.

"Ibrahim," she repeated the name.

A week later, wearing the felted indigo jacket she had made him that fit him perfectly, he was ready to leave. Bina handed him a woolen satchel containing bread, carrots, and seeds.

"Among the seeds," she said, smiling, "are those that can be seen and those that cannot."

One of those seeds, he believed, was a new awe for the healing power that may be hidden in the least expected place.

Crossing the meadow under an overcast sky, he looked back once to see the Alta kneeling forward, bowing to the fragrant lavender. He did not need to be at her side to know her pleasure. When she lifted her head for an instant to look in his direction, he knew this would be the last time they would see each other.

2

It rained heavily on the way to Horodenka, causing the horse to lose its footing, which woke the wagon driver from his half slumber to find Srolik still sitting next to him.

Earlier, the farmer had been surprised by Srolik's strength as he helped the man load the wagon. They stacked bag after bag of grain that would be used for making schnapps in one of the many breweries belonging to the nobleman Potocki, who owned Horodenka.

Thankfully, the bags were covered with boards now, so they would not spoil in the rain. The farmer and Srolik, however, were not as well protected. The autumn rain penetrated their clothes, and its chill entered their bones. Hunching against the heavy rain, neither complained.

Srolik was taken by surprise when the farmer slid out of his woolen coat and with one hand on the reins, wrapped the coat around Srolik's shoulders.

"Take this," the farmer said, the coat already in place.

Srolik wanted to give the coat back, feeling no more worthy of warmth than the farmer. But he did not shrug off the coat. Something so natural in the tired man's determined action, like a father protecting his son, led Srolik to leave the coat where the man had placed it. The wagon driver sat up straighter, facing the rain resolutely.

This time, it was Srolik awakened from sleep when the wagon finally reached its destination, the shelter of a large granary where their cargo was to be stored. Srolik returned the farmer's coat and helped him unload. The two bid each other farewell with silent nods. Srolik carried

the farmer's unexpected kindness with him along with the Alta's gifts
and a vague sense of being guided on his journey.

Srolik recognized quickly that Horodenka was larger and more prosperous than Okup, its roads traversed by more carts, its goods and stalls
more plentiful, with a greater number of them appearing permanent
rather than set up and taken down weekly.

It was just a few days before the new moon marking the *Rosh Hashonah*, the celebration of the New Year. The rich and less rich crowded
together in the marketplace shopping for holiday dates, pecans, pickled
herring, and the versatile new vegetable known as "potato." For the few
who could afford it, there was the extravagance of silver candlesticks or
fine quality goose feathers. Not only coins but ample patience was needed
by those crowded around the ritual slaughterer in hopes of a tender
chicken or a good, thick piece of beef. Those awaiting bones for the soup
of the poor required even more patience.

Srolik wondered if all this excitement and activity distracted from
the seriousness of inward preparation. His teacher at the cheyder in Okup
described the High Holy Days of *Rosh Hashonah, Yom Kippur*, and the
Ten Days of Repentance between them, as "the season of awe," the time
to repent for having turned away from God. Srolik had wondered where
one could possibly turn that was *away* from God? His father had taught
him that the *Shechinah,* God's Presence, is everywhere. But Srolik had
said nothing to challenge his teacher's words. Instead, Srolik began to ask
questions silently of a presence he increasingly felt with him. He liked to
imagine it was the presence of his father, although often it felt unfamiliar. But even then, the presence was comforting. Answers did not come
in words, but in feelings, a sense of things, like a gentle urge to move
towards or away from someone or something.

Srolik was grateful for the bustle of the marketplace, knowing that
with visitors arriving to be with family for the holiday, he would likely go
unnoticed. He wandered among the throngs of people, his pockets empty

of coins with which to purchase onions, parsnips, or a cabbage, not to mention having no place to cook them.

Srolik spotted a bright-eyed young boy, one hand holding down the cap perched over his curls, his other hand grasped by an older boy, probably his brother, who guided him through the current of townspeople. When a sudden gust of wind blew the cap from his head, peals of laughter erupted as he took off in chase of his cap.

"Don't leave us behind, Samuel!" a tall, slender woman called, laughing with the boy. "Gedaliah, follow him!" Honey-colored curls escaped her scarf, framing her face. Was it the angle of the afternoon sun or the woman's own radiance Srolik saw?

A peasant boy pulled two scrawny goats in front of Srolik, who backed out of their path. When he looked up again, the woman and the boys were gone.

Srolik felt carried by the undulating, thrusting waves of industrious citizens. A momentary parting of the crowd in front of the baker's stall revealed an array of sweet pastries. Surprisingly, his body did not clamor for one. Srolik had become able, despite his hunger, to witness food without being overcome by desire. In Okup, people had reprimanded Srolik for not showing normal, sensible yearnings. They admonished him for being drawn instead by foolish, even dangerous desires like his yearning to walk in the forest.

"Here, please."

The voice was sweet and came out of nowhere. Srolik saw the small palm extended with three figs in it before he saw the girl. Her head was level with his heart, beating a little quicker now than a moment ago. She urged the figs in her palm towards him.

"Take them. Please. My name is Rifka and my aunt just bought them."

For an instant Srolik hesitated before stretching his arm towards her. He took and ate one fig slowly, looking at her. The girl was perhaps six years old with deep brown eyes and dark hair tucked under a white woolen shawl that covered her head and shoulders. Her complexion was dark, her cheeks apple red. She smiled and did not look away the moment that Srolik accepted the first fig. Srolik did not look away either.

Despite the whirl around her, the girl did not move until Srolik had finished the last of the figs. Then she nodded her goodbye and disappeared, swallowed up by the sea of villagers that had briefly yielded her up out of its swell.

As Srolik continued to ease his way through the crowded marketplace, he passed an elegantly dressed spice trader questioning a fishmonger about where he might pray on the holiday. The fishmonger's lack of response made Srolik wonder if the man was deaf. No sooner had Srolik thought this, than the fishmonger looked directly at Srolik—his eyes so piercing Srolik looked away and rested his gaze on the glint of fish scales in the bright afternoon sun.

"The *shul* is not far from here," a neighboring vendor called out as she gestured towards the far edge of the marketplace beyond its bustle. "Down that cobblestone street. But be prepared, kind gentleman: Horodenka's synagogue is a humble one. Ours is a small wooden building not crafted in the fashion of large synagogues you might have seen somewhere like Warsaw, where even the banisters of the women's balcony have been ornately carved."

"We Jews of Horodenka consider ourselves lucky to have a place to pray at all," she bellowed, tossing a cabbage to a customer. "Our request for a House of Prayer was granted only three years ago by the nobleman Potocki who owns this town. You're welcome, of course, to pray with us. You can find lodging in a small inn near the shul, leased from Potocki by a Jew. Say Zelda sent you, for what it's worth."

The few to whom Srolik spoke the name of Ibrahim showed no sign of recognition, perhaps unable to hear him clearly above the din of the marketplace. In the meantime, Srolik would find a place to sleep—not under the innkeeper's roof like the wealthy spice merchant but under the stars. He would, however, accept the welcome to Horodenka's shul.

L EYA HOPED THAT SHE WOULD HAVE TIME TO FINISH the repair of Dovid's boot before closing the cobbler stall early for the holiday. She was relieved that it was no longer unusual for the citizens of Horodenka to see a woman cobbler bent over the stitching of a new sole to one of their worn shoes. At first some of the villagers had resented and even feared Leya taking the place of her dead husband Ber. What was she trying to prove, they insisted, by defying tradition and ignoring the reasonable limits of a woman?

But Leya was not to be deterred. Gradually the villagers began to bring their shoes and boots to her, as they had brought them to her husband. Some came out of pity, others with respect. All had to be patient while her skills rose to match her determination.

Leya sang as she worked, often not hearing a customer enter until he called her name or cleared his throat loudly, as Zelda the cabbage vendor did now, waiting for Leya to notice her with yet another worn out boot in hand.

"Zelda, I did not hear…"

"Yes, of course, Leyalla. How could you hear me? They say I am the loudest woman in Horodenka, but here are you singing louder than all the women in the synagogue wrapped into one shameless voice. What if it were one of our distinguished community leaders like Reb Wolf who had entered while you sing your heart out? *Oy*, poor men, forbidden to hear a woman's voice raised in prayer and song!"

"To any man entering, Zelda, I would say the same: 'What is it that needs mending today, kind gentleman?' As I will ask of you, dear woman, who wears through more than any woman's quota of soles, while digging, plowing, and tending your fine vegetables—not to mention peddling them at such favorable prices."

Zelda smiled an almost toothless grin at the one she called her favorite shoemaker, and exchanged her overworked boots for a restored pair. Leya's good-natured humor, uninhibited singing, and oddly enough, her disinterest in gossip, seemed to give Zelda pause.

Zelda had proven herself not only the loudest of the vegetable hawkers in the marketplace, but also the most irrepressible of the town's gos-
sips. It was somewhat astonishing to Leya that while Zelda made so much
noise, she managed to hear pieces of stories from lives all over Horodenka. She kept these tales piled up in her mind like the beets, onions,
and cabbages stacked high for her customers—only the stories she gave
away cheap. Leya, unlike most others, never asked for these bargain tales,
which made Zelda want to offer them even more.

"Leyalla, have you seen the stranger?"

Leya shook her head, wiping her hands on the heavy leather apron
that she had inherited from Ber. It was her habit not to look at Zelda
when the hawker embarked on one of her unwanted revelations. Instead,
Leya busied herself, hoping the *yenta* would excuse her and continue on
her way.

"Little more than a boy he is, but already as odd as the horse that,
since the day its mother was shot, wanders near my field like it doesn't
know if it's coming or going. This horse doesn't eat like a normal animal
or sleep like one—yet, strong *it is*, and impossible to harness."

Leya sighed, wishing Zelda might take her tales of the misfortune of
others and turn them under the soil with the dried stalks of her harvested
crops.

But Zelda persisted.

"The rumors from his native Okup follow him like a swarm of flies
around rotting fruit. I heard that his mother died with him in her arms
the very day he was born, having conceived him in the dusk of her life. His
father died soon after, leaving him nothing but a pinch of madness—and
maybe more than a pinch. I saw him yesterday, wandering not far from
where I was harvesting cabbages. He walked at the edge of the field with
his head down, probably afraid I would see the madness in his eyes. But
the simple boy cannot hide who he is. Is that what he thought when he
came here? I thought to call to him. But why? What conversation could I
have with one who doesn't speak?"

Leya was listening now, her curiosity and compassion sparked by the mention of a child. It was Leya's habit never to ask Zelda questions that might encourage her to adorn her "stolen goods." But this time Leya couldn't resist, asking without lifting her head from her work.

"What does the boy look like, Zelda?"

"He wears a woolen jacket, an unusual blue that changes like the sky. And boots—you, the cobbler maven should only see them—tied together with rope, which, of course, does not help with the holes. In a hard rain, his feet must swim. His hair is thick and honey-colored like yours and Samuel's, but redder, like buckwheat honey. It waves down over his shoulders as if never touched by a scissor. I couldn't see his face well; I think he's a little older than your Gedaliah, twelve or thirteen maybe. He has thick wrists and big hands. The time I saw him in the marketplace, it was his neck that surprised me—wide, as if he's used to working hard."

Leya stopped stitching, staring down at the leather without seeing it. Zelda's description confirmed what Leya had begun to wonder.

Leya had glimpsed the boy the day Samuel nearly lost his cap in the marketplace, when she had gone with the boys and Rifka in search of figs and other delicacies for their holiday table. She had seen him again the following day on her way back alone from the marketplace where she'd procured leather from a Warsaw skin trader who finally deemed her a reliable risk for buying on credit. Her market basket swinging, Leya strode quickly, enjoying the invigorating chill that hinted at winter. Ahead of her, she noticed a peasant child leaning intently over what she guessed might be a tower of stones he'd been constructing. The bright afternoon light played in the waves of his long hair. Leya put her basket down to tighten her scarf under her chin.

When the boy shifted his position, she saw what lay before him.

It was a large bird, a stork lying awkwardly on its back with its wings splayed apart. One of them, which appeared to be bleeding, looked partially torn from the bird's body. Leya saw blood on the boy's hands. She wondered if the creature were still alive until she heard its faint squawk.

It was common for storks to injure themselves on the thatch of cottage roofs. But it was not common for someone, especially a child, to stop to tend to one.

Leya watched the boy reach under his jacket to locate a small pouch that hung from a rope at his waist. He drew from it a tin containing a salve that he applied gently to the injury while murmuring something Leya could not hear. His fingers moved, nimbly and confidently, as he tenderly ministered to the bird. After tucking the salve back into its pouch, the child held his hands palms down just inches above the torn wing. He bent forward, closer to the bird. Leya wasn't able to make out the words of the boy's whispered song or if there were words at all. As she listened, she had the sensation of something exceedingly delicate being brushed along her spine—a sublime caress. Leya did not move.

She saw a subtle tremor travel through the bird's body, followed by a barely perceptible attempt to flutter its wings. The movement of the stork's wings gradually became more vigorous. The boy, arched over the bird's body, continued his whispered incantations. Leya watched with amazement as the stork struggled to stand, wobbling on its slender hinged legs and looking dazed.

The bird took a tentative step towards the child. The unintelligible, soothing utterances that Leya could not help but associate with prayer continued steadily.

With a forceful flap of its wings, the stork rose into the air, landing only a short distance from where it had taken off. Then the stork lifted itself again, this time gradually beginning to soar overhead until it was lost to sight.

If the boy sensed Leya's presence, he did not look at her.

Leya had picked up her basket and continued making her way towards the cobbling stall, her gait slower than before. She did not look back at the boy, but continued to hear his soft prayerful sounds long after. She would see the child again, she hoped, if only to offer him boots.

Now, as Zelda prattled on, Leya continued cutting the leather for the new boots she planned to make for Gedaliah's friend Dovid in time for the start of school. Leya would need to work steadily. Classes would begin not long after the holidays.

"Leyalla, I finally did call out to the strange orphan when he passed near my plot of vegetables. I motioned that I was leaving him something to eat. *Don't be ashamed to take*, I hollered to him, in case he could understand me. He didn't show that he heard, but later the few radishes, carrots, and crisp green beans were gone."

After Zelda finally left her shop, Leya's thoughts focused on the child. How would he sustain himself? Though he seemed self-sufficient, he was after all only a child. It was not likely a family in Horodenka would take him in, hard as it was for laboring villagers to feed and shelter their own children. Leya hoped that the boy had at least by now been directed to the village poorhouse for shelter and food. Pushing her steel needle through the leather of Dovid's boot, Leya wondered how she might render the child some measure of the tenderness she had seen him bestow upon the injured stork.

Leya looked up. Absorbed in thought, she had not realized how close the sundown was and with it the start of the holiday. She must set down her stitching along with her thoughts and head home to her cottage.

She bolted the door of her stall behind her and hastened the kilometer distance to her cottage. Aryeh would be arriving soon from Okup. Since his wife Dvorah's death, her brother and niece Rifka had been coming from Okup as often as they could to spend the Sabbath and holy days with Leya, Gedaliah, and Samuel. Rifka, who usually traveled back and forth with her father, had remained in Horodenka for the past two weeks. Leya, the boys, and Rifka had been preparing the cottage and cooking special foods for the New Year holiday all week.

THE MOMENT Aryeh entered, he delighted in the irresistible fragrances that greeted him: noodle kugel seasoned with the cinnamon obtained from a Turkish spice merchant, a bean and barley stew, its aroma blending with the round golden bread Rifka had helped to braid, and Samuel's favorite: sweet pastries coated in a glaze of mahogany-colored honey. The food was arrayed on Leya's special lace tablecloth spread over the long walnut table that filled much of this central room. He could imagine Rifka, Leya, and the boys diligently working at the hearth, the dry sink, and the large table to prepare this holiday feast. But where were they now? Normally, Rifka and Samuel would be climbing his legs in greeting.

Leya, so still that he had not even noticed her at the hearth, rose now and came to embrace Aryeh, a mischievous gleam in her eyes. Samuel's laughter came next as he jumped down from the makeshift couch in the corner, Aryeh's bed when he visited.

Then, as if timed, Rifka emerged from behind the curtains of the sleeping alcove—one of two alcoves that extended like bumps off the central room, each large enough for a narrow bed or two, a chamber pot, and small cabinet. Only after she had intently set down the brass menorah she carried that had belonged to Leya and Aryeh's mother did she run into her father's open arms.

The only one missing, Gedaliah, came through the front door moments later, arms filled with wood that Aryeh helped him unload.

At the setting of the sun, Leya, with Rifka at her side, stood before the three-branched menorah and lit the candles. Leya slowly recited the blessing that heralded the start of the holiday, waiting for Rifka to repeat the words. Then Leya made wide arcs with her arms pulling the light of the , the Sacred Presence, into her heart before bowing her head into her hands. Now she would whisper her own private prayer, which Aryeh was close enough to hear: *May we know Your Love even in our losses.*

SROLIK ENTERED Horodenka's modest house of prayer and stood against the back wall, directing his eyes downward. He knew no Jew would be excluded from today's service regardless of how poorly garbed or ignorant he was. The straight-backed pews were crowded, the room filled with the steady rich drone of prayer. At the eastern wall, a tall wooden ark housed the Torah scrolls. Srolik neither held a prayer book nor joined in the prayers.

As the collective murmur washed over him, Srolik felt the intense longing in one voice among the others. He knew its source—not from whose body and throat the prayer issued, but rather the condition of the heart filled to breaking with sorrow. That he could know this surprised him.

LEYA SAT with the other women in their own section of the House of Prayer, a separate room resembling a low-ceilinged shed built onto the wooden shul as if an afterthought. A few boards had been removed from the wall between this room and the larger men's area, which allowed the women to hear the men's prayers. Leya could not see her brother or sons, but she thought she spotted an indigo sleeve then the bowed face of the boy who had healed the stork.

Mothers and daughters crowded together as tightly as they could fit, the youngest on laps. Rather than praying from the official Hebrew prayer book, the few women who could read prayed from small booklets of Yiddish prayers written by women for women, supplications arising from their daily life and struggles. Others murmured prayers they had memorized, careful to keep their voices low, since it was deemed a distraction for a woman's voice to be heard by a man absorbed in prayer.

Leya had learned to read Hebrew from her grandfather, so she held the same book as the men held, the booklet of women's Yiddish prayers tucked between its pages. Rifka peered eagerly into the prayer book that her aunt held open, waiting for the strange code to reveal itself to her.

"*Shalom Aleynu*, Peace be upon us," Leya whispered into Rifka's ear, moving her niece's thick black hair aside in a gentle sweep with one hand, and pointing to the words in the prayer book with the other.

"*Shalom Aleynu*," Rifka repeated.

Rifka's appetite for learning reminded Leya of her own as a girl. Like Rifka, she had lost her mother early. When years later, Leya's beloved husband Ber was thrown from his wagon to an instant death, she was reminded of how easily those she loved could be taken away. She might have been overcome by her grief had it not been for her sons, Samuel, then a newborn, and Gedaliah, five years old; her duties as a mother kept her from sinking into despair. When her dear sister-in-law Dvorah had died, two years after Ber, Leya's support of her grieving brother and niece buoyed not only Aryeh and Rifka, but Leya as well.

Leya closed her eyes now and let herself be rocked by the women's whispered prayers, weaving with the men's voices. Suddenly, she was curled again in her grandfather's ample lap on a chilly, predawn morning. A blanket over the woolen prayer shawl was wrapped around them both. He swayed as he prayed, rocking Leya gently as he did, not forgetting her even when he seemed to forget everything else. He became lost in melodies that Leya imagined would carry the two of them away to a place without danger.

"Is it almost time, *Tanta* Leya?" Rifka's question summoned Leya from her reverie.

Aryeh, although not a resident of the town, had been offered the honor of blowing the ram's horn, the *shofar,* in honor of his brother-in-law Ber. Ber's muscular build and extraordinary vitality had made him a natural, chosen year after year to blow the shofar on the High Holidays. While Aryeh did not have the apparent confidence or the muscles of his brother-in-law, he had shown himself capable of many vigorously short and long blasts from the curved ram's horn.

Wearing the customary long white robe over his clothes, Aryeh climbed the steps to the *bimah,* the raised platform in the center of the synagogue, and received the ram's horn from the rabbi. He positioned himself facing the Holy Ark, its velvet curtains pulled aside to reveal two Torah scrolls. Each was dressed in embroidered velvet and embossed silver crowns covered the scroll's handles. The time had come to awaken the slumbering souls of the Jews: to wake the dead and free them to move on, but above all to stir the living.

Aryeh picked up the horn and put it to his lips, waiting for the rabbi to intone the name of the sound.

"Tekiyah," the rabbi called out.

A long sustained blast on the horn, ending abruptly.

"Truah."

A moan from the shofar.

"Shvarim."

A piercing series of staccato blasts.

"Tekiyah." Again the plaintive wail.

Finally, it was time for the last, the *Gedolah,* or "big" *Tekiyah* that only few men could blow and hold. Those who could often trembled as they did.

"Tekiyah Gedolah," the rabbi intoned.

Rifka drew in her breath just as her father did, and took hold of Leya's hand.

A sustained blasting wail emanated without cease from the horn—penetrating deeply enough to shatter the strongest walls of disbelief.

"MAY GOD give you strength," echoed among the men, as one-by-one they shook Aryeh's hand on his way back to his seat.

After the service was over, the handshakes continued.

"From your mouth into God's ears," Levi the soap maker said.

The milkman, whose humor was delivered daily along with the milk, slapped Aryeh on the back, "May God give you good health, Reb Okupnik, and send you to live with us in Horodenka. We need another loud mouth."

The boy that Aryeh had glimpsed in the back of the shul walked past him now. He was somehow familiar in his blue jacket, his long hair the color of honey pouring out from under his small cap and hiding much of his lowered face. Then Aryeh remembered.

This was the son of Sarah and Eliezar.

When after Dvorah's death Aryeh had gone to help Alta Bina chop and carry wood, the old woman, who usually said little, had talked about the boy. She said that Dvorah would have recognized something in him because of her ability to see goodness even when disguised. Then

Bina, looking across the field, said: "That one has set out on a journey to discover *and to reveal* what is hidden."

The words had not made sense to Aryeh then, nor did they now.

"Father!"

Rifka was calling his name and running towards him. Aryeh set down his ruminations, lifted Rifka, and spun her.

He was relieved and grateful that his sister and daughter had consented to his suggestion that for now Rifka remain in Horodenka and live with her aunt instead of traveling between Okup and Horodenka. Praise God, no danger had come to them on the roads between the villages, but the risks of such travel were not to be ignored. Although Leya worked all day, her cobbler stall was a more hospitable place for Rifka than where Aryeh toiled at the heat of his forge. Rifka would benefit more from being in Leya's company than surrounded by men in Okup—friendly men, yes, but always preoccupied with their troubles, which they regularly cursed. Most important, Rifka would not be surrounded by Aryeh's grief, which accompanied him like his shadow.

He should be free of his sorrow by now, he knew. The shy tailor in town had taken a new wife not even two years after losing his first, and regularly counseled Aryeh to do the same. But although almost three years had passed since Dvorah had been taken from them, Aryeh could not even imagine marrying again, even though the opportunity—as some thought of it—had presented itself.

The widow Yitta with four sons and no daughters showed great affection for Rifka, inviting her from the heat and soot of Aryeh's work into her small house where hot tea and sweet rolls were waiting for Aryeh when he came for his daughter.

On one of his visits to Horodenka, Aryeh had confided in Leya about Yitta's attentions. Leya, feigning the wide gait and affections of the overly friendly widow, had waddled over to Aryeh and teased him with a broad seductive smile.

"Oh, gentle blacksmith with such strong hands," Leya pronounced with exaggerated sincerity, stroking his cheek, "You have not yet been a widower as long as I have been a widow. There has not been enough time for your coals to cool."

It was impossible for Aryeh not to laugh.

"A kind man like you," she continued, "could be a jewel in a woman's crown. So, my *good, good* friend, when the time comes that you are ready to end your loneliness and give your dear Rifka a mother—who God knows could never replace your Dvorah, *Peace be Upon Her*—do not forget the widow Yitta who keeps a steady fire in her hearth."

His sister Leya seemed able to touch his wound the way no one could, whether with compassion or tender humor. And Aryeh felt more hope of it healing when she did.

There is no allotted time for grieving, Leya had said so many times.

But despite his sister's consolation, Aryeh felt shame and even fear that his grief might never leave him. And if he did not overcome this grief, what kind of father would he be to Rifka? It would not be easy to be apart from Rifka between visits to Horodenka, but he knew that she would be well cared for and that she would learn at her aunt's side. As busy as Leya was, she had promised to teach Rifka to read. He would feel Rifka's absence, yes, but how much sweeter the Sabbath when they re-united.

At sundown, concluding the holiday, Aryeh would return to Okup alone.

RIFKA WALKED beside her father to the wagon that was bound for Okup, her tanta Leya a short distance behind them.

"Would the sun burn my hands if I held it?" Rifka knew the answer but asked anyway, pretending to reach for the glowing orb to stop it from gliding down behind the rows of black trees. For a little while after her mother had died, her father had continued to bring her to the hill of the abandoned fortress in Okup where they watched the sky change colors as if it was undressing and dressing itself in different gowns. Rifka would be wrapped in the thick, blue shawl that had been her mother's favorite, a gift from Alta Bina, the old woman with silken white hair who lived by the woods and brewed healing teas. But her father had stopped taking Rifka to watch the sun set. Perhaps it saddened him to think of her mother, who, bright like the sun, had disappeared forever, not just until the next morning.

"If the sun were the warmth of your cheeks, that would be the perfect temperature," her father said, gathering her up and pressing his face against hers.

Watching her father ride out of Horodenka with the other tradesmen, Rifka touched her finger to her cheek, hoping to find one of his hidden tears.

3

In the crowded marketplace, Leya knelt to help retrieve the rolling onions an old woman had dropped. Leya was surprised to find the boy Srolik on his knees too, helping to gather up the onions. When the youth saw Leya, a smile formed on his lips and in his piercing blue eyes.

By the time they were upright again, an idea had hatched itself in Leya's mind about how to help the stranger—and not only him.

What if he, who must be at least thirteen, were to lead the village boys, some as young as five, to their morning study each day? Two kilometers and a small forest separated the boys' small schoolhouse from the Jews' other communal buildings. The community would have preferred the cheyder to be closer. But when the Polish town magistrate offered to rent the Jews the deceased coppersmith's shed, Reb Wolf, the head of the Kahal, gratefully signed the lease. If Srolik were to accompany the younger boys, he could ensure their safety. Leya drew closer and shared her idea with Srolik. He nodded silently.

Now Leya would have to convince the Kahal, the handful of prominent Jews elected by their brethren to administer the Jewish community and report to the Polish authorities. She hoped they would agree to her plan for the boy and in return would yield him just a few *groschen* from the communal taxes. But first Leya would confide her idea to her dear friend Gittel. Leya knew that some of Horodenka's Jews were confused by and even fearful of Srolik's behavior. If her closest friend said no to the proposal, there was little chance that the other villagers, much less the Jews' governing council, would accept it.

A TAUT ROPE of silence stretched between the friends within the whitewashed walls of Gittel's small cottage. Leya had shared her idea, but Gittel, as yet, had said nothing. Leya sat on the short, three-legged stool that Jacob had made, peeling spirals of potato skin. These she dropped into a pail balanced between her linen-draped knees.

It was rare for the two friends to share silence. Dovid and Nessa had gone with their father Jacob to deliver a wheel for a cart. Gittel's youngest daughter Tanya, exhausted from her ceaseless attempts to walk, had fallen asleep at her mother's breast. She now slept peacefully in the wooden cradle, also crafted before it had become difficult for Jacob to manage his tools. With Jacob and the children gone, it would be some time before the cottage was full of voices again.

Leya cast a glance at Gittel before reaching into the barrel of cold water for another potato. Leya had introduced the potato to Gittel, who had been hesitant to use it, shortly after a Warsaw merchant first brought the highly adaptable vegetable to the village marketplace. The two women often joked about their differences. Gittel was quiet, reserved, and slower to change, Leya, ardent and often defying convention. These differences enhanced rather than lessened their appreciation of each other. Leya had come to value the gradual way Gittel greeted new ideas in contrast with Leya's instinctive spontaneity. But now, waiting for Gittel's response was not easy.

Gittel added a log to the fire in her hearth.

"Leya, are you suggesting this young stranger lead our sons despite the fact that he is reputed to be simple-minded and reckless? Could it be that your generous heart is leading you astray, my friend?"

"Gittel, almost as certainly as I can predict that these potatoes when boiled will not become rocks, but will add flavor to your soup, I am convinced that Srolik can be relied upon to nourish our children and not lead them astray. In fact, although it may surprise you to hear me say this, I believe his presence will bless our sons. I can't convince the others to employ the boy based on my inner feeling. But Gittel, you of all people might find this adequate."

Gittel trusted Leya more than she trusted anyone. True, her dear friend was often a challenge to village authorities, who considered her far too independent. Many of Horodenka's Jews judged Leya harshly for assuming roles not rightfully hers. And they couldn't understand why an attractive widow would be indifferent to any available suitor.

Leya was at once so gentle and so fervent. She never compromised her vision of the truth, a vision that had never harmed or misled anyone. So, as she had before, Gittel would again trust her friend.

"Yes, Leyalla," Gittel said, approaching her stubborn, fiery companion whose curls were like soft flames. "We will send Dovid to cheyder with Srolik. I speak for Jacob, too."

Leya rose so enthusiastically from the stool, she tipped her pail of potatoes. Laughing and waving a half-stripped potato, Leya crossed the room in two long strides to embrace Gittel, who couldn't help laughing with her.

LEYA WAS RELIEVED when Reb Jeremiah, the boys' teacher, readily embraced her suggestion that Srolik be employed as his assistant. "The children will be more likely to come and their parents to send them," he confirmed enthusiastically. "Srolik could help the youngest to dress. He could also tell me upon the boys' arrival who might not have eaten and needs a bowl of hot cereal."

Reb Jeremiah expressed no concern about Srolik's questionable qualities, heartening Leya to seek approval from parents before approaching Kahal members. She would steal minutes where she could after a day's work to visit and try to persuade families, especially the parents of boys who were strangers to books.

As she expected, fathers whose sons assisted in the family's livelihood resisted her entreaties immediately. When Leya asserted that his sons would return from their studies ready to resume their tasks with more vigor, the milkman's forceful opposition surprised Leya, given his characteristic humor. With great vehemence, he challenged the value of his boys receiving instruction in a classroom.

"Tell me something, good wife of Reb Ber, Peace be Upon Him," he began respectfully. "Can learning kindle or sustain a fire in one's hearth? Do words feed hungry children, clothe them, or keep them safe from persecution or sickness?"

Other protests echoed the milkman's. "What use the alphabet and Torah study when my boy has lost his leg to infection?" the glazier argued. "Did knowledge help the learned Jews when Cossacks ravaged their towns?" the salt dealer demanded.

Leya knew that knowledge of the alphabet and the ability to study did not in themselves assure a kind and generous heart. But she believed that all should be entitled to learn. She also knew that few of Horodenka's sons aspired to study in a *yeshiva* where they could learn Talmud, the basis of Jewish law and ethics. These academies for young men past the age of bar mitzvah were scattered throughout the commonwealth, mostly in larger towns and cities. The yeshivas prepared young men to be rabbis, judges in rabbinical courts, or perennial students and interpreters of Jewish law and tradition. The majority of the boys in Horodenka would follow the labors of their fathers, which was all the more reason for them to study now, when they could. Leya was convinced that even a small, true taste of learning could affect the children forever. To all who would listen, whether in their homes, the marketplace, outside the shul, in her cobbler stall, or in other artisans' stalls, Leya urged that the children of the Jews of Horodenka be allowed this time to know both the power and the curiosity of their minds.

"Learning when they are young can invigorate our sons for the rest of their lives, "she asserted. "They will gain strength from study, especially study together. Communal prayer and study unites us; none of us can be truly free or strong alone. Through study, our children can connect with a power greater than muscle or money," she encouraged.

Several of Leya's neighbors opened to her words, particularly the mothers. Most dared not speak their acquiescence directly to the "obstinate cobbler's widow." But a number of them, Gittel told Leya, had approached their husbands in the wake of Leya's visits to ask that their young sons be permitted to go to cheyder.

LEYA FINALLY would seek approval from the Kahal to hire the orphan not only to guide the village sons to school but also to serve as caretaker of the synagogue. Levi the soap maker had been caretaking the shul, but with a newborn fourth daughter and a sick wife, he had little extra time for such duties. Srolik, since he had no home, could spend his nights in the shul. He could make a strong fire before dawn, warming the small building for early morning prayers. Following his morning duties with the boys, Srolik could sweep, mop, wipe the benches, and wash the synagogue's two small windows before the evening service.

Reb Wolf, the Kahal's head, was the hardest to convince, his pomposity as difficult for Leya to penetrate as her tenacity was for him to tolerate. What finally swayed him was the argument that the boy's presence could protect the sacred Torah scrolls from vandalism. Throughout Poland, in truth, in every country where Jews had been fortunate enough to build synagogues, and even in the Holy Land itself, there had been attacks against synagogues. Miraculously, no desecration had yet occurred in Horodenka's prayer house.

Reb Wolf finally succumbed to offering a few coins as salary to the "pitiable orphan," making the Kahal's vote unanimous. The community council had come to its verdict.

Leya saw Srolik when she came around the corner of the *Beis Midrash*, the men's communal House of Study. His back was to her and his head bowed forward. He was so still, he barely seemed to be breathing. Leya drew closer, stopping instantly when she saw a purple butterfly on the toe of his boot. Watching the delicate creature open and close its wings, Leya fell again into timelessness. Only when the butterfly flew upward in a spiral from Srolik's shoe did Leya return.

The boy turned to face Leya, his gaze meeting hers.

"You shall lead our sons, Srolik."

He said nothing, but Leya thought she saw pleasure flash in his eyes.

"Levi the soap maker has been cleaning our House of Prayer, opening its doors for prayer and locking them again in the evening. Now *you* will take care of Horodenka's prayer house. The Kahal will pay you a small salary, enough for your food and clothing."

"Tonight you can begin to sleep in the shul," she continued. Leya didn't know where or if Srolik had laid his head down at night in the weeks since his arrival. Even if he were comfortable with the earth as his bed, soon it would be far too cold to sleep outside or to take refuge in a barn or granary. Now he would have a warm, safe place to abide in.

SROLIK WAS GREETED by Levi waiting at the open door of the small wooden building. He gave the boy a key to safeguard, a tall broom, a mop and pail, sheep's wool for dusting, and a bag of torn rags for cleaning the windows. Srolik followed him, listening. Levi showed him the store of coal and how to load the stove properly and get the coals to glow. He explained when to bolt the doors at night and when to unbolt them in the morning.

After the soap maker had left, Srolik lay down on one of the hard benches. It was the first time since he'd arrived in Horodenka that a roof, and not the night sky, would hover over his sleep. A knock summoned Srolik from the prayer he was about to recite.

At the door stood the boy Srolik had seen in the marketplace holding the hand of his younger brother, sons of the kind woman with iridescent eyes and fire in her heart.

"My mother sent these for you."

Srolik reached to take the handle of a cast iron pot that protruded from beneath the quilt that filled the boy's arms. A simple tunic, two pairs of socks, and a tin cup were wrapped in the quilt.

The young emissary placed everything on one of the wooden pews and turned to leave.

"Thank you," Srolik said. "Please thank your kind mother, too."

Alone, Srolik partook of the warm beet borsht and the kugel. Then he lay back down again, grateful for the warmth of the food and the quilt.

Closing his eyes, he whispered the sacred syllable of the prayer of unity: *Sh'ma*, Hear, Our God Is One, which his father had instructed be his last words before sleep, the nightly journey of his soul.

If his soul travelled during the night, Srolik certainly could not recall the details of any of those journeys. His father had taught him that the soul cannot be destroyed, not even by death. Did his soul travel nightly to meet with the souls of his deceased parents? There was much his father had explained that Srolik had not understood. But oddly, he could now remember many of Reb Eliezar's words, like the time on the banks of the Dniester River when his father told him: *Trying to hold the mysteries of life in one's small mind is like trying to contain the ocean in a thimble.*

IN THE MORNING, Srolik stood close to the stove whose warmth radiated from its belly full of coal. He bent over the pail Levi had left him, splashing water on his face. According to custom, Srolik poured water over each hand three times with the tin cup as he recited the blessing for hand washing. Then came the blessing to recite before his first bite of leftover kugel.

Levi had cautioned Srolik that this particular morning was not a typical weekday morning when one hoped at least the ten men needed for a prayer quorum would come for the morning service on their way to work. Today the shul would be filled. It was *Simchas Torah*, the holiday celebrating the completion of the reading of the entire Torah, before starting over again for another year. Levi had implored Srolik to do a good job.

With a clump of sheep's wool, Srolik began to wipe the benches. He cleaned the three stairs, their banisters, and the railings and the balustrades of the bimah, the platform on which the Rabbi and Torah readers would stand.

Srolik paused in front of the Holy Ark that housed the Torah scroll. The Ark seemed to have been carved by a different hand than the rest of the platform; its graceful simplicity was captivating. The cabinet's legs, solid yet flowing, were like roots. The delicately carved letters, *Bes* and

Heh, over the curtained Ark soundlessly issued praise: *Baruch Hashem,* Blessed is the Name. The oak seemed to breathe with the longing of its humble artisan to express beauty and harmony beyond his reach.

Srolik cleaned the women's section, swept, mopped, checked on the stove, and finally, seeing the morning light wash the room, unbolted the door.

The earliest of the congregants gathered in the sanctuary.

"God should only have pity on him," one of the men muttered under his breath.

"God forbid this should ever happen to one of my own," a second replied.

Srolik realized they were talking about him. Like the residents of Okup, these men acted as if Srolik were not there. Maybe they thought him deaf because of rumors that he never spoke. The words floated over and around him. In Okup, men and women had spoken hopelessly, angrily, and, at times, with such piercing sympathy, Srolik had wished he could ease the speaker's pain. He was pitied and blamed for being "abandoned," "desolate," "a poor orphan without shelter."

But Srolik did not feel abandoned or desolate. While his father still lived, Srolik had felt protected. He thought it was his father's presence. But after his father died, Srolik's sense of protection did not vanish as he thought it might. The feeling of being protected came from within him.

Although his father had instructed Srolik not to feel afraid, he did feel afraid at times. But his fear would dissolve like ice melting into the water around it. Maybe this is what his father meant when he said Srolik would not be alone. Srolik liked thinking of God as a moving current carrying him always, even when he couldn't see the water.

Horodenka's Jews of all rank gradually filled the synagogue for the Simchas Torah holiday. The annual cycle of Torah reading would end with the last words of Deuteronomy and immediately start over with the first words of Genesis: *In the beginning.* It was a sacred duty to be joyous on this day. Even those with heavy hearts rejoiced. *Men who do not know how to read can offer their hearts to Her,* his father had said, explaining to

Srolik that the Torah was referred to as She. He also said: *When we dance with the Torah, we give Her feet.*

The moment the last words of Deuteronomy were read, Reb Wolf, who had been given the honor of holding the Torah, lifted the scroll high like a great lantern while all sang to Her, the Tree of Life. Srolik knew the Jewish people referred to themselves collectively as the Bride of God, their faithful Bridegroom. Dancing now as if they were grooms at their own long-awaited weddings, the congregants followed behind the Torahs, circling the bimah platform first, then going outside to circle the House of Prayer itself. Reb Wolf led the men in circling the building seven times—each procession a holy pilgrimage that did not require men to be citizens of status or yeshiva scholars. Humbly dressed laborers danced behind the Torah in jubilation. With dancing feet and waving arms, they offered their unrestrained, untrained love for the Beloved. Today, a man's tithe was his joy.

Srolik did not really understand the covenant between a man and wife. But he had begun to sense the difference between a Jew who gives his whole heart to an intimate relationship with God and one who holds back. Those who felt loved by God appeared to suffer less than those who felt betrayed, even when the circumstances of their lives differed little.

In Okup, and again tonight, Srolik observed those who could not abandon themselves to joy—or would not. He had heard people argue that it was dangerous to have too much faith, *to love God without caution.* Almost as proof, men recounted countless tragedies, such as the Cossack massacres that Jews had endured and in whose aftermath thousands of Jews had limped behind the false messiah Shabtai Tzvi, who had then shattered their hopes. But now, simple, unlettered men and the congregation's women trailing a distance behind in the shadows of the night danced with unfettered hearts. So-called ignorant men and women were becoming the teachers of others who were more elegantly dressed but poor in faith.

As the men emptied the prayer house, one stopped and stood in front of Srolik. He was a hardy, broad-shouldered man whom Srolik had seen carrying a yoke with heavy milk pails on either side. His critical glance swept Srolik from boots to cap and back again. Then, looking bewildered, the man scratched his head.

"If this is a teacher's assistant," he bellowed, "then I am the szlachcic Potocki's long lost cousin. You'll excuse me, I left my silk tunics and fur-lined cape at the palace."

A few men laughed and looked at Srolik as if waiting for him to reply. But he could not find the right words, or any words, and remained silent.

∾

WEEKS LATER, BEFORE THE FIRST OF THE QUORUM of men needed to pray the morning service had stepped into the shul, Srolik heard an unfamiliar voice whispering his name. Looking around the empty prayer house, he saw no one, nor had he heard anyone enter. Had he imagined the subdued voice? And what of the sudden scent of fish that wafted through the room?

Srolik looked towards the door, slightly ajar. In the bright morning light that poured in, he saw the silhouette of a tall figure. When the man drew closer, Srolik thought he recognized the brilliant eyes, but was not sure why.

The towering stranger broke the silence with a single word: "Ibrahim." This was the name of the man the Alta said would be awaiting him.

The white-bearded man with piercing eyes instructed Srolik to lock the door after the evening service, as usual, but instead of remaining inside, to come outside and stand in front of the small synagogue.

"I will be waiting," Ibrahim concluded. He turned, walked to the open door, and stepped back into the light out of which he had come.

That evening in the chill air, Srolik awaited Ibrahim. He smelled the man before he saw him—the same scent of fish he had detected in the morning. Without speaking, Ibrahim walked rapidly until they were swallowed by the darkness of the moonless night. Slowing his pace, Ibrahim stopped at what seemed to be a barn or stable.

Once inside, Srolik's guide kindled an oil lamp, finding his way to it as if he had done this often. He carried the lamp to a small table upon which lay an open book. The intense Ibrahim gestured that Srolik sit on the bench near the table. He sat down next to the youth. Then Ibrahim pointed to a place on the page.

When Srolik leaned forward, he expected to find the small black marks moving as they had whenever he looked into a book. But instead the letters remained still, still enough for his teacher to point and begin to name them. Reb Ibrahim took his time, introducing the characters one by one, asking Srolik to repeat the letters' names and the sounds each made. By the end of their study session, Srolik had greeted each of the twenty-two letters of the Hebrew alphabet.

"The building blocks of creation," Ibrahim concluded, closing the book that Srolik now knew to be Genesis, the first of the Five Books of Moses.

They walked back in the darkness to the small house of prayer.

"Tomorrow night," Srolik's guide said softly before vanishing into the dark.

They studied together this way each night, making their way to and from the place of study with the stealth of creatures familiar with the night. Before long, Srolik was able to make his way alone, knocking three times on the door that even on a moonlit night looked like the stable wall, not an entrance.

When, in the marketplace a few hours before the start of Sabbath, Srolik overheard a small group of women joking about a certain fish vendor's devotion to his fish, he became curious.

"He's so devoted, he never takes his gaze from his fish even to look at his customers. Just watch, he'll barely look up when he hands over that herring." The speaker gestured towards a man bent over his fish. Srolik recalled the fish vendor. He was the one who months earlier declined to answer the spice trader's question about where to pray on the High Holy Days.

As if hearing Srolik's thoughts, the fish vendor raised his head and looked in Srolik's direction for a moment before lowering it. Srolik's teacher by night was a fishmonger by day!

SROLIK LEARNED with Ibrahim how the letters combine to make the sacred roots of words. He learned that most Hebrew words have a three-letter root that contains the essence of that word's meaning. The addition of suffixes, prefixes, and vowel sounds beneath the three consonants change the nuance of the word. For centuries, rabbis and others have studied and interpreted these roots to elucidate deeper meaning in the Torah.

Srolik was thrilled when, after several weeks, his mentor found him ready to study rabbinical interpretations using roots to illumine a word or phrase's meaning and significance. The first word the two studied was *Torah*. Srolik asked eagerly if *ore,* a root meaning light, was the root of *Torah*. It was the first time that Srolik saw his teacher smile.

"*Torah Ore: The Torah, the Teaching, is Light,* it says in Proverbs. She is the Light that shows the way to life. But there is more that can be discovered here," Reb Ibrahim said enthusiastically. "Another root word is hidden in the word Torah, one which means *to shoot, to point, and also a direction being pointed out.* The word *moreh* derives from this root; *moreh* means teacher and also archer. Thus it can be said that Sacred Teachings are the Light pointing to and lighting one's way."

If Srolik could have smiled with his entire body, he would have. How thankful he felt to his moreh for having pointed to the very first letter on their first night together and all the letters after that. Ibrahim was illuminating the darkness that the Okupniks claimed had swallowed Srolik's mind.

THE FIRST MORNING of classes, Samuel announced to Leya that he would be the one to greet Reb Jeremiah's new helper at the door when he arrived to take them to the small cheyder building. Not able to bear waiting until he was seven, Samuel had pleaded to begin sooner; waiting until he was almost six had been long enough. The moment he heard the knock, Samuel jumped up from the table, ran to the door, and opened it.

When Srolik did not step in, Samuel pulled lightly on his sleeve.

"Come in, Solik! We have kasha to warm your belly so the coldness does not make you too cold."

Srolik smiled in response to the boy's enthusiastic welcome, not noticing or not minding Samuel mispronouncing his name. Srolik's gaze met her older son's through a veil of steam rising from Gedaliah's steaming groats.

"Solik, please come in, *now*," Samuel pleaded.

The shy youth entered, wiping the bottoms of his worn boots with a cloth he seemed to pull from nowhere. Leya could not help staring at the boots and vowed inwardly to replace them.

Srolik sat down on the bench where Samuel pat an insistent hand.

"Solik? You do like kasha, yes? And barley tea, too?"

At Srolik's nod, Leya placed a clay bowl of hot buckwheat groats and a cup of tea on the table in front of him.

They ate together without speaking except for Samuel's outbursts asking "Solik" if everything was delicious enough to which he received nods that satisfied him, at least until he asked again.

After the three boys had left, Leya watched them stop a distance down the dirt road just before they were to turn to Dovid's home and disappear from sight. Srolik knelt to help Samuel with the top button of his jacket, which he had left unfastened in his exuberant haste to leave. When Srolik stood, Samuel slipped his small, gloved hand into the older boy's bare hand. Leya nodded, tucking a wayward curl into place under her headscarf before going back inside to rinse their bowls and cups in a pot of heated water.

Walking to her cobbling stall, Leya wondered if Dovid's father would be at home when the boys arrived. These days Jacob was often asleep in the middle of the morning after coming home late and so full of vodka that Gittel wondered how he had made it home at all. She had even begun to worry that Jacob might hurt himself with his own wood-working tools.

Lately, Gittel had become more concerned about Dovid, too. Dovid had always been a serious boy, more withdrawn than his friend Gedaliah. As quiet and contemplative as was Gedaliah's temperament, it had never been flavored by melancholy like Dovid's. Dovid's somberness had deepened the more that drink pulled his father away from the family. He had even begun speaking of stopping his studies to learn a trade. In this way, he said, he could help his mother, whose lace-making business would not be enough to sustain the family without his father's earnings.

Gittel did not want Dovid to stop studying even if it meant accepting the help offered by Gittel's well-to-do cousin Batya who lived miles away in Tluste. Batya, whose husband's inherited wealth had made her life very comfortable, was aware of Gittel's trials and had offered not only financial support but even the shelter of her home should Jacob and Gittel no longer be able to pay their rent. Until now, Gittel had thanked Batya but declined any help. Leya hoped Gittel might become willing to accept her cousin's assistance if only for the purpose of Dovid's studies.

"Dovid has a good, strong mind and loves learning," Gittel had said to Leya recently. "I want him to continue his studies. If he must learn a trade, he can do that later. Jacob wanted to study in a yeshiva," she added ruefully, "even dreamed of attending university where so few Jews are admitted."

Leya knew that Jacob's father Shlomo had impeded his studies but little more. Leya also knew that Jacob and Gittel together had fostered a love for learning in Dovid since he was a very young boy, a boy who had asked more questions than they could possibly answer: *Do beetles have souls? Who gives the sun its light? Why is Challah braided? Why do people kill animals when there are so many other things to eat?* When a wagon loaded with logs ran over his friend Benjamin's leg, for days afterward Dovid asked why God let accidents happen that caused people to cry out in pain.

Dovid's questions had been a welcome fountain in Jacob and Gittel's life. Now the fountain, although most certainly not dry, no longer flowed as it had. Although Leya had not said so to Gittel, she hoped Srolik's presence would hearten Dovid.

GEDALIAH SHOOK his friend's hand when Dovid joined them on their way to the cheyder. Dovid glanced at Srolik but said nothing, hanging back as they continued on to gather the other students. Dovid did not step forward when Srolik, Gedaliah, and even Samuel coaxed their fellow students to finish their simple breakfasts and prepare to leave. Given Dovid's playful tenderness with his sisters, Nessa and Tanya, and with Samuel, this new sullen retreat was hard for Gedaliah to watch. His best friend was carrying some unseen burden. Gedaliah tried to meet his friend's gaze, but Dovid kept his head down, kicking a stone ahead of him.

The caravan of fifteen boys, led by their tattered, humble shepherd, made its way to the forest through which they had to pass to reach the small schoolhouse on the far side of the village. When Dovid kept himself several meters behind the last child, Gedaliah went to walk beside him.

A melody like a thread carried by the wind began to weave through the caravan, making its way to the tail of the line. At first Gedaliah thought it might be the peculiar sighing of the late autumn wind. Then he realized it was a voice, a single voice carrying the tune, lifting it and lowering it, so that it was at once playful and tantalizing. Gedaliah looked around, almost expecting to find the melody visible among the boys.

Clearly, his fellow students were surprised and delighted, too. The strange melody hid and then revealed itself like an exuberant child unable to remain hidden for more than a moment.

What a surprise then to discover that Srolik was the source of the tune that wove among them, teasingly inviting the boys to join in.

A few followed Srolik's lead when he added syllables that made no sense to ride on this melody: *ya-da-dye-da-da-dye-dye-dye-dye...* Srolik with his voice, eyes, and gestures coaxed the boys to join him.

Samuel was the first to find the invitation irresistible. Although he could not match the syllables, or the tune, his own sounds added to the strand of Srolik's compelling melody.

Soon most of the boys were humming melodies that wove through one another. Entranced by the spell cast by their odd shepherd, the boys alternately imitated Srolik then let go into their own melodic variations, always returning to the central cord, the *niggun* that wrapped them all together without binding them too tightly. They laughed as they walked, taking hands and beginning to skip. Even the older boys, too self-conscious and embarrassed at first to act carefree, gradually abandoned their seriousness—all except for Dovid, who was seemingly indifferent to the delight around him.

But among the rest, Srolik's joy was contagious. Gedaliah, humming now, was not even sure when he had started weaving in and out of the melodies. How could it be that Srolik, so passive and unable to express himself, had kindled such joyous expression? Dovid appeared even more serious and indrawn than he had at the beginning of their expedition as if trying hard to resist the contagion. But, at least Dovid was here; at least they were together. Perhaps the joy, spreading like summer heat among them, would eventually warm and soften Dovid's heart.

DIGGING RADISHES next to his father, Simon heard the boys pass along the edge of the field. He wished he were among them, but knew that even wishing so was a betrayal of his father, who had denied him permission to attend classes. His father knew what was right. Where would it get Simon to think differently? How many times had his father repeated the same warning and just recently barked it in the wake of the visit of the cobbler woman.

Simon knew the words by heart he had heard them so often. *A boy who disobeys his father is like a colt refusing to be trained. A horse that is impossible to ride or hitch to a plow is of no use to anyone. The same is true of a son who thinks he can live free of the reins of his father.*

Were the boys singing? Simon could not help stopping to listen, sitting back on his heels. How pleasing the sound, he thought, then quickly reprimanded himself. If they were singing, all the more reason not to be among them rather than here where he belonged. Better to be useful, ridding the soil of rocks and clumps of knotted roots that would keep the seed from taking root. Every day of labor in the fields was crucial now. Soon they would seed the winter wheat, hoping for enough time for the seeds to germinate, the crop to root and form tillers before deep cold set in. There was no time for such foolishness as singing.

THE BOYS' teacher, Jeremiah, was perhaps the first to see the change in the boys. It had become a delight to teach them. Even the most passive among his students displayed a new curiosity and the desire to learn. In addition, more village boys were attending cheyder than ever before, including those who had never expected to learn to read, let alone study. Whatever the reasons for the change in Horodenka's sons, it didn't matter—even if it was the influence of his inscrutable assistant and the mysterious joy derived from the playful melodies laden with nonsensical syllables. The boys were learning.

The children's parents, the members of the Kahal, the vendors in the marketplace, even the yenta Zelda hawking her vegetables noticed the changes. The boys displayed a lightheartedness not seen among Horodenka's Jews for as long as could be remembered. And not only did the boys study with zeal and focus, they had begun to treat their sisters, parents, animals in the village, complete strangers, and each other with kindness and patience that astonished the citizens of Horodenka. Even relations between Jewish and Polish Christian children of the village were friendlier, a change welcomed by the children although greeted with a measure of caution by the adults.

Had the children neglected their responsibilities at home, their parents might have regarded the spiritedness of their sons more suspiciously, judging it to be an almost dangerous levity. But this did not happen. The boys were as hardworking and responsible at home as their parents could wish. Even the fathers who had initially been most hesitant no longer protested.

Winter settled over the village with its usual ferocity. The boys walked to and from the schoolhouse, huddled more closely together, singing ever more heartily, their voices muffled in scarves, and coats pulled up over their mouths. The older boys surrounded the youngest to break the impact of the wind.

The colder and more harsh their passage became, the more determination the children mustered and the louder they tried to sing, even when it seemed the sounds might freeze in the icy air the moment they left their mouths.

∾

A YEAR AFTER SROLIK HAD BEGUN LEADING THE boys through the forest to cheyder, Moreh Ibrahim told him it was to be their last lesson together.

In the lesson, Ibrahim explained the four levels of meaning in the Torah as described in rabbinic literature, using the letters of the word *PaRDeS*, meaning orchard. "The Torah is compared to an orchard because the deeper you enter and the longer you linger, the more likely it is that you will harvest even Her hidden fruit."

"The first level of meaning, *Peshat*, is the simple straightforward literal meaning," Ibrahim taught. "This is the story contained in the Bible as passed down through generations from Moses at Sinai. At this level, we study events occurring in time; we describe God as King and the Hebrews as the chosen people."

"The next level, *Remez*" he continued, "is the Torah's symbolic, allegorical meaning. For example, the Song of Songs appears to be a love song between lovers, but can be understood more deeply as the relationship between the Creator and creation."

Srolik was enthralled.

"*Derash,* moral interpretation is the third level. This is the level of the volumes of rabbinic commentary, generated in dialogue among rabbis and scholars. Torah study is a lifelong, communal pursuit. Therefore, if you do not grasp the significance of PaRDes now, Srolik, you will have plenty of time to do so."

"The word *Sod* for the fourth level means mystical or secret." Reb Ibrahim lowered his gaze and his voice, his reverence tangible. "This is the innermost level of meaning for which one must be prepared not only by studying the other levels but also by living with respect for all life."

The moreh paused, now looking intently into his student's eyes.

"When you are ready, Srolik, another teacher will appear who shall lead you into these hidden levels of meaning. You will then embark on your study of *Kabbalah* whose root is to receive. One must be ready to receive these understandings, which is why they have been guarded so carefully, generation after generation. Eventually, you will be introduced to the *Zohar,* the Book of Splendor—the greatest of all Kabbalistic texts. The Zohar illumines the unrevealed dimensions of Torah. Beyond all this, my son, you will find one day that it is no longer enough just to study, to point to the Light. You will have to become the Light."

4

It was still dark outside, the sun not up yet even though Rifka was. She was thinking about something that troubled her. Rifka, already seven, knew that being envious was a sin. The widow Yitta had told her. Back in Okup, the loud widow had invited Rifka to her house often, insisting it was good for her to leave her father Aryeh's "filthy" blacksmithing shop. When the widow Yitta first talked to Rifka about sin, she had whispered like she was telling Rifka a secret.

"A sin," she said solemnly, her mouth close to Rifka's ear, "is doing what is not right."

Watching the never-ending mischief and disobedience of Yitta's four sons, Rifka wondered sometimes if their mother had ever talked to *them* about sin.

Envy, the widow Yitta warned her, was a particularly bad sin. "Beware, Rifka, not to want what you cannot have. Envy is a thief," she would say, squinting as if she had seen the thief with her own eyes and he was exceedingly ugly. "Envy steals happiness."

Rifka had not known what *beware* meant, nor had she asked.

Now she did know, and more than that, she also knew now what it was to want something she could not have.

Tanta Leya had never warned about envy or a thief who steals joy— not even when Rifka told her that she wished she could go the school like her cousins. Her tanta did not say that Rifka was wrong to wish it. In fact, what her aunt did say made it seem that Rifka was not sinning at all.

"Your desire to learn is beautiful, Rifkalla, like a strong fire burning. Such a fire can bring you and others great light and warmth."

Rifka was even more surprised when Tanta Leya agreed that it was not fair that there was no cheyder for girls. Maybe Yitta the widow was wrong about envy, just as she had been wrong when she said Rifka would enjoy herself more in Yitta's house than in the cold and noisy blacksmith shop.

The day Tanta Leya put a drop of honey on the page and started teaching Rifka the alphabet was one of the best days in Rifka's seven years. The moment she tasted the honey on her tongue, she felt so happy that even if a thief *had tried* to steal some of her happiness, there would have been so much left over. Leya promised to teach her every single letter until Rifka had learned each letter's magic. Some day, Leya told her, Rifka would be able to use the letters to compose her own poems and prayers.

Because Tanta Leya was so busy making shoes, fetching water, collecting firewood, cooking, and washing, Rifka could not study as her cousins did every morning. Rifka could feel the thief of envy creep in and take away some of her happiness each day that she watched Srolik and the boys leave her behind. She was not only learning the magic of the letters slowly, she was also learning she was not good at being patient. Now not only did Rifka have envy, she had other things the widow Yitta might call sins: impatience and sometimes anger.

Despite the quiet of the early morning, Rifka might not have heard Dovid's knock if she had not been listening, so lightly did he tap on the door of her aunt's cottage.

When she opened the door and greeted him, Dovid did not look into her eyes. She had not expected him, too, of course, although she had not given up hoping that he would, one day. Rifka knew it was not unfriendliness; it was just his way of being.

Dovid was holding a fragrant kugel his mother Gittel had made for Justyna's family. Because Dovid and Gedaliah were eleven now, they had begun to go alone to Justyna and Dominik's farm. Leya and Gittel got milk and cheese from Justyna, paying the kind peasant family with new soles for their shoes, new boots, a special lace collar on Easter for Justyna, and most weeks with a kugel or two and a loaf of braided challah, which the family liked even though these were Jewish foods. On Sundays, like today, the boys needed to set out before sunrise to arrive before the family would leave for their church. There would be plenty of time for the boys to be back in time for cheyder.

Rifka wanted to invite Dovid, who shivered by the door, to stand closer to the hearth while he waited for Gedaliah. But she knew Dovid would prefer to stand and shiver rather than be noticed. Dovid reminded Rifka of a turtle. All she needed to do was barely touch him with her glance, and he would pull into the shell of himself. Sometimes, she secretly wished that Dovid would smile at her the way he smiled at Samuel and his sisters Nessa and Tanya. But girls and boys did not play together unless they were very young, or sister and brother. Even so, Rifka wished she and Dovid could be friends.

After Gedaliah slipped his arms into his jacket and took the loaves from Dovid's arms, Rifka surprised herself by asking, "May I go with both of you to the farm?"

Tanta Leya was the first to respond.

"Not such a bad idea is it, Gedaliah and Dovid? Come, Samuel, put on your jacket and with those strong arms come to carry wood in with me." Taking his hand before Samuel could insist he wanted to go along too, Leya walked out of the cottage.

Rifka did not waste a single moment while bundling herself up to accompany the boys.

When Rifka had walked before to Justyna and Dominik's farm with Tanta Leya, it had not been this dark. Even so, she could feel when they started to climb the hill. She knew the tiny cottage by heart: the way its thatched roof reminded her of a straw hat pulled down over a squat person. There were six, almost seven people living there: Dominik, Justyna, and their four, soon to be five, children. Tanta Leya had explained that the family farmed for a nobleman, master to thousands of peasants. After years of their ancestors' service to his family, the nobleman had granted Justyna and Dominik a small parcel of land of their own to farm, a tired cow, and, recently, an old goat. The family sowed wheat and grew beets, cabbages, peas, and onions for their own table.

It was on the way to the farm with her aunt that Rifka had first seen the girl Marishka, Justyna and Dominik's daughter and Rifka's own age, running in the fields behind a herd of her master's goats. Rifka did not know her name then or that the girl had eyes the color of a bright clear sky and plump cheeks like two blushing apples. Rifka could only see her back and the way her long yellow braids bounced under her brightly colored scarf when she ran, reminding Rifka of her own darker braids, and how she liked to run fast, too. It was a few days later, when Marishka came with Justyna to Leya's cobbler stall, that Rifka saw how Marishka's eyes smiled.

Marishka did not seem to mind at all having a Jewish friend. That was how it had felt right away—that they would be friends. And neither Leya nor Justyna was against their being friends, despite the warnings and taunts that came whenever they walked in the marketplace together, a Jewish girl and a Polish peasant girl, holding hands. Not only did Leya and Justyna not mind, they seem pleased about the girls' friendship. Rifka decided to be more pleased than afraid.

What she and Marishka enjoyed most together was climbing the hill overlooking the szlachcic's vast wheat fields. Once there, they would wrap themselves in burlap feed sacks and watch the tasseled golden wheat being waved by the wind. After awhile they would lie down, look up at the clouds and talk about learning.

Marishka wanted to learn to read as much as Rifka did. Now that Rifka was learning the alphabet, she wished she could teach Marishka. But it would be even better if Gedaliah, who knew more, could teach Marishka along with her brother Patryk, who was Gedaliah's age and wanted to learn, too. But Gedaliah and Rifka were studying a different alphabet than the one Marishka and Patryk needed.

By the time Gedaliah, Dovid, and Rifka came over the hill, their eyes had adjusted to the dark. They were able to see the strand of smoke curling up from the small cottage that seemed to crouch like a frightened animal in the pre-dawn valley.

"Who can make it down the hill first?" Gedaliah dared.

Pails, kugel, bread loaf and all, the three charged down the hill. At the very moment Rifka arrived breathless at the bottom of the hill, the littlest of Marishka's brothers burst half naked from the door. Following close behind, Justyna caught him and swung him up over her shoulder. Her swift graceful movements made it look almost like she was dancing.

"May God Bless You," she said, reminding Rifka of Tanta Leya always saying *Baruch Hashem*, Blessed is the Name, upon Rifka and her father arriving safely from Okup.

Bowing her head slightly, Justyna gestured them to enter.

Gedaliah thanked her, saying they would come in only for a moment to set down what they had brought since Justyna's hands were full. It was not one of the visits when they could stay to drink the fragrant, sweet tea made with Justyna's own herbs and honey. Patryk said he would lead them to the barn where Marishka was milking the family's cow.

Marishka's braids were tied together over her head; she wore no scarf. Her cheeks were even rosier than usual, probably from the cold. Without taking her hands from the teats, Marishka looked up to greet them, flashing a smile at Rifka.

"Hojny's milk is *not* flowing like a river. Patryk chose her name, which means bounteous, hoping it would increase her flow. Bring me your pails and I will fill them with as much as Hojny will offer. We will get the rest from Dar the goat."

Gedaliah offered to help with the milking of Hojny, but Marishka declined, laughing warmly.

"She is used to my hands; not even my brother can get her to yield her milk."

Gedaliah laughed in response, louder than usual, Rifka noticed, his cheeks flushing red. Rifka was surprised to see her cousin not take his eyes off Marishka as she lovingly coaxed and admonished Hojny. Dovid helped Patryk bring hay to the small stalls that housed Hojny and Dar. Rifka shuddered with cold, but knew that she would not choose to be home by a warm hearth instead of here in the warmth of this circle of friends.

RIFKA AND THE BOYS made their way home with only the slightest hint of dawn on the horizon. They walked briskly, huddled against
the cold wind that faced them now. Dovid and Gedaliah were planning
a game of stickball to play after cheyder, when Rifka looked up to see
soft light illumining the small window of the shul. She pulled on her
cousin's sleeve.

"I want to look in that window."

She pointed to where light shone through the small panes.

"Why do you want to look there, cousin? Anyway, the window is
too high."

"If only you will lift me for a moment, Gedaliah—just for a moment—
I promise to come down and walk as quickly as I can the rest of the way
home."

Appearing amused by Rifka's insistence, Gedaliah agreed to help her.
In just moments, Dovid had gotten a distance ahead, kicking a stone,
catching up to it, then kicking it again, all the while trying not to spill
any milk from the pail he carried. When Gedaliah called to Dovid they
would catch up to him, Rifka put her finger to her mouth.

"Someone might be sleeping, Gedaliah," she said, keeping her voice low.

Gedaliah looked at her questioningly. He settled his pails and walked
with Rifka closer to the building. Below the window, he turned his palms
up, weaving his fingers together to make a place for Rifka's foot, and
hoisting her up onto his shoulders. But even sitting on Gedaliah's shoulders, Rifka was still not tall enough to see into the window, so she stood
up. Startled, cautious Gedaliah held tight to her ankles.

Edging her way from the corner of the outer sill, Rifka peered inside.
She saw no candle, no lantern, but there *was* light—a sphere of light radiating from Srolik's face, the boy she had first seen in the marketplace
when she suddenly wanted to give him her figs. Since then she had seen
him often, coming for her cousins to lead them and other village boys to
cheyder. He was standing on the platform where the rabbi and the Torah
readers usually stand, a book open before him.

Was the soft light surrounding him just her imagination? It seemed to be coming from Srolik's own face. Rifka closed her eyes for several seconds. But when she opened them she saw the same thing: Srolik's face was illumined as if from *inside him*.

He did not look up. Nor did he appear to sense that he was being watched. Rifka's eyes watered from staring so hard. Standing as still as she could and holding her breath, she tried to hear the sounds coming from Srolik's moving lips. She leaned closer, pressing her ear to the cold pane. She could hear a melody, barely audible, its syllables rising, dipping, then soaring once more. Rifka straightened and looked again. The light was becoming stronger. Not believing her eyes, she searched one last time for the candle or the oil lantern that brightened the room, but could see none.

When he lowered her, Gedaliah saw that Rifka was crying. He spoke softly.

"You were hardly breathing. Were you frightened, cousin, by what you saw?"

"No." That was all she said.

They came upon Dovid leaning against a tree. Without any words exchanged, he reached for the handle of his pail and the three walked on together.

As she walked, Rifka pictured Srolik's face filled with light. She would never forget what she had seen.

❧

DOVID WALKED BEHIND THE YOUNGER BOYS, THEIR capped heads bent into the assaulting wind. They huddled close behind Srolik, moving in one mass, hunched against the cold. As had become customary, a few of the older boys walked at the head of the line to lessen the impact of the wind. Others, Gedaliah and Dovid among them, walked at the tail to make sure that none of the smaller boys lagged behind. Gedaliah walked close to Benjamin, whose lame leg had been reason enough for him not to attend school until recently. More than once, Gedaliah stopped to secure Benjamin's boot to the foot that dragged along the ground. When Benjamin became too tired to continue, Gedaliah carried the thin boy on his back.

The children moved slowly forward, all the while sustaining a niggun, at times barely audible over the whipping wind. The niggun had become an indestructible rope woven more thickly over time, binding them to each other and to a cheerful spiritedness that uplifted them. Dovid watched Srolik pull the students forward with a strength that was not physical. Reb Jeremiah's odd helper never seemed to tire or show discouragement. Srolik's energy and enthusiasm, strangely disguised when he was among adults, was contagious among his charges, spreading to even the most sluggish and slow learning among them.

This morning, the claws of the cold reached mercilessly under the boys' scant layers and through their lean bodies to grip their bones. Crossing the open field, there was no shelter from the ravaging wind. The shrouded sun withheld what little warmth it might have given.

When they finally reached the arch formed by heavily laden evergreen branches and entered the dark woods, the trees burdened with ice offered little reprieve from the battering wind and cold. As Gedaliah and Benjamin, the last two in line, entered under the ominous canopy, the group was assailed by something worse than the fierce wind. A heartwrenching moan made the boys freeze in their steps. The agony sounded human but not possibly human.

When the moan stopped, the boys stopped holding their breath. Dovid wondered if it had been a rare piercing cry of the wind that had terrified them. But when it came again—a tortured howl as if from the intestines of the earth—they all knew it wasn't the wind. The angry, twisted groan sent chills through them all.

Srolik, farther in front of the line now, continued walking. Afraid to follow, but afraid to hang back, the boys moved forward slowly, taking small steps, their legs trembling as they moved, some of the youngest sobbing. Walking behind them, Dovid imagined the questions they might be too numb or afraid to ask. *Why was Srolik walking forward? Why did he not turn around and lead them back where they had come from? Why did Srolik not say he heard the cry, or assure them it was the wind shrieking between the icy trees?* But Srolik did not turn around. Dovid and the others followed him, not knowing what else to do.

The desperate shrieking pierced the air like a sword slicing what thread of courage still united them. The boys were no longer able to move forward. Srolik stopped as well.

When he turned to face them, he was still humming softly. Dovid was not the only one surprised to hear him, most having forgotten the melody in their shock. Srolik sang with a tremor in his voice that Dovid had not heard before. He stepped forward close to Srolik and, for the first time in all the months that they had walked together, Dovid gave his voice to the niggun. Gedaliah joined, then Benjamin, young Samuel, and a few others.

When a sudden wail shattered the air, several of the younger children in terror gripped the legs of their older brothers. Motke, often teased for his uncontrollable wheezing, fell to his knees gasping for breath. Dovid knelt beside him. He took Motke into his arms and gently stroked his back as he had seen the child's mother do to calm him.

What could their shepherd, barely fourteen, do in the face of this danger? Dovid wondered suddenly if Srolik's behavior—going towards rather than away from this nightmare—was a sign of the unpredictable madness the villagers had been warned about early on. Perhaps Dovid and Gedaliah along with other older boys should lead the tribe of students away from this danger. When Dovid sought Srolik's face and eyes for some sign, Srolik appeared suddenly much older and more resolute than Dovid had ever seen him.

Meeting his glance, Srolik said, "Do not stop singing, Dovid. Sing as loud as you can—with great tenderness—as if you are singing to someone who is suffering."

Dovid was not sure if he could do what Srolik asked. Then he heard the change in Srolik's melody and within it a depth of compassion that took his breath away. Feelings buried so deeply within Dovid that he would not have been able to name them if asked were stirred by the unceasing niggun that poured from Srolik.

Dovid heard the mournful wails, saw the terror of the boys, felt his own buried pain, and began to sing to all of it. As he sang, he recognized the power of the niggun to comfort fear. Was it not affecting him this way? Gedaliah joined Dovid, singing as loudly and unfalteringly as he could.

Srolik instructed Dovid and Gedaliah to continue to sing while caring for the younger ones.

"I will return," he told them. The stunned flock of boys watched as their shepherd walked forward into the heart of the forest without looking back. Soon he was out of sight.

Dovid supposed he was not the only one who considered fleeing.

But they did Srolik's bidding, taking shelter in his faith in them and in their strange faith in him. The boys sang as forcefully, yet tenderly, as they could, not an easy combination. The continued wracking cries broke into their fragile niggun, threatening to shatter it completely. But by helping each other whenever one hesitated, they mended the melody, making it whole again and stronger for having been restored.

The boys remained where Srolik had left them, under solemn clouds in a forest penetrated by dread, listening between syllables for any sign of Srolik's encounter with the source of the agonized howls. Then something changed.

The unleashed, monstrous sounds of pain and rage became deep moans of pure sorrow. The boys softened their niggun. Benjamin asked if Srolik had sacrificed himself to save the rest of them. No one could answer. They waited, humming, listening, and shivering in their skin.

Dovid gently released Motke, whose breathing had become more even. Then, astonishing himself, Dovid suddenly started jumping up and down and running in loops making the number eight over and over. He encouraged the younger boys to do the same to keep their feet from becoming numb. Dovid's words rode the boys' melody as he told them to move their fingers and hands, the toes inside their boots. Several of the boys, despite themselves, began to laugh. It distracted them to hear the niggun now instruct them to wiggle their toes, and they were further distracted to see the usually serious Dovid behaving this way.

When Srolik suddenly appeared in the distance, several of the boys cried with relief. He made his way towards them, his face pale, eyes red and puffy as if from crying. Dovid searched his face. Srolik looked neither serene nor distressed; he appeared awestruck.

SROLIK SAID nothing, moving silently among them, placing his hands on their heads, warming their hands in his own, caressing their faces.

He wondered how to talk to them. He would seek guidance from the inner Presence his father had assured was always there. From this Source, Srolik had drawn the strength to move forward. When he had first heard the inhuman cries, he had felt great fear. But he also felt called to walk towards the cries, not away. As Srolik did this, the fear weakened and something else began to reveal itself. How could he explain this to his charges?

Srolik stood before them without words until the words arose.

"Thank you," he finally said slowly, his voice rising from deep within. "You are all—each one of you—very courageous. I could hear and feel your love and your tenderness."

He usually spoke to only one or two at a time; he had never spoken to all of them at once.

"When I left you, I was afraid. I felt called to walk towards the source of the wailing without knowing what I was to do. I sang as you sang, hoping our niggun might bring blessing and comfort. When I drew nearer, I saw a man humped over a freshly dug grave surrounded by other new graves. The grievous howling was so great it did not seem possible that it was coming from that lifeless body, cast over the grave like a worn coat. I took hold of the melody more strongly, telling myself what I had told you: to sing to someone suffering. I lifted my voice, imagining your voices braided with mine."

Srolik paused, his glance resting on the boys one at a time before he continued.

"I learned that the man, a hunter, had lost his youngest child to illness three weeks ago. The same illness then took his four sons and his remaining daughter, leaving only his wife. The hunter had just finished burying his wife near the graves of his children. So great was his despair that, after covering her grave with a last shovelful of earth, he was preparing to take his own life."

Srolik let out a long breath, looking directly at the boys who steadied him as he tried to steady them.

"The man's sorrow had taken on a life of its own, joining with the universal sorrow that has no face or limbs, sorrow that roams desperately over the face of the earth bereft of love. Such heart-rending sorrow pours forth in our world all the time, but only sometimes are we able to hear it. When we entered the forest, we heard the unrestrained despair of a human heart feeling abandoned and believing life to be only suffering."

Srolik paused. They all breathed in, then out, as one body whose heart beat a little less thunderously now.

"Unable to bear his pain, the hunter lost consciousness. The anguish of his soul found a voice and released itself into the forest. When our tender love touched that grief, it was transformed into grief a man can bear, grief that will open his heart rather than destroy it. This is the power of compassion.

Motke, short of breath but filled with urgency, asked, "What we hear now—are they the sobs of the hunter who did not die?"

"Yes, he weeps, Motke. Pain that we cannot contain escapes as our tears. That a man can weep is a blessing."

"Will he cry forever?" urged forth from Samuel, his face revealing how greatly it saddened him to imagine this.

"No, dear one, he will not cry forever. Do not worry. He will not live locked inside of his own pain. When a man or woman's heart is broken, more love may enter."

Srolik knelt and extended his arms, the youngest entering his embrace.

"Because we did not flee but approached the man's torment, it was no longer the only force in the hunter's life. The force of love was present as well. We were the messengers of that love—small lights in the complete darkness enveloping the hopeless father. Although it was the time for those he loved to be taken by Malach Hamoves, the Angel of Death, it was not yet his time."

Srolik saw that weariness pressed the boys' shoulders down and added weight to their eyelids. Just an hour earlier their shoulders had been lifted and tightened in terror, their throats constricted and eyes pinned open. Their bodies had endured a great deal. He wished he could touch and soothe each one of them.

"Despite the terror you faced, you were able to find and share your courage with each other, and with a man lacking all hope. Unimaginable power dwells in each of us, power that is magnified—made greater—when we unite. You have made a miracle today, the miracle of life raising life. It is our time, dear ones, to leave this place and continue to the cheyder. You have been lending each other warmth that is beyond the body."

They walked slowly, their shepherd and his tireless niggun again pulling them forward.

JEREMIAH, concerned about his students' lateness, had begun making his way to meet them. Even from a distance, he sensed that something weighed on them.

After they were settled in their seats, some shivered, unable to become warm. Others laid their heads on their desks. Jeremiah's inquiries were greeted with silence. Neither could Srolik, responsible for their safe arrival but so poor at communicating, explain.

Jeremiah had learned to expect little from his strange assistant beyond rounding up the boys in the morning, leading them home, and the task at which Srolik excelled: brewing the barley tea. Srolik would add ingredients the teacher had long ceased to question, so nice a flavor and fragrance did they bring.

Today, Srolik's ignorance was close to infuriating.

The teacher dismissed his class earlier than usual, watching his students hesitate as if stopped by a wall before finally entering the woods.

Parents became troubled by their sons' changed behavior of sleeping long hours or being unable to sleep and by the absence of appetite and normal conversation. They feared a dangerous illness was spreading among their sons and their suspicions were confirmed when fevers and coughs began to emerge. But not all the children had symptoms of illness.

The boys' reticence to talk about what had occurred rekindled the villagers' initial skepticism about the odd stranger in their midst. Many kept their sons home. Attendance at cheyder diminished greatly and remained that way even after all signs of sickness had vanished.

OVER TIME, as the boys' apparent dejection lifted, Jeremiah was not the only one to notice surprising changes in their demeanors.

Almost overnight, Horodenka's sons seemed to have inexplicably matured. Most showed greater compassion, patience, and kindness in their homes and in the larger community. Even the youngest boys, while still playing freely, displayed an attentiveness beyond their years.

One by one, the boys approached their parents, asking to be allowed to return to the cheyder with Srolik. Gradually, they were permitted to do so.

Jeremiah noticed how his charges sustained the niggun they brought with them each morning with deeper joy and abandon than ever before. He did not call attention to this. He chose instead to start walking home with his students and to join in the compelling melody and its variations, which became for him a path whose destination was unexpected peace.

5

It was a night like many others in Dovid's small home. His mother Gittel crocheted lace in the circle of light cast by an oil lamp while Dovid's sisters slept. His father Jacob was out drinking in a barn or in one of the woodcutters' huts where the homemade whiskey was cheaper than the tavern's. What would make this night different, however, was that tonight Dovid would break his silence.

A week ago, he had listened to Srolik speak about secrets. One of the boys had questioned Srolik about why he behaved differently with adults from the way that he behaved with children. Srolik said that some things remain secret simply because they are not ready to be understood. "But," he added, "there are also deadly secrets that, when guarded too long, rob one of life." Since hearing Srolik's words, Dovid had been summoning the courage to bring his own secret out of its darkness.

"Mother?" Dovid started softly, so as not to startle her from her deep concentration.

Gittel lifted her face and turned towards him. Her eyes were red as they often were, from ceaseless stitching, crying, sleeplessness, or perhaps from all three. She was the gentlest person he knew. Would it be better, he wondered, to leave his questions unspoken after all?

Gittel stopped crocheting and set aside the lace collar for the well-to-do wife of Reb Wolf. She motioned Dovid closer. As he moved towards her, he felt the distance being spanned between them as far greater than a few meters. He had pulled so very far away.

"What is it, Dovid?"

"Mother, I want to know… I need to know…" The questions stirred inside him like a boiling soup; how he could pull anything out of this burning confusion?

"What is happening to my father?"

Tears came that Dovid had not let escape before. He was kneeling before her, head in her lap where the lace had rested. He should not be pulling her from her work, every one of her minutes was so precious. She removed his cap and rubbed his head.

"Your father is suffering a great deal. Jacob has fallen into a dejection so deep, he cannot lift himself from its depths. Nor can I."

Dovid looked up into her moist eyes. "Why does he stay away from us?"

"Your father assures me we are his solace, not the cause of his pain." She drew in and let out a long breath. "He has pulled away in shame. As his despondency deepened, he tried to numb his pain with schnapps. He says he cannot bear for us to watch him drowning in both his pain and the drink with which he tries to erase it."

Memories Dovid kept at a distance surfaced: his father rocking little Tanya on his lap and asking animated questions about Dovid's studies. How honored his father had felt when he had been asked to carve the Holy Ark, crowned with the letters *Beis* and *Heh* for *Baruch Hashem*, Blessed is the Name. When was the last time Jacob had made a wheel or even thought about carving something beautiful?

"Why did this happen?" he asked, unable to fathom the darkness that had swallowed his father.

"You may remember witnessing some of what I am about to tell you, Dovid," she began, her hand firmly on his shoulder.

"Four years ago, a frail old man came to our the door, so weak he could barely keep himself standing. Hair matted, clothes ragged, he appeared malnourished, and smelled of tobacco and schnapps."

"I called to your father, home early from his labors. As soon as he approached and saw the man, he turned without saying a word, suddenly pale. He did not ask the stranger to cross our threshold. He just stood staring down at the floor, looking suddenly lost."

Jacob? the stranger rasped. Your father showed no surprise when the man used his name. *Jacob?* the old man wheezed again. When your father said nothing, the stranger summoned him a third time with more effort, stretching out his frail, trembling arms as if he had come a great distance just to reach out like this. When I turned my head to look at your father, his eyes were pooled with tears, his face ashen. I looked at the emaciated man breathing roughly. It was then I realized."

"*Reb Shlomo?* I asked, fairly certain by now this was the living ghost of Jacob's father. The old man did not nod or respond in any way, except to look as if he had finally arrived at the end of his journey, the place he could die. I could not close the door in his face. I led him shuffling and wheezing to the hearth to warm himself."

"Dovid, what follows is not easy for me to tell you; it was not easy for your father to tell me. When your father was a boy, his father beat him. Reb Shlomo's mind and morale had been destroyed by the violence he had witnessed against his wife in the Chmielnicki uprisings. He could not bear the sight of his surviving son, beating him as if this might bring back what had been lost. Reb Shlomo became mad with grief and vodka."

Dovid wanted to both hear every word and not one more.

"When your father was just a little older than you, he escaped his father's brutality to find a new life. A carpenter, taking pity on him, made Jacob his apprentice. Jacob did not see his father Shlomo again. He imagined him dead—until the man found his way to the son he had not seen in decades. Right or wrong, I could not send the old man away. He died here under our roof."

Dovid was suddenly aware of a strength he had never seen in his mother.

"I hoped that your father might find peace after that, but instead he became more restless, more ill at ease with himself and with everything around him. As odd as it sounds, it was as if something passed between the men as Reb Shlomo was dying, as if Jacob took on his father's restless torment."

Dovid's memory of his grandfather was vague, but he did remember the old man staring up for hours on end, as if what he saw terrified him. Dovid also recollected his father acting as if the old man were invisible. Yet it was when Reb Shlomo appeared that Jacob had begun to disappear.

DOVID SAT WAITING to be called up to the Torah as a bar mitzvah who from now on would be expected to uphold the sacred duties of a Jewish adult.

Red-eyed but sober, Jacob sat on Dovid's left side, next to Gedaliah's uncle Aryeh. Gedaliah sat on Dovid's right. Aryeh and Leya had invited Jacob to Leya's cottage for the past several days; they had bathed him, fed him, dressed him, and kept him from heavy drink. Wide-eyed Samuel sat on the other side of his uncle Aryeh, leaning forward frequently to look at Dovid and wink. At least Samuel had enough fervor and good cheer for two.

Today, Dovid would be welcomed as one of the people of the covenant. From now on he would be counted as one of the quorum needed for prayer. He would be encouraged to attend as many of the day's prayer services as possible and to fulfill many other sacred duties around which his life would revolve. Dovid knew that he should feel proud, honored, and elevated by this day. Was it not a pinnacle in the life of a Jewish boy to become a man among his people? That he felt little enthusiasm disturbed Dovid; his indifference seemed an unseen sin on the very day he was to take on the yoke of greater righteousness.

Dovid stole a glance up into the women's section to see his mother, a newly completed lace shawl draped over Gittel's head and shoulders. He had spotted her before the service had begun, rocking gently, absorbed in her book of Yiddish prayers. He knew how much she loved these prayers composed by women. He also knew how much she struggled to read them. She had only learned to read as a grown woman with Jacob's patient help. As his bar mitzvah ceremony approached, a quiet peace had begun to settle over her like one of her delicate and lovely lace shawls— so different from the harsh burden of Jacob's anguish. Since there was no change in his father that Dovid could discern, his mother's serenity puzzled him. Had her quiet joy been precipitated by today's long-awaited event? Had she also noticed Dovid's lack of glad anticipation? The last thing he wanted was to rob her of even the smallest pleasure.

RIFKA COULD NOT see Dovid from where she sat in the women's section between his mother Gittel and her tanta Leya. Rifka was very pleased with the small triangle of lace on her head that she had stitched mostly by herself under Gittel's guidance.

But Rifka stopped thinking about stitching as soon as she heard Dovid begin to chant blessings on the Torah. She tried to imagine how he must feel. In three years, when Rifka would turn twelve, she would be considered a woman according to Jewish law, but there was no ceremony to mark this. Rifka wanted to be called to the Torah to read, too, and to be counted in the quorum needed for prayer. She'd wished this on the day of Gedaliah's bar mitzvah ceremony, too, when he, like Dovid, passed through an invisible portal she was not allowed to enter.

Thank goodness Tanta Leya was not a stranger to such thoughts. Recently, Rifka's aunt had approached the Kahal with a proposal that most Jewish citizens of Horodenka, even the women, found outrageous. Leya had proposed that a suitable instructor be found and that a cheyder for girls be started.

Leya had given Rifka permission to accompany her to the Study House where the Kahal was meeting. Gittel had told Rifka how rare it was for a woman to attend a meeting of the community leaders, let alone address them. But Leya did not seem afraid at all, so Rifka tried not to be either. She was right next to her aunt when Leya stood up and cleared her throat loudly. The head of the Kahal, Reb Wolf, ignored her at first.

When Leya started speaking, his face showed great annoyance. Rifka could remember almost every one of her tanta's magical words that night.

"A daughter's hunger is as important to feed as a son's." Leya had raised her voice so that it could not be ignored.

There were whispers, outcries, and even laughter until Reb Wolf—as if Tanta Leya's request were a mere piece of dust—swept it away with his declaration. "Much more urgent matters than this are facing the Jewish community in Horodenka." None of the other Kahal members protested his gesture. Rifka wished she were older. She would have stood up beside her aunt and insisted loudly that her tanta was right, even if they ignored her, too.

Dovid, saying the blessing upon completing his Torah portion, brought Rifka's attention back to the present. Through the missing boards between the men and women's sections, Rifka could see Dovid's father Jacob stand and embrace his son. Rifka looked up to see Gittel's eyes filling with tears.

Rifka did not really want to trade places with Gedaliah or Dovid—to be a boy instead of a girl. She wanted to keep being a girl and become a woman, strong like Leya and Gittel. But she wished she could also stand and read from the holy Torah scroll and study day and night in a *Talmudic* Academy when she was older. There were many such academies for boys, but not a single yeshiva anywhere for serious girls. There was not even a classroom for young girls, to prepare them, and Tanta Leya had not been able to convince the Kahal to allow one.

AS DOVID left the House of Prayer, Srolik offered him the blessing for continued strength, not with words or a handshake. Instead, Srolik looked into his eyes.

Dovid felt time stop. In Srolik's eyes, Dovid saw the unbroken continuity of a luminous chain to which he had just been attached as a new powerful link. He had no idea how long his gaze remained locked with Srolik's before he finally turned away, found his legs, and walked on.

JACOB REMAINED in the sanctuary after everyone had left and went to stand before the Holy Ark. It comforted him to run his hands over the smooth corners. He could remember the concentration he had summoned and the prayers he had uttered so that he could exceed his skills and create a space sacred enough for the repose of the Torah. He had been a different man then, someone able to surrender himself to earnest effort, rather than the embittered, fearful man he had become. Jacob knew that he had lost himself along the way.

"This Holy Ark was fashioned with great love."

"There *was* love," the carpenter replied.

"There still is."

Jacob turned to look at who had spoken. It was the stranger who shepherded his son, a sturdy young man of maybe sixteen. He had penetrating eyes, surprisingly free of judgment.

"There still is love," the youth repeated. "The love in the heart of the man who crafted this holy cabinet has not been destroyed."

Jacob listened, his senses clearer than usual.

"Now the craftsman must craft himself with the same patience, and again find his fierce yearning to go beyond his limitations."

Jacob was stunned. Had this reputedly ignorant youth just told him it wasn't too late to save himself? If Jacob didn't know better, he would think this a drunken hallucination. But no hallucination had offered such a lucid message nor reached him in his exile, until now.

Jacob looked up at the letters he had carved to crown the Ark: *Beis Heh*.

"Baruch Hashem," Jacob said aloud for the first time since Reb Shlomo had come back into his life. When he turned his gaze from the Holy Ark back to Srolik, there was no one there. But Jacob knew he had not imagined the shepherd and his gift of hope.

᠓

GITTEL'S COUSIN BATYA WAS DELIGHTED TO BE IN Horodenka. Given her son Naftali's condition, Batya rarely left her

home in Tluste, despite her husband's wealth. But she had been determined to visit Gittel and her family, if only briefly. Batya regretted having missed the ceremony honoring Dovid becoming a bar mitzvah. But
at least now she was the bearer of good news, news that could change
Dovid's life.

Batya informed her cousin's family that her husband Meir, the rabbi
of Tluste, had arranged for Dovid to study at a yeshiva in Polnoyye. A
modest room had also been found. With Jacob and Gittel's permission,
Dovid would attend the Talmudic Academy under the direction of Polnoyye's Rabbi Lazer. Batya and Meir would gladly pay for Dovid's travel
and provide for his meals and any other expenses.

Batya thought she spotted a gleam in serious Dovid's eyes as he
listened.

"Polnoyye is a distance from Horodenka," she explained, "two hundred kilometers. I am sure that we all wish it were closer. But the rabbi
there knows Meir, which enabled us to make this arrangement."

Batya was relieved when Gittel did not protest. Batya had more
resources than her less fortunate cousin; she wanted to be generous with
her means, which derived not from Meir's humble work but from his
father's success as a ruby merchant. She had tried to help Gittel many
times before during her cousin's many years of struggle, including suggesting more than once that Gittel and the children come and live with
her in Tluste. But only when Jacob's condition became dire had Gittel
become willing to accept just enough help to assure that her family would
not go hungry.

Jacob was the first to show his enthusiastic acceptance of Batya and
Meir's offer. Nodding heartily, he rose to his feet and grasped both of
Batya's hands. Then he moved to embrace Gittel and finally Dovid, holding his son tightly in his arms. Batya looked away, certain she had not
imagined the tears filling Jacob's eyes.

She had been quite surprised and pleased to find Jacob sober. He
appeared to have returned as if from a long trip, bringing gifts of laughter
and tenderness.

Gittel's eyes met Batya's and she, too, nodded.

"Dovid?" Batya asked, although she thought she had glimpsed an answer in his eyes.

A single resolute dip of his chin sent handsome Dovid's coal black hair falling forward.

"*Mazel Tov!*" Batya called out, putting her hand firmly on the somber young man's shoulder before pulling him into an embrace.

IN THE MARKETPLACE that afternoon, Batya was introduced to Srolik, the shepherd about whom she had heard praise from Gittel and Gittel's friend, Leya. The celebrated teacher's assistant stood with his gaze directed downward. He appeared not to think as highly of himself as others did. Swallowing his mumbled greeting as soon as he spoke it, he did not impress Batya as someone capable of inspiring others. But she kept this to herself.

Batya happened to see the youth again the following morning with some of his charges. Watching him interact with a young boy who had fallen, Batya noticed the gentle attentiveness with which the teacher's assistant tended to the child. After Srolik wiped the distraught boy's tears, the two boys walked hand in hand, singing a soft melody. Srolik's mindfulness of the child reflected both a confidence and skill Batya had not discerned in their meeting the previous day, as if this weren't the same person.

This young man might be the one she was looking for. Batya had heard talk about the youth's presence benefitting Dovid and inspiring ardor in the sons of Horodenka. Perhaps Srolik could awaken the flames of desire for learning in her son Elias and even feed the small quiet fire trapped in Naftali's twisted body.

And so it was later that day that Batya confided to Gittel that Meir had finally agreed to employ a tutor for their sons and that after observing Srolik, she was considering offering him the work. Elias, almost thirteen, was too restless for learning, though his intelligence was not something to be wasted, and Naftali, ten, was too crippled to attend the village cheyder. Meir would have liked to be the one to educate his sons. But he was a man who knew his limits. He had extensive duties as the spiritual and administrative head of a sizeable congregation, yes. But the greater unspoken obstacle to educating his own sons was Meir's lack of patience. Thus the rabbi had granted his wife's wish.

Batya also knew that while Meir did not oppose the education of girls, if it were not for his sons, he would not hire someone merely to teach their daughter Zofia. It was Batya's intention that their tutor would teach them all—Batya included. Although it had been assumed Meir would choose the tutor, Batya was convinced he would not protest her choice of tutors if she found a suitable one first.

When Batya spoke of the advantages of Srolik coming to Tluste, Gittel agreed that the youth would benefit from the opportunity to earn a greater livelihood and to live in a home, instead of sleeping on a bench and eating somewhat sporadically. If Srolik were to consent, he would be missed in Horodenka, she said. But regardless of anyone's opinion, it was his decision to make.

WHEN BATYA addressed Srolik with her invitation, he stood before her silently. She was uncertain if his slight nod had in fact been his consent to her invitation. *Was she making a mistake?* Perhaps this odd young man was not what her family needed, but instead might prove to be a burden not a boon. Yes, Gittel had spoken highly of him. But Batya and her cousin were so different. Having lived so long with Jacob, Gittel was forbearing in ways Batya was not.

"With the will of God," Batya suddenly heard the young man state, "I will satisfy your need for a tutor." He had not looked at her when he said it, and for a moment, Batya felt confused, doubting he could have been the source of the quiet, clear words.

Srolik's direct glance—lasting just an instant like a sudden bright flash of light—compelled and reassured Batya.

"We will welcome you, Yisroel. From now on," she said, regaining her composure, "I shall address you by your given name: Yisroel, not Srolik—a nickname belonging to a child."

BEFORE THE RABBI'S WIFE had invited him to tutor her children, Srolik had given no thought to leaving Horodenka. But as soon as he heard her offer, he knew he was to accept. The tall, apprehensive woman, rubbing her hands together as if she were washing them without water, appeared to regret her decision only moments after asking. He had looked into her eyes to relieve her doubt.

It was agreed that he would remain in Horodenka after the rabbi's wife returned to Tluste so that he could gradually take his leave of the boys he had grown to love. For now, he would keep the name by which they knew him, taking leave of "Srolik" for "Yisroel" when he left them.

He spent time with each of his charges individually. He went with them for long walks, sometimes talking, mostly singing familiar and new melodies braided together. When Samuel, Motke, and others expressed sadness about his leave-taking, Srolik asked them to talk about what they were feeling. Each reply included something the child imagined would be lacking: laughter, courage, adventure, or the answers to their questions.

"What you imagine might be missing," he replied, "is actually within you and within each other." When Motke looked puzzled, Srolik added: "Remember, when you think something is missing, look with curiosity into yourself and into each other. There are treasures just waiting to be found there."

THE NIGHT BEFORE he was to leave, Srolik saw Rifka standing outside of her aunt's shoemaking stall, watching the sunset. Since that day almost four years ago when she had greeted him in Horodenka with three figs in her outstretched hand, he and the girl had only spoken a few words to each other. But he had felt her heart and the yearning it contained for something she feared would be denied her. Srolik stopped and stood near the girl, both facing the setting sun. He thought to tell her not to fear her longing. But he said nothing, nor did she. Both allowed the farewell to be wordless.

Later, Srolik awoke from a dream on his hard bench in the shul. His dream, still quite vivid, was of the woman cobbler who had been the first in Horodenka to trust him. In his dream, she had entered the House of Prayer, hooded as if to conceal her identity. Srolik watched from inside the Ark, leaning against a Torah scroll, unseen. With a look of anguish on her face, Leya knelt in front of the Holy Ark, looking anxiously from side to side as if she had lost something irretrievable and the loss was unbearable. Suddenly she faced forward, straightened her back, and prostrated herself fully. Forehead to the floor, she whispered prayers Srolik could not decipher. When the cobbler widow lifted her head, her anguish was gone.

6

Batya's son, Elias, met Yisroel in the square where the wagon from Horodenka had left him. Tall like his mother, Elias extended his hand warmly. Seeing only the small satchel in Yisroel's hands, he looked around for the tutor's other bags.

"Is there something I might carry for you?"

Yisroel shook his head, smiling.

Elias gestured in the direction they would be walking. He led Yisroel to a wide cobblestone lane where brick houses, unlike the more common wooden and stucco cottages on the surrounding narrower dirt roads, reflected the more ample means of their inhabitants.

Yisroel heard the girl's laughter before he saw her. She seemed to be enjoying repeating his name, which she pronounced *Sroel*. A lively girl of perhaps six years, she positioned herself directly in front of him, as he stood still holding his bag.

"Zofia," she said definitively. "That is me. And you, you are Sroel."

He looked down at her.

"Yes. That is me."

Pleased by his answer, Zofia stayed right where she was, staring up at the new tutor.

"You already know my brother Elias. But you do not know my brother Naftali. He is over there and even though he cannot say hello like I can and like Elias can, Naftali is very happy you are here because he wants to learn, too. I know it because he told me."

Zofia's self-command and earnest directness warmed Yisroel's heart. He looked in the direction she had pointed and saw a boy of perhaps ten whose limbs did not seem to be under his control. His head, atop a permanently twisted neck, was tilted forward and to the right; he appeared to be looking up at something he could not quite see. His hands were bent towards him at the wrists, his feet turned toward each other, all of him trembling as he made the effort to communicate. With a kneading motion of his contorted lips, he urged forth one labored syllable, then another.

"He said, '*So-el*,' Zofia interpreted enthusiastically. "He is saying hello to you." She ran over to kiss her brother, slouched in the wooden chair. "My mother's cousin Gittel has a husband Jacob who made this special chair for Naftali a long time ago. Naftali has grown, so it is almost too small." Taking both his flapping hands between her small hands, she said tenderly, "Yes, Naftali, this is Sroel who has come to teach us."

The moment she said the word "us," she let go of her bother's hand and covered her mouth as if she had let something secret escape. But behind the hand she kept over her mouth, Zofia's remorse instantly turned to giggles, eyes twinkling.

"Welcome, Yisroel," the familiar voice drew his attention away from his arresting young hostess and her hard-working brother to their mother, the rabbi's stately wife Batya.

"We are glad you have arrived safely. I know the route from Horodenka and that it can be quite dusty when the roads are dry. A washbasin awaits you in the room you will be sharing with my sons. We hope you will be comfortable here."

Zofia nodded in spontaneous agreement. Then exaggerating the gesture for Naftali's sake, she nodded again. Yisroel wondered if the boy welcomed his energetic sister's persistent initiatives or whether he would rather not have her hover so devotedly?

Yisroel had the poignant answer to his question after only a few days with the family. Naftali wanted so much to learn that he heartily embraced *every* opportunity to do so. When Zofia stood in front of her brother, intending to teach him a new word or phrase, Naftali tirelessly attempted to follow her instructions. Each day, Yisroel witnessed the perseverance of the determined pair, Zofia and Naftali. Neither ever showed defeat or discouragement. His new students would also be his teachers.

THEY STUDIED TOGETHER every day, even on *Shabbos,* the Sabbath. As Batya had hoped, she and Zofia were welcome to the feast, which was how it felt to learn with Yisroel.

When introduced to the alphabet, Zofia became instantly swept up in the adventures of the letters. The letters' journeys made her laugh, worry, and celebrate—as when *Yud,* the smallest letter of all and shaped like a tiny flame, proved itself to be the most powerful because two Yuds side by side formed the never-to-be-pronounced name of God.

Batya reveled with her children in Yisroel's stories about the essence and personality of each letter.

"*Aleph,* the esteemed head of the alphabet is deeply silent. When other letters surround the aleph or when vowels are written below her only then will sound emerge from her vast silence."

"Think," he said, "how important each letter is. There is no other just like it. Even those that make the same sound cannot take each other's place."

"Long ago," he explained, "these gracious letters agreed to gather two or three at a time to create what would become the roots of other words. Then, joined by other letters in a great variety of combinations, these roots formed longer words with an array of meanings. The letters standing together form the words we use to speak our feelings, to ask for help, and to express gratitude. Words serve the One who created them from an infinite silence; they carry the energy of that great silence."

The morning Zofia had finally learned all the letters, she jumped to her feet and ran over to her brother Naftali. She proceeded to recite the alphabet slowly and deliberately, raising her brother's arms up then bringing them down like two exclamation marks with the naming of each letter. Naftali's limbs trembled with excitement, his face growing more and more animated until the grand finale of the final *Sof.*

"Sroel," she said after only a moment of respite, "is it really true that these very same letters make Hebrew *and* Yiddish words?"

Yisroel nodded. "Zofia, Yiddish, the language we speak every day, is our mother tongue, while Hebrew is the language of formal prayer and Torah, also called The Holy Tongue. Over the years, countless Hebrew words have made their way into Yiddish. But each language has words of its own that are not shared."

After a moment of pondering, Zofia winked at Naftali and addressed her tutor. " I know another tongue, Sroel," she announced like it was a secret. "Do you wonder what it is?"

Yisroel nodded as did Batya and even Elias, head down, drawing pictures at the end of the table.

"It is Naftali's tongue that he speaks with his hands!" she said triumphantly, bringing her cheek next to her brother's, whose eyes shone.

Batya could see that her husband was both pleased and confused by the new tutor. Meir had witnessed the undeniable enthusiasm under his roof, but whenever he addressed Yisroel directly, he told Batya, it seemed as if the mind so instrumental in inspiring the rest of his family, abandoned Yisroel's body.

While he did not understand this, neither would Meir challenge the tutor, given the joy that he saw in his children and wife. Even poor Naftali seemed more controlled. This all helped a grateful Meir to focus on his responsibilities, which had recently come to include his participation as a judge in the Rabbinical Court.

Batya was pleased to learn that when Yisroel had asked her husband if he might study in the rabbi's library, Meir had granted permission. "I doubt that our simple tutor will spend much time there," Meir told his wife. Batya disagreed but said nothing.

YISROEL WAS GRATEFUL for Batya's suggestion that he avail himself of Rabbi Meir's books. He rose at midnight and studied each night until the dawn, as had been his custom in Horodenka. Here among the rabbi's ample library, in addition to volumes of Talmudic legal tractates, were Kabbalistic books that Yisroel had heard Ibrahim speak of, but which Yisroel had not seen until now.

Yisroel ran his hands along the spines of these volumes, recalling his teacher's warning. The fish-vendor moreh maintained the importance of having deep roots in the ground of Judaism before entering the carefully guarded mystical teachings. This ground was the Torah, the Five Books of Moses, and the Talmud, the compilation of oral teachings, centuries of rabbinic commentary and interpretation inspired by the Torah and passed down from generation to generation.

"The Torah and the Talmud are life-giving and life-sustaining sources," Ibrahim explained. "You will drink from them your entire life, and you shall bring others to drink."

Ibrahim taught that flowing from these oceans of wisdom are rivers of Kabbalistic writings, among them the unparalleled waterfall known as the Zohar, the Book of Splendor, to which Yisroel would be brought when he was ready. At just the right time, another teacher and guide would come and lead Yisroel to drink at the springs of Kabbalah.

Yisroel was eager for this to happen. Given that his last teacher smelled of fish, Yisroel knew that his next teacher could emerge from the least likely of places. In the meantime, he would continue his nightly rendezvous in Rabbi Meir's library, meeting, through their commentaries, rabbis who had lived two thousand years ago.

IN PREPARATION for the Passover holiday, Yisroel and his students discussed passages from the book of Exodus about the Jews leaving their slavery in Egypt, the land of *Mitzrayim*, to be led through the desert to the Promised Land.

"The root of the word Mitzrayim, '*tzr*,'" he told them, "means *narrow, tight, and constricting.*"

"It was not very long after leaving Egypt," Yisroel explained, "that the Jewish people became afraid and wanted to return."

"But why?" Zofia asked, perplexed. "Why would they want to be slaves again?"

"If you had been a slave—in bondage your whole life— and your parents before you and their parents before them," Yisroel addressed Zofia and his other students, "might it be hard for you to imagine being free?"

"Bondage?" Zofia's brow wrinkled. "What is bondage?"

Naftali, eyes on fire, began to move energetically in his seat as if he wished to answer his sister's question. Clearly, he had something to say and did not stop trying until he forced out a rough approximation of the syllables: *Mitz-Ra-Yim.*

"Praise God!" Batya called out as she bent to kiss Naftali's cheek. "And praise our dear Naftali who makes such effort to be free from his own bondage, his own Egypt."

Yisroel found he loved teaching as much as learning. In fact, the two could not be separated. When he introduced a single letter or read a passage of Torah, his own understanding deepened, as did his awe. Yisroel was continually reminded of what he had begun to observe in Horodenka—students differ, a fact that calls upon a teacher to study his students.

Some, like Zofia, were like bottomless pails asking that more and more be poured into them from the well of knowledge, even when what is being given overflows them. To Naftali, learning was sustenance for his body and soul. Elias hovered, at once drawn to the lessons and holding back. Their mother Batya was almost as shameless in her quest for knowledge as her daughter.

FOR BATYA who had never studied like this, the lessons were more wonderful than she could have imagined. As the months passed, her joy was compounded, watching Elias draw closer and closer to the table of learning. Although he did not participate, he was clearly listening.

Sitting still anywhere, let alone in front of a book, had always been hard for her firstborn. This had come to a head as Elias was preparing to read the Torah portion for his bar mitzvah ceremony. The more difficult it became for Elias, the more frustrated his father became. Meir expected nothing from Naftali; Elias, he believed, had no excuse. Batya knew that her husband was greatly disappointed in his elder son, and she sensed Elias knew this, too.

So Batya was delighted to see Elias gradually become absorbed in writing, head bent intently over his quill, gaze moving between an open prayer book and the parchment before him, mysteriously able to focus his attention when doing this work.

One day after several months, Elias announced that he had been copying blessings from the prayer book. When Zofia asked if she might look on as he wrote, Elias agreed.

Zofia sounded out the words *Baruch Ata Adonai Eloheynu Melech Ha'Olam*, recognizing the phrase beginning the blessings recited over wine, bread, and the Shabbos candles: Blessed are you, Lord our God, King of the Universe.

"If God, *Adonai,* is not a person," Zofia began with concern, "then how can Adonai be called a king? A king is a man."

Batya, noticing that Elias had stopped the movement of his quill but did not look up from his writing, was not entirely surprised when her son, distanced not only from study but also from prayer, challenged their tutor.

"I never liked hearing God compared to a king." Elias stated with more than a hint of anger in his voice. "Kings are distant and uncaring. I have heard traveling merchants talk about Poland's King Augustus. While kings and sultans live in grand palaces protected by high walls, the people they rule suffer. Most of their subjects have no food; others, not even a home. What matters to a king is his own comfort and power. Why then is Adonai called a king? Is power and glory most important to God? Are we supposed to fear and obey God as people do King Augustus?"

"Elias," Zofia reasoned with her older brother, "I don't think Adonai is like those kings. Kings die but Adonai can't ever die, right? That's

one difference, a big one. And I don't think God cares about being rich."
Her brow wrinkled. She turned to Yisroel. "Sroel, why *do* the prayers call
Adonai a king?"

Yisroel preferred to guide his students to seek and find their own
answers. But he would offer some response now, so that they would know
they had been heard and their questions honored.

"Perhaps Adonai is called a king in order to serve as an example of
a just, loving ruler for kings on earth," he began. "A true king uplifts
those in his kingdom by assuring their safety and sustenance. A good
king brings and guards peace for his people. But Adonai does not do this
alone. We help to create the kingdom. You could say that we are Adonai's
body: we are God's voice, hands, and feet. We can protect each other's
freedom; we can make sure that each person has food and shelter. We can
become Adonai's messengers of justice and peace."

"Yisroel," Elias began, looking at his tutor now. "When you talk
about the letters and the creation of our world, you make it seem that
God creates out of joy." At this point, Elias rose from his chair and began
circling the table, opposition now softening into enlivened curiosity.
"The Creator *you* describe has great patience, a huge imagination, and
loves what has been created. You never talk about God's punishments or
strictness. What's the truth?" For a moment, Elias stopped circling and
looked intently at Yisroel, "What *is* the *truth* about God?" he insisted.
But instead of waiting for an answer, he continued, resuming his walking as he spoke.

"You describe Adonai as not only full of pleasing surprises, but as
close to us—even inside us. The God you describe isn't seated high on
a faraway throne surrounded by important angels who act nothing like
us. You make it seem as if God is playful and even mischievous, and that
God hides from us, secretly wishing to be found."

Elias suddenly stopped moving and smiled broadly.

"The pleasure that God takes in making small, unimportant things
like ants, bees, and tiny vowels is making me think that God and I have
a lot in common."

7

Aryeh worked longer hours now that Rifka was staying with his sister Leya. He hoped to earn more and perhaps become able to make a home and practice his trade in Horodenka. It was rumored that there might be enough business there for another blacksmith. The szlachcic Potocki who owned the village was acquiring new lands, and more horses would be needed to work them.

Aryeh would rather fashion iron implements for village families than work for the szlachta. But he was willing to do whatever work would bring him closer to his daughter, sister, and nephews.

He knew that Rifka missed him, but she was clearly happy and thriving with Leya. He was glad not to burden Rifka with his prolonged grief over the loss of Dvorah. Once he arrived in Horodenka, he would, again, do his best to conceal his melancholy.

When Rifka drew close after the midday Sabbath meal to ask Aryeh what troubled him, he suspected his efforts to mask his sadness were not succeeding.

"Rifkalla, do you remember Shayna, the graceful black horse you've watched me shoe? The one Reb Mosha let you ride?"

Rifka nodded, curious.

"Shayna has died."

Rifka leaned her head against him, and he wrapped his arms around her.

Few horses were as charismatic as Shayna, and it was rare for a Jew to own a horse let alone to have developed such affection for one, as Reb Mosha had for Shayna. But, although it was true that Aryeh was grieved by the horse's death and moved by his good friend Mosha's sorrow, what

Aryeh didn't say was how intensely this death stirred the feelings of loss he carried within. Nor would he admit how being apart from Rifka made everything harder to bear.

Rifka asked many questions about the horse's death. Aryeh wanted to answer without telling the true story of how the horse had died. He would not even share the truth with Leya, lest Rifka overhear.

"What happened *after* Shayna slipped on the ice and broke her back?" Rifka insisted with great concern. Leya, Gedaliah, and Samuel were now listening intently, too, as Aryeh continued.

"Shayna stopped breathing. Reb Mosha said the mourner's prayer. A local peasant who had offered his assistance when he saw us kneeling by the horse, held his cap over his heart."

Rifka curled herself tighter into her father's lap, pressing her head against his chest. Samuel had so serious a look that he did not resemble himself. Gedaliah's head was bowed. When Aryeh saw Leya searching his face, he lowered his gaze.

That Shayna had slipped on ice and tragically broken her back was true. That Reb Moshe had prayed while a local peasant had bowed his head, held his cap over his heart, and wept at Shayna's side was also true. But that the poor horse's death was an unfortunate accident was not. Mosha would never have worked Shayna when the ground was treacherous. Instead, that night the horse had been forcefully led from her stall by a group of drunken peasants. It was one of those peasants who afterwards came to Aryeh just before sunrise to tell him, deeply remorseful, sobered and shaken by the cruelty in which he had participated. The youth had seen Aryeh fitting Shayna for shoes when he had brought one of his master's horses to the Jewish blacksmith. Aryeh had seemed mild-mannered, which made it easier and safer, the peasant said, to confess to him what had transpired.

A group of peasant farmers full of vodka stirring up their hate for "the stinking Jews" had decided to take a little revenge on a Jew who thought he was good enough to own a horse. At their head was Kovel, a large, brutish man proud of feats that intimidated even the Polish authorities. As before, Kovel boasted of murdering animals with his bare hands with and without vodka goading him.

"So why not people, too, for a good enough price—and even without a price!" Kovel shouted, rousing his comrades in the tavern. "We all know that Jewish bastards collecting taxes for the szlachta bastards are responsible for our rotten lives. Tell me: what's the difference between one set of bastards who strut with nobility up their asses, and the other set of bastards, the Jews, who lick those asses?"

"No difference, Kovel," his comrades bellowed.

"That's right. No difference. So why not teach the ass-licking bastards a lesson? Tell me: what Jew deserves a beast like that horse?"

Blind with drink, they lured Shayna out, the repentant youth recounted to Aryeh. The horse did not trust them, resisting as fiercely as she could, which made them more determined to overcome her. They pushed and whipped her as she bore them one by one, trying not to fall on the ice crusted over Okup's unyielding soil. Shayna buckled under their weight when four of them whipped her sides.

She finally collapsed with the men on top of her, her back broken.

Warmed by the horse's dying body and by the fiery *schnapps* in their bellies, the drunken men had fallen asleep draped over each other. In the morning, those who had not vomited the night before did so then, reeling away from the dead horse. They stumbled away laughing and cursing the Jews who made so much trouble for them. One of the men wondered aloud if the Jewish bastard who owned the horse would retaliate, at which Kovel laughed so hard, he retched.

Aryeh thanked the young informant for his honesty and courage, assuring him this visit would not be mentioned. Moving quickly to gather his hat and coat, Aryeh was surprised when the young man did not move from the door, even after Aryeh explained that he wished to hasten to the horse's owner. He put his hand on the young man's elbow, hoping to lead him out. The youth straightened.

"I am Stanislaw," he said, removing his cap in a sudden gesture of deference, and bowing his head. "The least I can do is take you and the horse's owner to the poor animal."

Returning to the present, Aryeh held Rifka's head next to his heart and rocked her for quite a while until she was ready to climb down. He watched Leya slice the apple cake her friend Gittel had sent as a Sabbath treat. When she served the children, she did not serve him a piece.

"Come, my brother," she said, hooking her arm into his, "we need a refreshing Shabbos walk."

Once outside, but not until they were far enough from the cottage not to be overheard, Leya stopped to face him.

"Aryeh, do you want Rifka to come back?"

He shouldn't have been surprised; his sister had always been able to see into his heart.

"Aryeh, I am concerned," she continued without waiting for his response. "Your sorrow was lifting and now it seems to have settled back, leaving you in its shadow again. Maybe having Rifka live here was the wrong decision."

Aryeh wished she weren't saying this. He preferred Leya's comforting certainty. Her faith, especially when he lacked faith, buoyed him just as it buoyed him to hear her remind him of all there was to live for. He almost could not bear her concern.

"Leyalla," he stopped and turned towards her, "I do miss her. Greatly. Some days, it feels that the light is gone from my sky. First it was my Dvorah's light taken, now Rifka's."

Leya did not take her eyes off her brother.

"But I do not want Rifka to return to Okup. It is good for her to be here. I long for her at times, yes, and there are days when I feel lost. But someone very wise," Aryeh touched his finger to Leya's temple, catching a curl, "told me that to love so deeply is a blessing."

He stepped closer, whispering. "I will tell you a secret, Leyalla. Sometimes to love strongly seems more a curse than a blessing."

"I know," Leya said.

⤳

TRAVELING TO BRODY WITH HIS SISTER A MONTH later, Aryeh was still uncertain of the purpose of this trip. When Leya had first requested his company, she said it was to seek the advice of a rabbi there.

His sister was so resolute and asked so little of him that Aryeh had agreed. He made the arrangements for a wagon in which they would travel early on the morning after the Sabbath. Young Stanislaw, Aryeh's new apprentice, would tend his blacksmithing stall in Okup. In Leya's stead, Gedaliah would receive the shoes and boots in need of mending, and though not skilled enough to mend them, he could cut leather, sweep, and otherwise act like a cobbler. He had asked to work at his mother's side until he left to study at a yeshiva in Mezritch, so he had already spent hours in the cobbling stall. The boys and Rifka would remain under Gittel's care while Leya and Aryeh traveled.

Now, reins in hand, after over two days of travel, Aryeh directed the wagon to Brody. Aryeh assumed Leya's secrecy was due to the fact that she was holding the confidence of someone in the village who was unable to travel on his or her own behalf. It did not surprise him that his sister would consider it imperative to be an emissary for someone seeking spiritual counsel. But why they should be seeking counsel in Brody, a hundred and fifty kilometers from Horodenka, perplexed him. Leya addressed him now as if he had spoken his question.

"We are going to see Rabbi Elijah of Brody to seek his understanding of death and his blessings in the healing of grief," Leya said.

"His understanding of death, Leyalla?"

"Aryeh, I want to talk to Rabbi Elijah about you and about me, about the losses we have endured and about how we are living in their wake. The rabbi is older than we are and known for his great compassion. Many years ago, he lost his wife. Batya has described his love for her as that of the rain for the earth."

Aryeh did not lift his gaze from the horse whose reins he gripped more tightly.

Aryeh and Leya's wagon entered the city, moving slowly along a wide cobblestone street, crowded with peddlers pulling carts behind them.

Brody, although not as large as Warsaw, was a prosperous city into which a steady stream of commerce flowed. Aryeh knew Brody was owned by one of the commonwealth's richest and most powerful noblemen, who was said to control more of Poland than its king and who had bestowed upon Jewish and Gentile traders many privileges and protections. It was the nobleman's intention that the trade between the Ottoman Empire and Western Europe pass through Brody instead of along its current route through the city of Lemberg.

Here in Brody, Jewish vendors were scattered throughout the city, rather than clustered in a designated marketplace once a week as they were in Horodenka and Okup. From the wagon, Aryeh and Leya could see that Jews and Poles here also peddled a larger amount and wider array of wares, including bolts of fine cloth, gems, silks, and furs. Brody's artisans worked in larger stalls with numerous apprentices and finer materials at hand. In addition to numerous tinsmiths, there were several silver and goldsmiths. Furriers and perfume and silk merchants wore their fine black coats that were usually reserved by village Jews for the Sabbath and their shtreimels, the wide black hats trimmed in fur that only the rare village Jew could afford. The thriving Jewish merchants paraded and conducted business as if they were part owners of Brody.

Aryeh watched a wealthy Jew enter a stately brick house along the main thoroughfare as if it were his own. Surely this couldn't be. But as their wagon rolled past the towering three-story house, Aryeh spotted the *mezuzah* at its entrance, indicating this was indeed a Jewish home. Surely, Aryeh thought, there must be was a sector of Brody in which the majority of Jews lived, crowded into homes that were neither brick nor so stately.

When Aryeh saw a tiered roof visible over the other buildings, he guessed it was the roof of Brody's renowned synagogue. This was their destination. The synagogue shared a courtyard with Brody's largest Beis Midrash. Leya had been instructed that it was in this House of Study that Rabbi Elijah performed his duties.

The highly esteemed Rabbi Elijah was chief judge of Brody's Rabbinical Court, where all manner of religious and secular disputes, including tax collection issues, crimes, and divorce matters, could be settled instead of in the courts of the Polish monarchy. Brody's Rabbinical Court was the most influential in the commonwealth; its rulings interpreting Jewish law had impacted the lives of Jews throughout Europe and beyond.

As they drew closer to the imposing structure, Aryeh was astonished. The staunch wooden building with its three-tiered roof was the height of perhaps seven or eight men standing on each other's shoulders. With carved double doors and a carefully crafted balcony, the full width of the front of the building, this House of Prayer exuded none of the self-effacing meekness of a village shul tucked out of sight. Instead, the synagogue had the bold stance of a church whose dome and spire could be seen from a distance.

They decided to enter the synagogue before seeking Rabbi Elijah in the neighboring House of Study. The doors were unlocked, though it was not the hour of a prayer service. Aryeh encouraged Leya to enter with him through the main doors, not the side entrance that led directly to the women's section. With no caretaker to deter them, Leya took Aryeh's arm and crossed the threshold. They were instantly struck by the beauty and scale of what they beheld.

The sanctuary was larger than any prayer hall either had seen. Four massive, carved pillars framed the platform in its center. The banisters and balustrades surrounding the bimah were so intricately carved that the wood, Leya whispered, reminded her of lace. Most compelling was the Holy Ark at the Eastern Wall in which the Torah reposed. The Ark was tall and elaborately carved with figures of fish, intricate vines, deer, and eagles in flight.

They climbed the stairs of the platform. Aryeh slowly ran his hands over the carvings of half men, half fish on the wings of the Ark.

"The labor…" he whispered, his voice trailing.

Looking up, their marvel expanded. Over the bimah, a vibrantly painted canopy crowned the sanctuary as if heaven and its contents lay open above them. Living letters and passages of the Torah had been painted between the carved arches of the pillars. Aryeh and Leya, riveted by the astounding artisanry surrounding them, did not move.

Finally, taking hands, they walked slowly towards the door. At the threshold, they turned around almost as one, and stood in silent awe to take in the hall of prayer once more before leaving.

"Aryeh," Leya whispered gently, "As stunning as this sanctuary is, I believe the sanctuary of the heart is even more wondrous."

Moved by her unexpected words, he turned to face his sister. Light filtering through a patch of blue-green stained glass made Leya's tears glisten with color. Aryeh touched his finger to her cheek.

"And this tear, Leyalla, is this one of the heart's jewels?"

They stepped from the grand synagogue into the bright afternoon light.

In the courtyard, they learned from a yeshiva student coming from the Beis Midrash that Rabbi Elijah, not feeling well, had left and gone home. Perhaps in response to their looks of disappointed surprise, the student said quickly that he would lead them to the rabbi's house.

"But might it be an imposition on the rabbi? If he is not well, then…"

"Not an imposition at all," the young man interrupted Aryeh. "Rabbi Elijah welcomes visitors! *One must consider a guest as God himself,* he likes to say. Come, I will show you where the good rabbi lives."

The distance warranted horse and wagon. On the way, their lively host answered questions they had not asked as if they had.

"The rabbi has a distinguished son named Gershon who is likely to follow in his father's footsteps. He makes his home in Kuty but is presently visiting his father. Rabbi Elijah also has a daughter whom few have seen. Because she lives a somewhat secluded life, rumors grow around her like weeds around a rare flower."

The moment they arrived at the rabbi's home, the young scholar jumped down, saying he would care for the horse's needs. He directed them to the door and quickly led the horse away. Aryeh was not accustomed to such a talkative yeshiva student. On the way to Rabbi Elijah's door, they could hear the young man, still continuing his lively conversation, now with the horse.

Aryeh knocked at the rabbi's door while Leya ran her hand over the silver mezuzah on the doorpost, embossed with the letter *Shin* standing for *Shaddai,* one of God's names. She smiled. "One with *so many* names, yet impossible to ever really describe."

The young man who answered the door was close in age to the student who had led them, but seemed as shy as the other had been outgoing. He averted his gaze as Leya explained who they were and the purpose of their visit. His reticence seemed, at least in part, a response to the fact that a woman was addressing him.

"Rabbi Elijah was informed of our visit, although no specific time was established," Leya told him, "He wrote us that we should come when we were able and then, once here, seek him out. We went to the Beis Midrash, but were told he had returned home."

With a subtle gesture of his thin hand, the young man invited them to cross the threshold and remain just inside the door. He bowed his head, burying his chin and beard in his neck, and hastened down the corridor, disappearing from view.

Within moments, another young man, perhaps seventeen or eighteen years of age, walked towards them, his posture erect. He extended his hand to Aryeh and without looking directly at Leya, tipped his hat in her direction.

"I am Rabbi Elijah's son Gershon. I welcome you to my father's home."

Gershon inquired about their trip, apologizing for any difficulty they may have encountered in finding his father. There was something unusual about Gershon's manner. Was it his uncommon blend of confidence and humility? The way young Gershon held himself and spoke, even the quality of his voice, bordered on arrogance, but it was not. He seemed to have no doubt that he belonged here—at this time, in this place—as if he knew and accepted his destiny as the son of Brody's most renowned rabbi without a trace of personal pride.

They followed Gershon into a small sitting room where he asked them to wait for his father.

When the silver-haired rabbi entered alone, Aryeh and Leya rose. Aryeh immediately sensed the same confidence he had seen in the man's son. The older man, however, offered Leya his hand with a direct and warm glance and a sincere smile of welcome. He shook Aryeh's hand firmly. Before sitting down, the rabbi motioned to his guests to sit in two chairs across from his.

"Rabbi Elijah, as you know," Leya began, "it is for your counsel that my brother Aryeh and I have traveled here."

The rabbi nodded, leaning forward attentively.

"Almost five years ago my husband Ber died in a sudden and unexpected accident when his wagon overturned." She turned to her brother. "Aryeh, if you allow, may I speak for a moment on your behalf?"

Aryeh nodded, relieved not to speak.

"My brother lost his wife Dvorah a little more than two years ago. I have two sons, one, thirteen and the other, seven. I live in Horodenka, Aryeh in Okup. Aryeh's nine-year-old daughter Rifka has come to live with me. All three are sensitive children, each feeling the loss of their missing parent as well as the sorrow of the one remaining."

Leya paused, looking pensive now, as if not sure what she would say next. The rabbi watched Leya with a delicate smile. She was put at ease by this attentive, gentle confidante.

"I have felt very close to my late husband Ber, Rabbi. Perhaps too close. I feel him around me at times, comforting me with a voice that seems to come from my own heart. All this has been a great consolation. I have invited his presence eagerly."

Leya paused for a moment then spoke again softly.

"Rabbi Elijah, is it possible for me to keep Ber's spirit, his soul, tied to the earth and in this way not allow him to move on? Is this what I am doing? When I encourage my brother Aryeh to reach to his Dvorah, to invite her spirit to soothe him, am I doing harm?"

Aryeh was taken aback. Leya had received so much solace from feeling Ber's presence; sensing him close had strengthened her. She had confided to Aryeh that some times she felt Ber guiding her when she stumbled in her knowledge of shoemaking. And the rare times when Aryeh sensed Dvorah close, had he not been filled him with hope, as if soothing waters had been poured on the searing fire that consumed him? Why would Leya imagine this could be wrong? How could something so filled with blessing and beneficence possibly cause harm?

Aryeh leaned forward, face down, not certain that he wanted to hear the rabbi's answer to Leya's question.

"Your love for your departed husband does not bind him," Rabbi Elijah began, the compassion in his voice palpable. "Do not worry."

"But," he went on," if over time your sense of Ber's presence changes, you must allow it to change. Your love for him and his for you shall never end. But you may find as time passes that the loving presence you experience as Ber no longer feels to be that of an individual man. He will have merged completely into the Source of Love from which all human love arises."

Aryeh lifted his head from his hands. It seemed the man was looking right through him, waiting for Aryeh to speak. Aryeh had nothing to add to what his sister had said. It had not, after all, been his idea to come for this meeting. But in the next instant, Aryeh was speaking.

"I miss my Dvorah greatly. At times, my desire to live is like a weak flame being swallowed by darkness. I call out like my sister—but I call out with anger, despair, and futility to a God I have judged cruel enough to steal the life of the innocent. I have hurled insults as if I knew better than God what should come to pass. I have no right to question the will of God so severely as if I were the only man to ever lose what was precious to me. Instead, I should..."

"You *are* the only man," Rabbi Elijah interrupted.

What had the Rabbi said? That Aryeh was the only man to have lost someone he loved? What could he mean by that?

"You are the *only* man who can feel what it is to lose this particular woman you love so dearly. No one else can know what that pain is. This is your pain. And you must feel it as only you can feel it."

Aryeh, not having expected any of this, fixed his attention on the rabbi.

"Although you saw her suffer, Dvorah does not feel pain any longer. Know this, Aryeh. Do not add to your suffering by reliving hers or pitying her. She has been freed from the bondage of the body's suffering. Her soul's wish is that you not suffer unnecessarily. But there *is* such a thing as necessary pain that cannot be avoided, which is why there is a time prescribed for mourning."

Aryeh immediately felt his familiar shame for mourning well beyond the prescribed time. As if knowing Aryeh's unspoken feelings, Rabbi Elijah continued.

"This does not mean that each man and woman is to measure and count their days of mourning. We do not cease to grieve by the power of our will alone. To find peace in the face of loss is the work of grace more than individual will."

The rabbi spoke without pedantry. The intimate, genuine manner in which he addressed them evoked Aryeh's trust.

"My wife Dalia, *Peace Be Upon Her,* died when our children Gershon and Channa were very small. I could not imagine raising them without her. It was difficult just to raise myself from my bed without her. It did not matter that I was a noted rabbi by then, a competent and respected judge in the court of Brody, schooled in the laws of burial and called upon to counsel my fellow Jews when the much feared Angel of Death came for their loved ones."

"Suddenly I was not able to speak about death with anyone. All my knowledge was like dust under my shoes. I had nothing nourishing to give as spiritual food when men and women came to me. Some days, like you, dear Leya, I called out to my Dalia, begging her for advice, for words to cross my mind and fall from my lips—words I could apply like a balm to the suffering men and women seeking my help. Sometimes when I felt my wife close to me, I would think: *Yes now, she will inspire me with the words to speak.* But, instead the grief would intensify, swelling in my chest with so much force that I could barely breathe. She did not bring me hope to give to others; instead she showed me the way deeper into my grief."

Aryeh was intrigued by the rabbi's words.

"Finally, I yielded. I stopped seeking words to give others that might still the tremble of their shoulders and hearts. I had no drink for their thirsty souls. I could only sit with them, cry with them, shake with them, call out to God for mercy, and thirst with them. I could only *not understand* with them. I stopped looking for answers. And I still do not have them today, years later."

The rabbi fell silent, continuing to look at Leya and Aryeh with his radiant eyes. No one spoke. Aryeh felt words clamoring inside him like people in a building on fire, caught in a narrow passageway through which none could exit.

"Aryeh, there is no end to the sorrow of losing one who can never be replaced. But there is an end to the sorrow that makes one wish not to live. Sorrow and love can live together in one man's heart. *They must.*"

"Are you saying, Rabbi Elijah, that I do not need to fight these torrents of grief?"

"You *cannot* fight them. Tell me, Aryeh, what if you simply saw your grief as love?"

"I would not feel shame," Aryeh answered immediately. "And I would fear my grief less, and its power to harm my daughter Rifka."

"Aryeh, when you know that your grief is rooted in love then you will feed yourself and your daughter with the power of this love. Feel the loss, but do not let it destroy you. Trust that you are being called to even greater love."

Aryeh felt both tender embrace and challenge in the rabbi's powerful words.

There was nothing more to say or ask; he felt strangely emptied— a welcome sensation, different than the customary hollow of his grief.

The three sat in silence.

~

Leya watched a girl of perhaps twelve or thirteen enter the room almost soundlessly, carrying a tray of tea and other refreshment. Her long thick hair, the color of cocoa beans, cascaded in long waves down her back. The girl moved as if she wished to be invisible, almost floating through the room. But far from being invisible, her presence was compelling, her movement eloquent.

She paused, holding the brass tray in front of Leya, who lifted one of the delicate china cups and took a piece of the fragrant, golden honey cake. The girl served Aryeh and lastly, Rabbi Elijah. She then glided out of the room, leaving Leya feeling as if an enchanting breeze had just swept over her.

Several moments passed while the three drank the hot cinnamon tea and ate the welcome delicacy.

"Was that your daughter, Rabbi Elijah?" Leya asked, aware of the strong impression the girl's brief appearance had made.

"Yes, that is my Channa." The rabbi appeared pensive when he said it, as if something preoccupied him concerning her.

Leya did not feel it her place to inquire any further although she would have liked to. Perhaps sensing her interest, the rabbi continued.

"My daughter has been promised to a very serious, dedicated student in the Brody Yeshiva. She will become his wife when she is fourteen. Reb Mendel would have her sooner, but her marrying even at fourteen seems young to me. I have refused to approve an earlier marriage. It is the custom to marry our daughters and sons at young ages, but I question the wisdom of these practices."

Leya nodded in agreement, relieved to hear the rabbi doubting the customary age of marriage, which Leya also thought too young.

No more was said about the age of marriage, about the good rabbi's daughter, or about grief. Leya offered a silent prayer that Channa be blessed with a good marriage.

As the three were leaving the sitting room, the rabbi's son Gershon entered the corridor. Rabbi Elijah, turning towards him, requested that

Gershon assure their guests' comfort for the night and that they be supplied whatever might be needed for their journey back to Horodenka.

Gershon attended them, performing his duty with a reserved kindness.

In the morning after Leya and Aryeh had eaten, he led them to their wagon. Leya realized she had been wishing for another glimpse of Channa. Even as Gershon bid them a courteous farewell, Leya looked past him, hoping the girl might appear.

8

Yisroel continued living in Rabbi Meir's home in Tluste, tutoring the rabbi's children and his wife Batya, and being present when the rabbi and his wife received distinguished guests.

Tonight, Rabbi Meir and Batya's guest was an emissary between the Jews of Poland and Jewish settlers in the Holy Land. Rabbi Ezra had just returned from conveying funds from wealthy Polish Jews to their brethren in Palestine. When the family sat together to eat, the visitor spoke of his experiences in the Holy Land.

Yisroel listened ardently as Rabbi Ezra described the Negev, the expanse of desert leading to the Dead Sea, so dense with salt that nothing could survive in its waters. Yisroel and the children marveled to hear how Rabbi Ezra had sat upright in the Dead Sea waters as if sitting on its shore. The family was enthralled by his descriptions of Eyn Gedi, a lush oasis where mountain goats grazed between olive and eucalyptus trees flourishing close to the Dead Sea.

Their guest spoke reverently about entering the holy city of Jerusalem. He described kneeling, when he arrived, to kiss the soil "saturated by tears and unimaginably sweet..." Rabbi Ezra's attention seemed to wander from the library towards somewhere distant, his voice drifting.

When he resumed, the rabbi described the growing numbers of Sephardic Jews from Spain, Turkey, Italy, Greece, and Egypt settling in Jerusalem, Hebron, Jaffa, and Gaza. He spoke of his surprise at how the Sephardic prayer service differed from the Eastern European tradition more familiar to him. Prominent Sephardic rabbis had established flourishing academies for the study of Torah.

Every night, the visitor transported his hosts, their children, and their tutor to that captivating land of stunning contrasts. On the last night of his visit, Rabbi Ezra began speaking about Safed, a village in the Galilee valley.

"I will take you there," the gentle-mannered rabbi announced. "We will travel back two hundred years, to the early 1500s. Here in Safed, a number of men with their families have settled to study and practice Kabbalah. Close your eyes; it will help you to see."

Yisroel settled back into his chair and, like the rest, closed his eyes.

Slowly and deliberately, the congenial rabbi led them on an ascent to the mountaintop village and its sacred atmosphere. They were guided through narrow cobblestone streets to the blue door of one of the prayer houses. The blue door opened onto a room with four painted arches, also of blue. Beneath the arches sat men of all ages, dressed in white— immersed in a stunning silence. Rabbi Ezra, now speaking very softly as if not to disturb the congregants, whispered that the men were meditating on the names of The Nameless One. Some had eyes closed, others sat with eyes wide open; each was absorbed in the particular name of God that he was contemplating.

At the heart of the room in the center of the rings of men was a very tall, thin man of about thirty-five, olive-skinned with a thick, wiry black beard and penetrating black eyes. This was the Kabbalists' teacher, Rabbi Isaac Luria, known as Ha'Ari, the Lion. He was reading a passage that Rabbi Ezra recited now as if repeating what he had just heard.

"You cannot find anything that exists apart from the Ayn Sof, the One Without End. *There is nothing but God.* Everything that exists, large and small, exists solely through the divine energy that flows to it, and that clothes itself in it. This Presence fills the world."

Listening, Yisroel felt as if he was returning to a home he had been seeking, not knowing he had been seeking it. He was struck by the power of his longing.

Suddenly, Yisroel envisioned Ha'Ari stepping forth toward him with a golden key in his extended palm. The key was being offered across a distance at once vast and intimate. No sooner had it been offered than it vanished. Ha'Ari drew even closer and stepped *into* Yisroel, who felt an indescribable impact in his heart that left him breathless.

Yisroel felt as if he were catching up when he heard Rabbi Ezra describe Ha'Ari leading his disciples to welcome the Sabbath in a large field overlooking the Galilee valley. The Kabbalists were singing *"L'Cha Dodi," "Come, My Beloved,"* a prayer composed by one of their community, Rabbi Ezra recited some of the prayer's words.

"Come my friend to greet the Bride, to receive the Presence of the Sabbath. She is the wellspring of blessing. Leave your turmoil. Free yourselves. Dress in garments of splendor. Rouse yourself, your light is coming, rise up and shine. Awaken. Awaken."

"What is Kabbalah, Rabbi Ezra?" Zofia asked. Her high voice abruptly brought Yisroel back from the mountaintop field to the book-lined room.

The kindly rabbi smiled and looked directly at Zofia.

"Imagine, dear child, that you are an open bowl, a vessel and that your Creator is a Source of never-ending light who wants only to fill you up." Yisroel watched Zofia draw in a deep breath then close her eyes, probably trying hard to imagine being a bowl.

"Kabbalah, my child," Rabbi Ezra said, "means that which is received."

Zofia opened her eyes, looking puzzled, as if she could neither see nor feel any "kabbalah" filling her.

"Kabbalah," he explained, "also refers to texts that contain teachings such as the words of Ha'Ari that we heard earlier. The Creator wants only to give, to bestow all manner of blessing, the way the sun gives its life-giving rays to every growing thing. Our human purpose, Kabbalah teaches, is to receive blessing and to become able to bestow it. Most Kabbalistic texts are ancient ones that were copied by scribes and available only to very few people."

" In the 1500s, shortly after Jews were expelled from Spain," Rabbi Ezra went on, "the young Luria's mind and heart were pierced by the radiance of the Kabbalah. At the age of fifteen, he retreated to an island on the Nile River where he immersed himself in the greatest of all Kabbalistic texts, the Zohar.

Elias, pacing the room as he did each night—which seemed to make it easier for him to listen—slowed now to ask a question.

"Ha'Ari was only fifteen? Did he live there by himself?"

"It is said that he was visited by rabbis of ancient times and prophets, and that it was the prophet Elijah who finally guided Luria to move to Safed."

"He wasn't much older than I am." Elias commented more to himself than to anyone in the room. "But I would not be able to concentrate that way ..." he added, voice trailing.

"Don't be so sure, my son," their guest replied, looking not at Elias but at Naftali whose eyes were riveted on Rabbi Ezra. "Never imagine yourself less capable than you are."

LATER, YISROEL thought he heard a soft knock at the door of the library where he now studied every night between midnight and dawn. Without waiting for an answer, Rabbi Ezra entered, closing the door quietly behind him.

Had Rabbi Meir and Batya become aware of Yisroel's nightly explorations and informed Rabbi Ezra? Or had the good man merely risen early in anticipation of his morning departure and made his way to the library?

The rabbi, saying nothing, drew near to where Yisroel had been leaning over a volume of Genesis. Rabbi Ezra put his hand firmly—fingers spread wide—on the open book, his hand resting there as he spoke.

"The Zohar speaks of the stories in the Bible as garments. These garments cover the Torah's soul, its underlying revelations."

Yisroel recalled his moreh Ibrahim in Horodenka speaking of the four levels of meaning.

"It is warned that we not mistake the garments for the soul. Would you like to penetrate the layers, my son?"

The wise fish vendor had promised that a teacher would come when Yisroel was ready. Was this his next teacher and guide?

As if he had heard the wordless question, Rabbi Ezra replied. "I have come to walk with you deeper into the orchard."

The following morning, Batya told Yisroel that she and Meir had invited Rabbi Ezra to remain in Tluste. Yisroel was surprised and not surprised. He was becoming more accustomed to events unfolding as if destined. Their guest had been offered a room in the large home and was welcomed to abide there until the time came for his return to the Holy Land. Yisroel did not think that Rabbi Ezra had informed Rabbi Meir and Batya of his intention to guide Yisroel. Had this rabbi known when he came to Tluste that he was to find Yisroel?

RABBI EZRA and Yisroel studied and practiced Kabbalah, night after night in Rabbi Meir's library.

"*Sefer Yetzirah*, The Book of Creation," Rabbi Ezra stated, drawing the volume from the shelf, "was written anonymously in the third century." He read from the book's introduction. "When one gazes into Sefer Yetzirah, there is no limit to his wisdom."

The root of the word "gaze," Rabbi Ezra pointed out, denotes more than physical gazing; it suggests mystical meditative insight. Sefer Yetzirah is a meditative text on the sacred letters, leading one to experience the alphabet's inner significance and the power of words to create. The Book of Creation also reveals the relationship of the letters to the earth's elements and to the planets," he explained.

It intrigued Yisroel to learn that many of the text's mysteries and revelations were attributed to the astrological teachings of Abraham. He had not known that Abraham was a practiced astrologer.

At another of their rendezvous, Rabbi Ezra introduced the three categories of Kabbalah.

"The first branch of Kabbalah is the theoretical, based largely on the Zohar. Here questions are raised and answers posited about the dynamics of creation, such as the emanations of Light from the formless Ayn Sof into the differentiated world. The Zohar also speaks of angelic realms. This form of Kabbalah reached its zenith among the Kabbalists of Safed, Ha'Ari's community, in the sixteenth century".

"The second aspect of Kabbalah," Ezra went on, "is meditative Kabbalah, presented in texts such as the Book of Creation. These texts introduced the use of divine names and letter permutations to reach mystical states of union with the divine."

"The third category—closely related to the meditative—is the magical. It consists of various signs, incantations, and divine names through which one can influence and alter natural events. Magical Kabbalah, also known as practical Kabbalah, has been the easiest to popularize, as is happening now in Poland. I will explain the reasons for this popularization another time; it is important that you understand them."

Rabbi Ezra promised his pupil that he would gain a deeper understanding of each of these realms with time, reminding Yisroel that it meant little to have knowledge of the types of Kabbalah or the names of treatises without direct experience of these teachings.

"Experience will come," Yisroel's guide assured him, "through practicing as the seers who authored these books did. The great Kabbalists can lead us to expanded understanding of the outer world and of our inner worlds."

Reverently, Rabbi Ezra invoked the presence of ancient and medieval Kabbalists.

He instructed Yisroel to listen not just with his ears, but also with his heart to Abraham Abulafia's writings about "unsheathing the soul." Ezra read the words of the thirteenth century ecstatic Kabbalist Abraham Abulafia, slowly and deliberately.

"Prepare to devote your heart. Select a special place where you can be totally alone. Empty your mind. Wrap yourself in your prayer shawl so that you will be filled with the awe of the Sacred Presence."

Closing his eyes, Yisroel felt Abulafia's words circle around him, each word a sentry sheltering him. He kept his eyes closed even as felt Rabbi Ezra wrap him in a tallis.

> "Take hold of ink, pen, and tablet. Realize that you are about to serve God in joy. Now begin to write the letters, a few or many, in any order, revolving them rapidly until your mind warms up. Delight in how they move and in what you generate. When you feel within that your mind is very, very warm from combining the letters and that through these combinations you understand new things, then you are ready to receive the Abundant Flow from the Source."

Yisroel proceeded to write the letters on the page in various combinations. He turned the letters on their sides like tumbling children frolicking in defiance of convention. Then he combined letters to form as many names for God as he could summon until his arm then his entire body began to feel molten and fluid.

It was when Yisroel loosened his grip on the pen that the names began to write themselves effortlessly, flowing like thin strands of solid light from the tip of his quill. Finally, he released the quill altogether, swaying in the embrace of a palpable peace. This peace, he realized, enveloped and pervaded the entire world at *all* times; its presence was just not usually perceived.

WHEN YISROEL returned to the library before dawn one morning after just a few hours of sleep, he was surprised to find Rabbi Ezra already there, seated at a table in the center of the room. It was the first time the teacher had arrived before his student.

"I told you, Yisroel, that I would speak about the popularization of magical, "practical" Kabbalah in our time. I will do so tonight. There are several factors, which have led to the embrace—and the fear—of Kabbalah among our people."

"I am sure you have seen Yiddish booklets like these?" He held up one of the many Yiddish booklets Batya had brought to Yisroel's attention, asking him to help her become able to read them. The booklets prescribed Kabbalistic practices such as incantations of God's names to prevent or confront adversities like fevers, diseases, insomnia, sterility, and even thieves or poverty. A great many pages were devoted to curing barrenness and assuring healthy childbirth, including practices to ward off stillbirth, hemorrhage, and birth defects. Yisroel had also discovered a number of pamphlets whose purpose was to outline "ethical behavior" based on Kabbalah. Readers were instructed that each one of their actions played a crucial role in deciding the fate not only of their individual lives and families but of the universe.

"The widespread distribution of booklets such as these, not too long ago, would have been not only unthinkable, but impossible. So, why now?" Rabbi Ezra asked.

Yisroel, with no ready answer, listened with interest.

"The printing press is part of the answer, but only a part, Yisroel. These booklets and the practices they contain have blossomed from seeds planted by Ha'Ari long ago in Safed. But Ha'Ari's seeds were also watered by tears following the tragic heresy of Shabtai Tzvi." It was the first time Yisroel had detected sadness in his teacher.

"But let us explore one factor at a time. As I have taught you already, Yisroel, Ha'Ari after entering the depths of the holy Zohar, expounded the story of creation to his disciples in Safed. He taught a three-fold process: the withdrawal of the Infinite to "make space" for the finite world; the shattering of the vessels that could not hold the Infinite Light poured into them; and the ongoing repair of these vessels—finding the shards and releasing the hidden sparks that their light might be unified with its Source."

Yisroel recognized that it would take years, if ever, before he fully grasped the significance of Ha'Ari's cosmology. Rabbi Ezra smiled and nodded, appearing to read Yisroel's mind.

"Ha'Ari's teachings include myriad, complex details explaining the actions that must be taken to bring about the repair of our broken world.

He taught that every sacred commandment in the Torah, even the most basic such as washing one's hands before eating, has a mystical meaning. Each sacred action corresponds to a particular aspect of the Divine—aspects such as wisdom, beauty, and kindness, which he elaborated in a complex system known as *sefiros*."

"One way to understand the sefiros," Rabbi Ezra instructed, "is as rays emanating from an unknowable Source. To name these rays as they appear in creation helps us approach the unknowable. Ha'Ari instructed that a simple action can have a cosmic impact when performed with awareness of its correspondence to a divine quality. With ceaseless, intense rigor, the Safed Kabbalists studied the precise intentions taught them by their master; they performed each action hoping to contribute to the redemption and repair of the world."

"Elite groups have formed in Poland to emulate the great piety of the Kabbalists in Safed. In these elite academies, supported by private benefactors, men gather for the purpose of doing Kabbalistic practices day and night to effect unity on cosmic planes. These exclusive academies are known as *kloiz*; the most renowned of these is in the city of Brody."

"Ha'Ari's cosmology and teachings have proven in large measure too complex for the majority of Jews to follow precisely," Rabbi Ezra explained. "However, the belief that captive divine sparks can be released by human deeds—and that the world is improved in this way—has given countless men and women hope and a sense of sacred power. The popular Yiddish publications you have seen are filled with practices founded on the belief that one's deeds can impact the larger scheme of things. One can invoke desired outcomes and avert others rather than being a mere victim of fate."

A shadow crossed Rabbi Ezra's face.

"Tragically, the hope and pure power derived from Lurianic Kabbalah were exploited by the self-proclaimed messiah, Shabtai Tzvi."

Yisroel had heard the name of Shabtai Tzvi spoken disparagingly and even fearfully, but never with such deep sadness.

"To speak of Ha'Ari's influence would not be complete without mention of the aberration of Lurianic Kabbalah by Shabtai Tzvi and his 'prophet,' Nathan of Gaza."

"In the late 1600s," Rabbi Ezra went on, "the self-proclaimed prophet, Nathan of Gaza, hailed Shabtai Tzvi, a Turkish Jew, as the long-awaited Redeemer not only of the Jews, but of all souls. Shabtai Tzvi claimed to be the fulfillment of biblical messianic prophecy and promised to lead his followers to the World to Come. There they would finally experience the freedom and higher justice for which they longed."

"Jews of all social classes, from Amsterdam to Egypt, were inspired by the vision of a final and lasting peace in the paradise he predicted. Throughout Poland and, particularly in our region of Podolia, many took refuge in Nathan and Shabtai Tzvi's promises of relief. Vivid in everyone's memories was the brutal devastation endured at the hands of Ukrainian and Polish peasants led by the Cossack Chmielnicki."

"*The Savior*, as Shabtai Tzvi referred to himself, assured the Jews that their suffering had meaning; the ancient biblical messianic prophecies had, after all, warned of utter chaos before the end of time, had they not? The Savior's mission, he proclaimed, was to lead his flock to the freedom promised in the World to Come. His followers, who became known as the Sabbateans, merely had to do what Shabtai and his prophet Nathan prescribed—which was, primarily, to intensify the chaos."

"Your life will provide you with much more education about this, Yisroel. For now, suffice it to say that Shabtai Tzvi and his movement stole power from the teachings of the Ha'Ari *and* from the countless Jews who relinquished their inner power. The Sabbateans' hopes of being rescued by their "Savior" ultimately brought upon the Sabbatean flock further suffering when their savior abandoned them to save himself from the Sultan's gallows."

"But how did Shabtai Tzvi use Ha'Ari's teachings in his mission?" Yisroel held up a booklet exhorting men and women to ward off evil spirits with select angelic names. "And how has all this influenced publications like these?"

A rueful smile, not his usual amiable one, appeared on Rabbi Ezra's kind face.

"A good question. In fact, more than one good question." He lowered his gaze as if searching for the way to begin. "This, too, I shall relay somewhat simply for now."

"At the time of Shabtai Tzvi's emergence, Ha'Ari's teachings and his community were revered. This respect derived largely from descriptions in manuscripts that had made their way back to Poland and other nations about the piety of the brethren on the mountaintop. Their prayers and carefully applied intentions, it was heralded, could bring imminent change to the world."

"Shabtai Tzvi arose one hundred years after Ha'Ari, in a world of Jewry that because of Ha'Ari's cosmology believed redemption possible in their lifetime. The false messiah claimed his revelations were based on secret teachings of Kabbalah to which he, but not the masses, could gain access. Using Ha'Ari's teachings, Shabtai Tzvi spoke of the light trapped in shards of the shattered vessels—the good hidden in evil. But his interpretation of the Lurianic teaching that *Godliness exists everywhere* was to teach his followers to commit immoral and licentious acts in order to free godliness from where it is concealed in evil. He commanded those who worshipped him to free good by penetrating evil. He himself regularly practiced countless defilements in the name of liberating the purity confined there. The perpetration of illicit actions and the violation of all *mitzvos* governing moral and ethical behavior became commonplace."

Rabbi Ezra's caving shoulders belied the burden of a painful weight. Yisroel thought to comfort the man, but not sure how, remained rooted where he was. After some moments, the rabbi straightened and, regaining his customary demeanor, continued.

"When we began our studies, I spoke of the Torah's stories being the garments concealing its essence. This is a Kabbalistic perspective derived from the Zohar. From this teaching, Shabtai Tzvi and Nathan formulated a central doctrine of Sabbateanism: to violate the moral mandates of Torah and Talmud is to hasten revelation and the heavenly World to Come. Chaos and heresy must reign to precipitate redemption."

"Of late, there has been a proliferation of booklets filled with magical formulae, angelic names, and spells used for protection, all of which derive from ancient Kabbalistic practices. The majority of men and women who perform these practices are not seeking mystical insight into the nature of the Infinite. Many rabbis and scholars, as a result of Shabtai Tzvi's abuse of Ha'Ari's teachings, want to guard the ancient mystical texts and practices by limiting their proliferation."

Rabbi Ezra placed his large hand on Yisroel's shoulder.

"There is more for you to learn about the venerable Ha'Ari and the madman Shabtai Tzvi. Your life will bring you these and many more lessons. The Holy Zohar is a book that you will study for the rest of your years. But more than this: to *live* the Torah and the Zohar's essence is your destiny, my son."

At his moreh's words, Yisroel felt a palpable heat rising from the base of his spine to the crown of his head. Yisroel did not know that he had closed his eyes until he opened them and saw that Rabbi Ezra had left the room.

The next morning, as suddenly as he had entered Yisroel's life, Rabbi Ezra announced his departure. He would travel over land to Constantinople from whose shore he would cross the Black Sea and continue by land to Palestine.

ᚦ

"OUR DAILY EXPLORATIONS WITH YISROEL ARE wondrous journeys, are they not?" Batya exclaimed after a morning lesson, feeling tempted to clap her hands like Zofia and Naftali. "Perhaps Yisroel will join us on a journey to visit Gittel, Jacob, and their daughters? It has been some time since we all went together to Horodenka."

Zofia ran into her mother's arms, repeating *Yes* so many times that Elias teased her, asking if she was really quite sure that she wanted to go.

"And Naftali?" Yisroel's question stunned every one including Naftali.

Speechless, Batya wondered if Yisroel was serious about Naftali coming with them? The only journey her Naftali had made was the journey from her womb into the world where she had imagined at the time he would reside only briefly. But he had remained, his soul making its home in a body that miraculously did not diminish its light. To consider subjecting him to a discomforting wagon journey was out of the question. That Yisroel would even consider otherwise and now stood gazing at her reminded Batya that this young man of eighteen was not to be underestimated. And now, Naftali, attending to their conversation, strained to discipline his uncontrollable muscles.

"But Yisroel, surely—" Batya protested.

"I would very much like to accompany your family and to bring Naftali with us," Yisroel stated unequivocally. He had never interrupted her before.

"With Elias' help, I will lift him into the wagon and if need be, hold him during the ride. Should it be necessary to stop to attend to the needs of his body, I will carry him to a field and assist him in privacy. Once in Horodenka, I believe that the cobbler Leya will help to accommodate us, should we be too many for your cousin Gittel."

Seeing the expectant look on Naftali's face, Batya reluctantly agreed.

What lay before her now was to convince her husband. Although not a considerable distance, the twenty-five kilometers between the villages crossed through dense forests. Meir had routinely cautioned against travel to Horodenka because of the well-known dangers of the highwaymen, and this was without even considering the added burden of a disabled boy. But Meir did not like to refuse his wife, and Batya knew this.

Batya's request met with Meir's concerned opposition.

"Perhaps," asked Batya, who knew her husband very well, "if you came with us, you would feel more assured of our safety?"

"My dear, I would like very much to travel with you," he responded, "but I have certain duties here in Tluste that I cannot leave."

Moved by his children's eagerness, especially Naftali's, in the end Meir conceded to their trip, arranging for two wagon drivers, brothers reputed to be formidable in the face of attack.

The morning of the family's departure, in lieu of the two brothers who had been hired, a third appeared to replace them. His brothers, he reported, had been involved in a brawl the previous night and hence were not available to offer their services. Removing his hat, the fellow bowed from the waist with an almost comical flourish.

Batya was relieved that Meir had been unexpectedly summoned to the Rabbinical Court that morning; if he were there, he would likely have refused the unimpressive man's services. Batya would do nothing to put her family in jeopardy, but, surrendering to the perhaps irrational feeling that they were as safe with Yisroel as with any driver her husband might employ, she proceeded. Batya instructed a servant to inform Meir when he returned that his wife had hastened the family's departure to assure travel in full daylight.

DESPITE THE JOSTLING RIDE, Naftali fell asleep in the back of the wagon, his head resting in Yisroel's lap. The sleeping boy's countenance had a subtle radiance Yisroel had noticed before. It had begun to happen more often of late that Yisroel could perceive light emanating from people and even objects, as if each carried an essence that could be seen as light.

Batya's scream shattered his thoughts.

Yisroel looked up to see Batya pull Zofia close on their wooden seat behind the driver. The wagon stopped abruptly, horses rearing as the driver pulled the reigns taut.

Yisroel heard the raucous laughter before he saw the three men approach, knives drawn.

Swiftly and with minimal movement, Yisroel lowered sleeping Naftali's head from his lap, covering him with a blanket, head to toe. He signaled to Elias with his glance and a slight nod in Naftali's direction that this passenger was not to be mentioned.

A large man with stained teeth and yellowed eyes ordered everyone down from the wagon. Zofia clung to her mother as the two stepped down, taking the trembling hand of their driver. The terrified driver had not stopped begging for mercy since seeing the bandits, who now threatened to cut out his wagging tongue if he did not stop.

"You—fine Jewish bitch," the man giving orders demanded, "you must be carrying money and probably other things of value. Give it here—that is if you wish to keep your life and spare your precious children." He took a step toward towards Batya, his knife drawn in one hand, his other hand extended palm up.

Batya dropped a purse of coins on the ground in front of her.

"Come now, let me have the rest." The man stepped closer, his voice a mixture of threat and taunt. "Surely you have more concealed where you would not want me to search?"

A second man, younger than his cohorts, and eager to serve his master's whims, stepped forward, putting a blade to the staunch woman's neck. The third, a stocky man with one closed eye sucked back in to his skull, pulled Zofia away from her mother. Yisroel watched the child bite her lip but not cry out, following the example of her mother. Elias stood as unmoving as the wagon.

Yisroel stepped forward, impelled by an irresistible force, although he had no idea what he would do.

"These people have done you no harm."

Yisroel walked to within arm's length of the hulking man who had threatened the rabbi's wife. The burly, foul-breathed bandit laughed mockingly, then, staring straight at Yisroel, spat at him. The slimy bead of saliva hit the ground just in front of Yisroel who stepped over it and drew closer.

"For your own sake, do not harm them. What harm you do will be returned to you a thousand fold." A fearless certainty had possessed him, his own voice almost unrecognizable.

The brash leader, scratching the crown of his matted hair looked his unexpected opponent over. Instead of striking him down, which would have taken only one good thrash, he bellowed, "Who are you?" Then, appearing to regain his senses, he lifted his arm to strike.

Meeting his challenger's gaze, Yisroel did not move or speak. What he'd said earlier had been given to him; but no words came now. Instead, a mounting, forceful compassion enveloped Yisroel. He felt it flow from his eyes and unmoving limbs toward the furious man whose arm remained raised.

"Put him in his place," cheered the one-eyed thief hoarsely.

Instead the large man lowered his broad hand, suddenly appearing to have forgotten his reason for raising it.

"Go home," Yisroel spoke quietly. "Revive yourself as men. You are not ruthless thieves."

Disarmed without having been touched, the abashed leader looked confused. He turned to his comrades.

"Put your knife away, boy," he commanded the youth who had been gripping the gleaming weapon held at Batya's neck.

"And you," he gruffly ordered the other, "let the girl go to her mother. Leave these Jews. They have nothing to offer us."

The highwaymen retreated into the dark woods as suddenly as they had appeared.

Once they were out of sight, the wagon driver, who had not stopped trembling—although he had stopped begging—fell to the ground as if his fear had been holding him up.

Batya squatted to embrace Zofia, who had not taken her eyes off Yisroel. Elias climbed back into the wagon next to Naftali who, astonishingly, had not been awakened.

Yisroel was as stunned as the others by the drastic change in their fate. He had merely followed an inexorable guidance that directed his actions, words—even his silence; the Ayn Sof had taken the reins. Now what remained was to take the reins from the unnerved driver, obeying Batya's request to lead the horses home.

When Batya asked Yisroel what he had done to send their attackers away, all Yisroel was able to say was to ask her not to speak of what had happened to anyone.

WHEN MEIR questioned why the family had returned to Tluste, Batya replied that she had recognized the dangers of travel and thought it better not to continue on to Horodenka. After hearing their mother's response, the children, though they had not been asked to guard the secret, did not speak of the encounter either.

A fortnight later, when a teacher in one of Tluste's cheyders became ill, Meir asked Yisroel to take over the position. To appease Batya's concern about losing instruction for the children, her husband suggested that Yisroel continue to live with them and offer the family instruction after his hours in the schoolroom.

The following week, Yisroel assumed his duties as teacher in the Tluste cheyder.

"The cheyder students are humming melodies on their way home from school," Meir announced a few weeks later at the end of a family meal. Batya said nothing, waiting to discern if her husband, whose demeanor was, as usual, quite serious, was pleased by this or judged it as somehow frivolous.

"One of their favorite activities has become "singing God's glory," her husband continued, "which they do by reciting verses from psalms that they have memorized, as well as by making up new exclamations of praise such as *Praise the One who causes stones to be kicked farthest by me* or *Praise the One who sweetens wild blueberries*." Meir cleared his throat, patted his mouth with his napkin, and allowed his nascent smile to become quite broad—neither it nor his pleasure the least bit disguised.

"A slow-growing, steady respect for the new teacher is spreading among the Jews of Tluste," Meir nodded, looking at his wife, who could not help but smile back.

∾

RABBI MEIR'S comment about the community's growing respect for Yisroel was proven true only a few weeks later, when the fathers of two of his pupils came to him for help over an unsettled debt. The men asked Yisroel to counsel them so they would not need to make their dispute public by going to the Rabbinical Court. Yisroel was not sure what to do. He had never arbitrated a dispute. Was he capable of the task? When something within him, greater than his limited knowledge, acquiesced, he consented to hear what concerned them.

Adam the bricklayer was angry with the potter Moses. Two years earlier, the bricklayer Adam had agreed to rebuild Moses' kiln without being paid, knowing that the potter had just buried his wife and oldest son and did not have the means to pay.

"It was an act of trust, not of charity," Adam stated indignantly in the small, empty classroom. "I expected that he would repay me when he could. This was made very clear between us. It cost me many days to rebuild the kiln. Now, since injuring my arm, I am unable to lay bricks. I need the money owed me to feed my family until my arm recovers and I can work again."

"I do not owe the irate bricklayer any payment," the potter responded. "Some time ago I provided him with a multitude of bricks. I am free of debt to the good bricklayer," he concluded firmly, as unmovable in his conviction as his friend.

"His second-rate bricks cracked apart and were useless," the brick-layer contested hotly.

Moses turned his head in Yisroel's direction. "It is not my responsibility to guarantee that my bricks last an eternity. In this world of change, what can we be certain will endure?"

Yisroel, listening to the Moses the potter's certainty of his position, wondered why he had even consented to come.

As if he had heard Yisroel's unspoken thoughts, Moses added, "I came not because I think I have committed any wrong, but because Adam was my friend." Yisroel could feel the potter's sadness; the loss of his friend Adam was a chasm he didn't know how to cross.

"I am only seeking justice," the frustrated Adam asserted, wincing from the pain in his arm. "Had Moses' kiln not endured, I would have returned to repair it." He dropped heavily onto one of the classroom's low benches.

"I want justice, too," the potter said stubbornly.

Silence hung between the two men who seemed to have said all there was to say and now awaited their arbiter's response.

"You are friends."

These were the first words Yisroel had spoken since greeting the two at the door of his classroom. Unlike true judges, like Rabbi Meir, Yisroel was not schooled in the ways of commerce and in rabbinical wisdom governing the ethical and spiritual conduct of a Jew. He would call on whatever within him had led him to accept their request for counsel, and wait. Thankfully the words came soon and were clear.

"The loss of your friendship is the greatest loss. What you owe each other is to restore your friendship."

Neither man protested. The rigidness in Adam the bricklayer's shoulders lessened. The potter Moses, still standing, looked down.

Yisroel addressed him. "Moses, your friend needs your help now. When you worked beside him to rebuild your kiln, you gained some skill in bricklaying, did you not? You can repay Adam now by offering him your arms as his own arm heals."

Yisroel paused for a moment before turning to the bricklayer. "Adam, receive Moses' help and in this way allow your friendship to be rebuilt just as once the two of you reconstructed a kiln together."

The potter, as if he had been just waiting for an opening that might lead to reconciliation, took a step toward his friend, the bricklayer, where he sat, kneading his painful shoulder. Moses placed his hand gently on top of Adam's. Adam's hand stopped moving and for a moment, it looked as if he might pull it away, but instead Adam let his hand rest under Moses' hand.

What had occurred flowed from the men's mutual intention, even if unconscious, to find harmony. The power of their desire had led

Yisroel to surrender to not knowing—and to allowing grace to speak through him.

Was there deep within all men and women a core desire for peace? Was this present even in the highwaymen who had unexpectedly withdrawn their weapons and aggression? It was not Yisroel that had deterred them, but the presence of true compassion that had moved through him.

He would leave the friends alone now. At the door, Yisroel looked back to witness the embrace of two men who, having come for judgment, had finally stopped judging each other.

OTHERS BEGAN to come for the schoolteacher's judgment, although Yisroel knew it was not *his* judgment being dispensed. Merchants came with outraged patrons; wives, with their husbands. A peasant farmer sought Yisroel together with his neighbor who had allegedly damaged the farmer's plow while borrowing it and then refused to help with its repair. Even Christian neighbors approached when they learned of the gentle Jew who helped people mend broken promises.

In each case, Yisroel was careful not to form an opinion. He knew there was so much he did not know about the law or about those before him. Instead, he listened intently to the appeals and invited the guidance of One who exists beyond the grievances that separate men and women from each other.

Each night, after his duties as schoolteacher and arbiter were done, Yisroel returned to the family. There Zofia's voice singing psalms formed a quilt of light over the household. When Naftali tried to sing with her, the family welcomed his effortful grunts graciously. Zofia delighted in the steady music of her brother's eyes.

Elias had become something of a scribe, copying passages from books in his father's library. The opening of the book of Genesis, *In the Beginning God Created*, had become his favorite. He reveled in the creation of letters, words, and phrases coming through the tip of his quill onto the blank parchment where an instant before there was nothing.

∾

RABBI ELIJAH, CHIEF RABBI OF BRODY, WAS GRATEFUL to be welcomed as a guest in Rabbi Meir and Batya's home whenever his travels brought him to Tluste. No matter how demanding his schedule, he always enjoyed spending time with Meir and Batya's children, each so delightfully distinct from the other.

It did not take long for Elijah to hear and feel the enthusiasm Elias, Zofia, and even Naftali expressed about their new studies.

"The credit must be given to Yisroel," Rabbi Meir replied quickly when Elijah commented on this, "Tluste's schoolteacher who inspires not only the sons of Tluste, but also my daughter and even my wife."

Batya smiled. "The gifted teacher of whom my husband speaks is usually at our table. But, equipped with ointments he prepared, Yisroel has gone to visit a bricklayer whose arm is injured."

Rabbi Meir, appearing amused, continued. "Our noted tutor has many gifts it seems. Not only has he proven himself a good teacher, he also seems to have a surprising intimacy with plants and their secrets. But most notable, I would say, is Yisroel's unexpected ability as an arbiter. As a result of his successful arbitrations, the Rabbinical Court has fewer cases to review."

Only once before had Batya heard her husband speak of Yisroel's role as an arbiter. It had relieved her then and did again now that her husband, a respected judge in the Rabbinical Court, did not disapprove of Yisroel's arbitrations.

Elijah realized that he had already heard a story about the "peacemaker" Yisroel. A Jewish leaseholder of a small inn where Elijah had stopped for refreshment had called him aside, eager to "tell the good rabbi about a small miracle" that changed his life for the better.

The man confided that it was his wife who insisted they travel to the reputed arbiter. She had been threatening to go to the Rabbinical Court for a divorce decree based on her husband's inability to fulfill his intimate duties as a husband. The innkeeper further confided to Elijah that he had, in fact, been more than willing to act as a husband in all manners prescribed by Jewish law. But his increasing difficulty in sustaining his organ as needed for his wife's fulfillment and in order that they bear children had become a disturbing obstacle. He had not wanted to go to the young mediator, having little confidence that an unmarried young man would know about such matters, but he had reluctantly agreed knowing this would bring less shame than if the matter were to be brought to the Rabbinical Court.

The innkeeper spoke with awe as he described Yisroel asking delicate questions that helped him and his wife open to each other rather than separate further. His wife's suddenly unrestrained tears moved him deeply as he recognized the sorrow beneath her anger and how much she actually loved him. For the first time, the innkeeper spoke openly to his wife about his shame; he admitted an unspoken, haunting fear that he might *never* be a proper husband. He wept with his wife, who appeared to see him with new eyes and a changed heart.

The innkeeper, who appeared grateful for the chance to talk about the miracle, reported that Yisroel also spoke to them about specific plants and herbal teas whose properties might help the man—counseling that their mutual love and patience would have a bearing more powerful than any herb. Yisroel also counseled that regardless of his organ's behavior, the innkeeper could still express his great love for his wife. He could do so with words and touch. This was the tenderness for which his wife longed and from which he had withdrawn in shame.

Listening, Elijah witnessed how deeply Yisroel's encouragement had impacted the humble innkeeper—whose wife, he said, had since begun to ripen with child.

"Kind rabbi," the innkeeper implored, as Elijah was taking his leave, "While it is true that the young teacher is unusual, he is not to be distrusted. I urge you not to accept adverse judgments rendered by those who do not know him."

Intrigued by the innkeeper's tale and by Meir and Batya's regard for Yisroel, Elijah decided to meet the unusual arbiter. There was a matter at hand that had been part of his purpose in coming to Tluste. He would present this to Yisroel and observe his response.

AFTER BATYA introduced Yisroel to Elijah, she left the two alone in her husband's library where she assured them that they would not be disturbed.

It took only minutes for Elijah to sense something out of the ordinary about the young man, although if asked, he might not have been able to describe what he felt in Yisroel's presence.

"I have a complex and difficult matter," Elijah began, "about which I would welcome another perspective."

After Yisroel nodded silently, the rabbi began to unravel the details.

"A man named Saul who made his home in Tluste now resides in Brody. He left Tluste almost three years ago, just before you came to live here. Saul owes money to a number of Tluste's citizens. Merchants in Brody have learned of his debts and no longer are allowing him to purchase their goods or services without the needed money in hand. Generally, as you must know, it is customary to extend a certain amount of credit upon a man's word. The merchants argue that this man's word is not to be considered a worthy exchange for food, clothing, or rent. He was residing in one of Brody's shelters for the poor, but was asked to leave in order to make room for those more needy— widows with children, the elderly, and the infirm. Wherever he seeks to be hired, Saul's reputation precedes him and he is turned away."

Satisfied that he had Yisroel's full attention, Elijah drew in a breath and continued.

"I came to Tluste to learn more about Saul's history. From the baker here I've learned that Saul's wife and two sons perished in a sudden fire. The blaze destroyed the family's home and a shed that housed the pamphlets that comprised their business. Saul and his wife collected pamphlets of Yiddish prayers and rare collections of stories written in

Yiddish. Although their means were modest, they managed to feed and shelter their family."

"After the fire, Saul took up residence in the Tluste poorhouse," Elijah continued. "From there he drifted to the shelter of an unattended barn. He stopped paying his debts, which, at first, was forgiven—after all, his fellow villagers were not inhumane. They knew the man was suffering the loss of his family and livelihood. But when Saul continued to wander, making no attempt in their eyes to improve his lot, their patience withered. Even the baker no longer offered bread. The marketplace vendors stopped giving him vegetables, beans, and grains. The baker also told me that until Saul vanished, 'the rabbi's tall wife with the long strides, mother of the lame, spastic child,' as he described Batya, continued to offer Saul warm stew every week on the eve of Shabbos 'with no questions or expectation of repayment.'"

"When I heard all this," Elijah went on, "I asked the baker if he knew why Saul did not seek some kind of employment."

"'No one is certain,' the baker replied. 'Who can live in another man's mind?' Then, with a sprinkling of compassion added like a few pinches of precious cinnamon to his sweet rolls, he said, 'Myself, I think his despair overcame him. When his wife, his sons, and his precious pamphlets all turned to ashes, so did his will to live. He wandered like one who has already died. After a while the only food he ate was the stew the rabbi's son Elias set out in the barn each week, at his mother's request. It did not surprise me when Saul disappeared from Tluste.'"

Elijah took in and let out a long breath, regarding the youth before him now. "Yisroel, the Jews of Brody are confronted by a dilemma: here is a man in need, but unwilling to help himself. I am curious what light you might shine on the matter."

Yisroel remained silent. When he spoke it was to answer with a question.

"Good Rabbi Elijah, what is it *you* believe about Saul and the response of the Jews in Brody?"

"Some days it is my opinion that we should assure Saul shelter and feed him. But I also think it beneficial to require him to find a way to feed himself. Unlike many of my fellow Jews in Brody, I feel neither resentment nor impatience with Saul. I feel compassion. But there is a difference between compassion and pity. Pity can destroy a man. Saul *must* do for himself what he can."

"What do you believe he can do for himself?"

"He can find work. Although somewhat gaunt now, he is still a healthy man."

"I wonder, Rabbi Elijah, if Saul also wonders what he can and cannot do for himself. He may also be deeply troubled by what he thinks God has done to him and more importantly, to those he loved."

Elijah looked into Yisroel's eyes. Yisroel met his gaze and kept it as he continued.

"When Saul believes that God is not punishing him—but in fact that he is loved by the very One who appears to have abandoned him—then he may find the spirit to live again." Yisroel smiled. "One way for him to feel this love is through the love of his fellow Jews. Does he come to the synagogue to pray among the congregation?"

"Never."

"Have you invited him?"

"All Jews are invited to pray. No one needs a direct invitation!" For an instant, the usually unruffled rabbi felt exasperated. Then, almost immediately, a curious realization settled over him. "Perhaps some Jews *do* need an invitation issued to them when they cannot hear God's constant welcome."

Yisroel nodded.

In an instant, Elijah knew what he would do. He would offer Saul temporary physical shelter in his own home and spiritual shelter in the House of Prayer. He would also offer his unconditional love and acceptance, which eventually might enter the hollow space from which Saul's heart had been torn. The rabbi could not be sure that the stranger would accept this, but he would offer it wholeheartedly. Saul's loneliness felt vast to him, perhaps as infinite as God's promises had once felt to Saul before they were broken. Feeling this in another, Elijah understood with an even greater sense of peace the blessing of his own belief that God's promise of love is never broken. But he would not try to convince Saul of this; he would just love him.

Yisroel had been a catalyst for his clarity of heart. Elijah stepped forward and embraced the young man. Then acting on a surprising impulse, he brought his lips to Yisroel's forehead in a kiss of blessing as if the one before him were a son, not a complete stranger. At the instant of the kiss, Elijah pictured a door into the future opening—just enough for him to glimpse something that astounded him.

Elijah's attention was immediately drawn deep within himself as if pulled by a spinning vortex at his core. He could not resist closing his eyes. Behind his eyelids was an endless, almost luminous, blackness. Spiraling deeper and deeper within he came to a stillpoint that felt like the point of his very origin.

When Elijah opened his eyes, not knowing how much or how little time had passed, he saw Yisroel looking directly at him. Although it had probably only been moments, Elijah knew that he had been lost in eternity.

The next morning, before leaving Tluste, Elijah invited Yisroel to join him in Meir's library. He confided to Yisroel what he had seen with irrefutable clarity beyond the open door in his vision the evening before. He then drew from the pocket of his long black traveling coat a folded piece of paper, which he placed on Meir's desk and then signed.

Elijah handed the paper to the son that fate had revealed to him. "I trust that you will know when to make this known; in the meantime let it remain only between you and me."

As Elijah took his leave, he wondered if Yisroel suspected, as he did, that the two would not see each other again.

❧ 9 ❧

Although Rifka missed her cousin Gedaliah, a very good thing had happened since he had left to study. Her father Aryeh was extending his Shabbos visits to Horodenka so he could help Leya with anything she might need.

This morning her father would be going to Dominik and Justyna's farm with Rifka and Samuel to deliver Leya's noodle pudding and Gittel's braided Challah and to bring back milk and cheese.

Rifka was delighted by the wind that met them at the top of the hill with a slight hint of spring on its breath. Her friend Marishka and she had names for the wind, welcoming it as their playmate even when it was a fierce companion. Now Rifka eagerly pulled her scarf back to let the wind play with her long, unbraided hair. Ten-year-old Samuel, imitating her, pulled off his cap, his curls dancing in the wind. She watched her cousin run ahead, milk pail swinging. Rifka ran to catch up with him, her father trailing behind them both.

They paused to wait for Aryeh on the hill overlooking the valley where Marishka's small cottage squatted at the edge of the szlachcic's extensive fields. No sooner had Aryeh arrived alongside Rifka and Samuel than did he surprise them by breaking into a run down the hill, despite the pudding he carried.

Marishka's father Dominik looked relieved to see Aryeh. The hoof of a nobleman's mare had been damaged by her shoe, and he hoped Aryeh, who had shod so many horses, might be able to help. Dominik led him to the animal. Samuel followed, dragging his milk pail.

Inside the small cottage, Marishka, who had been sitting at her grandmother's feet, jumped up to greet Rifka and receive the offerings she held. Marishka's grandmother nodded without interrupting the prayers she uttered over the beads she moved between her fingers. Justyna, nursing Marishka's baby brother, smiled warmly, acknowledging Rifka and the food.

"Peace of the Sabbath," Rifka managed in the midst of Marishka's embrace. Although the Jewish and Christian Sabbaths were not on the same day and were honored differently, Leya had taught Rifka that all Sabbaths were worthy of respect.

Marishka had told Rifka about her family's worship of the Son of God, Jesus Christ. Jesus had sacrificed his life for all people—"which means for you, too, Rifka," Marishka added gladly. Recently, Marishka explained that she had been named after God's mother and that her grandmother prayed to "*Matka Boga*," God's Holy Mother, as she touched the beads of the bracelet that she never let out of her sight. Although Rifka had heard the words *God's children,* she had never heard of God having a mother.

She had asked Marishka how God could have a mother if God was the first thing that ever existed, the beginning of everything. Marishka did not know the answer to Rifka's question, although she had not minded at all that Rifka asked. When asked if God has a father too, Marishka answered that God *is* the father. On this, the girls were relieved they could agree. Later, when Rifka questioned Tanta Leya about God having a son and mother, her tanta replied: "Most important is to love God. Marishka's family loves God. What matters is to love the Source of Life with all one's heart and soul. To love your neighbor as yourself is one of the things God asks of us. When you respect Marishka and the way her family worships, although it is different from what you know, you are fulfilling God's commandment to love your neighbor."

Dominik's piercing cry of "Justyna!" startled Rifka. Justyna jumped to her feet and handed the baby to Marishka's grandmother. Lifting her long bright skirt, she ran towards the barn from where Dominik's frightening summons had come. Marishka and Rifka ran behind her.

Closer to the barn, Rifka heard her father calling Samuel's name urgently, and then she saw him kneeling, bent forward. Dominik called out to Justyna, who, seeing what had happened, hastened towards a small shed where she made what Marishka called her magic potions. Rifka was close enough now to see Samuel on the ground, eyes closed, his mouth hanging open.

What was wrong with Samuel? What had happened? Why did her father look so afraid? Why did Samuel seem so far away even though he was lying right there?

Rifka felt Marishka take her hand and squeeze hard; Rifka hoped she would not let go.

Dominik and Aryeh made room for Justyna to kneel close to Samuel. Justyna put her fingertips lightly on Samuel's neck. Then with those same fingertips, she made a cross on herself.

"He is alive," Marishka whispered to Rifka, then made the sign of the cross on herself with her free hand. Rifka knew that Marishka was thanking God's son and God's mother, because she heard their names. Dominik and Patryk also touched the tips of their fingers to their foreheads, chest, right and left shoulders.

Samuel was not moving at all. Instructing Dominik how to help her, Justyna lifted Samuel's head as carefully as if it were something very fragile. She wrapped a wet towel with a strange smell around Samuel's head. *She would not be doing that if he were dead*, Rifka thought. *But if he wasn't dead, then why wasn't he waking up?*

Rifka squeezed her friend's hand for a long minute before she let go and went to her father, who held out his arms to receive her. Curling into him, Rifka listened to him whisper over and over, *Please, Adonai, spare him. Please.*

Still, Samuel did not open his eyes

"What happened to Samuel?" Rifka asked into her father's chest, finally finding the words.

"He was kicked by a horse, Rifkalla. In his head."

"Will he open his eyes soon?"

"We must believe that he will. He is in a deep, deep sleep right now; but he will wake up. Soon." She could tell when he said *but he will wake up* and *soon* that her father wasn't sure, even though he tried to say it like he was.

Dominik secured a wagon to a mild-mannered horse and lined the back with straw over which he placed a wool blanket. Moving very slowly, Dominik and Aryeh, with Justyna's help, lifted Samuel onto the straw. After covering him with another blanket, Aryeh helped Rifka into the back of the wagon where they sat together beside Samuel. The whole way back over the hill, her father did not take his eyes off Samuel except once to look at Rifka so tenderly that she could not help crying despite having tried so hard not to.

LEYA, WALKING HOME from the cobbling stall, saw Dominik approaching from a distance. Was Aryeh in the back of the wagon? She almost had not recognized him hunched forward, shaking—was it with laughter? Pulling her shawl tighter around her shoulders, she walked down the dirt road in the direction of the wagon that was moving unusually slowly.

As the wagon drew closer, Leya saw Rifka. The child's eyes were pinned open with fear, her lips pressed together. Dominik pulled back the reins, his face tightened in pain.

Where was Samuel? What had happened? She rushed closer. When Aryeh raised his head and met her gaze, Leya faltered. Aryeh had not been laughing but crying. *Samuel! Had something happened to Samuel?*

As soon as Leya saw him, she was mute with shock. Samuel's face was colorless; he wasn't moving. Leya felt her legs start to give way. She held onto the edge of the wagon. No. How could this be? *Dear God!*

Aryeh's hand rested lightly on Samuel's chest. Was her brother's hand rising or was she imagining it? Leya focused more intently. Yes, Aryeh's hand was being lifted by Samuel's breath.

"He lives! Aryeh, he lives!" Tears not released in Leya's shock came forth now.

Aryeh helped Leya into the wagon. She knelt beside her son, bringing her face close to his. His breath was so thin as to almost not be there. Leya turned towards her brother, imploring.

"A horse kicked him in the head, Leyalla. He has not opened his eyes since."

Leya looked back at her son, hovering so precariously on this side of life.

"Aryeh," she found her voice. "Help me bring him into the house."

With Dominik's help, they lifted the child, Leya supporting his head. With slow deliberate steps, they carried him to his narrow bed. The men left Leya alone.

Sitting next to Samuel, she took her son's small hand, barely warmed by his faint life force. *If only holding his hand would assure that he stay.* Dizziness came over Leya again, a feeling of being pulled away. Her eyes closed as she started to fall back.

"No!" Leya called out, opening her eyes. She took in a breath and straightened her back. She needed to remain present and strong, an anchor tethering her son to this world. Samuel had saved her life when he was only a tiny baby. With each suck on her nipple, he had summoned Leya back to her body and to life after Ber's sudden death.

She invoked Ber's blessings for their son. She stroked and kissed Samuel's forehead under his curls and begged the One beyond time and space to let him live.

Maintaining her vigil, Leya was joined by Rifka and Aryeh, until Rifka could no longer keep her head up and Aryeh carried her out of the room.

The hours passed and Samuel's strange sleep seemed to deepen. As Leya watched, his eyelids stopped their fluttering. Was this a rest that would restore him, or a final rest from which he would not return? Only one answer was bearable.

Samuel's pallor became greater until his face was ghostly white. His head rolled to one side and his mouth dropped open. Terror rushed like ice water through Leya's veins.

"Samuel, don't leave us!" she screamed, pressing her hand to his cool cheek. Her mind felt like a trapped bird desperately hurling itself against the bars of its cage. Leya took in a long breath. *She must pray.* She must pray wildly that the Ayn Sof fan whatever tiny flame of life still flickered in Samuel.

Finally, she slept. She dreamt she stood on a mountaintop watching the setting of a blazing sun. Her husband Ber and son Gedaliah stood behind her, laughing, as she hurried towards the sun intending to catch it in her hands and stop it from setting.

Leya awoke to Aryeh's voice calling her name. Abruptly, she left her dream and the burning sun and was thrust into the living nightmare in which her son's body lay lifeless before her. She was surprised to feel a sudden surge of anger.

"I cannot understand God's will."

"Of course not," Aryeh said softly, embracing her. She shook so intensely in her brother's arms, she felt as if she might break into pieces.

"Dear God," she called out, "I do not understand Your will. Can you hear me? *I do not understand!*"

Leya was gripped by a sudden, shocking desire to die with Samuel— if he left, to leave with him. She wasn't used to feeling such defeat or such anger at God.

Aryeh held her firmly. He did not toss hollow, dry words on the fire that burned her. She knew he could not revive Samuel, take her pain, or explain God's will. But he would not leave her alone.

ARYEH WAS AWAKENED in the middle of the night by the sound of the door opening, and recognized Yisroel as he entered. He was surprised, but also relieved that Yisroel had let himself in so that Aryeh had not needed to stand and disturb Rifka, asleep with her head in his lap. The two nodded a soundless greeting.

Watching Yisroel cross the room slowly, Aryeh realized how much time had passed since he had seen the young man, who must be close to twenty now. If Yisroel had visited Horodenka since his move to Tluste, Aryeh had been in Okup and missed his visits.

Yisroel had become a man. Under thick auburn eyebrows, his blue eyes shone more brilliantly than Aryeh could remember them. Aryeh was struck by the compassion apparent in those eyes and on his face. Clearly, there was no need to explain what had happened to Samuel; Yisroel knew. Perhaps word had spread in the village, or Dominik, keeping vigil outside Leya's house in his wagon, had informed him.

Yisroel's tender compassion was apparent even in his touch, when for a moment he placed his open palm on the crown of Rifka's head. He turned and went to the room where Samuel lay.

In the wake of Yisroel's passing, Aryeh was aware that everything seemed to have slowed, in contrast with the accident, which had happened almost too fast to believe, and its heightened aftermath. An unexpected peace overtook Aryeh, soothing his body and even his mind. He felt himself yield, as if letting go of his moorings in Samuel's tragedy, and he drifted into the harbor of sleep.

LEYA, SINGING SOFTLY to her son, had not sensed anyone enter, so it surprised her to hear Samuel's name uttered by a voice she recognized as both strong and sweet at the same time. Before she could turn around, Leya felt a large hand on her shoulder.

"Yisroel," Leya said gratefully without turning to look at him. Although it defied custom for him to touch her, she hoped he would not move his hand. Leya continued her watch over her son with the solace of the broad hand steadying her. Yisroel must have just arrived in Horodenka. He had not been expected as far as Leya knew. How quickly he had learned of the accident—or had he known without anyone informing him.

In his silent presence, Leya felt the almost unbearable burden begin to lighten. Nothing had changed with Samuel. He looked closer to death than to life. Then why this lightening?

She heard her niece's voice from the other room. Leya was not able to make out Rifka's questions to her father, but could feel her urgent concern.

Leya realized Yisroel had withdrawn his hand, perhaps in the instant she was distracted by Rifka's voice. When Leya turned around, he was no longer there. Had she been so absorbed that she had also not heard him leave?

Leya brought her gaze back to Samuel, thinking she saw his head move, so slight a movement as to be almost imperceptible. No movement followed; most likely she had imagined his stirring. But now, a coin-sized flush blossomed on Samuel's cheek. A hint of pink tinged his bluish lips. His eyes began to move like two smooth stones rolling under his eyelids.

"Dear God," Leya whispered, leaning closer.

"Sro-lik." The raspy, tentative voice came from so deep inside him, it seemed a place beyond life.

His eyelids rolled slowly up, revealing a glazed expression, then closed, and Leya felt him withdrawing again—hopefully not to go as far away as before. Rifka stood at the door of the room. Leya motioned her closer and wrapped her arms around her niece.

"Samuel just opened his eyes, Rifkalla, did you see? I think he is returning to us."

The girl pressed her lips together hard, as if struggling not to let something in or out.

"Rifka, do not be afraid to feel all that is in your beautiful heart. Our hearts are big and strong enough to hold love and fear at the same time." Leya, Aryeh, and Rifka sat together at Samuel's side all night, sometimes one or two of them falling asleep, but never all three at the same time.

In the middle of the night, Aryeh brought hot barley and rye bread to Dominik, who sat bundled up in the wagon outside their door, keeping his prayer vigil there. Leya imagined Justyna on her knees in their cottage, her face illumined by the soft light of a votive as she beseeched the Sacred Hearts of the Holy Mother and Her Son.

At dawn, Samuel opened his eyes for just the smallest bit of time and asked again for "Srolik." He slipped back into his deep rest, now clearly slumbering on *this* side of life.

AS THE DAYS and weeks passed, Samuel stayed awake longer, until he was able to sit up, take water, and eventually to eat. Justyna sent herbal broths; Gittel, softened rice and other easily digestible foods.

When he was able to stand, his legs were weak and shaky.

Samuel continued to look for and inquire about his former shepherd and seemed surprised not to see him.

"Srolik led me back," he said often.

When he was able to stay awake for longer and to talk, he told them all that happened.

Samuel recalled falling from a high place; he did not know where. He fell without stopping into a thick, dark blackness. Afraid, he had called to his mother and Gedaliah to try to catch him, to stop the falling. When they did not come, he was sure that they could not hear him. So Samuel had given up calling for help, continuing to fall, terrified.

He landed in a totally dark place where he could see and feel nothing. He could hear a faraway murmuring of voices but felt completely alone. Then suddenly, Samuel had heard Srolik's voice singing the first melody he had taught the boys on their way to school. After that Samuel heard Srolik calling to him.

"Srolik told me: '*Open your eyes now, Samuel, even though it is dark. Open them and wait.*' So I opened my eyes. He told me soon I would see a light. It was tiny at first like a star."

"'*Walk towards it,*' Srolik said. So I did, taking a few small steps and stopping because my legs felt weak. Srolik walked with me. The light became brighter and brighter—almost too bright to look at. I had to squint my eyes."

Samuel paused in his telling, falling back as if the weight of his head had suddenly become too much for him. Leya moved to sit behind him and support his weight. It was clear he wanted to continue his account.

"Walking towards the light, I saw a man standing on the other side of a gate. The light passed right through him. When I came closer, the man smiled at me—so kindly. He did not say anything to me, but I think he wanted to."

"Then Srolik told me it was not meant for me to come closer to the blinding light—that it was not time yet for me to go through that gate to the man. He told me you were all waiting for me, and he asked me if I wanted to return. It felt sad to leave the kind man who wanted to embrace me with his arms made of light, but I took Srolik's hand to come back."

Samuel paused and sat up straight, leaving Leya's support. He looked around, searching as he often had since regaining consciousness.

"Where is Srolik? Why isn't he here?"

In the silence that followed, Samuel did not persist. Tired from telling the story, he leaned back again into his mother. He told them that Srolik, when he came, would explain about the falling, about the dark place and the blinding light. Srolik might even tell them who the kind man at the gate was.

The miracle of Samuel's return to life, his tale and all the unspoken questions it called forth, hung in the small room. If such silence could be weighed, Leya thought, it would be the weight of gold.

❧

RIFKA WATCHED WITH GLADNESS AS HER COUSIN'S cheeks showed red again. He had not looked like himself for such a long time. He was walking more without leaning on his mother or Rifka, except when he became dizzy. But Samuel could not run, not yet. Though some parts of him were coming back, important ones like running, spinning, and laughing for no reason were not back yet. Could the hard kick of a horse separate a person from parts of himself forever?

The night of Samuel's accident, Yisroel had stood beside her while she slept on her father's knee. His touch had let her know not to be afraid. But when she woke up, he was not there. Had she just dreamt he had come to the cottage?

When Rifka asked her tanta and father, they told her they, too, had seen Yisroel. He had come into the house quietly and made his way to the room where Samuel lingered between life and death. His visit was brief; neither her aunt nor her father had seen Yisroel in the days that followed. Nor had they heard anyone mention having seen him in Horodenka. Dominik, outside in his wagon, had seen no one enter. But, he thought, it was possible he had drifted off to sleep during his vigil, though he did not think he had closed his eyes all night.

Aryeh suggested that Rifka not try too hard to solve the mystery. Yisroel's visit had blessed them all and that was what mattered.

Yet, Rifka continued to think about Yisroel often. In the early morning at the well, she pretended to find secrets that he had left for her to discover in the water she drew. She recalled the radiance of his face at night in the small shul. She wished she could be one of his students in Tluste. She was almost twelve now, old enough to study on her own when her aunt could not study with her.

This very morning she had been wondering what Yisroel might say about a passage Leya had given her to ponder from a book called *Ethics of Our Fathers*. The words were: *It is not in our power to explain the prosperity of the wicked or the sufferings of the righteous.* If Rifka were Yisroel's student, perhaps they would discuss the passage for hours like yeshiva students did, until things that were hard to understand finally revealed even just one secret. Right now, the sufferings of the righteous seemed impossible to understand. If Samuel had died instead of lived, Rifka was not sure she ever would have stopped asking why.

By the second full moon since Samuel's accident, Rifka's beautiful body was initiated into womanhood, as Tanta Leya had said it would months earlier when she explained to Rifka the changes a young woman's body undergoes. So Rifka was not shocked when the blood showed itself and she felt the urge to fold in on herself. Parts of herself to which she hardly had paid any attention were suddenly so important, like her nipples, suddenly sensitive to even the slightest rubbing of her linen tunic.

Tanta Leya guessed right away. When Leya knelt beside Rifka and put her hand lightly on Rifka's abdomen, their eyes met, and without words it was confirmed. Leya said later she had observed Rifka's uncharacteristic slowness and what she called 'the mixture of fire and water in Rifka's eyes' as Rifka, stroking her belly, stared at nothing. Leya boiled the dried yellow hearts of the daisy-like chamomile blossoms from Justyna, and offered Rifka tea.

Rifka did not want to be ungrateful but found herself wishing to be alone: to hide under her blankets or to stand alone by the rushing Dniester River after completing an errand with her aunt. Leya understood and stepped back, leaving Rifka to throw stones from the riverbank, and moan at the unreachable pain deep in her belly, which the fragrant chamomile tea could ease but not erase.

~

L EYA WAS NOT THE SAME AFTER ALMOST LOSING Samuel. She awakened every night. Initially, it had been because she was unable to sleep. Now she woke intentionally at midnight to study, a practice that was the custom of the Kabbalists, although she knew that as a woman, she could never study among them.

Shortly before Yisroel left for Tluste, Rifka had confided in Leya about Yisroel studying in the dark by the light of his own radiance. Leya had convinced Aryeh to accompany her to the shul after dark so that she might witness for herself what her niece had seen. The sight of Yisroel reading by the light of his own ardor had kindled a longing within Leya that felt ancient. Since the miracle of Samuel's return to life, she had begun to fulfill this longing with hours of nightly study.

GEDALIAH RECOGNIZED the change in his mother within hours of his return from his yeshiva in Mezritch. It had taken weeks for word to reach him about his brother's accident and then days more for him to travel the two hundred and fifty kilometers between Mezritch and Horodenka.

His second night home, Gedaliah woke in the middle of the night to see his mother studying intently. Her long honey-colored hair poured over her shoulders and hid her face. Gedaliah felt certain she did not sense him watching as she rocked, murmuring passages of a book spread open before her.

After his mother had gone to her cobbling stall the next morning, Gedaliah looked at the text that had so compelled her. It was a portion of the Zohar, the Book of Splendor, described in his yeshiva as forbidden fruit.

He and his fellow students had been warned against plummeting into texts for which they were not sufficiently prepared—Kabbalistic texts like this one warranting the most caution. The dangers were exemplified in the fates of four rabbis who, in their desire for mystical knowledge, had entered the Divine Orchard, a metaphor for pursuing esoteric knowledge. Ben Azzai glimpsed, and died. Ben Zoma beheld, and went mad. Aher became a heretic. Only Rabbi Akiva emerged in peace. Those under forty—or a Jew of any age who had not studied Torah sufficiently, which included all women—could expect the fate of the three rabbis: to be destroyed by the power of Kabbalah.

Gedaliah's teachers also spoke solemnly of the widespread devastation that had occurred little more than fifty years earlier as a result of Shabtai Tzvi's abuse of Kabbalistic teachings. To avoid further travesty in the name of the Kabbalah, rabbis throughout the commonwealth and beyond were trying to ban study, especially of the esoteric Zohar, by all but the most adept of scholars.

Now, here was Gedaliah's own mother nourishing herself with forbidden fruit.

Two weeks after his discovery, walking back from the Shabbos morning service with his uncle, Gedaliah asked his uncle Aryeh if he knew about Leya's late night study and prayer. He also asked if Aryeh found Leya changed since Samuel's accident.

"Are you worried about your mother?"

"My mother seems more indrawn than I've ever known her to be. I worry that she's withdrawing in ways that will leave her more alone. Will she become less involved in the affairs of the town, less a spokeswoman for the women of Horodenka and reforms in the Kahal? This may surprise you, Uncle, but since leaving home I've had thoughts of my mother remarrying. I know she treasures her independence and has never expressed any desire or interest in marrying again. I know how close she feels to my father, May He Rest In Peace. I am probably thinking thoughts like these because I'm living so far away and unable to help her, just when I have become a man and could help her more."

Aryeh smiled, putting his hand on Gedaliah's shoulder.

"Your mother has always been like a horse not easily tamed. In fact, she has *never* really been tamed. She submits her will only to her understanding of God's will. Gedaliah, your mother is remarkably strong. Keep offering her your love and respect, not your worry. Your mother never needed or wanted pity, even when she was left a widow with two young sons. She only wished for respect, the same respect she shows to everyone."

Gedaliah realized how relieved he was to be talking with his uncle.

"Not long after Samuel's accident, your mother told me she wished to fathom the deeper mysteries of life and death. When Samuel almost died, your mother became angry with God and fearful of being abandoned. Although the experience was short-lived, never had she felt her faith so shaken. Since then she has said numerous times that she wants '*to draw close to the Fire that can never be grasped.*'"

As the two came nearer to the house, they could hear Leya singing "L'Cha Dodi." It had never mattered to his mother that the customary time to sing this hymn was at sunset on Friday to usher in the Sabbath

Bride. Leya sang it whenever she felt moved to sing, arguing that there was never a wrong time to welcome the spirit of Sabbath.

Aryeh, surprising Gedaliah, winked and gestured him towards a small window of the cottage that stood slightly ajar. Arms around each other, they leaned forward to look in.

There was Samuel kneeling in front of Leya. Rifka sat on Leya's right as if under her protective wing. When Leya came to the verse during which it is traditional to stand, turn, and bow to the entering bride, Leya leaned forward instead and kissed Samuel lightly on his forehead, whispering, "Welcome, dear Presence." Then to Rifka, "Welcome, dear Bride." Then his mother straightened, closed her eyes, and sang, "Come, Shechinah, into our hearts."

The men stepped back from the window. Aryeh embraced Gedaliah, holding him longer than usual.

"Your mother is not withdrawing from life, dear Gedaliah. Trust that she is finding the Shechina, God's Indwelling Presence, shining in the hearts of those around her as brilliantly as in the Holy Book of Splendor."

"THE ONE WHO counts the stars," Leya spoke the words of the psalm slowly.

It had become Rifka and Leya's practice to study the psalms together every Shabbos after lunch. Rifka loved how Leya could dwell on one phrase, sometimes just a single word, and be dazzled by what she had found. Rifka worried about how long it would take to make their way through the psalms, if they took this long to study each one. When she expressed her concern, her tanta laughed warmly.

"Rifkalla, there's great treasure to be found here, some that glitters and is easy to behold, but most of it, hidden. Only when we search, often where we have looked already, can we discover what is concealed."

Rifka was puzzled. "But why should the treasure be hidden?"

"So that we may make the effort to find it—and delight when we do. Come, Rifka," Leya motioned, "sit closer and let us go deeper into this psalm." Her aunt wrapped an arm around Rifka as she repeated softly, "the one who counts the stars," then fell quiet, closing her eyes.

Rifka was used to her aunt becoming quiet like this and even closing her eyes when they studied. Tanta Leya had explained that silence gives space for understanding to come.

"Think of the night sky, Rifkalla," Leya said when she next spoke. "Can you imagine counting its stars? *Every single one—not one of them ignored?*"

Rifka shook her head. She had started to count the stars many times but had never been able to finish. She could not imagine anyone able to count them all without falling asleep first.

"No woman or man is capable of such vast perspective. Only the One who created the stars can know each star. But what does it mean to *count* the stars? The Ayn Sof is not a person with a finger like you or me that points and counts. It is miraculous enough that each star is counted, but as the next words say: *to each one is given a name*—this is unfathomable! That all the stars are named reflects that *each one* is valued, that each has a purpose. If the Creator accounts directly for each star, then it must be true that each person and every aspect of creation is cherished."

Rifka looked up, not surprised to see Leya's eyes gleaming with tears.

"The daily prayer book says: *In goodness, each day is renewed, continually.* What this means to me is that the counting and naming did not happen just once in the remote past. The stars are counted and named each day."

Leya leaned forward towards the open book. "I have recited this psalm countless times, Rifka, hearing its praise for the abundant goodness of the One *who causes the rain to fall, the raven to cry, the wind to blow, and the rivers to flow.* But right now, I am discovering something I never grasped."

Leya's excitement felt like heat.

"We read the stars were *given a number.* Then just a few lines below that, it says, *To God's understanding there is no number.* And the psalm continues, *More than the number of stars, are the ways God understands.*"

The tears now overflowed her aunt's wide eyes. "Oh, Rifkalla, this means that the ways we are understood are beyond counting; they are infinite. The Shechinah, the Sacred Presence of Love, blesses us with understanding more times each day than there are stars in the firmament. No matter what our failings, no matter how deep our sorrow, how gripping our anger or our sadness, we are counted. We are named and we are blessed." Leya drew in a deep breath and closed her eyes again.

Rifka had seen her aunt reach this point of speechlessness before. Leya's headscarf had slipped to her shoulders. Her thick hair, released from its bun, spread wild and free. What Rifka loved best about studying with Leya was watching her catch fire. Even Rifka's father had teased: "On the Sabbath while one is commanded to refrain from building a fire, Leya's inner fire blazes."

Leya opened her eyes and looked down at the open book. She pointed, beckoning Rifka to look.

"Rifkalla, do you see the word *Ayn* in this phrase, *Ayn Mispar, There is no number?*"

Rifka leaned forward. Pleased to recognize the letters, she nodded.

"This is the same *Ayn* as in *Ayn Sof,* the One With No Limit, the One who cannot be known no matter how many ways we name that One. There is no way to describe the Indescribable. Yet this psalm tries to do so. Its composer reaches for the Unreachable, praises the love and attention of the Infinite for each particle of the created world."

Rifka felt, once again, as if she were being left behind on a path—a feeling that had once been uncomfortable, but was no longer. She could see and feel her tanta ahead of her, and was sure that she would turn around and come back for her. Eventually Rifka would walk with her, taking the same big gliding steps.

After Leya lay down for the nap, as was the Sabbath custom, Rifka sat alone at the table, the book still open. Suddenly, Rifka had an answer to questions that she had heard whispered in the marketplace and in the women's section of the shul: *Wasn't the cobbler's widow lonely? Why did she not remarry? She was an attractive woman, after all.* Maybe Rifka understood now. What beloved could ever compare to the One who had captured Leya moments ago in the psalm, the One in whose embrace her aunt rested peacefully now?

10

In the Brody marketplace, a hawker of cauliflower and cabbage overheard the stranger asking directions to the home of Rabbi Elijah. Dressed like a peasant farmer, he didn't look like someone who would have business with the chief rabbi of Brody, but who was she to judge.

A thick-necked neighboring vendor set down his large bag of parsnips and answered that the esteemed rabbi, *Peace Be Upon Him,* had died during the winter.

"A peaceful death," the burly woman added quickly, "Sudden, yes, but peaceful. My nephew who had the occasional fortune to assist the noble rabbi told me the virtuous man died with Adonai's name on his lips. A good death."

She watched the stranger close his eyes and move his lips silently.

When he was finished, they directed him towards Rabbi's Elijah's house where, they explained, he would find the rabbi's son Gershon presiding over the Rabbinical Court. Upon his father's death, Rabbi Gershon had moved back from Kuty to Brody to take his father's place as Chief Rabbi and Judge. Although not as congenial as his father, the parsnip vendor emphasized, Rabbi Gershon at the age of twenty-five had become quite accomplished in his own right.

"Surely," the hefty woman called out, knowing from her own experience, "you will find what you seek there."

The courteous stranger nodded his gratitude and began to walk in the direction indicated.

Curious, the woman watched the red-bearded, handsome Jew. Wearing the tall boots, short jacket, and thick belt of a peasant, he crossed the marketplace in no hurry. Laughing to herself, she turned back to the stacking of cabbages. Although most people would not compare a cabbage to a rose, she could see how the two resembled each other. Perhaps it was the way each one had many layers. This peasant Jew had struck her as being like both. Sturdy and earthy like a cabbage, the young man possessed some of the fineness of a rose. *Ah, back to work, foolish woman,* she reprimanded herself, tossing a cabbage to a customer impatient with this daydreaming.

RABBI GERSHON'S attendant opened the door to a shabby beggar. The poor wanderer had surely come to solicit the rabbi's well-known generosity. The attendant bade him wait outside.

When the attendant returned, he was taken aback to see that the stranger, covered by the dirt of the road, had crossed the threshold and brazenly entered the house. Nineteen or twenty years old, he stood now in the narrow corridor, humming a barely audible melody.

"Here you are," the young assistant said, extending the awaited coins.

When the pauper declined the generous charity, and instead requested the rabbi himself, the dutiful young servant was angered. He quickly reminded himself that it was not his place to determine the alms offered by the rabbi, nor was it his place to judge the need of this or any stranger. He turned on his heels to request of the rabbi a higher sum for the man at the door who appeared not to have eaten or bathed in days.

When he returned with a larger sum, the man again refused. "Thank you, good sir, but please take me to Rabbi Gershon."

"The honorable Rabbi Gershon is involved in the proceedings of the Rabbinical Court, and I cannot interrupt him again."

Surely, even an ignorant, illiterate Jew like this would grasp the import of the rabbi's time, take what been offered, and depart, if not with gratitude, then at least with the coins.

"I will wait here, then, for the esteemed judge," the persistent stranger said.

Yielding, the attendant left him standing in the corridor where the presumptuous beggar resumed humming the odd melody that seemed to keep him company.

GERSHON WALKED towards the purportedly implacable intruder.

"Did you find our charity lacking?" Gershon asked, more curious than irritated.

The man shook his head and muttered something Gershon could not decipher beyond the words "I seek."

"You seek what of me? Please speak up, sir, I could not hear you."

"I seek a word alone."

It appeared to Gershon painful for the vagabond to say what he wanted. He hardly seemed the demanding Jew his attendant had described. If the stranger wanted to speak to him alone, perhaps it was a matter pertaining to the court that he did not wish to confide in the corridor. Even a poor, simple Jew had the right to appeal to the Rabbinical Court.

Gershon acquiesced, leading the stranger to a small chamber where the rabbi's desk was piled high with books. The two remained standing. Gershon nodded to his guest, indicating that he should speak. The threadbare Jew drew a folded piece of paper from his tattered jacket pocket and extended it to his host. The judge slowly unfolded the wrinkled page. It took a moment to recognize it as a contract.

What was he seeing? Gershon couldn't believe his eyes. He read and reread what appeared to be contract betrothing his sister Channa to a man named Yisroel ben Eliezer. Wasn't this man before him little more than a beggar? What jest was this?

Gershon looked up to see the stranger nod, as if he had heard Gershon's thoughts. The discomforted rabbi continued to read. Astounding as was the notion of his sister marrying this stranger, more shocking was the signature on the contract—his father's? Who was this man standing before him and where had he attained such a document? It was impossible that Rabbi Elijah could have executed this agreement. He had never spoken of making such an arrangement for Channa.

Slow to wrath, the Gershon said nothing. But despite his efforts at restraint, the normally contained judge felt anger overcome him in response to the scandalous proposition.

"Do you expect me to honor this contract that my father, *Peace Be Upon Him*, is purported to have signed? If he had made such an agreement, he would have certainly informed both my sister and me. My father never spoke a word about the existence of such a contract."

"My agreement with your father was that this contract not be revealed until the time of my appearance at his home."

Gershon was stunned. He looked at the paper again. It was his father's writing—not only the signature, but the entire contract seemed to have been penned by his father. It was impossible that this Jewish peasant could have created so perfect a forgery.

"Although this appears to be Rabbi Elijah's handwriting, it is too preposterous to even imagine that he would arrange such an unlikely matrimony. I deny this as a binding agreement. "

"Does your sister have the right to speak for herself?"

The question startled Gershon, as did the clarity and confidence with which it had been spoken.

"My sister will have no more part in this than I."

"Should she not be asked?"

Gershon was about to insist that the audacious stranger leave, when he saw his sister Channa at the door. Gershon seemed more surprised than his guest to see her. How long had she been standing there? Had she heard what had transpired between the men? Channa, looking neither at her brother nor at the stranger, remained silent at the entrance to the room, arms wrapped around her slender body. She looked up pensively towards the right as if hearing or seeing something, a gesture that puzzled her brother. Without lowering her gaze, she spoke softly, yet audibly enough for both men to hear.

"I will honor the promise of my father."

Her words astonished Gershon.

"But, Channa," he implored, walking over to her. "How can you explain that our father would have wished you betrothed to a man such as this? You could have chosen from among the most renowned scholars of Brody—despite what occurred in the past—if you had consented to marry. For you to accept this proposal is more than foolishness; you will be throwing away your life."

Channa, almost seventeen now, had been reclusive even before her great misfortune, and Gershon had not tried to change this. He respected her wishes, just as their father had.

"My dear brother," Channa interrupted his thoughts tenderly but firmly. "My father's reasons do not have to be known to me. I trust his choice."

Channa did not look at either man before she turned and left.

Gershon sat down, dropped his head into his hand, and closed his eyes. It did not matter what he thought; this was not a case he had been asked to judge. Neither his father nor his sister required his ruling.

For an instant, Gershon wished to find the stranger gone when he lifted his head, to find the whole incident a hoax. But Yisroel ben Eliezar stood before him dressed as poorly as the poorest of Brody's Jews and was perhaps even more lacking in learning. Gershon didn't have the power to change what was unfolding. His sister had made her decision. The towering judge, defeated, addressed his unlikely victor.

"Yisroel ben Eliezar, you shall be granted the hand of my sister, Channa, daughter of Elijah and Dalia."

"I will return after the next Sabbath to discuss arrangements," Yisroel replied.

"After the next Sabbath," Gershon repeated absently, already beginning to grieve the loss of his sister. He did not extend his hand to his future brother-in-law and left the room, the bizarre contract crumpled in his fist.

∼

CHANNA WISHED her dear brother were not suffering so about her impending marriage. But she knew that she could not remove his misgivings. Perhaps her father would not have been able to explain, any more than she, why he sensed the rightness of this union.

The day before their wedding, Yisroel approached Channa quietly to entreat her patience.

"Your brother has instructed that there be no music or dancing at our wedding., When the time is right, dear Channa, we will dance together joyously in the embrace of the Shechina."

"Yes," was all she said, believing him.

The wedding of Yisroel, son of Eliezar and Sarah, to Channa, daughter of Elijah and Dalia, was a modest celebration not only because the couple wished it so, but also because Gershon saw little to celebrate. The *l'chaim* toasting the couple's future was to be made by the bride's brother, given that her father had passed away. When Gefrshon rose and raised his cup, it seemed to Channa that he was trying to summon even a small measure of genuine respect for his new brother-in-law. "L'Chaim," was all he ventured, looking only at her.

As customary, the wedding day had been chosen with consideration of the cycle of Channa's monthly blessing, so that she would not be forbidden to her husband. The date selected had to be at least seven days since her last stain of blood, thus allowing her to purify herself in the *mikveh*, the ritual bath, before consummating her marriage. Channa had only recently begun to menstruate again after more than two years without bleeding.

The night they were married, Channa waited for Yisroel to enter. He opened the door quietly. The candle burning at her bedside allowed her to watch him move across the room towards her. It would not be the first time she had been with a man. Yisroel knew this; she had made sure to tell him the day that he had returned, a week after first presenting the contract that had infuriated her kind, upright brother. That she had been married and divorced was considered a rare and shameful history for a woman to bring to her marriage bed—yet it seemed that Yisroel did not judge her for this.

He stood at the foot of the bed where she lay wearing the white linen nightgown that her mother had worn on her wedding night.

"Channa, I wish to request something of you."

She liked the warmth of his voice.

"Yes?"

"I ask your permission not to consummate our marriage tonight."

Channa laughed. Had he heard her own thoughts without her having said a word aloud? Although it was the permitted time in her woman's rhythm and it was expected that she lie with him, Channa preferred not to, not yet. This was not because of the repulsion she had grown to feel at the thought of a man approaching her. She simply preferred their intimacy to develop first outside the walls of a dark bedroom.

Yisroel sat down on the side of her bed and blew out the candle. He was close enough for Channa to feel his hip next to her breast. She was surprised to feel his presence stir desire she had thought long buried. When Yisroel placed his large warm hand on her cheek, the tenderness of his touch brought tears to her eyes. He would feel her tears in his palm.

In the dark silence that embraced them, the couple breathed together until Yisroel spoke again.

"Your brother's heavy heart, plus my sense that we will not remain long under his roof, bid me wait until—"

Channa reached her finger to his lips. "I also prefer to wait, Yisroel." She was relieved to feel the unity of their hearts even before the union of their bodies.

"Did my father inform you that I cannot bear you children?"

"No," Yisroel whispered. He leaned over to kiss her forehead then the corners of her eyes. "He must have understood that it would not prevent our marrying."

Channa felt the urge to protect herself, to withdraw, but she did not. How deep was the fear she had come to harbor.

When Yisroel gently cupped her face between his two hands, Channa felt something at once unfamiliar and familiar, something she could not name at first.

Then she realized. It was trust. She could trust this man. Channa was safe with Yisroel. She could let herself be held. It would be safe now to draw close and to be drawn close. To be seen, to be touched, and to be loved... by this man.

Gershon prayed for relief from his disdain for his brother-in-law. He sought the grace to surrender his pride, if pride was playing a role in his resentment of his sister's new husband.

For Channa's sake, he invited the couple to remain in the house where Channa and he had lived together since their father's death. For her sake, too, Gershon offered her husband employment as his carriage driver. The rabbi had many calls upon him to travel. It took little brains to lead horses. If her groom could do that much while the couple continued to live under his roof, perhaps Channa would be spared an impoverished life.

The first time Yisroel held the reins, Gershon's carriage went off the side of the road. If Gershon had foreseen the accident, he might have tried to take the reins, but all had happened so unexpectedly and unaccountably. Just moments before, they had been proceeding at a steady pace on a flat road, and then—as if Gershon had dozed for a moment and missed the cause—the carriage lay tilted on its two right wheels, the horse mired and frightened.

Yisroel, the reins dropped in front of him, appeared neither shocked nor dismayed. Nor did he seem capable of taking any useful action to extricate horse and carriage.

"Is there absolutely nothing at which you can succeed?" the distraught Gershon accused, knowing there was little point in admonishing a fool. Complaining to a man who might as well be deaf would bring no relief.

Gershon climbed down from his seat and spoke comfortingly to his horse. He tried to pull her out of her predicament, but couldn't. Even when Gershon managed to direct Yisroel where to stand and how to pull, in the attempt to free the horse's front right leg, there was little they could do together.

To send Yisroel for help was to risk none being found. Better he remain with the horse and coach—what additional harm could be done?—while the rabbi walked to their destination to entreat the aid of the citizens there. Thankfully, there was ample daylight and the road was open, not forested. Perhaps Gershon would be fortunate enough to encounter passers-by generous enough to offer some assistance.

The walk to the nearest town was much longer than Gershon had anticipated, and more exhausting. Finally there, the fatigued rabbi made his way to the Jewish sector. A dense gray layer of dust from the dry road coated his boots, trousers, and black coat. Grit collected in his nostrils and lay on his eyelashes and the brim of his hat. His face was smeared with a blend of perspiration and dirt. When Gershon located the rabbi with whom he was to meet, he declined the offer to refresh himself. Gershon preferred, he told his host, to return to free his horse, and make his way back to Brody before nightfall. The rabbi of the town arranged for a coach led by two horses, accompanied by two large, burly men. Gershon would be brought back to his own carriage and helped on his way.

As they rode, Gershon was surprised to feel more anger rising now than at the moment Yisroel had absentmindedly led his horse into the ditch. With the matter almost resolved, should Gershon not feel relief, rather than the futile rage gathering like a dark storm inside him? Praying to subdue his anger, Gershon looked up and saw in the distance a carriage coming towards them.

"It is him," Gershon stammered.

"Rabbi Gershon, sir?" one of the men queried. "Is that the man who steered your horse off the road?"

Gershon did not answer, his rage suddenly displaced by an overpowering exhaustion. When the horses stopped and the carriages were side by side, Gershon summoned his voice to address Yisroel.

"Did help come to free the horse?"

His impenetrable brother-in-law shook his head.

"Then how is it you ride here now, the horse free, the carriage aright and undamaged?"

"I withdrew the horse and righted the carriage," Yisroel said, adding, "Adonai gave me the strength."

Dismounting one coach and mounting the other, the weary Gershon did not take note of Yisroel's words until after he had taken the reins from his brother-in-law. When Gershon glanced at him, the bewildering Yisroel appeared hollow and impassive. No further words were exchanged between them on the ride back to Brody.

No words the next day either, or the next.

A FORTNIGHT LATER, Gershon requested that his sister and her husband leave. He had leased an abandoned inn located in Zabie, a mountain village in the Carpathians. Gershon knew the Jew from Kuty who had run the inn and left. It needed repair but would provide adequate shelter. Channa and her new husband could earn a meager livelihood by mining limestone in the hills and giving shelter to occasional travelers. It troubled Gershon that it was over two hundred kilometers from Brody; Channa would be so far from him. But, at least, the two might be able to make a life there.

When Gershon approached his sister to ask her forgiveness, he saw a gleam in her eyes that took him by surprise. Channa looked neither sorrowful nor afraid. She seemed almost pleased to be going to the forsaken inn. When she embraced him, he lingered in her embrace, fearing he was about to lose a part of himself impossible to reclaim.

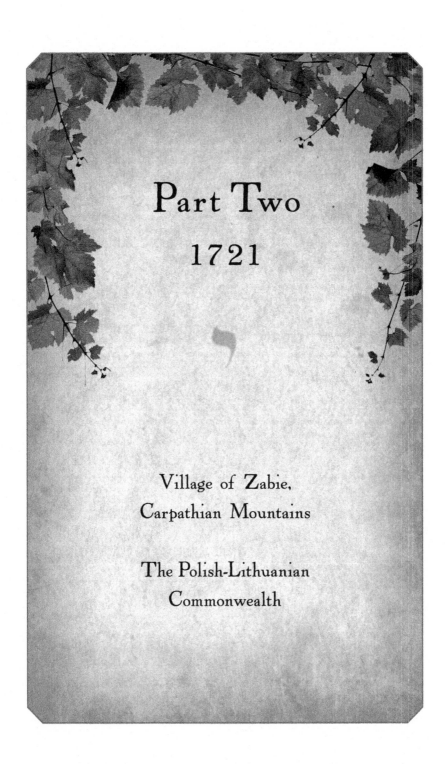

Part Two
1721

Village of Zabie,
Carpathian Mountains

The Polish-Lithuanian
Commonwealth

11

Gershon had employed a driver to transport the couple, their wagon filled with bags of grain, a loom, and simple furnishings.

The ascent into the mountains and the pure chill mountain air, while invigorating for Yisroel and Channa, was demanding for the horse. Yisroel asked the driver to stop and rest the animal. He then spoke tenderly to the horse, removing her harness. Channa listened as her husband thanked the "hardworking, devoted creature" for her labors, stroking her head and sides as he led her down a gradual slope to a mountain stream.

Seeing the clear sparkling waters made Channa thirsty. Lifting the hem of her woolen skirt, she made her way to the shimmering stream. She knelt and cupped the cold, clear water in her hands. The current was stronger than she had imagined, eager to reach the larger river beyond. Or was the stream, she wondered, eagerly hastening *away* from the river that had spawned it? The difference between moving towards and moving away was not always possible to distinguish.

Channa climbed back up to the narrow dirt road barely wide enough for one wagon. She took in a deep breath. The air was scented with a delicate, sweet fragrance she could not name. It must be these tiny wildflowers at her feet. Blossoms blanketed the hillsides, at the feet of staunch armies of firs.

The sentinels of tall firs seemed to guard Channa and Yisroel's passage into their territory: the mighty Carpathians. The mountains of the range hulked like slumbering animals in the distance. Veins of snow streaked their massive bodies. But perhaps she was mistaking the same lacy net of blossoms for snow—could it be those delicate wildflowers that coated the mounds in the distance?

The wagon driver stretched out on the ground among the tiny flowers, cap over his face, and dozed. Yisroel coaxed the horse to rest, drink, and graze.

Channa was grateful to stand and breathe in the vast expanse. Gershon had spoken only of the inn's desolate isolation. He had not mentioned the beauty embracing their new home.

Resuming their journey, the wagon climbed another hour before arriving at a plateau. A cluster of houses circled a well not far from where a small herd of goats grazed. This was the village of Zabie, their driver told them.

They travelled several more kilometers uphill, passing an occasional log house or barn, and came to a narrow road, more like an overgrown path, that forked to the left. The wagon made its tentative way uphill on the rutted road, which was overhung with tree branches. The encroaching dusk darkened their way. Channa wondered how the man knew the route to this remote inn.

When the wagon finally stopped and pulled off the road onto its stony shoulder, Channa worried that the horse had been harmed on the steep, uneven path.

"We have arrived at your destination," the driver announced.

It took her a few moments in the gathering dark to discover the inn. A tangle of brambles and low-hanging evergreen branches had almost swallowed the neglected building crouching beneath them. The forlorn inn was set back from the path that continued past it—to what possible destination Channa could not imagine. A fence close to the road was in the same disrepair as the inn itself whose double wooden doors were barred by a thicket.

Channa stepped down and followed Yisroel through the gate that hung by one hinge. Yisroel wielded a small knife with which he cut and tore at the thick growth. When he turned and gave her another blade, Channa was delighted and joined him in challenging what was likely to be the first of many obstacles they would face together in their new life here. They cleared enough of a path to reach the inn's creaky door, which thankfully had remained solidly on its hinges and opened easily.

With the driver's help, they carried in the contents of the wagon. Tipping his cap, the man declined Yisroel's invitation to stay the night. It was less than three kilometers distance to his brother Ambrozy's farm, further up the mountain. Ambrozy and his good wife Pela would be glad to see him, he assured Channa and Yisroel before taking his leave to continue his climb in the thickening darkness.

The doors of the inn opened onto a large room with an ample stone hearth, where Yisroel set about making a fire out of some of the brush they had cleared. There were several dry logs, too, buried in the tangle that had greeted them. Channa kindled a lantern Gershon had given them. She saw a narrow corridor extending from the hearth room, along which branched two small rooms on each side. The roof over the few small rooms farther back had caved in.

It looked as if a drunken brawl had taken place just before the inn's door had closed to further guests. Yisroel and Channa righted two chairs and freed them from the sticky filigreed nets in which they had been bound up by resident spiders. They carried the chairs to the end of a long oak table.

Yisroel wiped a patch of the table clear of dust, and set down a loaf of bread and a handful of dates. He pried open a handful of walnuts with his pocketknife, adding these to the feast. Channa was glad they had refilled their water jug at the stream. She set two tin cups down next to it.

After the ritual rinsing of hands and blessing of bread, they ate and drank silently.

Yisroel rose and came back to the table with a shawl he wrapped gently around her shoulders.

"Channa, we are both tired from our journey. I will set down a straw mat a safe distance from the hearth, cushioned with the blankets your brother thoughtfully sent. In the morning, we'll begin to make this abandoned shelter our home."

THEY WORKED diligently together the next day. Channa was grateful for the grain Gershon had sent to sustain them until they were able to grow their own. She kneaded and baked bread while Yisroel collected edible plants. He found these in abundance in the forest, and growing near the stream that ran behind the inn. They had heard the stream the night before and discovered it in the daylight at the bottom of an overgrown hillside meadow that slanted down to the sparkling water.

Channa was removing two fragrant rye loaves from the bread oven built into the side of hearth when she heard Yisroel call to her. She turned to see him making his way somewhat precariously through a narrow side door. His arms were filled with roots, stems, and large leaves. His pockets bulged. His cap, balanced on top of the greens he cradled, was filled with seeds. Channa laughed as she helped Yisroel empty his arms. His cap and pockets were filled with wild berries. He was a boy sharing his scavenged treasure.

When Channa handed Yisroel a cup of hot barley tea, her fingers brushed his. Touching him, rather than placing the cup on the table, let him know she was not menstruating and could be approached. She had immersed herself in the ritual bath before leaving Brody and could be with her husband.

Yisroel, holding his tea in one hand, pulled two long stems of rhubarb from inside his jacket, making Channa laugh again. As he gave her the magenta stems, his hand lingered, touching hers. Her breath caught and Channa's laughter stopped. When her gaze met his, she saw her laughter reflected in his brilliant blue eyes.

At sunset, a sword of light cut across their table. In the slice of this light, Channa placed a bowl of steaming buckwheat groats boiled with dark greens Yisroel had brought her. Dipping a small cup into the pail of water he had carried from the river, Yisroel poured a cupful of water three times over his right fist, then his left, letting the water collect in a wooden bowl under his hands. Channa did the same, reciting the blessing upon the washing of hands so that one may eat in cleanliness, awareness, and gratitude. They sat down opposite each other, heads lowered, reciting the prayer in praise of "the One who draws grain from the earth." When Channa raised her face about to take the bread to her lips, she saw Yisroel's hand extended towards her, holding a small bite of bread between his fingers. She leaned forward and parted her lips to receive his offering, his finger lingering for a moment inside her lips.

The two ate then cleared the table in silence. After their meal, they entered one of the small rooms. Two wooden pallets rested on legs that Yisroel had repaired during the day. Channa helped Yisroel pull the pallets together. As soon as she could, she would make mattresses out of dried grasses covered with fabric Gershon had sent along. For now they unrolled the narrow straw mat and blankets they had used the night before.

Yisroel left the room to feed the fire in the hearth.

Channa undressed in the dim light. She loosened her hair, letting it pour over her bare shoulders then slipped under the blankets. Hearing Yisroel enter, she rolled shyly to her side, facing away, listening to him undress.

He lay down beside her, close enough for her to feel his warm breath on her neck. Gently, he drew back the thick curtain of her hair, circling the strands behind the soft shell of her ear. She held her breath when his tongue, unspeakably light, then becoming firmer, traced the inside of her ear.

"I am grateful you accepted me, dear Channa. Not only was our union your father's wish, it also fulfills a longing I didn't know I had."

Channa leaned back into the crescent of Yisroel's body. She could feel his strength, the lean muscle of his arm wrapping around her. The power she sensed in his body made the gentleness of his touch more surprising. Yisroel's tenderness, so unlike Mendel's avaricious hunger, reassured her. With each moment, the reality of Yisroel replaced the dark specter of her first husband.

As Yisroel traced her neck with kisses, bestowing each like a jewel, Channa tried to let go the thought of Mendel. She tried to settle into her own body as she had not done since it was last ravaged.

Channa rolled over and faced her husband. His eyes glistened in the moonlight. Channa reached her hand to his cheek. Were these tears she saw or light? Both tears and light, she realized as Yisroel slowly filled her hand with his kisses. Channa closed her eyes and inhaled his breath, fragrant as a sweet herb. Yisroel appearing in her life and all that followed had been so unexpected. She had not wished to wed. One marriage, with all its attendant pain, had seemed enough for many life-times. How extraordinary that her father, who knew what her life with Mendel had been, had promised her to a stranger he had encountered in his travels.

Yisroel drew her close, her bare breasts pressing against his wide chest. She could feel her heart beating in her throat as Yisroel touched his hand to the soft curve of her buttocks and began walking his fingers up her spine, one step at a time—at once a reticent and a passionate explorer. She thrilled to his fingers traveling her, surprised at the sudden image that came to her of a tightly closed rosebud. It was bowed at the neck as if its stem were broken. As Yisroel's fingers made their way up her spine and reached the very top of her neck beneath her hair, Channa watched the rose's stem strengthen and regain its upright graceful posture. When Yisroel placed his lips on her lips, the bud opened into full blossom.

After an exquisite dance of their tongues, Yisroel leaned his head back and looked into Channa's eyes. Seeing his smile in the moonlight, she realized she was smiling, too. He kissed her chin then the hollow in her neck. His body seemed to glide as he made his way down, pressing his lips between her breasts, pausing to suck lightly on each nipple, then threading kisses to her navel. Yisroel's tongue lingered in Channa's navel before he trailed a silk ribbon to the opening of her other mouth.

Gradually, Channa let go into the almost unbearable pleasure of Yisroel licking her moist, parting lips, then the most delicate of places within her. As if hungry for her, he sucked, his lips and tongue enticing her juices into his mouth, ripening her. She ascended a ladder to jeweled castle doors. The next lick of Yisroel's firm broad tongue opened the doors to a limitless realm of blinding white light.

"Oh, Yisroel…Yisroel…"

He kissed her to sleep.

She dreamt of a bird soaring, joined by another. The birds soared gracefully, weaving patterns only their Creator could discern, their flight an ecstasy of secrets revealed to them.

CHANNA WOKE in the middle of the night and beckoned Yisroel to enter her. His organ swelled under her touch. Entering, he moved slowly at first, coated in her juices as a pressure mounted so great, there came no choice but to let go into a release so complete, his body and soul streamed into her. The sighs and exclamations that escaped him felt like a new kind of prayer.

Morning entered tentatively. Yisroel opened his eyes and looked at Channa asleep beside him.

It had not been a dream: the softness of her skin, the closeness of her breathing—the miracle of her presence. How astonished he had been when her tongue met his in a dance he had never even imagined. Her mouth was a world, her body, a universe. Yisroel had lost and found himself inside her.

Channa smiled in her sleep. Yisroel reached to touch her hair but withdrew his hand not wanting to wake her. He had touched the silken strands in the darkness, but now, in the dawn light, he marveled at the sight of the thick dark brown waves that were usually tucked under her scarf.

Before putting his feet down from the bed, Yisroel silently recited the simple and intimate prayer whispered each morning: *Modeh Ani...I give thanks to You for so generously returning my soul to me. Your faithfulness is abundant.* His father had taught him the prayer as a young boy, at the same time that he had instructed that the "Sh'ma" prayer proclaiming God as One be the words on Yisroel's lips as he fell asleep each night.

Covering his eyes, as was the custom, Yisroel would whisper the Sh'ma in bed next to his father, anticipating his soul would soon be taken. He never lifted his hand to peek despite being deeply curious to see the special angel assigned to the nightly collection of souls. He imagined his soul round and luminous like the full moon, though a lot smaller, somehow taken each night and put back in the morning. He believed that like the moon his soul was impossible to hold with human hands; only the Ayn Sof's unseen hands could carry his soul, which possessed a particular light visible only to the Creator.

Now Yisroel rinsed his hands over the bowl of spring water close to the bed. He stood to recite additional morning blessings, keeping his voice as low as he could, so as not to wake Channa.

"Blessed are You, who directs the steps of man..."

It moved Yisroel how repeating the same words could be so different from day to day, even though the words themselves, offered to One with no need for words, did not change. Some days the vessels of prayer seemed inadequate to contain all that Yisroel needed and wanted to pour into them. Other times, the prayers were so vast he could lose himself in their embrace, as he had in the prayer of lovemaking with Channa.

IN THE DAYS that followed, grateful for the warm and pliant earth, Channa and Yisroel worked together clearing the land of wild, untamed vines, then loosening the soil to prepare for planting. They created their first gardens in a meadow on the west side of the inn bathed in benevolent sunlight. Following Yisroel's suggestion, they waited until the moon waxed to plant the seeds that Gershon had thoughtfully supplied.

When Channa saw the delicate seedlings' first tiny leaves pressed together as if praying, she enthusiastically summoned Yisroel from his work at restoring the inn's dilapidated roof.

She was delighted by her husband's surprising intimacy with roots, succulent stems, leaves, berries, and even the bark of humble unassuming plants surrounding them. When she dropped a heavy log on her leg, Yisroel had a thick balm ready to rub on her thigh. He added fragrant infusions to the water he heated to pour over body and hair when she bathed.

Their secluded life suited Channa. She felt more at home here in this remote place than she had ever felt in Brody. But her preference for solitude, as before, met with self-judgment and struggle. Had she removed herself, and allowed herself to be removed, from where she belonged? Was she abandoning her duties as a member of a community of Jews? Was she wrong to prefer her simple life here in Zabie to a life among other women serving the poor and performing other charitable deeds. She had never lacked for food, shelter, or clothing. Was it not her duty to serve those less fortunate? And given her childlessness, should she not seek to be of service to children in some manner, such as attending to widows left alone with many children. Was Channa escaping her proper duties by living here?

CHANNA HELPED Yisroel move rocks to dam the stream in order to create a pool deep enough for the ritual immersions that he would make each day, and Channa weekly before the Sabbath, except when she was menstruating. They sheltered their mikveh within four simple walls and a roof, and created a space in the corner of the hut for the burning of hot coals in the depth of winter.

Only occasionally did someone pass by the inn, but rarely did anyone stop to seek refreshment or a night's lodging.

The couple subsisted primarily on money earned from the limestone Yisroel mined in the hills and brought to the village of Zabie every fortnight in a borrowed wagon. The wagon belonged to a neighboring farmer, the kind and generous Ambrozy who lived further up the mountain, brother of the steadfast wagon driver who had first delivered them to the inn. In return for the loan of the wagon, Ambrozy, surprised and grateful for his Jewish neighbor's knowledge of Polish and ability to write, requested that Yisroel pen letters of supplication on behalf of his sickly daughter to be retrieved by his brother and delivered to a priest in Kuty.

Ambrozy's wife Pela, a midwife and weaver, taught Channa how to weave. Yisroel traded unguents and herbal cures for Pela's needed fleece.

As their daughter's health improved, Ambrozy and Pela told other families in Zabie and its surroundings about Yisroel's healing potions. In exchange for providing families with cures, Yisroel and Channa were offered tin plates and cups, goose feathers for blankets, the milk of a neighbor's goat, then a goat kid of their own, as well as other materials and services the couple could not provide for themselves.

Yisroel slept no more than three or four hours nightly, waking before midnight to pray and study until dawn. Channa, drifting in and out of sleep, could hear Yisroel's murmured prayers. They comforted her like steady rain. Often she would wake at dawn to a stunning blend of yearning and ecstasy in those prayers that could rend the heavens. Such sublime supplication did not seem meant for human ears.

Thus, Channa understood his desire when Yisroel told her that he had found a grotto on the other side of the river partly up the mountain where he wished to retreat to study and pray. The grotto was tall enough to allow him to stand in its center. He would make a fire pit not far from its entrance. Channa helped her husband construct a bridge of logs and stones to arch over the river. When she saw him carrying several thick volumes to his grotto, she was surprised not to have noticed them among their possessions in the wagon from Brody.

Yisroel remained dedicated to the daily tasks of their life together, otherwise immersing himself day and night in prayer, contemplation, and meditation. When Channa needed him to help attend to a rare guest or for some other purpose, she could easily call or seek him.

Channa was content to spend time alone. Her daily tasks were her prayers. It was in the unhurried rhythm of harvesting and preparing food, spinning, weaving, and washing that she worshipped. She felt closest to her Source when alone, singing prayers and reciting psalms as she worked close to the earth. Channa was relieved that women were not mandated specific times for formal prayer as were men. It suited her to pray with her hands and body as she carried wood, washed their clothes in the river, harvested beeswax for candles, or collected wood ash to make their soap.

∾

YISROEL, DERIVING NOURISHMENT FROM HIS CEASE-less prayer, study, and the ineffable fruits of his meditations, had to remind himself to eat to sustain his physical body during his seclusion in the cave. Sated by the teachings and revelations of the sages, rabbis, and prophets, and by his own visions and realizations, he was left with little appetite for physical food, which seemed dense by comparison with the substance of inspiration.

But Yisroel's cave was not always alluring. The sublime absorption he experienced in his isolation could be glorious: piercing luminosity, fiery dancing letters, spheres of many colors, and spirals of light transported him. But these experiences also brought with them the terror that Yisroel would not be able to return to a normal state of consciousness, might lose himself in uncontrollable madness.

The threat of madness was not the only terror he encountered in the crucible of his cave. Sleepless nights followed tumultuous days, his body a battleground where the despair of centuries warred against faith, leaving him hollow and weak.

He faced the suffering to which his Jewish and Christian brethren were as bound as to their shadows. For most, there were only brief respites from the struggles and loss that dominated their lives. Prayer and Torah study were such places of peace for some, where they felt held by God and community. But for many, suffering had dried up their faith, and left them feeling betrayed. What reason did they have to believe in a merciful God when the unyielding claws of illness, poverty, plague, or hatred seized so many lives, among them untold numbers of innocent children? Countless men and women felt like victims of an unfathomable, punishing God, rather than a beloved partner in creation.

Yisroel understood the despair so widespread among his people. Their oppression had weakened and even broken some of them, leaving them with neither faith in a greater power nor faith in themselves and in each other. Even among the devout and spiritual leaders were many who found no comfort in a Sacred Presence.

Yisroel had witnessed such fear-filled doubt among Jews ardently praying on the High Holy Days in Horodenka. He had perceived it again in Talmudic scholars hosted by Rabbi Meir and his good wife Batya in Tluste. He had felt it in the meritorious, learned guests of his brother-in-law in Brody. These men worshipped a distant God rather than One they recognized in each other and in all of creation. For many, even God as a distant monarch had ceased to truly exist. Some of these disbelievers became gods in their own lives and in the lives of others, wielding power and control in order to secure themselves.

How could parents or teachers inspire faith in a Presence they did not know, feel, and trust? Yisroel could understand the grave disillusion of Jews and Christians who felt they prayed to a blind and deaf God. How difficult to heal and restore trust when broken promises had closed so many hearts.

Now Yisroel understood that he, too, had begun to feel crippling despair, the serpent of doubt writhing in his own body—the grief, hopelessness, and fear that consumed his fellows wracked him, too. Doubt had begun to devour him from within like a parasite, leaving unanswerable questions in its wake. There were hours, even days when Yisroel felt disconnected from any notion of sacredness. At other times, the serpent of doubt derided him, accusing him of blind, even dangerous faith and hypocrisy.

A battle waged between well-reasoned doubt and Yisroel's innate, undefended faith. He felt buried under the pain of centuries, pinned to the floor of his cave without the will to lift his head. His heart was breaking, crushed by the weight of injustice and shattered from within by unspoken sorrow. No tears could wash away the blood spilled in vain; no words of prayer could voice the lament of the suffering men, women, and children he saw lined up since the beginning of time.

But despite the heavy darkness filling and surrounding Yisroel, the light of a greater Presence was never completely extinguished.

～

Channa's presence helped Yisroel draw closer to the Shechinah. He watched his wife now in the glow of the setting sun. It was one of the cherished times in their week, the ephemeral moments at sunset when they stood together, dressed in white to welcome the Sabbath. Channa, facing the horizon, was luminous. Waves of dark hair, unbound, framed her sun-golden skin and flashing eyes. He perceived not only the beauty of her face but of her soul.

Their blended voices sang "L'Cha Dodi." How thrilling to watch his resplendent bride greet the Sabbath Bride, one a reflection of the other. Yisroel thought of the moon reflecting the blinding light of the sun, making its radiance easier to gaze upon.

As they walked slowly from the meadow towards the inn, Yisroel began to sing verses from the Song of Songs.

"An accomplished woman, who can find? Her value is far beyond pearls. With the fruit of her hands she plants a vineyard. She girds her loins in strength, and makes her arms strong."

A flush rose to Channa's cheeks, as he continued.

"She opens her mouth in wisdom, and the lesson of kindness is on her tongue... Strength and honor are her clothing. She smiles at the future. Her candle does not go out at night—"

Channa winked and, taking him by surprise, lifted the hem of her long white skirt and took off in a run. She turned her head once to look back at him, laughing and challenging him to arrive at the table before her.

They arrived as lighthearted to start their meal as if they had already drunk several cups of wine.

Channa kindled the Shabbos candles, afterwards drawing close to Yisroel and brushing her lips on his bearded cheek.

"Good Shabbat," she said softly.

"Good Shabbat, *Ahavah*," he replied, calling her by the word for *Love*. "Ahavah," he whispered in her ear.

That night they made love.

Afterwards, Yisroel spoke softly, his head resting on her breast.

"How wondrous, Ahavah, to know that the joyous union between a man and woman, especially on the Sabbath, is said to cause rejoicing throughout the cosmos."

"Wondrous indeed," Channa laughed warmly, weaving her hands through his thick hair.

The drifted together in and out of a light sleep, which returned them again and again to the land of each other's bodies.

Lightly, Yisroel sucked Channa's nipples, one and then the other.

The silence mounted with heat. When his organ throbbed against her thigh, Channa whispered into the crown of his head: "Come into my cave, so heaven and earth can rejoice once more."

Afterwards, they sank together into the peace that follows deep release.

CHANNA LAY with her head on Yisroel's chest and his arms around her. She pictured the vast cavern with shimmering walls in which his splendid heart resounded. Hot unexpected tears flooded her eyes—and with them a searing longing to bear a child.

The next night, with the appearance of the first three stars in the sky, they carried out the *Havdalah* ceremony that concluded the Sabbath. Just as the Bride had been welcomed with reverence, so was her leaving honored.

Yisroel held up the ceremonial braided candle that Channa had made and she kindled its light. With his other hand, Yisroel waved a tin box filled with fragrant herbs and spices harvested from their own gardens. As was the custom, they held up their hands, turning them and gazing at them in the light of the flame. Yisroel spoke the blessing that marks the separation of light from dark.

"A good week," Yisroel wished her, crowning her head with kisses.

It was not only their farewell to the Sabbath, but also to each other. Yisroel would make his way that night to his grotto, bringing with him a loaf of dark bread, a handful of dates, and her blessing.

~

After Yisroel left, Channa lay awake, watching the full moon through a small window high on the wall. How she loved lying in the moonlight with Yisroel. Being with him could not be more different than being with Mendel. With her first husband, her woman's body had been more a curse than the blessing, a place of dark struggle and unwanted intrusion. Her body still held the rough memories of a hard table or wooden floor when Mendel was in the mood "to generate a son."

With Yisroel, her body was safely awakening. Yisroel approached her the way one studies a treasured, sacred text. Only after revering all there was to be found on the surface—after he had moved his lips and fingers timelessly over all of her—the arch of her foot, the inside of her leg, the tip of her nipple and curve of her neck—only then did he plummet into the depths of her, her inner secrets. In order to survive Mendel's assault, Channa had done her best to escape her own body. Now, she was learning to trust Yisroel to travel the terrain she had once wished never to inhabit again.

Had her father sensed any of this when he arranged this marriage to Yisroel? He had been the one to whom Channa had finally confided the truth about her life with Mendel. He had welcomed her confidence, deeply remorseful for not having recognized the danger before agreeing to the marriage.

Mendel had approached her father, the notable Rabbi Elijah, Chief Rabbi of Brody, for his daughter's hand when Channa was eleven. He asked with an intensity that matched the passion he brought to his studies. He had been watching her serve refreshments to Rabbi Elijah's students, he told her father, and was enthralled. Rabbi Elijah said it was too early, and Mendel had reluctantly agreed to wait until she was fourteen years old before taking her as his wife.

She was not at all drawn to the large, loud student who never smiled. But listening to him debate Talmudic points with rigor, Channa saw that he was one of her father's bwest students. Perhaps this was why she agreed that it was a sensible match, when her brother and father asked her opinion.

After Channa disclosed Mendel's abuse of her to her father, Rabbi Elijah begged his daughter's forgiveness for his lack of discernment.

"I can see now that Mendel approached the Torah with greed," he told her, "which I mistook for an admirable zeal for learning. I saw his avid dedication and imagined that he would be as dedicated to you. I see in sorrowful retrospect that Mendel's desire to master Torah was the desire to dominate what can never be owned or mastered. Mendel sought power, not true knowledge. I was blind to this."

Channa was moved by her father's insights as he grappled with Mendel's transgressions and his own failure to prevent what had unfolded. With profound remorse he shared what he had only afterwards fathomed.

"The way a man approaches the Torah is likely to be the way he approaches his wife. Like Torah, a woman embodies impenetrable mystery and power. If a man comes to the Torah with respect and gratitude, knowing that he walks on sacred ground and that what he is about to receive is holy treasure, he is more likely to a be a humble and grateful husband and lover. But to use something as the means to power is *not* to respect the true power at its source."

"Mendel is afraid of you, my child," her father finally said one morning, looking into her eyes. "You will always elude his grasp. This fear is one of the reasons he seeks to control you. But his fear of you is also your ally."

Her father promised his support, knowing the dissolution of the marriage would not be easy, since divorce could only be granted upon a man's request. A woman, in rare circumstances, could appeal to the Rabbinical Court for a divorce decree on the grounds of being mistreated. But if her husband denied her claim, her appeal would be dismissed. Rabbi Elijah and Channa both acknowledged that Mendel was likely to become more abusive were Channa to approach the court for a divorce. She asked her father not to confront Mendel on her behalf, at least not yet, nor to inform her brother of what she had confided.

What finally freed Channa from the prison of matrimony was her barrenness.

Mendel desperately wanted a son and felt less of a man without one. When Channa did not conceive, Mendel accused her of being barren. Channa also believed she was barren. But just in case she was not, she did what she could to diminish the likelihood of conception and to feed Mendel's doubt in her ability to conceive. She feigned exhaustion and illness when she could use these to abstain from intercourse. Knowing that Mendel's fear of conceiving a deformed child kept him from forcing himself on her during her time of bleeding, Channa extended the length of her uncleanness by delaying her immersion in the ritual bath.

Finally, Channa felt certain that Mendel, convinced he would never conceive a son with her, would not obstruct her request for a divorce and so she appealed for a decree, which the Rabbinical Court, presided over by her father, granted.

After the divorce, Channa returned to live under her father's roof. When Rabbi Elijah died not long after her return, Channa was deeply saddened. The noble man died smiling, attentive to an unseen presence with which he engaged in a private and amusing dialogue. Even after his death, the spirit of the great rabbi's kindness continued to fill his home and Channa's life.

Channa was comforted by the knowledge that her brother Gershon agreed not to impose the burden of matrimony upon her again. Then to her amazement, Yisroel arrived, and overhearing the purpose of his visit, she had felt not even a moment of doubt.

Channa could not have explained then, nor could she explain now how she knew the poorly dressed stranger facing her outraged brother was her *basherte*, her destined one. Surprised by her own inexplicable knowing, she had come to stand at the door of the room. And so, encouraged by her father's presence—which she sensed as a subtle light hovering high in a corner of the room—she had acquiesced to the stranger's shocking proposal.

Yisroel did not want a wife as a servant or possession. He welcomed a partner with whom to nurture faith and revere life. Channa had found a home in Yisroel's embrace and in these mountains.

~

Channa woke before dawn and crossed the room to the small window left slightly ajar the night before. The morning's cold air greeted her brusquely.

She could hear Yisroel's chanting in the distance. In the thin strand that reached her ears now, Channa perceived a weave of joy, gratitude, and yearning with which Yisroel seemed to be reaching to the Infinite. But she also discerned something else she had begun to sense of late: a more urgent, almost fierce longing, tinged with pain. *He was holding nothing back.* Sorrow was carving within him a greater capacity to hold love; Yisroel was being formed into the vessel he was meant to be.

12

Nothing had been the same for Justyna and Dominik since Samuel's accident. What mattered most to them was that Samuel had survived and was recuperating, but what mattered most to their neighbors, and many of their relatives, was that their friendliness towards Jews was leading to problems. Justyna's cousin, Olga, above all, never ceased to express her embittered opinions. She harangued Justyna in the marketplace and after church, loudly enough for all to hear. Justyna had given up trying to talk sense into her.

At the recent seasonal planting festival, a number of drunken farmers and their wives had cursed Justyna and her family more viciously than ever before. A rock hurled from behind a wagon had barely missed Marishka's head; but the bitter rebuke hurled with it struck its target: "Stupid girl, when you find her Jew-devil horns, then you'll see what kind of friend you have!"

Justyna and Dominik had not planned to attend the festival, but they knew that to set themselves apart by not going would make their relations with their own people even worse. Both farmers' festivals, one at the time of planting and the other at harvest, were to Justyna's thinking degrading celebrations, the szlachcic's way of prolonging his serfs' slavery. First, the nobleman drowned the peasants in enough "free" vodka to stupefy them. What he asked in return for the free flowing drink was not money, which the peasants lacked, but instead that they pay with their very lives. The peasants promised the szlachcic further indenture: farming his land, tending his animals, working in his breweries, and whatever else might be demanded. The women, in addition to working the fields, were to attend the nobleman's wife, be nursemaids to her children, and serve as the szlachcic's unofficial mistresses.

Justyna understood how easy it was for peasants, encouraged by noblemen, to blame their poverty and suffering on the Jews, used as middlemen and portrayed as the true enemy of the disenfranchised peasants. It was not apparent to those fueled by schnapps that the majority of their Jewish neighbors were no freer than they, with little more material resources. At least a farmer could be assured enough to eat and a roof over his head as long as he fulfilled his obligations to his szlachcic.

Justyna knew that her friend Leya was not allowed to own her house or her cobbling stall. No Jew, even if affluent, could own property. Leya's cottage and livelihood could be taken from her at any time, the Polish authorities using the simple excuse that Leya had not paid her taxes, even if she had. It was common for false charges to be levied against innocent Jews who were unable to contest them. The Jews had their courts, yes, but these were for matters that concerned their own religious laws. The Jewish courts had no power in the face of Polish "justice."

Justyna's cousin, Olga, of course, denied and dismissed these realities. Olga, and others like her, found relief in having someone to blame, someone who could not dare punish them for their anger or rebellion.

Justyna and Dominik had taught their children that the Jews were *not* responsible for the inequality that existed between those who owned the land and those who worked it. It was by the szlachta's decree that families like theirs remained little more than slaves paid with heads of cabbage they themselves had raised, a fraction of the wheat, corn, and barley they had tended, and enough fermented liquor to keep them blind.

Justyna was disturbed by the increasingly virulent warnings that she not sell milk to Leya or Gittel and that she not "risk being poisoned by eating the red-haired Jew-devil's bread." Above all, she was harshly cautioned that she must stop acting cordial with "the cobbler demon." Her cousin Olga, drunk at the festival, called Justyna close to loudly inform her that she hated not only Leya and Gittel, but all Jews.

JUSTYNA WISHED that she could have protected Marishka from yet another bitter taste of the hostility that now consumed the local peasants. Making her way home from the riverbank, Marishka had repeated to herself the terrible and confusing words she had overheard so that she would be able to report them just as she had heard them.

Marishka told Justyna that as she was approaching the riverbank, she saw two peasant girls, younger than she and both very pregnant, washing their clothes in the river. They seemed not to notice Marishka. Hearing the words, "those stinking Jews," Marishka had stopped and moved behind a bush to listen.

"You do know never to let a Jew near your baby, right?"

When no reply came, the expert on Jews continued.

"They are sly, those stinking Jews. Doing business with them is one thing, but *never* invite one into your house or go into theirs. Jews *must* have the blood of pure, innocent Christian children to make the strange flat cracker they eat on that holiday of theirs that comes close in time to our Easter. They will do whatever is needed, including showing kindness to our children, to lure them to their death and get their blood."

What Marishka heard made no sense, but it frightened her. The one guiding her companion continued.

"You are new in Horodenka, but you know Justyna, right? The foolish woman has allowed her daughter Marishka to befriend a Jewgirl named Rifka from Okup. Now listen carefully: the Jewgirl's aunt Leya, of course, favors Marishka and her family. This means that when she and her people come for the blood they need, it will *not* be to Dominik and Justyna's cottage. They will come to our homes. Justyna's family will be spared. Justyna's cousin Olga has warned us all. When the time comes, it will be our blood the Jew devil and her people will seek."

Marishka wanted to scream out in protest, to tell them that they were wrong. But instead, she covered her mouth.

Justyna was enraged to hear what Marishka relayed. She was also frightened by the hatred gripping her people. It terrified her that hatred was finding a target in her dear Leya.

It was not the first time Justyna had encountered such accusations. As a child, she had heard the rumors about Jews needing Christian blood for their unleavened bread. Justyna had never believed that Jews practiced such heinous actions. Men and women who stood to benefit from scapegoating others regularly generated false accusations. Her father had been denounced by the aristocratic wife of a nobleman for committing unthinkable depravities with the nobleman's horse—false charges that exacted outrageous fees or years of labor in exchange for the alleged harm done the animal. Not long after that, Justyna's mother was accused of engaging in black magic, used to confound and paralyze the master's children.

Justyna crossed the room and knelt in front of a small altar over which hung an image of the Black Madonna of Częstochowa. She looked up at the Holy Virgin's sorrowful eyes. "*Matka Boga,* Holy Mother," Justyna implored, "in the name of your Son, open those hearts closed by hatred and fear." She remained on her knees, praying for protection for of her friend Leya.

Dominik entered and touched her lightly on the shoulder.

"I am troubled, Dominik," Justyna said after telling her husband what Marishka had confided earlier. "I think it best for us to withdraw from Leya and the girl and to warn them not to come here. One of our people might attack Leya or harm Rifka in their drunken stupidity."

NINETEEN-YEAR-OLD PATRYK was disturbed by his mother's words. He, too, had heard the warnings from parents to children, from protective older brothers and sisters to younger ones, to stay away from the Jews. "*Jew Devil*" had become a recitation. Patryk, like his mother, thought these ideas ridiculous and was worried for the safety of their Jewish friends.

Patryk had confided to his sister Marishka how greatly he missed Gedaliah and Dovid since both had gone off to study. The three boys had shared laughter and discussions of life as they worked together plowing and sowing seed, skills Gedaliah and Dovid had been eager to learn from

Patryk. Patryk had learned from them in turn not to fear talking about his thoughts.

Since their departure, Patryk had been accompanying Marishka to meet her friend Rifka. Even before hearing his mother's words, Patryk had begun to feel protective of Rifka. He tried to discourage her from walking alone even part of the way between Leya's cottage and his family's. But she insisted that she was no longer a girl but a woman, and could decide for herself what to do. He gave up trying to convince her, but just made sure to get to her aunt's cottage with Marishka before Rifka had set out and then to accompany her to the farm, all three walking together. This way, he joked, he and Marishka could help carry her pails empty in one direction and full in the other.

The discussions he shared with Rifka and Marishka were unlike any Patryk had ever had, even with Dovid and Gedaliah. Questions overflowed their minds as did milk at the lip of their pails. Many of the questions and topics were ones that Patryk had considered, alone behind his plow. *Was there one God, or different Gods for the Jews and Christians? Why had God created suffering? Why do innocent children die?*

Patryk explained to Rifka that his religion teaches there is everlasting life, but he wasn't sure what that really meant. Did people only *seem* to die? Was his baby brother alive in heaven, and, if so, where was heaven? Patryk felt afraid of losing those he loved. Was it wrong to fear death? What he did not say was that he felt afraid of Rifka dying, or at least her being badly hurt.

Patryk's peasant comrades would judge it foolish, even sinful, to have such conversations. They would think it especially foolish to talk with a female, knowing girls and women inferior in all ways. But to talk like this with a Jewess—they would think this not only foolish but detestable. And dangerous.

WHEN LEYA opened the door, she was surprised to see Patryk and to see him dressed so differently. She had only occasionally seen him dressed in clean woolen breeches and a shirt, almost white, stitched by his grand-mother. He was dressed as if about to accompany his family to the church for worship. Patryk's head was uncovered, his wool cap in his hands. To the Polish peasants, unlike the Jews, it was removing one's hat, rather than covering one's head, that showed respect.

When Leya gestured for Patryk enter, he declined.

"With great sorrow, *Pani* Leya, I must tell you not to come to our farm anymore. If my parents no longer greet you, Rifka, or Samuel with kindness, please know this is not due to their lack of respect or because we have lost our affection." He paused and looked down.

Leya followed Patryk's gaze to his hands twisting his cap as if he were wringing out a wet rag. She had never seen the youth this distraught.

"There are rumors, Pani Leya, dangerous ones. You must not allow Rifka to come anymore. And you must not come yourself. I will bring you the milk."

Patryk turned and left quickly, giving Leya no chance to respond. But she had no words anyway, just an uneasiness that twisted in the pit of her stomach.

Leya closed the door and crossed the room slowly to resume prepar-ing beet soup for the sick wife of Levi the soap maker. Leya stirred the red liquid.

Blood! That was it! That must be it. The rumors had reached her ears, but she had not wanted to pay them heed. The Passover holiday was approaching. In the marketplace, fear had been mounting among both peasants and Jews concerning "blood libel." For at least a decade, no Jew in Horodenka had been accused of charges of harming or, even worse, murdering a Christian child to obtain blood for making matzo, the unleavened bread baked for Passover. Now the subject was on the lips of many. Sparks were flying that could lead to fire.

Leya did not want to abandon her friendship with Justyna or with the numerous other Christian peasants and artisans she had befriended. Nor did Leya want Rifka to be less trusting of their Christian neighbors or to lose her closest friend Marishka due to primitive fears. But the danger could not be ignored.

∾

GEDALIAH ARRIVED IN HORODENKA FROM HIS yeshiva too late to help bake matzos, but in time to help his mother in other ways. Together with Samuel and Rifka, he would deliver the Passover meals that his mother and Gittel had prepared for several village widows and their children.

Before they went out, Leya reminded him of what she had been teaching him since he had first started helping her this way as a boy of five. *They must offer the food, aware not to shame the recipients in any way, even indirectly.* According to Rabbi Maimonides' ladder of giving, the highest rung, corresponding to the highest form of giving, is to give what can lead to self-reliance, to give something that helps a person help him or her self. The lowest was to give begrudgingly or to make the recipient feel disgraced or embarrassed.

In the many years that Gedaliah had accompanied his mother to homes in Horodenka, he had watched her help others to help themselves. This often took the form of acknowledging a woman heartily for an accomplishment that she had not even recognized. Leya managed to find and praise the skills of each woman she visited.

On their outing today, Gedaliah listened to his mother praise a widow for the crafting of a beautifully braided Havdalah candle. Leya asked the surprised woman if she had ever considered offering her exceptional candles in exchange for a reasonable fee, or for services that might help her family. When the young widow smiled shyly, looking intrigued, his mother encouraged her to start with one or two candles; if she felt wary of selling her candles in the marketplace, she should bring them to the cobbler stall where Leya's customers could see and buy the candles.

His mother spoke to another woman about her rare voice, saying her presence in the women's balcony added to the pleasure of the other women. Leya encouraged the blushing woman to consider teaching the daughters of Horodenka to lift *their* voices in song. Perhaps she could do this in return for wood to warm her oven, for a chicken, or perhaps for soap made by Reb Levi, father to four daughters.

Gedaliah and his family continued to make their way, offering *matzos* wrapped in muslin, clay pots of thick soup, and two pairs of small boots.

ARRIVING FROM OKUP, Aryeh was happy to find that his nephew had made the long trip from his yeshiva in Mezritch. Just a few hours remained before Leya and Gittel's families would squeeze into Leya's cottage for the Passover ritual meal.

Aryeh looked on quietly as Rifka supervised the making of a mixture that symbolized the mortar used by Jewish slaves to make the bricks of the pyramids. Samuel was instructed to pour a small amount of sweet wine into the nuts and apples that she and Nessa had finely chopped. Rifka coaxed ten-year-old Tanya, more shy and retreative of late, into the honor of sprinkling the ground cinnamon Aryeh had procured just for this purpose. Samuel stirred the mixture. Then he offered a small taste to each of the cooks. Leya had him spoon some of the sweet mixture into a small clay cup and bring it along to the marketplace.

In the marketplace, Aryeh enjoyed watching his sister haggle good-naturedly with Zelda about horseradish root.

"I will not charge you for bitterness," Zelda insisted.

"Something sweet in exchange for taking away some of the bitter?" Leya said, taking the cup from Samuel's hands. "How can you resist such a deal?"

Smiling her toothless grin, Zelda conceded.

It heartened Aryeh to watch his nephew Samuel laugh at the haggling between the women. Since the accident, the boy's laughter no longer erupted as spontaneously as once it had. Samuel's light-heartedness had become buried under the weight of fearful anticipation. He dreaded being "taken away" by yet another sudden attack, something that had started after his recovery that he could not predict or stop once started.

"Suddenly everything disappears into blackness," thirteen-year-old Samuel told Aryeh. "Then somebody's voice or hand reaches to me from far away and brings me back. Sometimes, it feels as if I have been gone a very long time; other times, as if I was hardly gone at all, no one but me even noticing that I went away. Each time an attack happens," his nephew confided, "it feels as if the cloth the day is made of is torn and cannot be made whole again."

But right now, Samuel laughed freely, watching Zelda give his mother the root then pull it back again, the two women partners in a strange and humorous dance.

At the Passover meal, Rifka seemed delighted to have a turn reading from the *Haggadah*. She stood to intone the ten plagues, in as grave a voice as she could summon.

"Blood. Frogs. Lice…"

As she named them slowly one by one, everyone dipped the tip of their fifth finger into a nearby cup of wine, letting the drop fall onto a plate before them.

"Each drop is meant to also recall, with compassion, the spilled blood of the enemy," Leya explained.

Hearing the quivering in her voice, Aryeh looked over at his sister.

"May it be God's will that no more blood be spilled by man against man," she added, eyes brimming with tears. The worried look on his sister's face startled Aryeh.

AT THE END of holiday, Aryeh offered to take Gedaliah back to Mezritch where he lived with his father Ber's cousin, who was also a blacksmith. Aryeh had learned from Gedaliah that Ber's cousin had need of a new forge. Aryeh had procured one and looked forward to delivering it.

A sturdy wagon and horse had been made available to Aryeh in return for shoes he had fashioned for the horse. It would give Aryeh pleasure to thank Ber's cousin for his hospitality to Gedaliah.

Aryeh had considered bringing Rifka along. She spoke often about missing their travel together between Okup and Horodenka, watching the Dniester River disappear and appear again along their route. But in the end, he decided it best that she remain in Horodenka safe with her tanta.

THE MORNING of Aryeh and Gedaliah's departure was not an easy one for Rifka. No matter how often she had done so, it was difficult to part from her father. In addition, she had to say goodbye to her cousin for an indefinite time. After the wagon had left for Mezritch and Leya went to her stall, the cottage felt suddenly terribly empty.

Benjamin's whistle summoned Samuel from the table. Rifka went to the door and watched the two walk side by side, Benjamin dragging his leg and Samuel, his invisible burden.

After cleaning up, Rifka put on the shawl she had proudly crocheted with little help, and set out for Gittel's cottage where she went daily now to stitch at the new widow's side and keep company with Nessa and Tanya.

Jacob had died not long before the holiday. Gittel had told Leya how grateful she was that Jacob had been able to return to life from that living death before the Angel of Death finally came to take him. It was a disease of the liver that finally took Jacob, his body weakened by his years of drinking. Jacob had died in Gittel's arms, whispering both apology and gratitude. She consoled her daughters, allowing each her sorrow. Gittel clearly carried sorrow, too, but she also seemed at peace with Jacob's death.

Rifka learned much under Gittel's gentle guidance. Rifka had become so skilled in crocheting that she now fashioned most of the lace cuffs. Initially worn only by noblewomen, the lace cuffs had recently become common additions to the dresses of prosperous merchants' wives. Traveling merchants, buying them from Gittel, sold them in Warsaw and Lemberg.

Rifka's work left Gittel free to repair men's coats. It had proved a boon for Gittel the first time she was commissioned to fix such a coat. Word of the quality of her work and its reasonable cost—much cheaper than the village tailors—spread quickly. She asked those who sought her services to be discreet in speaking of her work, so the tailors' guilds would not accuse her of stealing their business.

This morning, Gittel had a surprise. In honor of Rifka's turning fifteen, Gittel would now pay Rifka something each week for her work. Before she could refuse, Gittel, eyes gleaming, placed a bill in her hand, closing Rifka's fingers around it.

Rifka welcomed the feeling of responsibility that came with her duties. As well as crocheting, she often helped Gittel prepare food, and most recently, had begun teaching the girls to read. On top of all this, she occasionally was able to assist her tanta Leya with shoemaking.

But what Rifka loved most was the time she spent learning. Every spare hour that she was not engaged in other tasks, Rifka hurried to the beloved texts that had become her friends: the worn book of Psalms, the Song of Songs Dovid had given her before he left, and most valuable, the Yiddish prayers that her mother Dvorah had composed. Rifka had even begun to compose her own prayers.

On her way home from Gittel's, Rifka started writing one in her mind, saying the words as she walked: "*Dear Source of All. Please open my heart wide enough to hold all of your opposites without breaking: Laughing and Crying, Knowing and Not Knowing, Living and Dying.*"

Rifka saw confusing opposites everywhere, like Samuel who used to be lighthearted and now was heavy hearted. The lightheartedness had not left him altogether; Rifka could still see signs of it, like a secret, in his eyes. But with each unforeseen seizure, heavy clouds rolled in that darkened his eyes, at least for a while.

Samuel had returned from his morning duties at the cheyder by the time Rifka returned.

Together, they brought water from the well. They rinsed and cut vegetables for the evening meal's soup.

"Cousin," Rifka said, taken by an idea, "why don't we go meet your mother at the cobbling stall and accompany her home?"

Samuel was clearly pleased.

The walk to the cobbling stall was at least a kilometer. The weather was becoming milder and the green greener as spring spread across Horodenka. It was the kind of weather that used to make Samuel run freely, and then wait for Rifka to catch up. Rifka did not expect him to do that today, but hoped that Samuel's inner joy might venture forth in some other way to greet the afternoon's playful breezes.

As they approached the cobbler shop, its heavy door was ajar. Leya, too, must be enjoying the spring air.

Samuel put his finger to his lips. They would surprise Leya.

When they entered, they were the ones surprised.

"Tanta Leya?"

Rifka called to her, hoping her aunt had stooped behind the counter the way she used when they were younger. Samuel had loved hiding.

But Leya was not in the stall. Had she gone to a neighboring shop and left the door open?

"Look, Rifka," Samuel called out. He held up his mother's leather apron.

Rifka searched around the bench where Leya did her cutting and stitching. On the ground, she found a boot with a partly sewn sole, Leya's needle and thread still attached. Leya would have set them down on the bench if she had stopped to tend a customer, not thrown them down in this manner.

Something was wrong.

Rifka took the apron from Samuel and placed it on Leya's bench. Rifka tried not to let her voice show her fear when she spoke.

"Samuel, come, we'll go to Gittel's home right away and see if she knows where your mother is. But first, we must lock the door. Help me find the key to this padlock. I don't think your mother has taken it."

On their way to Gittel's, Rifka tried to veil the foreboding mounting inside her. She resisted the urge to break into a run, which might have not only frightened Samuel but taxed him, too. She was not sure just what brought on his attacks. Ever since seeing Samuel nearly dead on the ground near Marishka's barn, Rifka had been protective of him. She would do anything to shield him from harm.

"When we see your mother, we'll tell her this was her best ever hiding," she told him.

Samuel laughed weakly; he, too, was worried.

13

G ittel did not know where Leya was.

"Please stay with the girls and Samuel, Rifka." Gittel pulled a shawl from the back of her chair and with one quick look back at the children, left in search of her friend.

The knocking at the cottage door a few minutes later surprised Rifka. She heard someone call her name then knock again insistently. Rifka recognized Levi the soap maker's voice and opened the door.

The hunchback soap maker remained where he was. Awkward as usual, he stared silently at Rifka—his face strained. It seemed that he wished to tell her something but could not get the words out. Directing his gaze towards the ground between them, the soap maker finally began to speak.

"Your aunt's friend Gittel, she, she… wants you to wait here… here in the cottage… you must stay here until she returns. You see, she came to me looking for your aunt… I told her that your tanta Leya… was taken… the Polish police… they took her… there are charges… they took her for charges."

"Charges? What charges?"

He looked up at her, kind and pained, as if his words were too many delicate objects to hold in his clumsy hands.

"They say your aunt… of course, it is not true… they accuse her of… "

His head hung down as if it might fall off his neck and roll across the threshold. Rifka leaned forward, looking up into his face, desperate for him to explain.

"Who are '*they*'?" Rifka tried to control her voice, terror overcoming her. "*Who* thinks something not true about my aunt? And exactly what do *they* think?"

Reb Levi pushed the words out of his mouth.

"They say she has killed a Christian child. To take his blood. That is what they say she did."

Rifka could not speak. What had he said? Leya accused of killing a child? No one could possibly believe such a thing! He must have heard wrong!

The man straightened as much as he was able. Fear mixed with anger in his voice. "They say we Jews need the blood for our matzos. An excuse to accuse and punish us…"

Samuel and the girls had come to stand behind Rifka. Even if they had not heard or understood Levi's words, they must feel his urgency. Rifka turned to face them. She could see by the look on Samuel's face that he knew or at least suspected that his mother was in danger.

Rifka could not leave them alone and even if she took them with her, where would she go to find her tanta?

She turned back to look at the large awkward man before her, who stood frozen now.

"Reb Levi," Rifka implored, "when Gittel comes back, will you take me to my tanta?"

"I must say something to you alone." He motioned that Rifka step outside the cottage with him, gesturing toward the younger ones as if to make sure not to be overheard.

Rifka turned, putting one hand on Samuel's shoulder and the other on Nessa's. "Look after Tanya, please," she gently commanded them. "Comfort her; she looks frightened. I will return in just a moment." Before they could protest or ask anything, Rifka stepped forward, gently closing the door behind her.

The distressed Levi looked at her directly. His words came in a torrent now.

"Your tanta Leya is a strong woman. I heard her protests from my stall, and when I came out, I saw one man, a Polish official, holding her hand behind her back while another spat on her. When this same scoundrel, curses be on his head, raised his hand to slap your tanta's face, from out of nowhere a third guard stepped forward. He told the one with his arm in the air not to dare touch the prisoner.

'She is to be treated with respect,' he commanded.

I don't know where this sympathetic Pole came from. Dressed in the same uniform as the other two, he did not appear to have a higher rank than they. The first two grumbled but did not hit her again. Your aunt kept her back straight and did not scream out in fear. I do not know where they have taken her. I am so sorry."

Rifka's mind and heart raced. Leya, who had never harmed anyone, was being harmed. Rifka wished for her father. Surely, if he were here, he would let no harm come to his sister.

Rifka thanked the despondent messenger. Straightening her back like Leya, she opened the door of the small cottage to comfort the younger ones.

WHEN GITTEL returned to the cottage, she could tell immediately that Rifka had been informed of her aunt's capture. Gittel went to the girl and held her close.

"Leya has been imprisoned in a cell under the town hall," she whispered into Rifka's hair.

It had not taken long for the news of Leya's capture to spread among the town's Jews.

Gittel had learned that a six-year-old peasant boy named Henryk had disappeared the week before Passover; his body had been found last night, washed up by the Dniester River. The child's parents carried their son's bloated body to the local parish priest along with a vile accusation against the hateful *Pani* Leya.

They claimed that the "Jewdevil cobbler" had been seen with the child just before his disappearance. Using the large needles of her trade, they accused, she had obtained from him the blood needed for baking her matzos. Then, assisted by a Jewish kinsman, the diabolical Pani Leya had thrown the small child's body into the river. The Jewish witch was avenging the injury and near death of her own son at the hands of peasants. The river had returned the boy Henryk so that the evil woman's crime would not be buried.

The Jews of Horodenka were all too familiar with such accusations. They knew that Jews had been tortured, hung, and burned at the stake throughout the Polish Lithuanian Commonwealth on charges of blood libel. Unfounded charges of ritual murder had been levied against Jews for centuries. Irrational fear and superstition moved among their Christian neighbors, deeper than reason and justice would reach.

The village Jews also knew that once a ritual murder charge was issued, it was a common occurrence for many more Jews to suffer. Businesses and synagogues might be destroyed, Jewish homes seized and their residents banished. It was not unusual for the accused, under torture, to implicate other Jews in return for saving their own lives.

Those accused had succumbed to Christian baptism to be spared, or had begged to be murdered quickly rather than by slow, gruesome means.

Gittel knew that the majority of Horodenka's Jews were paralyzed by fear of the consequences should they speak up. Gittel also recognized a painful irony. If it were Leya receiving news of such charges against a fellow Jew, she would do whatever she could to challenge the injustice. Leya would not remain passive, even if it meant risking her life.

"How could anyone say that Tanta Leya would hurt a child?" Rifka cried in Gittel's arms. " What will they do to her?"

"We will do whatever we can to protect and free your tanta. I am going to the head of the Kahal, Reb Wolf. Despite his disagreements with your mother, he will recognize that a great injustice is being carried out. As both the head of the Kahal and a prosperous Jew, he has relations with the Polish magistrates and with the noblemen who control them."

Gittel cradled Rifka's face in her hands. "God will protect your tanta, Rifkalla."

Gittel did not want to leave the children alone, but she had no choice.

"I must go. There is some *chulent* left over from Shabbos. Feed the younger ones and take for yourself. I will return as soon as I can. Bolt this door behind me and do not open it to anyone unless you know who it is. *God protect you.*"

REB WOLF told Gittel they must wait until the morning.

"It would only endanger Leya and others of our people, as well as arouse the wrath of our Christian neighbors, were we Jews to begin clamoring for her immediate release. To whom would we direct our demands now anyway? A trial will be organized, but not tonight. Once the Polish authorities have announced the proceedings, the Kahal, as representative of the Jews of Horodenka, will ask to be involved in the case."

"How can we let the night pass without doing something to assure Leya's safety?" Gittel protested. She could not bear to imagine the torture that might begin at any time in the dank dungeons beneath the town hall. The officially sanctioned, brutal means of "obtaining proof" in such cases was infamous.

Unexpected and of some consolation was Reb Wolf's report that Father Amadeusz, the parish priest who had received the child's body, had tried to calm and dissuade the drowned child's parents.

"Father Amadeusz said that he knows the woman being charged and is certain of her innocence."

"Then why was she taken?" Gittel asked, stunned.

"The parish priest confided to a member of the Kahal that the desolate parents, overcome with grief, were incited by certain of their neighbors. These neighbors seized the boy's bloated body and, carrying torches, incited other peasants until the authorities had no choice but to seize and imprison the accused."

Reb Wolf paused. "There is nothing to do now, dear woman. I am sorry." His voice was tender; his genuine compassion almost pierced her resolve not to weep.

"There is nothing for us to do but pray," Reb Wolf concluded.

Despite the danger, which was greater during the night hours, Gittel risked making her way to Justyna and Dominik's farm. Wrapping her shoulders and head in a black shawl, hunched over like a peasant woman with a basket, Gittel hurried the distance.

When Justyna saw who it was at their door, she ushered Gittel in quickly, concerned for her safety. Dominik motioned for Gittel to sit. Gittel acknowledged his courtesy, but remained standing.

Marishka and Patryk, who had been sitting close to the hearth, stood now, each with a small child in their arms. Gittel could see that none of them knew what had happened, but they feared that something had.

"Leya has been accused of blood libel and imprisoned."

"*Jesu!*" Justyna called out, grasping the back of a chair.

Patryk stepped forward.

"When was she taken?" he demanded. "What did her accusers say?"

"A young boy disappeared whose body was washed up by the river," Gittel replied, her voice shaky. "They are blaming Leya. They say she is responsible for his death."

Dominik directed an imploring gaze at his wife. Patryk, as if hearing his father's unspoken message, knelt in front of Justyna.

"You must go and talk to your cousin Olga," Patryk urged his mother.

"Even if she shuns you, you must try again," Dominik said.

They did not explain, and Gittel did not ask.

Patryk accompanied her home. When they arrived, she invited him to enter for a moment to receive a small bundle of clothing she had set aside for his little brothers. Removing his cap, he followed her into her cottage.

Patryk recognized Rifka even though he could not see her face, hidden by the cascade of her thick black hair as she leaned over the children asleep around her.

When she turned towards him, Patryk was saddened to see her eyes so red and swollen. His urge to embrace and comfort her, to ease her sorrow, took him by surprise. If only he could do something to help.

～

L EYA SQUATTED ON THE PACKED DIRT FLOOR OF THE underground cell that was little more than a crawl space. Wrapping her arms around her shivering body did nothing to fend off the damp and cold. She was thankful for the young guard who had stopped his comrades from beating her when she was first seized. He had stayed their violence twice more since then. Now, bent over, he carried a small bowl of broth into Leya's cell, setting it down on the packed-dirt. As if addressing his own mother, the young man spoke with a concern that shocked Leya.

"Please eat, Pani Leya. I am sorry there is so little, but it is all they will allow. Please eat, Pani Leya," the gentle guard urged sincerely before departing.

He closed the heavy wooden door of the cell slowly.

She guessed that several hours had passed since she had been led to the bowels of the municipal building. It had been afternoon when she was shoved through the building's heavy double doors and down its narrow, winding stairs to this pit. For a while, Leya heard muffled voices and the pounding of heavy boots above her. Then quiet. Perhaps most of the Polish officials left the building at night, leaving her guarded by one or two until their return.

Leya thought again about the compassionate guard, whom she had heard called Dobry. When she first saw him enter her shop with his storming comrades, he looked as if he wished he were not on this mission. He was perhaps sixteen or seventeen. She thought she recognized him as one of Patryk's friends, a peasant farmer's son. Perhaps he had even worked side by side with her own son when Gedaliah and Dovid had joined Patryk to plow.

Leya sat on the damp ground. She pulled her draped knees close to her body and began to rock, more for comfort than for warmth. She thought of Rifka and Samuel. Rifka would have gone to Gittel who would look after them, thank God. Her friend would ease their fright—as best she could.

LEYA DID NOT KNOW how long she had been lying on the damp cold dirt when she was roused from a nightmare into this waking one. Had hours or days passed since she'd been confined to this dark pit?

Breathing in the foul mustiness, Leya felt a sudden rising panic that made the dank room feel smaller and airless. *She had to breathe fresh air or she would die in this merciless crypt.* She tried to stand. But she hit her head on the low roof of her cell. The clammy walls she found on hands and knees, closed in around her. Dark and fear were swallowing her.

She had to calm herself.

She would take God's name, that's it. There were many to choose from. She would repeat them out loud—one by one, slowly, over and over again. *Adonai. Ayn Sof. Shechinah. HaShem. Breathe through me!* She must feel God's love around her—in her. She would think of God's love as the air she breathed.

Suddenly, Leya heard angry shouting. A cacophony of voices. Coming from a distance. She heard the words *Jewish Witch,* then other Polish curses amidst a clamoring of what sounded like sticks hitting tin. A herd of angry men.

Leya stood as best she could, hunched under the low ceiling. She tried to listen more closely. The sounds were advancing towards the cell.

The men were drunk.

She did not know if the sympathetic Dobry was on the other side of the thick door or if he had been replaced by one of his ruthless comrades. Even if it were he, there was little he could do in the face of a horde of drunken men seeking revenge. Leya banged on the door and called to him anyway.

As the board was forced from the small window, Leya held her breath—releasing it when she saw young Dobry. She watched the boy's eyes dart fearfully as he listened to the riotous band screaming for justice. For an instant, his eyes locked on hers. His compassion overpowered the hatred of his peers. Leya felt God in him.

When glass shattered above her, the moment was shattered, too.

Dobry looked up.

Leya tried to breathe in God's love.

Another window was shattered. Dobry spoke now, assuring Leya that the men had not entered yet. It would not be easy to do so.

"A large window on the second floor has been broken, but it is too high to allow entry. There are windows on the first floor, but they are too small for a man to climb through."

A thunderous banging on the doors began and the curses grew louder.

Leya closed her eyes. "Protect me, Adonai. Surround me with your love." The violent mob grew louder. Leya drew in her breath. "Preserve my life, Adonai, for my son's sake, for Rifka and Aryeh." She heard the doors groaning as if they could not much longer resist the weight against them.

The doors were forced open.

At the thunder of boots above her head, Leya began to whisper the *Sh'ma* prayer. *Sh'ma...Adonai Echad.* Hear! Our God is One. She had not imagined dying this way, but now that the time had come, she would not be separated from her faith. She repeated the prayer louder until she found herself intoning just the single the word for "Hear"—*Sh'ma*—as long as her breath would carry it. The syllable seemed to extend infinitely, beyond Leya's ability to breathe it.

Suddenly, Leya felt vast black sky over her. No heavy boots or storming drunks, just a black void. A familiar voice joined hers, intoning the single boundless syllable. The voice carried the sound when hers faltered. It was Aryeh! Aryeh's voice joined with hers! His voice urged hers forth so that it grew louder, firmer, more resolute. Then, as suddenly as Leya had felt Aryeh join her, he was gone.

Leya heard Dobry's voice rise above the clamor of the others. She stopped chanting and listened. He was pleading and commanding at the same time.

"Bolek!" Dobry bellowed the name forcefully above the raging voices, summoning the attention of the swarm. "Bolek! Does your young brother still wear the boots the cobbler woman made for him? She would take no payment because of your father's accident in the fields, do you remember?"

Yelling as loud as he could, Dobry challenged another.

"Anzelm, after your young wife almost lost her life in childbirth, a gift was left at your door. Do you recall how the tiny shoes heartened your bride?" "And you, Kasper," Dobry called out with a hoarse voice, "was it not the woman's son Gedaliah who put his shoulder to the plow with you and our friend Patryk?"

The deafening clamor had become a rumbling over which Dobry could be heard more clearly, but he spoke no less forcefully.

"And how many of you were served over the years by the woman's brother Aryeh, the generous blacksmith from Okup? The Jewish blacksmith took your tools to his village, repairing them on his forge when the szlachcic who owns your land and your labor would not help you!"

Was the mob's turbulent rage subsiding? They could easily have taken Dobry's life and then hers. But the men did not press on. Despite being lost in their drunkenness, they had heard the young guard, whose courage was quelling the vicious fire raging out of control.

Leya wrapped her arms around herself, only now aware of the trembling throughout her body like a tree in a storm. "Adonai," she whispered to calm the trembling. "My dear God." Legs folding under her, she fell to the ground. "My dear God, thank you. And Dobry, dear Dobry..."

PATRYK WAS DISTURBED to hear Olga's accusations and demands for justice grow louder and more insistent after Leya's arrest.

Her mindless rage did not decrease nor her demand for Leya's death cease, even after the drowned child's body had been fully inspected by Father Amadeusz and an autopsy performed by the barber-surgeons. Both revealed no reason to suspect anything other than accidental death by drowning. Enlisting the support of those she could rally, Olga insisted that the priest's determination did not make Leya innocent.

Father Amadeusz counseled Olga to release the poison in her heart and in her words through prayer and confession. In response, Olga ridiculed the earnest priest, saying his backbone had been sacrificed to the Jew's Seder plate.

~

Patryk could not imagine how his mother finally was able to elicit her cousin Olga's boastful admission that she had gone to the bereaved couple and given them someone to blame for their tragedy.

Upon hearing Justyna's report, Patryk immediately went to Henryk's parents, imploring them to withdraw their charges against Leya. It was not until Patryk returned with his mother that Henryk's parents would even consider Leya's innocence. But even then, they were unwilling to withdraw the accusation of blood libel.

Finally, the decision was made to drop the charges.

Dobry's courage, Justyna and Dominik's ceaseless petition of the Polish authorities, and the declarations of the kind Father Amadeusz to his parish members and local church officials had all united to spare Leya. But Patryk knew that it was truly Pani Leya's goodness and devotion to her neighbors that had saved her life.

᪐

L EYA WAS RELEASED ON A FRIDAY AFTERNOON. She did not know what day it was. Justyna, offering her hand to Leya when the cell door opened, told her she had been set free in time to greet the Sabbath.

After the darkness of the cellar, the light of day hurt Leya's eyes. They walked slowly, Leya leaning heavily on Justyna's arm.

Samuel ran to his mother the moment he saw her in the road and embraced her tightly. Rifka and Gittel met her with silent embraces when she crossed the threshold of her cottage. They had been preparing the Shabbos meal in anticipation of her arrival.

Leya sat. Few words were exchanged—perhaps because all of them still inhabited the strange dream that had swallowed Leya whole.

Smelling the golden raisins Rifka had added to the Challah, Leya welcomed the fragrance of the bread into every pore of her body. She breathed in the flavors of the soup simmering on the hearth—parsnip and broccoli, a favorite of Aryeh's.

She was relieved for his sake that Aryeh was far away in Mezritch and that he and Gedaliah thus had not suffered her imprisonment.

Leya kindled the Shabbos candles. She looked up and saw the dancing flames reflected in her niece's eyes. Leya had prayed in her cell to live to see the eyes of her beloveds again. Embracing Rifka, Leya's knees almost buckled under the realization that she might never have welcomed another Sabbath again. Leya wished Aryeh the Peace of the Sabbath wherever he was, picturing his dark intent eyes reflecting the flames. When she next saw her brother, she would confide how she'd felt his spirit unite with hers to sustain her when she had almost succumbed.

LEYA WAS SUMMONED from sleep by the loud calling of her name. Was it Gedaliah? The neighing horse that she could hear now, pulling a wagon, had been in her dream. But the voice could not be Gedaliah's—he was back in Mezritch. He called again.

Leya made her way to the door.

Gedaliah walked towards her slowly, eyes glazed, stunned.

"Why have you returned," she asked, "and where is your Uncle Aryeh?" Leya's heart raced.

Gedaliah straightened with some effort. He looked directly at her for a long moment, tears overflowing his eyes, before wrapping his arms around her and pulling her close.

"Mother, Aryeh is dead."

Gedaliah was kneeling beside her when Leya opened her eyes. As his face came into focus, so did his words. She had fainted at the news. When she tried to sit up, a pounding inside her head pinned her to the ground.

Gedaliah supported her to sit.

"We were several kilometers from Mezritch when Uncle Aryeh let go the rein he was holding and brought his hand to his chest." Gedaliah's voice quavered. "He leaned forward in great pain. When I asked if I could help him, he lifted his head for a moment and looked at me as if he wanted to say something but could not. Clutching at his chest, he lowered his head, let go the other rein and fell forward into my arms. With the little breath he could summon, he whispered "Sh'ma," closed his eyes and did not open them again."

Aryeh dead. Was she trembling or was it Gedaliah, holding her?

"I led the horse and wagon back to the tiny village through which we had just passed. A compassionate Jew offered me shelter and offered to shelter my uncle's body. He was a woodworker. The kind man summoned the *Chevra Kadisha,* those Jews entrusted with preparing a body for burial, from a larger village. This handful of men came and performed the ritual cleansing of Aryeh's body. They shrouded him in white linen before putting his body into a simple wooden coffin the woodworker had nailed together.

Leya stroked her son's face as he spoke. How good to have him here, so solid to touch.

"Aryeh's coffin was then taken by wagon to the larger village, since there is a Jewish cemetery there. We lifted the coffin high to walk to the cemetery as an act of honor. As we took our first slow steps, I suddenly recalled my father's coffin being carried—Uncle Aryeh was one of its bearers. I was such a young boy then, I couldn't help carry my father's body." Gedaliah stopped, swallowing hard. "But I helped carry my Uncle Aryeh to his grave."

Gedaliah fell silent, tears streaming from his eyes as he wept in Leya's arms.

WHEN RIFKA returned home from the Shabbos morning prayer service, Leya held her niece and told her that her father had died.

Rifka appeared to feel nothing, not the touch of Leya's hands, nor the blow of her father being taken from her. She stiffened and stared straight ahead, as if her ears refused to hear and her heart refused to be broken.

In the days that followed, Rifka moved as if she wished to be lifeless, too, but her dispirited body had no choice but to live on. At a memorial service held for her father in his home village of Okup, Rifka neither prayed nor spoke. She had not cried a tear as far as Leya could tell.

Leya implored the Shechina and her brother Aryeh, for the strength to bear her grief and to help Rifka bear hers.

"RIFKA'S GRIEF weighs heavily on her," Leya shared with Gittel when her friend came with one of her nourishing broths to strengthen Leya's lungs, which had not yet recovered from her underground confinement. "Rifka has locked herself in a room that none of us, not even her own feelings, are permitted to enter—"

Leya's cough interrupted. She pressed her hand to her chest, then continued.

"Gedaliah and Samuel are each finding solace and have reached out to their cousin. But she does not let us touch her."

"How are the boys finding solace?" Gittel asked.

"Gedaliah goes to pray each morning with a quorum of men at the shul. Then he makes his way to rob me of my cobbling duties. I have finally given up trying to convince him to return to his studies and have reluctantly surrendered to his staying in Horodenka to repair shoes."

Gittel appeared less disturbed by this last news than Leya, who had wished so strongly that Gedaliah would not abandon his studies.

"Samuel speaks often of missing Aryeh. It consoles him to recall the angelic presence at the gate that welcomed him after his accident. Samuel imagines his uncle to be in a place of beauty and peace."

"But Rifka? She is so angry, Gittel, towards her father, her mother, me—and God. Maybe this anger is what she needs now to protect her from the pain she cannot bear. But anger will not always protect her. If she does not allow herself to feel the pain beneath her it, her anger will destroy her life."

"And you, Leyalla, what are you feeling since losing your beloved Aryeh?"

Leya set her bowl down on the table. She untied and removed the scarf covering her hair, letting it fall over her shoulders.

"I miss him greatly, but I also feel my brother's spirit. Some might say it is my imagination, as many would have said had I told them about Ber's visits after he died. I can feel Aryeh's love and there is great solace in this, even as I long to hear his voice, to laugh and cry with him. But what astonishes me most is to feel Aryeh light-hearted again. I pray that Rifka will open her heart to her sorrow and to the mysterious power of love to reach us from beyond death."

✥ 14 ✥

"Take my hand!" The sound of his own voice calling out with urgency woke Yisroel in his cave. Seeing the embers of the night's fire, he was reminded of where he was.

In his dream, he had been calling to Rifka. She was drowning. He swam to her as rapidly as his arms could propel his body; Rifka had little strength left. They were in a turbulent sea under a foreboding sky. Icy waters, the color of tin, lifted and dropped Rifka who appeared to be losing consciousness. Rifka, reaching towards him, had not yet taken his outstretched hand.

Yisroel stared at the glowing coals. Closing his eyes, he decided to complete his dream in meditation. After taking in and releasing a few deep breaths, he was in the steely sea once more. Yisroel swam towards Rifka, drawing close enough for her to grasp his right hand with hers. She held on for a few moments, then let go of Yisroel's hand and began to swim—not towards the safety of the shore, but into deeper shimmering waters. Rifka swam with slow, sure, graceful strokes towards the pale violet horizon and disappeared.

Yisroel opened his eyes and stepped out of his cave into the warming spring air. The sky that had been overcast for days was clear. His days in the cave were as different from each other as the sky. Sometimes the horizon of his mind was completely clear: a radiant sun inside of him illumined his studies and meditations. Light and harmony flowed from the unseen worlds into his physical reality. He felt on fire with the ardor of learning. But there were many days when the sky of his mind was as dark and foreboding as it had been in his dream that night and when his mind was as agitated as the sea that threatened Rifka. On those days the Ayn Sof was like a sun obscured by menacing clouds.

Yisroel recalled how as a very young boy, on deeply overcast days, he worried that the sun might not return.

'The sun is *always* here!" his father had assured him. "The clouds are hiding the sun from you. But they only do so briefly. Enjoy the sun *and* the clouds, Srolik." Reb Eliezar encouraged. Another time, kneeling by a small wildflower, his father explained that it was by the sun's light Srolik was able to perceive a flower. But if Srolik were to look directly at the sun he could blind himself. 'In the same way,' Reb Eliezar continued, 'it is not possible for woman and man to look at God, but only at the emanations of the Divine. This tiny flower is one such emanation. You, my son, are another.'

Yisroel thought of one of the blessings he had prayed earlier that morning, its words lifted from one of the psalms: *Blessed are you, Adonai, Who gives strength to the weary.* Like the psalmist, Yisroel knew what it was to feel weary, to feel the need to be strengthened and straightened by grace. Was Rifka feeling such deep weariness now?

∾

K NEELING IN THE GARDEN IN THE LATE AFTERNOON, Channa heard a wagon stop in front of the Inn. Yisroel had gone to study in his cave; if there was no reason to summon him, she would not. Channa rose to approach the wagon.

"Surely you do not tend the inn by yourself, Frau?"

The suggestive tone of the man's voice gave her pause. The older of two well-dressed Jews descended the carriage. Channa did not look directly at him, although she sensed he was staring at her and that in his eyes would be found the same impropriety she detected in his voice.

"We have been traveling many long miles and are in search of the comfort we hope you can offer us."

"My husband is close by. I will let him know that we have guests." Changing the heavy basket of cabbage and beets to her other hip, she led the two men to the door.

"*Eager* guests, Pani. Tell him you have *very eager* guests: Otto Frank and his traveling companion, two men in need of food, drink—and warm beds." He laughed derisively at the mention of the last.

Channa looked up for a moment to see the men exchange looks. They seemed to share some unspoken understanding, maybe even a plan. The younger of the two, a tall man, moved towards Channa. When she reached to open the door, he placed himself in her path. Instinctively she stepped back a few steps, feeling her heart beating hard in her chest.

The coarse-voiced older man intervened. "I am certain you will extend your utmost hospitality to my companion Leon and me *later*, once we've made ourselves more comfortable." The emphasis on "later" thankfully moved his comrade out of Channa's path. The younger man's retreat at the other's bidding reminded Channa of a performing monkey she had once seen doing the bidding of his master.

"We find the remoteness of this inn quite suitable for our purposes, don't we, Otto?" Leon said in a cheerful high-pitched voice.

"Yes, my friend, quite suitable. But for now, let us prepare ourselves for the afternoon prayers," he added, addressing Channa again. "Is there a place, my lovely Pani, where we can wash?"

"I will ask my husband to bring basins to you," Channa said quietly, opening the large front door and pointing towards two doors at the end of the narrow corridor. "You will find bed sheets, feather blankets, and washing towels. Please excuse me. I will inform my husband that we have guests."

Yisroel attended to the men. The two spoke animatedly throughout the meal. They demanded wine, expecting that "even such humble innkeepers will have wine on hand, if only for the Sabbath." They insisted on as much wine and vodka as the couple could spare; they would "pay well."

Yisroel brought them one bottle.

When it was finished, Yisroel informed them there would be no more.

"We will not go dry," Otto bellowed, dispatching his companion to go in search of "the bottles that accompany us for just such emergencies."

The two drank until their speech slurred. Frequent belches insinuated themselves into their conversation along with indiscriminate words. The more they drank, the less guarded was their speech.

"Gentlemen." Yisroel interrupted the stream of curses issuing from Otto's mouth. "You have imbibed enough. I ask for your own sakes, as well as for my wife's, that you stop your drinking now."

Channa, sitting close to the hearth, was relieved by her husband's interception and uneasy about the men's response.

Otto scoffed. "Oh, but dear innkeepers, we are freeing the holy sparks in every drop of this holy schnapps." His head dangled between his shoulders as if it were loosely attached.

"This is our Godly work," said Leon, burping loudly. "We are liberating the sparks in us, too, not just in the drink." Leon stood, barely able to balance himself, and stumbled from the table. "Innkeeper's pretty little wife, where have you gone?"

"Yes, where is our charming hostess?" Otto echoed, knocking over his chair as he rose and squinted towards the hearth to where Channa sat.

"My wife is resting," Yisroel asserted, standing in front of the men who leaned into each other. Yisroel stretched his hand out for the half-filled bottle that Leon grasped at its neck. As if under a spell, the man handed the bottle to Yisroel, turned around, stumbled back to the table, and sank into his chair.

Yisroel, turning Otto's fallen chair right side up, pointed to it, wordlessly commanding him to sit back down. As Otto made his way to his chair, Yisroel removed an unopened bottle of vodka from the table. He placed in its stead a ceramic jug of ruby red beet juice. Yisroel emptied what vodka was left in the men's cups into the fire, and filled the emptied goblets with the beet borsht.

"You'll forgive that we have no more sour cream."

Channa was amused to hear Yisroel say it and sound genuinely apologetic.

"I have a matter of more importance than sour cream, dear innkeeper," Otto said, trying to regain his composure. "My companion and I are impressed with your hospitality, we would like to make a proposition..."

"Yes, a proposition," Leon interrupted, raising his goblet of borscht in the air.

"We would like to reserve your inn for a gathering," Otto continued. "We want to arrange a holy convocation of our colleagues, distinguished Jews like ourselves who are devoted at all costs to bringing the messiah faster."

An enormous belch erupted from Leon, followed by an enthusiastic outburst. "We're disciples of one no longer alive who guides us from other planes. We know he will soon be sending a living messenger in his stead." As if he had squeezed out the last bit of coherence left him, Leon fell forward, his head landing hard on the table.

"We have a secret society," Otto's words came emphatically. He straightened in his seat. "You will see, you will all see," Otto warned. He was no longer focused on Yisroel. It was as if he addressed a vast, unseen audience.

It appeared to Channa that Otto's imaginary audience was skeptical about his message, which made him all the fiercer in his delivery. He banged his fists on the table to call the masses to attention.

"I tell you the long-awaited messenger is coming. In the meantime, don't hold back. Our master Shabtai Tzvi taught that the shattered sparks of the divine can be found everywhere. And we must free them wherever they are hidden—like here." He picked up an empty bottle, waving it over his head. Instead of hurling the bottle, though, as he was preparing to do, Otto suddenly fell forward. His head, like Leon's, hit the table. A twisted smile remained.

As the two began to snore, Yisroel stirred them and led them to their rooms.

That night Yisroel slept in the inn close to Channa.

When the men woke midmorning, Yisroel cordially served them dark bread and tea. Otto ordered his young traveling companion to get some vodka in which they might dip the pieces of bread. Yisroel put his hand on Leon's shoulder when he rose, returning him to his seat.

Otto, recalling little of the prior night, asked if he had remembered to reserve the inn for a gathering of their colleagues. Channa smiled when Yisroel affirmed that the men had remembered, but that the inn could not be made available.

Just before climbing into his carriage, the elegantly dressed Otto Frank drew something from his pocket with an exaggerated gesture. Channa saw from the door of the inn what she guessed to be a finely embroidered silk handkerchief. He leaned toward her husband conspiratorially, unwrapped the silk and extended his open palm.

"Fire opal," Otto proclaimed. "And we can get many more gems like it. Also, the finest of textiles from the Ottoman Empire," he gestured toward a crate in his carriage. "They are worth enough to transport you and the pretty wife from your dreary inn to a splendid palace. Are you still sure that your inn can't be made available to us?"

Yisroel said nothing. Stepping back, he motioned Otto to mount.

YISROEL SENSED Channa's uncharacteristically heavy heart following the visit of the disturbing guests. Rather than returning to his grotto, he sat with her after their midday meal. Her face was the closest he had ever seen it to despair.

"Yisroel, I believe that Otto Frank and his companion are part of the Sabbatean underground. As a girl, I heard about of the cells of hidden Sabbateans. I saw the shudders of fear in grown men, guests in my father's home, as they spoke of the Chmielnicki uprising and of the self-proclaimed messiah that rose from the ashes of those Cossack massacres. My father wanted to spare me the horrors, but it was impossible for me not to hear some of the stories. I pretended I wasn't listening, but I was—attentively—to men much older than my father recounting monstrosities perpetrated by the peasant army incited by Bogdan Chmielnicki. What I heard terrified me."

Yisroel reached across the table for Channa's hand, not saying anything so as not to interrupt the words and feelings pouring from her.

"Men choked on their tears, describing the enraged Cossacks goaded into attack, discharging their wrath upon every Jew and nobleman they could hunt down. I listened, holding my breath, to descriptions of men forced to bury their wives and children alive then thrown into the same pits on top of their loved ones. They recounted the nightmare of pregnant women cut open, cats sewn into their wombs and mothers forced to watch their infants cut into pieces. I could not distinguish which of the tales might be exaggerated and which, just as terrible, were left untold."

Channa brought her free hand up to her throat.

"Hearing about these horrifying acts of savagery, I found it hard to eat or sleep. I became haunted by the question of whether I would have been able to maintain my faith in a loving Creator if had I been forced to witness my mother or brother tortured before my eyes."

Yisroel tightened his grip on Channa's hand.

"Yisroel, these visitors stirred questions in me I have not asked myself for a long time. Would I, too, have put my faith in Shabtai Tzvi in the wake of such devastation? Shabtai Tzvi promised more than relief; he said he had come to bring the *end of all suffering*, a final peace for our people. Would I have believed and followed him? And when this savior abandoned his mission and betrayed his followers, would I have betrayed my faith in God? Would I, disillusioned, have abandoned my faith in a benevolent Source of life?"

Yisroel heard the fire in his wife's voice and had no desire to quench its flames.

"Those who put their faith in the false messiah must have felt their wounds reopen when he abandoned them," she continued. "A deeper, blacker, thicker despair must have filled the caverns of their hearts where they had made room for hope to live."

Yisroel leaned forward and lifted his hand to Channa's cheek, holding it there until he felt his beloved's body soften and her breath deepen.

"Ahavah, both Chmielnicki and Shabtai Tzvi preyed on followers who saw themselves as victims. The shepherd Tzvi promised his flock that their losses and anguish in this life would bring otherworldly gains of infinite measure. He commanded "his sheep," as he called them, to surrender all power to him, which included committing the moral travesties he counseled would hasten the Messianic Age. Chmielnicki assured his armies of peasants that they could redeem their losses by avenging themselves against their Polish and Jewish persecutors. In both cases, the end justified the means; all the followers needed to do was follow."

Channa stood. "How is it possible that there are those who still worship Shabtai Tzvi as the Messiah? The men who just left our table proclaim there is one who shall come in Shabtai Tzvi's stead, the soul of their revered master returned in a new body. Have they not learned? It terrifies me to imagine how we can blind ourselves in order to follow flawed leaders."

She crossed the room, opened the door, and drew in a long, deep breath of the fresh spring air. When he spoke, she turned back to look at him.

"Shabtai Tzvi convinced himself and others that he held the key to unlock the door to God's everlasting love," he said. "He was the intermediary for those who forgot or perhaps never really knew that the key must be found in one's heart."

He stood and drew close to Channa. "To discover that we each hold the key, Ahavah, isn't this the sacred challenge and invitation God has given us? This is the holy opportunity to know the *I AM* within ourselves— a life-changing mandate."

Tears collected in her eyes.

"Yisroel, I have one more question for now," she said, her voice lower and calmer now. "Do you believe that unimaginable suffering must precede the coming of the messiah?"

He had asked himself the same question, searching for his own interpretation of biblical references to the messiah and an age of peace.

"I believe that we hasten the coming of an age of peace by practicing peace now," he replied. "Will an individual arise to lead us into a realm where, as it is written, 'the lion can lie down with the lamb'? I don't know. Might 'The World to Come' be our physical world transformed by our love and respect for one another? What if the messianic age of peace is actually a way of being with each other *moment to moment now*?"

∽

CHANNA ENTERED THE RITUAL BATH A SHORT TIME before sundown in preparation for *Shavuous,* the Festival of the Weeks. She lowered herself into the water, holding the customary intention of immersion: to emerge new and without blemish as if from the womb.

Leaving the mikveh, she saw Yisroel walking towards her. Shavuous commemorated the time of covenant, the giving and receiving of the Torah. The holiday was celebrated with reflections of beauty. Her husband carried several boughs of lilac and a cluster of meadowsweet to add to the fragrant creamy-white blooms that Channa had collected that morning to adorn their home for the holiday.

They made their way together up the hill towards the house.

After finishing the last preparations for their meal, they watched for the first three stars in the night sky, signaling the time for Channa to light the candles and welcome the holy day. When she lifted her face from the cradle of her hands, Channa blushed to see Yisroel watching her intently. He drew close and traced the rose she had embroidered on the sleeve of the dress for the holiday.

"A blessed holiday, Ahavah," he whispered, his breath warm at her ear.

Channa placed her hand on the side of his face, combing his beard with her fingers.

"Yisroel," she whispered, "how I wish for *every* soul to feel loved and to know the blessing of loving. I wish this also for our child." She put her hand upon the barely visible mound of her belly.

When his gaze met hers, she wasn't sure if she saw a gleam of surprise or knowing delight in his eyes—perhaps both—as he placed his large warm hand over hers.

A HINT OF DAWN slipped in unnoticed to conclude the all-night vigil held on the first night of Shavuous. This vigil was another of the practices, now mainstream, that had been introduced by Ha'Ari in Safed.

Yisroel was savoring the sound of Channa's voice reading from the Book of Ruth, one of the scriptures customarily read during the vigil along with chapters from Exodus, Ezekiel's vision, passages from Isaiah, and selected psalms. Listening, he imagined them joined by the unseen spirit of their child.

When Channa went to rest, Yisroel remained awake, drawn to meditate in the afterglow of their study together. In the days between Passover and Shavuous, Yisroel had thought continually about the journey out of slavery into the wilderness. Yet again, he was inspired by the wise injunction to view the exodus from bondage to the Promised Land as one's personal journey. This was the journey of freedom not only from outer enslavement, but also from inner bondage, fear being the greatest shackle of all.

Yisroel sensed that like the Jews being led to Sinai, he was being guided through the wilderness of the Carpathian Mountains in preparation for a new level of covenant with his Creator. Had the great emissary Moses also feared what might be revealed to him and wondered if would be able to bear it? Had he doubted that he could fulfill the mandate given him, to carry the truth to his people? Yisroel witnessed in himself the same struggles and failings that had possessed his ancestors in the wilderness. He often wished to remain in the safety of the known rather than risk entering the unknown. He could be content as a simple farmer and itinerant healer offering his services, with little attention drawn to him.

But Yisroel could feel something calling him forth, although to what was still shrouded in mystery. He apprehended, not through spoken words, but through the inner stirring that had always guided his way, that the time would come when he would be called to leave this refuge in the mountains. He would enter the world of endless human suffering, fear, greed, and loss in order to bring a message. It would be one message garbed in many different ways of offering it. Before that time, he would need to become certain of the message, to know and breathe it like his own breath. That he did not know the one message he was to carry did not plague him, but doubt that he could fulfill this destiny did.

After his morning prayers, Yisroel lay down quietly next to his wife, moving carefully so as not to wake her. Sleep did not delay in taking him.

WHEN CHANNA AWOKE, she lay without moving. If she had not felt Yisroel's leg against hers, she would not have known he was there, so subdued was his breathing. When she rolled to her side and looked at her husband, his pallor alarmed her. Channa sat up, hoping when she looked again, to see the color returned to his face. But instead he resembled a corpse, no life force animating its body. She put her hand to his cheek. It was cold.

"Yisroel! " she cried out. She would have shaken him hard, but he looked so fragile. "Yisroel!" He did not stir. When she lifted his arm, it dropped quickly as if lifeless. She had seen Yisroel meditate when it appeared he was not breathing. Surely this must be what was happening now.

"Yisroel," she implored, "Please, are you all right?" When there was no response, she turned his head slowly; when she let it go, it dropped heavily to one side.

"Dear God!" she exclaimed, not taking her eyes off him. *What could have happened while she slept?* She leaned forward and brought her head to his chest. Not able to hear his heart, she pressed her ear closer to his chest. Surely, she was just too distraught to hear.

"Yisroel," she part pleaded, part commanded, "Come back! Adonai, bring him back!"

She kissed his face, her tears wetting his cheeks until she fell into chanting his name over and over—the only supplication left her. Placing her hand on her abdomen, Channa silently reassured their child all would be well—as if some greater force were guiding her hand and abating her terror. She leaned forward to kiss her husband's eye, then his lips. "My love," she repeated, pleading.

Yisroel's head turned slightly towards her. "Yisroel!" An eye rolled under his eyelid. When her husband's eyes finally opened narrowly, he seemed not to see; he looked confused as if he did not know where he was.

"Channa?" The intoning of her name was so quiet it seemed more an exhalation than a word. "Ahavah?"

She nodded, suddenly unable to find her voice. She stretched out next to him, her face close enough to feel his breath, her arm over his chest. She would not ask him what had happened, not yet.

Yisroel regained his strength over the next few hours. Warming his hands by their hearth after their meal, he finally spoke.

"When I opened my eyes, Ahavah, I saw your terror tempered by relief. I am sorry for the fright you endured. I will try to describe what words cannot truly contain."

Yisroel drew two chairs close to the hearth. Channa sat facing him. He leaned forward and took her hands in his.

"I ascended to a place I have never seen or even imagined. I saw a gate and beyond it light more radiant than any I've ever beheld. In the heart of the light was an assembly of rabbis and sages studying together. I felt certain that among them were the prophets, forefathers, and foremothers, although I could not yet see them clearly. I wanted more than anything to go through the gate and join their assembly. I knew beyond any doubt that the knowledge there exceeded any I could possibly grasp on the earth."

Yisroel paused, staring into Channa's eyes. "The condition for entering was to give up my life. My yearning to enter, to merge with the light on the other side of that gate, overwhelmed me. At that moment, the cost did not matter."

"My soul was severing its connection to my body when I heard my name called by you. In that instant, I was reminded of my love for you. I felt the pull of love in *both* directions—towards my life here and to the heavenly realms. The syllables of my name became thunderously loud; they reverberated in my body. The summons of your love compelled my soul to retreat from the gate. The gate and the brilliant luminosity behind it disappeared. I understood that my time would come, but that it was not yet. Then I awoke here."

It tool several moments for Channa to find her voice.

"Yisroel, if I had not called you… if I had remained asleep or awakened without looking at you and left the room…?"

"I do not know, Channa."

Had she summoned Yisroel from a glory he should not have been asked to relinquish? But before she could ask, Yisroel spoke.

"It was not the time for the Ayn Sof to harvest my soul, my love. Do not regret your summons. All could not have been so without God's will." He turned toward the flames dancing in the hearth. "I will not forget the light that awaits us beyond this world."

Then looking at Channa again, he reached to touch his finger to the corner of her eye, lifting a single tear to his lips. "It tastes like longing, Ahavah," he whispered.

"Yes, longing," she whispered back, "my longing both for you and for the light that you glimpsed."

❧ 15 ☙

L eya's persistent cough, the pain in her chest, the aching in her back, and an overall fatigue had all begun and worsened since her return home from her imprisonment. It was becoming increasingly difficult for her to make and repair her customers' shoes and boots. Gedaliah was almost always at her side in the cobbler stall these days and sometimes Rifka and Samuel came to help as well. It was rare now that Leya was alone.

Today, a few hours before the descent of Shabbos, Leya felt better than usual. She implored Gedaliah to leave early. "If you leave now," she suggested, "you can go to the mikveh in preparation for Shabbos."

He protested as she expected he would. But when Leya did not yield, he reluctantly put down his awl and removed his leather apron. Smiling, he glared at Leya through narrowed eyes.

"The victor," he said affectionately, bowing his head in her direction.

Leya smiled back. She was grateful for her older son's help and caring. Nonetheless, she wished he had not left his studies to assume the obligations of shoemaker, dutiful son, brother, and cousin. At the door, Gedaliah turned to look at Leya. She dismissed his concern, waving him on.

Only after Gedaliah had stepped out and closed the door behind him did Leya realize how long it had been since she had been alone in the stall just before the descent of Shabbos. This had always been her favorite time in the shop when, after locking the heavy door she would commune with her beloved Ber. Today, she would have a conversation with her brother— out loud, not just in her mind.

"I know that our Rifka is in God's hands, Aryeh. I know also that we are meant to serve as God's hands, to comfort and console one another. Rifka has been enclosed in a shell of pain. How can I help her? How can we soften her hardening heart? Sometimes I wonder if she fears burdening me with her sorrow and if this is causing her to retreat further."

Leya was surprised to see Yisroel's radiant face appear in her mind's eye. She closed her eyes to feel his presence more deeply. "Yes, Aryeh!" she exclaimed out loud, opening her eyes. "Yes!"

AFTER THE Sabbath midday meal, Leya suggested to her sons and niece that they make plans to travel to the Carpathian Mountains to visit Yisroel and his wife.

"It will do us all good to be in his company," she said. She looked at Gedaliah. "Our apprentice Dobry has received enough training; he can be trusted to watch over the cobbling stall while we are away."

Her sudden decision to visit Yisroel surprised them. Gedaliah clearly was trying to restrain himself and not give voice to the concern apparent on his face. His concern, Leya knew, was not about the cobbler shop but about her.

But Samuel's face was exuberant. He had frequently reported "visits from Srolik, like dreams but more real." The thought of seeing his beloved Srolik in the flesh clearly thrilled him.

Rifka showed a veiled curiosity.

Gedaliah stood to address Leya. "I am concerned, Mother, about you taking a journey like this. It is at least a hundred kilometers to Zabie. You have not been well, although we rarely speak of this. But it is a fact, and we would not want to cause you further discomfort or injury, even for such a good purpose."

Leya appreciated her son's concern. But she was determined to make this journey and would not allow her health to be a deterrent. Gedaliah would put down his protest in the face of her resolve.

She looked at Rifka now, not wanting to pressure her for a response, and wondering what stirred under the surface of her almost impenetrable countenance. It was hard at times to believe that she was the same Rifka as before. But Leya knew she was; it was to that Rifka she spoke now.

"Rifka, my heart stirs me to go to see Yisroel. Will you help with the preparations for the trip?"

Rifka kept her eyes lowered and said nothing. Then to Leya's immense relief, she let her gaze meet Leya's in a manner that for some time she had been carefully avoiding. Eyes locked on Leya's, Rifka nodded.

॰∿॰

A FORTNIGHT LATER, THEIR WAGON STOPPED UNDER a strong sun in front of the inn. Leya was grateful for the mountain air that tempered the heat of the day. The trip had been exhausting. Along the way, she had given up trying to restrain her coughing so as not to worry the others.

Gedaliah helped her descend from the wagon and walk slowly with his support towards the wide door of the inn. No sooner had Gedaliah unhinged the wooden gate than Samuel darted past the two of them like a flash of light.

Reaching the door, he began to knock enthusiastically, accompanied by chanting "*Srolik, Srolik,*" the name he had never relinquished. "Where are you?"

A man with a full auburn-colored beard opened the door. Leya stopped to regard him. He must be twenty-five by now. Leya saw the power coupled with humility that she had first seen in him as a boy. Smiling broadly, he embraced Samuel firmly.

"I didn't know how much I missed him," Gedaliah whispered under his breath.

Rifka had not stepped down from the wagon yet, as if to resist the magnetism of Yisroel's heart.

A young woman Leya guessed must be Yisroel's wife appeared behind him. Leya was immediately struck by her grace and presence as she came forward to stand beside her husband. She was twenty at most, Leya guessed, just a few years older than Rifka. *Why did she seem so familiar?*

Then Leya remembered. This was Channa, the daughter of the kind Rabbi Elijah whom she and Aryeh had visited in Brody some few years earlier. Leya hadn't seen her since the day Channa had served them tea in Rabbi Elijah's home. Channa's presence had captivated Leya then and did again now, not only Channa's physical grace but also her spiritual poise.

But something had changed, too. Observing her now next to Yisroel, Leya thought that the strength and serenity she had sensed in Rabbi Elijah's daughter all those years ago had been deepened by suffering. Perhaps Leya recognized this because it was true of herself, too. Her own faith had grown more tenacious roots as a result of losses that had almost uprooted her. Whatever Channa had endured, she had clearly done so with humility and faith; both sustained her now.

As Channa reached out to embrace her, a deep gladness filled Leya about Yisroel's union with this woman. Leya felt the swell of Channa's belly, slight as yet, and knew that she was pregnant.

RIFKA HAD watched Channa usher Leya into the inn then come back out. Now Channa walked in Rifka's direction like a strong river current flowing toward her with intent and power. Rifka was bewildered by the strange tumult within her, like a flock of birds, each clamoring to take flight.

Rifka stepped down from the wagon. When Channa took Rifka's hands lightly between her own, the frenzy inside Rifka quieted. She met Channa's dark eyes, surprised by the strange sensation of looking at her own reflection. Surely the two were more different then alike—Channa's apparent serenity in such contrast with Rifka's turmoil.

Rifka had not let herself think much of Yisroel after his departure from Horodenka. When the news arrived by way of Gittel's cousin Batya that Yisroel had married, Rifka had simply refused to believe it. Imagining him with a wife roused more anger than his leaving them to live in Tluste. If Rifka had been confiding in her tanta Leya, she might have shared her confusing feelings, knowing that Leya would not judge her as unkindly as Rifka judged herself. Her tanta would have been likely to receive Rifka's stormy feelings with compassion, even her inexplicable and shameful jealousy.

But why *was* Rifka jealous? She had not really imagined marrying Yisroel. She had not pictured Yisroel marrying anyone for that matter. She'd believed—or had she hoped?—that he would never choose one person to love, and thus risk being stolen from the rest.

Rifka mind was summoned back from its wandering by Channa's gaze.

Rifka realized that she liked Yisroel's wife. She more than liked her. Channa, like Yisroel, could bring blessings to people's lives, maybe to Rifka's, too.

THEIR DAYS TOGETHER were filled with activity that was wrapped in the vast silence of the mountains that surrounded them. All coaxed Channa, ripening with child, to allow her guests the privilege of taking over some of her duties.

Leya delighted in watching Samuel work beside Yisroel, digging lime, cutting firewood, and foraging ingredients for mysterious remedies. He woke early to join in the pre-dawn baking of bread and eagerly participated in the transformation of parsnips and carrots into delectable soups with esoteric seasonings. He learned how to milk a sinewy, lactating goat, a gift from a grateful farmer, and to churn milk into creamy butter.

Channa made a chair of willow for Leya, who, despite initial protests, accepted the respite from working in the garden and took refuge in the shade not far from where Rifka worked along side Yisroel's wife.

They prepared for Shabbos together. Rifka baked next to Channa. Samuel gathered wood enthusiastically, after which he and Gedaliah were invited to immerse themselves in the ritual bath, then pray the service welcoming the Sabbath.

Samuel could not stop smiling, even during the solemn Prayer of the Eighteen Benedictions. He stood close to Yisroel as they prayed very much as he had attached himself to his shepherd on their way to and from the cheyder, wishing never to be separated from him.

Leya and Channa both kindled Sabbath candles.

Afterward Channa lifted her head and looked at them one by one. She placed her hand on the rise of her belly. "What great fluttering," she laughed, "I believe this new life is celebrating its growing family!"

CHANNA SPOTTED Leya sitting on a small boulder, one of many Yisroel and she had unearthed when making their gardens. Leya sat remarkably still, wrapped in a woolen shawl despite the late spring warmth. Her face was turned up towards the sun, eyes closed.

Were it not for Leya's frequent coughing, Channa might not have noticed her there. In the stillness, Channa could hear the wheezing in Leya's chest. She watched a smile part Leya's lips as if she were recalling something pleasant. Then suddenly seized by a deep cough, Leya's back rounded and her head lowered as the coughing racked her body. Leya's eyes remained closed; when the coughing released her, she straightened. Her will, it seemed to Channa, was remarkably strong.

At forty, Leya was a few years younger than Channa's mother Dalia would have been if she were alive. Based on stories her father Elijah had told her about her mother, and stories Yisroel had shared about Leya, it seemed that the two women had some rare qualities in common. Channa recalled a story about Dalia trying to convince members of Brody's Kahal to build another shelter for the homeless. "Do you imagine, dear rabbi's wife, that we have unlimited resources?" someone had challenged. Her mother had replied, "Yes, actually. We do have unlimited resources when each of us, especially the wealthy, look deeply enough into our pockets and our souls." Both Dalia and Leya's convictions were fueled by their profound respect for life—and their fearlessness.

Channa had been harboring a question that she wanted to ask of Leya when no one else was around. Although reluctant to interrupt what appeared to be Leya's meditation, Channa spoke Leya's name softly as she lowered herself to the ground at Leya's feet.

"Leya, Yisroel and I have a question."

Leya smiled at Channa with her eyes.

"We would like to invite Rifka to stay with us until—"

Leya's cough interrupted, her chest caving as the coughing seized her. Regaining her breath, Leya placed her hands behind her on the rock to steady herself. "I am fine now," she said, stretching out her hand to keep Channa from standing.

"We would like Rifka to stay with us until our child is born."

Leya nodded slowly, looking over Channa's head as if seeing someone approach. "Rifka is happy here. Something captive within her is being freed." She looked back at Channa. "Have you spoken to her of your invitation?"

"We wanted to ask your permission first."

"It is given gladly. I cannot imagine a greater blessing at this time."

Channa was relieved. But there was another question she hoped would be as welcome.

"Leya, Yisroel and I want *you* to stay as well, to be the grandmother to our child."

Leya straightened, staring into the distance again, silent except for the wheezing in her chest.

"That is generous of you, my dear Channa, very generous of you both. But—" she took another long, labored breath, "I must return to Horodenka."

Channa thought to ask why and almost let the word escape into the widening silence between them.

RIFKA AND CHANNA were walking arm in arm to prepare lunch when Channa invited her to remain in Zabie through the autumn harvest and the baby's birth.

Rifka stopped walking. Had she heard Channa correctly? A song thrush in playful flight alighted on a branch so close she could see its spotted underbelly. As swiftly as it had landed, the bird launched itself again into the air. Rifka felt a sensation she had not felt since skipping with Marishka. She turned to face Channa.

"Your tanta Leya has given her heartfelt blessing if you choose to stay," Channa added before Rifka could ask.

"We invited her to stay, but she said she must return to Horodenka. She told Yisroel that her friend Gittel and other neighbors would assist her, should there be need, while Gedaliah is working and Samuel assisting at the cheyder."

Neighbors? Most of the village women had withdrawn from Leya. It was only in part because of the blood libel charges. Facing Leya reminded them of all they had lost or might lose: husbands, brothers, safety, health. Rifka sometimes wondered if Leya's persistent faith and love for life, despite all her trials, had also caused the citizens of Horodenka to pull away from her. People preferred to cling to their complaints, self-pity, and disappointment with God. Rifka recalled something Zelda the vegetable hawker had told Leya gruffly one morning, though she had said it with obvious admiration.

"There are people who don't recognize when they have run out of blessings to count. They just keep counting like fools. God forbid we should mention anyone in particular."

Rifka did want to remain here, but she did not want to leave Leya with less help at home. She and Channa walked on in silence. Rifka recalled a moment, earlier that morning. She and Channa had been on their knees, shoulder to shoulder, laughing as they sowed onion seed. When Rifka looked up, Leya was watching them with a delight Rifka had not seen on her tanta's face for a very long time.

"I'll stay," Rifka said finally. "Perhaps my tanta will change her mind."

GEDALIAH KNEW WELL the strength of his mother's convictions, so he would not contest her decision to return to Horodenka. But he did harbor concern about his mother's well-being there. Even in Rifka's despondency, her presence had supported and heartened his mother. Together, he, Rifka, and Samuel had been able to take care of many of the tasks Leya would otherwise have insisted on doing. It was not easy for Leya to be inactive, although it had become easier as her pain and fatigue increased. Although quite healthy for her almost forty years, Gittel could not look after two households.

Gedaliah also understood how beneficial it might prove for Rifka to stay. His cousin was blossoming like the small plants she now tended so diligently in the light of the sun. The tight bud of her heart was opening. He was glad she had made this choice.

In the midst of his musings, Gedaliah remembered something Gittel had humorously announced at their Passover meal several weeks earlier. A conversation had started about God's faithfulness as a Beloved in the face of how often his Bride, humanity, lost faith in Him. Perhaps it was the effect of the wine at the ritual meal that led to jesting about Gedaliah, Rifka, and even absent Dovid, finding their earthly beloveds. Completely unexpectedly, Gittel had lifted her cup and proclaimed, "I propose that Leya and I—who are both already betrothed to Adonai—be betrothed to each other!"

Gedaliah had never seen Gittel so outspoken.

"God knows neither of us plans to marry again," she continued. "Perhaps we can be a comfort to each other." Her toast was greeted by laughter and a hearty L'Chaim, and the meal moved on.

But what if Gittel would actually consider *living* with his mother? Gedaliah knew her older daughter Nessa had been promised in a marriage that was to be arranged by Gittel's cousin Batya. The wedding would take place in the coming months. Batya had invited Nessa to live in Tluste, inviting Gittel and Tanya to also make their home there. Gittel had sent her daughters with a glad heart, but had declined her cousin's generous offer.

A plan was hatching in Gedaliah's mind. He smiled, wondering if, being his mother's son, he could match her strong will.

That evening when the blessing after the meal was complete, but before anyone else moved from the table, Gedaliah cleared his throat. In a voice that compelled all to listen, he announced that during dinner he had received guidance. He stood.

"The guidance I have received," he said dramatically, "must be the result of my cousin Rifka's sublime beet soup. The vivid, scarlet color of the exquisitely prepared beets seasoned with a perfect dose of caraway seed has roused in me," Gedaliah paused, trying to maintain his serious demeanor, "immense delight."

He had engaged their complete attention. They were, after all, not accustomed to Gedaliah seasoning his words with humor.

"I have a match to propose between two people who are clearly basherte." It had not occurred to Gedaliah until now, seeing their faces, that they would think he was talking about himself. He decided to sport with them.

"Sometimes even those destined for each other do not suspect their destiny."

"Gedaliah," Samuel interrupted, unable to tolerate anymore. "Have you found someone to marry?"

Gedaliah smiled at his brother and raised his glass. "The match I am proposing is that of our mother Leya and her friend Gittel. May God grant them long life together!"

Gedaliah saw the smile in his mother's eyes before it revealed itself on the rest of her face. He continued, but now with the staid intent more characteristic of him.

"Mother, Gittel lives alone, having renounced her cousin's invitation to move to Tluste. Why then don't you and your best friend live together under one roof, either you in her home or she coming to live in ours? I will work cobbling shoes and provide for us as best I can. We may be able to add to this Gittel's earnings from her sewing."

Leya turned her gaze from her son to the hearth. The room was quiet except for the hiss of the fire. When his mother looked at him again, he knew that he had matched his mother's determination with his own.

THAT NIGHT, when all were gathered near the hearth, Rifka knelt in front of Leya and rested her head in her tanta's lap. After a few moments together this way, Leya gently pulled her niece up and wrapped her arms around both the girl Rifka and the woman she was becoming.

Leya's heart suddenly raced. She knew that she would not see her beloved Rifka again.

Leya, Gedaliah, and Samuel left at sunrise in the wagon that had brought them.

"*Imyirtze HaShem*, God willing," Gedaliah said to Leya and Samuel as he guided the horse down the mountain, "we will return in the autumn for the Feast of the Tabernacles, and to greet Channa and Yisroel's child."

❧ 16 ❧

T oday the words in the prayer book were rote syllables, hollow vessels emptied of meaning. Yisroel felt unable to pour meaning into them.

It humbled him to confront the closed fist of his heart. How impossible it could be at times to move from feeling limited and unworthy to an expanded awareness of oneness with all that is. He was like a wave convinced of the truth of being separate from the ocean. But all he could do right now was surrender to this sense of separation, while longing to feel his oneness with the ocean of all life—from which surely his own mind, above all, was keeping him separate.

Yisroel stepped out of his cave and sat down on the ledge already warmed by the late spring sun. He dipped a piece of challah into the thick honey Channa had sent with the bread. that Yisroel had seen traded in the Brody marketplace. Savoring the taste of the aromatic honey coating the braided bread, he thought of Channa harvesting the honey from the hives she tended with such reverence. *More precious than rubies and gold* was she to him, as he sang to her each week from the Song of Songs.

Yisroel closed his eyes and turned his face up towards the sun. Its rays warmed his cheeks and forehead. A breeze moved through his beard. He felt the heat of the solid rock beneath him, supporting his weight under a great dome of sky. There were so many gifts in this single, ample moment. Gratitude filled Yisroel like a bucket at a well being filled with sweet, fresh water. The vitality missing during his prayers was returning. Gratitude was coaxing open the fist of his heart reminding him that Shechinah was always close, even when he forgot that, believing that he had to beckon Her to appear. And with that image, Yisroel thought of how he had beckoned Channa closer with his love, his words, his caresses, his lovemaking. And then a new thought appeared in his mind. What if he were to allow his love for God to overtake his body and mind the way his love for Channa could? Would his presence and passion for God also fulfill his deep desire to unite with the Shechinah? He had known limitless ecstasy in his union with his wife. Could he be as faithful and attentive in his intimacy with the Shechinah?

What would it be to live in oneness with the boundless Ocean of Love, remembering that even as an individual wave, he carried the essence of that ocean?

ALTHOUGH CHANNA had come to embrace her solitude while Yisroel dwelled in his grotto, it delighted her now to share her days with Rifka. It was like having a sister close enough in age that they could enjoy much together.

Channa taught Rifka all that Yisroel had taught her: how deep and far apart to place seeds, what plants made good companions, what to harvest from the meadow and forest for nourishment and for healing. Rifka had become an avid gardener and although a less avid cook was nonetheless a competent one. Daily, the two women walked arm in arm to tend what was cultivated or to forage in the forest or on the riverbank. They utilized every root, leaf, and seed that they carried back from their daily excursions. Rifka brought to Channa the seeds of inspiration in the prayers she composed and read to Channa when they rested in the garden or by the hearth at night. In her prayer poems, Rifka harvested her sorrow, longing, delight and gratitude, offering these to Adonai in basket upon basket woven of her words. The two women thrived, with the growing baby a continuing source of wonder and speculation between them.

~

WHILE CHANNA and Rifka were praying the afternoon service, each on her favorite boulder, Channa's prayer book slipped from her hand. To spare her bending, Rifka moved quickly to pick up the book and hand it back to Channa. Nodding her gratitude, Channa returned to her prayer.

Rifka did not turn back to her book; she could not take her eyes of her friend's round, full silhouette in the afternoon light. Even Channa's lips had become fuller in the two months since Rifka had first met her, as if all of her were ripening. Her cheeks maintained a permanent flush; her eyes, a perpetual gleam. Not only was her child blossoming into perfection with each day that passed, Channa was, too.

Tears filled Rifka's eyes. She could barely contain a sudden, almost unbearable protectiveness.

Channa finished praying and closed her prayer book, kissing it lightly on its front and back cover, then resting the book on her thigh. Wrapped in the quiet aura of her prayer, she turned her face toward the radiant morning sun and closed her eyes. Channa's hand slowly circled the sphere in which her child grew.

It seemed not to startle but please her when Rifka placed her hand on top of Channa's for a moment. Eyes still closed, Channa smiled.

Rifka poured them each a cup of the lemon verbena and mint tea whose leaves had been steeping.

"Channa, do you feel afraid?"

"Afraid?"

"Afraid to love your child with your whole being, knowing that you might lose her or him? God forbid," Rifka added—not having intended for her words and fear to pour out like this.

"The greatest sorrow is to keep from loving because we are afraid of losing," Channa replied with her equanimity.

Now Rifka felt oddly relieved to have let the question erupt.

"I have lived distrusting human love, " Channa went on. "I learned to trust again. The most tragic loss, Rifka, is to hold back from loving."

∾

GEDALIAH DECIDED TO LEAVE THE SHOP IN DOBRY'S hands again and accompany his mother and Gittel to Tluste for Gittel's oldest daughter Nessa's wedding. Batya's generosity had allowed them to hire a comfortable wagon and driver for their journey. Batya also assured Gittel and Leya that she had enough room not only for the two women but also for Gedaliah and Samuel to stay with her in Tluste and that it would please her if they did.

Within hours of their arrival in Tluste, Nessa was overtaken by an intestinal affliction that then felled Batya, but, thankfully, spared the others. It was decided that the wedding must be postponed—first only by a few days, and then, when Nessa and Batya's fevers lingered, by a full month, in order that Nessa not be menstruating and thus be able to consummate her marriage. Batya encouraged her guests from Horodenka to remain nonetheless.

Gedaliah, concerned about being away so long from his work, was reluctant to remain beyond the three or four days he had anticipated being in Tluste. What convinced him to stay a few additional days turned out to be Naftali's animated pleas. The boy's irrepressible spirit had captivated Gedaliah within moments of their meeting. Naftali expressed himself with tireless vigor.

Gedaliah was equally enthralled by the care fifteen-year-old Zofia showed her brother. Gedaliah was intrigued to see Naftali's spirits soar despite his constricting body and chair, and to witness Zofia, so joyfully and faithfully tethered to her brother. Zofia's ardor made Naftali's blaze; Naftali's enthusiasm increased Zofia's. Gedaliah was convinced that Zofia, as beautiful as she was in all ways, had not married because she would not leave her brother's side. Naftali was the one to whom she had taken vows of loyalty.

GEDALIAH JUDGED by the deep quiet in the large house that everyone was asleep. But sleep eluded him as he lay reflecting on the affinity he felt with Zofia despite their differences. Her animated nature was more akin to the spiritedness of Samuel, Rifka, and his mother Leya. Gedaliah was restrained by nature, like a beast of burden moving through his days steadily, plodding and reliable, never too fast or impetuous.

Zofia's presence had such a strange effect on him. Hearing Zofia laugh made him want to stop his plodding and find what had made her laugh, to see how her eyes looked when she did, and to watch her toss her head as if throwing off unnecessary burdens.

But there was also something very alike about Zofia and him: their sense of duty. The difference was that Zofia carried hers with lightheartedness, as well as with zeal.

ZOFIA, STANDING QUIETLY at the entrance to the room, watched Gedaliah and her brother, who were unaware that they had a witness to their laughter and playfulness. Gedaliah was tickling Naftali, whose body trembled with joy. Naftali tried to direct his fitful gestures so he could tickle his new friend in return.

She felt a rare pleasure watching them together. When Naftali, filled with delight, reached a tremulous hand to Gedaliah's shoulders, Zofia fondly recalled Yisroel, the gentle tutor in whose company Naftali had always been an honored guest.

Zofia had also witnessed Gedaliah anticipate and respond to his mother Leya's needs with consistent patience and deep love. He did this so unobtrusively and sensitively that his actions did not compromise his mother's independence. Gedaliah's attentiveness to his brother, during one of Samuel's falling attacks, reflected the same care.

Zofia also noted that her extreme devotion to Naftali did not perturb Gedaliah but instead pleased him.

LEYA WATCHED Gedaliah discover Zofia. Batya watched her daughter read psalms to the gentle, serious Gedaliah— Naftali always in their midst.

So it came as no surprise when Gedaliah and Zofia called together Leya, Batya, and Rabbi Meir to ask if they might marry.

"We asked Naftali first," Zofia said, the joy in the room palpable as Naftali nodded his head giving his blessing again and again.

It was decided that the two weddings, Nessa's and Zofia's, be held together within the month.

In the meantime, Gedaliah and Samuel would return to Horodenka to their work, leaving Leya and Gittel in Tluste until the weddings. An invitation would be sent to the inn at Zabie with little expectation that either Yisroel or Channa would be able to come, given Channa's pregnancy and the risks to her of travel on the mountain roads. Whether Rifka would come remained to be seen.

A WEEK AFTER Gedaliah and Samuel had returned to Horodenka, Gittel opened the door to a messenger sent by Gedaliah to Batya's home.

"I carry a message for the cobbler's mother," the man stated, indicating the message was a serious one.

"I am the cobbler's mother," Leya replied, beginning to rise from her chair. Gittel gestured that Leya remain sitting. The swelling in her friend's legs had worsened.

"The cobbler Reb Gedaliah wishes to inform you that two Polish farmers by the names of Justyna and Dominik are dead—stricken down by pneumonia, which has also taken their young sons."

Leya gripped the arms of her chair. She coughed the deep, thick cough that had started underground and had now become a force in her life. When Leya finally caught her breath, the man continued.

"Reb Gedaliah asked me to convey that the illness has not found its way to the heart of the village. There have been fewer deaths than feared, even among other farmers."

"Have you any news about the rest of the farmer's family?" Leya asked.

"Reb Gedaliah said the peasants' daughter Marishka is alive but very ill. A message has been sent to her brother Patryk, a seminary student studying some distance away."

The merchant, appearing relieved to be unburdened of his message, bowed his head and took his leave.

When Leya rose several moments later, it seemed she lifted a greater weight than that of her own body. "We must send a message to Rifka in Zabie," she commanded. Rifka must know that her dear friend may be dying."

⁓

THE NEWS OF THE JUSTYNA AND DOMINIK'S DEATHS and of Marishka's illness arrived at the inn along with news of Gedaliah's wedding.

Rifka had an immediate, strong desire to travel to Marishka, which she questioned almost as quickly. Even if she could travel to Horodenka and then make it to Tluste in time for her cousin's wedding, what might be the risks of bringing illness back to Channa or others?

When she asked their counsel, Channa and Yisroel replied almost as one that they would help her prepare for the journey to Marishka's side.

The three worked long hours gathering and preparing herbs that might alleviate Marishka's pain, lower her fever, nourish, and strengthen her. When Channa tired in the heat, she left Yisroel and Rifka to continue working in the small hut built for preparing remedies.

The two worked side-by-side deep into the night. Rifka concentrated on Yisroel's instructions. After it had steeped long enough, she would strain the blessed thistle to complete the infusion. To prepare the butter-bur extract, she measured alcohol to add to the butterbur rhizomes that they had harvested on the riverbank and chopped into pieces.

Rifka marveled at Yisroel's unwavering, intense concentration and sense of purpose. When her legs and back begged for relief, Yisroel still showed no sign of tiredness or distraction. He hummed or sang softly as he worked, one of the melodies that so often accompanied him.

She watched him carefully pour boiling water over the fresh angelica root that he had bruised to extract its honey-colored juice. When the water had boiled down enough, she was to strain the angelica and add honey to make a syrup. In the meantime, she would resume crushing the feathery blue-green rue leaves to begin the preparation of a poultice.

"Rifka," Yisroel said as they both worked. "When you are with Marishka, remember: it is not in your hands that Marishka live or die."

Rifka realized that Yisroel was giving her the unseen ingredients she would need in Horodenka. He was preparing not only the herbal remedies but her heart as well.

"What you are bringing your friend is more potent than any of these preparations. The essence of these roots, leaves, and seeds will bring relief and perhaps strengthen Marishka. But greater than the effect of these plants is the gift of your love for your friend. It is the essence of your love that shall bring the greatest healing—healing that will have taken place even if you should see her die. You have the capacity, Rifka, to love your friend without conditions, even the condition that Marishka survive."

"But, Yisroel, how can there be healing in death?"

"There is so much to understand about healing and about death. If at the time of death, a soul is no longer shrouded in fear, a great healing has occurred. Your unconditional love will cradle Marishka's soul the way your hands cradle her head. When one has glimpsed the true face of love, one's dying journey is blessed."

A wagon and its driver, a stout, trustworthy man, came for Rifka the next morning. He would take no payment, offering his services in exchange for Yisroel having recently freed his wife of her tormenting headaches.

Rifka embraced Channa. Then she took a step back and placed her hand lightly on the sacred mound rounding with life. Rifka lowered herself to one knee and whispered, "I will return to Zabie before your arrival, little one. Two full moons remain before we shall meet face to face."

About to mount the wagon, she heard Yisroel's benediction.

"Rifka, go with faith in yourself and your beloved friend. Call upon the One who created both of you, though you invoke that One with different names."

RIFKA WAS let into Marishka's family cottage by a neighbor, a white-haired, stooped peasant woman who promptly scurried out as Rifka removed her shawl.

Rifka walked slowly towards the bed where her friend lay sleeping, her cheeks flushed with fever, not exuberance as they had been when Rifka had last seen her.

When Marishka finally opened her eyes, they were watery and glazed. In them Rifka could see her friend's gratitude—and her fear. A smile made its way to Marishka's lips, lingering there even after she closed her eyes and seemed to drift away, a raft with nothing fastening it to the shore.

Rifka fed her the remedies and maintained her vigil at Marishka's side, as her friend seemed to float between life, where Rifka waited for her, and realms beyond, where Rifka could not follow. She never complained, despite her obvious pain. Gaining Marishka's silent permission, Rifka applied compresses to her damp, clammy forehead and chest.

Marishka's brother Patryk entered quietly after dawn the next day. With his full dark beard and intense blue eyes, he looked much older now. Rifka moved away from the bed to allow Patryk time alone with his sister.

Later, Patryk supported Marishka while Rifka held herbal teas to her lips and helped her to drink. Her harrowing cough and chest pain seemed to be relieved by the infusions, syrups, and poultices.

For the next four days and nights, Patryk and Rifka took turns holding vigil at Marishka's side. On the fourth night, Marishka managed to inform Patryk that her mother Justyna, father Dominik, and her two younger brothers had returned to the cottage to "fetch" her.

Marishka died the following morning, Rifka and Patryk on either side of her when she drew her last strained breath. Patryk gently folded his sister's hands across her chest, then lowered his head and wept. Rifka brought her lips to Marishka's forehead and whispered a promise.

PATRYK ARRANGED for his sister's burial, officiated by Father Amadeusz, the priest who had challenged the false blood libel charges against Rifka's aunt Leya. At the funeral, Rifka, standing behind those gathered, saw several farmers' wives she recognized. The women acknowledged Rifka's presence with a mixture of surprise and what appeared to be gratitude.

"I no longer have roots here," Patryk told Rifka after the funeral, "The szlachcic who owns our land is reclaiming the farm. He has sent word that he plans to occupy our small cottage with a 'fruitful' family eager to serve him."

Rifka heard the anger mixed with Patryk's sorrow, and for some reason, this pleased her. In the wake of her father's death, her anger had fueled her life when she could feel little else.

"When I complete my seminary studies, it is likely that I will become a parish priest. There is an old priest in a village north of Horodenka, who can use the assistance of a younger man."

"Patryk extended his arm and uncurled the fingers of his cupped palm, revealing something colorful. Rifka recognized it immediately as a flax belt Marishka had woven and worn around her waist. Their eyes met before Rifka reached to receive the precious gift. For a brief moment, Marishka was vibrantly alive again between them.

"I am glad that you are able to study, Patryk. I know that your parents and Marishka would be proud of you."

He bowed his head, choking back tears.

"Patryk, I promised your sister that I would fulfill our dream of educating girls as hungry to learn as we were."

"Amen," he said, lifting his head, eyes brilliant. "Amen, dear Rifka—and Amen, my dear Marishka."

Rifka knew that Gittel and Leya were in Tluste in anticipation of the two wedding celebrations. On her way to Horodenka, she had learned from a passing wagon driver that Gedaliah and Samuel had traveled to Tluste just days earlier. When Patryk offered to arrange travel for Rifka to Tluste, Rifka decided, given the date of the weddings, that there was ample time to return to Zabie and then travel from there to Tluste. Hopefully Channa would be safely able to make the journey and they could all go together to Gedaliah's wedding.

Patryk found a reliable driver to take Rifka back to Zabie.

∾

HER FIRST NIGHT BACK AT THE INN, RIFKA SAT WITH Channa on their favorite boulders under the light of the waning moon. It lightened Rifka's heart to speak of her love for Marishka, of her sorrow, and about seeing kind, earnest Patryk at his sister's side.

Later, in the thickening darkness, they laughed together when Channa told the moon it was becoming more slender as she was becoming more full.

IT WAS WHEN the moon had become a barely visible hint of itself that Rifka first felt weak. She thought little of it at first, imagining it to be the residue of her exhaustion. When Channa commented on Rifka's increasing weakness, uncharacteristic lethargy, and almost complete lack of appetite, she dismissed Channa's concern. She was just recovering from the fatigue of her journey to Horodenka, she assured Channa, until one morning she could barely lift herself from her straw mat.

It was agreed that Rifka would stay in the hut where Yisroel concocted his remedies, so she would keep some distance from Channa. By her fifth day there, Rifka could no longer lift her head without searing pain. Fiery liquid she feared might leave her blind burned her eyes. A mounting, relentless fever, then delirium, overcame what was left of Rifka's denial.

YISROEL AND CHANNA made the decision that Yisroel would tend to Rifka. Were they to seek the help of local women, none would come, fearing Rifka the victim of a disease that could endanger them and their families. So Yisroel, trusting he could protect himself and Channa, began to care for Rifka despite the prohibition about touching a woman who is not one's wife or daughter.

Yisroel applied herbal compresses to Rifka's forehead, the bottoms of her feet, and along the inside of her wrists to quell her high fevers. He raised her burning head enough to bring decoctions to her parched lips. He invoked the Supreme Healer.

Rifka's eyes rolled up into her head so that only the whites showed. Her limbs trembled as if she were possessed. Disease had seized Rifka so completely, Yisroel was not sure it would let her go.

On his third night at her side, Rifka sat up suddenly and opened her eyes wide, looking like a madwoman. She seemed not to recognize or even to see Yisroel, as she reached out her arms and called to her mother Dvorah. She repeated, *I am ready, I am ready.* Then as suddenly as she had sat up, Rifka fell back unconscious.

The next night, just after midnight, Rifka began to weep, this time calling her father's name. Eyes closed, she wept until the dawn, repeating Aryeh's name over and over with unbearable yearning, as if she were reaching with all her strength for something that remained just beyond her reach.

Yisroel, sensing Rifka's heart breaking, wept with her. He did not feel pity or sorrow as he wept. Rather, he felt awe at the purity of her love and desire.

By morning, Rifka's fever was gone.

Assured that Rifka was beyond danger, a kind widow consented to take Yisroel's place and care for Rifka for a period of days.

Some days later, after thanking him yet again, Rifka asked Yisroel what had saved her. He did not know if she would understand or accept his response, but he could offer no less than the truth.

"I believe that your heart needed to break when you were not strong and determined enough to defend or protect it," he told her. The grief held captive there was released to become one again with the pure love of which grief is made. Now you cannot help but pour this great love into the world; there will be no stopping this flow."

17

When Gershon heard that his sister was with child, he had dismissed it as rumor. There had been so many rumors about Channa, after all.

He was familiar as a rabbi and judge with the disdain harbored against divorced women. Some citizens took it upon themselves to judge a woman more harshly than the law. After Channa's divorce, there had been many pronouncements about his sister's failure as a wife because of her inability to conceive.

In the wake of Channa's leaving Brody, there was more talk about her failure. This time it was not only her deficiencies, but also her brother Gershon's failure to have found a sensible husband for her second attempt at marriage. Her pauper fool of a husband was ridiculed. So it did not surprise Gershon when a rumor sprung up about the supposedly barren Channa being with child. The rumor not only mocked his sister, it also derided the haughty Mendel, cuckolded by an inept Jew with no learning.

Ignoring the rumor, and trying to ignore the constant feeling of loss associated with his sister, Gershon focused his attention on the many duties before him. Having married, he spoke often with his cherished Bluma about his concern for his sister. Not a day passed without Gershon wishing Channa well from the depths of his heart. Nor did a month pass without his sending supplies she might need, as well as ones she might not need but would very likely welcome. Just a few weeks earlier, he had sent rare seeds for Channa's garden, a bar of halvah, and an embroidered shawl that had belonged to their mother. Gershon had persuaded and paid a merchant with business in Kuty to assure that these would reach his sister.

It was from this merchant, on his return, that Gedaliah learned it was not a rumor that Channa was pregnant. Channa's child was expected during the Feast of the Tabernacles, the *Succos* holiday.

Gershon knew immediately that he would travel to see her. He wanted to be close by when the child was born. He would make the arrangements needed to free himself from his duties, so he could leave for Zabie before the holiday.

GERSHON'S WAGON slowed down in front of the inn. The forlorn premises had been transformed. The roof no longer caved in upon itself; its thatch was thick and healthy. The walls had been whitewashed. The windows shone. An innocent building seemed to stare back at him with its own eyes. Despite the chill in the autumn air, an abundance of vivid blooms flourished, flanking the inn and the path leading to its rebuilt door.

When the door opened, Channa, round as the fullest moon, tears in her radiant eyes, opened her arms wide to her brother.

"Gershon!" she cried as he embraced her. "How good that you have come, my dear brother!"

Channa seemed content—in fact, remarkably happy. She had never been one to reveal her joy in an exuberant fashion, which was true of Gershon as well. But Gershon could feel her great joy now, as undeniable as the new life she carried.

WITH THEIR GUEST Rifka's help, Yisroel had built a *Succah*, the traditional shelter in which to take their meals and, if possible, to sleep during the holiday. The roof of the small tabernacle, open to the sky, was formed of branches and woven grapevine from which hung dried gourds, drying herbs, and flowers.

Gershon elected to sleep there. The nights were colder here in the mountains at this time of year than in Brody, but he would make do. He had brought a goose down quilt, not thinking of his own comfort but his sister's, which Channa now urged him to use.

Gershon was immensely relieved to discover that his sister lived comfortably, though simply, with her husband. Yisroel appeared neither negligent nor unkind with regards to Channa, removing a burden from Gershon's shoulders and heart. Nonetheless, he intended to have little to do with the man. He hadn't come this far for Yisroel's company, but despite it.

TWO DAYS AFTER her brother's arrival, Channa woke in the wetness of her own inner waters. She had been dreaming that she was bathing naked in the unusually warm waters of the Cheremosh River behind the inn.

Channa called out to Rifka, asleep on a mat at the foot of the bed. Rifka rose quickly, kissed Channa lightly on the forehead, squeezed her hand, and set out to call Yisroel.

AS WAS the plan, Gershon took the wagon to fetch Pela, the midwife, while Yisroel and Rifka tended Channa, awaiting the midwife's arrival.

When one of the wheels of the old wagon cracked on Gershon's way up the mountain, he had to rein in not only the weary horse, but also his own agitation and worry. He dismounted and began to walk the remaining distance as quickly as his legs would carry him. Were his sister giving birth in Brody, a physician would have attended her, as was becoming more customary among the prosperous citizens of larger cities. But this was not the only thing that distressed Gershon. When his sister told him that Yisroel might be called upon to assist during the birth, it had only been Channa's penetrating glance that prevented him from expressing his shock and indignation.

Drawing closer, Gershon suddenly heard shrill cries coming from inside the farmers' cottage. A tall, lanky man Gershon assumed to be the woman's husband Ambrozy appeared at the door, his face marked with concern.

"I am so sorry, good sir, but my wife Pela is in great distress and cannot help Pani Channa as was hoped." Pela's anguish was palpable, her cries coming from behind a curtain of burlap. The farmer, glancing over Gershon's shoulder and seeing no wagon, pointed to a horse grazing not far from the hut.

"Take my horse. She's a good old mare. Tell Pani Channa, please, that we are deeply sorry," he concluded, tipping his cap with deference as he retreated to his afflicted wife.

Gershon had mounted a horse only once before. But this was no time to hesitate.

Riding the animal warily over the uneven road, Gershon recalled another episode of a wagon gone awry. But rather than allow frustration to overtake him, Gershon directed his thoughts to his sister and her safety. Making his way, he prayed for Channa's strength and well-being.

THE STORM in Channa's body threatened to overcome her only when she resisted it. Her travail was more bearable when she breathed rather than held her breath against the tightening that gripped her every few moments. Each time a wave of pain ebbed, she was left dazed and exhausted on an unfamiliar shore. She reminded herself that the swell of the relentless, hard waves was ultimately benevolent—that she must yield, not struggle. When she opened her eyes in the decreasing moments of respite, she saw Yisroel and Rifka close by.

Yisroel brought a cool cloth saturated in restorative herbs to Channa's lips for her to suck. Rifka rubbed her back and feet with oils prepared for this purpose. They were with her when the waves peaked with enough power to tear her open and when she rested for seconds on the shore.

"Soon, Channalla, soon, your child will be in your arms," Rifka, her lips at Channa's temple, cooed. "So soon, so soon," Rifka repeated, gently wiping the perspiration from Channa's brow. When a wave of almost unbearable force crested, it drowned out Rifka's assurances.

Pela the midwife did not arrive.

Yisroel was attentive to Channa's every exertion. Called to bring remedies, he had been present at a number of difficult births. Channa would trust his care now in Pela's absence.

She was relieved when finally—*had it been hours or minutes?*—Yisroel instructed her to bear down. "The baby's crown is at the sacred gateway. You can push now, Ahavah," he coaxed in a deep calm voice. "Help her to sit up, Rifka; it will help her to bear down."

Relieved that she no longer needed to hold back, Channa bore down and pushed their child into the world. The small body slipped through her and was released. Channa felt as if she had birthed the world.

"We have a daughter," he told her as he held up the infant, "dressed in the rich oils of birth." Rifka placed the blanket Channa had woven into her arms and Yisroel handed Channa her daughter.

Channa smiled while Yisroel wiped the tears that veiled her view of the small orb of head and the miraculous body in her arms.

Yisroel looked at Channa and the infant, his eyes brilliant. "As I cut this holy tether between mother and child, I pray that the unseen cord of light between mother and daughter may nourish you both eternally."

UPON RETURNING to the inn, Gershon had heard Channa laboring from the small shelter where he waited under the open sky. Having failed in his mission to bring the midwife, he tried to absorb himself in prayer for Channa and her child, rather than let his mind wander somewhere less useful.

When Yisroel entered the Succah, looking serene, his lightheartedness made Gershon question if the simple man had felt any sympathy at all for his wife's tribulation.

"A daughter has been born to our Channa," Yisroel stated, looking straight at Gershon, which he rarely did. Yisroel's strength and directness impressed Gershon as quite different than usual. "Mazel Tov, Rabbi Gershon," Yisroel continued, extending his hand and smiling at his brother-in-law.

Gershon was further taken aback when his enigmatic brother-in-law stepped closer and wrapped him in a strong embrace. He was not at all prepared to feel Yisroel's strong and unmistakable love flowing towards him. Gershon had rarely encountered what felt like such pure love.

Two days later on Simchas Torah when men ordinarily dance with the Torah, Gershon danced with his niece. He held her close to his heart, as he might embrace the most sacred of scrolls were he back in the ornate Brody House of Prayer. On this holy day of rejoicing, Gershon swayed, embracing this holy bundle at once tiny and unfathomable.

A week after her birth, Gershon was invited to recite the customary blessings on the occasion of using his niece's name for the first time.

"*The One Who blessed our foremothers Sarah, Rifka, Rachel, and Leah, may that One bless this beloved girl and may her name be Dalia.*" Gershon paused after pronouncing the name Channa had chosen, their mother's name. Then he continued with the rest of the official prayer.

"*With providence and in blessed time, may she grow up with good health and tranquility. May her father and her mother see her joy and be present at her wedding. And may she be blessed with sons,*" Gershon cast a glance at his sister, "*and daughters,*" he added as Channa and Yisroel had instructed. "*May this be the Divine Will! Amen.*"

"Amen!" Yisroel, Channa, and Rifka exclaimed. In the meantime, little Dalia had found and was sucking on her uncle's finger in search of nourishment. The rigor of the infant's sucking brought a broad smile to her uncle's lips as he delivered his niece back to her mother.

As he watched his sister, he could see clearly how contentedly Channa embraced her role as a mother. But Gershon also detected an unprecedented peace within his sister that derived not only from this. It seemed to him that living in this remote place had led Channa to feel more at home in herself.

Gershon understood now that although he had always deeply respected his sister, he had pitied her the ordeal of her marriage to Mendel.
He also realized that while their father had felt remorse for not recognizing Mendel's avarice and violence, Rabbi Elijah had never shown a trace
of pity for Channa, nor had Channa pitied herself.

THE DAY BEFORE his intended departure at dawn, when Gershon
was preparing to pray the morning service alone in his room, he was surprised by the sudden impulse to ask Yisroel if they might pray together.

The two had never prayed together before because Gershon assumed
his poor brother-in-law was illiterate. One of the reasons that Gershon
had so adamantly protested his sister's betrothal was thinking that Yisroel would stare blankly at a prayer book with little regard for its inesti-
mable value. Gershon hadn't wanted to verify his suspicions. But during
this visit, Gershon had come to know that Yisroel studied assiduously in
a grotto behind the inn.

"May I join you in the morning's prayers?" he asked, when he found
his brother-in-law splitting firewood.

Yisroel smiled his consent. Gershon filled his arms with logs and followed Yisroel to the inn's large front room where they stacked the wood
near the hearth. Yisroel added a log to the morning's fire to displace the
autumn chill then got his prayer book from where it rested on the large
dining table. Had he guessed Gershon would ask that they pray together?
Gershon pulled the small prayer book with which he traveled from his
coat pocket. The men faced east and began to pray.

It took only moments for Gershon to feel something he did not typi-
cally feel when praying: he felt himself to be *inside* the prayers. Gershon
was accustomed to uttering the words on the page and directing them to
some "destination" beyond him. Now, standing with Yisroel, Gershon felt
as if he were inside the very syllables, which, as they were pronounced,
dissolved into a soft, expanding light that enveloped him. As this continued, the light not only surrounded Gershon but entered him. By the time

Gershon lifted his heels to repeat *Holy, Holy, Holy,* his entire body felt like a prayer being offered.

In the silence following the Prayer of the Eighteen Benedictions, Gershon saw that his father and sister had not been deluded. Gershon had been the fool. Finally, he, too, was able to recognize the holiness of his humble brother-in-law.

Had Yisroel hidden his light so that Gershon would be reminded not to judge a man by his outer appearance, whether a pauper or a seeming man of stature like Mendel? If so, the lesson was an especially worthwhile one that Gershon realized he might not be finished learning.

CHANNA RETIRED with Dalia shortly after the evening meal. Rifka followed not long after. Gershon was glad for this time alone with Yisroel, who now knelt to add more logs to the fire. There was a subject of great concern that Gershon wished to address.

Given the inn's isolation, Gershon was uncertain if Yisroel knew of the threatening actions being perpetrated throughout Podolia by followers of Shabtai Tzvi. For some time, there had been evidence of secret underground cells in Turkey, particularly in the cities of Smyrna and Salonika where Shabtai Tzvi had spent most of his time. But now cells of men and women adhering to Sabbatean teachings and practices were being discovered throughout Poland. That the self-proclaimed messiah Shabtai Tzvi should still have a following, seventy years after his apostasy and betrayal, astounded and disturbed Gershon.

As a young boy, Gershon had listened to the heated discussions among the rabbis and scholars of Brody about Shabtai Tzvi's ecstatic pronouncements and mesmerizing charisma. But Gershon had also heard tales of the man's paralyzing dejection. Shabtai Tzvi traveled to the infamous doctor of souls, Nathan of Gaza, seeking relief from this crippling despair. Shabtai remained in Gaza long enough for Nathan to behold his ungovernable mania and the perverse grandeur that accompanied it.

Nathan convinced Shabtai Tzvi that he had been sent to embody a diabolical struggle between good and evil on behalf of humanity. His despair, Nathan declared, reflected the power of demonic forces to overcome a soul; his exaltation, the power of the soul to defy and triumph over this demonic grip. Precisely because he embodied this diabolical struggle, Nathan professed, Shabtai was uniquely equipped to redeem the world from the grip of evil. Nathan's prophecy attributed nobility to what Shabtai had feared was intractable madness. Nathan's diagnosis also offered hope that, in the World to Come, Shabtai Tzvi would finally overcome his agony and abide in ceaseless exaltation.

During his next prolonged period of "divine exaltation," Shabtai Tzvi embraced Nathan's prophecy that he was the long-awaited messiah—the redeemer not only of the Jews but of all men. When Shabtai entered his next attack of self-degradation and withdrew into implacable self-flagellation, Nathan praised his humility. Nathan, proclaiming himself a prophet, went on to promulgate Shabtai Tzvi's divine destiny.

At first, Shabtai Tzvi and his followers had vacillated between extremes of ascetic self-denial and unbridled licentiousness in the name of freeing sparks of holiness from their shells of evil. Over time, the "King," as Shabtai Tzvi titled himself, had denounced any adherence to morality, arguing that complete and total chaos was needed to hasten the messianic age. The recent discovery of secret cells in Podolia revealed the discouraging and dangerous reality that the Sabbatean movement was not simply an historical anomaly.

The loud crackling of the fire interrupted Gershon's thoughts.

"My brother…" Gershon paused, about to add "in-law" and then refrained from doing so. "My brother, Yisroel, are you aware of the presence of Sabbateans in our very own Podolia?"

"Yes," Yisroel's nodded, now sitting opposite Gershon at the table. "How extraordinary, Rabbi Gershon, that hope can be so easily kindled in despairing hearts and that once kindled, it is not easily extinguished."

Gershon was astonished by what he heard. Was Yisroel, God forbid, condoning the appalling actions of the Sabbateans? Gershon stood up, shaken. Could it be that his sister's husband was himself a hidden Sabbatean? Gershon's mind raced beyond any words it could formulate. He began to pace.

Yisroel's hand on his shoulder stopped Gershon's racing thoughts. He sat down.

"Hope is as vital to life as breathing," Yisroel continued. "Thus, it is a profound transgression to inspire hope in what is false." Yisroel spoke slowly and deliberately. "As it turned out, the faith and fervor aroused by Shabtai Tzvi served to restore to life many who had become debilitated by hopelessness."

Gershon's suspicion flared again.

"This does not condone a single of Shabtai Tzvi's words or actions, nor those of the equally deluded Nathan of Gaza," Yisroel went on emphatically. "These men endangered not only those they claimed to be liberating, but also the collective spirit of a people. Shabtai Tzvi proved to be a fraudulent messenger of redemption. His betrayal extinguished the embers of faith that his claims kindled in the wake of the Chmielnicki massacres. But yet again the people survived their own despair and, although it may not have appeared so, they were strengthened by their ordeal."

"But, Yisroel, how do we respond to renewed belief in Shabtai Tzvi's imminent reign?" Gershon insisted. "In the name of future redemption, Sabbateans are again violating morality with their practices of liberating the "holiness hidden in evil." Clandestine sexual orgies have been reported in which women of all ages, including the young and unmarried, are passed around like merchandise at a market fair."

Gershon had not intended to raise his voice. In truth, what Yisroel had said about hope being life-giving had moved him. But Gershon was fearful of the destructive impact of Sabbateanism; he felt confused and troubled for his people. He and his fellow rabbinic authorities were charged with being guardians of moral conduct and behavior in accordance with Jewish law. What were they to do?

"Yisroel, the Sabbatean cells are proclaiming it virtuous to denounce all prayer and study. Do you not fear for our people? The

Sabbateans, focusing on The World to Come, advocates abandoning all decency in this one."

Gershon suddenly felt exhausted.

When his eyes met Yisroel's, he was overcome by the compassion harbored in this mysterious stranger's gaze.

"My esteemed Rabbi Gershon, there is no assurance from the Ayn Sof that our journeys in this world will be free of great trial. What is assured is that we don't have to traverse our journeys alone."

Gershon lowered his shoulders that had been hunched like a frightened animal. It had become a common posture, Gershon realized. *When had he become more afraid than comfortable in God's world?*

"Gershon, my brother, to have faith is not to accept passively everything we behold. The behavior of the Sabbateans defies respect for the sacredness of human life. To challenge such behavior and the beliefs that fuel it is a sacred duty."

"How is our protest to be effective?" Gershon responded immediately. "As you may know, just months ago, a group of distinguished rabbis gathered to preside over the Rabbinical Court in Lemberg. Flagrant defilements have begun to occur there, and in other Polish cities and towns. The rabbis issued a *cherem*, a ban decreeing that a Jew who engages in depraved behavior shall be shunned and excluded from his community. He is to be barred from commerce of all kinds and from participation in the synagogue. The rabbis hope the ban will deter further Sabbatean immoralities. Others argue and fear that it will, as before, simply lead to more secrecy."

"Honorable Gershon, while you protest the actions of those who debase themselves, I beseech you also to imagine their hearts that long for freedom from suffering. This is not to condone the manner in which they seek freedom. But I invite you, even while condemning their behavior and banishing them, to embrace these men and women with compassion, with prayer, and with the breadth of your love."

Was Yisroel actually asking him to respect men and women who were practically defecating on the Torah? Suddenly, Gershon thought of his father Rabbi Elijah. When Elijah had been preparing Gershon to serve as a judge in the Rabbinical Court, had he not also cautioned to always unite censure with love?

THE NEXT MORNING before mounting his coach to leave, Gershon leaned as close as he could to the tiny round face of his niece. He inhaled the sweet fragrance of her milky breath. Gershon would bring the memory of Dalia's purity with him.

He would also carry another memory wrapped in the sublime fragrance of truth: to bring love to what he judged.

Descending the mountain in his wagon, Gershon thought about what he had not said to Yisroel when relating the ban against the Sabbateans. He had not spoken of the incongruous, disturbing actions of Mendel at whose hands Channa had suffered such abuse.

Gershon had been mystified by Mendel's behavior at the time of the Ban of Lemberg. At first, Mendel forcefully opposed *"such harsh consequences against those whose mission was the elevation of Jewish men to their rightful place as Kings of Heaven."* But when accused of harboring Sabbatean sympathies, Mendel quickly shifted his position. He became one of the bitterest proponents of the ban and of punishing clandestine followers of Shabtai Tzvi.

Gershon could not help but suspect Mendel's motives. Mendel often cited his membership in the Brody Kloiz—whose purpose was to provide a haven for the serious study of Kabbalah— as evidence of his being one of the elect and deserving of being shown greater honor than other Jews, an attitude that dismayed Gershon. What pleasure did Mendel derive from claiming his superior status to those with less learning and opportunity to study? Within the Kloiz itself, Mendel frequently denigrated the contributions of his study companions.

Gershon had long wanted to expose Mendel's true character and insist that the man be excluded from the Kloiz. But to keep his promise to his sister, Gershon had refrained from doing so. Channa had beseeched her father and brother to allow people to believe that her divorce from Mendel had been precipitated by her inability to bear children—preferring this to it becoming known what had actually transpired. To honor her, Gershon resisted his impulse to denounce Mendel publicly.

As demeaning as Mendel could be with his fellows, his contempt and scorn for women was much more severe. Mendel had married again immediately after divorcing Channa and although his new wife had born him a son, Mendel nonetheless humiliated her. When Gershon saw Mendel and his young wife together in public, Mendel derided her for the slightest of her "constant transgressions," such as requesting a few groschen that she might purchase fish for their Shabbos meal.

Since learning of Channa's pregnancy, Mendel's bitterness had been directed toward Yisroel, who Mendel degraded in Gershon's presence every chance he could. Most recently after a gathering of the Kloiz, the corpulent Mendel had collided with Gershon on their way out. Gershon could see the mockery in Mendel's expression as he apologized for the "unfortunate mishap."

"So, esteemed judge," Mendel bellowed. "I hear your sister has been impregnated by your useless brother-in-law. I am surprised that his organ was able to rise to the occasion and penetrate the impenetrable…"

Gershon had walked away briskly. "Useless" was to engage with this deplorable man.

Gershon thought of Yisroel's entreaty to feel compassion for that which he condemned. He found it difficult if not impossible to summon compassion for Mendel. Would Yisroel be capable of feeling compassion for such a man?

Gershon *could* feel compassion for Mendel's wife and two-year-old-son Amos. He wondered if there were some way that he could assist them without Mendel unleashing violent repercussions upon them. If Channa and he had been able to converse the way they used to, she might have advised him.

Gershon shook his head to dispel at least one thought for now: he would no longer wish his sister back in Brody because he didn't believe that she would wish this for herself.

18

Batya stood very still, watching from the entrance to the small, softly lit room. Behind her in the dining hall, the Sabbath candles she had kindled still burned.

Leya's head rested in Gittel's lap. No more tying back and modestly concealing Leya's abundant red hair, now threaded with white strands. It spread in waves framing her weary face and draping over Gittel's black linen knees. Gittel ran her fingers through Leya's wild mane, stroked her forehead, and occasionally leaned forward to kiss the top of her friend's head in the silence they had become accustomed to sharing.

Batya had called in a physician who confirmed that Leya's lungs were filling with fluid. Her breathing was labored most of them time now, except when it became inexplicably still. Batya had felt alarm several times, believing Leya had stopped breathing. But Gittel showed no sign that her friend might be taking leave of her life; this was how Batya had come to determine that Leya was still with them.

Batya allowed the two friends uninterrupted time, only occasionally entering, like now, to ask if there was anything she might bring them. Perhaps it was more for her sake than theirs that she wanted to enter. An aura of great peace surrounded the two friends. Elias spoke too of the great stillness radiating into the house. He told Batya that he felt as if a warm, steadying hand were resting on his shoulder, quieting his all-to-familiar restlessness. As Leya gradually became more still, so it seemed did his body and mind.

Batya stepped into the room, suddenly drawn to wish Leya the peace of the Sabbath. Gittel, eyes meeting Batya's, nodded, beckoning Batya closer. When Batya whispered the words, Leya turned to look up at her, eyes burning with startling clarity. Batya recognized Leya's profound serenity despite the battle being fought within her languishing body. Leya held both within her unconquerable spirit: victory and defeat.

Leya smiled weakly and turned her head to the side.

Batya backed up, rather than turning around, pausing at the entrance to the room. She prayed for Leya's relief from the suffering she was enduring. She also prayed that at the threshold of her own death, she might find the serenity in which Leya seemed now to abide.

Gittel began to sing "L'Cha Dodi." When she sang the prayer's refrain, *Come my Beloved, to greet the Bride, Let us Welcome the Presence of the Sabbath*, and bowed her head, Batya felt as if her cousin was bowing to the Sacred Presence not only in Her form as the Sabbath, but also in Her form as Leya.

Batya bowed her head, too, stepped back, and closed the door.

GITTEL DID NOT NEED to hear Leya's words to feel her gratitude. As long as Gittel had known her, Leya had been able to find God in the midst of affliction. Even when Leya faltered, Gittel had watched her summon an inner strength to elevate her spirits. Not only this—Leya's spirit strengthened others, her sons, niece, neighbors, and friends, including Gittel, in their affliction and grief.

Gittel stroked her friend's hair and face. She had continued singing "L'Cha Dodi," although the Sabbath Bride had swept in a while ago, dusk having become night. Gittel stopped singing, thinking Leya asleep.

"May God bless this night of your life, Leyalla," she whispered.

"A sweet and welcome night," Leya replied, in so hushed a voice that Gittel just barely heard her. Surprised to hear Leya speak, Gittel bent forward to meet the words being uttered.

"This night, Gittel, is luminous. I see a path of light to walk.

Leya paused. Timelessness spread between each breath. Her eyes became riveted on Gittel's.

"There is such an embrace now. Such an embrace." Leya closed her eyes. One more breath. Then there were no more.

"God gave and God has taken away." The words spoken aloud sounded like someone else, not she, had spoken them. "Oh my dear Leyalla." The tears that Gittel had held back flowed now as she touched her lips to her friend's forehead. "May the love you have given be the chariot of your sweet soul."

∾

RIFKA WOKE ABRUPTLY. SHE SAT UP, LOOKING FOR WHO it was that had summoned her. Her small room at the back of the inn was enveloped in deep night. There seemed to be no one there in the cold dark. Who then had wakened her? Or had the summons come from her dream? She wished she could recall who or what had needed her attention so desperately. Rifka slipped back down under the sheltering feather quilt and pulled it up around her shoulders.

Later, as she made her way through her day, she was surprised that the compelling feeling of that summons remained. Kneeling to harvest the cool-weather herbs, she tried to ignore the bewildering, persistent pull—to what? The feeling lingered on the edges of her awareness: a mysterious incompleteness.

Rifka looked up from her writing, several days later, to see Channa approaching the table. Absorbed, Rifka had not noticed that dusk had come and with it, the time for the evening meal. She gathered her loose papers and closed her book, noticing only now that Channa was empty-handed. She held neither her daughter nor the cauldron of fragrant stew that had been simmering for hours over the hearth. Did Rifka imagine the grave look on her face? Was Dalia all right? Rifka rose to her feet in concern and glimpsed Dalia in her cradle not far from the hearth, peacefully asleep. What then was prompting Channa's somberness?

Yisroel came in from the chill air with reddened cheeks, put down his armload of logs and came to the table to stand beside Channa. He gestured that Rifka sit.

"There are some lights that when extinguished give more light," Channa said.

Her words were perplexing. Rifka looked at Channa questioningly then at Yisroel. The compelling uneasiness, which had been with her for days, now filled the room. Channa placed her hand on Rifka's shoulder then sat down beside her, looking into her eyes.

"Leya has left this realm, Rifkalla. She left in great peace, the peace she earned."

What? What did Channa mean? Rifka felt suddenly breathless and dizzy as if she had received a blow to her chest.

"What did you say?" Rifka's voice seemed not to belong to her. "*Leya dead? I'll never see my tanta again? No!*" Her throat locked. When the trembling in her shoulders started and tears began to rise, Rifka straightened and tightened. She must brace herself. If she allowed herself to cry, she might never stop.

"Who told you?" she asked, her voice rigid. "When did you find out?" Rifka felt the numbing start.

"A messenger on his way from Tluste met Yisroel bringing lime to the village."

Rifka felt herself slipping into darkness, that familiar endless void. When Channa called her name, a gentle pleading invitation, Rifka opened her eyes, not even aware that she had closed them. Meeting Channa's compassionate gaze shining with tears, Rifka let go into her friend's embrace, crying until she could barely breathe. Then, catching her breath, Rifka heard Dalia's voice, as if summoning her from drowning. Rifka looked up to see Yisroel approach holding the baby.

Kneeling, he extended the baby to Rifka. Without thinking, she received the child into her arms. The trembling that Rifka could not control and the tears that now wet the infant's cheeks did not keep tiny Dalia from cooing.

It was not true that all light had been extinguished in Rifka's world. Great light yet remained: Channa, Yisroel, Dalia. Samuel and Gedaliah. Gittel. Even Dovid. Each had brought light to her life. Rifka would not descend into the black pit that opened before her. She would resist the pull of that endless darkness.

In her arms, Dalia had begun to search avidly for nourishment. Rifka stood and brought the child to her mother. As she did, a tidal wave of grief washed over Rifka; she felt exhausted.

"I cannot imagine Tanta Leya gone," Rifka said weakly.

Channa settled the baby at her breast and reached her hand to Rifka. As Dalia nursed then dozed in her cradle, Channa kept Rifka close.

IN THE MORNING, Ambrozy's brother, who had been visiting Zabie, arrived at the inn, to transport Rifka to Horodenka.

Leya's burial had already taken place. Rifka arrived in Horodenka in time to join the family for the last two days of *shiva,* the seven-day mourning period that had begun immediately after the funeral.

Despite how old her cousins were—Gedaliah, twenty-one and Samuel, already fifteen—Rifka could feel the boy in each, now motherless.

The small cottage was crowded with neighbors who had come to offer condolences, food, and prayer. Rifka kept expecting Leya to appear among them.

With Meir and Batya's financial help, a small alcove had been added to the house in Horodenka to accommodate the growing family that included Zofia's brother Naftali and now Gittel. Originally, it had been agreed that Gittel and Leya would remain in Tluste for several weeks after the wedding to allow the "children" to settle into their new life together. Then, the two women were to follow before the onset of deep winter. Instead, Gittel had returned alone.

It took several moments before Rifka found her way to Gedaliah's new wife Zofia. Zofia was carrying Leya's first grandchild, Rifka saw, and immediately imagined Leya's delight. She knew that according to Jewish tradition if a wedding and a funeral procession meet on the road, the wedding procession takes precedence. In this spirit of honoring life, Rifka asked Gedaliah and Zofia to speak of their wedding when the cottage had finally emptied of its stream of visitors.

Gedaliah described his veiling of Zofia, symbolizing his commitment to clothing and protecting her. He talked about the wedding canopy, its poles decorated with living vines, and spoke of the shattering of a crystal glass, the reminder that love can be fragile and must be protected. "Don't forget the delicacies from Turkey!" Samuel inserted. As Gedaliah continued, Naftali danced in his chair at the mention of the Klezmer musicians. Rifka was most moved by Zofia's description of the pomegranate that Gedaliah had carefully opened, which he held as Zofia took a single tart seed, nestled among the others like jewels, and fed it to him. Zofia described the brilliant, scarlet interior and her wonder at the multitude of seeds. The two fed each other more seeds, representing both the promises their future held and their desire to nourish each other and their union.

Gedaliah, on behalf of the rest, invited Rifka to remain in Horodenka. She knew even before he had said it that if she chose to stay they would make room for her in what had been Leya's bed. She said she would let them know the following day, although she knew the answer within seconds of being asked.

Rifka would return to Zabie. She did not know for how long. But for now Zabie was her home.

∾

THE NEWS OF LEYA'S DEATH, PENNED IN GEDALIAH'S hand, had been delayed in reaching Dovid in Polnoyye. Gedaliah's letter included a prayer composed by "*Rifka bas Aryeh*, Rifka daughter of

Aryeh" in honor of her tanta Leya. Dovid unfolded the Yiddish prayer in
the privacy of his cell-like room, reading it in a whisper:

Dear Source of All That Is,
May my days strung together
Be a garland placed lovingly
On Your throne—
As you reveal Your throne to be
My own Heart.
Grant me the strength to endure,
Remembering Love.

To endure remembering Love, Dovid repeated.

What did Rifka understand when she spoke of "Love"? What was
it that helped Dovid to endure? He rarely thought about loving God or
being loved by God. What helped him endure was remembering his commitment to endure.

Dovid folded the paper, placing it between the pages of his prayer
book. He would go to his teacher, Rabbi Lazer, head of his yeshiva and
Chief Rabbi of Polnoyye, to ask permission to travel to Horodenka.
Although he would arrive after the initial seven days of mourning, Dovid
could offer his condolences to Gedaliah, Samuel, Rifka, and to his mother
upon the loss of her dear friend.

Dovid hoped Rabbi Lazer was not secluded in his chambers, which
he often was, no one knowing when he might emerge. Dovid could knock,
but he would not want to disturb his teacher's seclusion. Fortunately,
Dovid found Rabbi Lazer on the bimah in the synagogue, addressing a
number of students congregated there.

Slightly hunched, Rabbi Lazer appeared to be constructed of long,
frail bones attached to each other by taut strings that kept him from breaking into sharp, brittle pieces. His face was drawn and gaunt, his sparse
wiry beard threaded with white. Most compelling were the rabbi's eyes,
black and flashing. They were large for his face, bulging and so intense

that Dovid's sullenness seemed but a feeble attempt to emulate his rabbi's solemnity.

"Your will must be the indomitable ruler of your body," the rabbi cautioned those before him. "Your body will learn this when its appetites for food and sleep are denied and its demands for comfort overridden. To pray upright for hours despite one's legs weakening or eyes burning from the effort is to triumph."

Pacing back and forth, he spoke forcefully, his frailty enhancing his power.

"Eventually we become elevated above all desire for comfort, and only then may we be blessed to experience a holy trembling. The goal of all these austerities," he insisted, "is to teach the body to crave spiritual sustenance, not material sustenance. Only by practicing rigorous and relentless self-denial can one eventually conquer the lower demands of the body and truly serve the Divine. We must make of ourselves instruments able to vibrate in response to the call of God."

Rabbi Lazer was like a sheath of wheat trembling in a furious, divine wind. By the time he concluded, the gray tinge in the hollows of his cheeks had reddened. He was burning with a fire that consumed him from the inside out.

Dovid waited, approaching Rabbi Lazer when he finally stepped down from the bimah. He granted Dovid permission to travel, counseling him to maintain his austerities while away from Polnoyye.

IN HORODENKA, Dovid recognized that his mother was enduring the loss of her dearest friend with both surrender and great sorrow. Witnessing his mother's quiet restraint, Dovid realized she been his first teacher in renunciation, although her manner was by far gentler than his.

Dovid learned that Rifka had come and gone, making her home now in Zabie with Yisroel, his wife, and daughter. He could not recall clearly the last time that he had seen Rifka. His visits to Horodenka had been rare since leaving for Polnoyye seven years earlier. He had not even returned for his father's funeral.

Jacob had died soon after Dovid's departure for Polnoyye, though in truth his father had seemed dead long before his body had expired. Jacob had been sober for a brief spell before Dovid left to study. But Dovid had been too afraid that Jacob would abandon them again after giving his mother and sisters hope. Dovid could not—or would not—open his heart.

Now, back in Horodenka, Dovid could feel his guarded heart. There seemed to be within him a door that he could not permit to open, a door to which he had somehow lost the key. He could not feel the depth and immediacy of his love—or of his grief—and did not know how to change this. His compassion for his friends and even his tenderness towards his mother felt distant. The news that Rifka had almost perished after attending to Marishka, whose entire family except for Patryk had lost their lives, pierced the uncomfortable numbness only briefly. Dovid wondered if his mother perceived his lack of feeling. If she did, she didn't speak of it.

Nonetheless, Dovid was relieved to see that his mother, although quiet, was allowing her grief, as were Gedaliah and Samuel. Dovid could see the sadness in their eyes and hear it in their voices. He perceived it in the way each of them moved through the cottage, even in the way they walked to the well. Leya's absence was as tangible among them as her presence had been. But Dovid imagined they would not continue to carry her absence as a burden. He knew, as did they, that Leya would not want that; she would want them to live with joy. However, if Leya were to ask this directly of him, Dovid would not have been able to grant her wish. He endured, focusing neither on joy nor love.

He would be relieved to return to Polnoyye where thoughts of unlocking the doors of one's heart were a foolish, even imprudent, indulgence.

∾

ON THE NIGHT OF THE LAST CANDLE OF CHANUKAH, Rifka received Dalia from Channa's arms. *Chanuka* had been Rifka's favorite holiday as a child. She'd loved hearing the story about a small tribe of courageous fighters who against all odds succeeded in reclaiming their people's desecrated temple. There had been only enough oil to last one night but the oil had miraculously lasted for the full eight nights of the siege. Referring to the miracle of Chanukah throughout the year, Leya would say: "When we fear we won't have enough love, patience, or courage, we are reminded that the supply is infinite."

Rifka also knew that Chanukah was a time of rededication. She had been experiencing rededication to her own life since almost losing it and truly, since coming to the inn. Leya must have sensed this when she suggested they all go to Zabie. Rifka had closed her heart to protect herself from more pain, but in doing so, had separated herself from the love that would heal her. In Zabie, she was learning to be loved and to love with less fear.

Holding Dalia now, the joy she felt was unencumbered. The familiar, subtle fear of losing Dalia—always woven into her love for the child—was not present. At least not in this moment.

Yisroel had explained, when Rifka recovered from her fever, that a broken heart is a heart broken open to more love. Perhaps she *could* fearlessly grieve Leya's death. What if she could not only survive Leya's death, but could also honor Leya by keeping her heart open?

Rifka carried Dalia swaddled in sheepskin along a path that had been cleared in the warmer months. Sunlight filtered through the canopy of hemlocks, the light dancing around them.

She appreciated how readily Channa and Yisroel shared their precious daughter with her. They had even begun to refer to her as Tanta Rifka. Although Dalia could not speak or walk yet, she had already become Rifka's teacher. In Dalia's presence, Rifka was reminded of the eternal, that which is before birth and after death.

Dalia blinked her tiny eyes against a sudden burst of cold wind. Rifka pulled the infant closer in to her chest. She made her way forward slowly, not to slip on an unseen icy patch. One step, then the next, then the next. If grief came to walk with her, she would allow it, alongside her faltering hope. There was room here for both.

19

C hanna heard a wagon stop in front of the inn, a rare occurrence. She put down her knife next to the small discs of carrot mounded like some strange orange currency. Rifka had gone walking with Dalia, both bundled against the cold. Yisroel was behind the inn, removing the feathers of a chicken for their Shabbos meal. Channa made her way to the door.

The tall, somber stranger, whose knock she answered, was clearly a Jew. His demeanor and respectable dress led her to wonder why he was traveling alone. Where were his driver and his carriage? The stranger seemed perturbed and, of course, did not look directly at Channa when he asked if the innkeeper was at hand.

"Do you seek accommodations?" she replied, hesitant to summon Yisroel if he was not really needed.

"Yes...yes...I do now," he stammered. "With hopes of reaching my destination before the start of Sabbath, I tried a new route and have lost my way."

"There is place here for you to spend the Sabbath, if you wish," Channa replied to put the man at ease. "You would be welcome to join us. My husband is removing the feathers of a chicken then was going to gather the wood for our fire. When he returns, he will care for your horse."

The man let out a breath of relief. "Thank you." Then as if recalling courtesies left behind in his worry, he cleared his throat and tipped his hat. "I am Rabbi Avner." He took a few steps backward. "I will just get some belongings. Perhaps then your husband will have returned." He turned and walked the short path to his wagon.

HOW FORTUNATE, Avner thought, having washed and prepared for the evening meal. What was the likelihood of finding Jewish innkeepers in these remote mountains? Simple Jews, but hospitable enough. They had even said they could provide kosher wine when Avner requested it.

Avner, of course, obliged the couple when they asked him to recite the prayer to sanctify the wine. Without them even asking, he then offered the blessing over the small challah that the innkeeper's wife and the other woman, perhaps her sister, had baked and braided quite nicely. It seemed perfect now that he had become lost on his way, he mused, once again appreciating God's cleverness. As a result of losing his way, Avner had been led to this destitute, remote inn where he could carry out the proper observances for those who might otherwise have passed the night unable to honor the sanctity of the Sabbath.

It still surprised Avner when he encountered among his people those who did not know even the letters of the alphabet—Jews unable to express their praise and thankfulness with the words the Holy One had given them for this purpose. Clearly, God had ordained that Rabbi Avner was to bring some measure of holiness to these simple innkeepers. Perhaps after his visit, they would adopt the custom of washing their hands before breaking bread as they had seen him do, even if they could not remember the words of the blessing.

Satisfied with his devotion and satiated with his meal of surprisingly tender chicken and potatoes seasoned with—rosemary had she said—Avner retired to his room. His exhaustion was so great that the sparseness of straw in his mat did not keep him from falling into a deep sleep.

AVNER WAS startled awake by the smell of something burning. The rabbi jumped up from his mat and quickly dressed.

Stepping into the vestibule, he could hear the fire blazing. Then, from the end of the short corridor, he saw flames in the hearth room. No longer contained in the hearth, the fire burned dangerously out of control.

Translucent flames surrounded Avner's very seat from the night before, the chair oddly whole in their midst.

Avner saw no sign of his hosts.

"Fire!" Avner screamed as loudly as he could, again and again. When neither the innkeeper nor his wife or the other woman appeared, Avner banged on the door closest to his room. He was shocked to hear the calm voice of the innkeeper's wife inside.

"Rabbi Avner? Do you need something?"

If he did not know better, he would think she was amused.

"Can you not smell the flames?" he responded incredulously. "We are all in danger; your inn may burn to the ground! Where is your husband? If he is not awake, you must rouse him immediately!"

Avner was breathless and terrified. What could he do? Should he run out and save himself only? What of the helpless infant? It shocked him further when the woman opened the door and spoke as if commanding him.

"Go then, Rabbi Avner, and put out the fire. Go to the room where we sat for our meal and extinguish the fire."

What madness was this? Not sure why he was obeying, the rabbi walked towards the large room from which long tongues of flame extended.

At the room's threshold, Avner was stunned by what he saw.

Before him stood the innkeeper wrapped in a large white prayer shawl that was draped over his forehead. Avner could make out the man's eyes, rolled up so that only the whites could be seen. The mad innkeeper was murmuring unintelligible syllables as he rocked in the center of a circle of flames that did not burn his prayer shawl or his clothing. The flames, as if obedient to a master, circled the man lost in prayer. The innkeeper's ardor seemed to at once be creating and taming the blaze.

Avner felt suddenly dizzy. Balancing himself against the wall, he closed his eyes. If this was not a dream, then surely the strange couple had put something into his wine; he had heard of such things, tinctures that cause hallucinations.

When he opened his eyes, the fire was gone.

Avner's seemingly ignorant host, who throughout the evening had avoided his glance, now turned and looked directly into Avner's eyes. The innkeeper's eyes were glazed with tears, his cheeks wet with them. Had he put out the fire with his tears?

Speechless, Avner knew instantly that he had not been hallucinating. He had beheld a power he might never understand.

"The fire?" he stuttered.

Yisroel looked at him with compassion.

"What was it then?" Avner ventured.

No answer came. Avner heard the gentle laughter of the man's wife behind him.

"Rabbi Avner," she said, "I see that you have found the fire."

Without turning, he nodded.

"This is not an ordinary fire nor one easily extinguished," she said. "Its danger is only to those who fear it. At times, when my husband prays, his heart catches fire with longing and his ardor manifests as flames. You were meant to see this fire, since your eyes were able to behold it."

Her husband now began to speak, the first words Avner had heard from the man since his arrival.

"What you saw, Rabbi Avner, is a reflection of your own longing— otherwise you would not have been able to see the flames. Consider it a blessing to have witnessed the fire." Yisroel stepped closer. "I ask you, please, Rabbi Avner, not to speak of what you saw to anyone. We have no desire to draw attention." Without waiting for a response, the innkeeper and his wife left the man.

Avner went back to his room and lay awake until just before sunrise, when he too rose to pray. When he had finished washing his face and hands in the basin of water provided, he thought he heard melodious chanting. Knowing by now to take nothing for granted, he followed the melody's source to the room where the circle of fire had captivated him.

In the same place where the innkeeper had stood enveloped in fire, he stood praying now, wrapped in the same prayer shawl. But this morning there were no dancing flames accompanying him.

Avner's pride dissolved in the presence of the holy man and his wife. For the rest of the Sabbath, Avner allowed the couple's humility and kindness to nourish his spirit just as the three meals he took with them strengthened his body.

When it came time for Avner to take his leave, the innkeeper's wife gave Avner a portion of challah and a handful of dates. Her husband blessed the rabbi's journey, not with formal prayers or gestures but with a prolonged embrace. Avner departed from the inn laden with provisions and the incomparable sustenance of a vision he knew would remain with him until his death.

~

OF LATE, YISROEL HAD FELT AN INEXTINGUISHABLE fire burning within him, even when he was not praying. He thought of the fire never consumed in the bush on top of Mt. Sinai. Should Yisroel's attention or physical energy wane, both were soon revived. His ardor kept him upright night after night as he leaned over the flaming letters in his holy books—black flames emerging out of white fire then merging back into it.

As he read, he escaped Egypt, wandered in the wilderness, feared and embraced freedom. The voice of Adonai boomed within him and around him, commanding his faithfulness and that he have no other gods. He heard the shattering of the tablets and the golden calf echo through the ages and in the cavern of his own chest. He helped to build the Temple and then, one with the Temple, was destroyed. He was rebuilt as a Sacred Portal for the Holy Spirit. The more Yisroel lost his sense of his own beginning and ending, the less separate he felt and the more filled by an Infinite Presence.

Yisroel entered where initially he had not even perceived a place of entry. Locked passages of Torah, Talmud, Mishnah, and the Zohar opened to him, as well as locked rooms in his own being.

Fierce battles began to rage within Yisroel's body and mind, his faith ravaged by doubt. Yisroel's entire body writhed yet again with the pain of his brothers and sisters who cried through him that God had forsaken them and that there was no true peace to be found. He called out, demanding explanations, revenge, relief. How could ages of human suffering possibly be justified? Where was a loving and faithful God when evil continued to lay waste to goodness and innocence? What was illusion and what was truth? What was blindness and blind faith—and what was seeing clearly? His doubts arrayed themselves like mobilizing armies to prove that his joy, his ecstasies and encounters with the sublime were not only delusion, but dangerous escapes from the reality of evil.

Despite the ravages of his nightly battles, Yisroel greeted the new day feeling stronger not weaker. Like Jacob wrestling with the angel, he was left not vanquished but blessed. Yisroel gave up trying to either understand or control what was happening. He could only surrender.

IT WAS NOT ONLY in his cave that Yisroel learned great lessons. He found his teachers everywhere, often among the humblest and most destitute of people. Yisroel was learning much about humility and generosity from his neighbors in the foothills of the Carpathians. The lives of these peasant farmers and their families who endured great hardship and deprivation showed how one's attitude could lessen or increase suffering. Some, like the wagon driver Ambrozy and his wife Pela, seemed to possess indestructible faith.

Pela and Ambrozy's unfailing hospitality was rooted in their conviction that God would provide for them. When the couple barely had enough for a simple meal, still they invited less fortunate neighbors and even wanderers to their table. There would somehow always be enough, the scant portions offset by the couple's ample warmth and kindness. Ambrozy and Pela welcomed entire families to take refuge in their home, even when it meant that the two of them sought temporary shelter in the horse barn or slept under the stars. After Pela lost her third infant during childbirth, she became determined to help others not endure the same loss. With her husband's blessing and help, she sought and found a skilled midwife many kilometers from her home from whom she could learn to serve her neighbors as a midwife.

So of course, Yisroel was moved when Ambrozy, frightened and bewildered, approached him for help. An assault, which he and Pela had kept hidden in their shame, had taken place the night before Dalia's birth. It was this that had kept Pela from assisting Channa and that continued to cause her suffering. Returning from midwifing at a neighbor's child-birth, she had been attacked in the forest and violated. Because Pela's assailant was hooded and had not said a word in the thick darkness, she had no idea who had attacked her. Since then, Pela suffered fevers, abdominal pain, and tormenting dreams of being attacked by a creature part man and part beast.

While Rifka remained with Channa and Dalia, Yisroel, with Pela and Ambrozy's permission, climbed to the tiny farmhouse to maintain an all night vigil at Pela's side. As before and most recently during Channa's birthing of Dalia, Yisroel would align with a Source beyond his limited experience and allow his actions, silences, and words to be guided.

He returned each night for a week. He circled the small cot, holding his hands above Pela's body, while asking her terror to abandon its host. Yisroel instructed Ambrozy to place his large hand on his wife's abdomen so that its warmth and protection could penetrate her. Yisroel also spoke directly to the afflicted woman, assuring her that she was safe and did not need to live in fear. When the full moon rose on the fourth night, he coaxed Pela to drink a bitter tonic made from an aromatic plant with feathery silver stems that grew close to her home. Guided by Yisroel, Ambrozy gently coaxed open her fists and rubbed oils into her palms.

When Ambrozy finally took rest and slept, Yisroel prayed.

By sunrise on the eighth morning, Pela's fever, abdominal pain, and her terror were leaving.

After a time, and finally herself again, Pela approached her mid-wifery with even more zeal. She also sought to minister to the mountain village women who, like her, had been violated, knowing these experi-ences would be shrouded in secrecy and shame. She would be patient, she told Yisroel, as patient and fearless in the face of others' anguish as he had been in the presence of hers.

Overcome by gratitude, Pela found for Yisroel not only an old wagon that Ambrozy restored, but a capable horse as well, so that this Jew "with hands and heart of gold" would be able to travel freely to others who might benefit from his healing.

Upon Pela's recommendation, Yisroel was summoned to the side of a girl of thirteen. An inner demon was starving the girl. She had wrestled for two years with the affliction. Her despairing family received Yisroel with hope that he could tell they were afraid to feel. For four consecutive nights, he applied amulets, prayed, and addressed the spirit possessing her. The girl awakened the fifth morning noticeably changed. She began eating again. By the third full moon, the blood flow of the young woman was restored.

∾

RIFKA WAS AWARE THAT REPUTE OF YISROEL'S HEAL-ing power was spreading among the mountain villagers. Hearing about these miraculous healings from Pela and others, Rifka recalled the first time she heard about possession by a *dybbuk*. She had overheard Dovid talking to Gedaliah about a soul without a body wandering the earth looking for someone to inhabit. When the dybbuk took possession of its host, the possessed man or woman became split between warring parts of themselves. In such cases, there was no more powerful source of protection and healing than calling the Names of Adonai.

Rifka had learned much from Yisroel and from Channa about the healing properties of plants. But she knew that while Yisroel profoundly respected these healing powers and was able to apply them in an astonishing variety of ways to serve his family, neighbors, and even their animals, the primary power that Yisroel revered and used for healing was the Name.

Her father Aryeh had told her about "masters of the name" when she was a girl.

It was when they were returning from one of their visits to Alta Bina, the mysterious white-haired woman whose small hut and large meadows Rifka remembered well. Rifka accompanied her father to the Alta's hut in the days preceding each of the holidays and sometimes before their Shabbos trips to Horodenka. Rifka was captivated by the towering, leather-skinned, but surprisingly gentle old woman who helped Okup's villagers. The Alta seemed both invincible and frail, which confused Rifka. Her father assured her that she needn't worry about Alta Bina; the Old One knew how to take care of herself.

It was toward the end of one of their visits that Rifka overheard her father call the Alta a "mistress of the name." Rifka did not recall Alta Bina answering him with words, but her flashing eyes had responded. On their way home, Rifka questioned her father about what he had said. He explained that *baal* means master, and *shem*, the name, so the meaning of *baal shem* is master of the name. "A master of the name, a *baal shem*," he said, was someone who in addition to balms, poultices, teas, and countless other natural remedies also uses the name of God to heal. Though he had referred to Alta Bina as such a healer, in truth, he said, he had only known of a man being called a baal shem.

Her father went on to explain that a baal shem could be a learned rabbi, but most often was an itinerant healer skilled in nature's ways who also employed the name of God for healing and protection. It was a common practice of a baal shem to write the letters of particular names of God on parchment or small dried pieces of calfskin tied together with a string, and to put these into a small pouch. Called *amulets,* these were placed on particular parts of the body, kept beneath the mat on which one slept, worn around one's neck, or hung in one's home to ward off evil spirits.

After one of their last visits to the Alta, Rifka had asked her father if Alta Bina had ever given her mother Dvorah such a special pouch.

When Aryeh told Rifka that the Alta did not use amulets, she had become angry, arguing that if her mother Dvorah had been given one upon which to rest her head, or to hold close to her chest, she might have survived. Her father stopped walking. Rifka could almost recall his exact words as he knelt before her.

"Rifkalla, Alta Bina sows each seed with God's Name. She lives with God's Name in her heart, on her lips, and even in her silence. She sees all the growing things as made by the Love that is their Source. This is why her remedies offer such great protection and blessing."

"Then why didn't her herbs save my mother?" Rifka insisted.

"Bina gave your mother herbs so that her last days and months would be comfortable, so she would not suffer great pain," her father said. "I believe the Alta saw that the time for your mother Dvorah's soul to depart her body was drawing close. A wise healer knows she cannot impose her will to change what is meant to be."

Rifka could see now that some of her questions had been her father's, too. His eyes were moist when he told her, "We must believe there is a purpose for suffering that cannot be understood."

Over time her father told her more about the masters of the name. Most were looked down upon as practitioners of magic, he explained. They were not only disrespected but also often feared in part because of Shabtai Tzvi's abuses of practical Kabbalah. Shabtai Tzvi and his followers had used names of God and other Kabbalistic invocations to induce trances and carry out heresies, her father explained. In his shadow, many of those using the Name were suspect and denounced.

Despite this, many Jews and even non-Jews sought the services of these healers, especially when other forms of healing failed. Rifka witnessed this now as Yisroel's practices more valued among their Polish neighbors.

RIFKA WAS DELIGHTED when early one morning Yisroel invited Channa and her to witness the preparation of an amulet. They crossed the small bridge to Yisroel's cave, with four-year-old Dalia holding Rifka's hand.

Yisroel's parchment was spread on a rock so flat and smooth that it hardly seemed natural. It was as if the earth herself had offered him this sacred table for the preparation of the sacred amulets. Yisroel explained that as well as using the names of God to alleviate physical and mental suffering, particular psalms might be chosen as well.

"The scribing of the Name or verses from a psalm," he said, "is done in the ancient style prescribed for the Torah's parchment scrolls and for the small scroll in a mezuzah affixed to a Jew's doorpost." Quill in hand, Yisroel began to form the letter *Aleph*, the first letter of Adonai, the name of God most often used for protection.

He scribed with astonishing intent and precision, pausing to explain the formation of Aleph according to sacred tradition. "Each letter has precise dimensions," he said slowly, "the Aleph has three distinct parts and ten laws concerning its form. For example, the size of the *Aleph* should be three times three widths of the tip of the quill." He breathed slowly and deeply with each stroke, as if his breathing was part of the process. Rifka could not imagine carrying out such a task. But what mesmerized her even more than his strokes was Yisroel's awe, as tangible as his parchment, quill, and ink. Surely, the inherent power of the sacred names and prayers he scribed were being enhanced by Yisroel's faith in their power.

She knew Yisroel used these amulets even with peasant neighbors who had no connection to the Hebrew Holy Names. He did so, he said, because they had beseeched him to bring whatever he considered most effective to heal conditions that their own herbalists, priests, and others had failed to alleviate. Yisroel attended to them with all manner of restoratives—seen and unseen—not the least of which was the power of his intention.

Rifka hoped no danger would befall him in his unusual ministry. He could be accused of conspiring with the devil. Or someone, having had too much to drink, could claim he had worsened a condition. If so, what might his adversaries do to him and to his family? False accusations had shortened Leya's life.

Rifka excused herself to make her way to the solitude of the garden in hopes of relieving her disquiet.

❧

IN CHANNA'S DREAM, SHE WAS IN A WAGON TRAVELING slowly along the road in front of the inn. Channa seemed to be invisible to the other passengers, three young men. Yisroel, holding the reins, knew that she was there, but did not address her. No one spoke.

When the wagon began to ascend, Yisroel held the reins as if nothing unusual were happening. One of the young men began to tremble, repeatedly looking over his shoulder toward the back of the wagon. Channa turned to look as well. The wheels of what was now a chariot had become spinning flames, spinning fires upon which the chariot seemed to be propelled forward. The fire illuminated what had been a black—now jeweled—sky.

The fierceness of the flames might have frightened her, but didn't. She wondered if there was a destination to which they were bound, knowing at the same time that they were traveling outside of time and space.

The second of the young men stuttered prayers, fear jumbling the syllables emerging from his lips. When the third young man stood, about to hurl himself into the mercy of the starry void, Channa placed her hand on his shoulder to stay him. He sat.

Yisroel's head was surrounded by an aura of blue-tinged light. Beyond the hiss of the fires upon which they rode, Channa heard another of Yisroel's irresistible melodies. She could not make out the words or even if there were any. The fires continued but were now like tamed animals, not wild with rage as they had just been. The three young men, captive to their fear, did not stir.

"We enter," Yisroel said, although to Channa's perception, the mysterious, seamless blackness had not altered at all. A passenger in timelessness, she needed to know nothing.

The chariot landed abruptly on a bumpy road filled with rocks, the dust of the dry road filling Channa's nostrils. The dark sky no longer enveloped them like an endless drape of black silk. Where there had been spinning fires, now there were ordinary wheels and a trail of dust. And Channa's hands, resting on the heavy brown linen of her dress, were not covered with the dust of the road as she expected. The three young men had fallen asleep. Yisroel pulled back on the reins. When the wagon stopped, they were in front of the inn. Yisroel turned and smiled at Channa.

It was then she awoke.

It had become fairly common for Channa to be awakened before dawn by the sound of Yisroel's wagon's departing or returning. She and Rifka had become accustomed to Yisroel's comings and goings, often not knowing where he was going. He did not always seem to know either. He embarked not only in response to summons from others but also to summons from within.

Channa knew that though Yisroel's unpredictable and uncommon guidance was becoming familiar to Dalia, too, it was less easy for her to accept; she didn't like not knowing when her father would return to her. It helped though that no matter how urgent the summons, Yisroel never rushed his farewells to his young daughter.

This morning, Channa watched him kneel to receive Dalia, whose most recent joy was running into her father's waiting embrace. Yisroel stood and spun Dalia, whose long copper-colored waves, so like her father's, lifted in the breeze.

"*Livovi*," he sang into her ear his special name for her: *My heart*. "Livovi, I will carry you with me." He said the phrase each time he prepared to leave; it was their ritual.

After singing this promise, Yisroel gave Dalia into her mother's arms. Then, the final part of their farewell dance: Yisroel cupped his hands over his heart as he backed away slowly. Dalia, mirroring her father's love, cupped her small hands together, too.

CHANNA WATCHED her daughter delight in harvesting the young spring beets. Dalia was enthralled, digging her fingers into the loose soil until she could not see them. She curled her small hand around one of the ruby orbs, pulled, then fell back with her deep red prize in hand. She repeated this as quickly as she could, amazed and laughing as if each beet were the first—a completely new discovery.

Dalia listened attentively to her mother's instruction to harvest only those the size of her own fist.

"Look, Mama, another little girl beet," Dalia exclaimed, pulling yet another of the small burgundy spheres from darkness to light. "I am adding one more and one more to the mountain of baby beets I am making."

So absorbed was the child in her search for more hidden treasure that she did not notice when Channa gestured to Rifka to take her place at Dalia's side, allowing Channa to take refuge from the midday sun.

Channa walked to the far end of the gardens, a secluded, shaded spot. She wiped the perspiration from her forehead then brought her soil-stained fingers to the back of her neck to tighten the knot of the kerchief that covered her thick hair. She could feel the sweat trickle between her breasts and for a moment imagined her body shiny, oiled by the sweat that soaked her linen dress.

She smiled, recalling what Rifka had said just a few days earlier. Hoeing at Channa's side in the afternoon heat, Rifka had encouraged Channa to imagine they were with Eve in Eden, that first unimaginable garden. To amuse Channa, Rifka had woven an outrageous tapestry. She described a measureless expanse of garden tended only by women: mothers, daughters, and even grandmothers. If a man happened to come near inadvertently, the garden would not be visible to him. The plants and seeds in

Rifka's prodigious garden grew only at the hands of women. In the blazing heat, the women would first remove their shoes, then take off and set aside other layers of clothing and undergarments, allowing the sun's rays and warmth to pour over the soft roundness of their breasts, the curves of their shoulders and hips. The warm soft earth would come up between their toes, yield easily beneath their knees, and then, yield to the kneading of their hands.

Channa passed her arm across her forehead with a sweat-dampened sleeve. How Rifka's imagination could take flight, she mused, recalling the legion of naked women deeply content in a garden invisible to men. A thought scurried through Channa's mind like a field mouse making a dash beneath the grasses: *What would happen if she were to peel off her heavy dress now?* She could drape it over a low-hanging branch where the sweat could evaporate. Why not?

Channa hesitated long enough to laugh out loud before lifting her dress up over her head. Her kerchief dislodged, the thick chestnut-colored hair poured over her shoulders to her waist. Channa draped the wet linen over a branch extended like a waiting arm. She would keep on her white linen slip and other undergarments.

The weighty air, which had been completely stagnant, now stirred. A breeze arising from nowhere greeted her, brushing lightly over the exposed hairs on her arms and along her neck.

Channa bent to untie her right shoe, then her left. She removed the brown hose and tossed these towards the branch. One caught there, the other landed on the ground beneath her dress. Then, with a sudden change of heart, Channa removed the white linen that always sheathed her body—exposing the skin of her belly, her breasts, her back, hips, and thighs. As the breeze caressed the length of her body, her toes dug into the soil. Channa had never before stood naked under the sky like her dear plants.

Channa knew she could have felt ashamed, foolish, even sinful. But she did not. Instead, she felt free and content.

Rifka would laugh to see her. And Dalia? If the child approached, hands stained by the buried treasure of beets, she would undoubtedly be surprised, but then, in all likelihood, she would hasten to remove every thread of her own clothing, too.

FIVE-YEAR-OLD DALIA was becoming one of Yisroel's most delightful companions and teachers. Returning from his cave one afternoon, he found her busy on the riverbank.

"Livovi," Yisroel called.

He was not surprised when Dalia did not reply, so absorbed was she in her pursuits. Now, with intentness so like her mother's, she dug her plump fingers into the yielding soil, singing.

Dalia had consecrated particular melodies to the earthworms, others to the birds, and yet others for herbs depending on their tenacity when yanked from the earth or their bitterness when the leaves touched her tongue. With great reservoirs of patience, the child spent hours watching the activity of small insects burrowing or clinging to the underside of leaves. She was enthralled should a creature with a multitude of legs alight on her arm, holding her breath so as not to disturb its adventures.

"Livovi," Yisroel sung.

Dalia looked up to see her *abba* sitting on one of their favorite rocks and went to him. Wordlessly, he lifted her to his lap. She was comfortable with his silence and had learned to sit very still with him.

Sometimes, her father whispered to Adonai as if Adonai was as close to him as she was. She wanted to be friends with God the way her abba was. She had decided the best way to learn would be to watch her abba very closely, even to breathe with him when she could.

"*Blessed are you, my God...*" he began then paused. He was going to recite a blessing; she could tell by the way it began. There were *so many* blessings. She knew only a few like the one for washing hands, taking the first bite of bread, or drinking water. Dalia looked at him questioningly, wondering what he was about to bless now.

"Did you know, Livovi, that there are *b'rachas*, blessings, for behold-
ing something beautiful for the first time after a long time, like the first
cherry tree in blossom, or the first rain after a long time without it?"

She shook her head.

"There's great wonder in seeing as if for the first time. *Blessed are you,
Adonai, for opening my eyes to see my beautiful daughter as if for the first
time*," he prayed, looking right at her, then kissing her on the forehead.
She wondered if there really was a b'racha for seeing a daughter after a
long time or if her abba had made it up.

"When you look so carefully at the beets, worms, ants, or beetles,"
he went on, "you are blessing each without words. Close attention is a
silent blessing. After watching you watch the creatures, I feel more ready
to pray."

How glad she was to see him pull a small prayer book from his pocket
and began to pray right there on the big rock. Dalia watched him turn the
frayed pages of the book. But he did not seem to be really focusing on the
words. Suddenly, his eyes rolled up backwards under his lids and disappeared as if he were looking inside himself.

Dalia was not afraid. The first time she had seen this happen, she had
been frightened, wondering if she should call her mother or Tanta Rifka.
But she had waited instead, and, sure enough, her abba changed back
into his usual self again when he was finished praying. She was becoming *almost* used to such things happening. Anything might happen when
her father prayed or meditated. Sometimes he trembled. Other times he
laughed and laughed until his eyes watered. Or he cried over his prayer
book as if he might never stop. Probably, she thought, if she asked him
why, he would tell her. But she didn't ask.

Maybe when she was bigger she would ask. For now, she just watched.
And when he came back, she would be here, waiting for him.

❧ 20 ☙

Yisroel received a message from Elias telling him that his mother, Batya, had died. Yisroel had not seen Elias for at least seven years. Travel between Zabie and Tluste was a significantly greater distance than he customarily traversed in his healing and lime selling. But feeling an inner prompting, he conferred with Channa, who readily agreed he should go.

Yisroel arrived in time to join Elias for the last of the seven days of shiva. His sister Zofia, in Horodenka and pregnant with her second child, had not made the journey, but was honoring the seven days of mourning there with their brother Naftali. Yisroel knew that Rabbi Meir had died a year earlier. With Zofia and Naftali not in Tluste, Elias was the only immediate family member mourning in the large house. Upon receiving the news of Batya's death, Gittel had come from Horodenka and, with her daughter Nessa, who resided now in Tluste, had taken charge of receiving visitors.

Yisroel sensed despondency in Elias that did not derive solely from his mother's death.

Elias had not married and did not have his own family, he reported almost apologetically. He was certainly of age, he added, being twenty-six, just three years younger than Yisroel. But thus far marriage had not been his destiny. It relieved Elias to no end that his mother's cousin Gittel had been gracious enough to manage the stream of visitors to the house.

It relieved Elias even more when the formal period of mourning was complete and he could return to the small room that had become his cloister.

Elias explained that ever since Yisroel had introduced him to the letters, his life had not been the same. "Surely you, our resourceful tutor, must have noticed my delight and then obsession with the alphabet," Elias challenged warmly. "Before you came, I was incapable of sitting still—to my father's great distress—and I certainly showed little promise of following in his footsteps."

Yisroel easily recalled young Elias' delight in meeting then forming each letter until they danced across his pages in a never-ending stream.

"It's still true that only when I write can I overcome the restlessness that ordinarily plagues me," Elias confided. "Until his last breath, my father Rabbi Meir judged my affinity for the letters a lesser accomplishment than had I become a rabbi or scholar. On the other hand, my mother Batya was grateful that I had found so pleasing and engaging a vocation. Over time, my love for letters led to my employment as a scribe. Shortly after my father's death, my mother offered me a small room on the top floor of the house for my work. I rarely leave the room now."

The night after the seven-day mourning period ended, Yisroel climbed the narrow staircase to the small room. He knocked lightly on the door and, after Elias invited him to enter, he pushed the door open slowly. Yisroel expected to find Elias carefully fashioning letters by lantern light. Instead, the young man sat with shoulders hunched on the edge of his bed, his quills idle on a wooden board.

Yisroel drew closer, seeing the quiver he had noticed earlier in Elias' right hand. Elias stretched out his arm, not lifting his gaze. When he spoke, his voice was subdued.

"It has been a year since I have been able to work as a scribe. The tremor in my hand prevents me from forming the letters with the perfection required."

Yisroel crossed the room, knelt, and picked up a piece of parchment that lay crumpled near the leg of the table where Elias had worked previously. He spread the wrinkled parchment on the table. Yisroel motioned Elias to approach.

Reluctantly, Elias crossed the room and sat in the chair he no longer came to regularly.

"Pick up your quill, Elias."

Perhaps because he was used to following the directions of his former tutor, Elias did what was asked of him. He murmured that he had picked up this quill less than a handful of times in the past year. When he now failed to control the movement of his right hand, he put the quill down.

"In the right corner of the page," Yisroel told him, ignoring Elias' reluctance, "make the smallest of letters: *Yud*—a single flame with immeasurable power to ignite."

Elias slowly opened a jar of ink with only a very small amount left in it.

"What makes the *Yud* perfect is not its shape or that you write it without trembling," Yisroel said firmly. "What makes the letter perfect is the intention with which you write it."

Elias put the point of the quill to the paper, his arm trembling so much that he feared tearing a hole in the page. After making a small mark where Yisroel had asked for the *Yud*, Elias, discouraged, let his arm slacken.

"Now the letter *Heh*, Elias. Be less concerned with controlling your hand than with directing your mind and heart. What I am asking for is not the perfection of your previous work, but a different kind of perfection."

When Elias finished the *Heh*, Yisroel asked that it be followed by a *Vov*, then another *Heh*. He was instructing Elias to form one of the ineffable names of God, *Yud-Heh-Vov-Heh* whose syllables are never to be pronounced as written, but instead spoken as *Adonai*.

Yisroel smiled, placing his hand lightly on Elias's left shoulder. "Perfection is a pure heart willing to write the names of God, despite doubting one's ability to do so."

The two spent the entire night together, Yisroel intoning the names of God, which Elias then wrote.

Adonai. Ayn Sof. Elohim.

Some were written with great hesitation. Others poured out of the tip of Elias' quill almost as they had before the trembling had begun.

Shaddai. Eloheynu. HaMakom.

AT DAWN, Yisroel asked Elias to become his scribe. Under Yisroel's guidance, he would write the contents of amulets beneficial for healing the body and mind.

Elias was not surprised to learn of Yisroel's work as a baal shem, using the name of God to heal. Although it had rarely been spoken about in his father's company, Yisroel's knowledge of herbs and healing had been amply demonstrated within the walls of Rabbi Meir's household as well as in other homes in Tluste.

Elias recalled something else now. After his father's death, he had asked his mother about the small pouch she had placed on his father's chest that had seemed to ease his agony. Batya had explained that it was an amulet made by Yisroel, containing holy names.

If Yisroel thought him capable, then Elias would try to surrender his doubt. He nodded his agreement: yes, he would scribe for Yisroel.

In the silence that followed the sounds of Yisroel descending the stairs, Elias felt an inexplicable, joyous anticipation like that which had overtaken him after leading Yisroel to his home in Tluste ten years ago. A decade ago, Elias had met the teacher he did not know he had been waiting for. Apparently, there was still more for Elias to learn from him.

∾

GITTEL'S DEATH TOOK HER SWIFTLY. STRICKEN WITH a piercing pain in her head and great dizziness, she had gone to lie down and not risen again.

Nessa and Tanya, Gittel's daughters living in Tluste, made their way to Horodenka as soon as they heard. Gedaliah sent a message to Dovid, too, but given the distance to his yeshiva in Polnoyye, Gedaliah did not expect Dovid to arrive until after the seven days of shiva were over.

Gedaliah wondered now if a premonition had led Gittel to his cobbler shop a few weeks earlier. She had come to ask if her daughter Tanya could live with them. Tanya's debilitating headaches had worsened in Tluste; at least in Horodenka she had sometimes been able to find relief in the woods and meadows surrounding the village. There, at the first sign of an impending headache, she would make her way to as open a space as she could find near her home. Tanya had explained to her mother that in the open space she pictured the thoughts in her head escaping, running wild and unrestrained—no longer trapped.

Dovid had mentioned little about his sister's headaches. Over the years, Gedaliah had wondered if it was because of her headaches that Tanya, who possessed the pleasing appearance and mild manners of her mother, had never been betrothed. But perhaps her headaches were not the reason at all.

Tanya had maintained the shyness Gedaliah remembered from her earliest years. He would kneel in front of Gittel to greet young Tanya, tucked behind her mother, and offer the girl a bite of honey cake or some other holiday treat with his eyes closed so that she could receive the gift without being seen. As far as he could tell, Tanya's reticence had intensified, not diminished. Before moving to Tluste to live with her sister, Tanya had rarely left home. Gittel's lifelong acceptance of Tanya's temperament and her retreat from life reflected that she understood what stirred in her daughter's heart and why it was that Tanya kept so separate. If Gittel had confided more about this to his mother, Leya had never mentioned it.

Gedaliah had only seen Tanya two or three times in the five years since his marriage to Zofia. Should she come to live with them, he could accept her reticence as he had before. When Gedaliah informed Zofia of Gittel's request, she eagerly consented to welcoming her cousin Tanya, now seventeen, into their home.

DOVID LEFT as soon as he could after receiving news of his mother Gittel's death.

On his last visit to Horodenka shortly after Leya's death, Dovid's grief had been mysteriously absent. All feeling had been dulled. Now as before, there were no tears. Instead, Dovid's grief was taking the form of a storm of anger that had started shortly after leaving Polnoyye to travel to the village of his childhood.

Bitter protest raged in his mind. Why had a gentle soul like his mother had to work until her fingers swelled or bled? How had his father Jacob dared to abandon himself and the rest of his family for so long? Would his mother know peace or was there no peace to be known after all? And what had Dovid truly done to help? Had he, too, abandoned his mother?

It was not the first time that Dovid felt attacked by his own mind. His thoughts routinely railed against human ignorance and selfishness, most forcefully condemning his own. Now again, his mind turned on itself, attacking his foolish sorrow in the face of the inevitable: who was he to challenge Malach Hamoves, God's emissary of death? Didn't he know by now the foolishness of clinging to the temporal world when all that mattered was the eternal?

Dovid tried to quell his rage. One the one hand, he was filled with accusations against fate, God, and himself. On the other, his mind condemned its own outcry as senseless and futile.

By the time Dovid had arrived in the village of his childhood, his anger had turned into a fury that consumed him. Mouth dry, stomach knotted, muscles taut—all of him braced against the rage overtaking him.

As Dovid approached his friend Gedaliah's cottage, he prayed for the strength to suppress his agitated thoughts or at least contain his feelings.

Tanya greeted Dovid at the door. Surely his sister, who had always been so sensitive, would sense his turmoil immediately. But Tanya's deep eyes held neither judgment nor apprehension as she gestured him to enter. He lingered long in Tanya's embrace; it seemed to cool the heat in his body. He could not remember the last time anyone had touched him.

More than a week had passed since their mother's burial. Dovid learned that his sister Nessa had returned to her family and that Tanya would remain to live with Gedaliah and his family in Horodenka. Dovid was glad to hear this, knowing that his sister's delicacy would be well tended to by Gedaliah. How generous of his friend. A glint of gratitude pierced him like moonlight entering the cracks in a stone wall.

When Tanya knelt and opened her arms, only then did Dovid become aware of the child's presence. The boy began to limp across the room. He led with his left side, the right dragged along, arm dangling as if loosely attached at the shoulder. His lip and the right side of his face appeared pulled down by an invisible string. Although it seemed to require great effort for him to maneuver his body, Tanya, in her affection for the child, did not intervene nor did she show any signs of pitying him. The boy stopped in front of Dovid and smiled a crooked smile.

"Me-ir," he pushed the syllables out through his drooping mouth, while lifting his left arm bent at the wrist as if perpetually pointing at himself. "You?"

"Dovid." Dovid realized this must be the child with whom Zofia had been pregnant five years ago when he had last visited.

With Meir now settled on her lap, Tanya told him that Samuel would be back after helping in the cheyder, and Gedaliah, shortly after sunset from his cobbling stall. "Zofia," she said, pointing to a closed door, "is suckling her daughter Batleya, eighteen months old, named for both of her grandmothers, Batya and Leya."

In the stillness, Dovid heard Batleya's voice, and was softened for the third time that day.

Suddenly, a thought rigidly summoned him like a stern commander on a battlefield: *Some men, like your friend Gedaliah, are destined for familial life. But you, Dovid, are meant to renounce everything but God.*

Dovid managed to suppress his inner uproar, although he suspected that his old friend Gedaliah could sense the struggle within him. Had he tried to speak to Gedaliah about what roiled within him, it would not have been easy to find the words. How dare Dovid feel angry with God when his goal was unquestioning surrender? His anger was unacceptable, but he felt powerless to rise above it.

When Gedaliah suggested they visit Yisroel in Zabie before Dovid's return to Polnoyye, Dovid hesitated. To go to the Carpathian Mountains would take more time away from Polnoyye. As difficult as Dovid found it to consent, it was more difficult, as it turned out, for him to refuse, not because of pressure from Gedaliah, but because of Dovid's own pull to Yisroel.

Dovid noticed how graciously Zofia encouraged her husband to go. Samuel and Tanya offered to help Zofia with Naftali and the children. Dobry, the man who had protected Leya in jail, now worked hard at Gedaliah's side. Their business included more peasant boots alongside the shoes and boots of Horodenka's Jews. Dobry could be trusted to tend the stall while Gedaliah traveled to Zabie.

With no further obstacles except for Dovid's vague trepidation, the two friends embarked on the hundred kilometer journey to Zabie.

DOVID HAD MET neither Channa nor the lively young Dalia, whose unrestrained questions amused him. But to see Rifka was perhaps the biggest surprise of all. It had been at least seven or eight years since he had seen her. She must be twenty-one now.

It didn't take more than a few minutes for a new battle to mount within him. It was not rage, this time, but something else perhaps worse.

Dovid was glad when Rifka turned away; he should, too, but instead, he watched her cross the hearth room to add logs to the fire. There was something about her that had always captivated him. It had not only been her outer beauty: her gleaming blue-black hair, the smooth dark complexion that he imagined felt like silk, and the piercing blue eyes she occasionally directed at him. Even more compelling was her indomitable spirit so like her tanta Leya's and yet carrying its own unique force. Just these brief moments in her presence had shown him that her spirit was as vital, if not moreso, then when she was a girl. She was old enough to have children now, but he knew from Gedaliah that Rifka hadn't married though she covered her hair as if she were a married woman. Why would someone so beautiful, inside and out, not have married?

~

In the late afternoon, Dovid saw Rifka from a distance, kneeling on the bank of the Cheremosh River behind the inn, washing clothes. She had removed her kerchief and let her hair fall free. Dovid remembered being mesmerized by its luster all those years ago. How unbridled was his mind. He rebuked himself and looked away. It displeased him that he could still entertain not only the recognition of a woman's beauty, but, worse, the desire to draw close to her. He must resist these feelings with vehemence so as not to weaken the rigor of his discipline. If he was to become pure enough to serve selflessly, like Rabbi Lazer, he could not permit himself such thoughts.

He tried not to sleep that night lest an undesirable dream pierce his willed renunciation.

Early the next morning, Yisroel invited Dovid to join him in his cave for prayer.

During the Prayer of the Eighteen Benedictions, Dovid was swallowed by a swirl of images and sensations. He felt his hands guided by his father Jacob's, helping him make his first stool; his father's delighted patience and his mother's contented presence were palpable and heartwarming.

With great effort, Dovid clamped down on the images and feelings. He would not allow such abandon to continue. He opened his eyes.

Dovid watched Yisroel finish the Prayer of the Eighteen Benedictions. He appeared to be praying with great joy. Dovid knew Yisroel was well aware of the sly Evil Impulse and the ease with which one can be distracted from prayer. But Yisroel did not appear fearful that feeling joy might undermine the seriousness of his worship.

Waiting for Yisroel to return from his immersion, Dovid watched a butterfly dance in the sunlight at the opening to the cave. For an instant, he saw in the creature a glimpse of his own joy taken wing, bidding he follow. Dovid shook his head and turned away. It was not that simple. When he looked again, the butterfly was gone.

~

GEDALIAH PRAYED the afternoon service with Yisroel in his cave.
At his side, Gedaliah experienced the prayers as a vast river into which
he wanted to dive. But he held back, remaining on the banks—sensing
the current and its power as if from a distance. He could see Yisroel surrendering to its deep pull. Yisroel moved vigorously as he prayed, rocking, swaying, then closing his eyes and remaining completely still before
moving again. His entire being was engaged. He voice made the syllables
and the words of the prayers come alive.

When Yisroel turned unexpectedly to Gedaliah, the compassion in
his gaze was startling.

"There is a fire that burns in you, Gedaliah. Why do you fear it?"
There was no censure in Yisroel's words or tone. "You do not need to fear
your ardor, Reb Gedaliah."

Gedaliah felt like he was being beckoned into a room he had not
known was there. Yisroel was waiting at the entrance, gently beckoning, and powerfully summoning at the same time. Gedaliah knew that
he would follow.

"You have learned, Gedaliah, to walk steadily. Your steadiness has
been a great support for your mother, your brother, cousin Rifka, and
now for your new family. But there is also a great yearning in your spirit
and your very limbs to run free, to be unbridled. Although neither your
father nor your mother intended that you bear this burden, you have
worn the noble yoke of responsibility, believing you had to do so."

"I invite you now to experience another truth," Yisroel continued.
"Constancy and freedom can exist in the same heart."

Was Yisroel suggesting that Gedaliah relinquish being responsible in
order to live his life fully? The risk seemed too great. Laid out before him
were times Gedaliah had forcefully maintained self-control: when his
father Ber was thrown to his death by a horse, when Samuel was kicked in
the head, when Aryeh died, when Rifka almost drowned in grief, and, of
course, when his beloved mother Leya, not long after her unjust imprisonment, died. Each time, he had resisted feeling the piercing depths of
his love. A vivid memory appeared to Gedaliah now. He was five years

old—not long after his father had died—and his mother was reassuring him that he did not need to hold back his tears.

Gedaliah feared the fire within that Yisroel might succeed in kindling. He yearned for it, too.

AFTER GEDALIAH and Dovid left Zabie, Rifka wondered if she had imagined the changes in her cousin and his friend by the end of their short stay. Had she been asked to describe it, she might have used one word for both of them: longing. But longing for what? Had they, like she, perceived themselves in the mirror of Yisroel's presence? Did they also now long to unite with all they could be?

Although Gedaliah and Dovid differed in their demeanors and in their outer lives, there was something alike about them. Since childhood both had been reserved, certainly more than Samuel and she. Rifka had admired this. But Dovid's restraint now seemed to harbor restlessness and even discontent, as if he were not comfortable in his own skin. She could remember him playing freely. Where was the joy she had witnessed in him as a boy? Did Dovid now find this joy in his studies? Certainly centuries-old commentaries and ancient prayers were far more reliable and less likely to disappoint than a father fallen victim to his own despair. Was this why Dovid appeared to find more comfort in books than in people?

Perhaps she was not so different from Dovid. She found herself increasingly drawn to study rather than to the vocation of wife. Though she knew scholarly pursuit was not a sanctioned choice for a woman, the intimacy and caress of study beckoned to her.

In the two years since Tanya's mother's death, the kindness of Gedaliah's family and the gentle attentiveness Samuel expressed towards her were creating a foundation of well-being and safety Tanya had believed she would never feel again with Gittel gone.

For as long as Tanya could remember, her mother had been her shelter. Gittel did not know the nature of Tanya's wound, but she knew that there was one. She never pressed Tanya to explain the terror and shame that were her constant companions. Tanya couldn't have explained had she tried; the events were too buried. So, Tanya accepted living with an invisible wound that might never heal. Her mother's unconditional love was a balm—making it possible for Tanya to survive the nightmares and haunting images by day of violations that now seemed to have happened to someone else. It no longer mattered if there were or were not a God as long as she had her mother. Then her mother died.

For a while, Tanya imagined dying in her sleep, too, like a plant dried up for lack of water. Her mother must have known, when she approached Gedaliah, that the love in his home might keep Tanya from withering and even help her grow new roots.

Zofia, Gedaliah, Meir, and little Batleya had welcomed Tanya with open arms and hearts. The small cottage, filled with the presence of children, left little space for loneliness. Although there wasn't anywhere Tanya felt truly at ease, she found comfort in the embrace of familiar routines, even those that took her out of the house like going to the well or to the marketplace. It helped to know she would be returning shortly to the refuge of her new home.

It also helped to have known Samuel all her life. His kind, undemanding presence was sheltering. Perhaps, Tanya dared to believe, her understanding comforted him as well. She saw how he had pulled away from people, fearing that one of his attacks might descend at any moment. In this way, he was not like others around him. Tanya was not like others either. She recognized and understood Samuel's retreat to an inner cave and, without speaking of it, she felt as if the two of them met there.

GEDALIAH KNEW that Samuel had hoped to accompany him to pay a mourner's visit to Reb Jeremiah's widow. The old teacher who had taught Gedaliah and Samuel in cheyder twenty-five years earlier had been buried two days before. But when dizziness deterred Samuel, Gedaliah went with Zofia and a cabbage stew that Tanya had prepared.

When the two returned, Tanya was kneeling by Samuel, tilting his head back as she had seen others do. The attack had been a massive one. Gedaliah saw the tears in Tanya's eyes as she cradled Samuel's head.

"Perhaps," Zofia whispered later that night when they were in bed together, "our dear Tanya and Samuel will help one another relinquish the shame each seems to bear."

Within just a few weeks of what Gedaliah now regarded as Zofia's benediction, Samuel and Tanya approached Gedaliah and Zofia with their request to marry.

In the time his brother and Tanya had been living under the same roof, Gedaliah had seen little more than a reserved kindness between them. It was rare that they even spoke directly to each other. Zofia, however, had sensed the tenderness between them and recognized what the two seemed to share.

Tanya and Samuel asked that their wedding be at home and very simple. Those family members not in Horodenka—Dovid, Nessa, Rifka, and even Yisroel—would be informed later. The couple would continue to live with Gedaliah, Zofia, Naftali, and the children.

~

On the day before their wedding, Tanya was surprised—and very pleased—when Samuel asked to assist her in preparing the simple wedding meal.

And on the wedding day itself, Gedaliah surprised everyone when the door opened to a fiddler he had employed for the celebration. When the fiddler began to play, Naftali and Meir clapped along gleefully. Batleya danced, first in the bride's arms then in her uncle Samuel's.

"L'chaim to my brother and his new bride," Gedaliah toasted. Tanya, then raised her glass high: "And l'chaim, too, to Meir, Batleya, and Naftali, whose laughter is wedding music from the angels."

SAMUEL AND BENJAMIN, who had been assisting at the cheyder, took over Reb Jeremiah's duties. This way if Samuel were to suffer one of his attacks, there would always be one adult with the boys. "What a pair we are," Samuel joked, "you who drags your foot and me who comes crashing to the ground."

Samuel remembered well their cheyder days when Benjamin, called "the crooked one," was teased for his limp and Motke for his wheezing. He also recalled how after Yisroel became the boys' shepherd, all insults ceased. This was not because Yisroel had spoken sternly to those doing the taunting. He had simply begun to walk beside Benjamin or Motke, singing cheerfully, reflecting that walking with each was a great privilege. When either needed to pause from the effort of walking, Yisroel paused with him. The melody weaving its way through the line of boys would slow, too, and then resume its jauntiness only when the boys were ready to walk again.

Samuel's nephew Meir had also been a target of ridicule when he began attending cheyder, despite the fact that Samuel was at his side. Samuel suspected that he, too, was being laughed at, just more covertly, as an authority figure among the young boys. At first, Samuel lamented that he lacked Yisroel's instincts, patience, and courage, believing that if he had these, he would be more skillful and successful in quelling the ridicule of the unruliest students. One morning, after several weeks, Samuel had decided to walk with his charges *as if he were Yisroel,* wondering what he might feel.

It did not take long for Samuel to realize that his most sacred duty as the boys' guide, and in every encounter, was to be fully himself. This was the essence of Yisroel's courage, the courage to be himself. What would it be like, Samuel pondered, if he were to embrace his condition with neither shame nor apology? This would convey a message more powerful than any words he could say. Young Meir at his side, moving forward with great effort and awkwardness, served as Samuel's teacher. When he was teased, Meir responded with kindness, which surprised his taunters. Meir laughed with the gibing children as if their laughter was not mockery, but a lively gaiety he could join. Meir, not Samuel, was transforming the way the others treated him.

So Samuel began walking, not like Solik, but like Samuel—whole and worthy even if an attack might descend and separate him from himself. Recalling Solik, witnessing Benjamin stand tall despite his crookedness, and walking with Meir, Samuel began to assume a new inner posture from which he could teach.

∾

D OVID WAS NOT QUITE THIRTY YEARS OF AGE WHEN his revered teacher, Rabbi Lazer, died. Despite the fact that the exacting rabbi had numerous students more advanced in years and learning, no one but Dovid seemed surprised when the stringent rabbi, on his deathbed, named Dovid to succeed him as leader of the synagogue and yeshiva of Polnoyye. There was little enmity among those who might have been chosen, since all could see that Dovid's asceticism had almost exceeded their teacher's. There was no risk of laxness or of personal pride in assigning him the role. If pride *were* to arise within Dovid, everyone knew he would exercise the requisite severity to root it out.

This morning, the austere new rabbi of Polnoyye was lost in study. Or so it must have appeared to the yeshiva student at the door of his dimly lit study, come to remind Dovid that soon it would be time for the afternoon prayers. Although the punctual rabbi did not need reminding, this particular student had taken it upon himself to do so regularly in addition to offering more than reminders. As usual, Dovid did not look up, nodding slightly to indicate that he had heard and would soon make his way across the courtyard to the synagogue. When the messenger remained at his door, Dovid lifted his gaze.

"Dear Rabbi, I do ask your pardon. The baker's wife has sent over a freshly made noodle casserole, still warm. I did not have the heart to deny her. It is only a small piece I have brought you. Please," he pleaded as if this time his solicitation might be accepted. Dovid knew it was the young man's concern for Dovid as well as his lack of experience in the dangers of indulging desire that prompted his daily beseeching.

I ask your pardon, Honorable Rabbi, he would say, "*but you are so pale.*

Or, *Your skin, dear Rabbi—you will forgive me, I hope—has begun to resemble that of a man twice your age.*

I beg your pardon, Master. Might I bring some butter for your bread?

Please, Sir, it will only take me a moment for me to fetch a blanket to wrap around your shivering shoulders.

As always, Dovid waved the youth away impatiently, ignoring the rumbling demands of hunger, which had thankfully become less powerful over the years. To eat as little as possible had been somewhat difficult in the beginning. But now, fifteen years had passed since he had come to Polnoyye and Dovid's body had accustomed itself to the meager rations it received each day at the noon hour: two slices of dark bread, not too fresh, a small piece of dry meat, a few radishes, an occasional potato. Dovid's discipline had triumphed in other realms as well. His rebellious body had finally learned to require as little sleep and rest as he allowed it—no more than three hours each night before the midnight hour. Each night at midnight, Dovid rose to study until dawn with the students he was teaching to also overpower the distractions of their bodies and minds so that they might study seriously and live righteously.

"In order to draw close to the Creator," Dovid taught, as Rabbi Lazer had, "one must renounce the body's desires until its only desire is to serve God. The mind, however, is a more formidable enemy than the body. When desire does not gain entry through the body, it will seek to do so through one's thoughts."

"Vigilance, constant unyielding vigilance," Dovid preached to his students night after night and to the villagers who gathered in his synagogue for prayer. Some days it required great effort for Dovid to summon the hoarse, but thundering voice from his thin body. To speak forcefully was crucial to the well-being of his students. Whatever could be done to dominate the body's needs and intercept its cravings would lead to *higher* pleasures.

Fear had been his master's weapon. Now Dovid wielded it against himself as much as against the others who gathered around him.

ALMOST OVERNIGHT Dovid had inherited dozens of disciples of all ages who believed that renunciation was the key to opening the door to higher states of consciousness and unity with God. Dovid's students, as young as seventeen and as old as seventy, rose before midnight to gather in the Beis Midrash. They remained standing in a narrow room intended to be too small to hold them comfortably, a room deliberately not heated well in the winter and with only a single small window for air.

For hours each night, the students recited Talmudic passages, debating their meanings, analyzing the interpretations of the ancient rabbis, and interrupting each other to amend the commentaries with their own interpretations. The students abandoned themselves to legalistic, hairsplitting arguments in their scrupulous search for truth and adherence to the Torah's moral code. At sunrise, continuing to forcefully deny any summons from their bodies, they put on their prayer shawls and prayed the morning service.

Those new to such austerities found their exhaustion and hunger made it impossible to resist extraneous thoughts during prayer, especially those that intruded during the silent recitation of the Prayer of the Eighteen Benedictions. Dovid would remind them that relentless battle was required so as not to yield to base impulses. As part of their rigor, Dovid's students were exhorted to admit their temptations. When his wife might conceive was a distraction for one student; how he would earn a living troubled another. All manner of sensual, mercenary, and prideful thinking stirred in the serious, young scholars, who aspired to match Dovid's unwavering concentration and abstinence.

His followers did not know that a profound conflict waged in Dovid, which he experienced as actual physical pain in his heart. He believed the pain to be a reflection of the terrible division he felt within himself, a division resulting from his contact with Yisroel and the very different and confounding way Yisroel drew close to study, prayer, and to his wife and daughter. In addition to this, when he visited Zabie, Dovid had felt stirred by Rifka's beauty and vitality. Dovid tried to subdue his confusion by cleaving more ferociously to his austerities, which in occasional lucid moments, he considered might be contributing to his despair.

Dovid was thankful that the students who emulated him and sought his counsel remained ignorant of the menacing questioning and confusion that threatened the foundation of their rabbi's world.

Dovid rarely questioned his choice to abstain from marriage. He had chosen not to marry in order to devote every waking and sleeping moment to the Source and Goal of his life. Were he married and a father, he would have less of himself to give his followers. This was not, however, a value or choice he recommended to his students. Marriage was extolled by Judaism. Many of his students were betrothed or soon to be. It was important to prepare them for their duties as husbands. If married, it was a sin *not* to engage in the sexual act with one's wife. To fulfill one's wife in this manner and to father children was a sacred duty. Dovid had no intention of misleading his students by his example. But while he did not counsel abstaining from marital relations entirely, he did counsel that his students not take undue pleasure in the conjugal act.

Not only had Dovid elected to refrain from sexual intercourse, he guarded against the temptation to give himself pleasure by arousing his organ. No mention was made against the act of self-pleasuring in the Torah or the rabbinic commentaries. But Dovid believed this behavior, too, could result in his becoming more attached to his body and to life here on earth. The only allowable pleasure was the pleasure derived from renouncing pleasure in order to cleave to the Formless One.

A FEW DAYS LATER. Dovid was pulled from his thoughts yet again by the self-assigned guardian angel calling through the door.

"It's time, Rabbi Dovid, for afternoon prayers."

When Dovid opened the door to the House of Prayer, instead of finding at least the quorum of ten men needed to pray, he was surprised to see the sanctuary nearly empty except for two elderly men. The young man who had summoned him stood in the corner, looking embarrassed. Since Dovid had been leading services as the Rabbi of Polnoyye, there had always been at least twice the required quorum of ten, not only on Shabbos but also on weekdays like this one. Never had the sanctuary been as empty at the hour of prayer.

Dovid crossed the room to address his student whose unusual, almost shamed expression suggested that he might know what had occurred. Before Dovid even asked, the youth began to jabber, his words like anxious horses galloping from their corral.

"When I entered and saw the synagogue empty, Rabbi Dovid, I was bewildered. So, I walked out of the building and started making my way through the town, hoping to see some of those who pray here each day. In the square at the center, I saw a large crowd, Jews and Gentiles among them, all unusually quiet as if listening to someone in their midst. I couldn't see what it was that drew their attention, so I pushed my way into the throng. I heard his warm laughter before I saw the stranger in the center—a man I have never seen in Polnoyye. Gathered around him were yeshiva students, water-carriers, members of the Kahal, peddlers, tinsmiths, farmers, and even a few daring women. The simply dressed man is quite unlike the customary itinerant preachers. He speaks of God's closeness, addressing each one in the crowd there as if he or she were the only one there..."

The enthused narrator looked off into the distance now, as if a pleasing memory were beckoning him. Then he added with a rueful look on his face, "He told the townspeople not to judge themselves as sinners or to fear God's disapproval."

Dovid thought the report finished. It was not.

"Rabbi Dovid," the youth continued, avoiding Dovid's gaze now as he spoke. "The stranger said not to condemn ourselves, thinking we lack learnedness, devotion, or purity. 'Focusing on your sinfulness can lead to melancholy,' he said. As I was turning to leave, he called out with light-heartedness: 'We serve each other with our joy.'"

When his eyes met Dovid's, the young man's expression changed to a somber one, as if he were suddenly aware it might be wrong to be so enthusiastic.

"Perhaps, Rabbi, this stranger is one of the Sabbatean underground, one of those who, in the name of elevating the holy sparks, preaches indulgence?"

Dovid had heard quite enough. He put hand up to silence the repentant youth who had tried to turn the tide of his unbridled excitement. Had Dovid not been making an effort to curb his angry outbursts, he would have interrupted long before.

"Return to the square," he commanded his student now, "and summon this presumptuous itinerant to the Rabbi of Polnoyye at once."

Then, despite not having a quorum of ten, Dovid prayed with the two old men, grateful to find himself able to do so for the most part without his thoughts wandering to the market square.

As the last words of the concluding prayer were recited, the door of the shul opened.

Dovid raised his head and saw Yisroel standing at the threshold, smiling broadly. The astonished rabbi of Polnoyye instantly squeezed his eyes closed. It wouldn't be the first time his senses had deceived him; lack of food and sleep easily produced a measure of delusion. But when Dovid opened his eyes, he saw that it was indeed Yisroel.

"You wished to have a word with me, esteemed Rabbi?" Yisroel asked. Dovid heard the respect in Yisroel's voice, perhaps seasoned with amusement, but no mockery.

Dovid led the way to his small room, entering first when gestured to do so by Yisroel, who then closed the door behind them. When Yisroel said nothing, Dovid also remained silent, feeling suddenly like a young boy rather than the leader of a community of serious adherents.

So Yisroel had been the stranger in the square? If so, why hadn't Dovid ever felt Yisroel's disdain before, given that what Rabbi Lazer and now Rabbi Dovid of Polnoyye taught was the opposite of his own teachings. It occurred to Dovid now that he had never witnessed *any* disdain in Yisroel's manner—neither towards him, nor towards those who had distrusted and humiliated him all those years back in Horodenka.

Dovid, on the other hand, realized, as if suddenly faced with a mirror, that he himself donned this disdain like the tight, threadbare jacket in which he wrapped himself daily and even slept in, slouched over his books. Then, as spontaneously as it had appeared, the reflection of Dovid's disdain in the mirror of Yisroel's silent presence was gone. Instead, Dovid saw only Yisroel's unconditional compassion.

Dovid fell into his chair, trying to resist the tears collecting in his usually dry eyes.

Yisroel placed his hand on Dovid's shoulder. Just as there had been no reprimand in Yisroel's demeanor, there was none in his touch. Dovid was overcome by emotions surging in him like a forceful river flooding over a dam. Was it Yisroel's tenderness that unleashed this flood, or the piercing realization that his own tenderness towards himself had been absent for so long?

Dovid looked up to meet Yisroel's luminous eyes. It felt to Dovid as if the veil of tears obscuring his physical vision was somehow yielding greater clarity within.

"Rabbi Dovid," Yisroel spoke slowly and softly. "It is not your suffering but your joy that will draw you closer to that for which you long."

The words were as penetrating as Yisroel's gaze.

"Your body is not your enemy. Even your mind with all its wanderings and frightful desires is not your enemy. *You* have become the enemy of both your mind and body. You wish to keep anger, fear, and lust captive. But when locked in a cage these become more vicious and consuming forces. Your body and mind exist in order to bring you closer to the Source of Being and to be vehicles of that Source. There is nowhere that God does not abide."

Dovid received every word as if being fed something for which he was starved.

Yisroel kneeled down before him, peering into Dovid's eyes and heart simultaneously.

"Love yourself, Rabbi Dovid. Love your students. Allow your discipline to flow from love rather than fear."

Dovid could feel Yisroel's words flowing from the love he was urging Dovid to find. Yisroel was plucking strings taut in Dovid's heart, making them quiver; he was gently tuning the dissonant rabbi to the spheres of Boundless Love.

❧ 22 ❧

While four-year-old Elijah slept under the watchful gaze of his devoted sister Dalia, now almost twelve, Channa made her way deeper into the garden. She removed her leggings, for the weather was mild enough, and pressed her knees into the warm soil. She leaned forward to weed between the stout cabbages.

She could admit now without shame that she found more comfort and joy being surrounded by plants than by people. It had been many years since Channa had sat among women in the balcony of a house of prayer. Now the house of her prayer was this garden, and her worship was tending it. That a tiny seed, little bigger than one of the dots appearing under the letter in a prayer book, contained the essence of cabbage was a miracle.

She felt freer and closer to her Creator in nature than within the walls of any building, including the prayer house. It had always been this way, but her acceptance of this had not. During Channa's thirteen years in Zabie, in the presence of her husband, the generous earth, and the flowing, luminous Cheremosh River, her self-accusations had finally been silenced. Now, so close to the earth's body that she and it could breathe as one, Channa no longer felt divided.

Talking with Yisroel about living conscious intention, whatever one's circumstances, helped Channa make peace with how she might serve others, even while she lived in so isolated a place. Trusting in the power of intention, Channa prayed under an unlimited canopy of sky that love radiate throughout the world, that the earth and its inhabitants experience well-being and care for each other. Sometimes she did this holding a prayer book and uttering the formal prayers contained there. More often, though, she prayed spontaneously while planting, harvesting, caring for her children, or kneeling on the banks of the river. It was becoming natural for her to greet the infinite in a tiny seed and in the tears or laughter of her children.

While she remained secluded, Yisroel was being summoned from greater distances to respond to increasing needs for healing. Horses and wagons were often sent so that he might embark on a journey to this or that farm, to the village of Zabie, or to another mountain several days' journey away. It had stopped being necessary for Yisroel to mine and sell lime. Although he didn't charge a fee for his healing services, he was compensated, if not with coin, then with milk, coal, fleece—and, recently, animals: two healthy goats that had taken the place of the scrawny one that had just died. Word was spreading, even among peasants who lived a good distance from Zabie, about this healer who, though a Jew, could be trusted to perform miracles.

On his most recent visit, Gedaliah had spoken of word reaching Horodenka, perhaps traveling on the lips of highwaymen or farmers bringing their goods from the Carpathian mountains to the villages of Podolia. A highwayman's daughter had been extolling the man who had challenged her violent father on the road between Tluste and Horodenka and had ended his illicit pursuits forever. Zofia, it turns out, had actually witnessed the extraordinary encounter when Yisroel was her family's tutor.

Poles and Jews of solid and of questionable morals were seeking Yisroel as healer and miracle maker. He declined no one whose motives were pure.

Among the reports were outrageous stories and rumors: lost limbs or vision spontaneously restored; herbal brews sweetening mean-spirited relatives; highwaymen returning stolen goods to those they had robbed. Yisroel attributed these uncanny miracles to the longing and faith of those he had served. Never did he credit himself.

Channa's thoughts were interrupted by Elijah's laughter. She looked up from her weeding to see her son running behind a brilliant orange butterfly, weaving among apple trees ripe with fruit. A free-spirited soul, Elijah seemed happiest when running. Dalia, feigning breathlessness, was not far behind him. Her body hinted at womanhood, but Dalia relished being outdoors no less than when she was younger. The orchard into which the children now disappeared had been long abandoned by the time Yisroel and Channa had arrived here. Now it thrived. They were all thriving.

Elijah bounded out from between the heavily laden apple trees. Channa smiled. There certainly were many ways to pray. The fruit trees offered praise by bearing their fruit. Elijah's prayer was to run joyously, squinting in the light of the sun, in pursuit of a dancing butterfly he could not catch. His delight did not wane though the object of his quest eluded him. This just made his pursuit more captivating.

With her children's laughter encircling her, Channa finished her weeding and rose. Resting her basket on her hip, she began the walk to the inn. A sudden thought overtook her like a stranger drawing close out of nowhere: *her family's precious days in these mountains were numbered.*

TONIGHT AS USUAL, Yisroel prepared to rise while everyone slept. It was the midnight hour, the portal through which Yisroel was accustomed to enter his hours of study and prayer until the dawn. More and more often, he woke feeling as if he had not spent any time asleep or, more accurately, as if he had been in two places at once: both dreaming in bed *and* present at the destination to which he had been summoned. These nightly healings, rather than occurring with herbs or amulets, appeared to take place in a realm other than time or space as he knew them. He travelled with no conveyance, neither wagon nor horse, as if his soul were the vehicle. Yisroel often perceived himself as a body of light before those who summoned him. Sometimes he did not appear to them at all, but healing transpired nonetheless.

Questions swirled in the firmament of his mind. *What was dream and what real? Was the dream state more real than he'd ever supposed?*

Did his soul take leave of his body while he slept and don a subtle body in order to minister to those seeking healing? Did he appear to some persons as a body of light, to others as the sensation of presence, and to yet others in in his physical form—in response to what they could believe and accept?

That all this might be madness occurred to him, too. But he was becoming less afraid of what he could not fathom. It was helpful to be able to speak to Channa of these new capacities that baffled him. She never responded fearfully, but rather held his questions in the ample container of her love for him.

As time passed, Yisroel was regularly summoned from sleep to travel to those in need. Most nights, this was unlike any travel he had known. Yisroel did not decide where to go, nor whom to seek once there, how long to stay, or when to leave. Time and space seemed to collapse, so that the call to a distant village and his arrival there were no longer separated by the days of travel normally required to span the distance. An inner knowing guided each of his journeys and directed what transpired at each destination—in concert with the particular yearnings that had summoned him. It awed and humbled him to surrender to healing on planes other than the seen—to be able to touch lives with his spirit, not only his hands.

The shell of Yisroel's understanding about what was humanly possible in time and space was shattering. The confines of life were being challenged; what was possible was being revealed. As Yisroel journeyed beyond the boundaries of time, he received more frequent unbidden visions of the future, such as seeing the unborn children of a couple still under their wedding canopy. He could explain none of this, including his increasing lack of fear. He also knew that he could not will these encounters were he to try. Something larger than his personal will was directing him, as it had since he was a boy.

~

ALONE IN HIS CAVE, Yisroel closed his eyes to meditate. It didn't take long to feel a familiar pull beckoning him to the center of his being. He floated in the lush inner darkness until the pull grew in such intensity that Yisroel sensed that one of his ascents might be unfolding. The first time he had ascended, when he had almost relinquished his life, he had been summoned back by Channa. Since then he had returned from his ascents on his own.

Yisroel did not invite the ascents. He would feel a vortex of energy pulling his awareness as if through an unseen portal and then, he would find himself in a column of light. He had been shown visions of angels, ancient sages, and prophets gathered around heavenly tables studying, praying, and meditating. He felt humbled by the grace, the mysterious benevolence that yielded these wondrous experiences. He recognized that it was not his will, pride, or desire that elevated him, and was grateful that the gravity of doubt had not kept him from ascending. Nor had doubt or fear ever forced his descent from these unanticipated revelations. Over time, Yisroel had learned to let go of his fears and resistance and to relish these mysterious journeys. Perhaps because of his willingness, the ascents had become more frequent.

Now again, Yisroel felt himself drawn up through a pillar of light. Free of his physical body, it was his consciousness—his essence—that ascended. He made his way through what seemed a number of levels until a swell of outcries stopped him, imploring with great force. What did they want of him? Yisroel saw that these were prayers, suspended in the pillar of light. The prayers begged that he take them along as he made his way to the higher realms. They had been stalled here for untold time. Yisroel was stunned and had no idea what he could do.

Behind the prayers, he saw shadows. These were the doubts of the men and women who had offered the prayers, uncertain there really was a divine destination for their prayer. The lingering prayers and shadows of doubt pressed upon Yisroel so forcefully, he thought they might swallow his soul. Suddenly Yisroel heard a voice louder and more commanding than the rest.

"*Stop!*"

It was *his* voice. "*Stop!*" he compelled the distraught prayers and doubts. "*Stop and remember.*" The words thundered through him. "*Remember your Source and your Destination!*"

Before him now were rows of transparent veils. He knew that if it were it not for the veils, the light beyond them would be blinding. Within the scintillating light, Yisroel glimpsed an assembly of men and women, their faces radiant as full moons. These were the ancient matriarchs and patriarchs. Beyond them, more beings of light extended into infinity, the souls of great luminaries who showed the way to peace. Some had lived, others had not yet walked the earth garbed in physical bodies.

A gate appeared. From the other side of the gate, a single luminous form moved towards him. Wordlessly, Yisroel offered a question: *Will there come a time when the lion will lie with the lamb, when men and women will live together in peace?* He could feel the question reverberate in a void without beginning or end.

An answer rose from the ocean of silence: *Peace shall be with us when we know who we really are.*

The figure of shimmering light passed through the gate and drew closer with a message: *When men and women learn to drink from the inner wellspring of Love, their deepest thirst will be quenched. To guide others to this wellspring is your sacred duty, Yisroel ben Eliezar. When the world refreshes itself from these living waters, the Age of Peace will be upon us.*

Returning to his body, a tremble of love moved through Yisroel, leaving no part of him untouched.

∾

OVER THE COURSE OF THE NEXT TWO YEARS, DALIA watched the increasing flow of guests. Instead of a rare traveler stumbling upon the inn as before, at least one or two and sometimes as many as three or four men came each week now to spend the Sabbath. These were not travelers who happened to be passing through Zabie, but men who had come specifically to meet her father. The visitors were men of all ages, among them established rabbis.

When Dalia first asked her mother how these men and the few bold women traveling with them had come to know of her father, Channa had smiled and replied, "Destiny."

Dalia listened as strangers arrived asking for "the miracle worker," to which her father sometimes answered, *"That must be you. Are you not a miracle?"* Often, her abba would even invite the confused guest to sit and tell him the wondrous miracles in his or her life. Some said they felt mocked by his behavior. Dalia knew her abba did not intend this, although at times she did wish he would not answer a question with another question.

It intrigued Dalia to watch her father behave differently with different guests. He was completely unpredictable. A number of indignant visitors, calling her father "charlatan," "trickster," or "impostor," complained that they had not traveled all this distance to be greeted like fools.

As Dalia observed what went on during these visits, she couldn't help feeling protective of her abba. Some men seemed to have come to test him, to prove that Yisroel was ignorant, even dangerous, and that he didn't deserve his good repute. He never argued, nor did he engage in any overt actions to prove himself worthy of his guests' respect. And to Dalia's amazement, no matter what went on, he seemed unperturbed. Instead he offered only patience to those who became red in the face in response to something he had said, or to the ways he prayed.

Most of those who visited were outraged by the way her father regarded the women around him. Some said they had been warned about Yisroel behaving as if women were equal to men. No matter who or how many people came, Channa, Rifka, and Dalia were never asked to leave the large hearth room where the prayers, meals, and conversations took place, nor did Yisroel ask them to subdue their voices during times of prayer. A sheath of muslin stretched between two posts was put in place, in deference to the visitors as well as for the women's sakes. Dalia learned that this piece of cloth was a much less substantial means of separation than the more common division of women and men into separate rooms or different floors of the synagogue. Before the visitors had begun to come, Dalia had no idea that a woman's voice raised in prayer was not to be heard by men praying in proximity. Her abba had never asked her, or her mother, or her tanta Rifka to restrain their voices. Now, Dalia was getting used to heads turned and scowls because men were "being forced to hear women's voices" as fully a part of the prayers as their own.

But not all who visited were blinded by prejudices and pride, and not all basked in their holiness, comparing it to Yisroel's ignorance. There were also those who came openheartedly, curious about the man who had caused their neighbor or relative to change: to regain his faith, to act scrupulously in his business affairs, to become kinder to his wife and children. These guests observed and listened earnestly. Some engaged in dialogue, prayer, study, and meditation with Yisroel, and seemed to leave changed. She noticed this especially in those who came carrying unnamed burdens. Men arriving with caved shoulders stood more upright, as if the weight they bore had been lifted.

Today, again, Yisroel was urging those who could receive his words to put down their burdens in the refuge of the inn, trusting they could reclaim them upon leaving if they wished to.

"Our burdens," he told three men, two seated at the large table, the third pacing, "grow heavier with the weight of worry. So for now, release your troubles into the hold of your Eternal Companion and see what happens."

"Even if you have stopped believing in God," he added, "put down your burdens as if you did. Just for a while."

Dalia watched and listened as his guidance was met with a mix of responses: relief, confusion, and, sometimes, outright hostility.

She left the room to try what her abba had suggested in a way she had not thought to do before. Dalia made her way down to the bank of the Cheremosh, closed her eyes, and imagined putting down her worries about her father's safety as if they were a bundle of wet clothes wrapped in a sheet.

She waited. It didn't seem enough to have just set the bundle down on the ground. What did her abba mean by, "release your troubles into the hold of your Eternal Companion?" Dalia picked up the bundle of worries in her mind and this time dropped it into the air for it to be caught by unseen hands. What happened next surprised her: she was the one who felt caught—and held.

Only when she heard Elijah call her name, did she realize that she had forgotten all about her bundle of worries.

DALIA GREW to dread the visitors less. Over time, her apprehension was even replaced by excitement, as she anticipated who would be at the table for the next Sabbath. She became curious about the diverse minds and new voices joining for prayer services and study sessions. She found herself more interested in the lively conversations, even when these included challenges for her father. She looked forward to the debates over the interpretation of the law laid out in the Torah.

Her father did not dominate but rather invited many points of view, allowing everyone to have a voice. This, too, some guests, who deemed themselves more knowledgeable, might sometimes criticize and even condemn.

After the Havdalah ceremony concluding the Sabbath, Dalia watched a somber youth of perhaps sixteen approach her father, who was kneeling at the hearth. The young man had traveled a long distance alone, she knew, arriving shortly before the descent of Sabbath. Upon overhearing him tell her mother that he'd come fffrom Brody, Dalia had instantly felt a surge of missing her dear uncle Gershon, whom she'd last seen almost five years ago when her brother Elijah was born. When, at the evening meal, she asked the youth if he knew Rabbi Gershon, the boy, who had seemed unsettled from the moment he arrived, acted as if he had not heard the question.

The youth, waiting for her abba to stand, stood stiffly, shoulders back and chest expanded, as if his body were saying *I dare you,* even before a word had crossed his lips. He scowled as he addressed her father.

"I was warned of your behavior before traveling here. But only now, after praying under your roof, do I see how completely you abandon all caution concerning women and the dangers they pose." The irate guest went on to quote a rabbinical commentary concerning distraction during prayer. Dalia looked at her father, who stood now facing the youth. He was smiling.

How could her father not feel even a trace of annoyance, she wondered. Even she felt annoyed. It astounded Dalia that her abba never responded in the manner in which he was attacked. In the face of defiance, hostility, and now, youthful arrogance, he only smiled and otherwise acted completely unassailed. How gracefully did he step out of the path of an arrow, leaving it with no target!

The young man took a deep breath. Keeping his gaze directed to the floor, he turned in Dalia's direction. Without waiting for her father to signal her to stay or leave, she slipped behind the muslin divider that had been moved to the side of the room. She heard the boy draw a long breath and then continue speaking.

"My father, a rabbi of great renown, has impressed on me since I was a small boy how carefully I must protect myself from the evils of women, including my mother and sisters. You have allowed women to invade the hallowed sanctuary of men's prayer. How can you permit this?"

When her abba still made no comment, despite the gravity of the violation being pointed out to him, the agitated young man continued more vehemently, raising his voice.

"My esteemed father was right about you. What you are condoning prevents a man from offering himself fully to his prayer. To hear the voices of women joined with ours makes it impossible to shun images of other kinds of joining with them. Women steal the minds of men away from the divine mandate to focus on holy texts and perform other sacred duties."

When Yisroel still did not respond, Dalia pictured the silence shattering into shards like a fragile cup unable to contain its contents.

She heard Yisroel draw in a deep breath and she did the same. But, despite pausing and breathing deeply, Dalia felt her anger growing. This belligerent boy's "esteemed" father had apparently taught him little or nothing about speaking respectfully.

"My father, the honorable Rabbi Mendel, is the head of one of Brody's yeshivas," he went on. He teaches the importance of dominating one's thoughts regarding the female gender and cautions us to dominate our wives when we marry lest their powers of seduction deter—or, worse, destroy—our passion for study. Rabbi Mendel warns of the countless ways women so cunningly arouse men's passion and lead them astray."

"What is your name, my son?" Yisroel interrupted, his voice steady and calm.

"Amos, son of Mendel," he answered, as if his father's name were a shield protecting him.

"Are you married, Reb Amos?"

"No...," he stammered, "but soon to be."

"So you are betrothed?"

"I will be soon."

"What is your basherte's, your destined one's, name?

Dalia could hear a tremor in the student's voice as he replied, "I do not know. My father will choose, not I."

"Reb Amos, it is natural for one's mind to wander towards union with one's beloved. The pleasure that God has ordained between a man and his beloved is not sinful but holy. You are right that thoughts of such union may distract a man or a woman reciting words of prayer. But this can be an opportunity, Reb Amos. We can feel grateful for the pleasures available to us, then offer our gratitude and sing God's praises with even more ardor."

Dalia wished she could see the face of Amos ben Mendel as her father spoke.

"My good Reb Amos, when you hear the voices of women expressing their devotion and those voices press upon your thoughts, you can bind your voice to theirs as the divine Bridegroom binds himself to his Bride, the Jewish people. In the joy of such unity, continue to pray. The struggle to deny the beautiful aspects of creation can be even more distracting."

Dalia thought she heard the young man sigh, but not one of his earlier sighs of disgust. Had he become able to listen?

"Women are not to be dominated by men, my son. On the contrary, we men have much to learn from women. Because a woman is a vessel for life, she is more capable of surrender, and her heart is more readily stirred to compassion and tenderness. To dominate women is to destroy the tenderness that seeks to take root within us as men. It is true that women may seduce us, but this can be a holy seduction: women beckon us into our hearts."

Dalia risked peering over the top of the divider. The youth's taut neck muscles had loosened. Amos said nothing, and lowered himself into a chair. At least for now he had stopped fighting.

"Do not wage war against your instincts, my son," her father's voice consoled. "It is not women who threaten harm. The deadly serpent is your fear of women, not women themselves."

Pain flashed across Amos face.

Dalia wondered if this was "breaking the shell of his pain," as Yisroel described it. Breaking open, her father often said, did not happen through force, but through love. Such opening, although it might appear to be against a person's will, was always aligned with that person's deeper longing. With his shell broken, Dalia thought, perhaps the tenderness hidden within Amos could be expressed, and the tenderness of others like her abba, and even women, might be allowed to enter his life. Then she thought about Amos' father and what he taught. Would Amos harden his shell again when he returned home?

AFTER THE NEXT DAY'S evening meal while Rifka and the children gazed at the full moon, Channa and Yisroel cleared the table.

"Young Amos is no longer holding himself captive," Channa told her husband, having witnessed the changes in their young guest from a distance.

Yisroel stood still and turned to face her. "Channa, he is Mendel's son," he stated softly, as if setting something very delicate down on the table.

Stunned, Channa said nothing. The man who had treated her violently had been rearing his son to be the same. Had Yisroel's loving wisdom changed this course of events? Would Amos's betrothed be spared the harm and shame she might otherwise have endured?

Channa stepped close to Yisroel who wrapped his arms around her. In his embrace, she wept with compassion for what the younger Channa had suffered and with wonder at life's inscrutable plan. She also prayed for Amos along with his mother and sisters, that they might all be somehow protected from Mendel's cruelty. And Mendel, could she pray for him? Could she—within the safety of Yisroel's arms and the protection of his love—actually pray for Mendel?

Not yet.

When she brought Mendel to mind, her body recoiled. She burrowed more deeply into Yisroel's arms. He tightened his embrace. Closing her eyes, Channa drew in a deep breath. Suddenly in her mind's eye, she saw Mendel's heart pierced with arrows as if it were a creature that had been hunted and captured. She opened her eyes quickly.

That was enough for now. She did not want to summon him even in her imagination. It was easier to pray for his family. She would leave Mendel to an invincible enemy: the truth.

Dalia knew that several visitors to the inn had approached her father to ask for Rifka's hand in marriage. Dalia had also learned that a prospective husband rarely went directly to the woman in question, but rather to the man believed to have the right to give her away in marriage. If a father could not be found, then he went to the woman's brother, which is what they must have assumed Yisroel to be—Tanta Rifka's brother.

It had come as a shock when fathers, traveling with their sons, beardless yeshiva students of fifteen or sixteen years old, also went to Yisroel to discuss betrothing their sons to Dalia. Recently, two widowed men, when their request for Rifka was turned down, had asked after Dalia! She was not much past fourteen now and relieved that her father and mother had no plans for her to marry as young as was customary.

Dalia would tell Rifka about the men, and they would laugh as they had about other betrothal inquiries. Not long ago, they had fallen into each other's arms following the departure of a petulant, bald widower, blind in one eye, who had made it very clear that he was equally disposed to marry either of them.

RIFKA KNEW that it would be her permission, not Yisroel's or any other man's, that would lead to her betrothal.

She had not discussed her feelings regarding marriage with Channa or Yisroel. Despite knowing they would not judge her, she had tried to keep her confusion from them, perhaps the way she had kept it from herself. Men's interest in marrying her was bringing her confusion to the surface. She could not imagine marrying any of them and had told this to Yisroel when he asked. But, it was even worse than this. She felt no desire to commit her life to *any* man.

Rifka heard a knock, then Channa asking if she might enter. Had Channa somehow sensed her turmoil?

If Channa was surprised to find Rifka in the dark, she did not show it.

"What is it, dear friend?" Channa asked in a whisper, remaining just inside the closed door. Rifka kindled the oil lamp. Channa drew closer, a circle of light illumining her face. "What I am most drawn to, I also fear," Rifka began. "I fear defying what is prescribed as the highest duty for a Jewish woman. But I cannot imagine myself bound by oath to one man and one family, Channa. God forgive me; I know this is not the way of our people."

Channa sat down at the end of Rifka's narrow bed.

"It is as if I was already betrothed, but my betrothal is not an accepted one," Rifka continued. "I feel drawn to a different life, not alone, but one joined with many other lives—although not a husband's. I want to commit my life to girls and women who wish to learn. Although they may never have the privileges and freedom of their brothers, they *can* enter realms from which they have been barred. I want to feed them knowledge and inspire them to succeed."

Rifka had never stated her heart's desire so clearly. She could trust there would be no admonition, even unspoken; no scriptural excerpts quoted punitively, citing commandments about marriage and procreation. Channa and Yisroel would not condemn Rifka the way she had been condemning herself.

Rifka looked into her beloved's Channa's eyes. She saw no argument there, no challenge.

Channa moved closer and took Rifka in her arms.

Her heart pressed close against Rifka's, as if their two hearts might become one, Channa's breath warm on Rifka's neck. Rifka felt the longing that had first stirred in her as she watched Channa ripe with child, praying on a boulder in the garden. Then and now, Rifka yearned to cherish this woman until only death parted them, to protect and comfort her, to hold and be held by her. But this could never be in the manner of man and woman, cherishing each other's bodies as well as souls. Although she had withheld nothing else from Channa, Rifka had not and would never burden her with this desire.

They had found their way to being companions of the soul. This would be the fulfillment of their destiny.

❧ 23 ☙

"Livovi?"

Her father's voice little more than a whisper broke into her thoughts.

"May I sit with you?"

He always asked first. Dalia nodded, her eyes still closed.

The large boulder had become one of Dalia's favorite places to be alone, especially since Tanta Rifka had described to her the beauty of her mother praying on this boulder, pregnant with Dalia. She could think here—all kinds of thoughts, including those she wished she didn't have. Despite her acceptance and even growing enthusiasm about the swelling stream of visitors to the inn, she often wished for the simplicity of life with her parents, brother, and tanta. Her father was traveling more now. She wanted to feel deep gladness, knowing that he was bestowing blessings wherever he traveled. But that was not all she felt.

After a few moments of silence, Yisroel gently swept aside a few strands of Dalia's hair that the wind had tossed in front of her eyes.

"I will be traveling soon to Brody to spend Yom Kippur, the Day of Atonement, with your uncle Gershon."

"But you have never been away from us for any part of the High Holidays." The words escaped quickly along with her disappointment and even a trace of accusation. Dalia wished she could inhale what she had just said, along with the tone of voice, and say it all differently. She straightened. She would speak more respectfully, more maturely.

"Please convey my love to Uncle Gershon, Abba."

"You can convey your love directly, Dalia."

"What?" She looked at him with surprise.

"I would like you to come with me to Brody. I have spoken with your mother and she has given her blessing. Now I need your consent."

Her father was serious; he would not tease her in this way. Dalia pretended to consider his proposal. She wrinkled her brow thoughtfully, tilted her head, and narrowed her eyes.

"Hmm" she said, and "hmm," again before jumping up and exclaiming, "Of course, Abba! How could you wonder?"

"Your will must always be your own, Livovi. We have each been given free will to use wisely. Come, let us tell your mother how you have decided to use this will of yours."

IT SURPRISED DALIA, but did not seem to surprise her father when, shortly after their arrival in Brody, her uncle Gershon invited Yisroel to lead the closing prayers of the Yom Kippur service. This was the most auspicious holy day of the year, The Day of Atonement. Her abba said yes without hesitation.

Dalia entered the Brody synagogue through the door designated for women and began to climb the stairs. This would be her first time in a women's balcony, praying with so many women. She ran her hand over the smooth, sinuous banister as she climbed.

Once seated, Dalia was astounded. She had never seen even a small house of prayer let alone one of this size and grandeur. Arches framed high ceilings, colorfully painted. In the center of the huge synagogue, four steps led to a raised platform on which there was a table. Four towering columns, one on each corner of the platform, stood like sentinels. She had never seen such deep burgundy wood or such carving. On the eastern wall, also on a raised platform, an ornate cabinet housed the Torah scrolls.

Her father had explained on their trip here that every shul, no matter its size, had a Holy Ark that housed at least one Torah scroll, meticulously scribed on parchment with not even a single error. The scroll was tied with a strip of silk and usually robed, too, in silk or velvet, on top of which hung an ornamental breastplate crafted by a silver or goldsmith. Placed over the scroll handles was a crown also finely crafted of silver or gold. In wealthier congregations, each scroll handle was adorned with its own crown. These crowns might be finely filigreed and set with precious gems. The *sacred vessels,* as the adornments were known, honored the Torah, whose wisdom and beauty were priceless. In the huge and elegant Brody synagogue, he told her, there would be several scrolls, each dressed uniquely and the sacred vessels adorning them quite elaborate.

Dalia wished she was close enough to get a good look at the golden brocaded letters on the Torah's mantle and at the delicately filigreed vines that formed Her crowns. She hoped she would at least be able to hear the tiny bells, which she'd learned were often attached to the tops of the crowns and rang delicately when the Torah was carried among the congregants. Even though the Torah would not be carried among the women, maybe she would still hear the bells.

Some hours later in the service, Dalia watched her father climb slowly up the steps of the bimah in the center of the huge synagogue filled with Brody's Jews. Every seat was taken. Men stood in the aisles and at the back of the room; their wives and daughters filled the balcony. If her father had known the size and grandeur of this synagogue, would he still have agreed to lead all these people in prayer? He had only conducted prayers with a handful of people, at most.

Dalia looked down at the platform upon which her father now stood, his large prayer shawl wrapped around him and draped over his head as he swayed from side to side. She heard the mounting fervor in his prayer. The entreaty in his voice stirred Dalia to tears.

When it grew long past sunset and the hour the service should have concluded, Dalia wondered if her uncle Gershon might be regretting his decision. Was it not well past the time for all to go home and break the fast with as much or as little as one had to eat? The sun had set nearly an hour earlier on the solemn fast day that had started at sundown the night before. Everyone, except for the old, the very young, and the sick had been standing for the past several hours, since the Ark had been opened. But still her father had not finished praying. The Shofar blast signifying the end of the holy day had not yet been sounded and the weary people had not yet been dismissed.

Dalia observed the congregants' increasing impatience, their restless movements and glances, their sighs as they gazed at their timepieces. Some had begun to mumble discontentedly. At least, the mumbling made it less likely anyone would hear the growling in Dalia's stomach. It was only her second full fast since she had crossed the threshold from girlhood.

Dalia knew that nothing her father did was unintentional. Surely he could feel the growing tension in the synagogue. But his head remained bowed. His impassioned and direct communication with the Ayn Sof had become more subdued.

Suddenly, a piercing whistle sounded. Dalia looked around, as did others, to find its source. A poorly dressed boy blew a second time on a small shepherd's pipe. Dalia saw the old man next to him, perhaps his grandfather, try unsuccessfully to capture the whistle.

She had noticed the boy earlier. He had been reluctantly approaching the House of Prayer led by the old and tattered man; both were wearing sheepskin vests. Curious about the two, Dalia had searched from the balcony to find them. The old man held no prayer book; perhaps he could not read. Dalia had thought it curious to see him stay the child's small hand with his heavy one whenever the boy reached into his pocket. The boy must have been seeking his whistle. Now, the weary shepherd tried unsuccessfully to wrest the small pipe from the boy. But in another swift, undeterred move, the boy blew into it with all the power he could summon.

Her father had straightened, pulled his prayer shawl back from his head, and turned to look at the boy. Refusing to yield the pipe, he sounded it again for the third time before restoring it to his pocket.

The silence that fell over the congregation amazed Dalia, given the restlessness just a moment earlier. When the boy noticed Yisroel looking at him, he bowed his head and muttered something. Was it an apology? Dalia strained to hear him. Her abba asked the boy to speak so all could hear.

"I blew my whistle to tell Adonai how much I love Him, because I cannot read the words."

Yisroel nodded, smiling broadly. He then proceeded to recite the last words of the closing prayer, lifted the Shofar, and sounded the final penetrating blast signaling the end of the holy day. Although all were hungry and had been so eager to leave, no one moved from his or her place. Transfixed, Dalia watched her father's compassionate glance sweep through the House of Prayer.

"We pray each day," Yisroel voice boomed. "*And you shall love the Lord your God, with all your heart, with all you soul, and with all your might.* Just now, a pure sound issued with heart, soul, and all the might of this child has lifted the rest of our prayers. The young shepherd held nothing back, wanting only to give his love. We can learn from him how to pray. When we offer our loving gratitude without holding back—just as we are—our prayers become irresistible."

THE EVENING AFTER his return from Brody, Yisroel went to find Channa, who had gone out into the night air that she so relished. The moon, waning from its Yom Kippur fullness, was still robust enough to allow Yisroel to find his way to her. From a distance, he saw her seated on the large boulder she favored at the center of the herb garden. Wrapped in a thick woolen shawl, she was looking up at the night sky. He would have liked to leave his wife's quiet reverie untouched, to protect her solitary meditation in these mountains not only tonight but for countless nights to come.

"Ahavah, I do not wish to disturb you," he said, as he drew closer, "but may I speak with you?"

Channa moved over slightly to make room for him on the large rock.

"Channa, Gershon has invited us to live with him in Brody."

If Channa was taken aback, she did not show it.

"Your brother urges that I join the Brody Kloiz, the elite academy of rabbis and Kabbalists of which he is a member. As you know, the rulings of this group of rabbis and judges impact Jews throughout the Polish-Lithuanian Commonwealth and far beyond. Gershon believes I can contribute to this noble body. Your brother and his wife Bluma have also invited us to live with them. He assured me that since they have borne no children of their own, it is with great pleasure that they welcome Dalia and Elijah."

Channa looked straight ahead, sitting so still she barely seemed to be breathing.

"Ahavah, I neither desire to leave Zabie nor to be a part of an elite group. Yet I sense it right to accept Gershon's invitation." He paused. "I will not make a decision, however, without knowing your response."

They shared the deep silence both treasured.

"Channa, there will be no gardens like we have here in Brody, nor such deep quiet. In the fifteen years since Brody was your home, it has become an even busier city."

Channa turned towards him, placing her hands on top of his. Her eyes shone in the moonlight. "We've both sensed that the time would come for us to leave here, Yisroel. I've cherished the vast quiet and beauty of this abode. Now it's time to carry this generous peace inside us to wherever we place our feet and lay our heads." She stood. "We will go, my love, to our new home."

YISROEL SENT a message accepting Gershon's invitation. Yet how easily Yisroel could imagine continuing to live at the inn. This would have been his personal inclination had he not glimpsed a different destiny even before his brother-in-law's invitation. The flow of guests to the inn, along with Yisroel's travels by day and his mysterious journeys by night had begun to send ripples to people and places well beyond Zabie. It was time to make the waves larger.

In Zabie, in addition to cultivating the land with Channa and Rifka, Yisroel had been cultivating a spiritual practice that had yielded rich fruit: the practice of *Devekut*, Remembrance of his closeness to God. His father had been the first to teach him this when he was on his deathbed; Reb Eliezar had instructed him to remember, assuring him that he would not be alone. To remember was to focus on the energy at the root of all life and to feel united with that energy.

For Yisroel, the practice of Devekut was not merely a mental activity, although it started with directing his mind. To remember was to *feel* the Shechinah close. Not only during meditation, prayer, and study but in his daily life as husband, father, farmer, and healer, Yisroel practiced remembering. He turned his attention to feeling and in this way to knowing the unknowable force called God and by many other names. What fueled Yisroel's impulse to love, learn, and laugh if not this Source? Adonai was his very breath. The Shechinah infused these very thoughts as he was thinking them. The Ayn Sof was present even in his doubt. To practice remembrance was to greet this Presence everywhere—starting with finding God in one's own heart.

Most beings lived unaware of the treasure they carried within. What if each woman, man and child became able to experience his and her life as the incomparable, unique gift it was meant to be? What a sacred opportunity each of us was given: to reflect to each other who we really are, reminding each other when we forget.

Remembrance was at once a path to awakening and the practice of remaining awake.

After hearing him speak about the practice of Devekut to their Shabbos guests, Dalia, with her usual intent curiosity, approached Yisroel, wanting to understand more.

"When I worry and become afraid, am I forgetting that God is with me?" she asked.

"You needn't worry, Livovi. It is very easy to find one's way back. You just can remember."

"But *what* should I remember?" Dalia, brow furrowed.

"It is not such hard work," Yisroel reassured her, smoothing her brow and touching his daughter's cheek tenderly. "Perhaps it will help to imagine it this way: imagine a river with many times the current of the Cheremosh—a river of love that you may not see but can *sense* flowing through every being and instant of life. You can draw power from this stream of blessing at any time. All that is required is to pause and remember it's always there."

Dalia's expression relaxed.

"Remembrance is a gentle, moment to moment practice, Livovi. When we have forgotten, a hint is that we feel less joy. When we remember, there is deep joy and even relief, the relief one feels finding one's way home after being lost." He paused.

"We are here together to help each other remember."

Dalia was especially pleased by these last words.

THERE WERE THINGS Yisroel left out of the conversation with his daughter. Many, if not most, would find it heretical to teach that God dwells within an individual as his or her own Self. At Yisroel's table, it had been hotly argued by some that "the Almighty" must be placed *above* man and must be greatly feared if we are to have order, not chaos and immorality. Some worried that to teach that God is within is to give people power that might have devastating consequences.

It did not call for fortune-telling abilities to predict that Yisroel's teachings and counsel could be misunderstood and denounced both by honest and unscrupulous leaders of his people. Some would protest because of their genuine fear that people might stray from holy texts and morally mandated actions were they to believe themselves the source of holiness. Others, who perhaps did not acknowledge their actual motives even to themselves, would challenge Yisroel because his belief threatened their personal power and authority. One such potential source of forceful opposition was Mendel, Channa's former husband.

On Yisroel's visit to Brody, Gershon had informed him that Rabbi Mendel was a member of the city's prestigious Kloiz. Over the years, Mendel had managed to amass significant wealth and status among his brethren, including a dominant role in the elite Kloiz. Mendel's genius as a yeshiva student, his ability to dominate Talmudic debates, his indomitable *chutzpah* when standing up to older students, and his relentless ambition had become known among Brody's Jews—but Mendel seemingly needed more than these talents had given him. So Mendel had glorified his reputation, Gershon asserted. Both in matters of commerce and communal leadership, Mendel had bribed, shamed, denounced, and threatened his way to the power and success he coveted. He had also managed to garner the respect and pity of his brethren for his "selfless matrimony to the mentally defective Channa," a marriage he proclaimed to have had the courage and decency to end on behalf of his future sons. Although Gershon had publicly confronted Mendel's narrow-mindedness in the Kloiz, he had remained loyal to Channa's request not to reveal what had transpired in her marriage to Mendel. Thus Gershon had never spoken out against Mendel's allegations about the marriage.

Yisroel's brother-in-law was deeply concerned that a number of his colleagues, honorable members of the Kloiz and conscientious guardians of their people's welfare, were swayed by Mendel's self-righteousness and claims to superior status. It troubled Gershon to hear these men concur when Mendel argued that "the holy role of the Kloiz is to protect the simple Jew from himself."

Gershon informed Yisroel that the misogynistic Mendel had sent his son Amos to the inn to glean more information about Yisroel. Following Amos's return, Mendel had confided his disgust to Gershon, believing Gershon to still harbor disdain for his sister's "ignoramus husband Yisroel" and even for his own sister. The outraged Mendel told Gershon that his son Amos had dared to question him about whether women could be trusted. Mendel was inflamed by his son's "first and last challenge" to his authority and worldview, explaining proudly that he had put his son in his place. Mendel vowed to silence Yisroel and any like him "who dare to poison our youth with such beliefs."

Yisroel believed Mendel would do whatever he could to defy and demean him. Yisroel didn't how he would respond. But to dread or even just to dwell on thoughts of Mendel's attacks could rob Yisroel of the strength he needed to step forth into his destiny. He would encounter whatever "enemies" awaited him as they appeared. There could be none more formidable than his own doubt and fear. Remembrance would be Yisroel's most powerful ally.

CHANNA TOLD RIFKA about the decision to leave Zabie and move to Brody. Channa wished it were possible for Rifka, who loved the gardens as much as she, to remain at the inn if she wanted to. But, in truth, a woman tending such a place alone, especially a Jewess, was out of the question. Rifka could neither provide for herself nor be safe there. Channa explained that Gershon had arranged dwelling for Rifka in Brody if she chose to go there, too. A kind elderly widow had already offered a room in her home.

Rifka's response to Channa's concerns was immediate and not laden with any sense of loss.

"I accept the widow's offer," she answered without hesitation. "I am thankful, my beloved friend, for your abiding love, and I appreciate your brother's kindness." Then Rifka added, "Our gardens, my sweet Channa, will be the wives and daughters of the men who come seeking Yisroel. In their hearts, we shall plant seeds."

Part Three

1736

City of Brody,
Podolia Region

The Polish-Lithuanian
Commonwealth

❧ 24 ❧

Given his initial judgment of his brother-in-law as an ignoramus, Gershon thought it ironic that he now strongly desired Yisroel's participation in the Brody Kloiz.

When the idea first dawned in his mind, Gershon had felt a strange mixture of eager anticipation and discomfort about inviting Yisroel to meet with the city's most illustrious and learned Jews. Ultimately, however, his conviction that Yisroel would contribute a unique and pure perspective, however unorthodox, won out.

What inspired Gershon to propose Yisroel's membership, despite his unconventional ways, was the integrity Gershon had witnessed during the Yom Kippur service Yisroel had conducted in Brody months earlier. Gershon recognized not only Yisroel's integrity, but also his courage when he risked the displeasure of the entire congregation to wait for a genuine, humble expression of prayer. So Rabbi Gershon had heartily recommended his brother-in-law as a future member to his brethren in the Kloiz.

Thus far the only reason the Kloiz was entertaining his recommendation was the regard in which his father Rabbi Elijah was held and the respect Gershon had garnered over time. Gershon hoped he could convince them of Yisroel's merit.

Gershon argued that there was precedent for men to join the Kloiz who were not residents of Brody. Yes, he acknowledged, these men from outside Brody had renown that had distinguished them and made them desirable members. But Yisroel's eminence was of a different nature. His authority did not derive from external status or scholarly ranking but from his commitment to the highest truth and essence of Torah: to value the life of another as you value your own. Gershon spoke of the unusual and rare compassion, vision, and courage of Yisroel ben Eliezer.

The assembly of noted rabbis and scholars greeted his words with skepticism and caution. They recalled Yisroel's unprecedented behavior at the Yom Kippur service, which all judged as extraordinary—some favorably and others quite the contrary.

In the end, even Gershon was distressed to learn that his own good name and well-respected judgment was not enough to convince his brethren on the Kloiz to welcome Yisroel son of Eliezer into their hallowed circle. Gershon had been defeated, his nomination rejected by a majority vote.

Gershon subsequently learned from a few of his fellow rabbis and judges in the Kloiz that Mendel had moved among them, discrediting Yisroel in every manner possible. This included accusations questioning his morality and mental acuity. Mendel claimed to be protecting his fellow Jews "from a serpent disguising himself as a Tree of Knowledge." Mendel's sabotage of Yisroel's membership dismayed but did not surprise Gershon. But why, Gershon wondered, had Mendel chosen to do so covertly? Why did he not denounce Yisroel publicly? Surely, Mendel had his motives.

YISROEL DID NOT seem at all distressed to have been excluded from the notable Kloiz. Within a short time of his arrival from Zabie with his family, he was in the streets, speaking directly to the citizens of Brody.

"I am learning a great deal from the unschooled citizens of Brody," Yisroel told his brother-in-law when Gershon questioned him. "Who can say if I would have learned as much meeting late into the night with the esteemed brethren of the Kloiz?"

Gershon learned that Yisroel listened intently to the hardships of his Jewish and Christian neighbors. His insight and compassion were becoming known among tradespeople, shopkeepers, peasants, and those forced to rely on the uncertain charity of others.

"This man can re-awaken joy and faith long gone. Hearts closed like fists in order not to feel more pain and misfortune are being coaxed open," a Brody ruby merchant of stature, paradoxically known for his closed fist in regard to charity, informed Gershon. In the next breath, the merchant, an embittered widower, told Gershon he would be giving funds to Brody's Kahal to build a shelter for widows.

Yisroel did not make it his habit to pray in the stately synagogue where the members of the Kloiz regularly prayed. Instead, he frequented the humbler prayer houses where he'd been invited to lead services. Gershon knew also that Yisroel had begun to teach in study houses where groups of men, less revered than those forming the Kloiz, gathered to study when they could. There, Yisroel celebrated the merits of diving into Torah study, while instructing that most important was living the Torah.

But Yisroel could most often be found in the bustle of the marketplace. Unlike the smaller towns and villages where the marketplace unfolded for a few hours a week, in Brody merchants of all sorts, from wealthy traders to simple peddlers, conducted business every day of the week.

Gershon's wife Bluma came home one afternoon, remembering words of an illiterate rag picker she had encountered while walking with Channa and Dalia. The grateful man had burst into an unexpected account when Dalia offered him a coin in exchange for a bright piece of cloth. *The new rabbi in the square*, he reported enthusiastically, *told me that if a rag picker and a judge were placed on two sides of a scale, it would be their deeds not the holy texts they've read that would matter in the court of God.*

Although Gershon said nothing to Yisroel or Channa, he felt conflicted hearing accounts of Yisroel in the streets like a commonplace itinerant preacher. But he restrained himself from rebuking or even from questioning his brother-in-law, surmising that Yisroel's actions held purpose even if Gershon could not discern what that purpose was.

Gershon was not surprised to glean from second hand reports that Yisroel was not summoning citizens in the manner of the itinerant preachers who traveled from town to town. In fact, Yisroel's messages were arousing great consternation among the itinerant preachers, similar to the reactions from members of the Kloiz. It was the mission of most of these preachers, who were often spokespersons for other religious authorities, to vehemently reproach their fellow Jews, instilling fear and shame in them for their grievous shortcomings. They warned of dire consequences for those not leading pious lives of regular prayer, study, tithing, and deference to established religious leaders.

Itinerant preachers barked endless "heaven forbids" should a man imagine himself worthy before his Maker. A man must never, they hotly exhorted, not even in his sleep, forget his inferiority and tendency to sloth. Knowing the tribulations in this life, such preachers spoke often of The World to Come in which a man with little in this world is likely to have a large portion awaiting him. But heaven forbid, if man should choose to set aside his shame before his Maker, for then he would also set aside his good portion in the World to Come.

Thinking about all this on his way from the meeting place of the Kloiz, Gershon practically bumped into one of these preachers, with a handful of men and some women gathered around him to listen.

"A man must keep his sins and weakness before him at all times," the preacher bellowed. "And know this, too," he wagged his finger, face reddening, "to think yourself able to overcome your failings *without* the piety of study and prayer is a certain road to hell."

Gershon continued walking. Preachers like this one prescribed actions that were difficult if not impossible for most Jews to fulfill. They demanded regular attendance at prayer services from laborers who worked long hard hours every day of the week, and diligent Torah study from men who could not read. Women were not even mentioned, there being little besides the bearing of children and the serving of their husbands and sons that could redeem them. For failing to fulfill the required, sanctified actions, punishment could be expected in the form of more hunger, illness, or even homelessness. Poverty and a lowly condition in life were cited as reflections of one's lack of favor in the eyes of the Lord.

These were not Yisroel's messages. But what *was* his brother-in-law saying? And just what was Yisroel hearing from the citizens of Brody?

By the time he arrived home. Gershon decided that he would go into the streets to observe Yisroel first hand. It was no longer enough to hear other people's reports.

GERSHON ARRANGED to leave his duties as rabbi and judge. He dressed simply so as not to call attention to himself, and set out early in the morning to find his brother-in-law. He had learned that artisans collected around Yisroel before their stalls opened and again at dusk after they were closed. Gershon stood unobtrusively among a growing number of men and women in whose midst he had been told he would find Yisroel.

Instead, Gershon spotted his brother-in-law a short distance from the crowd, kneeling and speaking softly to a lame child. Not far from where Gershon stood was a widow he recognized, wearing a coat his wife Bluma had given her to replace her threadbare one. Gershon looked away in case the woman might feel awkward as the recipient of his wife's charity. But he could not help overhearing what she was saying to several women facing her.

"All I had to offer him when he came last night at sundown was a bowl of thin broth, flavored only with bones bare of meat. "How gratefully, I tell you, did that humble rabbi receive my offering. How meager a reward for the consolation he bestowed so freely…"

"I beg your pardon, dear Hadassah," a second woman interrupted, an accusing edge in her voice, "but at that exact hour, the good rabbi was under *my* roof. It is because of that very visit that I stand here now, no longer hiding my face in shame."

Her voice softened as she continued. "Since my daughter suffered an unspeakable violation, we've been shunned, as you know. Even though she was an unfortunate victim, my daughter has judged herself hopelessly damaged. When the child she bore as a result of her rape was born dead, my daughter decided she was cursed. In Rabbi Yisroel's presence, my

daughter rose from the bed she has not left since her child's stillbirth. With
the good rabbi's blessing, she is unburdening herself of her shame. I'm daring to believe she will return to me and more importantly to herself. I do
not understand how the kind rabbi could have been with you, Hadassah,
and with us at the same hour?"

"Since the change in your daughter can be regarded as a miracle," the
widow Hadassah replied, "maybe we should also accept the miracle that
this man has the power to be in two places at once."

A cobbler who apparently had been listening to the women, called
out to Yisroel, now walking slowly toward the crowd holding the lame
child's hand.

"Hey, miracle worker," the man bellowed, "I dare you to admit or
deny that you can really be in two places at once! If you can, teach me,"
he laughed.

Gershon was relieved that the cobbler's challenge was not a hostile one.

Yisroel looked up for a moment, remaining silent. He appeared as
surprised by the allegation that he had been in two places at once, as were
those awaiting his reply.

Unable to fall asleep that night, Gershon remembered how the townspeople had referred to Yisroel as *Rabbi.* He was sure that Yisroel had never
referred to himself this way. It was the sanction of other rabbis, known
as *s'micha,* that ordained a man a rabbi. Here the people themselves were
conferring their s'micha upon Yisroel. A rabbi must be worthy of respect,
a wise and trusted teacher and spiritual guide. Yisroel, Gershon was
coming to see, was all of these.

EAGER FOR another opportunity to accompany his brother-in-law,
this time Gershon asked Yisroel if he might join him, to which Yisroel
readily assented.

Early the following morning, Gershon donned heavier than usual
boots, knowing that Yisroel had begun making his way to Brody's outskirts

by foot. After Gershon and Yisroel had walked quite a distance, it became clear that his brother-in-law had no particular destination in mind. He had heard from Channa and others who walked with Yisroel that this was often the case until a particular destination became apparent to Yisroel. Then, he would he make his way with clear determination and purpose to the person or place that had revealed itself.

Today Gershon was led to a hut, the home of Blind Enoch, who in his younger, more able days had been a peddler of tin wares. Enoch had not always been blind; he had lost his vision gradually. Once completely blind, the peddler made his way through perpetual darkness with his wares. Citizens joked that although everything else had disappeared, the tin man could always find himself because of the rattling cups attached to his rickety cart. Now an old man, Enoch lived by the charity of others. His neighbors brought him small meals, stews and soups, a fresh challah or bit of wine for Shabbos and whatever else they would spare.

When Yisroel knocked, a hoarse voice bade him enter. After greeting Enoch, Yisroel announced it was time to pray the afternoon service. Enoch said nothing, but a slight furrowing of the old man's forehead, barely distinguishable among the folds of his aged skin, suggested he had heard Yisroel and was uncertain or confused about what was being asked of him. Yisroel drew two small prayer books from within his woolen vest, handing one of the prayer books to Gershon. Then Yisroel, with Gershon following suit, proceeded to pray.

As Gershon had suspected, the simple tin peddler was ignorant of the words and remained silent. Not only this, the man did not even recognize the beginning of Prayer of Eighteen Benedictions and know to stand. Had they been in a synagogue then, at the moment when the curtains of the Holy Ark are pulled aside revealing the Torah, to remain seated would have been a transgression. Gershon looked up and was startled to see tears coming from Enoch's opaque, filmy eyes. But it surprised Gershon more to watch Yisroel draw close and touch his finger to the old man's cheek and tears.

"The longing of your heart is a powerful prayer, Reb Enoch," Yisroel chanted as if still praying. "The tears you offer your Creator are as holy as the words others offer. Your Creator is not blind, but it is not with physical eyes that he beholds you now and has beheld you every moment that you have longed for mercy in your dark hut."

The man wept, his soft whimpering reminding Gershon of a wounded animal.

"Enoch!" Yisroel's commanding voice shocked Gershon, as did the contrast with his preceding tenderness.

"You are *not* a beggar at the table of your compassionate Creator," Yisroel said firmly. "Your poverty, your ignorance of the words of prayer, even your anger when dragging wares that do not find buyers—*none of this* distances the One who created you and your tin pots and ladles..."

Gershon watched a smile begin to form on Enoch's dry, cracked lips.

Yisroel reached for the peddler's hands, taking both of them into his own. "Enoch, grant yourself peace in your final days. You are not alone and abandoned although it may seem so to you. The darkness in which you sit can be illumined by even the slightest flame of love."

The peddler's brow wrinkled though it seemed impossible for there to be any more furrows in his forehead.

"Love?" he repeated hoarsely as if hearing the word for the first time.

"Reb Enoch, now is the time to strike a holy bargain with God," Yisroel said.

Enoch looked even more bewildered.

"Give up your unworthiness as if it were a useless, battered tin cup. Let God purchase it. Payment shall be the only currency God uses: *Love*. Just a mere coin of divine love can fill your heart and your hut with the light you crave."

∾

GRADUALLY, GERSHON BECAME AWARE THAT THE wives of his brethren in the Kloiz were among those seeking

Yisroel's counsel and blessings. These women and others were approaching Yisroel for spiritual counsel, herbs, and amulets to heal themselves and their loved ones of ailments, sorrows, and possession by dybbuks. Channa and Rifka increasingly served as intermediaries so the women might feel more at ease.

There was rising concern among Kloiz members in response to Yisroel's unconventional behavior, which, they argued, could lead to upheaval among the large number of Brody's simple unlettered Jews. The Jews of Brody for the most part had managed to live side by side with each other with minimal disruption. It was feared that Yisroel's actions might contribute to unrest. The Kahal, the Jews' elected governing board that reported to the Polish authorities, had also begun to keep its eye on the stranger in Brody's midst.

When it was discovered that Yisroel had led prayer services in the homes of citizens unable to attend formal prayer services, and that he had counted women as part of the quorum of ten required for the recitation of certain prayers, both the Kloiz and the Kahal censured Yisroel's actions, forbidding such practices. Prayer services were only to be conducted with the proper quorum of *men* and under the roof of a synagogue.

At one time Gershon might have agreed with them. But now he could not concur with arguments that sought to condemn his brother-in-law's spontaneous prayer—prayer that had occurred not only in humble homes, but also in fields and stables.

Despite Yisroel's supplication that his brother-in-law not intervene on his behalf, Gershon could not resist.

"I am not defending Yisroel ben Eliezer merely because he is my brother-in-law," Gershon asserted to a group of Jewish leaders and scholars. "I speak on his behalf because he is being misjudged. Yisroel is not encouraging the violation of our sacred commandments. In actuality, he is restoring the morale of those defeated by the struggles of daily life. If anything, he is inspiring men and women to sacred deeds, deeds that are within their ability to perform. "

A few nodded in accord as Gershon spoke. But the majority rejected what had been designated as Yisroel's dangerous benevolence with regard to ritual observance. Gershon was stunned by the blindness of men he had previously deemed capable of reasonable discernment. Was Mendel furtively planting accusations and painting pictures of Yisroel in their minds so that the man they were condemning was not in fact the man Gershon saw in action?

When Gershon heard the murmured accusation of *heresy*, he was both astonished and frightened.

⌒

G ERSHON WAS SURPRISED AND AMUSED BY HIS NIECE Dalia's proposition.

For three days of the week she would receive the requests of citizens wishing to bring cases to the Rabbinical Court, and she would then present the information to Gershon. On the other three days of the week, she would continue to accompany Bluma, Channa, and Rifka to the new shelter that the Brody Kahal, with the help of funds donated by a miserly widower, had finally constructed for the city's homeless widows. While Dalia deeply enjoyed helping her tanta Rifka educate the widows' daughters, she was also ardent about the prospect of working for her uncle.

Gershon was skeptical about his niece assuming this role, but loving her as he did, he was willing to let her attempt it. He did not tell her, of course, that he expected she would rather quickly resign from these duties not intended for a woman.

Those who Dalia received on her uncle's behalf were disconcerted by the presence of the confident young woman who did not avert her gaze. Many hesitated to return Dalia's direct greeting, and looked over her head or through her, as if she were not there. But Dalia was undeterred. Gershon was captivated by Dalia's undaunted self-assurance. Watching his niece, he realized that his sister Channa and her husband had raised their daughter without the conventions and restrictions within which most girls were confined.

Gershon found he was delighted to be wrong when Dalia did not retreat, despite the affronts of numerous disgruntled claimants.

Dalia's duties expanded as the weeks turned into months. She asked to be present when the Rabbinical Court reviewed cases. Despite the disfavor of his fellow judges, Gershon granted his niece this privilege as long as she agreed to remain discreetly quiet behind a screen at the rear of the room.

Of late, Dalia had begun to come to Gershon's library where he frequently studied legal tractates of Talmud late into the night. Thankfully, centuries of oral law based on Torah had been codified, allowing a judge like Gershon to find a clear basis for his rulings. Dalia was curious and fascinated to hear how her uncle applied Talmudic debates and conclusions to his current cases. She would enter with great eagerness, often after the others in the house were asleep. It amused Gershon to watch her trying to remember *not* to seat herself until she was invited to do so. He always gestured for her to sit, regardless of the hour. Dalia would lower herself quietly into the chair closest to his desk, eagerly waiting for him to pause from his research and look up again, giving her the opportunity to question him about cases that had been considered that day. To appease his niece's appetite, Gershon had recently lent her an old volume of Mishnaic tractates that she could study on her own.

Tonight Dalia entered with such haste—peering down at a heavy volume in her hands—that she did not notice anyone sitting in the chair she usually took in front of her uncle's desk. Gershon laughed into his handkerchief to see his niece inadvertently collide with the tall, dark-haired Spaniard who had stood upon her entry but been pushed back into his seat, the heavy volume and Dalia both close to landing in his lap.

Standing before Gershon, guest and niece looked down, rather than at each other, until both, almost simultaneously, looked up at Gershon, awaiting his instruction. Gershon pointed to a chair against one of the walls, gesturing that the young man bring the chair closer. To Dalia, Gershon motioned that she now sit in her customary chair.

"Dalia," Gershon began as if she had just entered and nothing out of the ordinary had happened. "Although I feel as if I have met the honorable Reb Judah before, it is actually my first meeting with him, just as it is yours. Judah's father and his uncle Sadya visited my father Elijah many years ago. We have corresponded since. Judah is of Sephardic background; his family has resided for generations in Àvila, the province of Spain where the Zohar emerged. Most of Reb Judah's ancestors were killed or expelled during the Spanish inquisitions, but a handful later returned to Spain. Reb Judah, a dedicated student, has come to further his studies in one of Brody's renowned yeshivas."

Dalia, who had been looking intently at her uncle, lowered her glance. Was Gershon imagining the flush of her cheeks or was his intrepid niece, who *never* averted her gaze, doing so now—*and* blushing? It had always been his sister Channa, not he, who sensed things before they were clearly revealed. But in this moment, Gershon felt fairly certain that the olive-skinned, serious Judah was his niece Dalia's basherte, the one destined to share her life.

❧ 25 ❧

Amos had not been the same since his encounter with Yisroel at the inn in Zabie. Almost five years had passed since he had gone to spy on Yisroel at the bidding of his father Mendel. According to his father's tally, at that time, Yisroel had at least two grave flaws. First, the foolish innkeeper was reputed to regard women as equal to men and to treat them as such. Secondly, Yisroel had impregnated Mendel's purportedly barren, discarded first wife Channa. Wanting to learn more about this dangerous fool Yisroel ben Eliezar, Mendel had chosen his "prized firstborn," as he liked to call Amos, to travel to Zabie.

In Zabie, the disarming Yisroel had challenged Amos with a vigor equal to his—but without the arrogance and disdain Amos had displayed. Yisroel's perspectives, initially repelled by Amos, had ultimately become impossible for him to reject, even in the face of his father Mendel's opposing views. Amos never told his father about the seeds that Yisroel had sown in him, which had since taken such root in his life.

Not long after Amos' visit to Zabie, his mother had taken ill. When his father ignored this, Amos insisted on caring for his mother. As she became too ill to care for her daughters, Amos started fending for his sisters, too, whom he only then realized often went hungry. Until then Amos had ignored their plight, adopting his father's indifference and self-centeredness. It horrified Amos to become aware of his father's abuse of them and to face his own compliance with this cruelty. For the first time, Amos began to treat the women under his roof as worthy of respect rather than as his servants.

That his mother and sisters did not exude bitterness but instead retained the capacity to express love to him and towards each other reminded Amos of what Yisroel had tried to tell him. *Because a woman is a vessel for life,* he had said, *she is more capable of surrender. To dominate women is to kill the tenderness seeking to take root within us as men.*

Amos was stunned by his mother's persistent love up to the moment she drew her last breath. He witnessed the difference between humiliation—which men like his father feared at the hands of women—and humility. Genuine humility, he was discovering, was a virtue that could bring a man not only closer to a woman, but to God. Amos often recalled Yisroel speaking of woman's "holy seduction," as a call to the heart—not some vile temptation to be shunned.

Mendel begrudgingly allowed his son to arrange a dignified burial for his mother. Amos grieved her death secretly, not wanting to endure his father's censure on top of his grief. Amos felt more sorrow, but not surprise, when Mendel, arguing that his daughters would be great burdens without their mother to care for them, announced that he would be marrying them off as soon as the prescribed year of mourning had passed. Amos knew it was useless to try to intervene in the expedient betrothals his father was already planning with no regard for his sisters' young ages or desires. If anything, his father felt very proud of the alliances he had been forming with several influential widowers many times his sisters' ages.

His father's cold-heartedness, which had seemed natural and even necessary to Amos before his trip to Zabie, had begun to shame and anger Amos. He kept these feelings to himself, knowing it would do little but provoke his father's rage were he to speak of them.

Since learning about Yisroel's presence in Brody, Amos had maintained his distance. He did so not only because he dreaded his father's condemnation. Even more so, Amos feared that time spent with Yisroel would make it unbearable for him to tolerate his father's self-absorption and his misogyny. In Amos' eyes, Mendel's hypocrisy as a respected leader in the community had become excruciating to witness. But what could Amos possibly do?

Above all, what kept Amos from spending time in Yisroel's company was how costly the ramifications might be for Yisroel. Amos recognized that despite his father's hatred of Yisroel, Mendel was restraining the full force of his destructive power. Whatever Mendel's reasons and strategy were, if Amos became involved with Yisroel, the temptation *or need* to destroy Yisroel might become impossible for his father to resist.

AMOS WAS SURPRISED by his father's uncharacteristic hospitality when an old friend and fellow rabbi passed through Brody from Warsaw. Rabbi Avner and his daughter were invited as rare guests to Mendel's home.

The young woman's beauty and zest immediately disoriented Amos. He also could not help noticing that the lively Zahava seemed to be as indifferent to his father as Mendel to her. It was as if the two were not visible to each other. When Mendel directed his son to take Avner's companion to the women's room, Amos winced with embarrassment. It was not only the disrespectful manner in which his father had referred to his friend's daughter that was offensive, but also where he was sending her to sleep.

The door to the room in which his mother and sisters had lived had not been opened since his last sister had departed months earlier. Amos rushed ahead of the young woman, entering quickly to open the one small window and to gather the bed linens, hoping to find others with which to replace them. Zahava, clearly not one to swallow words as had the women in Amos' family, commented on the stale air.

"I'll sleep with the window open as far as its latch will allow and hope the night's fresh air will replace the air in this sad room. Thank you, Amos, for removing the linens."

Zahava's words about the sad room prompted Amos to tell her that his mother had died in the room and his sisters had suffered her loss deeply. Not waiting for her response, he hurried from the room, embarrassed by his excess.

RABBI AVNER and his daughter stayed for several days. Amos supposed the tie between his father and Avner to be a particularly strong one for this to be tolerated.

Early on the fifth morning, Zahava, defying conventional behavior between an unrelated man and woman, asked Amos if she might accompany him to the synagogue. Amos consented, relieved that his father wasn't present to hear her request and his response.

"I've overheard your father maligning the mysterious Rabbi Yisroel so fiercely that it's made me curious to judge him for myself," Zahava told him as they made their way towards the stately Brody shul. "The infamous rabbi is conducting a prayer service in the tailor's shul. Let's go there now."

Amos was astonished and even somewhat amused that this fearless young woman had learned where Yisroel would be and was now urging him to go there. He didn't refuse her.

At the shul, Amos once again found Yisroel's views intriguing. Undeniably intriguing as well was the presence of the beautiful and independent Zahava.

AT THE SHABBOS MEAL, Avner and Mendel announced to Amos and Zahava that their marriage had been arranged. Until now, Mendel had rejected proposals from the fathers of young women in Brody. Had he intended Amos to marry his friend Avner's daughter all along? The distinguished Rabbi Avner, as well as being a rabbi, was reputedly becoming a very successful textile merchant in Warsaw.

The match must be a prestigious one in his father's eyes, Amos concluded. Mendel had not of course, asked Amos what he thought or desired. But this time, Amos did not mind; he was thrilled with the match. Had Avner consulted with his daughter before making the agreement? Given Zahava's independent temperament, Amos suspected Avner would have asked, and thankfully, judging from Zahava's manner with Amos, she appeared to have given her consent gladly.

Mendel organized a lavish wedding feast in his firstborn son's honor, not even mentioning his daughter-in-law. Zahava's father Rabbi Avner contributed generously to the celebration, in addition to providing an abundant dowry, a matter Amos knew was of no small import to Mendel.

On the day of the ceremony and celebration, as Mendel toasted the couple, Amos could not help but notice the irony. The transformation that had begun in Yisroel's presence had made Amos worthy of such a wife as Zahava. Amos had never forgotten what he had been given to taste in Zabie. Mendel's new daughter-in-law led his son back to the fruit forbidden him by his father. Yisroel had prepared Amos for Zahava, and Zahava had led Amos back to Yisroel.

~

DALIA WOULD NEVER HAVE GUESSED WHEN SHE FIRST met Amos in Zabie, his face red with self-righteous anger, that he would one day call her father his teacher. But her father, given his ways of seeing into the heart, probably could have guessed.

It was easy for Dalia to embrace Zahava as a friend. It wasn't just their age, both of them almost seventeen; Zahava felt like a kindred spirit.

Zahava confided to Dalia that she had not enjoyed even a moment of Mendel's company. But she was certain that the heart of his son Amos was quite different.

She also said that she believed her father Avner was not of the same mind about Yisroel as the bitter Rabbi Mendel. Rabbi Avner had confided to his daughter that he could not harbor disdain against a man he had never even met. Zahava hoped that one day her father Avner would also come to value Dalia's father.

Dalia was relieved to hear this although she could not imagine how this would come to pass, since Avner had also said that out of courtesy to his host he would "not seek out the egregious baal shem." Had Zahava actually told her father that she had sought out Yisroel? And if not, would she tell him before Rabbi Avner returned to Warsaw? Dalia could not help wondering what the composed Rabbi Avner would say were he to learn that his daughter, son-in-law Amos, and a growing number of others had begun to value Yisroel as a revered teacher.

AS DALIA had gotten to know Judah more over the last two years, she discovered that he required immersion in the physical world to go along with his immersion in holy texts. Born into a line of woodworkers, Judah had been trained from a very young age by his grandfather and father and had come from Spain with these skills. It was important to him to maintain this connection to his family and to the pleasures of handling wood, two of many things that Dalia had come to respect about the tall, dark stranger from Avila who spoke Yiddish as if it were a song.

Most compelling of all was Judah's fervent desire to experience the Shechinah. He recognized her father as a guide; early on, Judah had described Yisroel as a "pillar of fire capable of leading men through the wilderness of their ignorance."

"It is not only your father's fire I admire," Judah had told her since, "it is yours as well. You've inherited not only your father's red hair but some of his fire, too. Both are beautiful to me—what I see with my physical eyes and what I behold with my heart."

Dalia and Judah approached her parents for permission to marry. Yisroel and Channa's consents came with unconcealed joy and gratitude.

Dalia sought Tanta Rifka first, then went to Zahava to share the news. Dalia and Judah would marry on Shavuous, the holiday commemorating sacred covenant and commitment, the perfect time to enter into the covenant of marriage.

HER FACE VEILED, Dalia circled Judah seven times, then came to stand on his right side under the wedding canopy. When all the elements

of the ceremony were complete, from the blessings to sanctify the marriage through the breaking of the glass, Dalia met Judah's warmhearted
gaze. How grateful she was for this union.

"Judah, Dalia…"

The two turned as one towards Yisroel.

"Each soul has its own light," he stated, his whole being radiating
love and delight. "When two souls that are destined to be together find
each other, their streams of light flow together and a brighter light is born
of their union. When this happens, as now, there is great rejoicing, not
only on the physical earth but in all realms…"

∽

ELIAS WAS SORRY TO HAVE MISSED DALIA'S MARRIAGE
to Judah, but was glad to be in Brody again. His visits to the family had been more frequent when Yisroel lived in Zabie, but the distance
between Tluste and Brody being so much greater, Elias had only come
twice in two years. But even one visit a year, he told Dalia after congratu-
lating her, was much better than none.

Now, as before, Elias came prepared to scribe amulets as directed by
Yisroel. He also brought with him the amulets he had been assigned to
scribe at home, containing the holiest of God's ineffable names, which
could be written but never pronounced.

On this trip, Elias also brought his wife Naomi.

Dalia, who knew a little of how Elias and Naomi had come to marry,
encouraged Elias and Naomi to share the story with Judah and Zahava
and Amos one afternoon after the six shared a meal together. Naomi
smiled and nodded that Elias begin.

"Some years ago, my parents met with the parents of a young woman."
Elias met Naomi's smile with his. "They arranged our marriage. But feeling unworthy because of my tremor, I declined the betrothal."

"I married someone else," Naomi continued. "Two years later, my
husband divorced me on charges of barrenness. Not long after that, my

grandmother initiated me into the practice of midwifery. I decided not to marry again."

Elias took over. "More years passed. My scribing having become known in Tluste, Naomi approached me for amulets to protect women during their pregnancies and birthing labors. She continued to come. I was deeply moved by her unflinchingly enthusiastic devotion to the families she served."

"The families have served me no less. My vocation as midwife has made it easier to bear my childlessness," Naomi inserted. "Each child I help arrive into this world leaves me feeling blessed, not deprived."

"Encouraged by Yisroel, I finally asked for Naomi's hand. I in my early thirties and Naomi in her late twenties, we were late to marry. But this has made it all the sweeter.

Elias turned to Dalia. "My choice to marry was yet another sacred choice and commitment inspired by your father."

While Elias spent his few days in Brody making amulets in a room offered by Rabbi Gershon, Naomi accompanied Bluma, Channa, Dalia, and Rifka to the shelter for homeless widows.

When Elias left his scribing work one afternoon to accompany Yisroel in the streets of Brody, he was stunned by the contrast of the warmth with which Yisroel was received at one moment and the hostility that greeted him the next. Elias was not surprised, however, by Yisroel's equanimity in the face of each; he showed no noticeable preference for kind regard over rejection.

Elias tried to describe his impression to Naomi on their way back to Tluste. "If Yisroel's encounters could be said to have different flavors—some sweet and others bitter to the point of searing the tongue—I would say that he finds the bitter no less palatable than the sweet."

"Or perhaps," Naomi added, "all tastes sweet to him. What if Yisroel finds nothing to shun in anyone he meets?"

❧ 26 ❧

For a second time, Dovid was surprised by an unexpected visit from Yisroel. He led Yisroel into the dimly lit chamber he had inherited from Rabbi Lazer. There was a dusty chair where an occasional visitor might sit, but Yisroel did not move towards it nor did Dovid indicate that he should. Except for books added to the piles stacked everywhere in the small, cluttered room, the room was much the same as before—and so was Dovid. Dovid had not forgotten Yisroel's last visit, with his words that had gently but clearly reflected how Dovid had made enemies of his body and mind, and had distanced himself from joy. The visit had plucked at the strings of Dovid's heart, but in response Dovid had tightened those strings, still fearful of losing the control he had strived so fervently to gain.

Dovid was not able to discern the expression on Yisroel's face. Was he struck by Dovid's appearance? Dovid was probably a good deal gaunter than when they had last seen each other over a decade earlier. Dovid was thirty-seven now, no longer a young man.

When Yisroel suddenly sneezed, Dovid shook in response—like a sapling in a strong wind, he thought, imagining Yisroel's observation. Such physical frailty was Dovid's goal, making him more vulnerable to the will of his Maker.

As Yisroel stood before him smiling but not saying a word, Dovid felt oddly anxious then startled by the strange and unexpected shift in perspective overtaking him over. He suddenly felt as if he were regarding his body from the unfamiliar vantage point of being deep inside it. He was wearing his body as one might a tattered, baggy overcoat. His arms were two long appendages hanging lifelessly at his side; his skin, a loose wrapping around brittle bones. He perceived the pallor of his skin and recognized the toll his hunger and exhaustion had taken on his organs.

Stunned, Dovid felt as if he were occupying a corpse—*his own*. Terror spread into his bowels.

Yisroel stepped closer and gazed into Dovid's eyes, which now felt to Dovid like portals through which streams of light were entering the shell of his body. This light reached the witness Dovid had become inside his own skin.

"Dovid," Yisroel began softly, "when an instrument's strings are pulled tight enough to snap at the touch of even the most skilled musician, it is impossible to make music. Your body is the instrument of your soul, the instrument the Creator has given into your care so that love's music may be played for you and for others. Your body is not an enemy unless you, who are its animating life force, turn against it. This choice is given along with the gift of the instrument."

Yisroel stepped closer and placed his hand on the crown of Dovid's head. Immediately, Dovid's consciousness expanded from the point deep within his core and filled his entire body. He felt his mouth and eyes soften, his posture become less rigid.

"Welcome home, great Rabbi Dovid of Polnoyye. Welcome home. Your beliefs and unnecessary fears have made the home of your body hostile to your spirit. There is no need to fear your body and its needs; they will not lead you astray. A man who shuns his body becomes a homeless wanderer."

Dovid sank into the chair he had not offered to his guest. He began to feel sensations, as if his body were waking up: a pulsing in his temples and neck, the throb of his heart, heat in his fingertips, and moistness inside his mouth.

Yisroel took Dovid's hands, pulled him to his feet, and embraced him.

"Rabbi Dovid, offer your soul *and* your body in service. When you restrain either, you restrain the power of both."

Yisroel's firm, warm strength wrapped around his frailness felt good. Dovid was grateful that Yisroel did not let go. Despite the urge to pull away, Dovid remained, surrendering to being held by more than physical arms.

That night, Dovid lay awake, but not because he was trying to conquer sleep. His sleep had washed him up on the shore of a new awareness, possibly a different life.

This is the Torah of Yisroel ben Eliezar kept repeating itself in his mind.

Dovid had locked himself out of this world, judging it a distraction from the pursuit of the Highest. Yisroel had invited him to return; he could show Dovid the way back to life. For the first time in years, Dovid smiled broadly, a smile he could feel in his eyes. Yisroel could show him the way to what he had been seeking by denying the world.

Dovid would follow.

∽

ALMOST THREE YEARS HAD PASSED SINCE YISROEL and his family had come to live in Brody. By now, it was not only the majority in the Brody Kloiz, but many others among the rabbinic and scholarly leadership of neighboring villages and cities who had become outraged by the rabbi speaking in the streets with both honey and fire on his tongue. Yisroel was accused of igniting fires and confusing ignorant men and women with his unwarranted praise for the simplest of actions and intentions.

Stories of Yisroel's travesties had earned him the extremes of both disdain and emulation. Tales about the impious rabbi abounded. One popular tale involved Fishke the comb maker. The distraught Fishke had not set foot in a House of Prayer for weeks. He had even stopped praying at home because his wife and mother-in-law had taken ill. The hours that the laborer was not attending to the women, he needed to invest in his work. The man's remorse had been great when he approached Yisroel. Yisroel instructed the forlorn man to *talk to God as he tended the women and to remember God* while he cut teeth for his combs. For now, this would be his daily prayer.

Yisroel's controversial guidance that "God has ears not only for the syllables in a prayer book but also for the unspoken yearning in a man's heart" was deemed by many of Brody's Jews as a pronouncement that threatened the very foundation of Jewish life: the sanctity of prayer.

Gershon had been present during Yisroel's exchanges with Fishke the comb maker, the blind tin peddler Enoch, and countless other Jews and even Gentiles. He was disquieted by the judgment waged against his brother-in-law. Thankfully, despite murmurs of heresy, there had been no formal rabbinic ban of excommunication or any overt violence directed at Yisroel. Were Jewish religious and political authorities exercising restraint because of Yisroel's popularity? Did they fear that charging him officially would win him even more attention? Whatever the reasons, Gershon was relieved and grateful not only for his sister's and her children's sakes, but also for the sake of the countless Jews whose lives were being uplifted by Yisroel.

But Gershon could not help but worry. For although no official sanctions had been taken against Yisroel, there had been increasing instances of venomous scorn directed towards him, and some of these had reached frightening proportions. Charges were borne by men Gershon knew to be close associates of Mendel's, individuals with few scruples whose services in the battle to discredit Yisroel could be purchased. Gershon was finding it increasingly difficult to contain his anger—and fear—in the face of these demeaning threats against his brother-in-law and sister and their children.

Gershon was mystified by Yisroel's apparent indifference to the scorn being aimed at him. Surely his brother-in-law must be aware of the spoken and unspoken opposition, the heated attacks and seething resentment? Gershon knew by now that it was not Yisroel's nature to be scornful in turn. But did Yisroel really not feel *any* justifiable anger in response to the bitter denouncing of his character and questioning of his respect for Jewish tradition? Although he had come to trust Yisroel's integrity regarding the sanctity of the sacred commandments, Gershon was not beyond entertaining doubt about Yisroel's discernment and common sense. Was Yisroel foolish enough to endanger himself and his family? Did he underestimate the power and influence of those demeaning him? But, no matter what Gershon thought, he knew better than to try to direct his "wayward" brother-in-law, who appeared to be heeding guidance that Gershon could neither discern nor fathom.

GERSHON FOUND HIMSELF leaving the Rabbinical Court and his duties there more frequently in order to accompany Yisroel. He wondered if this was to protect his brother-in-law or perhaps, to sanction Yisroel's actions in the eyes of others. Or was he doing it simply for his own sake? The truth was that Gershon felt awe watching Yisroel's simple acknowledgment and kindnesses change the faces and demeanors of those he addressed. He offered boundless appreciation as naturally and generously as rain, and with no apparent desire for anything in return.

It was not just "common folk" that were enamored of Gershon's uncommon brother-in-law. Many scholars and rabbis of stature, although they did not speak out in his favor, recognized Yisroel's integrity and regard for truth. Like Gershon, these men had come to realize that Yisroel was exalting *the essence* of Torah.

Today, Gershon trailed not far behind as Yisroel walked some distance with a rag picker, then wove his way among the vegetable hawkers. As Yisroel was admiring the care with which the onion vender's widow Hadassah had arranged her onions, a white-haired dung peddler toppled the onions. When the remorseful man bent stiffly to retrieve the onions, Yisroel placed his hand on the man's shoulder, motioning that he remain standing. Gershon watched Yisroel bend, then place several of the onions in the old man's stiff hands to return to the widow Hadassah. When the dung peddler prepared to take up the handles of his cart,

Yisroel stood in his path, staring into the man's eyes. While the bustle of the marketplace swirled around the two, Gershon witnessed a timeless encounter; he could almost see the burdens, far heavier than onions, being lifted from the shoulders of the weary old man.

Each time Gershon witnessed such an encounter, he was astounded. Suddenly a man or woman, Jew or Christian, appeared to be freed from under an untold weight.

Yisroel seemed to Gershon to leave a trail of light as he moved among the so-called insignificant men and women of the city. Not only did he look at each tenderly with no trace of condescension, he also remembered their names: *Hadassah, Zemel, Fishke, Yidl, Boaz.* It was as if he had known them all their lives, and they were very, very dear to him.

It was the tailor Zemel who first called Yisroel the *Baal Shem Tov.*

Gershon was standing close by when the simple tailor announced the title enthusiastically to a group of men and women gathered around him. For several weeks, Zemel began, he had been following Yisroel's prescription to Fishke to talk directly to his Maker. Until then, Zemel had never addressed Adonai except in the language of formal prayer, and he had done that quite haltingly.

"God—who I always imagined to be separate from me and *very* far, now feels as close to me as my own breath. You may think me mad," Zemel smiled an almost toothless grin, "I have come to feel that the God *is* my own breath, what gives me life. This baal shem Yisroel is unlike the others who travel from village to village to heal with herbs, potions, and amulets containing the Names of God. I tell you, Yisroel ben Eliezer is different. So I say we give him another name. He is no ordinary master of the name, he is *the Baal Shem Tov,* the *Good* Master of the Name."

"The Master of the *Good* Name," the onion vender Hadassah, called out.

"The Baal Shem Tov," Gershon repeated, nodding.

≈

FOR THE SECOND TIME, Dalia's uncle Gershon invited her father to lead the Day of Atonement prayer service, three years after he had led the closing service of Yom Kippur. This time, Yisroel would guide the congregation through the entire service, starting with the opening prayers at sundown on the first night of the holiday and continuing through the entire next day's services until the concluding prayer service. Determined, her uncle had prevailed over the opposition of a number of his colleagues. He had been both relieved by and suspicious of Rabbi Mendel's noticeable absence from the discussion about Yisroel assuming this responsibility.

From the balcony, Dalia could see the old shepherd Yidl, who had been so distraught by his grandson's outburst three years earlier, standing next to the boy who had blown his whistle with such fervor. The shepherd's grandson Boaz, now twelve years old, had learned to read, with Yisroel's help, and would soon become a bar mitzvah. There were many others tonight who had been in Brody's esteemed synagogue three years earlier when her father had conducted the now infamous closing service.

When her father began to speak of that night three years ago, Dalia was taken by surprise. Yisroel reconstructed the evening with empathy, even with some humor as he described the mounting hunger consuming the impatient congregants. Peering at some of the faces around her, she saw less consternation than she feared and *much* less than three years ago. Then, she had been in the balcony with women she did not know. Now Dalia stood with her aunt Bluma, her mother, and her tanta Rifka.

"Three years ago, a child's purity of heart ushered our prayers through the gate," Yisroel continued. "Until that moment, the prayers uttered here were lingering, unable to lift themselves. Weighed down by doubt, feelings of unworthiness, and judgment about the unworthiness of others, our supplications could not ascend. When the young Boaz, who did not know how to read or how to pray, sounded his whistle, his supplication was whole-hearted. He did not withhold in fear of being unworthy of God's presence. Instead, he fulfilled his yearning to express love and praise with unrestrained zeal. Not even fear of his grandfather's reproach stopped him."

Yisroel looked up and around at the faces turned towards him.

"I speak of prayer lifting itself. In truth, there is no distance between the One we invoke in prayer and those who are invoking. God is not a king sitting on a distant throne, a capricious power *above us* whose love and favors we must earn."

Channa took Dalia's hand. Yisroel continued, a smile spreading across his face that made Dalia smile.

"The gates of prayer are within us. We can enter through these gates and meet God in our hearts as our own love." Even this far from the platform where her father stood, Dalia could see the gleam of compassion in his eyes.

"We can always find our way back to love, no matter how far we've drifted." He spoke as intimately as if he were addressing her beside him on the bank of the river behind the inn. "When we make our way deep into our own hearts, we discover the infinite wellspring of Love within. Pray to find that spring and nourish yourself there."

Were there tears now in her father's eyes? It would not be the first time the spring he described overflowed his heart.

"As you refresh yourself at this inner wellspring, remember: there will always be enough. The more you draw from your inner well, the more abundant will be its flow. Receive and give freely."

IN THE MARKETPLACE, Channa stopped and picked up an unusually large beet. Yisroel had asked if he might accompany her to buy what was needed for a soup she planned to make. Now, he watched her become quite still, both hands cradling the red orb as if somehow rooting her.

"Ahavah, do you miss the life you so cherished in Zabie?" he asked when they continued walking.

She stopped and turned to look at him, serious for an instant before a smile started in her eyes. "I have no regrets, my love. There are seasonings one may add when cooking that can change the taste of the soup entirely. Regret is an ingredient I have chosen to forego, knowing it would sour my soup."

Channa stopped and gave a few *zlotys* to a vendor in exchange for two turnips she placed in the basket Yisroel carried for her. They walked on slowly, side-by-side.

"My time with the widows is nourishing me, Yisroel. I am grateful to be able to support women whose marriages have ended in unexpected loss, especially when for reasons other than death. In death, these women have our traditions to support them. But a woman whose marriage ended because of divorce or her husband's disappearance or abandonment is often blamed for her loss. How unexpected to be able to serve this way in the very city where before I did not know how to find my place. Every aspect of my journey, its shadows and its light, can be brought to bear on my relationship with the widows. I can understand firsthand the confusion and shame and fear of women who have been abandoned or abused. I can allow a woman her anger. And when the woman is ready, I can encourage her to forgive herself."

Except for negotiations with merchants, they continued their shopping in silence. Potatoes secure in the basket along with kidney beans, bulgur, and a kosher chicken, Channa and Yisroel made their way towards Gershon's house and Channa began to speak again.

"Spending time at the shelter with Rifka, Dalia, and Bluma makes all this even more fulfilling. Bluma knows so many of the wives of the more established and well-off citizens of Brody so she is able to ask for donations of money and goods for the shelter. Rifka, with Dalia's help, has begun to educate those women and their daughters who want to learn to read. The widows' sons are able to attend cheyder, but of course, there were no classes or opportunities for the girls to learn. At first, only a few of the widows accepted Rifka's offer to teach them to read. But now, more are coming and they're bringing their daughters, too. Gershon has helped to furnish a small room in the shelter with chalkboards and other materials needed for learning."

Channa smiled, hooking her arm into Yisroel's. "Do not worry about my happiness, dear one. I am cultivating contentment here in Brody and it is bearing fruit for me and others."

"YOUR SISTER was telling me she has been cultivating contentment here in Brody, my brother," Yisroel told Gershon as they walked together in the night air after enjoying Channa's soup. "Her words helped me to see that my contentment is deepening day by day. Right now, I am relishing this refreshing air, the movement of my limbs, and the pleasure of your company."

Gershon looked not only perplexed but troubled by Yisroel's words.

"Yisroel, you are being viewed unjustly by many powerful men in this city and beyond. Maybe you don't care, but *I* cannot feel indifferent to the insults and accusations they hurl. There are rumors that men have met to plot against you. You act as if this weren't happening. I don't understand."

"My dear brother, " Yisroel began slowly, "I *do* see and have heard the accusations that concern you. But such intrigue and drama are not of great interest to me. My focus is the man or woman before me: her anguish; his pain; their beauty—their need and desire to be reminded of who they are."

Gershon said nothing, but his telling glance implored Yisroel to help him grasp what he did not yet understand.

"There are many ways to dispel darkness, my brother. I judge none of them. My way to dispel the darkness has become to focus on the light. It is not merely my choice; it actually has become impossible for me not to see the light. In the darkness of despair, ignorance, hatred, vengeance, and even in violence—I see light."

"It is not news to me that one could find light hidden in darkness. But what of the danger of ignoring the darkness?" Gershon insisted. "When evil is ignored it gains power."

"That is what many believe."

"And you, Yisroel?"

"I believe the human soul is both a brightness more blinding than the sun and a tiny spark that can be swallowed by darkness. My attention to each spark adds to its light. The essence of this attentiveness is love; love feeds and amplifies the light. And love illumines the dark, whether the darkness of circumstances or the despair in a man's own mind. Is it not a comfort to know that darkness can only obscure light for a time but ultimately not extinguish it?"

Gershon stopped, turning to Yisroel. "Has it always been this way for you, Yisroel? Did you never feel threatened by the power of ignorance and evil?"

"No, it was not always this way, Gershon."

"When and how did it change then?"

"A good question, my brother. Are you ready for a long answer?"

Gershon nodded.

"On his deathbed, my father told me I would never be alone, that God was with me. Believing my father, but not able to *see* God, I decided that God must be hiding in the people of Okup, too. And if God was everywhere, then God had to be not only in their generous actions, but in their mockery, too."

"At times, it seemed as if I was just pretending, that I was merely imagining God's Presence. But the pretense allowed me to feel protected and less alone, so I continued it. It was much easier to feel close to God in streams, in trees, in silence, so I spent most of my time wandering in the woods and farmlands. There, I met a wise old healer. Watching her, I became convinced that she was seeing God in the growing plants and in the remedies she created from them. By then, I had already sensed that not everybody could see where God might be hiding. I wanted to stay around the Alta. She became my teacher."

"You must know, though, my brother," Yisroel continued, "that all that time and for years that followed, I also had doubt, despite my wanting to believe in God's presence. Doubt was a sharp, jagged stone in my boot. Was I creating a benevolent presence, not unlike my father, in order to feel comforted? Was the Alta really a madwoman like so many said?

Was I mad, too? After all, many of the townspeople of Okup thought me mad. What caused my doubt to cut deepest was when I saw and felt their suffering."

"From an early age without trying or wanting to, I found myself able to feel the anguish of others: gripping cold, hunger, a burning fever, heart-breaking grief, the terror induced by the Chmielnicki massacres. I couldn't help wondering why God would permit such brutality and human suffering?" He paused. "My doubt tore sharply at what I thought might be my illusion of God."

Yisroel put his hand on Gershon's shoulder.

"My doubt was finally vanquished in a crucible of suffering that almost vanquished me. I felt the torment of human suffering in every cell of my being, as if my body was humanity's body. I was burned from the inside out by a fire defying description. To be annihilated, I thought, would be a blessing. But something within prevented me from begging to be spared, even when it meant losing consciousness and waking to further anguish." Yisroel stopped. He was becoming breathless talking about the time of trial in his cave.

But Gershon's intent look urged him on.

"I faced the human capacity for cruelty and destruction. At the same time, I experienced the inherent desire of life to endure and flourish. Perhaps this is what a soul is: a spark of pure impulse to live and thrive. Nonetheless, we have to choose, again and again. A man can close his eyes and only perceive darkness; a woman can close her heart and only know hatred and terror. Or we can choose to focus on the light and increase it. This choice is at the heart of being human. I made my choice in that crucible."

Yisroel stopped walking. "Gershon, I do perceive darkness, but I no longer can perceive it without seeing the light. To see this light is to remember its Source; this Source is what allows us to see."

Gershon's gaze remained locked with Yisroel's.

"So my brother grew new eyes in his darkness," Gershon said finally. "Perhaps I can find new sight in the darkness that I fear."

27

When the tragic news from Horodenka arrived in Brody, Rifka was the first to hear and was so shocked that she could not speak about it for several hours. She had at least somehow managed to question the messenger enough to piece together what had happened, which she shared now with Channa and Yisroel. There had been a fire—a fire in the cottage that had been Tanta Leya's and where Gedaliah and Samuel now lived with their families. Gedaliah and Zofia had not been home. Samuel and Tanya had been exposed to enough smoke to almost kill them, but they had been spared. She stopped, her throat starting to lock.

"The fire claimed Naftali's life," she whispered.

Even when Channa drew close and the two held each other, Rifka did not cry. She felt stiff in Channa's embrace, numb. Within the shell of her silence, Rifka's thoughts pressed forward frantically.

There was no mention made of the children. Gedaliah and Zofia's oldest son Meir would be fifteen perhps by now. Given his handicap, he would not have escaped a fire with ease. Had he and any of the younger children perished but not been counted? What of Batleya, at least twelve, and her cousins Luba, Samuel, and Tanya's daughter, born—was it two years after Batleya? And what of Zofia and Gedaliah's two little ones, Ber and Reuben. Had they all survived?

Rifka was grateful when Yisroel said they would leave for Horodenka immediately. He would travel with Rifka. They would bring Judah, whose woodworking skills were likely to be needed.

They heard more of the story before the three arrived in Horodenka. When they stopped to refresh themselves and their horses, they met a fur trader who, when he learned of Yisroel and Judah's destination and that the woman with them was related to the cobbler, relayed what he knew as quickly as if his tongue were on fire.

"The cobbler and his wife were not home at the time of the fire, nor were their children. The cobbler's brother, suffering one of his attacks, had dropped a log onto the fire, which caused a burning log to roll from the hearth. As the fallen man's wife ministered to him, the hem of her skirt burst into flame. She managed, batting at her skirt, to extinguish those flames, then made her way to the one tied in his chair."

The trader paused to catch his breath and, perhaps, Rifka thought, because he was reluctant to continue.

"I heard," he continued, "that the valiant woman was rendered unconscious by the smoke. She was dragged from the cottage by neighbors. Her husband was pulled from the house as well. It is a wonder that the two survived and were not, instead, charred beyond recognition."

"And Naftali," Rifka asked, "the man in the chair?"

"His body was also not devoured by flames."

Rifka felt her heart race. Had he survived then? Perhaps the news of his death had really been of his *near* death.

"He was dead by the time the neighbors carried his chair out. The flames climbing the legs of his chair had not reached him. It's believed that his heart stopped in fear. The fur trader lowered his eyes now. "I heard that the cobbler's wife rocked her dead brother in her arms for hours," he added without looking up.

WHEN RIFKA. Yisroel, and Judah arrived in Horodenka, they learned that while their cottage was being restored, Gedaliah, Zofia, Samuel, Tanya, and the children had gone to live with Gedaliah's childhood friend Aleksander and his wife Tova, the son and daughter-in-law of the deceased Reb Wolf, former head of the Kahal. Rifka recalled the stately brick house belonging to the Kahal leader who had once disdained her tanta Leya.

When she finally saw her cousins, their wives, and children, Rifka embraced each one, her words tumbling over themselves in a moving stream of gratitude that they were alive.

It did not take Rifka long to learn that Samuel and Tanya blamed themselves for the tragedy and that Gedaliah seemed lost, not only deprived of his physical home but exiled from himself. Rifka had seen her cousin's despondency before in the face of his helplessness to protect those he loved: his brother from his kick in the head; his mother from her jail cell; his uncle from a failing heart. She wondered if he felt that way now, as if he had failed to protect Naftali and the rest of his family from this tragedy.

In Zofia, whose grief was apparent, Rifka witnessed a deep and wordless surrender. She saw what Yisroel had once described as Zofia's resilience as she now buoyed Gedaliah and the others in the ocean of grief.

After kindling the Shabbos candles, Rifka watched Zofia approach Gedaliah, putting her hand on his cheek. He had been staring vacantly. Startled out of his stupor, Gedaliah looked at his wife.

"Naftali would not wish us to live in mourning," she said, vigorous in her certainty.

She cradled her husband's face in both her hands, summoning him from wherever he'd been wandering, away from himself and the rest of them.

"Reb Gedaliah," she addressed him, uniting gentleness with piercing intention. "Naftali would want us to live in joy."

YISROEL WORKED with Gedaliah and Samuel under Judah's guidance to restore what had been damaged. Rifka, Zofia, Tanya, and even Batleya and Luba contributed, too. Gedaliah's sons, Meir, Reuben, and Ber, in spite of their youth, also found ways to participate in the rebuilding. Rifka witnessed not only the family's roof, walls, and furniture being rebuilt, but also their spirits.

In the midst of all of this, Rifka was grateful for the opportunity to spend time with Batleya and Luba. She accepted readily when one afternoon, despite the mounting cold, the girls invited her to accompany them to a spacious meadow still laced with wildflowers in spite of the change of season.

Running to stay warm, the three landed close to each other on the hardening earth and huddled together. Rifka cupped one hand on the side of Luba's eager face, the other on Batleya's cheek.

"When I was a girl and my cheeks were red from cold like yours are now," she told them, leaning in close, "your grandmother Leya would put her hands on my cheeks and whisper: *The Shechinah is using my hands to warm your sweet face.*" Batya reached a hand to one side of Rifka's face while Luba pressed her hand to Rifka's other cheek.

"Now the Shechinah is using our hands to warm you," Batleya laughed, joined by Rifka and Luba, their breath visible.

"If your *Buba* Leya were here now, girls, she might tell you to close your eyes and imagine this wind as the Shechinah's breath." Without her uttering another word, the girls closed their eyes. "Your grandmother was always reminding me how close God is," Rifka said softly, wrapping her arms around Batya and Luba.

"Your Buba Leya also told me that the Shechinah breathes the first breath into every new child and takes the breath away at the appointed hour." She paused, pulling the girls closer. "We cannot understand why, but it was time for Naftali to draw his last breath."

The girls leaned their heads against Rifka, who rocked them.

Walking back, Rifka began to hum a wordless melody. Like Yisroel, she added syllables to her niggun. *Ya-da, da da da, ya da da...* If the girls were surprised, neither showed it. At first, Rifka sang so softly the wind competed with her. But gradually the wind began to weave itself into Rifka's simple melody, as did her companions' sweet voices.

Strides widening and melody growing stronger, Rifka recalled something else Leya had told her, words she had not recalled until this moment: *One day, you will be a shepherdess, Rifka.* At the time, she knew that Srolik was sometimes referred to as a shepherd. She had wondered what her aunt meant using the word about her.

Right now, for the first time, Rifka did feel like a shepherdess. But not only that; she sensed that one day Batleya and Luba might be shepherdesses with her.

THE TRAGEDY of the fire and Naftali's death threatened to shatter Tanya's new world completely. Her fear of there being no real safety in this world was borne out—and even worse: she could not trust herself to protect life.

Samuel had yet again endured significant injuries to his head when he fell on the stone hearth. Although he was slowly regaining his steadiness walking, the bouts of dizziness persisted. Tanya also noticed the increased weight of discouragement and shame under which he struggled. It did not help when in a moment of despondency, Tanya unwittingly wished that she "could have been the one to die not Naftali." Right after letting the words escape, she regretted their impact on dear Samuel. But it was too late to take them back. Since then, Samuel had encouraged her tenderly to unburden herself of her guilt. Tanya could see that they probably both needed to do this, but she did not know how.

When Rifka approached Tanya with the suggestion that she compose her own heartfelt prayers "like you are writing a letter to Adonai. Tanya was dubious. For one thing, she did not know how to write. Rifka assured her that didn't matter; she could write her prayers in her mind. Tentatively, Tanya began to express her sorrow in private, unspoken prayers.

Slowly, Tanya's silent prayer and the steady love of those around her helped her recover from the shock of what had happened. Hearing Rifka and others say that Tanya had not failed those she loved became a lifeline for her. Perhaps she *could* forgive herself. As day followed day in the wake of the tragedy, Tanya relinquished more of her fear and self-judgment. What if her safety and life itself were not as tenuous as she feared, nor she as fragile? She could not control her world, but what if she could just love it—and touch by touch, let it love her.

AFTER THE SABBATH midday meal, Gedaliah asked Yisroel if they might walk together. They passed a number of small cottages and continued in the direction Gedaliah had taken so many times as a boy to his friend's Patryk's house.

"Yisroel, do you ever question if God is with us?" The query, long dormant in Gedaliah's mind, had been rekindled by the fire. "Why should the innocent suffer?" he pressed. "To tell myself that God's will is mysterious, no longer is satisfactory. I can mouth the words in the prayer book, but they don't ease my grief. Nor do my prayers restore the light to my Zofia's eyes."

He had buried the questions and tried to placate himself with the old words, *God gives and God takes away*, and *who was he to question God's will*? Yet it struck Gedaliah that his mother, in the face of considerable loss, had never placated him in this way.

Yisroel slowed his pace. He started across a wide meadow, stopping when he reached a large boulder, and lowered himself to the ground. He gestured that Gedaliah sit beside him.

No sooner had Gedaliah pressed his back against the solid stone then the sorrow he had worked so hard to hold back was unleashed. He felt choked by grief. He closed his eyes and surrendered to a raging current that dragged him beyond any bearings. When an uncontrollable trembling began deep inside, he did not try to resist it as it spread into his limbs.

The steadying hand on the crown of his head surprised him. He was guided to rest his head in Yisroel's lap, his body now stretched out on the ground. The trembling intensified.

Gedaliah did not know how much time had passed before his grief started to subside. He had the strange thought that he needed to find the pieces of himself that had become lost in a flood. But under the steady weight of Yisroel's warm hand, he did not rise; instead, he let his back soften into the warm earth. His breathing slowed and deepened.

Gedaliah began to feel as if he were floating. He was in a black void, a darkness that had no weight or density and was almost transparent, as if permeated with light. Then suddenly he was not *in* the void—he *was* the void. He was one with this luminous darkness. There was no separate Gedaliah. There was nothing separate, nothing other.

Then, as suddenly as he had merged, Gedaliah felt poured back into his body. The formless void filled his physical body, his legs, torso, and arms then his neck and head. Gedaliah blinked his eyes.

How could he explain what it had been to *see* in that darkness where *seer* and *seen* were one?

He sat up slowly with Yisroel's support.

What had been at the heart of his questions had been answered wordlessly. He was not alone, not separate from the Source of All. *No one was.* If Gedaliah's suffering had led him to this experience, then suffering could indeed be grace. And if death was to return to the Oneness that Gedaliah had experienced, then death was neither curse nor punishment.

On their walk back, he asked, "Yisroel, if before we are born, we know who we truly are, our unity with all that is, why do we forget?"

"So that we can remember," Yisroel answered, "and remind each other."

∼

A FEW DAYS AFTER YISROEL RETURNED FROM HORO-denka, Channa awoke from a dream, Yisroel asleep beside her. Seeing the position of the moon, she guessed that there was yet some time before the midnight hour when Yisroel would rise to study. She wanted to tell him the dream, but would wait. This was not a fleeting dream that would fade quickly.

When Yisroel stirred not too much later and opened his eyes, Channa touched the side of his face and turned his head towards hers.

"They are tears of awe," she told him when he showed concern. "It feels as if I have just fed the Formless One from my very hands." She sat up, her hands trembling as she held them open before her.

Yisroel sat up and faced her, taking her hands in his.

"In the dream, a hooded figure garbed in rags and light appeared at our door, seeking something to eat. I could not discern if it was a man or woman and whether hunched with age, illness, or shame. There was nothing to offer the beggar but the few potatoes being roasted on the hearth. No sooner had I thought this, than the calloused, bony hands reached out to receive my offering. The coarse skin was red, heavily wrinkled, and cracked from cold, laboring, age... all three perhaps? I took the hands in mine and held them. They were almost frozen." Channa squeezed Yisroel's hands. "I did not let go until the warmth of my hands flowed into the old one's, warming each rugged knuckle and stiff finger."

"As the figure raised its head," she continued, "a blinding light flashed. Where I would have beheld a face, I saw a featureless radiance. I let the hands go. The stranger remained with hands open. I hurried to gather the hot potatoes in a thick towel. Without thinking, I dropped them quickly into the open hands. But they did not burn them, and instead held the potatoes as if they were jewels. It was only when I awoke that I realized that the luminous beggar at the door was the Shechinah embodied."

Channa lay down, drawing Yisroel close. She had not expected or needed him to say anything. It was enough to lie with him in the shimmering silence. When Yisroel placed his hand gently on her rounding belly she smiled and covered it with her own. Channa closed her eyes and let go into sleep.

YISROEL WATCHED Channa fall asleep with a smile still on her lips. The first time she became pregnant, Channa, convinced she was barren, proclaimed it a most unexpected blessing, a promise being kept that she did not know had been made. She had lovingly chided Yisroel for not showing more surprise.

"Perhaps you are more accustomed to miracles," she told him, framing his face with kisses. "Then I, too, will learn to be accustomed to miracles." Now, after the birth of Dalia and Elijah, they faced yet another unexpected blessing: late in her childbearing years, Channa, at the age of thirty-five, was again with child.

Channa released a pleasurable moan in her sleep, her face bathed in the full moon's light. Yisroel had been about to rise for his nightly study, but he would remain a few more moments. For now, he would study the Torah of Woman.

He reached his hand to the silk of Channa's hair. God blesses a man with a head of hair, practical like a hat to keep him warm in winter and cool in summer, he thought. But a woman's hair is created for more than warmth and protection. Her hair was yet another place to become lost where touch becomes prayer. Yisroel rose on his elbow. It was not her hair that gave his cherished Channa her beauty, yet her beauty could be found in her hair as if her essence were contained in each strand.

Moonlight spilled even more generously into the room. The endlessly Creative One, who had perfected the moon, had fashioned this exquisite crowning of woman. There was no end to the delights of being human. How blessed they were to be welcoming *two* new souls to new bodies and to life here; Dalia, the first fruit of Channa's womb was with child also. He lay down again beside his Channa, her slumber beckoning him back to sleep.

A frightful dream woke Yisroel.

A menacing shadow had obscured the sun, causing terror and havoc, until the shadow slipped away as mysteriously as it had appeared.

Yisroel rolled to his side, placing his hand lightly over the waxing moon of Channa's body. But he did not fall back asleep.

BRODY FELT more like home now than Horodenka, Rifka realized. But home was not the city of Brody; it was the presence of Channa, Yisroel, Dalia and Elijah. They had become home to her.

It was Dalia who told Rifka, immediately upon her return, that Channa was pregnant. Dalia confessed her concern about her mother bearing a third child at her age.

"Do not worry about her," Rifka replied firmly, speaking to herself, too. "Your mother would not want our worry."

Now, watching the earnest faces of the widows' children she had taken on an outing, Rifka became aware that the presence of children also gave her the feeling of being home. A friendly gem trader had caught the children's attention with a large diamond held in his open palm. The jewel sparkled in the afternoon's bright sunshine. The trader explained that the diamond had once actually been sooty coal deep in the earth's belly. Incredulous, Rifka's charges listened as the man told them that unimaginable heat and pressure had turned the coal into something of immense beauty and value.

"What is most precious often comes from unexpected places," the gem trader said just before they left him. Rifka appreciated the kindness in his remark, which was as much about these children as the diamond.

Walking back to the shelter with the widows' young sons and daughters, Rifka added, "I don't think the coal could have imagined becoming so extraordinary—"

"Like us!" one of the older girls interrupted. To Rifka's delight the child went on to explain enthusiastically to the others, "We are coal becoming jewels, too!"

That night Rifka dreamt she was holding a diamond in her cupped hands. The dream's revelation was clear to Rifka upon awakening. A pure diamond of love had been mined in the dark recesses of her being. The coals of covetous desire had been transformed in the heat of her longing for release from such desire. She wanted nothing more than to be able to offer clear love to Channa. The many facets of her love had finally been unified into one radiant, enduring love for her friend. She would care for this diamond with the vigilance and caution it warranted.

"IS IT TRUE then that his wife Channa is fat with child again?"

Dalia knew she should walk on when she heard her mother's name spoken in the busy street, but shocked by the words, she remained rooted to the spot. The man slandering her mother was either ignoring Dalia or did not see her behind a tall butcher with a bloodied apron.

"Perhaps it's not a child, but a cabbage? Or maybe she's sheltering the carcass of some small, helpless creature?

Dalia felt sickened by the man's talk. She was relieved that her mother was far enough ahead with Tanta Rifka not to hear the insults. The mockery went on, a handful of artisans and others forming an audience around its source, whom she now recognized as Amos' father Mendel. Zahava had pointed him out to her before, always careful to avoid him. Was he drunk? How else could he, a rabbi after all, be so crude?

"Let us make no mistake about the magic powers of this peculiar baal shem," he shouted, evoking derisive laughter from his audience.

"Or maybe, it doesn't take magic," the butcher shouted. "Maybe what it takes is a sly organ." He pumped his hips.

"A versatile man indeed is this baal shem," Dalia heard someone else call out as she hastened away.

RIFKA WAS disturbed to hear Dalia's report, but was also relieved that Dalia had not kept it to herself. Though Rifka was not surprised to hear about antagonism towards Yisroel, the manner in which the degradation had been enacted and the shaming of Channa disturbed her deeply.

A growing number of people of all ages—men and women—had begun to consider themselves disciples of the mysterious and irresistible Baal Shem Tov. Many had begun to refer to Yisroel with affectionate reverence as their *"Rebbe"*—their teacher, their mentor, their guide. Rifka and Yisroel's other students could see clearly that the Rebbe did not elevate himself above them. Nor did he ever degrade his opponents. Despite this, outrage among his opponents flared. They attacked his arrogance, which they saw proof of in his disregard for established authority. They warned of his ruthless mission to empower those not deserving of power. Rifka knew that they had no idea who he really was.

28

C hanna agreed with Yisroel that the time had come to leave Brody. Yisroel needed a place where he could enter deeply into study and practice with those who were becoming his disciples.

Elias and Amos traveled upon Yisroel's request to explore Medzibocz, a city in the north of the Podolia region. Medzibocz, Yisroel told Channa, was a growing center of commerce. Not as large as Brody, still the city was of substantial size and population. Channa, not recalling the city of Medzibocz as one of Yisroel's physical destinations for his trips over the years, wondered if he had visited there in the course of his mystical travel. But she knew that either way, Yisroel would have experienced the essence of the place.

"Elias and Amos have found an abandoned house of prayer much in need of repair, Ahavah," he told her. "A quorum of congregants who remained faithful to the shul's elderly rabbi until he could no longer lead them in prayer left after his death to pray in a larger synagogue. Next to the modest shul—with a small courtyard between them—is another building with three very small rooms, which, Amos has suggested, might serve as our home. These rooms adjoin a large, narrow room with two south-facing windows that allow light to flood in and expand the space. This narrow room could be the communal House of Study."

Channa nodded again as she had throughout his account.

"Elias was informed that the Jews' governing council owns the abandoned buildings. The old shul's destiny is unknown; its fate is to be decided at an upcoming meeting of the Kahal."

Without hesitating, Channa suggested that Yisroel go to Medzibocz.

"I will be safe here," she assured him, placing her hand on her swelling abdomen. "Months remain before our child shall enter the world. Go to this place that may be our new home."

YISROEL TRAVELED to Medzibocz accompanied by Amos, who told his father Mendel he was going there to cultivate useful connections with Zahava's relatives in the promising commercial center.

Yisroel and Amos found the head of the Kahal on his rounds, collecting taxes from Jewish shopkeepers on behalf of the nobleman who owned the city. In response to Yisroel's inquiries, the man, curious, cited a time and place for a later rendezvous.

When they later met, Yisroel asked if he might rent the two buildings.

"The destiny of the old shul has not been determined. But," the Kahal leader added, "I can present you and your proposal to the members of the Kahal." He would gather the members the next evening for a special meeting.

"Tell me your name once more," he inquired of Yisroel.

"Yisroel ben Eliezar."

"Yisroel son of Eliezar," the man repeated, pausing to search his memory but showing no recognition of the name. When Amos cleared his throat, Yisroel smiled without looking at him, sensing Amos's relief.

The next evening, the Kahal members met the man introduced as "the pleasant rabbi inquiring about the old shul." After minimal discussion, the group deemed him a responsible man of his word. They offered a lease to be renegotiated after two years. When the head of the Kahal shook his new tenant's hand, he did not hide his surprise at the firmness of the Yisroel's grip.

ELIAS AND NAOMI had told Yisroel before their return to Tluste that if he chose to create a community of his students in Medzibocz, they wished to be part of it. They wanted to be closer to their Rebbe and trusted they could support themselves in a new city as scribe and midwife.

Yisroel sent word to Tluste confirming the move to Medzibocz. Naomi and Elias could occupy the three rooms adjacent to the shul until Yisroel and his family arrived. Yisroel and Channa would not travel for at least seven weeks following the birth of their child.

Then Zahava and Amos approached Yisroel and Channa with their decision to join the community in Medzibocz as well. Mendel's actions continued to disturb them. Most recently, he had broached the subject of imposing a cherem on the heretic Yisroel ben Eliezer. Advocating for the ban, Rabbi Mendel was making fierce claims against Yisroel's "masquerade of righteousness." Amos and Zahava had continued not to reveal their alliance with Mendel's enemy.

They explained their move to Medzibocz as the opportunity to live closer to Zahava's family. Mendel, believing these family members might one day become advantageous liaisons, had acquiesced as if the two had asked his permission. Yisroel could see that Amos and Zahava wished they did not have to conceal the truth, let alone lie, in order to create their lives apart from Mendel. But they had not sought Yisroel's counsel, just his blessing to be among his disciples.

When he was in Medzibocz the first time, Amos did in fact seek out a distant relative of Zahava's whom she believed resided there. Zahava's mother had spoken of her only once not long before her death. This cousin, advanced in years, said she would be pleased to offer Zahava and Amos shelter in her simple dwelling.

Eager to embark and assured of a home, Amos and Zahava would leave as soon as they could. Together with Elias and Naomi, they would prepare for the others to come.

On his recent visit, Elias had spoken to Yisroel on behalf of his friend Ezekiel who, with his wife Malka and daughter Kaila, also wished to join the community in Medzibocz. His tailoring skills would help him sustain his family in a new city. Ezekiel credited Yisroel with having freed him from "a prison of debilitating fear" where he had been trapped since he had witnessed a terrifying assault on his father. After spending time with Yisroel in Zabie, Ezekiel had for the first time since the attack felt safe in his body and in the world. He had moved his tailoring trade from the shelter of his home to the Tluste marketplace. Now, it was his great wish to serve others who might be trapped by fear so that they, like he, could finally feel the blessing of being alive.

Some, like Ezekiel and Elias and Naomi, asked the Rebbe's blessing to move to Medzibocz; others like Amos and Zahava decided for themselves and then told him of their plans.

The community would grow naturally like the gardens in Zabie. It would need cultivation and tending, with careful attention to the growing conditions. Although his students might imagine him to be the source of the light needed for their growth, in truth, each of them would bring light. The community would be the soil into which their roots could reach deeply and draw nourishment. Each member of the community, even the very youngest, would contribute to the flourishing of the whole. And as plants yield their vital and unique qualities in a garden, so would each man, woman, and child yield gifts to the whole.

Who else would root themselves and become more permanent members would be revealed. Some would just pass through, nourish themselves, and carry away a harvest in their hearts. These gleanings, Yisroel believed, would bless their lives and the lives of countless others who might never come to Medzibocz. And, so it should be. Yisroel was not meant to be the focus or the source; he was a reflection. Gradually his students would come to know themselves as reflections of love and light, no less great than he.

Gershon asked Yisroel if he was leaving Brody in order to get away from Mendel.

"If one has a chance to start a garden in rich loam, in deep, loose soil free of weeds and disease, isn't this preferable to a soil where weeds and disease might take their toll on young and tender plants? It will be easier and more pleasant to build a community in Medzibocz without the ominous clouds of judgment that have gathered on Brody's horizon. Once plants are strong, they can endure adversity. In fact, adversity can strengthen them."

"So, yes, for now, my brother, it makes sense to nurture community elsewhere—and no, escaping men like Mendel is not my primary purpose and never will be."

∽

G ERSHON'S LIFE HAD BEEN CHANGED IN THE TIME since his brother-in-law had come to Brody and had touched the lives of so many of its residents. Since Gershon had known him, Yisroel had never hesitated to follow his inner summons. Even when uncertain of the outcome or how it might offend those who would not understand, he always proceeded. Witnessing this over time, Gershon had allowed a longing to stir in him and awaken, a longing that he had harbored for years. He had not shared it with anyone, not even Bluma. He did not know just what had kept him from admitting his desire—perhaps the thought that his longing was in vain or that his desire was selfish? Gershon yearned to visit—no, not just visit—to *abide* in Jerusalem. And Yisroel's recent words to a widow of little means had spurred Gershon to turn towards his desire. The widow had asked Yisroel if it was Adonai's will that she grant her only son, and primary source of support, her permission to attend a yeshiva.

"Seek your heart's consent," Yisroel had replied, which puzzled the widow as it had Gershon. "To seek your heart's consent, you must enter your heart. You'll find your answer there. Patience and faith are required for this most sacred of pilgrimages: the pilgrimage to the heart."

"Let there be times when you sit quietly with yourself," he had instructed the widow, "whether among women in shul, in your home, or as you walk. In that inner stillness, ask to know what your heart contains. Ask not once, but again and again, with humility and surrender. *Then listen.* You will learn to recognize your heart's prompting, which will not always be in accord with the desires or judgments of those around you. The guidance that you seek from me now you can find in your own heart."

Acknowledging with his compassionate gaze the woman's efforts to grasp what he was saying, Yisroel then added, "If your heart urges you to let your son go, and you consent, then you will not lose the support you fear losing by letting him go. Instead, you will be blessed with the support you need in your daily life."

The widow had tilted her head questioningly.

"And if your heart tells you it is best that he not go but remain home, and you consent to this," Yisroel had continued, "your son will not lack what you wish him to attain in the yeshiva."

Yisroel's words encouraged retreat from the external world, even if only for a few solitary moments, but because of his many responsibilities, Gershon rarely found time to sit alone quietly. This evening, however, after the last judge had left the Rabbinical Court, Gershon went to his study, sat, and closed his eyes. As if tentatively entering a room, he imagined entering the space of his heart. Gershon felt his shoulders drop, reminding him again of the customary way he braced himself against the world, unaware he was doing so. His entire body and even his breath relaxed, as if given the space and time, all of him could dare be less guarded.

Feeling settled in his heart, Gershon then welcomed his desire to abide in the Holy Land, welcomed it to join him as he would a guest to his study. Almost immediately, thoughts invaded, assaulting him with reasons not to go. He struggled to keep the space of his heart clear of their grasping. He had heard Yisroel instruct that the wisdom of the heart had a different quality than the reasoning of the mind; the heart's call was subtler than the mind's insistence. He tried to quiet himself further in the presence of his desire.

Then, as Gershon sat, the seed of his desire blossomed. Gershon felt like a lover finally freed to whole-heartedly admit his love as he embraced his powerful yearning to make his home in the Promised Land.

Several minutes later, eyes open, Gershon was slow to rise from his chair. Could he surrender to an aspiration he had deemed impossible and even wrong for so long? Was this what it was to be in possession of his heart's consent—even without knowing what this surrender would mean?

Gershon approached Yisroel to speak of his wish to abide in the Holy Land.

"I have felt Jerusalem calling to me as if she were a living being," Gershon confided. "Despite the force of this yearning, I've tried to keep my longing hidden—even from myself. It seemed too grand an aspiration. Every year we say *"Next Year in Jerusalem"* at the end of the Passover meal, but every year I told myself that I belonged here in Poland, that this is where I am meant to serve my fellows. Then I followed your guidance to know my own heart more deeply."

"The Shechinah planted this seed in your heart, brother. But our will must be joined to God's Will. This is what it is to give your heart's consent. It is to say yes to destiny. This is not a passive act; it is to become a creator."

Yisroel put his arm on Gershon's shoulder.

"Now, go Rabbi Gershon, and seek your wife's consent."

AFTER BLUMA gladly consented to accompany her husband, Gershon informed the members of the Kloiz and his fellow judges of his intention to make his home in the Holy Land. His decision was greeted with consternation. Several challenged the indiscretion of the rabbi leaving his position in Brody for the uncertainties of a new life. But by far the strongest arguments warned of the dangers associated with life in the Holy Land, dwelling on the tension between Jews from different parts of the world. Gershon was cautioned about the low regard and disdain with which Eastern Europeans were held by the Sephardic majority in Jerusalem.

"Have you considered, Rabbi Gershon, that you might not be allowed entry to Jerusalem?" one member of the Kloiz warned.

It was well known that most of the Jewish settlers in the Holy Land, those who had created its communities, were from Turkey, Spain, North Africa, Greece, Italy, and Egypt—Sephardic Jews such as the family of Dalia's husband, Judah. Gershon had heard about efforts to ban Eastern European settlers—rabbis being no exception—from the Holy City. The differences in traditions, especially the contents of the prayer service, had been contested between the two sectors of Jewry, but never so hotly as when members of both communities were settling in the same land.

Despite the warnings, Gershon remained resolute. He started to relinquish his responsibilities in Brody. As if walking into his own dream, he began to study and investigate the route of his pilgrimage. Gershon would not leave however before greeting his newborn niece or nephew, Channa's third child.

An unexpected and fortuitous invitation came from Judah's Uncle Sadya, who had been visiting in Brody. The well-to-do Turkish merchant would be hiring a coach back to his home to Constantinople, which lay en route to the Holy Land. Sadya invited Gershon and Bluma to join him. Once they arrived in Constantinople, the kind merchant would make arrangements for the couple's travel on to Jerusalem. Gershon was grateful but reluctant. This would require leaving before the birth of Channa's child.

It was Channa who convinced Gershon that Reb Sadya's offer would make the trip considerably easier for him and Bluma. In addition, Gershon could conserve financial resources that would be needed to sustain the couple once they reached their destination.

"You will send blessings to this child from Jerusalem," Channa laughed, embracing him firmly. "Go on, my brother. Accept the invitation the Shechinah has offered through the hospitable Sadya."

Gershon would do as Channa counseled, although he felt it to be a bittersweet resolution.

"One day I shall meet this one in the Promised Land who I am not to greet on Polish soil," he told his sister, holding her hands in his. "And you, Channala, is it not possible that your heart shall lead you there, too?"

Channa's eyes closed slowly as she nodded. "I am certain, my dear brother, that we will reunite, if not in the Promised Land then in the promise of love."

It was not the first time his sister had said something enigmatic. He would not ask her to explain as he usually did; this time he would just accept the mystery.

What grace it had been to be with her these past years since she had come to live in Brody. He would miss her voice, the direct way she looked at him, her serene, sustaining presence. Gershon had suffered her absence when she was in Zabie. It pained him to imagine being distant from her again. When he told her this, she quieted him as only she could do.

"Please, Gershon," she urged. "Go with a glad and unified heart to your destination. I promise to do the same."

TO PRAY WITH his holy brother-in-law would be another blessing Gershon would miss. For the third and last time, Gershon asked Yisroel to lead the New Year prayer services at the large and stately Brody synagogue.

During the service, Yisroel did nothing to shield his sublime joy. Not a word, gesture, or sigh of intense longing was withheld from his communion with the Ayn Sof. Yisroel allowed his ecstasy to be evident.

When it came time to intone the auspicious Sh'ma, the prayer of unity, there was a tremor in Yisroel's voice. Gershon listened to Yisroel sustain the words, "God is One," and felt something burst in his chest. The sensation frightened him. Gershon brought his right hand from where it had covered his eyes to the center of his chest. When Yisroel whispered "Blessed is the Name," Gershon felt a geyser of joy rise up from deep within. The urge to laugh overtook him, but no sound came, just the continual fountain of an unencumbered joy he had never felt before. Was this joy the result of his impending departure to the Holy Land?

He looked at Yisroel wrapped in his prayer shawl, rocking back and forth. No, Gershon knew, this was not a conditional joy. What Gershon had just experienced was the joy that Yisroel described as man and woman's birthright.

"A divine gift with which each of us is born," Yisroel called it, "the pure joy of being alive, the same joy that Adam and Eve knew in their paradise in the Garden of Eden." Gershon remembered vividly what else Yisroel had said because it had shocked him and the others listening. "This joy," Yisroel had dared to assert, "was not lost when Adam and Eve left the garden. Rather it has been buried by the burden of false guilt. Pure joy is a perennial grace we are meant to discover and allow."

Gershon began to laugh aloud and could not stop. Only when he felt a pulling on his sleeve, did the thought arise that he was behaving without decorum, making him smile even more broadly.

"Why are you laughing, Uncle Gershon?" nine-year-old Elijah whispered.

Gershon opened his eyes and squeezed his nephew's hand tightly. He had no single answer. "Because I am so happy you are here," left his lips, and he knew the words were true, even though his joy arose out of a limitless source.

Gershon put his arm around his nephew and pulled him closer. He would miss this earnest child who found it easier to commune with the natural world than with people. He was a bird with nowhere to nest in the city. How much like his mother when she was a girl. Gershon would miss them all.

A FEW DAYS BEFORE Bluma and he were due to leave, Gershon learned that not only had Channa counseled their departure, but that she had also encouraged Dalia and Judah to embark sooner than later for their new home in Medzibocz. Channa's child was not due until Chanukah when winter would be well underway and travel more difficult. Dalia's child was not due as soon. It was better, Channa urged, that Dalia and Judah find a home before the birth of their child. How fortunate that Naomi, Elias' wife, was an experienced midwife who could watch over and assist Dalia.

Reluctant to leave her mother, Dalia had finally consented.

His beloved Dalia was the last one Gershon embraced the day both of them left Brody.

∽

C HANNA SAW HER MOTHER STANDING OVER HER, looking just as she had when Channa, just a girl, had last seen her. Her mother stood between Rifka and Leya, all three peering down at Channa. Had she fallen? She could feel the damp earth beneath her. They regarded her with great compassion, although no one reached to lift her. Her mother leaned forward for a moment but did not touch her.

Was she ill? Was this the reason they were surrounding her? The ground beneath her was so wet; it felt as if she were lying in the bed of a stream. Her nightclothes were saturated under her hips and lower back. If she were to stand, the white linen would be heavy with the weight of the water. But Channa was too weak to stand. She remained prone, sinking deeper into the cradle of sodden earth beneath her.

The figures above her become less solid and turned into translucent, delicate shafts of light. The darkness of descending night came through them. The three women began to sing softly and rock in prayer. Suddenly, Channa glimpsed her father Elijah praying silently behind her mother. Had he been there all along? As Channa listened more closely, she heard not one but several melodies weaving among the women as if each had her own unique melody. Channa's gaze rested on Rifka's face, which showed great pain. She reached her arm up to Rifka. It was time to rise.

Channa woke from her dream.

In her narrow bed, she was indeed wet under her waist and hips, as if something had spilled there. She rolled to face her newborn son, a little over a week old, swaddled in white, asleep. Eyzer, named for Yisroel's father, Eliezar, had been circumcised and given his name two days earlier. Channa slid one arm under him. She pressed her other hand to her abdomen where the cramping pain she had felt in her sleep was mounting. What did she smell now? She reached to the pool under her hips and drew her hand back. It was covered with blood.

Yisroel came quickly in response to her call. Channa removed her blanket to reveal the pool of blood. If he was alarmed, he did not show it. He pressed lightly on her abdomen.

"Ahavah," he said evenly, "the baby's nursing will help your womb return to its normal size and slow the bleeding." Channa nodded, but did not move. Yisroel bared her breast then brushed his finger over Eyzer's cheek to stir his desire to suckle.

The infant did not wake from his angelic sleep. Channa's mind, which had been sluggish, began to rouse. *Was the baby all right? Had he stopped breathing?* She tried to lift her head, but fell back dizzy, feeling a gush between her legs. She wanted to speak but could not find her voice. Channa slid her face close enough to her tiny son to detect his almost imperceptible breath. *Thank God.* Channa let her eyes close.

When she opened her eyes, not knowing if a second or an hour had passed, Yisroel's gaze met hers. He gently kissed her forehead.

"My love, I am going to raise your hips," he said, looking into her eyes intently as if doing that might keep her from drifting away. "It's best now that your hips be higher than your head." Channa felt his strong arms slide under her low back and buttocks. She thought to help him lift her weight, but she had become unable to will her body to do anything.

"Rifka has brought quilts, pillows, and overcoats," he said, "to help me support your hips." Channa felt the cushioning slide under Yisroel's arms. She was glad Rifka was here. Not yet having seen her friend's face, Channa wondered if it had the same anguished expression as in her dream. She watched Yisroel adjust his posture in order to sustain her weight. An unexpected tidal wave of love for Yisroel overcame her and tears brimmed in her eyes.

More gripping contractions seized Channa's abdomen. Warm tears slid from the corners of her eyes. She did not know if she had the strength to endure this storm. Her head, a moment ago too heavy to lift, felt weightless now. She was drifting, trying to resist the disconcerting lightheadedness that was making her lose her bearings. A cool wet cloth touched her lips and Rifka's voice urged her to suck water from it. Channa wanted to open her eyes and acknowledge her friend, but could not.

She felt a sudden surge of bleeding and a cold tremor shot through her body. Would this current of blood carry away her life force? Had the time for her death come? She had imagined that when the Angel of Death came for her, she would be ready. But Channa did not want to leave her newborn son without a mother, nor did she wish to leave her beloved Yisroel, Dalia, Elijah, and dear Rifka. Dalia would be bearing a child soon.

Channa felt another gush of blood and was engulfed by terror. As blood spilled from her, an icy coldness filled her veins. *Shechinah!* Channa screamed without sound. *Shechinah, surround them in love always!* Channa pleaded for the well-being of those she loved.

As suddenly as it had enveloped her, the terror left. In its place, a calm so heavy it felt tangible descended on the room and filled her. She could feel it in her veins. She looked at Eyzer, still asleep. This calm was the peace of eternity, Channa knew. She was being wrapped in it. There was no room for fear anymore.

Channa was aware of more wetness between her legs, but was unable to discern if these were trickles or gushes. The flow of blood had become a distant thing as if it were happening to a body no longer hers.

Channa opened her eyes or had they been open already? She watched Yisroel's arm—hadn't it been under her?—moving towards her so slowly that she sensed the air parting in its path. When she felt his finger pressed to the pulse of her neck, it was not *like* God's touch, it *was* the touch of the Infinite. Yisroel's hand was God's Love having taken the form of his hand. The shimmering rays of dawn entering the room were God's love having become light. Yisroel's tender whisper into her ear was God's whisper in God's ear. The rise and fall of Eyzer's tiny chest was God breathing through God's new body. The air, the walls, ceiling, sounds from the street—all was God's love having taken on form. The mat beneath her, the board supporting the mat, the window, and every element of the world beyond it— made of love. There was nothing else.

How could she not have seen until now? God's Love had become passionate Yisroel, loyal Rifka, and dear Gershon. Each of her children was Love. Channa, daughter of Elijah and Dalia, made of nothing but pure Love.

Channa's blood gushed more heavily now. The strange coolness returned to her veins, but this time she was not frightened. She could feel a thread of cool blue light escape the crown of her head like a strand of smoke from a candle just extinguished. Her life force was leaving. All Channa could feel was bliss. It filled her, the room, and the world.

"Ahavah?" Yisroel softly called her name.

Yes, she wanted to say or had she said it? She could no longer tell what was thought and what spoken.

Channa laughed. The joy surrounding them, the bliss of love, was infinite. Channa began to tremble with laughter. She did not know if anyone could hear the laughter or see her body moving. She would not be here with them much longer. She would never stop marveling. Channa closed her eyes—or were they opening? The light was dazzling.

ON THE SEVENTH NIGHT after her death, Channa came to Yisroel in a dream.

He was standing in a sun-filled field that appeared to have no end. Strong scents of chamomile, lavender, and other fragrant herbs coming on a welcome breeze reminded him of the herb gardens Channa had cultivated in Zabie. But everywhere he looked, the terrain and vegetation were foreign.

Suddenly, he saw Channa walking slowly towards him from a great distance. She was dressed in white and crowned with a garland of fragrant herbs. A breeze moved through her long, unbound hair and carried her fragrance to him. He waited for her, watching his beloved's graceful, unhurried movement towards him, knowing she was spanning a vast amount of time and space.

When she was almost within reach, Yisroel took a step towards her. He lifted his hand to Channa's cheek. She blushed and lowered her gaze then looked up and gazed piercingly into Yisroel's eyes. No words were spoken.

Whispers began to surround Yisroel, the way the fragrances had gently enveloped him. He tried to make sense of the hushed whispers, hearing letters and syllables that didn't seem connected. Then from the swirl of sound a single word emerged clearly: *promise*. He had not seen Channa utter the word but again he heard it unmistakably. *Promise.*

Yisroel felt heat building under his hand where he still touched Channa's cheek. She became more radiant as if illumined from within by a penetrating, immortal fire. He wished he could dissolve his body into hers. He could remember the joy of leaving the confines of an earthly body during the ascent when Channa had feared him dead. She had summoned him back to his body and life. Could he summon her back now?

Channa put up her hand, which he knew was at once her hand and the hand of the Shechinah, emanating an almost blinding light. Standing in the heat and light of her outstretched hand, Yisroel became aware again of the whispers. He heard the word *promise* repeated.

"Have you come to remind me of a promise I've made, Ahavah?" he beseeched.

Channa eyes blazed with intensity. Then, with no warning, his beloved vanished beneath his touch. Her heat and light lingered, as did the fragrance of her crown of blossoms before they were dispersed by his wakefulness.

~

DALIA HAD RETURNED to Brody as soon as she heard the news of her mother's death.

She listened now with tears in her eyes as her abba shared his dream. She wondered what the word *promise* in his dream meant to him, but when he offered no interpretation, she did not ask. There would be time for that. That her mother was dead seemed more of a dream than what her father had just recounted.

From the moment she had received the shocking message in Medzibocz through her travels to Brody, to joining her father and brother for her mother's burial and shiva, none of it seemed as real as the way she expected her mother to enter the room any moment. Were it not for her father, brothers, and the life she carried within, Dalia felt she might be doing little more than staring into space or weeping. Instead she attended to her brothers, one of them only weeks old, and to her dear abba, whose loss she could not fathom. Her mother had been his holy companion.

"Your mother taught me the essence of surrender," her father spoke into their shared silence, "along with so much more than my words can hold."

Clearly her abba had learned well; Dalia could feel his surrender. She felt it most strongly when she watched him with tiny Eyzer. His attentiveness to Eyzer's discomfort and crying, the tender, patient way Yisroel held the helpless newborn, his full presence with the baby—all this mirrored to Dalia how her father was being with his sorrow: attentive, tender, and patient. He surrendered to the needs and demands of the baby, whenever and with whatever force they came, surrendering and tending to his own grief in the same way. How much this taught her!

A light knock on the door, and Kaila entered with Eyzer. Kaila, her husband, and new infant had recently joined her parents, Ezekiel and Malka, in Medzibocz. Hearing about Channa's death, Kaila, who was still suckling her daughter Raisa, had offered to accompany Dalia to Brody, to nurse Eyzer as well. Kaila placed Eyzer in his father's arms and left.

Yisroel confirmed to Dalia that he would be waiting the seven-week period agreed upon with Channa before leaving for Medzibocz. He had not expected to go without her mother, he added quietly.

"I believe, Livovi, " he told her as he cradled sleeping Eyzer, "that there is more than one promise for me to fulfill. I do not know them all. For now, your mother's visit in my dream affirms the promise to go to Medzibocz to tend the growing garden of souls there."

DALIA LAY in the silent darkness of early morning, recalling the conversation between her father and brother the day before. Elijah had asked their father why, since he was able to heal people, he had not saved their mother.

"My love," Yisroel sat, gesturing that Elijah sit next to him. Her abba had wrapped his arms around her brother. "I know how hard it is to be without your mother. We miss her so. But as your mother was dying, I could feel that the time had come for her soul to leave her body. I know this may be hard to understand and accept."

Her abba brought his lips to the top of Elijah's head, speaking into the crown of Elijah's head.

"A soul takes a body to live in and to learn in on this earth. When the soul has learned what it came to learn here, it leaves the body it no longer needs. Does it help you to know that though we cannot see your mother, she is not gone from us?"

Elijah, eyes red and swollen from crying, turned his face up to look at his father who continued. "It is true. The soul does not die even though we no longer see the body it wore." Yisroel looked compassionately at Elijah. "At yet at the same time, she is gone as we knew her—her voice and touch no longer here. And missing her hurts so much, we can fill rivers with our tears."

Her father and brother had then cried in each other's arms, and Dalia had cried with them.

It was at dawn just before the veil of night lifted away that Dalia could feel her mother's presence most strongly.

Dalia placed her hand on the swelling mound that sheltered Channa's first grandchild. A tiny fist or foot greeted her touch. Dalia smiled, recalling a time in one of Zabie's gardens when her mother, pregnant with Elijah, had brought Dalia's hand to feel the baby's movement.

"In this temple," her mother had said, "the soul is forming the body in which it will clothe itself. The Shechinah breathes life into this new body." Dalia had asked if she had once lived in such a temple, too. Channa laughed. Dalia invoked the warmth of that laughter now.

"Dalia, my love, you are living in a temple *right now*—the temple of your own beautiful body. You did not leave the temple behind in here. " Channa patted the mound draped in brown linen. "Your soul has created a breathtaking temple through which it shines here among us." Then Channa guided Dalia to breathe in the beauty of her own self. Dalia did that now. She breathed in her beauty and also the beauty of the soul within her, creating its temple.

Since her mother's soul had left the temple of its body, her presence at times felt boundless—as if Channa's soul was sheltering Dalia as once her body had.

RIFKA WAS ALONE in her small room in the widow's residence.

She could not free herself from the weight of her sorrow. Since Channa's death, the familiar numbness had taken over her body and mind. She walked around almost without sensation. Everything seemed to be enveloped in a thick fog, robbing her moments of color and sound. She lacked the appetite not only for food, but also for study and discourse. She could find no meaning in the words of prayer. The Shechinah felt distant and withdrawn. Or had Rifka herself withdrawn?

She was grateful to help care for Eyzer and to prepare food for Yisroel, Dalia, Elijah, and Kaila. At those times, Rifka felt less numb and became more aware of how tightly despair gripped her.

Despite the losses she had endured in the past, Rifka had managed to find her way back to faith each time. But would she this time? Channa in her last moments had whispered: *Love. There is only love.* But Rifka did not feel this, although she longed to trust a creator whose essence was love. Would it be her life's work to keep faith alive in her heart? Perhaps only then could she fan this flame in others, especially in the hearts and minds of children. Children would not be deceived. Had Leya's faith not been so genuine, it might not have sustained Rifka.

Rifka had heard Yisroel speak often with great compassion about the anguish of those who feel abandoned by God. How great the burden of their hopelessness, he would acknowledge, without the slightest trace of judgment. What if Rifka were to witness her grief and despair with compassion now? It terrified Rifka that what she held most dear could be removed at any time. Could she hold her sorrow and her fear as Yisroel suggested—like one might hold a fearful child?

Rifka dropped onto her bed.

Channa, if she were here, would invite Rifka to enter the fire of her own love, not avoid it. Rifka would try to meet Channa in her heart now—even as she felt her heart breaking.

Suddenly, in the embrace of Channa's love, Rifka realized that it was not and never had been the power of her grief she had resisted. It was the power of her love that she feared.

29

The Rebbe arrived in Medzibocz in the second month of the year 1740. Rifka, who had waited and travelled with Yisroel and his sons, watched the poignant mixture of joy and sorrow with which Yisroel was received.

Yisroel and his sons would occupy one of the three rooms designated as the Rebbe's home. The second room was reserved for private meetings with him, and the third for Kaila, Eyzer's wet-nurse, and her daughter Raisa.

Channa, in her naturally welcoming and unobtrusive way had, at one time or another, made each of them feel at home. Her respect for life had penetrated her actions, words, even her glance. Now, as they made Medzibocz their home, the memory of Channa's strong, steady, and generous presence inspired them.

Many who knew Channa felt her presence especially strongly when they drew near to Yisroel. So closely connected was Yisroel's heart to hers that she seemed to live on in him. Some had worried whether Yisroel would continue to live with the same conviction and stamina without his adored wife. It did not take long for them to realize that, although he clearly missed her, if anything, their Rebbe's conviction had strengthened. Rifka, too, felt Yisroel propelled by his devoted Channa's life force, as if joined with his own.

She invoked Channa's life force to impel her as well.

WHEN THE COMMUNITY began to prepare its House of Study, Rifka knew that Channa would have been pleased with the purpose and camaraderie flourishing among them. Grief's heavy fog lifted, as Rifka worked with the others.

Judah led the rebuilding of a long, sturdy table for the room in which they would meet and study. The table was almost the full length of the narrow room. Around this table students would soon bend over their open leather bound books of Talmud, volumes containing centuries of rabbinic interpretation of the Five Books of Moses. Elias and Ezekiel helped Judah. Yisroel, Amos, and Naomi collected the scattered chairs, sticky with cobwebs, the legs, seats, and backs in need of repair before they would bear the weight of the students. Malka and Zahava washed walls; Dalia, full with child, the windows. Rifka dusted the shelves that would house the holy books. With Kaila's help, Elijah filled then stitched his own mattress with straw. Seeing the youth's satisfaction, Kaila guided him in filling another small mat with goose feathers for his baby brother.

Someone had collected coal for the stove in a corner of the room. Its warmth radiated into a room already warmed by active bodies—and now warmed further by singing. It was, of course, Yisroel who had started— one of those melodies that seemed to come through him rather than from him, as captivating and irresistible a tune as those he had introduced when shepherding the boys of Horodenka long ago. As usual the Rebbe's melody was composed of dancing syllables. It wove through each of them and through the room like a stream of light, knowing just which dark corners needed illumining.

It was always like this in the Rebbe's presence, Rifka thought, listening. He seemed to know just where light was needed, light that might come in words, in melody, in understanding, or even as a challenge. Often it seemed as if Yisroel did not decide or will this. Rather, he was like a prism through which the supreme Light poured and radiated into the world.

The community greeted bright red beet soup, Dalia's specialty, with enthusiasm, and the fresh rye loaves that accompanied it. Then Yisroel invited them to join him in singing the traditional blessings after the meal. The Rebbe surprised them by leading the group in rousing melodic

versions of the psalms and other elements of the grace. When he began
to clap, then bring his fist down on the table and stomp his feet to accompany the thanksgiving, the rest of them could not help but join in. One
did not need to know all the words to sing with abandon. At the conclusion of the prayers, Yisroel returned to one of his nigguns, *"ya da da
da..."* The melody rose and fell, washing over them. Rifka was not the
only one to become breathless from the energetic chanting or to interrupt
her singing with laughter.

Refreshed, they returned to their work.

Late in the afternoon, just before dusk, the group adjourned to their
small shul. The modest prayer house had been prepared by those who had
settled in Medzibocz a month or two earlier. The wooden pews shone.
Against the Eastern wall, the simple, unadorned wooden ark housing the
Torah also had been lovingly oiled. Students had rubbed down the four
walnut posts framing the table where the Torah scroll would be unrolled
and read. A narrow staircase at the back of the shul wound its way up to
a small balcony for women. Would there come a time when they would
need to enlarge the men's and women's prayer spaces and expand the
study room, Rifka wondered, amused at her thought. For now, there was
plenty of room, warmth, and none of the tension that had become so palpable in Brody and in Zabie, their last years there.

The Rebbe and his disciples prayed the evening prayers together.
Women were welcomed to pray with the men on the first floor, an
arrangement Rifka actually thought it best not continue for now, rather
than shock the citizens of Medzibocz by immediately challenging outer
conventions. She had no doubt that women and their daughters would be
given the opportunity to pray without suppressing their voices. But for
now, why argue for their right to sit among the men in the shul and risk
the consternation of their new neighbors?

As Rifka considered talking to Yisroel about this, she realized that
women's right to sit at the long table in the Beis Midrash was another
matter. At least in the House of Prayer there was a place for women, even

if it was a small, crowded balcony. But if women were excluded from the House of Study, as was traditional, they would have *nowhere* to study communally. Thankfully, she trusted their Rebbe to foster a woman's right to study just as he nourished that desire in men of all ages. She just wished she could trust the Jewish citizens of Medzibocz to accept this without bitter opposition.

RIFKA WAS glad to offer Dalia help in the small garden behind her cottage. Full-bellied as she was, it had become quite challenging for Dalia to move between kneeling and standing.

Feeling the generous sun on her neck, Rifka slowly placed the seeds she had been asked to sow. Kaila sat on a small bench, nursing her daughter Raisa in the slight shade of the cherry tree, Eyzer asleep at her feet in a cradle fashioned by Judah. Next to Kaila sat Tanya, who had come to settle in Medzibocz just a few days earlier with Samuel and their daughter Luba, now almost twelve.

"I have made a drink to refresh all of you," Dalia's voice interrupted the silence. Rifka received the tin cup extended to her and drank the cool brew, licking her lips to acknowledge how pleasing it was.

"I am after all the daughter of my father and mother," Dalia said with a smile. "The midwife Naomi, Judah, and I have been foraging in the fields just outside the city. What we don't have room to grow in my small garden, nature has planted and tends within comfortable reach. This brew," she added, winking at Kaila, "contains herbs beneficial to the production of milk."

Then, as if a cloud had shifted, obscuring the sun, Dalia's face changed expression.

"I feel afraid of this impending birth," she blurted out, her face flushing now, "even though I know I shouldn't be. Recently, Naomi instructed me in breathing to assist in the birthing of my child. But still I am afraid." Dalia looked down now as if ashamed of her confession.

Rifka felt a wave of compassion for the mother-to-be, burgeoning with questions and new life, and she gestured that Dalia sit on a large stump Judah had placed at the edge of the small garden.

After sitting down, Dalia continued, "I know that I should trust. I should trust the child within me to reveal its readiness to be born. I should trust my body to go through this process. And, of course, I must trust Adonai."

"It is natural for you to feel fear, Dalia," Tanya interrupted softly. " Your grandmother Sarah and your mother Channa's lives were lost bearing children."

Rifka was stunned by Tanya's directness and by the fact that she herself had not thought of this.

Dalia looked surprised, too, then relieved.

"Maybe this explains my repeating nightmare," she said thoughtfully. "In my dream, I am gripping a thick rope to keep from falling into a dark canyon below me. I am terrified I will not have the strength to keep holding on. Until now, I did not think of this rope as my life."

Seeds clutched in her palm, Rifka straightened to address the young woman she loved like a daughter. "Dalia, when your mother Channa was pregnant with Elijah, I asked her if she felt afraid. She was chewing on a stalk that dangled from her smiling lips, its stem succulent with what she liked to call *the earth's juice*." Rifka looked into Dalia's eyes, filling with tears now. "I asked her why it is that women are ordained to bring forth children in pain. I remember her words vividly."

" 'We have been taught,' your mother began, 'that Eve was a temptress and sinner—that it is because of her sin that women are made to suffer the pangs of birth. What if Eve's desire for knowledge had actually *blessed not cursed* the fruit of her womb for all eternity!' "

"Your mother grew so enthused as she spoke, Dalia, her eyes full of fire: *'What if it is truly a great blessing, not a punishment, that a woman can experience the exquisite pain and the supreme bliss of giving birth? Think about it: a woman is able to know firsthand—with her flesh, bones, breath, and beating heart—what it is to give life! Through bearing children, Eve's daughters know the pure power of creation.'"*

"This was not all that your mother told me," Rifka continued, feeling Channa's presence and conviction filling her as she spoke. "She said it is not a reflection of sin that women scream out in awe of the feelings in our bodies. 'Doesn't the earth when she is gripped by a turbulent storm call out in many voices? Women call out and reach out hands to one another—during the turbulence of birth. This is neither failure nor a lack of faith or courage,' she insisted. 'This is living as one with the Creator who brings forth creation in a totality of being.'"

Rifka scattered the seeds she had been holding into a small furrow, and rose to stand in front of Dalia. She cupped Dalia's lovely upturned face between her palms.

"What man has judged a curse, we women can celebrate. Your mother believed the journey of bringing forth life was the greatest and most mysterious journey of all. Let her wisdom be the boat that carries you now over the sea of your fear and anticipation."

Rifka watched the beautiful young woman's features and body relax.

"I almost forgot! There's something I brought for you." Rifka winked, taking one hand from Dalia's cheek and reaching into her pocket.

"I know that your legs have been aching. Your mother's ached when she carried you. Your father guided us in making a balm to rub into the aching places." Rifka held up a tin of lavender and rosemary balm, and knelt in front of Dalia. "May I?"

Dalia nodded, smiling as she drew her skirt up to her knees, and removed her hose.

"Tanta Rifka, this holy deed you are performing is not mentioned in the Torah."

"Perhaps that is because such forms of worship," Rifka replied as she kneeled, "are sweet commandments whispered only into the hearts of women."

∿

ELIAS WATCHED THE COMMUNITY GROW AS IT GATH-
ered around the Baal Shem Tov. Each new person and each new
family was warmly welcomed and helped to find a home and some form
of employment. Most had trades or skills that Medzibocz, a sizable and
growing city, could use. Elias' cousin Tanya and family had been the
most recent to make this their new home. Samuel had found employment
assisting an old cobbler. Tanya would stitch lace as her mother Gittel had
taught her.

Elias continued to scribe the names of God on small pieces of parchment and on dried lambskin for the amulets used by his Rebbe. But living
closer now, he could also accompany Yisroel regularly as he ministered to
those who summoned him. Some sent physical messengers seeking Yisroel's services as a baal shem. Others called out in pain for relief and were
surprised to find a stranger called the Baal Shem Tov at their door. Just
a few days earlier, Yisroel had awakened Elias and Naomi before dawn
to "cross an arc of longing into the heart of a mother" who was fearful for her feverish infant. And it was not just to people that the Rebbe
responded. This very morning he'd replied to the cry of two abandoned
kid goats whose mother had died birthing them.

"I watch Yisroel obey the moral laws and commandments that govern every Jew, at the same time that he is devoted to the highest of *unwrit-
ten* laws," Elias shared with Naomi at their midday meal.

"Most of those who called upon Yisroel's services as a baal shem
don't recognize his brilliance as a scholar of Torah and Kabbalah," he
continued. "But this seems of no concern to Yisroel. He offers a spoonful
of herbal syrup with the same reverence with which he offers a holy verse
for his students' consideration. To watch the Rebbe remove his overcoat
can yield a lesson as profound as an entire morning of study. He moves
without the urgency that divides most of us: our head leaning into the
future while our bodies, fueled by worry and regret, linger in the past."

∿

NAOMI, AS TAKEN WITH the Rebbe's presence as her husband, was thrilled when she was invited to join them on the dirt road leading to the countryside that surrounded Medzibocz.

In the surrounding villages, she was introduced to those who might benefit from her services, and Elias to those for whom he would make amulets.

Dumbfounded, the two watched Yisroel exorcise a dybbuk, an unwanted spirit, that possessed a new bride. The young woman believed the spirit was preventing her from conceiving. Afterwards, Naomi and Elias witnessed him banish another dybbuk, one that possessed an old woman who felt she was not being allowed to die. Both times, the Baal Shem Tov, with a formidable blend of power and compassion, confronted the alien intruder—learning of its purpose before expelling it. To enlist the help of the one held captive by the dybbuk was also essential. Naomi watched in awe. She listened now with the same awe as Yisroel explained.

"The dybbuk is born out of the fear of its host; it is congealed fear that has assumed a presence. Fear can grow until it possesses the mind and then the body of its host, be that man, woman, or child. Conviction rooted in unconditional love is required to dispel such fear. To approach the dybbuk with fear is to give it more power."

"Even a glimmer of faith, which is what I encouraged in both women today, has great power, " he continued. "The host's desire to be free of fear loosens the dybbuk's roots. The exorcist can then add the power of his or her faith to uproot the rest. Without the genuine willingness and earnest desire of the afflicted to let go, the dybbuk lingers."

Naomi, captivated, had never heard a dybbuk and its exorcism described this way."In a room with one afflicted, I perceive—or sum-mon—the Presence of Love as a luminous pillar of light, "Yisroel said. "I place myself in this pillar of light and pray. I imagine the light expanding to surround the dybbuk's victim and the congealed energy of the dybbuk. Such unconditional and enveloping love strengthens the captive who has unknowingly been clinging to the dybbuk. The dybbuk, freed from a host who has relinquished fear, can then dissolve in the Presence of Love."

Elias and Naomi noticed yet again that the Baal Shem Tov spoke of Love as the healer, not him.

Just as Rabbi Gershon had heard stories from Brody's Jews and Polish citizens about Yisroel appearing in two places at the same time, Naomi began hearing reports about the Baal Shem Tov being seen in different places at the same time in and around Medzibocz. Some accounts were offered with incredulity. Other reports were delivered with unspeakable gratitude, in the form of live chickens or freshly harvested vegetables. Stories proliferated in animated conversations at the well, in the lines that formed at the stall for kosher chicken, and even among children playing kickball.

Just the previous week at the precise time when Jewish women throughout Medzibocz were kindling the Shabbos candles, three citizens—a humble Polish clerk, the town drunk, and a reclusive widow—had each encountered the Rebbe in a different place as the sun set: the widow Zissal had been lighting her candles; Kaspar the clerk had been leaving his small office; and the town drunk, dubbed Schnappsnik, had been hoping as usual that a kind Jew would feed him a Shabbos meal. The synchronicity of the distinctive Rebbe's visits had been revealed to them when the widow and clerk came at the same time to thank Yisroel. Shnappsnik had already approached Elias with shock and confusion: all desire to drink had left him since the Baal Shem Tov had emptied his last glass of vodka. In fact, the former drunk had begun to ask that he be called Simon, his real name, rather than the well-earned epithet of Schnappsnik.

Jews and Christians arriving in Medzibocz from distant places recognized the Baal Shem Tov upon meeting him, supposedly for the first time. He had come to them previously in their fevers, dreams, prayers, and even, they swore, in person.

Along with admiration, there also came angry accusations. How was it possible for a man to be in more than one place at a time? What ludicrous claims these were, they challenged. Did this rabbi think the people of Medzibocz were fools? Naomi was curious to see if Yisroel would reply and, if so, what he would say. He had explained his exorcisms; surely he could explain these ineffable experiences, too.

Late one afternoon, returning from one of their trips to an outlying village, Yisroel replied to Naomi's unspoken question.

"Often when I walk alone on roads like these or find myself in the refuge of the forest, I feel called upon by voices of anguish, loneliness, grief, ardent desire.... Many lament their misfortune; others yearn for health, children, or livelihood. Fewer pray for wisdom, for humility, for endurance. I can hear, not with my ears but with my heart, the summons of men and women passionately seeking relief and support. Some call out in desperation, others in faith or with pure concern for another."

"It is not a simple man with four limbs and a temporary body who goes to them," he continued. "It is the love of the One moving through me. Unobstructed longing summons that Love to them—summons what is truly the Presence of their own inner Love. Some who have prayed fervently for relief, guidance, or even for release into death envision the form of the Baal Shem Tov. Others see no form, but feel joined. What matters is that the Love they sought is embraced."

Naomi was deeply affected by her Rebbe's wonder in the face of his experiences.

A week earlier under the light of a full moon that illumined their path, she and Elias had accompanied their Rebbe to a terrified peasant child cowering in the corner of a small hut. There had been no messenger or other form of summons. Yisroel had ended the morning prayers abruptly and invited Naomi and Elias to join him. Once they had made their way to the child, he cradled the desolate girl, whose parents lay dead meters from her. He held and rocked the child close to his heart until she fell asleep. Then he entreated Naomi to stay with the girl while Elias went to seek the child's relatives.

"How, Rebbe, could you have possibly known that this child needed help?" Naomi marveled.

"I can't explain how this occurs any more than one can *truly* explain the travel of our earth around the sun. There are scientific explanations, but the greater truth is that an unseen Source of Will and Love commands all life-giving movement."

Tears glistening in Yisroel's eyes made his awe palpable.

"That same Love that directs the earth and sun called to us through the heart of the abandoned child and guided us to her by the light of the miraculous moon."

∽

A LETTER ARRIVED FROM CONSTANTINOPLE. GERSHON and Bluma had stayed there longer than anticipated. But given the time that had lapsed since this letter had been sent, Yisroel wondered if Gershon might have arrived in the Holy Land by now. Yisroel had sent word of Channa's death with messengers who were making their way to Jerusalem. He hoped the news would eventually find its way to Gershon; he also wished he could be there to embrace Gershon when the news arrived.

In his letter, Gershon described the plight of the Jews of Constantinople, which he had not expected to find so dire.

> An edict has been issued that endangers every Jew in the city.
> The Jews are to be taxed to such a degree that even the
> wealthiest of the city do not have what is being demanded.
> Were the Jews to relinquish all their assets, to sell all their
> wares, and to borrow from Jews of other nations, they could
> still not render the tax. Homes and businesses are to be seized
> to compensate for what is not paid. Beyond that, Jews will be
> asked to pay with their very lives.
>
> The most powerful and controlling Turks are actively
> convincing their brethren not to regard Jews as fellow citizens,
> but rather as thieves, deserving of punishment. In this way,
> mass murders will be easier to condone.

Gershon explained that he had learned from Judah's uncle Sadya that over time significant wealth had been accrued by prominent Jews in the city and with it some measure of power. This had given rise to jealousy and rivalry in the Turkish royal court. Power-hungry advisors to the Sultan had made it their mission to eliminate the Jews of Constantinople. These men had declared that the Jewish community in its entirety must be destroyed *"so that not a single one of its roots will remain in the soil of the grand Ottoman Empire."* Thankfully, there was some dissension among the Turkish authorities, who recognized the Jews' contributions to the empire, particularly their financial and strategic military prowess.

Yisroel knew that the Ottoman Empire, since his father's time of enslavement there, had become more tolerant of Jews and of other faiths besides Islam. This had benefited the empire. Was the Turks' decline prompting these drastic measures to seize the property and assets of the Empire's Jewish citizens?

Gershon's letter continued:

> *Thank God, not all Turks are blinded by their fear and hatred. There is one man in particular who is risking his life to protest the injustices threatened against his neighbors. This man, Khalil, whose name means friend, is bringing forth teachings from the Koran like great swathes of light. The courageous Khalil has dared to enter the meetings of the highest court. But mostly, he stands in the streets among the common people, inviting them to return to a faith rooted in love. He repeats that the prophet Mohammed holds his heart— and all other hearts—in His Hands, and therefore he, as Mohammed's servant, must hold the Prophet in his heart. With compassion and fervor, he declares that the sacred Koran is meant to fan the flames of love not hatred. I have copied below a translation of a passage from the Holy Koran, verses spoken by Khalil:*

"You will not enter paradise until you have faith;
and you will not complete your faith until you love
one another... No man is a true believer unless he
desires for his brother what he desires for himself...
Better than charity, fasting, and prayer is keeping
peace and good relations between people, as quarrels
and bad feelings destroy mankind."

Several days ago, Khalil called me 'brother' despite being denounced for this by many of his Islamic brothers. His calling me brother has kindled something within me. I asked myself what would Yisroel do if he were here? The next morning, I went into the streets as you might have and as my brother Khalil was doing. I sought my fellow Jews. Of course, at first, I was regarded with suspicion. "A foreigner," they accused. What could I know of their lives and plight? But, just as I have seen you do, Yisroel, I listened to those before me, one by one, and after waiting for the words to come through me, I spoke. Above all, I encouraged the Jews not to give up faith, rather to imagine that they could continue to live and thrive in this city. I urged that they find ways to communicate with their Turkish neighbors, seeking those with whom they have daily commerce and have built some measure of trust.

There were moments when I felt like a fool—what could one man, indeed a foreigner, do in the face of such a threat? Nonetheless, I walked with Khalil as I imagined you might have. I kept going, reminding myself of your words about dispelling the darkness by focusing on the light. You said attention to each soul adds to its light. Together, Khalil and I have sought reasonable Turks we believed would favor peace rather than domination and encouraged them to speak to their rulers as well as to their Jewish neighbors and business associates. Word spread more quickly than I could have imagined about the Turk and Jew, urging peace together in the streets of the city, like brothers. The crowds around us grew.

Both Khalil and I noticed a hooded figure at the edge of the crowd day after day. When the mysterious figure finally drew closer, we were surprised to discover it was a woman, her cloak made of fine wool. She beckoned us follow her. How amazed we were to be led to the Topkapi Palace, the home of the Sultan and the meeting place for the viziers who are plotting the destruction of the Jews. Undaunted, she led us through broad carved doors into a tiled chamber bedecked with richly patterned, thickly woven rugs. After we were seated and all attendants dismissed, the woman finally let her hood fall back, removed her cloak, and began to speak.

She explained that her grandmother Khadija was the daughter of the Sultan Mehmed. On old Khadija's deathbed, she had confided in her granddaughter that as a young woman, she had risked her life for the love of a Jew.

Old Khadija had explained to her granddaughter that she had become intrigued by a learned and respectful councilor to her father Sultan Mehmed. One morning, she went soundlessly to the small room where the man, granted an hour of solitude each morning, prayed. She discovered him wrapped in the prayer shawl of the Jews. Captivated, the young Khadija promised to conceal and protect his identity as a Jew. But over time, she fell in love with the Jew and finally asked if he would marry her, swearing to protect his identity. At the risk of his life, the Sultan's servant confided to her his longing to return home to his wife and to the freedom to worship as a Jew. Khadija, moved by his rare purity and devotion, decided to help him escape his servitude. Knowing that her father would not grant the release of one so valuable, Khadija arranged the Jew's passage on a boat in the dark of the night, so he could return to his people.

Yisroel looked up from the page. When he was a boy, Alta Bina had told him that his father had become a trusted advisor to the Sultan Mehmed and that his escape was a mystery. *Could it be?* Was the Jew for whom the Sultan's daughter had risked her life his own father Eliezar?

Yisroel continued reading.

After confiding this to her granddaughter, Old Khadija asked her granddaughter to promise that if she were ever given the opportunity to help a Jew, or the Jewish people, she would do so. "The time has come," Khadija's granddaughter informed Khalil and me, "to keep my promise to my grandmother." She would speak first to the Sultan Valide, the Sultan's mother, known to wield great power over the Sultan and his advisors. The young woman would implore that the edict be rescinded.

After informing us of her intention, Khadija's granddaughter paused, but made no move to dismiss us. She then confided: "I have been afraid to speak on behalf of the Jews. Being reminded of the Prophet's words from the Holy Koran and witnessing your courage, I can no longer remain silent. May Allah bless my efforts." After that she stood and led us to the wide doors. "I will inform the Sultan Valide that we have met, but the rest of what I have shared must remain just between us."

I have waited to conclude this letter to you, my esteemed brother. The edict has been rescinded! As soon as possible, Bluma and I shall make our way over land to Jerusalem. I am entrusting this letter to Sadya, who has assured me he will guard it carefully. A successful rug trader and an earnest student of Kabbalah, Sadya is also an emissary, bringing funds from the wealthy to those in need in the Holy Land. He has learned how to protect that which must be delivered safely.

I cannot end without sending my warmest wishes to my sister Channa and the new child I have yet to meet. I can only imagine my sister's joy. It will be with great delight that I embrace each of you again..."

> *Your humble servant,*
> *Gershon ben Elijah*

Yisroel sat with the pages in his lap. He was grateful that Gershon had taken the time to write the lengthy letter. Someone who did not know Gershon's nature and seriousness might suspect that he had exaggerated elements in the telling. But Yisroel knew it was all true and no less miraculous for being so. Gershon's narrative revealed how an individual's courage and commitment could change what otherwise seemed destined, even creating a new destiny. Yisroel thought of his father's commitment to live with integrity, even as a slave, a commitment without which Yisroel would not have been born. He thought of Khadija's and Khalil's courage to risk their lives for justice, and of his brother-in-law's willingness to stand in brotherhood with them.

Yisroel folded the pages. Kaila was tending Eyzer. Elijah had gone to visit his sister Dalia and her newborn daughter Freyda. The quiet would continue for a while yet.

Yisroel closed his eyes and invited his mind to rest in his heart. There, he imagined being at Gershon's side, the two holding each other in their shared love and loss of Channa.

❧ 30 ❧

Rabbi Avner arrived in Medzibocz exhausted by his journey from Warsaw. His primary purpose in the city was to see his daughter Zahava and meet his grandson, now at least a year old. Knowing that the city was blossoming as a center of trade, Avner also planned to generate interest in some choice woolens he had imported from England. But first things first.

There being no self-contained Jewish neighborhood in Medzibocz, Avner had a difficult time trying to find the old aunt with whom he thought Zahava and Amos still lived. A Jewish baker finally showed some recognition when Avner said "Zahava, the wife of Amos." The man nodded, pointing.

"Go that way. You are most likely to find them in the small synagogue and study house of the Baal Shem Tov, or if not there, then out making miracles somewhere." The baker's laughter struck Avner as a strange blend of derision and respect, as if the man were not sure what he felt.

Surprised both to hear mention of the Baal Shem Tov, and that his daughter and son-in-law might be found in his company, Avner began walking in the direction indicated. He hadn't seen his daughter since her marriage to Amos in Brody, when he and his daughter had been guests in Rabbi Mendel's home. Avner recalled his friend Mendel's bitter defamations against a "baal shem posing as an example of piety" and his own decision not to seek him out in deference to his friend and host. Was Avner now to encounter the man Mendel had so hotly condemned as an imposter.

Arriving at his destination, Avner stood outside the building, listening to the morning prayers. There were many more voices than he would have expected on a weekday morning. When he stepped inside, he found the small House of Prayer crowded, everyone standing. Lifting himself to the balls of his feet, Avner saw the open ark. There was no raised platform like those found in most synagogues, no one higher than the rest leading the congregants. When everyone sat, Avner found space at the end of a bench. He looked up to see a man who had remained standing, his head and shoulders draped in a large woolen prayer shawl. Was this the notorious baal shem?

Avner watched the impassioned, energetic rocking of the shrouded figure. Was this the "unconscionable wildness" Mendel had denounced? Just as Avner had this thought, the man threw his head back, looked upwards, and cried out "Adonai!" with such intensity that his cry seemed as if it could summon the Unseen to appear before them instantly. "Adonai!" he called again. Avner's heart raced. When before had he witnessed ardor like this? The man, whose tallis had fallen back from his head, now turned to face the congregation.

Even as tears clouded Avner's eyes, he did not remove his gaze. This was the innkeeper in whose home Avner had long ago cried out, fearing the flames of an uncontrollable fire.

After the building emptied, the Baal Shem Tov walked towards Avner. He shook Avner's trembling hand, but instead of releasing it, held it in his grasp, staring into Avner's eyes.

Mendel was mistaken. This man was not an imposter. He was an illuminated and rare messenger of the truth. After several stunned moments, Avner found his voice.

"As you asked of me twenty years ago, Yisroel, I have harbored the secret of what I witnessed in Zabie. Since then I have been waiting for the day I might behold that sacred fire again."

～

DALIA LED Rabbi Avner to his daughter Zahava. They walked slowly to keep pace with two-year-old Freyda holding her mother's finger. Dalia was delighted to witness Zahava's joy upon reuniting with her father, and to watch her give Avner his grandson. Leaving them, Dalia and Freyda made their way to the field where they hoped to meet Elijah and Eyzer.

As they walked, a shy youth, a year or so past bar mitzvah, paused to inquire where he might find the Baal Shem Tov. Moved by his enthusiasm, Dalia told the young man who seemed vaguely familiar that his search was over.

Only later did Dalia realize the youth was Boaz, the boy in the Brody synagogue who had not been able to control his passionate desire to pray and had used his whistle to call to God. The boy, who could not be restrained even when his grandfather tried to stay his hand, was not dressed as a shepherd now, which is perhaps why Dalia hadn't recognized him. In Brody, Yisroel had taught Boaz to read and prepared him to become a bar mitzvah. Now Boaz had come in search of his Rebbe and found him.

AMOS BROUGHT his father-in-law Rabbi Avner and Boaz to "the Rebbe's table," as the table in the long narrow Beis Midrash was affectionately called. Here the community gathered to mediate, to study alone and, at least each Sabbath, to share a meal together followed by a rousing grace. The House of Study was open day and night, Amos told Avner and Boaz. Enough chairs had been collected so that twenty could sit at the long table, surrounded by volumes of holy texts including books of Kabbalah. No book remained on the shelves long enough to become dusty.

Amos saw his father-in-law's surprise upon hearing that women were welcome to the Rebbe's table—surprise replaced rather quickly by curiosity, as if this fact were more interesting than threatening. How Amos wished that his father Mendel could be more tolerant and see the Baal Shem Tov clearly, too. But maybe even then, Mendel would oppose him. The Rebbe taught that each being was unconditionally worthy; Mendel believed one's worthiness had to be earned, and that some people—especially women—were inherently unworthy.

Amos explained to Avner and Boaz that it was common for travelers to join the students gathered around the Baal Shem Tov, especially on the Sabbath. Recently, more travelling preachers had come to gather new stories at the Rebbe's table or to hear the same ones with new understanding. These wandering preachers left Medzibocz with parables they would later offer at their village pulpits. But most itinerant preachers kept a "safe distance" from Yisroel. Red in the face, these men stood on wooden boxes and warned about the dangers of idolizing a man.

Amos did not tell Boaz, nor had he told anyone, that just a week earlier a preacher had hurled a rock, not hitting but shocking Amos, which perhaps had been the man's intent. The aggression, he hoped, had only risen from one individual's momentary resentment and would not repeat itself. But Amos could not deny that in Brody an incendiary hostility had become widespread. Would a similar climate of misunderstanding overtake Medzibocz?

"IF HE IS such a great healer then tell me—why did his wife die giving birth?"

The question was followed by raucous laughter.

Samuel looked up to see who had asked the question, returning the book he had been holding to the bookseller's stall.

"You didn't know?" It was a sooty, inebriated coal merchant who spoke. "You didn't know that Rabbi *Big Healer* let his own wife die? My wife told me—God knows how she found out, but women have their ways."

Samuel looked at Elias and Ezekiel, whose faces reflected that they had heard the man, too.

"If he's such a *good* master of the name, why couldn't he save her?" challenged a second man, as intoxicated as his friend. "Maybe he didn't think she was worth saving?" he belched loudly, precipitating more laughter. The third, a younger man, did not laugh, but rather shifted his weight uncomfortably under the merchant's black-handed grip.

"I have a theory, gentlemen," the coal man slurred. "Maybe the good woman died because God's name was misspelled with crooked letters in the amulet under her pillow. The strange rabbi's poor scribe, have you seen him? His hand shakes so much, it's a wonder he can hold a quill at all. Imagine the name of God penned by *his* unsteady hand! A drunk could write better."

"Speaking of drunk," his companion interjected, "I don't think I can stand here much longer without pissing. The incompetent baal shem is nothing to be proud of, but the whiskey here in Medzibocz, well, about that there's nothing to complain!"

Samuel, Elias, and Ezekiel walked on in silence. After several minutes, the somber young man who had been with the other two overtook them, breathless. "Kind sirs, I believe you are students of the man my uncle was defaming?

Ezekiel nodded as they kept walking.

"I apologize for the behavior of my uncle and his companion. They've spent too much time in the tavern, which, of course," the red-faced youth added, "doesn't excuse them. Please may I walk with you?"

They continued on, the eager stranger in their midst.

"I've heard many stories about this rabbi of yours. Even when they aren't drunk, people make disparaging remarks about him."

Samuel began to feel impatient. Is this what he'd sought them out to say?

"Can your rabbi, in fact, make miracles?" Before any of them could say anything, the young man's questions barreled forth. "I am newly married and my wife, sickly all her life, has given birth twice to a dead child. She almost died with the second one. I know people come to your rabbi asking for miracles and that miracles have in turn occurred. Tell me please. *Please* tell me," he insisted, "can your rabbi's blessing grant children and protect a woman giving birth? Despite what my uncle and his friend claim, I believe in the rabbi's powers. At least, I *want* to believe in them. Please," he begged, "tell me about your rabbi's powers."

"Reb...? Elias waited for the young man's name.

"Daniel."

"It's true, Reb Daniel," Elias began, "that many have come to the Baal Shem Tov asking to be blessed with children. It's also true that some have then borne children and others have not. Our Rebbe does not claim to have magical powers or to divine the future. Nor does he control the destiny of other souls. We have heard him say that our love and our faith create the 'miracles,' and that love and faith protect us. Our faith and love also bring the strength to endure whatever comes—or does not come."

Elias smiled. "I am the one your uncle accused of misspelling God's name, the crooked scribe. I hid myself and gave up on scribing, which I so loved. I discarded my gift because it came in a package I found faulty. *Now*, even if Yisroel could remove the tremors in my hand, I don't know that I would want that."

Daniel looked at Elias with curious surprise.

"Now," Elias continued, "I am reminded daily that perfection is not in the precise proportions of my letters but in the loving intent with which I fashion the letters. As I tremble through writing God's names, I'm also reminded of something else: a perfect world isn't one without illness, trial, and loss; it's one in which we love despite these and because of them."

The men walked on until Ezekiel stopped and turned to young Daniel. "I, too, can share with you a story about the Rebbe's power to awaken healing.

"Please..." Daniel invited.

"After witnessing my father's murder as a young boy," Ezekiel began, "I felt terrified just to leave my house. I also lived with paralyzing shame. Years later, Yisroel led me into the heart of my fear. I allowed my grief and forgave myself for failing to save my father or truly comfort my mother. This has freed me to live a different life. But, thankfully, the Rebbe did not erase my memory of the past and of my fear. My humiliation was transformed into humility. Humiliation separated me from others; humility has brought me closer."

Samuel was struck by the openness of the stranger who had joined them and whose longing had, somehow, inspired Elias and Ezekiel to open their hearts to him. The young man listened as if at a tavern drinking his fill, glass after glass. Samuel put his hand on Daniel's shoulder.

"Our Rebbe doesn't decide what a soul needs; the souls he serves direct his course. Although he reminds us that the soul is eternal and does not suffer pain or death, this does not lessen his compassion for human pain and suffering. Nor does he ever say it is wrong to desire health or to wish to be spared tragedy, as you do now. Reb Daniel, you are welcome to accompany us to the Rebbe. There you may offer your prayers for the well-being of your wife, as well as your longing for sons and daughters. We can assure you that your *deepest* prayers—those not only grasped by your mind and uttered by your lips, but those known by your soul—will be met with grace."

༄

JUDAH'S UNCLE SADYA FROM CONSTANTINOPLE ARRIVED in Medzibocz unexpectedly. Asking if he might attend one of the Baal Shem Tov's study sessions, he was warmly welcomed. Yisroel saw immediately that the man was distracted by thoughts that weighed on him. When the session was over, Yisroel invited Sadya to share a meal and then to retreat with him into his private chamber.

Once in Yisroel's small room, the gentleman pulled out an ivory pipe and brocade sash from where they had been tucked under his own wide sash. No sooner did Reb Sadya offer his gifts to Yisroel than his concern poured forth.

"Some years ago, I had the good fortune to host your brother-in-law Gershon in my home in Constantinople on his journey to the Holy Land. During that visit, Rabbi Gershon said he would never have gone out among the people of Constantinople partnered with Khalil were it not for you. I asked him why and have never forgotten his answer." Sadya's gaze was riveted on Yisroel.

"The good rabbi described you moving among the souls of Brody one at a time offering pure water to the thirsty. He said you revealed the deep, inexhaustible well within each person, instructing each one to drink regularly from this Wellspring. Listening to Rabbi Gershon, I knew one day I would make a pilgrimage to meet you."

"So," Yisroel smiled, "you have come all this distance for me to tell you to drink from the well within you?"

"Yes and no, Rabbi. I have come also to draw from the well of *your* wisdom. There are questions that we Jewish leaders in Constantinople and other Turkish cities are struggling to answer. I believed it worth my time to digress from my usual trade route to meet you."

"I am glad that you have come, Reb Sadya, even at the risk of my telling you and your fellow Jews to find the answers you seek from me within yourselves."

Yisroel extended his right hand, palm up. Having already delivered his gifts, Sadya looked puzzled.

"Give me the questions, Reb Sadya, that you carry like a camel with a heavy load."

Appearing relieved, Sadya leaned forward and began to speak.

"Good rabbi, my questions pertain to the rise of the destructive Sabbatean movement. As you know, the heart of Shabtai Tzvi's movement in the 1660s was in the Ottoman Empire, particularly in the cities of Smyrna and Salonika. After Tzvi's betrayal and death, the blaze of Sabbateanism became a smoldering fire, but one that was never completely extinguished. It appears that a dangerous leader has emerged from these embers. This man, Jacob Frank, claims to be the reincarnation of Shabtai Tzvi. I had heard rumors of his activities from a few traders with whom I do business who have come to admire the young leader greatly. They say that he represents a break with the chains of tradition, and offers the promise of redemption."

Sadya's face became somber.

"This leader, Jacob Frank, is gathering a growing following in Smyrna and Salonika, the centers most active during Shabtai Tzvi's life," he continued. "Not long ago, he visited Constantinople to collect more "believers," as he calls them. I was present when he rallied support from the pulpit of a local synagogue. A young man in his twenties with dark penetrating eyes and a shrill, piercing voice, Frank is strangely compelling. He is fluent in several languages, though he claims with pride to be an ignoramus who disdains the value of Talmudic study."

"I've come for guidance, but also to warn you about this ominous leader," Sadya pressed on, clearly troubled. "Jacob Frank was born in a small town in Podolia, your region of Poland. His father Otto, a dealer in precious stones, and once an observant Jew, has long been suspected of having Sabbatean leanings and being part of an underground movement here in Podolia."

Yisroel, suddenly struck by a memory, put up his hand to interrupt his guest's narrative. *A dealer in precious gems. Otto.* This must be one of the two drunken men who had appeared at the inn in Zabie years ago. Otto and his companion had offered gems in exchange for the use of the inn for a gathering of their comrades. Channa had suspected the men of being Sabbateans.

Yisroel nodded and Judah's uncle went on.

"Jacob Frank's involvement with his father's business led him into the Balkans and eventually into contact with Sabbatean cells in Smyrna and Salonika. There, he studied the Zohar and subsequently made a name for himself as possessing special powers and inspiration drawn from this sacred Kabbalistic text. A growing number of followers are proclaiming Jacob Frank to be a prophet. He has recently left his trade to pursue his destiny as the Savior."

"Frank traveled to the grave of Nathan of Gaza, the self-designated prophet, who pronounced Shabtai Tzvi as the Messiah. Jacob Frank, after his visit to Nathan's grave, declared that he was the reincarnation of the 'Holy Redeemer.' He claims to have been sent to finish Shabtai's work of bringing a new age of freedom, the end of time as we know it. He argues that complete chaos, disregard of tradition, and immorality are required in order to destroy this world and give birth to another."

"What impelled me to finally come to you, Rabbi Yisroel, is what Jacob Frank declared in Constantinople. '*Salonika is an empty house*,' he told an astonishingly large crowd. '*The future of Sabbateanism lies in Podolia. It is my intention to cross the Dniester River and arouse there an army of believers.*' "

Sadya's head sank between his raised shoulders, like someone who had recently been struck, and fears being struck again.

Yisroel could understand why the news would disturb this man so deeply. In the name of mystical teachings, the codes of Jewish law and moral behavior as well as Polish civil laws were being ridiculed as being the temporary and confining laws of men. All laws on the earthly realm were not only to be questioned, but subverted. Women, children, and even animals had been abused in the name of creating a new order on the bones of this corrupt and incurable world.

The dismayed Sadya had more to say.

"Many of us are deeply troubled by the manner in which the sacred Zohar, the Book of Splendor, is being perverted by the Sabbatean followers of Jacob Frank. In the name of Ha'Ari, the great Kabbalist Rabbi Luria of Safed, the Sabbateans teach that our smallest actions can bring on the messianic age of freedom from suffering. But the actions Jacob Frank recommends debase; they do not elevate men. Among the many examples of Jacob Frank's perversions of sacred teachings is his explanations of Ha'Ari's teaching about the coupling of a man and woman. Union through the conjugal act, Ha'Ari taught, can bring about unification on higher realms and heal brokenness. The Frankists are using Ha'Ari's teachings to justify orgies. They employ Kabbalistic meditative practices and large amounts of whiskey. Then 'drunk on the Zohar,' they subjugate their wives and their own daughters in the name of sacred unification."

"Such practices are a mockery of Kabbalah," Judah's earnest uncle contested, rising to his feet. "Many distinguished rabbis and scholars, devoted Kabbalists among them, argue that it would be best if the Zohar were even more carefully restricted, and, with it, *all other Kabbalistic texts*. They urge keeping this sacred wisdom obscure. The only exception to this would be an elite group, such as the Brody Kloiz, who would be capable of discerning the Kabbalah's true intent and then use its practices for the benefit of humanity. Would it not be better that the Zohar remain a secret text?"

"Reb Sadya," Yisroel began, "one cannot keep knowledge hidden for fear of its misuse."

"But Rabbi," the protest came quickly, "what of the danger of corrupting ancient mystical teachings? The embers of the Sabbatean movement are becoming raging fires tended by men and women with undeterred conviction. These fires are spreading. It fills me with dread that the Holy Zohar may become tinder in this hazardous fire."

"Fear, my dear Reb Sadya, is tinder for the very fires you wish to put out."

The man looked questioningly at Yisroel.

"Your fear is natural. But I urge you, Reb Sadya, to strengthen your faith rather than your fear."

"I hear your words, Rabbi Yisroel. But what does this mean, practically? What are we to *do* in the face of the dangerous beliefs and actions Jacob Frank is promulgating?"

"How we should respond to depravity is a most serious question," Yisroel replied. "Surely, you recall the Ban of Lemberg against the Sabbateans, issued by a council of leading rabbis, more than twenty years ago?"

Sadya nodded.

"That ban just drove the movement deeper underground," Yisroel continued. "It was not effective in stamping out the Sabbatean infection— far from it. I agree with you, Sadya, that a disease with such crippling consequences cannot be ignored. I also believe, however, that the healthier we become, the less likely such contamination will be able to overtake us. I am not counseling passivity or indifference. I am counseling you to stand rooted in the truth you wish to protect, rather than bent over by fear. I urge you to strengthen your faith while remaining vigilant."

"How, Rabbi Yisroel?"

"Instead of focusing on the Frankists' misuse of power, employ your vigilance to go deeply into yourself to find *your* true power. Drinking from the Book of Splendor, The Holy Zohar, and other springs of wisdom will fortify your inner power. Rather than hiding the Zohar out of fear that its radiance will be darkened, invite its radiance into your heart and your actions. Instead of fighting the false, insidious interpretations of the Sabbateans, embody the sacred attributes revealed in the Zohar: understanding, wisdom, love, power, splendor, compassion, beauty, and endurance. The essence of Kabbalah is to receive the flow of light into our world. We can ask ourselves each moment what it means to be a vessel of this light?"

Yisroel paused, seeing the relief on Sadya's face and in his body.

"I know you know this, my friend."

"I needed to be reminded," Sadya replied. "Fear has taken me captive, and I was preparing to take the Zohar captive."

"Reb Sadya, look to your own heart. The most formidable force against Jacob Frank's delusion and abuses will be blazing clarity."

Rabbi Avner held the Torah scroll high. Rifka rose to her feet next to Naomi in the small women's balcony of the Medzibocz shul, and joined the singing. Rabbi Avner had just read the portion of the week. He lowered the scroll to the table where Amos would help wrap, garb and crown the Torah. Rifka and Naomi sat, as did the men in the congregation below.

Being childless, Rifka and Naomi were often the only women in the balcony on a weekday morning, like this one. Frequently, Naomi was not there either, but somewhere attending a birth, caring for a mother and her newborn, or resting after a long vigil at a woman's side.

Rifka looked at the men below, most of whom had come on their way to or from varied labors. Elias held his prayer book, fingers stained with ink. Boaz, who was apprenticing with a coppersmith, held his in blistered hands. Even from the balcony, Rifka could see the sawdust collected in Judah's hair and on the shoulders of his dark coat. The ritual slaughterer, a stocky man stripped of his bloodstained apron, prayed next to the milkman whose yoke and pails she had seen on her way into the House of Prayer. There were more men coming now, men she didn't recognize, or only vaguely.

Of late, there was barely enough room at the Sabbath morning service to accommodate all those coming to pray, even in in the women's section. For some time, there had been talk of expanding the shul. Then just last week, a large sum had arrived from Constantinople, donated by Judah's Uncle Sadya. Judah would lead the building project to make the shul larger.

Rifka watched Amos carefully belt the scroll and pull over it the velvet cover Tanya had made. He then positioned the breastplate over the cover and slipped the Torah's crowns over the scroll's dowels. To Rifka's surprise, Yisroel opened his arms to the scroll instead of allowing the Torah to be returned to Her place in the Holy Ark. Amos handed the Torah to Yisroel. Upon receiving Her, he drew the scroll close his chest.

The Rebbe began to sway with the Torah wrapped in his arms, then to turn in circles with Her. Like a man drunk, he danced to music only he could hear, holding the sacred scroll close. He began to spin faster.

Everyone, including Rifka and Naomi, got to their feet. No one spoke or sang blessings. Only the Rebbe's steps could be heard as he danced in silent ecstasy. He lifted the Torah above his head, his large hands clasping Her body then spun with Her held high before him. Even from the balcony, Rifka could see Yisroel's eyes gleaming. Watching, Rifka wished for just a taste of the ecstasy that overtook him there below.

Yisroel looked up at the Torah with a pure delight that suddenly seemed deeply familiar to Rifka. This was how she had seen him dance with his children in the gardens and meadows of Zabie and on the riverbank by the inn. When Dalia and Elijah were young, he would raise them up high over his head. His large, sure hands wrapped around their waists, he would spin with them—eyes laughing. Yisroel's joy had been contagious. Before long, Channa and Rifka would be laughing with him, taking hands, dancing and singing with abandon.

Rifka watched as something similar began to happen now. First Boaz, then Amos began to dance around their Rebbe. Although their movements appeared less abandoned and free than his, it delighted Rifka to watch them. Boaz, swaying, with arms spread into a wide "V," head back and eyes closed, reminded her of a vessel being filled up. A smile spread across his face. A soft melody wafted up to the balcony as other voices joined the niggun that Yisroel had started.

Rifka closed her eyes and did what she had seen Boaz do. She raised her arms high over her head, closed her eyes, and began to sway. Opening her arms wider, she imagined a stream of light flowing into her palms, down

through her arms, and into her heart. After just moments, the flow continued without Rifka's trying to imagine it. Light poured into her shoulders,
chest, abdomen, hips, legs, and feet. She felt made of light.

NOT ALL of the Rebbe's students were comfortable with his rapture,
with seeing him given over to ecstasy. It was one thing, some said, to dance
this way on the holiday of Simchas Torah, the day designated for such
rejoicing, upon the conclusion of reading the entire scroll each year. But
such abandon on an ordinary weekday? What other outbursts might await?

Although Rifka understood, she was surprised by the disciples' misgivings. Ezekiel and Tanya appeared almost embarrassed. Did they and
some of the others fear that a similar display of joyous abandon might be
expected of them?

Rifka heard Rabbi Avner, Amos, and others express their misgivings amongst themselves, concerned about the adverse judgment of others. They questioned if this was perhaps too great a violation of proper
conduct during prayer? The Baal Shem Tov and his disciples had already
been accused of undue exuberance and the lack of requisite seriousness
in their study and prayer. But to dance with the Torah like this, other
than on the holiday when it was sanctioned? This could mark the Baal
Shem Tov and his community as even more aberrant. The community
could not risk further ostracism. Perhaps his joy could be expressed less
publicly, they reasoned.

One afternoon, after there had been several more instances of the
Rebbe's dancing, Yisroel asked those present to speak openly about this
spontaneous rejoicing. Listening to the Rebbe's disciples, Rifka felt their
fears being pulled from a moist darkness where they had been festering
into the light of the Yisroel's unabashed joy.

Many revealed that they doubted themselves capable of the depth of
joy and devotion their Rebbe could so readily feel. Others spoke of the
imprudence of such expression given the risk of evoking censure from
the larger community. Yisroel greeted each remark with respect and

tenderness, not refuting any. Nor did he defend himself. His deep listening seemed to unburden his students.

Addressing those who feared that unbridled joy might lead to abandoning all discernment, the Rebbe assured them that joy and discernment could co-exist quite effectively. Facing life's challenges infused with joyful expectation would lead to much better results than looking at life's challenges joylessly, he asserted. A well-watered plant was able to withstand adverse conditions much better than one deprived of water and other nutrients. Joy was one of life's most vital nutrients.

THE BAAL SHEM TOV continued to dance as if he could not help himself, his joy filling every cell and spilling over. Over time, more and more of the disciples began to trust the bubbling up of their own unconditional joy. They also found more ease and freedom in expressing their joy.

Gradually, joyous gratitude infused more and more of the students' study and prayer together. If one of them felt despondent or weakened by fear, the spirit of the group buoyed him or her. The community was stirred to greater enthusiasm and to move with less inhibition during prayer. Their expanding joy infused their interactions with each other, their families, the visitors to the Rebbe's table, and the citizens of Medzibocz.

Rifka was dismayed to learn of warnings, in Medzibocz and beyond, about the dangers of being led into a trance in the unpredictable rabbi's "riotous" synagogue. The Baal Shem Tov, some said, stripped men not only of their reason but also of their dignity.

It was also accused that Rabbi Yisroel ben Eliezer was leading a Sabbatean cell.

❦

ELIAS RAN TO CATCH UP WITH THE REBBE WHO walked quickly on the road leading to the outskirts of Medzibocz. Once beside him, Elias adjusted his pace to match Yisroel's long quick strides. Elias had returned a few days earlier from Satanov, where he had traveled with Ezekiel and Malka to the wedding of Ezekiel's nephew. The trip had been a disturbing one.

"Rebbe, I can't free myself of what I witnessed in Satanov. May I speak with you?"

Yisroel nodded, slowing his pace. Elias began, not sure where to start, describing what had seemed a waking nightmare.

"I woke in the middle of the night and unable to fall back asleep, I decided to walk for a short time in the Jewish quarter where we were staying. It surprised me to hear loud, slurred voices mockingly reciting all manner of blessings. The strange invocations came from a large, brick house whose door and windows were open onto the street, so I could not help seeing some of what was taking place inside."

"There were ten or twelve men there with perhaps half as many women. All were intoxicated, the women no less than the men. A few with their heads tilted back poured vodka down their throats as if they were on fire and the vodka was water. Empty bottles were strewn about the room. One of the men saw me and gestured that I enter. My curiosity drew me despite my revulsion."

"We have the secret to freedom,' he boasted with a sweep of his arm. 'The long-awaited reincarnation of Shabtai Tzvi has finally appeared. Like Shabtai Tzvi, our Master Jacob Frank also teaches that holiness must be freed from where it is trapped. We serve humanity by engaging in the vilest of acts to free the goodness buried there.' The drunk pulled a woman over. 'My holy wife,' he called her. Her hair fell loose over her bare shoulders."

"'This one can teach you the secrets of the Zohar,' her husband bragged, 'Just let her show you. There are chambers within chambers; she can lead you there.' Then he pushed his wife towards me as if she were merchandise he was hawking in a marketplace. When I did nothing, he kicked her so that she fell against another as inebriated as she, and the two staggered away. Laughing, the man shoved me into the street."

Elias drew in a long breath.

"Rebbe, how can such practices be carried out in the name of bringing goodness into the world? How can Frank and his followers—"

A ragged peasant pulled his scrawny goat across their path. Elias tried not to feel impatient.

"Would the kind baal shem please help?" the farmer begged. "My goat has stopped giving milk. There are so many miracles the generous rabbi has performed. Surely he can cause a stubborn goat to provide again for seven hungry children?"

Elias nodded his assent that the Rebbe tend to the distraught farmer, his weary goat and hungry children.

Elias would make his way back rather than accompany Yisroel further. At least for now, he had let the horror of what he had seen and heard escape the confines of his mind. He would have the chance to ask his questions another time.

But on his way walk back, instead of relief, Elias was beleaguered by more troubling thoughts. For the first time, he actually grasped how Yisroel *could* be judged a source of Sabbatean blasphemies, and his influence be considered harmful. The Baal Shem Tov also counseled finding and freeing of love trapped in the shells of hateful actions. The spontaneous revelry in his houses of study and prayer could easily be considered blasphemy, as could much else in the Rebbe's behavior. And why did Yisroel never directly rebuke those attacking him?

Some of the disciples, disturbed by the shadow of disgrace over the community, wanted to challenge the accusations, while others suggested becoming "more discreet." Most tried to follow Yisroel's example and find compassion for their accusers.

Elias was confused. He felt uncomfortable fighting back, uncertain about becoming more discreet, and he was, as yet, unable to find compassion for their accusers.

When he heard the Rebbe call to him a few days later, Elias was relieved.

"You look like a man whose questions are weighing him down, Elias," the Rebbe said once they were side by side.

It wasn't the first time Yisroel had recognized Elias' agitation.

"Rebbe, I can see how those looking in at us from the outside might fear your being a Sabbatean."

Yisroel stopped walking and looked at Elias with a blend of amusement and curiosity.

"Rebbe, you've been charged with usurping the authority of tradition with your own authority. You praise the illiterate and elevate those who blow shepherd's whistles above the learned. You encourage women's voices to overpower men's in the prayer service and even worse, you encourage women to take roles not meant for them. You are accused of using names of God to induce trances, and of practicing witchcraft to confuse people into thinking they have seen you. It is even been alleged that, wandering the countryside, you are engaging the sympathies of the masses and recruiting them for Jacob Frank's *army of believers*—or for your own." Elias suddenly felt out of breath after reciting the list of indictments.

Yisroel nodded, amusement still his primary expression. "I have heard these, as well as other accusations."

"But, Rebbe, you appear oblivious to them, I thought that maybe you had not…"

"What I have not done," Yisroel inserted, "is let them guide my course." He turned and began the walk back.

"My purpose in this world is not to fight ignorance but to feed truth. We are here to meet God within us, as our own love. Sadly, Shabtai Tzvi lived exiled from the Promised Land of his inner love and could not find his way there."

The Baal Shem Tov, Elias realized, had found his way to the Promised Land of unconditional love. He was a rare guide who did not insist others follow him.

Elias would ask no more questions today. He had started out mired in fear. Now he felt as if he had been pulled out and pointed in the direction of his destination. If only, Elias wished, he could keep rolling forward without succumbing to more inner and outer enemies waiting in ambush.

∾

D OVID SAT ON THE WARM GROUND, HIS BACK AGAINST a stout oak. Had it been two months already that he had been coming to this field? The days had passed quickly since he had settled in Medzibocz to be closer to Yisroel.

Dovid watched the wind herd the wheat toward the horizon. He came to this field as often as he could to spend time in solitary meditation and reflection.

How Dovid had judged and punished himself was becoming more apparent each day in the company of the one who had shepherded him to cheyder, and was now a shepherd of souls. From the Rebbe, Dovid was learning that what he needed to renounce was not the flesh, but his false beliefs.

Dovid was troubled at first, watching Yisroel respond to the shortcomings and struggles of his students. Rather than rebuking, he responded with compassion. But his compassion could not be mistaken for either pity or indulgence, nor was it lacking in directness. He spoke of finding the power in gentleness, a concept and practice foreign to Dovid. The gentle vigilance that the Rebbe taught was so different from the harsh, relentless scrutiny that had driven Dovid's behavior for so long.

Dovid looked up, surprised to see Yisroel in the distance, walking briskly. He stood quickly to cross the sunny field, breaking into a run through the golden wheat, suddenly feeling that his Rebbe had been expecting him.

"May I join you?" Dovid called.

Yisroel nodded slightly, not turning around. Dovid fell into step next to his teacher.

"Tell me, Dovid, has your appetite for life grown?"

"My appetite, Rebbe?" The question surprised Dovid. Was Yisroel's inquiry really about food? To Yisroel, everything was holy, food no less. For many years, Dovid had eaten no more than one sparse meal a day: a slice of bread, handful of radishes, a cup of broth, occasionally, a small piece of chicken on Shabbos. But after his experience of his body as a corpse during Yisroel's visit to Polnoyye, Dovid had gradually allowed himself more ample meals. He could tell by the way his clothing fit that he had gained weight.

Yisroel's voice broke into Dovid's thoughts.

"Just as the body has an appetite, dear Dovid, so do the mind, heart, and soul."

"But surely, Rebbe, the appetite for learning is more meritorious than the appetite for food or other pleasures of the senses?" He was still trying to make sense of the Rebbe's values.

"Dovid, the body is no less a temple than the holiest temples of our people."

The Rebbe's statement stunned Dovid. *The body compared to the holy temple?* Once, Dovid would have argued vehemently against such blasphemy.

Yisroel continued.

"It's through the body and with the body that we are able to worship and to serve on this plane of creation. To weaken the body through austerities is to deprive it of its full power and radiance."

Dovid had been convinced that his austerities were feeding his ardor. Even when his short-temperedness, impatience, and irritation had intensified, Dovid viewed this as part of the purification process. He imagined himself on a faster, more intense route to union with God. Growing up, Dovid had witnessed the destruction caused by overindulgence. He had watched his father suffer from a ruinous lack of will and self-control that had led him to abandon his family. Dovid had vowed, without really knowing it, to make self-control his primary spiritual practice, underlying all others. Finally, thanks to his Rebbe, Dovid's grip on himself was loosening.

Yisroel stopped walking. Absorbed in his thoughts, Dovid hadn't seen or heard the approach of the tattered, old peasant farmer who now stood before them.

"Master, are you the one known as the Baal Shem Tov?"

In Yisroel's nod, Dovid recognized not pride but the knowledge that all was done through him. Dovid also perceived Yisroel's reverence for the soul of the old farmer. To the Rebbe, the one before him, regardless of his or her circumstances, was the true miracle.

"Master, I have been begging the merciful Lord to allow me to confess my terrible sins before my death. You appear now as the answer to my prayers." Although he struggled to remain standing on his frail legs, the old peasant began his confession right there without delay.

"I have lived my life as a Catholic peasant. But I was born a Jew. When I was an infant, my parents, fearing for their lives in a Haidamak attack, hid me in a bed of hay to save my life. A kind peasant farmer who knew my parents discovered me in the barn of the szlachcic that he served. The childless farmer and his wife got permission and even some coins from the nobleman to raise me as their own."

Yisroel extended his arm for the man to lean on. The peasant shook his head, clearly thinking himself unworthy. Wincing with pain, he shifted his weight and continued his narrative.

"The couple was devout and filled me with devotion to their faith. It was not until I was a young man that the farmer told me, on his deathbed, that I had been born a Jew and my actual parents had been massacred. By then, good master, I thought it would cause great pain to my wife, who was the farmer's niece and with child, were I to abandon her. Nor did I think it proper to persuade her to change her faith and adopt mine."

The man looked questioningly at Yisroel, whose nod encouraged him to continue.

"The years passed and, although I knew I was a Jew, I worshipped at my wife's side with our children. I prayed with my whole heart to the Lord Jesus Christ for blessing and protection and that none should suffer what my parents had suffered. I prayed for the Jewish people, knowing and rejoicing that Jesus, son of Mary, was a Jew, too. I must confess, Master," the farmer lowered his gaze, "that I even prayed for the Haidamaks, whose lives I imagined to be not so different from mine, as a landless peasant farmer. How abandoned by their God they must feel, to spill the blood of their brothers and sisters—sons and daughters of the same Holy Father." The humble farmer looked up, his face anguished.

"I have sinned… mightily, Master. I have dishonored the Jewish Sabbath not once but thousands of times. I did not circumcise my sons. My list of sins is as long as the list of commandments that a Jew must follow. My unworthiness has caused me great suffering. Now, I am an old man. My dear wife has died. My children are grown. The Lord knows I don't seek forgiveness, but penance. Your renown as a holy man has led me to seek you, that I might be told what penance I may offer until my last breath."

By the time he said the word breath, the weary man seemed to have almost none left. Dovid watched him lower himself to the dusty road. "Forgive me, holy Rabbi and companion," the man said, begging pardon, "I intend no disrespect. I am just so tired. I will stand again in just a moment."

Kneeling, Yisroel placed his hand on the man's shoulder to indicate that he need not rise. Yisroel reached under his caftan for a flask of water attached to a strap across his shoulder. The humble farmer hesitated until the Rebbe's nod and gesture persuaded him to drink.

"The thirst I witness in you, dear brother," the Rebbe began softly, "is not only for water. You have thirsted your whole life for closeness to God."

Dovid saw tears glaze the old man's eyes.

"You have lived all your days serving," Yisroel told him. "You served your humble parents and the nobleman to whom they were indebted. Then you offered the fruits of your labor and prayer to your wife and the children she bore you."

The farmer, hunched over, began to cry until his shoulders heaved.

After a few moments, Yisroel lifted the old man's chin so their eyes could meet.

"Do not punish yourself any longer. Recognize the pure heart you were given that belongs to no religion and to all." Yisroel wrapped his arms around the man. Dovid saw the farmer's thready muscles quiver in the Rebbe's embrace. "You never stopped being a Jew," Yisroel whispered. "What is your name, my brother?"

"Anatol," the farmer answered hoarsely. "The farmer who raised me told me it means sunrise."

"Anshel." the Rebbe said. "This shall be your Jewish name whose meaning is *blessed and fortunate*. You are fortunate and blessed, Anshel, to have lived your days with such devotion. Remember, dear soul, there is only one God who—like you—has more than one name."

Walking home with the Rebbe in silence allowed Dovid time to contemplate what he had just witnessed.

This was not the first time Dovid had seen Yisroel respond to someone's remorse for what they considered wrongdoing or sin. When Dovid's students had confessed their failings to him, Dovid reacted in the manner of Rabbi Lazer before him; he prescribed bitter remorse and increased severities. Rather than admonish men and women for their failure, Yisroel praised their desire to carry out good deeds. He focused on their longing for righteousness, not on their misdemeanors. The Baal Shem Tov forgave weaknesses; he chose instead to draw out strengths.

Recently, Yisroel had directed his students to search in the dark corners of their beings where doubt, fear, or envy might lurk. "Shine the light of your discernment there. And be willing to see," he instructed. "Enter your inner battlegrounds armed with lucid kindness. Such self-inquiry," he taught, "can bring awareness not only of your inner battles, but insight also into others' struggles."

Yisroel's laughter startled Dovid. Five-year-old Freyda, Dalia's daughter, was running towards her grandfather. With one hand, Freyda pulled her best friend, Raisa; with the other, Raisa's little sister. Dovid had learned from Dalia that Freyda had become inseparable from the two girls when their mother Kaila died shortly after her second daughter's birth. Yisroel knelt to catch the girls in his arms. But when all three children asked to be lifted, he looked up at Dovid with an amused gleam in his eyes.

"Will you offer your arms, good rabbi, to Raisa's sister who is asking to be raised up?"

Dovid knelt and extended his arms to the little one. Yisroel, holding Freyda and Raisa, stood and continued walking.

When they arrived at the Rebbe's small abode, Yisroel winked at Dovid. "Would you open the door for us all?"

Dovid reached for the wooden door handle. As he did so, Raisa's little sister cupped her small hands around his beard. *To open his arms to one asking to be lifted and to open the door of his heart*—perhaps this was the essence of what his Rebbe wished him to learn.

DOVID LEANED against the wall of the crowded Beis Midrash waiting with the others for the study session to begin. Yisroel had asked that just the men attend this morning, a rare request, which had left Dovid and some of the others curious.

Dovid was not yet accustomed to the presence of women in the study sessions. Even though he had heard, before coming to Medzibocz, that women were permitted to study with the male students, actually seeing this had surprised him. The biggest surprise had been seeing Rifka.

She had been offering a commentary when Dovid entered. He felt relieved that she was looking at Yisroel; she would not notice Dovid staring at her.

She hadn't changed as much as he would have guessed. He thought she must be past forty, just a few years younger than he. She possessed the radiance of the girl she had been, blended with the assurance and grace of the woman she had become. He watched Rifka's blue eyes open wide under the moving arcs of her thick, dark eyebrows. A few threads of her raven hair had escaped her headscarf and touched a small area of her neck beneath the knot of her scarf and the collar of her brown linen dress. When Rifka stopped speaking, her lips remained loosely parted in a smile. For the first time in his entire life, Dovid let himself imagine kissing a woman's lips. He looked away.

Dovid's thoughts were interrupted when the Rebbe began to speak.

"The subject of our conversation today, friends, is man's sacred duty to pleasure his wife. As before, we will use the Kabbalistic text, *Iggeret ha'Kodesh*, as our guide, a text that views sexual intimacy as holy."

Dovid straightened. He would not have attended had he known this would be the focus. Most of those present were married, or if not, had once been, like Rabbi Avner. Samuel and Ezekiel had been married long enough to have children of marriageable age. Judah, Dalia's husband, would soon complete a decade of marriage, as would Amos and his Zahava. Elijah and Boaz, at seventeen, were approaching the age to marry. Although Elias was childless, he was, at least, married. Dovid was fairly certain that the others at the table, most with substantial beards, were married or widowed. Dovid had no use for this type of knowledge; why hadn't Yisroel told him the topic in advance and spared him embarrassment? But, knowing by now that nothing happened randomly around the Rebbe, Dovid reluctantly surrendered to being where he was.

The Rebbe read from the text open before him. "A man approaching his wife in the darkness is likely to be aroused quickly without the need for tender, loving words to prepare him for sexual intimacy." He lifted his gaze, adding his own commentary.

"A woman must be approached in such a way that she feels cherished by her husband. For this reason, it is not respectful to enter her room with haste or insensitivity, let alone to expect to enter her body this way. When a man caresses his beloved with sincere and loving words, he opens her heart, which allows her body to open."

When the Rebbe stopped, the look in his eyes, not focused on anyone, made Dovid wonder if he were recalling intimacy with his beloved Channa. After their long marriage, Yisroel was a living text, Dovid mused. The Rebbe resumed speaking.

"But the communication of a man's love and respect for his wife is not to be reserved for the Sabbath or for only those times when his wife is able to enter into sexual union. This tenderness must pervade all the days of the month, even those when a woman is not to be approached physically."

In the lively discussion that ensued, Dovid learned that this was not the first time, nor surely would it be the last, that these topics were being addressed. Such teachings had been inspiring and challenging the men who came to the Rebbe's table for some time. Because the learning could always go deeper and because there were always new young men among them, man's sacred duty to his wife was a perennial and valued subject.

Now Yisroel directed his gaze at Dovid. Dovid wondered what in this discussion could possibly pertain to him?

The Rebbe looked down and read: "Even when a couple is unable to bear children or has passed the age of childbearing, a man's sacred duty to cherish his wife with tender words and touch remains the same."

Dovid was not sure why the words impacted him so deeply, but they did. Looking down, he fought the impulse to leave the room. Sorrow and longing filled his chest. This time, instead of resisting, he closed his eyes and let the feelings flood him.

❦ 32 ❧

I
n the years since a handful of students had first prepared the abandoned synagogue and study house, both had been expanded. Yet no more than a handful of women from Medzibocz had come to study.

What if there were a place where women could study and inspire each other? Rifka wondered. She went to the Rebbe with her idea.

With the Rebbe's hearty blessing, Rifka, assisted by Dalia, Naomi, and Zahava would create a study circle for women.

When a gold merchant's wife offered a room in her ample home for the women to gather, the wives and older daughters of the disciples were finally invited to their own table, a place of study for women. The women would meet once a month, at the time of the new moon.

At their first gathering, Rifka explained why the new moon had been chosen as the meeting time.

"According to a passage in the Talmud, women are exempt from all work on the new moon. A rabbinic commentary further explains that this time was awarded women for declining to offer their rings and earrings to be melted down for the fashioning of the golden calf in the wilderness. It was because of their faith in Moses' return that the women refused to contribute to this object of worship."

Rifka then read to those present a few lines of the ninth century Talmudic commentary.

"The Holy One, blessed be, gave the women their reward in this world *and* in The World to Come. What reward was given them in this world? Their reward is that they should observe the New Moons more stringently than the men. And what reward will be given them in The World to Come? They are destined to be renewed like the New Moons..."

"This study circle," Rifka went on, "will be our observance of the new moon."

In the next hour, the women explored their ideas about The World to Come and what it means to be renewed.

Dalia's story concluded the evening.

"When I was twelve," she began, "a visitor to our home in Zabie saw me running barefoot in the meadow. He told me that a girl my age ought to be more serious and responsible, lest I lose my place and reward in The World to Come. My parents had never cautioned me in this way, so after the guest left I asked my mother Channa about this."

"My mother explained that it is indeed true that my actions shape the world to come. I held my breath. But she went on to tell me that when I run barefoot in the meadow, happy and free, I am blessing the earth. 'Our generous home,' she called it. 'Your delight nourishes her like rain,' she said. I learned from my mother that my delight can nourish me and the world around me—both the world I see and worlds I cannot see."

IN ORDER to welcome more women to study, Rifka tried to meet with the wives of merchants, blacksmiths, tax collectors, tailors, ritual slaughterers, bakers, and more.

Many women on whose doors she knocked declined to let her enter. Unmarried and childless, Rifka was seen as different from them. Rifka was careful to let them know that neither she, nor a woman's study circle, repudiated men or marriage. When possible Rifka went accompanied by Dalia or Zahava.

The most common argument Rifka encountered was that such gatherings among women were a dangerous departure from tradition. She and her companions acknowledged that while study among women had never been recorded, this was not to say it had never occurred. Was it not conceivable that women had gathered in groups that were secret? The notion intrigued some women and intimated others.

She should perhaps not have been so surprised or so frustrated by the number of women who still believed that study and literacy were best reserved for a select minority of men. It was hard for Rifka to hear women defend the threatening outcomes that men associated with their becoming educated: *What if they were to become distracted from more important responsibilities? Worst of all, what if they should begin to consider themselves equal to men?!*

But as she proceeded, it intrigued Rifka to realize that along with their countless protests, the women actually seemed to wish that Rifka *would not* take "no" for an answer. Many who protested initially asked Rifka to return.

One or two at a time, women approached the open door of the place of study. Each was welcomed warmly, regardless of the poverty of her dress or the poverty of her knowledge or esteem for herself. Many brought young children, having been told that children, too, would be welcomed, fed, and cared for while the mothers learned together.

Rifka watched her new sisters embrace learning. It became a regular practice to study the weekly Torah portions and explore the ancient rabbinic commentaries on these passages. Study evolved from Rifka's teaching to dynamic conversations in which most of the women participated. Women even began to add their own commentaries and apply these insights to their daily lives. No topic was prohibited.

After eighteen new moons, the gold merchant's wife donated the funds to construct a large room adjacent to the Beis Midrash for a Women's House of Study. A wide window facing south would allow sunlight to bathe the room. This would be a place for women to come at any time of the day or night as their lives permitted.

WHEN RIFKA introduced the practice of meditation, she described it as sitting in silence with oneself and others. Many, if not most of the women, looked at her doubtfully. The clamor of children in the room, playing gaily or tugging for attention, made the idea of meditating together seem an unlikely one.

Luba, usually quiet much like her mother Tanya, surprised Rifka by speaking up. Betrothed to Boaz ten months earlier and soon to be a mother herself, Luba suggested that the women take turns caring for the children too restless to remain at their mothers' sides, freeing the others for their study and silence. In today's fair weather, the children could play in the courtyard. By the time the colder weather arrived, surely they could find another safe place for the children and one or two caregivers. Luba's suggestion was welcomed.

Women came in a slow, steady stream to the House of Study. Those who dared found themselves entering into not only a variety of sacred texts, but also into the mystery of their own beings.

Luba, holding her newborn Avigal, stood to welcome two young mothers who had paused reluctantly at the door, each holding an infant daughter. As Luba gestured for the women to enter, she repeated what Rifka had said to her just weeks earlier: "What could be more fitting than a child nursing at a mother's breast while a mother feeds her own hunger?"

In addition to learning together, the women had begun to celebrate life passages: birth, death, and all that came in between. The midwife Naomi had invited the two young mothers so that their daughters' births could be celebrated here. In the women's study circle, the births of daughters could be honored joyously and ceremoniously, as were the births of sons according to tradition. Malka, still grieving her daughter Kaila's death, finally came with her oldest granddaughter Raisa, after being encouraged to allow the women's circle to join in holding their sorrow. Soon the women would celebrate the first marriage among them. Gedaliah and Zofia's daughter Batleya had been betrothed to Yisroel's son, Elijah.

~

AT BATLEYA'S WEDDING, the women formed a circle and danced around the bride. Rifka saw Zofia leave the circle to rest. From the moment Rifka had first seen Zofia upon her arrival from Horodenka for the wedding, Zofia's pallor and uncharacteristic frailty had troubled her.

Rifka was delighted when, several days after the wedding, Zofia and Batleya came to participate in a women's study session. As the focus of study, Rifka chose a passage from Genesis about the creation of woman and the marriage of Adam and Eve. She had found a particularly inspiring rabbinic commentary on this section of Torah.

"The first man was called Adam, meaning blood and flesh and representing the solidly earthly and material," she read. "But after woman was created, both were referred to by a single word whose meaning was fire."

"Wait just a minute, dear Rifka!" interrupted the dressmaker Frumalla, who regularly spiced the study sessions with her uninhibited sense of humor. "We women were, after all, an early experiment. What else do you think God tried that didn't get recorded in Genesis, before he settled on what we now enjoy together in bed?"

"Who says we enjoy it?" an older woman interjected. "Speak for yourself."

"I would like to speak," Zofia's voice emerged over the laughter in the room. "I am familiar with this commentary and, as a contented wife and the mother of the bride," she smiled at Batleya, "I would like to add my commentary."

Rifka felt Zofia's weariness buoyed by her love for her daughter.

"Man and woman were ordained not just to be physical helpmates, but also spiritual companions," Zofia began, standing. "The Creator used the word *esh*, meaning fire—composed of letters from his ineffable name—for both man and woman. Then the Creator added other letters to *esh*, from the Name: the Yud turning it into *eesh*, for husband, and the letter *Heh*, to form *eeshah*, wife. So we can see that, *In the beginning*, Boundless Love entered the sacred covenant between man and woman."

Zofia's eyes burned with ardor even after she sat. Although Zofia's spirit was still strong, her body was succumbing—to what, Rifka did not know; she was weaker than Rifka had ever seen her.

TANYA HAD kept herself apart from the women's gatherings despite the welcoming invitations. But her distancing was not because she wanted to stay away. When Tanya confided this to Zofia on the eve of her sister-in-law's return to Horodenka, Zofia encouraged her to seek the Rebbe's counsel.

Tanya entered the shul a week later before sunrise. She found the Rebbe with lambswool in his hand wiping the benches before the others arrived for the morning service. Yisroel looked up briefly to nod his welcome then returned to his task. His greeting could not have been more perfect, she thought, making it easier for her to pose her question.

She drew closer and spoke softly.

"Rebbe, I've heard you say so many times that we bless the world with our joy. But regardless of what I do—even after the birth of my beautiful Luba and now my granddaughter Avigal—I feel a dark shadow over my life like a perpetual companion."

"Does the shadow ever leave?" Yisroel asked, not ceasing the rhythmic movement of his arm across the benches.

"Yes, there are times when for no apparent reason I feel unburdened. But banishing the shadow has not seemed a matter of will. How I wish it were. Some times hopelessness overtakes me so powerfully that I don't even want to leave my house."

"All this feels like an inexcusable failing, Rebbe. How can I still be subject to dejection given all that I've received from my mother, Samuel, Luba, you, and the community here in Medzibocz? I try to fight the gathering clouds by feeling gratitude. I recite psalm after psalm. But still the despondency comes. In its grip, I feel separate and far from myself, from those I love, and even from God. On top of this, I feel so ashamed that I am failing again."

Yisroel put down his dusting wool, picked up a broom and began to sweep, slowly and steadily. His lack of urgency surprised Tanya. She had expected him to treat her despair like something dangerous, urging her to shun and eradicate it like a contagion.

"When the shadow darkens your life, Tanya, what do you believe about yourself?" he asked.

What did she believe about herself? Didn't he know? Tanya felt annoyed at his question. She had come to the Baal Shem Tov for guidance. She wanted only to remove the shadow that oppressed her spirit. Did the Rebbe not grasp this?

"Tanya, what if condemning yourself separates you from love more than the despondency itself?"

Was he condemning her to an acceptance of her despair? She dropped onto a bench, discouraged.

Yisroel faced her now. "Tanya, the soul endures all manner of weather—arid seasons, turbulent storms, stretches of dense fog—during which we may lose our way. Instead of berating ourselves, it serves us to be forgiving, to pray for love to find us when we cannot find our way to love. Dear Tanya, can you accept, or at least not fear, the shadow?"

She shook her head.

"Tanya, if a horse upon which you were mounted strayed from the path, would you admonish it relentlessly and try to whip it into obedience? Or would it be more fruitful to speak encouragingly to the animal, to take its reins and steer it in the right direction, gaining its trust and cooperation. Our minds are like weary, oft-mounted horses in need of excellent care."

He took a step closer, his expression so tender it evoked her mother Gittel's tender and unconditional love.

"Yes, I counsel serving creation with joy. But like all teachings, this can be misunderstood and used as a weapon with which to punish oneself. There are times, my dear Tanya, when suffering comes unbidden. Our work then is to love, not abandon, ourselves during such trials." He opened his hand and rested it on her head, which she instinctively bowed. Was she imagining the heat that radiated from his touch?

"May you not fear the shadow when it hovers, dear one." He spoke the words so slowly and gently they caressed her spirit. "And may you find your way to the light of self-compassion."

ELIAS WAS AMONG those who rejoiced when Samuel announced that Gedaliah, Zofia, and their sons would be returning to Medzibocz to stay. An opportunity for livelihood had presented itself. The old cobbler in whose stall Samuel worked had begun to complain of great pain in his twisted fingers. Samuel had introduced Gedaliah to him. The two brothers offered the old cobbler a guarantee of livelihood for the rest of his days in return for his stall, his leather, tools, and customers.

Elias suspected that other factors had also compelled the move from Horodenka. For one, Gedaliah and Zofia's daughter Batleya had decided to remain in Medzibocz with her new husband Elijah. But most significant, Elias imagined, was Zofia's worsening condition.

Gedaliah would turn the cobbler shop in Horodenka over to loyal Dobry who had saved Leya's life in the underground prison. Meanwhile, Samuel, Elias, and a few others would ready Gedaliah and Zofia's new home, three small rooms that had been left empty after the death of the old cobbler's brother.

On the day of their arrival, Elias hastened to the wagon to greet his sister and her family. One look at Zofia's face revealed how frail she was, even before he saw her thin frame draped by her cape. Elias extended his hand to help Zofia descend the wagon.

The moment he wrapped his arms around what seemed like the bones of a bird, Elias was dazed by sudden grief. He thought of Naftali's death. He could not bear to lose his sister, too.

Releasing Zofia and facing her, he was relieved to find the same directness and delight he'd always seen flashing in her lively eyes. In some way, nothing was diminished.

Elias felt Gedaliah's broad hand on his back. He turned and gave himself to the embrace of his hardy brother-in-law, whose love for Zofia had been unwavering.

Samuel arrived to help Gedaliah and his family. Meir, now a man of almost thirty, did what he could with one hand to unload the wagon. The brothers Reuben and Ber assisted with the vigor of young men approaching twenty. The horses were tended, the family's possessions settled, and the community's newest residents well fed by Tanya.

As he took his leave, Zofia told Elias that she was relieved to be home.

RIFKA DID NOT KNOW what to expect from one day to the next in the Women's House of Study. This excited her. Women of all ages came and went, as they were able. Many had learned to read. Unlike the men, the women sat in a circle, often with children weaving their way among the chairs. It pleased Rifka whenever Zofia felt strong enough to sit in the circle. Despite the illness that seemed to be devouring her from the inside out, Zofia's spirit shone.

Today, Dalia opened the session. She read the words of Genesis, *In the beginning,* then stopped. With a twinkle in her eye, she asked, "Remember what happened in the beginning?" In reply to the questioning expressions that faced her, Dalia added, "It's said that every soul was present at the moment of the world's creation. We were each there, you know. So what happened?"

"Oh yes, of course, I remember exactly." The words came from Frumalla who could be counted on to be light-hearted. "I was the darkness, a happy, fat void spread out comfortably until an explosion of light made me gather up my skirts and make room for something else." The women laughed.

"What I remember," Zahava followed, "is just being. There was nowhere to go, nothing to add or to take away." She paused. "There were not even any questions—"

"Or any answers," Malka inserted.

"And then," said Naomi, in a suspenseful tone, "out of the limitless silence, like a seed sprouting, a single question formed."

"What was the question that formed from the silence?" a young mother, nursing her infant and new to the circle, ventured softly.

"*Was there a time that I was not?*" Zofia spoke the words with effort. "That is the question."

The evocative question was met with silence. Rifka suggested that the women meditate together. They closed their eyes.

One among them did not open hers again.

Zofia was lifted from where she had sunk in her chair, and laid on a bed of women's coats. Batleya knelt by her mother, kissing the limp hand she held in hers again and again.

Gedaliah was summoned.

When he entered, he walked towards Batleya, pressing his large hand to his daughter's back as he knelt beside Zofia. He reached his other hand to his wife's cheek.

"God bless you and keep you, my soaring bird," he whispered the words hoarsely. It struck Rifka suddenly that Zofia had perhaps been more prepared for this than Gedaliah. She had been speaking of retreating to a realm that she could not describe in words, but could feel beckoning. When Gedaliah began to tremble, Rifka knew his beloved's soul had fully released the garment of her body. This was the holy trembling of which the Rebbe spoke. Gedaliah dropped his head and wept.

RIFKA WAS GRATEFUL for the space and time to grieve and to allow others their sorrow. She was coming to understand that it did not help to rub the balm of comfort too heavily or too soon into the open wound of loss. The disciples had been reminded of this shortly before Zofia's death. The midwife Naomi, deeply shaken by the tragic deaths of a mother and baby at a recent birth at which she had assisted, had asked the Rebbe how to best console the children, husband, and parents of the young mother who had died.

Yisroel had begun his reply with a question.

"Have you forgiven yourself for what you were unable to prevent?" he asked Naomi. He let the silence deepen before continuing.

"When a wound is fresh and deep, it is usually neither the time nor a kindness to 'bestow wisdom' upon a mourner. Better to join the suffering ones. Allow your heart to break with theirs. But, as you open to another's pain," he cautioned, "remember to look for the light piercing the darkness of grief. It will help you not drown in sorrow; then as the mourners become ready, your love can help draw them back into the light of living."

Zofia's death evoked previous losses; waves of sorrow that had subsided were once more washing over Rifka, especially her grief at the recent loss of Channa, companion of her soul, from which she was not sure she would ever truly recover. The Rebbe's guidance helped Rifka be with Gedaliah in his immense sorrow, and with other family members who mourned Zofia's loss. Inspired by the Rebbe's teachings, she imagined sparks of love, long held captive in the shell of her grief, being freed to fuel the great fire of her life.

On the night of the new moon, a month after Zofia's death, Rifka sat to meditate.

As was her usual practice, Rifka closed her eyes, slowed and deepened her breathing, and gradually found herself feeling settled more fully in her heart.

Surprised by a triangle of light appearing in her inner vision, a short distance in front of her, she watched, eyes closed. Spirals of light spun at the triangle's three corners. From within the spiral at the peak of the triangle, Rifka saw Leya. It was her face, but more than that, her spirit that appeared within the spiraling light. Then from within the spirals of light at the corners of the triangle's base, first Channa's image and essence appeared, then Zofia's. Rifka was enthralled. Almost as suddenly as they had appeared, the brilliant lights softened. Just before the triangle completely disappeared, a thin beam emanated from its center. Rifka held her breath as she felt a delicate ray coming from her mother Dvorah's heart pierce hers.

~

The following morning, a seed long dormant in her heart sprouted. Rifka would create a cheyder for girls.

Several of the women who refused the invitation to the Women's House of Study had admitted they once harbored the desire to study. They simply had given up along the way. A common refrain was that even if it *were* possible to abandon other duties in order to learn to read, it was simply too late now. But over time, Rifka found that many who thought it was too late for themselves wanted something different for their daughters or, at least, for their daughter's daughters. The distiller's wife had mocked Rifka's suggestion that she could learn to read, but when Rifka was leaving, the woman implored Rifka to return the next day. When Rifka came back, the woman's married daughter, a young mother, was there. "Encourage her," the older woman whispered to Rifka, "even if she were to go once a month, that would be better than not at all."

When initiating the study circle for women, Dalia, Zahava, Naomi, and several other women assured Rifka that the aspirations she sensed in women—often hidden and even denied—were real. Rifka would trust this now, too.

Once again the Rebbe gave his blessing heartily when Rifka approached him. There would be a cheyder for girls!

No sooner was the idea shared with those meeting in the Women's House of Study, than the women banded together to raise money for materials and to find among their husbands, sons, and brothers the help needed to build a small room adjacent to the Women's Beis Midrash. Leya and Gittel's granddaughters, Luba and Batleya, whom Rifka had glimpsed as shepherdesses when they were just girls, would oversee the cheyder with Dalia and Rifka's support.

This seed that Rifka had carried for so long and had watered with longing and even with discontent was now breaking ground. Like all tender plants, it would need protection.

❧ 33 ❧

In the two years since Gedaliah had moved to Medzibocz, both love and opposition of the Baal Shem Tov had swelled greatly and had expanded beyond the borders of Medzibocz into other regions of Poland.

That they could neither predict nor control the Baal Shem Tov disquieted a growing number of well-established authorities. Many came to his table hoping to decipher whether he was cunning, or a fool. In either case, his popularity and influence, since he answered to no authority other than his own, made him dangerous.

Rumors more astonishing than ever wove a sticky web around the Rebbe and his disciples. Men and women traveled to Medzibocz expecting to see the Rebbe dancing on an open book of Talmud or howling madly in tongues. Visitors arrived on the horns of horrifying rumors, one being that the Rebbe forced his women disciples to fornicate with him. It was attested that children in the Baal Shem Tov's community were adorned and worshipped as idols, that men bowed down to women. Some had heard that the designated hours for prayer services had been abandoned in favor of being in the mood for prayer, that silent meditation induced trances that lasted for days and that dreams yielded more guidance than scriptural law.

Official allegations against the Baal Shem Tov had also become more astounding. After one of their fold had sat at the Rebbe's table, news came that some Warsaw rabbis had accused that "Rabbi Yisroel ben Eliezar chews on holy laws as if they were tobacco wads from which one sucks the juice and spits out what is unwanted." The pronouncements carried no official sanctions like the rarely issued ban of excommunication. None-theless, it carried a weight the disciples could feel.

Word had traveled all the way from Prague that a leading authority there, Rabbi Eybeschutz, had condemned the Baal Shem Tov from his pulpit for preying on lost souls. Eybeschutz alleged that the Rabbi Yisroel ben Eliezer was a Sabbatean, and his community a Sabbatean cell no lon-ger even attempting to be clandestine.

Gedaliah recognized the name of the Prague rabbi. Eybeschutz was the rabbi who had presided over clandestine gatherings in Prague so many years before. Reb Wolf, the father of Gedaliah's friend Aleksander, and the head of Horodenka's Kahal, had taken Aleksander as a boy to some of these gatherings. Aleksander had confided the incidents when Gedaliah's family had sought shelter in his home after the tragic fire that had claimed Naftali's life. Men, hailing Shabtai Tzvi, had rolled in the snow naked under a new moon and performed other "austerities" that had terrified and confused the young Aleksander. Was Eybeschutz accus-ing Rabbi Yisroel ben Eliezer of being a Sabbatean to deflect suspicion about his own allegiance to the Sabbatean movement and Jacob Frank?

Of late, there had been a number of incidents in which the Rebbe's disciples had been cornered, robbed, and even beaten, women threat-ened, homes ransacked. Several of the assaults had been accompanied by shouts decrying Yisroel ben Eliezer as a "pernicious servant of Jacob Frank." Would these attacks escalate? How could rabbinic authorities and others not recognize the difference between the Rebbe's teachings and Sabbatean practices? Or did they not want to discern the differences? And if not, why not?

Gedaliah and his fellow students tried to follow Yisroel's example of not contesting the accusations, regardless of how ungrounded they were. But it was not easy to resist clarifying the truth and defending the Rebbe.

The Rebbe intervened within the community with a reprimand at once gentle and firm. *An invitation*, he called it. Beyond defending them-selves and each other from physical attack, he urged that the community adopt neither an offensive nor a defensive posture toward antagonistic visitors, but rather focus on treating even the most hostile among their attackers with respect.

"To refuse to meet disdain with disdain, and anger with anger is not weakness," he instructed. "It requires great strength. Those opponents who are able to will recognize this strength; they will experience the power of your respect. Such genuine respect opens closed minds and hearts. It is not what you say or don't say; it is the condition of your heart that will be felt."

As always, there were many seeking the Rebbe who did not ridicule, degrade, or fear him, but rather received what he offered whole-heartedly.

Frumalla the dressmaker came with a satchel of worries about her simple-minded daughter, and traded it for the Baal Shem Tov's suggestion that she "offer a blessing to her daughter with every stitch." A week later, Frumalla confided to Gedaliah's Batleya that since she had seen the Rebbe, her tired hands stitched as if they had wings. When Alta Yankel came to share his shame after all these years for his limp and his inability to distinguish an *aleph* from a *bes*, Yisroel leaned close and put his arm around Old Yankel's shoulders. "Don't worry, Reb Yankel, were you to thank God with every holy crooked step, it would be more than enough." The Rebbe praised patient Lena, blind in one eye and soon to be blind in both, who was always accompanied by a caravan of stray dogs. "Your service to the four-legged creatures is a holy kindness," he told her. He urged that she show herself the same holy kindness and forgive herself for being a barren woman.

The messages were straightforward and simple enough. They did not violate the Torah's commandments or the Talmudic interpretations of those commandments. Nonetheless, it was asserted, by certain religious and civic authorities, that the stringency of the law was being loosened rather than pulled tighter, as it must be, to keep ignorant people bound to the law.

The Rebbe also spoke of binding, but he spoke of binding one's heart and mind to the Sacred Presence. To both the simple and to the learned, the Rebbe spoke ceaselessly of Devekut. "To wash rags with one's thoughts on the Ayn Sof, he taught, is of more value than to recite holy texts while one's mind strays like a dog sniffing everyone's garbage." From town to town stories traveled about the Good Master of the Name, the Baal Shem Tov who dares to teach that *a pure heart is the source and destination of prayer. To find out what he means by this, go and be with him*, they said.

They kept coming: those who approached with simple need and longing; others who brought suspicion and judgment; and still others who came with confusion about what to expect or believe. The Rebbe greeted them equally—but not identically. With some, he was exceedingly tender, with others fiery. He could be cryptic. Effusive. To each he gave "the medicine their soul needed."

Although there was much that Gedaliah did not fathom, his trust in Yisroel eased his disquiet in the face of the mounting attacks.

∿

"A SERPENT HAS EMERGED INTO THE PUBLIC TO BITE, inflame, and poison."

Zahava joined the others gathered in the courtyard to listen to Ezekiel. His voice quaked and his face burned red with an anger none had ever seen him express. It had been two or three days since he and Malka had returned distraught and withdrawn from Lanskroun where they had gone to visit Malka's relatives.

"A vile man who dares to call himself '*The Deliverer*' is inciting riotous followings in city after city in Podolia. Malka and I, searching for her relatives in the Jewish sector of Lanskroun, witnessed one of his gatherings when we were caught up in a crowd that swarmed around someone we couldn't see. A husky, bellowing voice commanded the disorderly throng to '*Be silent and pay homage to the venerable Deliverer, Jacob Frank, who walks in the footsteps of the Anointed One, Shabtai Tzvi.*'"

"Over the unruly screams of '*Long Live the Savior*,' we heard another voice, high-pitched and razor-edged." Eliezar reported. "It was their savior Jacob Frank, calling out to his 'believers.'"

"Frank told them that Shabtai Tzvi's blood and message pump through his veins and that soon it would be time to take flight from the nests in which the Sabbateans had been hiding. His sharp voice cut through the air like a blade: '*You will become an army—my army. I will lead you to victory you have not dared imagine*.' To deafening cheers, Jacob Frank promised '*only by throwing off all shackles of law and morality can you become your own masters*.' The crowd grew more frenzied. '*Only utter chaos would bring final freedom*,' he commanded."

Ezekiel stopped and looked at Malka, whose anguished expression reflected his. Malka shook her head no, as if cautioning him not to continue. When Ezekiel went on, Zahava sensed he was leaving something out of his narrative.

"Malka and I turned to escape the crowd. Ahead of us, I saw a large man who looked vaguely familiar. He stepped closer, blocking our path. Once in front of me, he spat on my shoe. When he spoke, I recognized the husky voice we had first heard."

"'*You are one of the sheep who blindly follows a blind shepherd*,' he hissed. "I worried for Malka, so I tried to keep walking. He pushed back hard against my shoulder; thank God, he did not touch Malka."

"'*You don't remember me?*' he insisted. '*Then I will have to make you remember. My name is Mendel, Rabbi Mendel of Brody*.' He tipped his hat like this were an ordinary, civil encounter. '*My mission is to support my master...*' he stopped and drew in a deep breath that he exhaled with a wheeze, '*and to destroy yours*.'"

"Rabbi Mendel, head of a yeshiva and member of the Kloiz, a Sabbatean?" Zahava's father Avner called out in disbelief. Zahava looked across the room at Amos. He was pale, leaning against the wall as if he would be unable to stand were it not there. It brought tears of gratitude to her eyes to see the Rebbe walk slowly towards her husband, nodding for Ezekiel to go on.

"Rabbi Mendel barked that a magician calling himself a teacher is seducing the masses with illusions of equality. *'Such self-righteous holiness is sugar on the wounds of our people,'* he accused. *'Violence is what is needed to overthrow injustice; force, not the docile passivity this holy herbalist feigns in order to rouse an army of fools.'* Rabbi Mendel went on to proclaim, less to us than to the group of Sabbatean followers who had gathered around us and were cheering his remarks: *'We Frankists are prepared to wage war against all that constrains us, including your rabbi.'* "

"'*We will triumph, you can be assured,*' he shouted, further rallying the others. *'The Baal Shem Tov's good name will be more smeared.'* With these last words, Rabbi Mendel spat again in front of us, rubbing his spit into the ground with the heel of his boot."

Weary, Ezekiel sat, his gaze directed downward, and said no more. Zahava was surprised when Malka stood.

"There is more," she said, "but it cannot be told now." Malka indicated with her eyes and the tilt of her head that this was because of the presence of the children.

In the evening, Zahava, standing close to Amos, was among the disciples gathered in the Beis Midrash to hear what had not been shared earlier. This time it was Malka who told the rest "the nightmare" that she and Ezekiel had seen in the broad daylight of Lanskroun.

"Blocking our attempt to leave, Rabbi Mendel insisted that we meet his Holy Master. Pushing Ezekiel, who did not let go of me, he forced an opening in the crowd until Ezekiel and I arrived at a wooden platform. There stood Jacob Frank 'the Redeemer,' half the size of Rabbi Mendel and with a slight hunch. His bony frame was draped with a huge velvet burgundy caftan lined with bright yellow satin. He was crowned with a turban of gold. Frank waved his gloved hands to silence his flock."

Malka continued without looking up.

"Jacob Frank waved his hand again, this time to summon twelve young women to surround him, a few of them little more than girls. He presented these as his Sacred Virgins. He then called Rabbi Mendel and eleven young men, his *Apostles,* to come and stand in front of his '*Holy Concubines.*' Among the young women were prostitutes. Jacob Frank reminded his followers that the great Shabtai Tzvi had found his wife in the streets—'*so destitute, she lacked even the dignity of a brothel roof over her head.*'"

When Malka's voice dropped and she appeared unable to continue, Ezekiel stepped forward.

"'*My brothers,*' Frank instructed the aroused crowd, '*no action of the holy Redeemer is in vain. Actions that appear heretical to the simple mind have mystical significance, which only The Deliverer can fathom.*'" The Savior commanded his army of believers to follow in his noble footsteps. "'*Whether betrothed or not, whether fathers or not, take mistresses to your beds,*' he told them. '*Send your own daughters into the streets.*'"

"As Malka and I turned our backs to leave, we heard Jacob Frank urge that everything known as holy be overthrown and that all that was deemed sinful, be revered. Only in this way, his shrill voice summoned, would the good hidden in evil be released and the truth beyond appearances be revealed."

No one spoke when Ezekiel finished. Zahava squeezed Amos' hand.

YISROEL PERCEIVED the discomfort and shock that moved through the minds and bodies of the disciples after listening to the account of what had occurred in Lanskroun. Several times during the narrative, one or another in the community had glanced over at him, looking for assurance or to find some bearing. What could he offer them now in the wake of the shocking rendition?

Yisroel began softly as if they were waking together from a collective dream.

"What we've heard is shocking and frightening. But right now, your children are eager to see and feel you. Without hearing what was spoken, even the youngest may sense a fearful shattering. They may or may not ask you what happened. Before you go to your children, bearing your own painful questions, while reaching for simple answers to theirs, I invite you to find one answer now."

They looked at him questioningly.

"Please, as best you can now, turn within." At these words, most closed their eyes. He did, too.

"Become aware of your breathing. With each long breath in and out, settle more completely in yourself." Yisroel waited a few moments before speaking again, letting the silence deepen. He breathed in a long breath and exhaled slowly then took several more long, slow breaths.

"Come to rest in the deep still space within you, beneath the roiling of waves on the surface," he guided. "You need not try to block out the disturbing actions of the Frankists. Just find your way to the place within you that is beyond fear. It is possible to find that place even now."

Yisroel gave his full intention to fortify them.

"When you are ready, open your eyes, keeping your heart open. Go to your children anchored in your heart. This will anchor and ease them in the midst of the turbulence they've sensed. In turn, your children will root you deeper in love, as you remain attentive to them rather than to distressing thoughts. What we are to do, if anything, will be revealed with time. We will better apprehend that call if we are settled in our hearts."

The disciples left the House of Study in silence.

Alone now in the Study House, Yisroel heard a gentle knock and watched the door open slowly. Five-year-old Avigal entered, gripping the handle of her basket. She had once again beseeched her mother Luba and grandmother Tanya to stay behind while she crossed the courtyard alone to knock at the Rebbe's door. Shyly, with a twinkle in her eye, the child crossed the room, one careful step at a time, holding on to the basket of warm rolls. When their gazes locked, Yisroel felt the smile in his eyes meet the smile in hers. Such silent encounters were common between them.

Avigal reached a warm roll up to Yisroel. When he cupped his hand around the roll and her rounded hand, a wide smile spread over the child's face. Yisroel was touched by her quiet wonder as if she possessed a secret she trusted her Rebbe knew without either of them having to speak.

After she left, Yisroel thought about Avigal's pure, uncomplicated faith. Many dismissed the shallow, untested faith of youth as naïve. But one's relationship to God did not have to be complicated and troubled. There was much to learn from the innocence and wholeheartedness with which children stand before life and God. What if one could stand in the presence of men like Jacob Frank and Mendel of Brody with pure faith— faith in life's goodness and in an underlying justice. Fear would call this foolishness; faith would know it as power.

AMOS KNEW RATIONALLY that he held no responsibility for his father's deplorable actions and beliefs. But the voices of self-reprimand, similar to his father's constant reprimand, did not let him rest.

How could he have remained completely ignorant of his father's sub- versive activities? If he had known, could he have somehow intervened? Could his influence as a son have curbed his father's loyalty to the per- verse Jacob Frank? The self-accusation became louder and louder until Amos confided his inner tumult to Zahava after their children slept.

Zahava's response was direct and perceptive. "The division between your father and you has become a division within you, Amos. Since news of the horrors of Lanskroun, your loathing of your father's actions appears to have spawned self-loathing. Is it possible," she asked, "to denounce your father's actions and to love the man at the same time?"

Love his father? Amos suddenly became overwhelmed by feelings he had been holding back. Shame, sorrow for his mother and sisters, rage at his father, and paralyzing fear swelled like a deluge of muddy waters and threatened to burst the dam of Amos heart.

The next morning, Amos woke in Zahava's arms. He felt exhausted by the battle he'd been fighting within himself. His father's persistent shaming of him as a boy, Mendel's harping on what it was to be a true man, and his deprecation of women, all had become demons caged in

Amos' mind. The effort it took for him to resist their clawing had never been so clear as now.

What was also clear was his knowing that he was not his father. He could begin to see and know himself through his own eyes, rather than his father's.

"Amos, can you see your father's hatred as a shield protecting his wounded heart? He cannot allow himself to be touched."

Amos had never considered that this man who did so much wounding might himself be wounded.

"Perhaps I can come to pity him, Zahava, but I don't know if I can find my way to loving this man whose actions are so treacherous."

"Start here," she pressed her hand to his heart, "by loving his son Amos."

∾

HAVING HEARD THE NEWS DURING HIS TRAVELS, Avner brought back word to the Rebbe and other disciples about the ban imposed on the Sabbatean followers of Jacob Frank. The cherem, issued by the influential Brody Kloiz of rabbis, scholars, and judges, had been precipitated by what was becoming widely referred to as "the Lanskroun Scandal." It condemned the Frankists as "impenitent heretics" and advocated that every possible measure be taken to expose and prosecute followers of Jacob Frank. Frankists were to be excluded from commerce, marriage, and even from being allowed to enter a synagogue. The Cherem mandated that adherents be treated "as vermin, but more vile and dangerous." Violent sanctions were condoned, if necessary, to challenge and uproot Sabbatean practices and the noxious influence of Jacob Frank.

Among the names of those responsible for issuing the ban of excommunication was the esteemed Rabbi Mendel of Brody.

∾

"RABBI AVNER!"

Avner turned toward the husky voice that had called his name in the crowded Medzibocz marketplace. He saw a hand waving, but could not see the face of the man that seemed to be pressing his way towards him.

"Avner!" the voice boomed more insistently.

Avner noticed the unusually fine shtreimel on the man's head. The shimmering pelt rimming the hat floated towards him above the other heads and hats.

Frozen where he stood, Avner watched Mendel close the distance between them. The elegant brocade cape framing Mendel's broad shoulders and the embroidered satin sash wrapped around his ample waist, both typical of Turkish dress, blended oddly with the fur-trimmed hat of a Polish Jew.

Mendel smiled broadly, extending his large hand. Avner lifted his stiffly. Mendel gripped it, slapping his "old friend" firmly on the back with his other hand.

""I did not expect to find you here, my good Avner," he bellowed. "What holy business brings you to Medzibocz? We rabbis trade in knowledge, but also in other precious merchandise don't we—like those fancy textiles of yours." He slapped Avner on the back again.

Avner was uncomfortable and unsure how to respond. This man had been his friend once. But Avner had been shocked by the news that this self-righteous, stringent defender of tradition was actually a Sabbatean. And Mendel would be as shocked to learn of Avner's involvement with the Rebbe. Or did he know already?

"Let's have a vodka together, my good friend," Mendel commanded, ignoring Avner's silence. Mendel's breath and demeanor revealed that he'd already had quite a few. Avner was actually relieved to find Mendel a little drunk; he would be more boisterous and likely to talk over Avner. Mendel extended his hand with a flourish, inviting Avner to lead the way to the tavern.

"How foolish of me!" Mendel blurted out as they made their way. "You must be here to visit your daughter—oh forgive me, her name, I forgot it. In any case, what doubly good fortune then, to find you! This Medzibocz is much bigger than I had imagined. You, my good friend, can lead me to my son Amos. Or if you, too, just arrived, we'll find them together! I should have come sooner, I know, instead of always insisting Amos come to Brody, but to tell you the truth, when he didn't give me any grandsons, well… let's just say, I lost some interest. You must understand. We're both busy men, you and I, are we not? That means sometimes we have to put first things first."

Mendel's ongoing one-sided conversation, now commenting on this building or that vendor as they walked, spared Avner saying anything. But at some point, Mendel *would* wait for a reply. It was not Avner's custom to conceal the truth, much less to lie. But if Mendel did not, in fact, suspect Avner and his son's involvement with Yisroel, Avner decided not to reveal it, at least not yet.

At the entrance to the tavern, Mendel leaned towards Avner, lowering his voice. "I know I can trust you," he confided, "so I will tell you, my friend. I have come to this city for business that does not involve my Amos. Although, of course, I want to see him and maybe finally the grandsons I asked him to promise me. Mendel's heavy hand at Avner's back pushed him through the door to a small table in the corner. The room was cloudy with pipe smoke to which Mendel added his own. No sooner had the men sat down than Mendel began.

"Surely you've heard about the Lanskroun Affair?"

Avner nodded.

"And the ban imposed by the exalted Rabbinic Court of Brody?"

"Yes." It was the first word Avner had said.

Mendel laughed. "My voice was the loudest among the exalted judges decrying the heinous scandal. I insisted the cherem be imposed on the impenitent heretics."

Avner could not hide his surprise. So Mendel had not only signed but initiated the cherem?

"Ah, you are surprised?" Mendel appeared amused. "Don't you agree that the Sabbateans pose a great threat not only in Poland, but beyond its borders as well? How can we tolerate events like those that unfolded in Lanskroun?"

Mendel, swiftly finishing his second glass of vodka, banged his fist on the table for the tavern keeper. "More for these two fine gentlemen," he bellowed then turned back to Avner. "It is my duty to protect the sanctity of our traditions, is it not?"

"Of course," Avner replied, growing more uncomfortable.

"Why, my friend, is your voice so without conviction then?" Mendel mocked, picking up Avner's glass still filled to its rim. "Ah, no wonder! Your tongue needs loosening. Drink up my friend!"

Mendel passed the glass to Avner who lifted it to his lips, but was relieved when Mendel looked away to pour another drink down his throat.

"I can trust you, right?" Mendel's slurred voice showed the vodka's effects. He leaned forward conspiratorially. "There's something we must discuss. A gift. A great gift that I would like to give my old friend Avner." Mendel looked through, not at, his friend. His drunkenness was making it less necessary by the minute for Avner to respond.

"I have a secret…" Mendel turned slightly to look over his shoulder then back at Avner. "I have found a hero among men. It is—*it will be*—your good fortune to meet him. Right now," Mendel bent lower and whispered, "he is in hiding in Turkey." He put his finger to his lips. "It's too dangerous for him to cross the border into Poland. Don't ask me how, but I managed to hide him and spare his arrest in Lanskroun!" Mendel seemed clearly proud and even somewhat amused by his success.

"With help," he pointed his finger straight up then turned it around and pointed it into his chest, "I have smuggled him across the Dniester River until the time is right for him to appear again in Podolia—next time welcomed by an even greater army of believers! But, the long-awaited King must be vigilant. He will stay in Turkey, except, of course, for when he crosses the border to meet with certain of his believers." Mendel winked and then reached for Avner's drink and finishing it, raised his voice in a sudden outburst of anger and irritation.

"Jacob Emden, prominent rabbi of Prague," Mendel scowled, "and opponent of my friend, Jonathan Eybeschutz, has gone to the ecclesiastical authorities in Prague. Emden has informed the church that Eybeschutz is promoting a new faith."

Mendel's indignant anger seemed to bring a greater clarity to his expression.

"Rabbi Emden also made a point of denouncing the "new faith" as a departure from Judaism. As such it is in violation of the church canon, which, as you may know, does not condone any new faiths in the commonwealth. Emden is asking for church persecution of those who believe in the new faith." Mendel banged his fist on the table "How foolish of Emden!" He stared intently into Avner's eyes, his focus surprisingly steadied.

"Avner, I have something very important to tell you," he said. "I've gone to Bishop Dembowski, the most powerful enemy of the Jews in the region of Podolia. The majority and the strongest of the underground cells are concentrated in his diocese of Kamenetz-Podolsk. I've asked his protection for the Sabbateans from the forthcoming, uncontrolled attacks of self-righteous Jews."

Mendel leaned back, his great pleasure displayed in the broad grin framing his teeth.

"I explained to Dembowski—who readily sympathized—that our Jewish brethren have attacked the followers of Shabtai Tzvi and now Jacob Frank because our beliefs are aligned with Christian doctrine. The fool believed me because he wanted to believe me. I have offered Dembowski our collaboration, in a manner yet to be determined by him, in return for his protection from those seeking to uproot us." Mendel threw his head back and, abandoning his previous caution, continued in a less subdued manner.

"Imagine, Avner! I convinced him we Sabbateans oppose the Talmud for countless reasons, thus separating us from other Jews. I also convinced him that we, too, believe that the Son of God has already come in human form, free of sin, to redeem all mankind. I did *not* tell him that we believe Jacob Frank to be that Son of God. I proclaimed our faith in the doctrine of the trinity, leaving out that we believe God the Father sent his Son, Jacob Frank, joined by the Holy Spirit of Shabtai Tzvi. May the zealous Bishop Dembowski believe what he will about his new allies, whom he has dubbed *contra-Talmudists*."

Mendel leaned closer. "I am confident that Dembowski and his associates will grant us the protection we seek. Those foolish rabbis and others who think they can quell or vanquish Jacob Frank, our Champion of Truth, will learn how futile their efforts will be to control their flock."

Mendel stood up. He appeared to be suddenly exhausted. "I have some business to conduct in Medzibocz before Shabbos. Seek me at the inn tomorrow night after Shabbos has ended. Then I'll be ready for the business of seeing my son before I leave the next morning. Maybe by then you will have found your tongue!"

Mendel slapped Avner one last time and stumbled out of the tavern.

Avner knew he would not seek Mendel at the inn after the Sabbath. In the meantime, between now and Sunday morning when Mendel would depart Medzibocz, Avner would stay away from the Rebbe's synagogue and Beis Midrash. He would even stay away from the section of the city in which both were located and where most of the community lived. He would somehow get word to Zahava or Amos that Mendel might be looking for them, and suggest they also stay away from the Rebbe's shul and study houses. The Rebbe would not ask this of them, nor even encourage it, but Yisroel did not make decisions for his students. Avner would do what he could to protect the Rebbe and the community—especially Amos, Zahava and their children—from Mendel's hostility.

When visiting Brody with Zahava years earlier, Avner had witnessed Mendel's bitterness more vividly than in any of their previous interactions. On his last night there, Avner, alone with Mendel, had expressed his sympathy about the loss of Mendel's wife, a subject he was surprised his host had not brought up. Mendel's lengthy denigration of the "worthless bitch and her equally useless litter of bitches" had horrified Avner. As if this were not enough, Mendel, steeped in schnapps, had come to denounce the vices of all women. He stopped abruptly, stood and put his hands and weight on Avner's shoulders, shaking him.

"I should know," Mendel hissed, "My mother used my organ as her toy."

No sooner had Mendel confided this than he collapsed into a chair, staring at nothing. A few minutes later he was snoring.

Avner was stunned and saddened by the violation Mendel had suffered. He had thought often since that night in Brody about the confession that poured out in his friend's drunken rage, wishing deeply that Mendel had not suffered as he had. Avner wished also that the vile mistreatment Mendel had endured were not leading him to mistreat others.

Would the Rebbe be capable of finding light even here? The only thing Avner could find in himself for the man was pity. Pity and grave distrust.

∾

THE WOMEN WERE GATHERED IN THEIR HOUSE OF Study when Dalia heard a scream. Fifteen-year-old Freyda was calling from the girls' classroom for help. Other screams joined Freyda's, summoning the women from their study room.

Dalia saw the flames the moment she entered. Freyda and Raisa were pulling and carrying the youngest girls out of the fire. Terror in their eyes, the girls escaped into the arms of their mothers, sisters, and aunts.

A number of the women and older girls ran with buckets to the well. The men not at their trades were repairing a shelter on the far side of town. Those few who were nearby joined the women's efforts to control the fire.

Water could not be brought fast enough to prevent the fire from spreading from the girls' cheyder to the Women's House of Study. There it burned more furiously upon contact with the many pamphlets, prayer books, and other sacred texts.

Before it was extinguished, the fire had devoured every letter and word in both the girls' cheyder and the women's study house. Remarkably, the men's study house had been left intact, leaving the community its meeting place.

Praise God, Dalia thought, *no life was lost.* Exhausted by efforts to combat the fire, Dalia stared numbly at the flakes of black ash that floated in the air. How could it be that what had been so solid one moment was now just—

When Rifka's arms wrapped around her, Dalia stopped thinking and let go into her tanta's embrace.

THE MORNING after the fire, leaflets began to appear throughout Medzibocz, denouncing the Baal Shem Tov and his followers in the name of the ban of excommunication issued in Brody against the activities of the Sabbateans. The burning of the girls and women's places of study was cited as the first of many warnings to the "zealous infidels" to stop the activity of educating women.

Rifka read from the leaflet to the handful of women gathered around her:

The infamous Yisroel ben Eliezar and his flock of zealous infidels have been punished for one of their many assaults on the ancient traditions protecting our people. To distinguish a room where women gather as worthy of the name Beis Midrash is an impiety and an incitement to action.

Woman has been fashioned to cherish her husband and children, not to run after what takes her from these duties. Innocent women and children are being pitilessly misled! In addition, the perverse magician, calling himself a rabbi, has knowingly allowed copies of the Zohar to fall into the hands of women!

The Cherem against the Sabbateans has restored the restriction, permitting only men over forty access to the Zohar. The travesty of putting the Zohar and other texts

into the hands of women has led to sacred books being
destroyed. This sin, too, is on the head of one known as
the Baal Shem Tov, destroyer of the holy.

IN SUBSEQUENT days and weeks, similar leaflets and letters appeared
in other towns and cities throughout the Podolia region and beyond.
These decried the Baal Shem Tov's pestilence and promulgated "*holy mea-*
sures" to be taken to quell the destructive Sabbatean fire. Severe reprisals
against "*these Sabbatean serpents*" were being condoned and encouraged.

Avner had said nothing to his daughter and son-in-law—who Mendel had not, it seemed, chosen to seek out after all—nor to any of the
other disciples about his sickening suspicions that the burnings might
have been "the business" that Mendel had come to conduct in Medzibocz.
What good would it do to tell them? Surely, even if true, there would be
no way to prove it.

Did Yisroel see through Mendel's duplicitous charade? Avner wondered. Did he suspect the violence of which Mendel was capable? Would
the Rebbe defend himself and the community? *Was it possible to protect*
the truth without defending it?

WITH FERVOR and the Baal Shem Tov's blessing, Rifka urged the
rebuilding of the girls' classroom and the Women's House of Study—
making each more spacious than before. Fear of further attack could not
deter the community from continuing to live its beliefs and ideals. "Even
if we are not free of fear," she encouraged, "we can move forward together
to take action."

It did not take much effort to convince her comrades. Once again,
the financial support for building materials came from the gold trader's
wife, but this time, also from other women of means. The disciples provided the labor, and even the children were given tasks so they would
feel included.

Rifka was heartened to see the building of the rooms—brick by brick this time—fortify the faith and unity of the disciples. The community's commitment to its values was being renewed, including the promise to educate its women and girls. The project was further blessed when citizens of Medzibocz who had never set foot in the Rebbe's shul or either of the houses of study approached to offer help and food.

What fear had dismantled, and tried to destroy, was being rebuilt more strongly than before. Not only was a more enduring foundation created for the building, the community as a whole seemed to be standing on more solid ground. It was not that every heart was free of trepidation at every moment. The Rebbe was clear that this wasn't even to be expected. But despite their fear, the disciples had marshaled their courage, not to fight evil but to protect peace. Their vision was not only to defend one community in one city in Poland, but also to bring the possibility of harmony and equality to the world. All this had become clearer in the wake of the fire.

Rifka suspected that this was why the Rebbe had begun to send disciples to cities and towns beyond Medzibocz. Judah and Amos had been sent to help restore a small synagogue damaged by a flooding river; Elias, to scribe in a city that had lost a Torah to fire. Naomi, accompanying him, had saved the lives of twins born to one who was little more than a girl herself. Malka and Ezekiel were sent back to Malka's relatives in Lanskroun with instructions to pray in the Lanskroun's synagogue as much as possible during the three days of their visit.

For certain trips, no specific purpose was given at all. Gedaliah and Dovid had traveled at the Rebbe's bidding to a string of towns, not knowing why they had been sent until they had spent time in each.

Rifka had begun to travel as well, sometimes sent by the Rebbe but, increasingly, led by her own desire. She journeyed in the company of one or several of the male disciples. Her chosen mission, upon arriving to a destination, was to speak with women, to encourage them to study together and to educate their daughters. She was greeted, most frequently, with suspicion, disdain, and even alarm.

Rifka was learning from her sisters in Medzibocz—Dalia, Naomi, Zahava, Malka, Tanya, Batleya, Luba, and even Freyda and Raisa—about the need to temper her zeal at times. They helped Rifka see how easily women could feel ashamed of their ignorance and their complacency, despite it being so contrary to Rifka's intention to never shame any woman. She was reminded that women—reluctant for whatever reason—needed to be met with genuine compassion as well as fierce conviction. She was grateful to her sisters' wisdom and courage; rather than weakening her resolve, their insight strengthened her.

As Yisroel sent out more of his students, each discovered where doubt or fear still lurked in his or her heart. Some struggled with sustaining faith in a benevolent Source in the face of bottomless human suffering. Others harbored doubts about their worthiness as the Rebbe's "emissaries." As they journeyed, each discovered more about living Love.

❧ 34 ❧

Disconcerting news came to Medzibocz on the lips of travelers. It concerned a bishop named Dembowski from Kamenetz-Podolsk, known for his disdain of Jews and the freedoms being allowed them by the Polish king.

Bishop Dembowski was demanding a public disputation to elucidate several key "principles of faith." The disputation was to take place between the contra-Talmudists, a group of Jews Dembowski had taken under his wing, and members of their own religion said to be victimizing the contra-Talmudists.

Dembowski would present the principles of faith to be debated between the contra-Talmudists and the Jewish authorities oppressing them. The Jews disputing the contra-Talmudists were to select a handful of rabbis and commanded to submit written documents proving or successfully disproving the tenets of faith being presented. This was to be done by the spring, just a few months away. The primary subject of the debate was whether man could possibly interpret the Word of God, the Holy Bible.

If it was determined that the Word of God could *not*, in fact, be interpreted by human minds then the Talmud, consisting of centuries of biblical interpretation, represented a grave transgression against Divinity.

The travelers relaying news of the disputation reported further that the esteemed Rabbi Mendel of Brody, renowned as one of Sabbateanism's fiercest opponents, had been elected the chief representative of Talmudic authority in the forthcoming disputation.

∽

BY LATE SPRING OF 1757, the outcome of the disputation reached Medzibocz as it did all the cities in the commonwealth: Bishop Dembowski had ruled in favor of the contra-Talmudists.

After reviewing the written disputations, Dembowski deemed that it had been proven impossible for the human mind to interpret the Word of God. To even attempt to analyze and debate biblical injunctions was a sin against the Lord's absolute authority. Therefore, the Talmud, consisting of centuries of rabbinic commentary and highly developed codes of conduct based on these interpretations, must be regarded as profane.

Severe penalties were to be imposed as a result of the rabbis' failure in the disputation. As the chief of these penalties became known, a tremor of shock and disbelief moved through not only the Jews of the commonwealth, but also among Christian leaders stunned by the bishop's decree: *the Talmud and all other books sacred to the Jews were to be confiscated and publicly burned.*

The first fire would take place in November at the seat of the bishop's diocese in Kamenetz-Podolsk to be followed by fires throughout the region. Dembowski proclaimed his intention that ecclesiastical authorities in the entire commonwealth and beyond respond in kind to the heretical Talmud of the Jews.

Dalia was with her father when he received the news of the bishop's decree. He said nothing, lowering himself slowly into his chair. Dalia could not recall ever witnessing the raw pain she saw in her abba's face now. How could he possibly find light and blessing in this curse? He covered his face with his hands. When her mother drew her last breaths, Dalia had seen her father's luminous blue eyes become radiant with tears, but now his face was sheltered. She couldn't tell if he was praying or crying.

Yisroel remained with his head in his hands. After several moments, Dalia heard barely audible utterances begin to issue from his lips; they seemed not to be formal prayers but rather his own words beseeching God, to whom he always turned. She could make out only an occasional word of the impassioned dialogue he was having. She moved back to sit on his narrow bed, allowing him the privacy of his supplication.

Feeling enveloped by her father's wholehearted absorption, Dalia closed her eyes. Almost instantly, an image of the golden calf arose in her mind's eye. She witnessed the frenzy of people regarding the molten figure of the calf at the foot of Mount Sinai. She recognized how terrified they were, how abandoned they felt without connection to the Source of true protection. They had resorted to idolatry, thinking this might protect them.

As the image of the calf and its desperate worshippers faded, Dalia kept her eyes closed, musing about the meaning of the idol's appearance. She thought about the bishop's edict. What was this nefarious bishop worshipping? And the contra-Talmudists—in what were they placing their faith, and from what source were they seeking protection? How challenging it could be in times like these for her and others in the community to sustain faith in the protection of an unseen Source of justice.

Dalia opened her eyes and looked at her father, his head still bent in prayer. Staring at him, she could feel her abba's supplication reverberating in her own body. His and now her own impassioned yearnings pulsed through her chest and limbs. This yearning was for love more powerful than fear. She was a vessel at once holding and being held in this love.

When her father looked up his eyes were red. The expression on his face had changed. Dalia still discerned pain but she saw something else, too. *Surrender.*

He was neither denying the gravity of the edict nor was he denying his pain. He had faced the edict and the evil behind it and somehow let this change him. The injustice and its horror had summoned an even greater measure of love from him—and from her, as well. The Rebbe taught his students that any so-called heights or depths they saw him attain, they could attain as well. She had not imagined herself capable of finding a compassionate way to 'hold' events such as those that had occurred in Lanskroun and Kamenetz-Podolsk. She understood more fully now than ever before that surrender in the face of injustice was not passivity. Her father was surrendering to unshakeable faith even in the presence of inhumanity. Could victory not be found in such surrender?

MAKING HIS WAY to the Beis Midrash, Gedaliah was hailed by two Christian clerics with whom he had engaged from time to time in enriching dialogues.

Greeting him somberly, the men informed Gedaliah that while on church business in Kamenetz-Podolsk they had witnessed the burning of Jewish holy books commanded by Bishop Dembowksi.

The kind priests, sympathetic to the plight of their Jewish brethren, and disturbed by the crime being perpetrated by the bishop and his cohorts, offered to share with the Baal Shem Tov's community what they had witnessed. To the men's knowledge no Jewish citizen had dared witness the burnings. If any had, they had remained well hidden.

The community gathered in the Beis Midrash to hear the account.

"Preceding the burnings, dozens of men were dispatched by Bishop Dembowski to raid synagogues, houses of study, and even the homes of the city's Jews," one of the clerics began. "This ransacking and gathering of books went on for several weeks. Jews who refused to cooperate were beaten. Members of the Kahal and religious leaders who dared to protest were imprisoned in the city's castle-turned-prison. The pile of books in the square outside the formidable cathedral of the diocese grew daily under the watch of guards armed with swords, lest any '*foolhardy Jews*' try to rescue even one. The burning was to take place on the Jewish Sabbath, a further affront."

"The morning of the burning," the second witness reported, "Bishop Mikolaj Dembowski emerged from the two enormous bronze doors of the ornate cathedral. The towering, thin man was crowned by a miter adorned with embroidery, rows of pearls, and discs of precious metals. The regalia of his vestments, the same worn to offer the Holy Eucharist, contrasted tragically with the ignoble task he was about to execute. The bishop, in his white-gloved hands, received a blazing torch from one of his clerics, knelt, and touched it to the bottom of the pile. It took only seconds for the flames to leap and begin to devour the holy books. As the fire raged, a smile danced on the bishop's lips until…"

At this point the man recounting the story stopped and exchanged looks with his companion.

"Bishop Dembowski," the second man, continued, "fell to the ground before the fire had consumed the books." Listening, the disciples held their breath.

"Efforts were made to resuscitate him, but they proved futile. The day chosen for the desecration of your people's holy texts was the day the bishop was doomed as well. We left before his burial, which was to be conducted with great pageantry."

Even before Gedaliah voiced his question, it was answered.

"The Edict that all copies of the Talmud be burned has been rescinded for fear that Bishop Dembowski's death was a Divine reprisal."

Relief spread through the room like a strong wind through a window suddenly thrown open. Some of the students wept. Others whispered prayers.

Gedaliah thanked the young priests and embraced them as they prepared to take their leave. "The Peace of God be with you," he spoke softly, words from their sacred Mass, taught to him by his friend Patryk so long ago.

"And with you," the men replied before retreating.

∾

THE PURPOSE FOR MEETING WAS NOT SPECIFIED, WHEN, on a snowy night not long after Chanukah was over, the Rebbe invited all the disciples to gather in the Beis Midrash.

Gedaliah watched his companions arrive with curiosity, excitement, and even trepidation. The Rebbe stood. With smiling eyes, he swept the room slowly with his gaze, his delight and appreciation for each of them apparent.

"Your wagons are full," he said.

The enigmatic words were greeted with puzzled looks. But a few students nodded as if they not only understood but had expected this.

Gedaliah glanced at Rifka, who like him did not seem surprised by their Rebbe's words.

"Now is the time to take your wagons into the marketplace," Yisroel continued. "Time to offer your riches. Some will know the worth of your treasure; others won't yet be aware of their value. Nonetheless, give freely the blessings you have received and receive freely from those before you and from your Source." He paused.

"It is time to live as teachers as well as students," he told them.

For some time, Yisroel had been encouraging them to embrace themselves as teachers, saying they would teach by living what they believed. But there was something different in the Rebbe's message today. What was different, Gedaliah realized, was not the Rebbe's message, but that he was preparing them to leave.

The Rebbe answered the unasked question hovering over the room.

"Some of you will remain here in Medzibocz; others will depart. All this will become clear as you are called from within by your destinies."

The Rebbe looked around the room, his glance resting on each one of them before continuing.

"I am not sending you into the world to rescue those who are suffering. I send you forth to see God in them and therefore to trust that it is God who will provide what they need. It is not yours to prescribe what a soul requires on its journey. Sometimes the soul's need is for hardship in order to deepen faith or develop courage, patience, or trust. When someone comes before you, what is needed from you above all is to be completely present. As you cleave to your heart, beneficial words and actions will arise naturally."

The silence in the room felt as fathomless as the Baal Shem Tov's love for them.

He would not ordain where his students were to go. He asked that they seek the counsel of their own hearts first then talk with their families and the larger family of the community. His door would be open as always to talk about the stirrings in their hearts and the practical considerations that might arise. Some chose their destinations readily. They would return to the villages in which they had been raised. Others would go to villages in which they had studied, where they had relatives, or where they might find the best prospects for earning a livelihood.

Tanya and Samuel would go back to Horodenka with their daughter Luba, her husband Boaz, and their granddaughter Avigal. Gedaliah's daughter Batleya, wanting to be close to her cousin Luba, would also return to Horodenka with her husband Elijah and their children. Luba and Batleya, thirty and thirty-three now, wanted to start a cheyder for girls in Horodenka. Samuel, who had loved helping in the boys' cheyder in Horodenka years ago, hoped to serve there again in some fashion. He had never made a good cobbler, he laughed. Elijah, so like his mother Channa in his love for the land, looked forward to life in the less populated village of Horodenka. He and Boaz, who had grown up a shepherd, were eager to link their livelihood to the farmlands surrounding that town.

Gedaliah felt torn. He could not imagine living far from Yisroel again after tasting the sweetness of his steady presence and inspiration. But neither could Gedaliah imagine being separated from Batleya and his grandchildren or from his brother Samuel and family. He liked imagining Zofia watching their grandchildren through his eyes. But Gedaliah would also have grandchildren in Medzibocz. His son Ber, married to a young woman from Medzibocz, had just become a father for the second time and would remain in Medzibocz. Gedaliah had trained both Ber and Reuben as cobblers, starting back in Horodenka. In their twenties now, the brothers were both skilled shoemakers. Ber would continue to work in the cobbler shop in which Gedaliah, Samuel, and his sons had been working in Medzibocz. Reuben had decided to return to Horodenka where he was confident Dobry would welcome him back to the cobbler stall. Gedaliah, a fifty-six-year-old cobbler now, was welcome to work as much or as little as he wanted either in Medzibocz or Horodenka or both. Meir, Gedaliah's firstborn, not able to live independently, had become inseparable from Batleya, who cared for him with devotion, the way her mother Zofia had for Naftali. Batleya had assured her father Gedaliah repeatedly that should he decide to stay in Medzibocz, she and Elijah would be delighted to bring Meir with them to Horodenka to live under their roof. Gedaliah's heart was divided between the two places.

When Gedaliah spoke of his dilemma to Yisroel, Yisroel counseled patience. Later that same day, the Rebbe reminded everyone, again, that to be close to him did not require his physical presence. Had they not, by now, experienced the unity of their hearts with his? To enter their hearts would be the same as entering his room. They could find him and each other there. That night, Gedaliah decided: he would spend a portion of the year in Medzibocz and the other months in Horodenka. In each place, he would have work, a home with his children and grandchildren, the company of other disciples, and the presence of the Rebbe, physically and within his heart.

A number of disciples would remain with the Baal Shem Tov in Medzibocz. Elias would continue as the Rebbe's scribe and assist Judah and Amos in maintaining the synagogue and Houses of Study. Naomi, at almost fifty, attended births only rarely now. Instead, she brought the vigor of her midwifery to the Women's House of Study—where many of the women, whose children she had ushered into the world, called her midwife to their learning. Together with Dalia and Zahava, Naomi would guide the Women's Beis Midrash and oversee the girls' cheyder.

Dalia's daughter Freyda, almost eighteen, and her dear, lifelong friend Raisa came enthusiastically each day to teach the girls. Some mornings, Raisa's baby, Kaila, named for her grandmother, captivated the girls more than the letters of the alphabet. But Freyda and Raisa knew that when the girls saw the magic of the letters becoming words and the words, sentences, they would not be able to resist the alphabet either.

IT WAS ASSUMED that Rifka would continue her travels, encouraging and supporting women throughout Podolia to establish places of study for themselves and their daughters. Dalia and Judah had begun to accompany Rifka with greater frequency, which pleased all three. Even on relatively brief visits to their varied destinations, Judah was able to find work as a woodworker, while the women encouraged their sisters in the region, one mind and one heart at a time.

For years Rifka had heard Yisroel inspire those who came to him, even the visitors listening with only one foot in the door, to meet their sacred destinies. Now he was inviting his students to be God's hands and heart in the world.

"There are countless people who suffer a hunger and need that they do not perceive as the hunger for God, as well as for food," Yisroel reminded them. "But it is *not* a gift to give a man or woman wise words when they come craving food. The words will provide sustenance in their time *after* the body has been fed, or the home provided. Assist your sisters and brothers in finding food and shelter for their families. Only then is a man, woman, or child ready to feed the deep hunger for closeness to God. And, please," he urged, "do not be condescending towards those whose yearning is for physical sustenance; this will only add to their burdens. Your love and respect, not your judgment, will bless those you encounter and will bless you as well. To receive another being fully is to give and receive the greatest treasure of all."

Rifka woke in the small room she now occupied, closer to the Women's House of Study and the girls' classroom. It was still dark outside. She had dreamt again about the Holy Land. She lay still, trying to keep the dream from dissolving.

In her dream, Rifka had been wandering in the desert alone, parched with thirst. Thin sandals kept her feet from burning on the scalding sand. She wore a hooded tunic, walking head down to withstand the sand that pelted her face. A girl of about twelve, she had escaped Egypt with thousands of other Hebrew slaves, but had become separated from the rest of the flock of Jews wandering the arid wilderness. She struggled forward with no sight of her tribe or any visible destination, impelled by something from within.

This was as much as Rifka could recall. The damp cold in her room quickly displaced the heat of the desert.

Rifka heard Avigal and Nava's laughter coming from the girls' cheyder. The two had made a pact to carry in coal for the stove early each morning before the others girls and their teachers, Freyda and Raisa, arrived. The camaraderie between Avigal and Nava, who had been named for her uncle Naftali, reminded Rifka and the girls' grandfathers Gedaliah and Samuel of the friendship between the girls' mothers Luba and Batleya. It was when Luba and Batleya were close to this age that Rifka had first spent time with them in Horodenka in the wake of the fire that took Naftali's life. In their company, she'd had the strange knowing that they, like her, would be shepherdesses one day. Soon Luba and Batleya would be welcoming young Jewish daughters to a new classroom in Horodenka.

Thinking of Horodenka's Jewish daughters learning to read, Rifka recalled Marishka's craving for knowledge, how she would have loved to create a place for peasant girls to come and learn. "The peace of God be with you, my friend," Rifka said aloud. "The peace of God be with you all," she repeated, hoping that dear Justyna, Dominik, Marishka, and her little brothers had indeed found peace. And Patryk? Gedaliah had learned from kind old Father Amadeusz, who had trusted Leya's innocence, that Patryk had finally become a priest, but Gedaliah did not know where. "Peace be upon you, good Patryk, wherever you are," Rifka said pulling the heavy linen of her dress over her head.

ON THE NIGHT of the new moon, Rifka remained in the women's balcony after the evening prayer service until everyone except Yisroel had left the shul. Descending the stairs, she drew closer to where the Rebbe stood on a small platform built when the synagogue was enlarged. Although Yisroel had not looked at her, Rifka felt suddenly that he had been expecting her.

She sat down on one of the benches and closed her eyes, seeking the connection with her heart to which the Rebbe never ceased directing his students. She breathed slowly, feeling each breath bring her more fully present. Her confused thoughts had created pressure that was being eased now as she breathed. Rifka heard Yisroel walk down the three steps. She opened her eyes to see him standing before her.

He seemed ready for her question.

But was she ready to ask the question her dream had helped her to find? She drew in a deep breath and let it out.

"Rebbe, I want to travel to the Holy Land. To learn—then perhaps to teach. Truthfully, I'm less sure of my purpose than of the call to go, which is very clear. Yet, I feel conflicted. My work in Poland is also very clear. There is much to do here; to leave Poland without really knowing why seems irresponsible, even selfish."

"What is it that calls you to go?" Yisroel asked, showing no surprise at her desire.

"There's a mountaintop village my tanta Leya spoke of often when I was girl. I have heard you speak with reverence about this same mountaintop village of Safed where a community of Kabbalists put down roots. Tanta Leya would say that she had lived among these mystics in a previous lifetime and joked about me being there with her. We were probably men at that time, she would surmise, allowed to enter the academies, perhaps even to study with Ha'Ari, the great Rabbi Isaac Luria."

Yisroel, attentive to Rifka, said nothing.

"I want to return there," Rifka continued, not having intended to say "return" but struck that she had. "I want to see the academies that remain, perhaps even to study in one of them. I know it isn't likely that they will admit a woman. But, what if, with time, I could open the door, making it possible for other girls and women to enter after me?" She paused. "It is so difficult, Rebbe, to imagine leaving Podolia and those I love here."

Rifka felt tears rise and her throat tighten against them.

"But the pull to go is also strong. I have sought and received my heart's consent as you instruct us to do. Now, I come for yours."

Yisroel directed his gaze above Rifka's head to the small window behind her. When she turned, she saw the moon, a narrow arc of light in the dark sky.

"Rifka," he said softly, "can you see the promise of fullness in the hint of moon?"

Rifka nodded. She remembered gazing at a slender crescent moon with Channa and discerning, for the first time, its shadowed fullness.

Returning her attention, Rifka realized that with his words, *the promise of fullness*, her Rebbe had just blessed her intention. She felt an unexpected surge of joy. When she looked up, Yisroel was smiling at her. "The Ayn Sof beckons us closer through our deepest desires, dear Rifka. But can we ever know the Infinite One? Your travel to the Holy Land is a step into the heart of that Mystery.

AFTER RIFKA left the shul, Yisroel sat down on one of the benches. It was quiet enough for him to hear the hissing prayer of the coal stove radiating its heat. These days he was seeing and hearing prayer everywhere. Sitting with dear, passionate Rifka, he had heard the yearning prayer in her heart. Then he had seen the prayer of possibility in the moon.

He, too, had felt a call to Safed, having recognized it as a home for his soul when he was perhaps sixteen, both a tutor and Ezra's secret student in Tluste. But as his life had unfolded, he had responded to other calls. In each place—Zabie, Brody, then Medzibocz—he had been where he was meant to be.

Now his disciples were embarking on their journeys, deeper into their souls. It was not just to this village or that city, to this role or that one that they were going; they were making the choice to be God's presence wherever they settled. This was the soul's most daring journey.

Yisroel would touch the Holy Land through Rifka's soul. Medzibocz was to continue as his home and, for at least a while longer, would be the hub in the wheels of his students' lives and the lives of those yet to become his students.

Of course, Yisroel's true home was his heart, where he united with the One whose Love fashioned all life. There was no greater honor or purpose than reflecting this Love. It was for this purpose that Yisroel was sending his students deeper into the world. They would reflect unconditional love to those who had lost their connection or perhaps had never known God's love in the first place. Darkness would call forth the disciples' light; ignorance would summon their knowing. Rooted in their hearts, they had ripened into teachers. They would teach love, faith, and courage just by being. Even for those who might not think themselves ready or worthy, it was time.

∾

M ANY OF THE DISCIPLES AND THEIR FAMILIES HAD crowded into the men's Beis Midrash for *Seder,* the ritual meal on the first night of Passover. Avigal slipped into her seat at the table between her grandfather Samuel and grandmother Tanya. Her gleeful search with the other children for the *afikomen,* the half piece of matzo the Rebbe had broken off and hidden at the beginning of the meal, was over. The Rebbe called them all winners, although it was Avigal's best friend and first cousin Nava who had found the afikomen.

"Thank you, my angels," the Besht said, glancing deliberately at each one of the children. "How beautifully you searched. Because of your efforts, the two halves are united."

"But Rebbe," Nava's little brother called out sincerely, "you were the one to hide the matzo. You could have found it without us. Why are you so excited then?"

Avigal could not help smiling. The Rebbe smiled, too. His joy being with them all was as real as the hands he raised now to bless them with. Avigal bowed her head. She was eight years old and would not peek like she used to. But she imagined what she had seen when she *had* peeked: the Rebbe stretching out his strong arms, palms down. Although not right near him, Avigal could feel the power of his blessing as if he were placing his large, open hands directly on her head. She had felt his warm hands many times when bringing him the rolls he received from her like they were made of gold not simple flour.

"May each one of you know what it is to be whole," the Rebbe said. "And may we each help to make whole what has become divided."

AFTER THE DISCIPLES had gone home with their children and grandchildren, Rifka and Dovid remained to clean with Yisroel. The three worked quietly together. As she swept, Rifka wondered if the children had understood the blessing and invitation to "make whole what has become divided?" *What, in fact, did these words mean to her?*

The theme of freedom was at the heart of the Passover holiday. The escaped Hebrew slaves had to learn what it really meant to be free. What about Rifka's journey to freedom? It would be freedom to go to the Safed, and once there to try to enter an academy closed to women. But these were outer events and, although important, not the deepest freedom to which the Rebbe wished to lead her and each of his students.

She stopped her sweeping of the last of the matzo crumbs and turned to Yisroel. "Would you say more, Rebbe," she asked, "about what it is to be divided and to become whole?"

"Let me ask you, Rifka," he replied, sitting down and motioning for Dovid and Rifka to do the same. "What does this mean to *you*?"

Why was she surprised? The Rebbe did this all the time: he turned a question back to the one asking it. She took a deep breath.

"I think the first thing we must do is heal the division inside," she finally said. "When I was as young as some of these children, as you know, Rebbe, I felt divided inside: my trust wrestled with my anger at God."

"And now, Rifka?" Dovid asked, the compassion in his voice apparent.

Rifka had gradually become more accustomed to Dovid removing the armor over his heart. Nonetheless, the tenderness with which he had addressed her took her by surprise.

"Is your heart still divided now?" he continued, imploring gently.

"My heart feels divided," she began slowly, "when my fear battles with my faith. When fear triumphs, I feel unable to find my way to love. I also feel more separate from other people. Rifka paused. "Trust quiets my fear and returns me to myself."

"But when in the grip of fear, how do you come to trust?" Dovid asked.

"Perhaps not unlike the way a young child stumbles one step at a time into the embrace of the one watching over her."

Dovid looked at her so openly, she looked away. Although Yisroel was not speaking, Rifka realized beyond a doubt that this conversation would not be taking place without the container of their Rebbe's love.

"Often I find myself taking tentative, awkward steps into my own embrace," she continued. "I reach to love myself just as I am, even when deeply afraid. God's love remains an abstraction if I am not intimate with myself. Loving myself is vital if I am to accept God's embrace through the love of others." As soon as *the love of others* was spoken, Rifka felt heat rise to her face.

In the gentle, undemanding silence, Rifka was grateful to feel the self-consciousness that had overtaken her slip away. Perhaps she did not need to understand the confusing feelings that sometimes arose in her friendship with Dovid. Living in the Baal Shem Tov's community, *not knowing* had become a more familiar and acceptable state of being. Impatience could still grip Rifka but was being joined by an odd, less familiar companion: surrender. Yisroel taught that one's troublesome and even unwanted qualities could yield gifts; he urged his students to peer into their own shadows to find the light hidden there. Rifka's impatience was one of these shadows; it had brought both pain and power. Impelling her since a girl, impatience had often separated her from solace; but it had also led her forward, clearing a path where there was none. What Rifka was moved to say next took her by surprise.

"I feel both faith and fear about my journey to the Promised Land." She was relieved to say this aloud. "But most of the time, more faith," she added, smiling, "which I suppose is why I am going." Perhaps it was thinking of forging a path that made Rifka recall a conversation she had once had with Leya about discouragement.

"Many years ago, my tanta told me lovingly that no matter what choice I make and even if I feel lost, I will not stay lost. As long as I seek guidance—remembering that I am not alone—I will be found. I have learned so much with you, Rebbe, about how to find myself."

"You have also taught others," Dovid whispered.

"Amen," Yisroel nodded, standing. "Amen, Dovid and Rifkalla. What was divided has been made whole."

DOVID LAY AWAKE unable to let go into sleep. Yisroel's enigmatic words were circling him. *What was divided has been made whole.* Was the Rebbe referring to Rifka and him?

If Dovid was to surrender to a much wanted sleep, he would have to replace these words and thoughts with others. There were so many other experiences during the evening that he could choose from: the Seder; the children's questions; the Rebbe and disciples' answers.

Dalia's daughter Freyda had raised a question during the meal about people being made in the likeness of God, asking the children what they thought it might mean, "to be like God?" The answers had come quickly and enthusiastically:

"I think to be like God is to be kind."

"To tell the truth?"

"Not to think you are better than another boy because you kick better than he does."

"I think," a sweet voice ventured, "that to be like God is to forgive mistakes." It was Avigal, Luba and the shepherd Boaz' daughter. Dovid could almost remember her exact words:

"Mistakes are a kind of forgetting. And being angry with someone who forgot doesn't help that person to remember. What helps them to remember is loving them, because what they forgot is that they are loved."

The memory evoked the same feeling now in the center of Dovid's chest as it had during the meal; he felt so open it almost hurt. *Whose mistake had Dovid not forgiven?*

Waking from a dream at dawn, Dovid knew that the question had prompted his astonishing dream.

In his dream, Dovid saw his father Jacob in the distance. Dovid's mother Gittel stood, transparent, between his father and him. Looking through her, Dovid's gaze met his father's. Dovid immediately looked away. Then he recalled the sweet voice: *Mistakes are forgetting. To be angry is not to help someone remember.* Dovid had still not forgiven his father's mistakes. Dovid lifted his gaze to meet his father's eyes again and instantly felt the shell enclosing his love break open. He realized that he had hidden his love so well, he had not been able to find it long after his father had died.

Suddenly, a blue light surrounded Jacob, who was turning slowly to his own father, Reb Shlomo, standing behind him. Jacob walked towards the man, touching his blue hand to the center of his father's chest. Instantly, both vanished, leaving a fading shimmer of indigo light in their wake.

Not long after Shavuous, Rifka gratefully accepted the opportunity to travel with a rabbi and his wife, acquaintances of Rabbi Gershon's, to Constantinople and from there to Jerusalem. Not only had Gershon helped to arrange her safe travel, he and his wife Bluma had welcomed Rifka to stay with them until she made her way to Safed.

The night before Rifka was scheduled to depart, a number of the women and their daughters gathered in the Women's House of Study. In the center of the table, usually covered with books, was a kugel, its plump soft raisins and fragrant cinnamon irresistible. Next to it, Naomi and Zahava had placed two clay pitchers of a cool tea, the fragrance of fresh mint and lemon verbena filling the room. Luba and Batleya, each holding a handle, carried in a cauldron of Tanya's nourishing stew. Freyda followed with two large freshly baked challahs. Several women and girls newer to the community arranged small plates, cups, and utensils collected from many households.

"A feast," Rifka said, not even trying to hold back the tears that overflowed her eyes. "Each and every one of you has nourished and sustained me with your spirits. Now you do so with this wonderful feast."

"I have an idea."

The voice was eager. Rifka turned to Avigal, whose red curls resembled her grandfather Samuel's, while her quiet intensity was so like her grandmother Tanya's. How greatly Rifka would miss her and her classmates. "Avigali, what is your idea?"

"That we study a little, all of us together, and then we eat and drink."

"A golden idea," Dalia smiled.

"This week's Torah portion, from the Book of Numbers," Naomi began, "takes place at the threshold of the Promised Land. How perfect for the week our beloved Rifka begins her journey to cross that threshold."

"Even the name of the portion: *Sh'lach*, Send, is so fitting as we send off our dear Rifka," Zahava added.

Naomi had spoken animatedly, but Rifka could hear her sadness. Zahava's voice had also contained a measure of heavy-heartedness. In the past days, much sadness had been surfacing about Rifka's departure.

"Who will remind us what happens in this portion?" Naomi invited.

"I will," Avigal ventured eagerly. "God told Moses to send spies to climb a mountain and view the Promised Land, then to come back, bringing news about what they saw."

"They didn't just bring news, you know," Nava chimed in. "They also brought a cluster of grapes, a pomegranate, and a fig." Nava seemed proud to have remembered so precisely.

"Just one fig?" Malka smiled.

"I think they were in a hurry to leave because they were scared," Nava explained. "So they only had time to get one fig."

"Why grapes, a pomegranate, and a fig? And why afraid?" Naomi asked.

Avigal spoke. "The fruit showed that the Promised Land had beautiful gardens and orchards and would always feed its people."

"And a pomegranate," Batleya added, "is a fruit whose seeds symbolize the many promises to be fulfilled."

The conversation continued a little longer until Luba, pensive and quiet until now, cleared her throat.

"This portion is so perfect for tonight because our teacher Rifka is going forward into the unknown. How brave she is. *How brave you are,*" Luba repeated, turning to Rifka.

"It is true that I don't know what to expect," Rifka responded, "but not true that I'm going without any fear."

"To be brave is not to be fearless," Tanya said firmly. Tanya's voice was rarely heard in a group, which made her conviction even more compelling.

"To move forward despite fear takes more courage than to act when one has no fear or doubt," Tanya added. Her direct gaze stirred Rifka, who could still easily picture this woman before her as a timid little girl hiding behind her mother Gittel's skirts. Tanya had traveled a daunting inner journey to become this steadfast daughter, wife, mother, and grandmother. These were her holy destinations.

"Now that we have feasted on delicious ideas, let's feast on this delicious food!" Dalia hooked her arm through Rifka's.

Rifka watched more than she ate. From women with white hair to babies at the breasts of young, dark-haired women who let their hair fall loose here, each one presented a miracle. How she would miss them!

"What if ...?" she called out. The room took several moments to become quiet enough for her voice to be heard. "What if my heart is a pomegranate and each one of you a seed in my pomegranate heart?"

"Would we be delicious?" a little one called out sincerely.

Rifka, overcome by emotion, was unable to answer.

"Very delicious," Dalia said, squeezing Rifka's hand.

❧ 35 ❧

Rabbi Avner was surprised to receive a letter from Mendel. He retreated to his small room to read:

My esteemed friend, Avner of Medzibocz. I hope that my missive finds your tongue looser that when last I saw it trapped in your holy mouth.

    I write to issue to you an invitation to join me in Iwanie, a city it will take some effort on your part to reach. The rewards of your efforts, I can assure you, will be amply repaid not with coins but with something worth far more than gold. The hero meant to lead men to final freedom has arrived in Iwanie, greeted with unabashed joy and gratitude by his Believers. This reunion has been awaited since I last saw you shortly after our Savior Jacob Frank was banished from the Polish-Lithuanian Commonwealth by a group of fanatic rabbis. I am greatly relieved that my posturing as one of these rabbis is soon to conclude. The Believers' burden of silence is soon to be lifted.

    You may recall that it was as a result of the ban and the persecution of the Sabbateans that the Redeemer crossed the Dniester to take refuge in the Ottoman Empire. What you may not know is that once there, he converted to Islam in order to assure the protection of the Turks for his movement. His conversion does not represent his allegiance to Islam anymore than my claims to poor Dembowski, and more recently to Poland's King Augustus, represent the Frankists'

*loyalty to the tenets of Christianity. When Dembowski ruled
in favor of the contra-Talmudists, the Believers rejoiced.
Plans were made to receive the Savior in Podolia. Dembowski's
death has delayed but not deterred us.*

*As the Savior Jacob Frank's secret emissary to King
Augustus, I secured favors and protection for the Sabbateans
targeted by the cherem. Home and property belonging to
Sabbateans have been returned to those of our sect who were
forced to flee Podolia in the wake of the Lanskroun affair.
Our ultimate triumph draws closer with the appearance of
Frank in the city of Iwanie, where our Redeemer will gather
his army of followers around him.*

*I urge you, my friend, to make your way here to Iwanie to
witness with your own eyes the Infallible One who is destined
to fulfill all messianic hopes. I will host you in a fashion that
shall meet all your needs for comfort, be assured.*

*I make one further request. When in Medzibocz, I sought
my son Amos but did not find him. I don't know if it is rumor
or truth that he is trapped in the web of the treacherous Yisroel
ben Eliezar.*

*Surely, had I seen you again after our encounter in the
tavern a year ago, you would have been able to lead me to my
son. I ask now, my noble friend, that you seek him and implore
Amos to accompany you to Iwanie. I am confident that when
he is in the presence of the long-awaited Messiah any delusion
that has kept him, or any others, bound to a false master will
be dissolved.*

Mendel, Humble Servant of the Saintly Jacob Frank

The letter felt like sugar laced with poison. Why, Avner wondered,
had Mendel not accused him more directly of being a follower of the
Baal Shem Tov? If Mendel knew that Avner had not been merely visiting
but resided in Medzibocz, he must know the rest, too. It sounded as if

Mendel actually believed the presence of his "savior" would wake Amos and Avner out of the dream of their devotion to their Rebbe.

Feeling a caution similar to what he had felt when Mendel came to Medzibocz, Avner made another decision he could not easily explain. He would go to Iwanie.

It was to Zahava that Avner confided his plans.

"Can you accept keeping something from Amos?" he asked her first.

Zahava hesitated, and not taking her eyes off her father as if he were a page she was trying to read, she nodded her agreement.

Avner told her about the letter and about his decision. He explained that there might be something to be gleaned in Iwanie useful to the Baal Shem Tov and his community.

"I am going for this reason alone. Rabbi Mendel will stop at nothing to attain the perverse victory he envisions. If he doesn't suspect my alliance with the Baal Shem Tov, he might yield information of benefit to us. It may serve our community for me to learn more about the Frankists and their leader."

Avner would not take Amos with him. This had also been clear right away.

Despite Zahava's misgivings—she would have preferred he tell Yisroel about his intentions and even ask his blessing—she finally consented to not reveal her father's destination. It would be assumed that he was leaving Medzibocz, as he frequently did, to trade textiles.

When they embraced at the end of his visit, Zahava said she suspected the Rebbe would know without being told about Avner's expedition. Then she added, "I will pray for you, Father—and also for the soul of my husband's father, the grandfather of my children, Mendel."

AVNER HAD BEEN surprised to hear that Jacob Frank was in Iwanie. He would not have expected to find him in a city this far west of the Turkish border, given Frank's apparent need to make quick departures from

Poland into the Ottoman Empire. The journey west from Medzibocz to Iwanie, covering a distance of almost three hundred kilometers, was long but not arduous. As Medzibocz thrived, the roads between this city and others were more traveled. Avner had the financial resources to travel comfortably and would be able to afford decent accommodations when he reached Iwanie.

In Iwanie, Avner found a comfortable inn run by a Jewish family, cleaned up, ate lightly, and entrusted the innkeeper's wife with the few wool rugs he had brought to sell.

When Avner asked if the couple knew of a Jacob Frank, a shadow crossed the woman's face. Keeping her gaze lowered, she indicated the direction in which he should walk. He would go some distance, she said, before finding what he was looking for, outside the city.

Forty-five minutes later, Avner approached a large dais blanketed with petals. Shouts and cries of "Long Live our Messiah!" swarmed like locusts. A figure, slight for a man, sat in the center, draped by so much finery that all Avner could see was his face, which was disproportionately small for his body. The chin and nose were pointed. He was beardless, his moustache waxed.

The Savior was garbed in the apparel of a Turkish sultan. His olive green robe, fastened at the sleeves with rows of tiny gold buttons, was bound at the waist with a crimson sash and draped with a crimson velvet caftan, its border embroidered with spiraling golden vines. Fine leather shoes, almost like slippers, peered from beneath the hems of caftan and inner robe. The Redeemer's head was capped by a tall cylinder wrapped in silk the color of his robe and adorned with three black feathers that had been attached to the top of the cylinder with pearl brooches.

Frank waved his white-gloved hands to silence his flock as he prepared to speak.

"The place to which we are going is not subject to any law," his shrill voice pronounced. "We honor the True Faith, my precious Believers, by breaking the dominion of all rulers and rules on this earthly plane. However, we must feign adherence to human law just a short while longer.

Our predecessors maintained secrecy for decades, but this shall not be our fate. Only for a short time longer do we need to shelter our faith from those seeking to undermine it. I ask of you, my precious believers, merely one further act of surrender to display your total submission to the True Faith."

Some of those in his audience appeared confused. Others were zealously eager to hear what more they could sacrifice.

"As you know, we have sought and gained privileges from your king, Augustus III. In turn, Augustus the Corpulent and members of his clergy are asking that we demonstrate our complete submission to the Christian faith."

Frank stopped and wiped his brow with a large, embroidered, silk handkerchief. Then with a flourish, he waved his handkerchief, gesturing to his right. Heads turned.

The proud Mendel strutted forward as Frank retreated into a throne-like chair that seemed to have appeared from nowhere, draped in heavy brocades.

Mendel bowed, pushing back the skirt of his forest green brocaded caftan. Mendel had become considerably more rotund in the year since Avner had last seen him. He spoke with authority, punctuating his proclamations with frequent bows in Frank's direction.

"When we first avowed our affinity with the Christian faith, we asked to continue to dress as Jews, to maintain our earlocks, to call ourselves by our Jewish names, keep our Sabbath, and not to be expected to intermarry. We argued that, in this manner, our fellow Jews would continue to consider us their brethren, and not suspect us, as we sought to bring them into the fold of Christianity. Of course, having our own True Faith, we had no genuine interest in being Christians. Jesus is the husk of which our Savior is the fruit." Mendel bowed again in Frank's direction, while holding onto the cone-shaped silk headdress that had replaced his sable shtreimel.

"But, my brothers," Mendel yelled above the crowd. "King Augustus and his church officials have decided to require our unconditional conversion if we are to continue to have their protection. They are demanding 'baptism without any precondition.'"

A low thunderous rumble moved through the crowd.

"Do not worry, my brothers," he cajoled. We have passed through the garb of Judaism then the garb of Islam when our King Shabtai Tzvi converted. Now we must simply wear the garb of Christianity before throwing off all garb."

Frank stood. Mendel bowed and backed away, relinquishing his position at the center of the dais.

"My faithful, devoted children," Frank shouted, his affectionate words contrasting with his caustic, shrill voice. "I shall repeat—so that your souls, as well as your ears, will hear the truth: *Jesus was the husk; I am the fruit*. But for now, we must avow to the Christian authorities that we believe Jesus to be our messiah. This will appease them, while we continue to collect the countless souls still hungering for the *True Faith*."

The self-proclaimed messiah began to laugh, a high-pitched cackle that startled Avner.

"Another doctrine we shall avow to our fellow Christians is our reverence for the Blessed Virgin. But we are blessed to venerate twelve, not just one," he said. He lifted and lowered his thin arms, resembling a strangely plumed bird. " Come now, my lovely virgins, and stand before these who crown you with their fealty."

Avner recalled Ezekiel describing Jacob Frank's Sacred Concubines, a number of them harlots. Avner watched twelve young women, aged perhaps twelve to fifteen, walk barefoot, heads bowed, to the center of the dais and form a crescent around Jacob Frank. The girls wore simple white tunics, their loose hair cascaded down their backs, and their faces were expressionless. Avner looked at the girls with pain and dismay. Three of the twelve bore visible bulges under their tunics, revealing their savior's violations. Avner overheard someone whisper that new virgins would soon replace those too large with child.

Frank snapped his fingers.

The twelve, as if one body, removed themselves.

"Now, come forth, my brave apostles."

From four directions twelve men climbed onto the dais. Each one was dressed in the elegant garb of prosperous Turks and was young, tall, and muscular.

"You will see new faces among my apostles," Jacob Frank shouted. "Those who failed my trials have relinquished their exalted status."

Whispers hissed through the crowd about the trials of the apostles: sexual acts with their Deliverer or with animals while he watched, and then mutilation of the creatures afterwards. Rabbi Avner, sick to his stomach, hurried from the crowd, found a narrow space between buildings, and vomited. He then hastened back to the inn, hoping Mendel had not seen him and would not follow. Although he had been in the city only briefly, Avner wanted to leave as soon as possible.

Paying the innkeeper generously, Avner implored the man to help him find a wagon or carriage leaving Iwanie as soon as possible. He was informed that the earliest and safest wagon would leave the following morning. Before retiring, Avner secured the innkeeper and his wife's promise that should anyone inquire about a stranger, they would not reveal Avner's presence.

Before dawn, Avner boarded a wagon departing Iwanie. Several kilometers from the town, the wagon driver spontaneously started praising "the Redeemer's divine strategy."

"He cares for us, his flocks, like a tender shepherd," the man raved. Without Avner saying anything, the driver continued proudly, "In order to assure the protection of the True Faith and of the Believers, the Redeemer is sending the esteemed Rabbi Mendel to meet with a bishop of great power in Lemberg. I know because I myself will be taking him there at the end of the week."

"What is the good Rabbi Mendel's business with the bishop?" Avner asked, trying to keep his voice neutral.

"You didn't hear?" the wagon driver exclaimed as if he had helped hatch the plan. "Rabbi Mendel is going to ask Bishop Mikulski to clear the name of all Sabbateans, especially to remove all stain from our leader.

This will allow the Savior Jacob Frank to travel freely through our country without problems from those holier-than-thou Jews trying to harm him and the rest of his faithful flock."

"To the Messiah!" The wagon driver lifted his fist in a gesture of toasting. "May the great apostle Mendel succeed in his mission to enlist Mikulski's protection without our conversion. But if we must hide behind the screen of Christianity until our Savior steps forth to reveal his full glory, then we will!"

SHORTLY AFTER his return to Medzibocz, Avner decided he would leave the city again without consulting anyone, except to inform Zahava that he might be gone for perhaps a fortnight. He did not inform his daughter of his destination this time, nor did she ask.

Avner planned to make his way to Warsaw, where he would seek the high-ranking church officials he had befriended while living and working there. In Avner's role as a rabbi, he was often consulted by the capitol's leading ecclesiastical authorities in matters pertaining to Jewish scripture and law. He had also come into contact with church officials through his textile trade. Avner had had occasion to procure exceedingly rare and exquisite fabrics worthy of the vestments and sacred altars of his Christian colleagues. Over the years, he had developed genuine, mutually respectful associations with a number of eminent church officials.

One priest in particular, a bishop whose given name was Patryk and who was of notably humbler origins than the others, had garnered the respect of his fellows as well as Avner's instant liking. Avner's intention and mission in going to Warsaw now was to inform Father Patryk, in particular, as well as Avner's other acquaintances in the church, of Jacob Frank's perfidy and of the duplicity of his claims. Frank was mocking the Christian faith and its representatives, as well as demeaning Judaism. Based on the fine men Avner had met, he was convinced there were far more devout men of integrity in the church than there were zealots like Dembowski. These leaders would want to be informed of Jacob Frank's clandestine ridicule of Church doctrine. Surely the Christian authorities in the commonwealth's capital city carried weight and influence enough to warn their fellow clerics in other cities and even to report the hypocrisy to Rome. Together, rabbinic and church leaders, even if not working side-by-side, could expose the fraudulent deceit promoted by the resurgent Sabbateans.

Avner's intervention met with favor, but also with troubling news.

After hearing Rabbi Avner's disturbing report, Father Patryk, now an Archbishop, convened a handful of other deeply concerned church dignitaries in Warsaw. The priests informed Avner that Bishop Mikulski was not a trusted guardian of the Sacred Gospel, but regarded by many in his own faith as a religious despot. He was known to be one of the principle promoters of blood libel accusations in the commonwealth. Dembowski had been one of his allies, as the two forged relentless campaigns to prove that Jews needed Christian blood for their matzos, and therefore, that each and every Jew must be considered a severe threat to his Christian neighbors.

Archbishop Patryk and the other forthright clerics expressed their fear that Mikulski, in granting protection to the Sabbatean sect, would exhort a return likely to be harmful to all Jews. In the meantime, the concerned priests assured Avner that they would alert fellow clergy whom they knew to be incorruptible. An emissary would be sent to Rome as well.

⌒

THE FINELY DRESSED, DIGNIFIED STRANGER IN THE Rebbe's courtyard introduced himself to Samuel as a rabbi from Brody with urgent business to discuss with Rabbi Yisroel ben Eliezer.

Samuel invited the traveler to enter the Beis Midrash where a small group of students had gathered. No sooner had the man stepped over the threshold into the large room, than he requested a word alone with their rabbi. It appeared to Samuel that the man carried his mission like a great weight. The Rebbe, whose head had been bowed as he pored over an open book, looked up now. Upon seeing the Baal Shem Tov's face, the man was clearly very moved.

"Esteemed Rabbi Yisroel, we have not seen each other in the twenty years since you lived in Brody. It is my honor to greet you now." The visitor awkwardly tipped his hat. "I humbly admit," he continued, sweeping the room with a sheepish glance before looking back at Yisroel, "that I was one of those who protested your membership in the Kloiz. I ask your forgiveness, and that I might speak with you privately about why I've come."

Yisroel smiled and stood, gesturing his guest to enter his small room.

When the two emerged a half hour later, Samuel noticed how different the rabbi from Brody appeared than when he had arrived. Was it the relief of having completed his task? Was it how the Baal Shem Tov had received him? In Yisroel's face, Samuel also discerned something—a look or maybe it was more accurate to call it a posture not there. Samuel watched Yisroel closely, detecting in his movements what he would have once suspected as defeat.

Through his years at Yisroel's side, Samuel had been discovering the difference between defeat and conscious surrender. *If I stiffened my back every time I am attacked,* Yisroel told them, *my back would have been broken rather than been made more supple.* Samuel suspected that the surrender he saw now was his Rebbe yielding his will to a greater Will.

After the dinner meal, the Baal Shem Tov invited his guest to speak to the disciples.

"I have come to Medzibocz on behalf of a delegation of rabbis who came to Brody from throughout the commonwealth and beyond." The man paused, straightening his back. Clearly this information was not easy for him to deliver, not the first time and not now.

"These rabbis have requested that your teacher, Rabbi Yisroel ben Eliezer, whom you and many others refer to admiringly as the Baal Shem Tov, speak at a Tribunal organized by the Bishop Mikulski. The Tribunal will take place in the city of Lemberg several months from now at the end of summer."

Ripples of discomfort and even dread moved through the room. Avner had informed the community about his encounters with Rabbi Mendel and Jacob Frank, and also about his intercession with the unnamed church dignitaries in Warsaw. He had also spoken of the churchmen's concern about Bishop Mikulski.

"In return for protecting the Frankists," the delegate from Brody continued, "Bishop Mikulski has required that they, the 'contra-Talmudists,' engage in yet another disputation with members of the rabbinate. There will be nine principles of faith argued. The most important of these—and the focus of the Tribunal—will be blood libel."

Samuel immediately exchanged glances with Gedaliah, thinking of their mother Leya.

"There are many in addition to Bishop Mikulski," the rabbi continued, "who yearn to hear Jews attest in a public forum that their brethren require Christian blood for the ritual preparation of unleavened bread for Passover. The testimony of the contra-Talmudists, who call themselves Jews, will be considered proof of the Jews' heinous need for Christian blood."

Dovid rose. "How was it determined that the Baal Shem Tov be invited to this Tribunal?" he demanded.

"The testimony in this Tribunal, unlike Bishop Dembowksi's disputation, is to be presented in person, not submitted in writing," the man explained. "As the most prominent rabbis and judges from throughout Europe were convening in Brody to determine who should represent the truth in the face of the contra-Talmudists' distortions, an urgent missive arrived from Jerusalem sent by the esteemed Rabbi Gershon."

"The letter was greeted with great eagerness. The honorable Rabbi Gershon's presence has been deeply missed in Brody. The good rabbi's letter stated that he had been informed of the disputation held in Kamenetz-Podolsk and of Bishop Dembowski's verdict. Having just learned of Bishop Mikulski's insistence on a tribunal whose primary purpose was to prove blood libel charges against Poland's Jews, Rabbi Gershon implored the council of Brody rabbis to "seek the Baal Shem Tov."

The emissary from Brody turned to face the Rebbe.

"He asked that we trust you. Rabbi Gershon declared that all rumors of you being a Sabbatean are false. *'Not only is he to be trusted,'* he wrote, *'it is probable that the Baal Shem Tov's presence at the Tribunal will profoundly impact the outcome for the better.'"*

The messenger paused. It seemed to Samuel that he was not finished, but had difficulty with what there was left to say. When he resumed, his voice was subdued and sounded pained.

"The last thing Rabbi Gershon's missive contained was a warning that came as a great shock to many, including me. Rabbi Gershon cautioned the assembly in Brody that the highly regarded Rabbi Mendel is not be trusted."

After several moments, he added ruefully, "To know a man for thirty years and not know him…" The drained messenger's voice trailed. Then, as if returning to the room from elsewhere, he concluded.

"As you may have guessed, your rabbi and teacher the Baal Shem Tov has accepted the invitation."

DALIA LAY AWAKE. She might as well give up sleep tonight with so many thoughts clamoring.

Did her father look weary—or had she been looking at him through the eyes of her own concern about the Tribunal? The task ahead of him was monumental. Thousands of Polish citizens of all social classes were expected to gather in Lemberg to witness the proceedings. Should the Baal Shem Tov transgress in the eyes of the power-hungry Bishop Mikulski, his punishment could be death.

He was to depart to Lemberg in the morning. Dovid and Gedaliah would accompany him; Dalia was glad of this, at least. None of the disciples had tried to dissuade the Rebbe, despite their concern. All of them, Dalia included, accepted his participation in the Tribunal as his duty. Uncle Gershon had been the first to recognize this. If anyone could bring light to the ominous shadows cast by Jacob Frank, Mendel, and their "army of believers," it was the Baal Shem Tov. *But what if even he couldn't?* Dalia worried.

How would her father feel facing Jews that were making a mockery of the Talmud—men at the same time covertly mocking the hallowed tenets of Christianity? The Frankists' claims would be rooted in betrayal; their arguments would be hostile. How was Yisroel to challenge Bishop Mikulski and the contra-Talmudists in this public forum where so much was at stake? Her abba did not greet hostile attacks with brute forcefulness. He would not respond to immorality with a corresponding disregard for human dignity, nor to power by seeking to control or suppress.

The students had been asking their Rebbe how they might support him.

"Hold to your faith that Truth is more powerful than untruth and respect a more forceful weapon than intimidation," he had told them. But if it is difficult for you to feel faith," he continued, "focus on whatever evokes your joy, then add your joy to my satchel for the journey to Lemberg."

IN THE FOURTH INN they tried, Yisroel, Gedaliah, and Dovid found one small room the three could share for the seven days of the Tribunal. Their host warned that meals would be very modest; the number of people who had descended on Lemberg had quickly depleted the marketplace of provisions.

"Vodka, however," a Polish guest inserted, "is flowing more abundantly in Lemberg than the Poltva River. The noblemen's distilleries have been preparing for months. The generous szlachta made sure enough rye was fermented to make a herd of elephants drunk, let alone a few thousand souls come to see a spectacle."

Gedaliah led the way the first morning. As they approached the site, Gedaliah saw the large raised platform that he had seen being constructed the previous day when he had gone to find the square in front of the majestic Latin Cathedral where the events would take place.

On the south side of the platform, facing the Cathedral, was a row of high-backed, carved oak chairs; the one in the center, flanked by three on each side, was taller, more ornately carved, and gilded. A pew, two meters or so in length, was positioned perpendicular to the chairs along the eastern edge of the platform; to the west, three pews had been placed, one behind the other.

Gedaliah had never been among this many people gathered in one place. As far as he could tell, the mass of people in the square was comprised mostly of Polish citizens. Nervous anxiety, curiosity, and impatience pulsed in those crowding around him, as they pushed their way closer to the platform. Since departing Medzibocz, Gedaliah had been trying not to feed his fear. He reminded himself now to take slower and deeper breaths and to see those around him as fellow souls, rather than enemies or threats.

Yisroel, standing beside him, appeared calm. But not only calm, Gedaliah realized. The Rebbe was watching the people gathering with a look of pleasurable curiosity. He stood straight with his chest open the way he welcomed strangers to his table at home—as if they were valued guests.

A thunderous salutation made Gedaliah turn from the Rebbe. Exiting through two cathedral doors twice their height, a stream of church dignitaries emerged in elaborate pontifical vestments. Three positioned themselves on one side of the doors and three on the other. Next, a short man more regally attired than the others stepped through the doors, moving slowly and ceremoniously. Crowned by a gold mitre that made him almost as tall as the men flanking him, the man Gedaliah supposed was Bishop Mikulski led the others, who fell into a single line behind him. The intent Mikulski, eyes narrowed under a furrowed brow, gripped his staff tightly and walked up the steps of the platform in front of him. Reaching his throne, he turned to face the Cathedral, waited for the others to do the same, and then lowered himself into his chair.

The crowd was remarkably hushed when the bishop began to speak, most of his audience behind him. Mikulski announced that an article of faith would be debated each of the seven days. He then summoned to the platform the contra-Talmudists who had been waiting. Twenty men seated themselves in the three pews to the bishop's left. The bishop then pulled a small scroll from under his robe.

"I will now read the names of those members of the rabbinate who are to take their seats today," he announced, gesturing toward the bench on the right side of the platform.

Yisroel ben Eliezer was not named.

YISROEL WAS NOT called to the platform for the next five days either.

Each of the days, after directing the contra-Talmudists and the rabbis to seat themselves, Bishop Mikulski presented a statement of faith. The Frankists, it turned out, had crafted the statements of faith to be debated. These principles of faith *appeared* to represent the tenets of Christianity, such as the tenet for debate on the fourth day: *Everyone should follow the teaching of the Messiah, for salvation lies only within it.* But in each case when mention was made of the Messiah or the Holy Trinity, no explicit reference to Jesus of Nazareth was included.

The rabbis were ordered to begin, their mandate being to disprove the truth of statements. The rabbis were deliberately cautious and respectful in their responses, choosing not to contest the tenets of Christian faith nor to directly challenge the ambiguous scriptural evidence presented by the contra-Talmudists to "prove the veracity" of principles such as: *All prophecies about the coming of the Messiah have already been fulfilled.* Nor did the rabbis assert their own messianic beliefs.

When the rabbis were finished—or told they were finished—the public ridiculed the failure of the rabbi's disputation. However, even graver than their failure in disputation, their audience accused, was the rabbis' failure to recognize and worship the True Messiah.

Bishop Mikulski did not disguise his satisfaction. Each day, after the rabbis' failure, he invited the contra-Talmudists "to prove as Jews themselves," the truth of each statement of faith. One contra-Talmudist after another rose to affirm the principles of faith and the validation of these principles in the texts holy to the Jewish people.

All knew that the seventh day of the disputation was the most significant. The seventh and final proposition being considered was the assertion that the Talmud mandates the use of Christian blood in the preparation of unleavened bread.

Unlike the preceding disputes, the final dispute was to be private. It would take place inside the Cathedral.

In the square on the seventh day, the bishop announced the fifty people who would be permitted entry: twenty contra-Talmudists, Rabbi Mendel's name among them; ten members of the rabbinate, including Rabbi Yisroel ben Eliezar; the rest, clergy selected by the bishop.

Dovid and Gedaliah, following Yisroel as he had requested, were stopped at the arch into the gilded room. Gedaliah did not hear the Rebbe's quiet, firm assertion that thankfully allowed him and Dovid to pass.

The carved doors of the ornate room were then closed.

The contra-Talmudists were seated at an enormous oval table below and to the left of the bishop's dais, the rabbis, in chairs across from the contra-Talmudists. The clergy in attendance sat further back on pews, facing the bishop's throne.

Bishop Mikulski cleared his throat, pressed his arms into the wings of his elaborate chair as if to rise, then settled back into the plush red velvet upholstery, as if having changed his mind.

"Our final gathering is to be devoted to the seventh proposition in our auspicious disputation." The bishop cleared his throat again before reading the statement crafted by the Frankists.

"'The Talmud teaches that Jews need Christian blood and whoever believes the Talmud is bound to seek it.' It is to argue against this fact that I summon Rabbi Yisroel of Medzibocz. His opponent, chosen to defend and to prove the truth as it has been stated, is to be the honorable Rabbi Mendel of Brody."

"But before we start our examination of the Jews' requirement for Christian blood," Bishop Mikulski addressed Yisroel, "I would like to pose a question, since this assembly has not yet had the privilege of hearing you speak, Rabbi."

The sarcasm in the words "privilege" could not be missed.

"Is it true that you and the majority of your brethren do not venerate Jesus the Christ as the long-awaited Messiah?"

Gedaliah looked at Yisroel's face. His thoughtful expression was one Gedaliah had seen many times when the Rebbe was confronted with a question burning in the hands of the one thrusting it.

Yisroel stood and looked directly at the bishop, but as he spoke, he swept the room with a slow, deliberate glance.

"The one you revere, whose given name was Yehoshua ben Yosef, was and is a pure expression of God's love. A soul such as his radiates its light eternally. Rabbi Yehoshua taught that the holy spark of God burning so brightly within him dwells in *every* being, did he not?"

The Rebbe turned back to the bishop.

"I believe, Bishop Mikulski, that we are each the long-awaited one. Each one of us must shine his and her great light in order to free our world from fear and division and lead us to true glory. I do not demean the great master Jesus; I affirm his message that each of us is the bearer of life-giving knowledge and love. We are *each* saviors. Our prayer and work together must be to live God's Love."

"What blasphemy! Your Holiness, allow me," Mendel struggled to stand, pushing against the heavy table to free his ample body. He walked to the center of the room and faced the bishop.

"Your Holiness, if it be your favor, please grant me a few words in relation to the sacrilege we've heard from the lips of this rabbi."

The bishop nodded.

"How can we who are *utterly fallible, weak,* and *impure,*" Mendel began, saying each word with great emphasis, "dare to blaspheme the Savior by comparing ourselves to him? What profanity to attribute even the slightest holiness to man, who is pathetically inadequate. Even to attempt such a comparison is obscene. A vulgar claim like this is inspired by the devil."

Mendel heaved a large sigh, appearing burdened by his body's weight. He swept a large handkerchief across his broad, perspiring forehead.

"Now let us move on to the matter at hand," he announced as if presiding, then catching himself, turned to the bishop and bowed his head deferentially. Mendel's gesture met with Mikulski's approval and a wave of the arm that he proceed.

"Venerable Bishop, you and your countrymen rightfully accuse the Talmud of mandating abhorrent rituals such as I cannot even bring myself to name. My fellow contra-Talmudists and I have severed our loyalty to the archaic practices hallowed by the Talmud." Mendel had begun to wheeze. "The old ways must be replaced by the living wisdom of the Messiah. We, the contra-Talmudists attest that the Savior *has* come in human form, and only this Savior is capable of leading sinful, despicable man from the pit of his infamy to the glory of his Creator."

"To glory!" Mendel raised a fist. The beads of sweat, collecting at his temples, streamed down the side of his face. "All that is needed now is to remove what stands in our Savior's way. Those who claim that man can approach the Savior's perfection defile the Son of God." Mendel looked with disgust in Yisroel's direction. "What brew have you, rabbi of ill-repute? What concoction made from boiling pods and seeds to confound and stupefy the minds of the righteous?"

Looking pleased with his taunting, Mendel nodded towards his benefactor, Bishop Mikulski.

"Have you anything to add?" the bishop addressed Yisroel curtly, looking over his head.

The Baal Shem Tov walked slowly to the center of the room and faced Mendel.

"The truth can be spoken simply. The ancient rabbis summed up the entire Torah in one phrase: *Love thy neighbor as thyself.* Is this not the essence of what the Rabbi Jesus taught as well? To take a life is in complete violation of this command. The accusation of blood libel is unfounded. It is that simple. One cannot argue a falsehood except to offer the truth."

Mendel began to laugh derisively.

"The truth illumines the lie, Rabbi?" he mocked, looking at the bishop.

Then Rabbi Mendel directed his piercing gaze at Yisroel. Starting to pace, like an animal stalking his prey, he did not take his eyes off his enemy. Mendel stopped, narrowed his eyes, and almost spat the words he aimed at the Baal Shem Tov.

"I have waited years to challenge you, the embodiment of falsehood!"

The dispute was no longer about the Talmud, blood libel, or the Messiah. Mendel took a step toward Yisroel and lifted his arm, as if preparing to strike his detested adversary.

Dovid rose to intervene. Gedaliah placed a firm hand on his shoulder and he sat.

"How dare you!" Mendel shouted, his arm held menacingly in the air. "How dare you come here to speak in the name of the truth!" Mendel's large frame shook with anger, but he did not strike.

Gedaliah knew his master well enough to recognize the genuine compassion with which he faced his opponent now. If it were any other man, Gedaliah would suspect him of feigning indifference or perhaps of being too afraid to defend himself. How many times had Gedaliah witnessed the Baal Shem Tov open his heart to someone who approached in anguish? Still, it was no less astonishing to watch now—that as Mendel's rage mounted, Yisroel grew more present, open, and tender.

"Your goodness and love are poisons," Mendel thundered. "*The truth?* I will tell you the truth. The truth is that life is suffering! The truth is that all our actions are in vain and meaningless. There is no compassionate source. That is the truth!"

Mendel stopped, appearing suddenly self-conscious. His back and neck stiffened. Directing his gaze towards the floor, his eyes darted as if frantically searching for something he had dropped. With a jerk of his head, Mendel looked up apologetically at the bishop.

"I ask your forbearance with my temper, Holiness. When I am confronted with evil, it is difficult for me not to oppose it with all my might."

"Your might, Rabbi Mendel," Yisroel interrupted firmly, "will never bring the peace for which you long."

Mendel lips twitched, but he did not move otherwise.

The Baal Shem Tov stepped closer and put his hand on Mendel's shoulder. Instead of shaking it off violently and striking Yisroel, as Gedaliah feared he might, Mendel shrunk back, looking more like a child, fearful of being struck, than the fierce contender he had been moments earlier.

Mendel looked imploringly at the bishop. "We aren't talking about me. We are talking about the truth, the desecration, the lie…" Mendel's voice faded. His shoulders hunched forward like an edifice shaken by the tremble of the ground beneath it and caving in on itself.

"Enough!" Bishop Mikulski intervened, bringing his staff down with force. The bishop rose to address the assembly.

"We now have proof from one who is unbiased," he announced, indicating Mendel. "The truth has been revealed that the Jews' Talmud calls for the sacrificial blood of our children. We need no further arguments."

The bishop clapped his hands. The doors of the room were thrown open. Rabbi Mendel was the first to leave.

∽

SEVERAL WEEKS AFTER YISROEL, DOVID, AND GEDALIAH returned to Medzibocz, a messenger arrived from Warsaw, saying he bore news about the Tribunal. Gedaliah ushered the gentle cleric into the courtyard where Dovid and Samuel were speaking with the Rebbe.

When the messenger announced that he had come on behalf of Archbishop Patryk, Gedaliah and Dovid exchanged looks. Could it be this was their old friend Patryk? Before the Tribunal, when Avner told the community he had met with high-ranking Catholic clergymen in Warsaw, he had not shared any names.

The messenger read Archbishop Patryk's message:

"Bishop Mikulski will not pursue his intention to indict the nation's Jews for blood libel as a result of the Tribunal held in Lemberg. Pressure from within the Polish church and, finally, word from the Vatican in Rome have halted the bishop's ambitions. The Baal Shem Tov and his community need not fear reprisals."

This was the second time that brave Patryk had acted to oppose the deadly charge of blood libel, Gedaliah mused; the first had been to challenge his aunt Olga in order to protect Leya.

"Before I depart," the emissary added, "there is a more personal message the Archbishop has given me to deliver to three men in your community, Rabbi. They are Dovid, Gedaliah, and Samuel."

The three introduced themselves to the messenger who greeted each one with a hearty embrace "on behalf of your old friend Patryk." The man then drew something from his pocket. When he opened his hand, three small rocks lay in his palm. He gave one to each of them.

"The good Archbishop did not explain the meaning of these. I trust you know?" he added, smiling.

Gedaliah's smile was met by his lifelong friend Dovid's. Kicking stones and throwing rocks into the pond near Patryk's farm had been among their favorite pastimes. Samuel had been too young to join them. But when Gedaliah and Dovid looked at him, he had the stone clutched tightly in his hand, needing no explanation.

∾

TWO MERCHANTS, PASSING THROUGH MEDZIBOCZ LESS than a month later, reported further news concerning the Bishop Mikulski and the contra-Talmudists.

In November, nearly three months after the concluding day of the Tribunal, Jacob Frank and a group of his followers had been baptized into the Christian faith. Bishop Mikulski had served as Jacob Frank's godfather. It was not known if Rabbi Mendel had followed his savior and also been part of the mass baptism.

Dovid asked his Rebbe what he felt upon hearing this news and what, if anything lingered in his heart as a result of the Tribunal proceedings.

"What lingers? A good question, Dovid," Yisroel replied. "Let's walk together into the answer."

It was early winter. The two dressed warmly, walking awhile in silence before the Rebbe began to speak.

"There is no getting used to the trespass one man can commit against another. Although one may feel compassion for the fear and pain at the root of destructive actions, the actions cannot be excused or go unchallenged. The suffering that Rabbi Mendel bears is deep and unconscious. But his pain cannot be avenged by causing more pain. One cannot bring justice through injustice."

Dovid recalled the last day of the Tribunal and how he had been moved to protect Yisroel, who had needed no defending.

"Mendel's desperation in the face of his own unexamined pain grieves me. Dovid, there are many who condemn others without ever seeking the root of their pain within themselves. Just one man—blind to what fuels his hatred and desire for control—can cause massive destruction and sorrow. *Just one.*"

And just one man, able to see into the heart, can free others, Dovid thought, looking at his Rebbe.

"Mendel and Mikulski's desires for vengeance may not be caused by the same events in their lives, but they spring from the same bitter poison of festering pain," Yisroel continued. "Both mistake their power for God's. But in truth, the power they wield derives from a desperate sense of powerlessness and renders them weak. No power these men wield will *ever* ease their pain. Harming others will bring no relief. This is what it is to be in hell: to find no relief from contempt. I pity these men, Dovid. I will continue to pray that they awaken. And if they cannot awaken, I pray that they and others like them cause no further harm."

∽

FOR THE FIRST TIME IN SEVERAL WEEKS, DOVID FELT well enough to sit up. The illness wreaking havoc in his chest was finally relinquishing its tight grip; the parching fevers that held his reason captive were retreating.

Tanya had been at his bedside steadily as he'd faded in andw out of awareness. She had applied compresses, brought herbal broths, and above all, offered the warming comfort of her company. He had not been this ill since the height of his deprivation in Polnoyye. Thankfully, Dovid had finally accepted, at his Rebbe's side, that when a body is vanquished, what heals is care, not self-punishing rigors. This had made it easier for Dovid to surrender to rest and to Tanya's nurture.

Tanya told him that in his delirium, he had called out to Rifka. He had muttered, too, about going to the Promised Land.

Almost a year had passed since Rifka's departure. In a few weeks' time it would be Shavuous, time once again to commemorate the receiving of the Torah, and his people's commitment to their Infinite Beloved. Before taking ill, Dovid, surprising himself, had begun thinking about forming a covenant with Rifka. There had been a kinship of spirit between them since childhood, as if even when they were children, he had recognized her soul. If she would not have him as a husband—they were, after all, old now, both nearly sixty—perhaps they could study and teach side by side in the Promised Land.

Dovid looked up as Tanya drew close with a cup of steaming broth. He felt oddly transparent. Had it taken being ill to leave him this vulnerable and undefended? In his sister's presence now, he was completely stripped of whatever armor had still shielded his heart. She set the bowl down and sat on the edge of his bed.

"Dovid," she asked warmly, "our Rebbe has directed us to listen to what calls us. Are you being called?"

For so many years, Tanya had been the "fearful one." Now, he was drawing courage in her presence.

"I will go to her, Tanya," he said.

❧ 36 ☙

The Baal Shem Tov became ill three weeks before Shavuous with symptoms resembling Dovid's. As soon as Dalia saw the unusual flush on her abba's face and heard the rattle in his cough, she urged him to retreat from his activities.

Those women who still remained in the community offered all manner of broths, asking Dalia for advice about which healing herbs to add to their soups and teas. She carried their offerings in and out of her father's room. Increasingly, she found him with his eyes closed, meditating. She had seen him in meditation often enough and could tell, even when he was lying down, that he was conscious and not asleep. What differed about his meditation now, however, was the labor of his breathing. Dalia had always been comforted by the circular flow of her abba's long deep breaths in and out as he meditated. Now hearing him wheeze with each breath, Dalia felt a tightening in her own chest.

Of course, her abba did not complain about the constriction or the sharp coughing that sounded as if it was going to tear his chest open. At those times when his breaths were quieter and easier, Dalia felt the relief in her own body, too. She prayed for more of the increasingly rare moments when his body found respite from its struggle to breathe. How it saddened her when another bout of coughing interrupted the brief stillness.

DALIA WAS GRATEFUL and relieved when her father's illness finally loosened its hold. His cough subsided and his breaths seemed to be drawn at less of a cost. His fever, although still present, burned with less intensity.

Word spread quickly that the Rebbe was better. Maybe by the time Shavuous came in two weeks, he would be well. The children who had been collecting in the courtyard outside his room with hopes of seeing their Rebbe clamored for his company. With more conviction than before, Dalia assured them it would not be long before he was out among them again. Soon they would hear his stories, his laughter, and his melodies. How happy he would be to take walks with them again!

Today, as Dalia emerged from her father's room, a very determined group of children between the ages of five and ten greeted her. They had just finished their morning classes. *"One story, just one story,"* they chanted sweetly as a unified chorus. *"One story, just one story from the Rebbe. Please."*

When they quieted, Nava stated on behalf of the others: "We won't tire the Rebbe. Maybe to tell us a story will help him to get better sooner. He told me a story once, and I felt better right away."

"Me, too! Me, too!" The words bubbled up among the children like *Amens.*

Dalia was clearly more surprised than the children when the door of the Rebbe's room opened, and her father stood in its threshold. His voice was hoarse and face pale. Dalia was glad for the children, but worried about her father's exertion.

"If you can be patient with me," their Rebbe told them, "and if you will sit far enough away from my coughing so it will not hurt your ears, I shall tell you a story."

The older children took charge quickly, gently coaxing the group back. They seated themselves on the warm ground, small ones on the laps of the older. Dalia placed a chair behind her father.

"It will be a short one, my loves," he began, the twinkle in his eyes not diminished by his illness. If anything, Dalia thought, his eyes were gleaming more brightly than ever.

"So, my angels, my beautiful flowers growing in God's beautiful garden, let us begin." The children nodded eagerly. Dalia saw in their faces what she knew so intimately: the feeling of there being nowhere else she would rather be.

"There was once a beggar who had very little, but nonetheless, he considered himself wealthy. Do you know what wealthy means?" he asked.

"Someone who has a lot of things," a boy stated confidently.

"A lot of money, not things," another interrupted.

The Rebbe continued in a raspy whisper.

"In truth, a person can be wealthy without having either money or things. This particular beggar considered his riches to be the moon, the stars, and the wind. They didn't belong to him, but, oh, how he could enjoy them! They were of greater value to him than things he could put in his pocket or keep in his house. In fact, he especially liked riches that couldn't fit into his pockets, his purse, or even under his roof. This beggar was a happy man, a very, very happy man."

The Rebbe paused and Dalia was pleased to see him catch his breath. A sudden outburst of coughing evoked compassionate looks from the children.

"As the days, months, and years passed, the contented beggar's beard grew white. Like mine," he laughed, stroking his beard.

"But your beard is gray not white, Rebbe!" one of the youngest children called out, quickly shushed by the others. The Rebbe feigned shock, lifting the end of his beard as if to verify this new information, then went on with his story.

"The time came when the joyful beggar could no longer walk as fast as he used to. But even this he considered a blessing because it was spring and walking more slowly he could notice more. He listened to the birds singing. He did not pass the flowers as quickly, leaning close to smell their exquisite fragrances, glad that these, too, could not be tucked away in a pocket. At night, he turned his gaze to the stars."

Dalia watched her father's vitality overcome his weakness.

"One day, the happy beggar realized it was time for him to stop walking. His body had become very tired. But his soul—who he was before he put on his body—was not tired at all and wanted to play more. So under the bright heat of the summer sun, the wise beggar lay down in a much-loved field where he was quite comfortable. He was among the tiny creatures with countless legs and feelers that can feel the finest of vibrations. There he let his soul soar, leaving his body to disappear into the earth and become part of the soil from which more flowers would grow."

The Rebbe drew in and let out a long breath.

"The children who had gotten used to seeing the beggar, to hearing the bell of his cart and his singing, felt sad that he no longer played among them."

Lips trembled as the children in the courtyard felt the hearts of the children in the story.

"Then one by one by one," the Rebbe's voice lifted, "the children started to notice—when they least expected it—the treasures the beggar had shown them. Some saw his face in the moon; others noticed the twinkle of his eyes in the stars. They began to hear his laugh in each other's laughter. Gradually, the children began to see with the beggar's eyes. They noticed all the riches around them and they, too, became wealthy."

He stopped, nearly breathless again.

"Among the dear children's riches," he continued, whispering now, "was the beggar's love for them and theirs for him. This love, like the beggar's joyous soul, always played among them."

THE SUN DESCENDED and candles were lit to welcome the first night of Shavuous. Her father's health had worsened again in the days approaching the holiday. During that time, he had grown increasingly silent. Dalia marveled that despite his difficult breathing and his fever, her abba did not seem to be in great discomfort and pain. He appeared to have retreated to a place so deep inside himself that his body's pain could not reach him.

Dalia knew he might be leaving them. But instead of being consumed by dread, she felt a strange grace that allowed her instead to be present moment-to-moment with her abba just as he was. She did what she could to assure his comfort. But she also knew that it was out of her hands to control his course. His soul would determine his course. It surprised Dalia not to be more distraught. She recognized this surrender as another of her abba's gifts.

Dovid, Gedaliah, and Samuel had received their Rebbe's permission weeks earlier to observe the holiday's all night vigil at his side. They were relieved to have asked before his retreat into almost complete silence. Dalia welcomed them now into his room.

She would leave them for a while. Perhaps she would go and take the infant Kaila, so that her mother Raisa could pray and study with the others during the vigil without her arms full.

IN HIS SMALL ROOM, Yisroel heard Samuel's earnest voice reciting verses from the Book of Ruth as if from a great distance. Gedaliah and Dovid joined Samuel, the three reading now in unison.

"Wherever you go, I will go..."

It was the holy night of Covenant.

How he loved them; their love would always summon his.

Now he felt the summons of all his beloveds as one, reaching towards him with arms of light. No—they were reaching with *arms of flame* to bear the fire of his soul from the earth of his body.

Soon there would be no more words.

"Wherever you go, I will go," he whispered with the little breath left him, hoping they would hear. "Where you dwell, I will dwell." If they had not heard him with their ears, they would hear with their hearts.

Light flooded the room, too bright for eyes to bear. Yisroel watched the walls of his small room dissolve, then the ceiling and floor all vanish into the boundless, brilliant light. Light was breathing him now, relieving him of the great effort to draw each stabbing breath.

"And God is a consuming fire..." Samuel read, his words rippling towards Yisroel on waves of light.

The waves rocked the vessel in which Yisroel now drifted unmoored on a sea of water and light.

Approaching the violet hues of the horizon, Yisroel blessed all that had tethered him to the shore: those he loved, those who had loved him, and those who cursed him. He let them all go. The current increased, carrying him more swiftly now to a portal in the horizon.

There, Channa stood on the threshold, her hand extended. She would pull him from his vessel through the dazzling portal. Behind her Yisroel saw spirals of light: his father Eliezar, Alta Bina, Leya, and Sarah, the mother he had never known.

Yisroel took Channa's hand.

LIST OF CHARACTERS

This is an alphabetical list of the characters in *The Tremble of Love*, along with a brief description of each one. Characters who are only named in one scene and do not appear again in the narrative are not named here. Note: "Reb," a word often found within the story with the names of male characters, is a title of respect before a name, e.g. Reb Eliezar, so look for characters by first name, e.g., Eliezar.

Alta Bina, *old herbalist*
Aleksander, *friend of Gedaliah's, son of Reb Wolf*
Amadeusz, *Polish parish priest*
Ambrozy, *farmer in mountains of Zabie, husband of Pela*
Amos, *son of Mendel*
Aryeh, *blacksmith, father of Rifka, husband of Dvorah*
Avigal, *daughter of Luba and Boaz*
Avner, *rabbi*

Batleya, *daughter of Gedaliah and Zofia*
Benjamin, *friend of Samuel's*
Ber, *husband of Leya, father of Gedaliah and Samuel,*
    namesake of Gedaliah's son, Ber
Batya, *cousin of Gittel, mother of Elias, Naftali, and Zofia*
Bluma, *wife of Gershon*
Boaz, *shepherd boy with whistle*

Channa, *daughter of Rabbi Elijah, wife of Yisroel*

Chmielnicki, *(Bogdan Chmielnicki) leader of Ukrainian Cossack uprising in late 1600s*

Dalia, *daughter of Channa and Yisroel*
Dembowski, *(Mikolaj Dembowski), bishop of the city of Kamenetz-Podolsk*
Dobry, *young Polish prison guard*
Dominik, *peasant farmer, husband of Justyna*
Dovid, *son of Gittel and Jacob*
Dvorah, *(deceased) wife of Aryeh, mother of Rifka*

Elias, *son of Batya and Rabbi Meir, husband of Naomi*
Eliezar, *deceased father of Srolik/Yisroel*
Elijah, *Chief Rabbi and Judge of Brody, father of Channa and Gershon, namesake of Elijah, husband of Batleya*
Enoch, *blind tin peddler*
Eyzer, *son of Channa and Yisroel*
Ezekiel, *friend of Elias, husband of Malka*
Ezra, *rabbi, Kabbalist, and teacher of Yisroel in Tluste*

Freyda, *daughter of Dalia and Judah*

Gedaliah, *son of Leya, husband of Zofia*
Gershon, *son of Rabbi Elijah of Brody, brother of Channa*
Gittel, *best friend of Leya, mother of Dovid, Tanya, and Nessa*

Ha'Ari, *"The Lion," refers to Rabbi Isaac Luria, renowned sixteenth century Kabbalist*
Ibrahim, *Kabbalist teacher of Yisroel in Okup*

Jacob, *husband of Gittel, father of Dovid*
Jacob Emden, *rabbi from Prague*

Jacob Frank, *self-declared messiah claiming to be the reincarnation of Shabtai Tzvi*
Jeremiah, *teacher in boys' cheyder in Horodenka*
Jonathan Eybeschutz, *rabbi from Prague*
Judah, *nephew of Sadya, husband of Dalia, father of Freyda*

Kaila, *daughter of Ezekiel and Malka, wet nurse to Eyzer*
Kovel, *violent Polish peasant*

Lazer, *rabbi and head of Polnoyye's Yeshiva*
Levi, *hunchbacked soap maker*
Leya, *widow, cobbler, mother of Gedaliah and Samuel, aunt of Rifka*
Luba, *daughter of Tanya and Samuel*

Malka, *wife of Ezekiel*
Marishka, *Polish peasant friend of Rifka's*
Meir, *rabbi, judge, husband of Batya, namesake for Zofia and Gedaliah's son*
Mendel, *Channa's first husband*
Motke, *schoolboy*
Mikulski, *bishop of Lemberg*

Naftali, *handicapped son of Batya and Rabbi Meir, brother of Zofia and Elias*
Naomi, *midwife, wife of Elias*
Nathan, *aka Nathan of Gaza, "prophet" who proclaimed Shabtai Tzvi to be the Messiah*
Nava, *daughter of Batleya and Elijah*
Nessa, *daughter of Gittel*

Olga, *cousin of Justyna*
Otto Frank, *visitor to inn at Zabie, Sabbatean follower*

Patryk, *son of peasant farmers Dominik and Justyna*
Pela, *midwife in mountains of Zabie*
Potocki, *nobleman, owner of village of Horodenka*

Raisa, *daughter of Kaila*
Ruben, *son of Gedaliah and Zofia*
Sadya, *Turkish merchant from Constantinople,*
    Judah's uncle

Samuel, *son of Leya, husband of Tanya*
Sarah, *deceased mother of Yisroel*
Shabtai Tzvi, *false messiah of the 1600s,*
    risen on the heels of Chmielnicki massacres
Shlomo, *deceased father of Jacob*
Srolik, *childhood name for Yisroel*

Tanya, *sister of Dovid, daughter of Gittel, wife of Samuel*

Wolf, *head of Kahal in Horodenka*

Yitta, *widow in Okup*

Zahava, *daughter of Rabbi Avner, wife of Amos*
Zelda, *vegetable hawker*
Zofia, *daughter of Batya and Meir, sister of Naftali and Elias*

GLOSSARY

Note: Hebrew, Yiddish, and Polish words in the novel's text are italicized the first time they appear and subsequently appear in Roman type. All the following (unless otherwise indicated as Polish) are transliterated from Hebrew or Yiddish according to the Ashkenazic pronunciation used in the Polish Lithuanian Commonwealth in the 1700s.

ADONAI: the name of God used most often in the Torah:
   the Tetragrammaton, *Yud Heh Yov Heh,* the ineffable name
   not to pronounced as written but rather as Adonai

AHAVAH: love

AFIKOMEN: a half piece of matzo broken off during the Passover
   ritual meal

ALEPH: first letter in the Hebrew alphabet

ASHKENAZIM: descendants of Jews from France, Germany,
   and Eastern Europe

ALTA: old or old one

AYN MISPAR: without number; cannot be counted; infinite

AYN SOF: literally, without end; a name for God, The Boundless One

B'RACHA: a blessing

BAAL SHEM: "master of the name"; one who brings healing using
   the Divine Name

BAAL SHEM TOV: "Good Master of the Name" and "Master of the
   Good Name"

BARUCH HASHEM: "Blessed is the Name"; also used as: "God Bless!"
   and "Thank God!"

BAS: daughter or daughter of, as in Rifka *bas* Aryeh

BASHERTE: destined or "destined one," often referring to a soul mate

BEIS MIDRASH: House of Study

BEN: son or son of, as in Yisroel *ben* Eliezar

BES: second letter of the Hebrew alphabet:

BES HEH: acronym for *Baruch HaShem*

BIMAH: raised platform in a synagogue from which the Torah is read

CHALLAH: braided bread prepared especially for the Sabbath
   and holidays.

CHANUKAH: winter holiday commemorating the rededication of the
   Holy Temple

CHEREM: Ban of Excommunication; highest ecclesiastical
   censure that mandates the total exclusion of a person from the
   community

CHEVRA KADISHA: "holy society"; the men and women who
   prepare a body for burial, performing the ritual cleansing,
   shrouding, and vigil until burial

CHEYDER: classroom where boys are taught until they turn thirteen

CHOLENT: stew containing meat, potatoes, beans, and barley

DEVEKUT: closeness to God; the practice of constant Remembrance

DYBBUK: in Jewish folklore, a malevolent, wandering spirit that
   enters and possesses the body of a living person

EEESH: man or husband

EEESHA: woman or wife

ELOHIM: a name for God

ELOHEYNU: "our God"

ESH: fire

GEDOLAH: big

GROSZ: (Polish) silver coin

HA'ARI: "The Lion"; refers to Isaac Luria, renowned sixteenth century rabbi and mystic of Safed in the Galilee Valley whose teachings are referred to as Lurianic Kabbalah

HAGGADAH: "telling"; a text that sets forth the order of the Passover Seder; reading the *Haggadah* is a fulfillment of the commandment to tell the story of liberation from slavery

HaMAKOM: literally "The Place"; a name for God

HAVDALAH: ritual that marks the end of Sabbath and ushers in the new week, performed on Saturday night after the appearance of three stars in the sky

IGGERET HaKODESH: "The Holy Epistle"; a Kabbalistic work written in the second half of the twelfth century that describes sexual intimacy between man and woman as sacred

IMYIRTZE HaSHEM: "with the will of the Name"; God-willing

KABBALAH: the ancient mystical cosmology that explains the nature and purpose of existence, including the relationship between an unchanging and eternal *Eyn Sof* (Infinite Source) and the mortal and finite created universe; referred to as "the soul of Torah."

KABBALIST: student and practitioner of *Kabbala*

KAHAL: governing body with regulatory control over Jewish residents in a locality, responsible for administering religious, legal, and communal affairs

KASHA: porridge of buckwheat groats

KLOIZ: elite fellowship of rabbis gathered to study Torah and Kabbalah

KUGEL: sweet or savory pudding of noodles

L'Cha Dodi: "Come, My Beloved," a prayer-song recited Friday
   at sundown to welcome the Sabbath

Livovi: "my love"

Matka Boga: (Polish) Mother of God

Malach Hamoves: Angel of Death

Melech Ha'Olam: "King of the Universe"

Mezuzah: piece of parchment (often contained in a decorative case)
   inscribed with specified verses from Deuteronomy and affixed to
   the doorpost of home or room

Mikveh: ritual bath

Mishnah: written compendium of Oral Torah; a compilation of
   rabbinic legal opinions and debates

Mitzvah: "commandment"; refers to a moral deed performed as a
   religious duty (one of 613 commandments in the Torah; has also
   come to describe an act of human kindness [pl. *Mitzvos*]

Mitzrayim: "narrows; constriction; constricted place";
   Hebrew for Egypt

Moreh: teacher

Nigun: improvised melody comprised of repetitive syllables rather
   than words

Nistar: one of the 36 hidden righteous ones in every generation

Ore: light

Pani: (Polish) salutation equivalent of Miss or Mrs. as in *Pani Leya*

Parsha: weekly Torah portion read and studied communally
   and individually

Pardes: "orchard"; written PaRDeS, an acronym for levels
   of biblical interpretation

Reb: salutation of respect before a first name or surname,
   e.g., Reb Eliezar or Reb Wolf (to be distinguished from *Rebbe*)

REBBE: Yiddish honorific deriving from Hebrew word rabbi,
   referring to a teacher of Torah, a spiritual master, personal mentor,
   and guide

ROSH HASHONAH: the Jewish New Year, a day of remembrance,
   described as the birthday of creation

SCHNAPPS: whiskey

SEDER: "order," the ritual feast that marks the beginning of the holiday
   of Passover

SEFER YETZIRAH: "Book of Creation" aka "Book of Formation";
   earliest extant Kabbalistic text

SEFIROS: Kabbalistic term meaning the emanations of the *Ayn Sof,*
   through which the Infinite reveals itself and continuously creates
   both the physical realm and the chain of higher metaphysical
   realms

SEPHARDIC: descendants of Jews from Spain, Portugal, North Africa,
   and the Middle East

SHABBOS: Sabbath

SHADDAI: one of God's names [see *Shin*]

SHALOM ALEYNU: peace upon us; part of a prayer invoking peace

SHAVUOUS: holiday commemorating the giving and receiving of the
   Torah at Mount Sinai

SHECHINAH: "dwelling"; denotes the Indwelling Sacred Presence

SHIN: a letter in the Hebrew alphabet, especially auspicious because
   it is the first letter of *Shaddai*, a name for God often seen on a
   mezuzah case

SHIVA: seven-day mourning period beginning immediately after burial
   for the family of the deceased

SH'LACH: "send"; the 37th weekly Torah portion (*parsha*) in the annual
   Jewish cycle of Torah reading, Numbers 13:1-15:41

SH'MA: "Hear!"; the first word and name of the Prayer of Unity: *Sh'ma*
   Yisroel Adonai Eloheynu, Adonai Echad, "Hear, O Israel: the Lord
   our God, the Lord is one»

SHOFAR: ritual musical instrument made from the horn of a ram,
　　　sounded on the High Holy Days of Rosh Hashonah and Yom
　　　Kippur to herald spiritual awakening

SHTREIMEL: large, round, fur-edged hat

SHUL: house of prayer, synagogue

SHVARIM: three medium wailing sounds blown on the *Shofar;*
　　　one of four different sounds associated with the blowing of
　　　the *Shofar*

SIMCHAS TORAH: "rejoicing with the Torah"; holiday that marks
　　　the conclusion of the annual cycle of Torah readings and the
　　　beginning of a new cycle

SUCCAH: "booth"; temporary hut used during the week-long
　　　Jewish festival of *Succos*

SUCCOS: "Feast of Booths" aka Feast of Tabernacles and Feast
　　　of the Ingathering; marks the end of the harvest time and
　　　also commemorates the Exodus, the period of wandering
　　　and complete dependence on the Unseen

SZLACHCIC: (Polish) nobleman [pl. *Szlachta*]

TALMUD: teachings and opinions of thousands of rabbis on a
　　　variety of subjects, including law, ethics, philosophy, customs,
　　　history, lore, and other topics; the basis for all codes of Jewish
　　　law and widely quoted in rabbinic literature; the *Talmud,*
　　　consisting of 63 tractates, has two components: the *Mishnah*
　　　(a written compendium of Rabbinic Judaism's Oral *Torah*)
　　　and the *Gemara* (an elucidation of the *Mishnah*)

TANTA: aunt

TEKIYAH: long sustained blast on the *Shofar;* one of four sounds
　　　associated with the blowing of the *Shofar*

TEKIYAH GEDOLAH: prolonged, unbroken sounding of
　　　the *Shofar*

TORAH: "Instruction"; "Teaching"; *Torah* can both refer to the
　　　Pentateuch, the first five books of the twenty-four books of

the Hebrew Bible or to the entire canon of the Hebrew Bible,
including the Pentateuch, Prophets, and other Writings of
Wisdom Literature; also a way of life

TRUAH: ten very quick, abbreviated blasts in succession sounded
on the *Shofar*; one of four different sounds associated with the
blowing of the *Shofar*

YENTA: a gossip

YESHIVA: *Talmudic* academies for men focused on the study of
traditional religious texts, primarily the *Torah* and *Talmud*

YOM KIPPUR: "Day of Atonement"; holiest day of the year;
day of purification, repentance, and forgiveness

YUD: tenth and smallest letter of the Hebrew alphabet

YUD HEH VOV HEH: the Tetragrammatron [see *Adonai*]

ZLOTY: (Polish) coins of a higher denomination than *Grosz*

ZOHAR: "splendor"; "radiance"; the foundational work in the
literature of mystical thought known as Kabbalah

ACKNOWLEDGEMENTS

Many persons have contributed welcome and needed reinforcement along the way from this novel's conception to its birth. I thank you each and all. I want to acknowledge here those without whom this book might not have seen the light of day. With great respect and love, I am deeply grateful…

…to my parents Esther and Arnold Tuzman, for their love in all its forms. May They Rest in Peace.

…to Bryan Hayward, who told me, when I thought I could not afford the time to write this book, that I couldn't afford not to.

…for the scholars and authors whose work was key in my research: Dan ben Amos and Jerome Mintz (editors and translators of *Shivhei Ha Besht, In Praise of the Baal Shem Tov,* for quite awhile the only book in English about the Baal Shem Tov); Gershom Scholem; Martin Buber; Aryeh Kaplan; Abraham Joshua Heschel; Gershon David Hundert; Adin Steinsaltz; Eva Hoffman; Immanuel Etkes; Perle Epstein; Jacob Immanuel Schochet; Yitzchak Buxbaum; Meyer Levin; Isaac Bashevis Singer.

…to Harold Grinspoon for generous support that came at a vital time, making it possible to keep going and follow the call.

…to Marti Reed, whose love of books and faith in mine were more sustaining than she might imagine.

...to Dagny St. John, who helps me drop sandbags of doubt and travel lighter.

...to Meg Fisher for steady friendship and deep listening.

...to Melissa Tefft, whose presence time and time again helps me find my way back to the wisdom of my own heart.

...to my editorial and design team, Alan Rinzler, Meg Fisher, Rosie Pearson, Laura Duffy, and Karen Minster, for such skillful and heartfelt collaboration.

...to Baba and Gurumayi, always guiding me to Remember.

And first and last: to *the Rebbe*, the Baal Shem Tov, who called me—perfectly imperfect vessel that I am—to write this book, and whose loving wisdom has inspired every step of this journey.

ABOUT THE AUTHOR

Ani Tuzman grew up on a back road chicken farm, the daughter of Holocaust survivors.

At the age of eight, Ani began writing to an invisible companion, filling page after page with her questions about a world darkened by the shadow of the Holocaust and the bewildering bigotry of her American neighbors. But there was also the ecstasy of rain, the dance of the willow in the wind, the stars illumining the night sky. Writing about it all—in the silent, unconditional embrace of nature—became Ani's path to the light.

Along the way, Ani became captivated by legends of an eighteenth century Eastern European mystic rabbi known as the Baal Shem Tov who valued all people as equal. A Kabbalist, he taught that divine sparks are hidden everywhere and it is one's sacred duty to find and free the energy in these sparks whose essence is love. When Ani turned 50, she experienced an inner call to write about the spiritual master.

The Tremble of Love, A Novel of the Baal Shem Tov is a testament to the inextinguishable fire of love. Although people and their institutions may be devastated, as was the case with Eastern European Jewry and with other cultures throughout history, the human capacity to love and to heal cannot be defeated.

An award-winning poet and a writing mentor, Ani Tuzman lives in New England, where she relishes long walks in the changing seasons, meditation, and her grandchildren's visits. To learn more about Ani and her work, please visit anituzman.com.

If you enjoyed this novel, please tell others about it.

You can also support a valued book by writing a review,
even a brief one, to Amazon and other online retailers.

Reviews offer a great service
to authors and to other readers.